THE LEW A

V

ROSS MACDONALD was born near San Francisco in 1915. He was educated in Canadian schools, and then travelled widely in Europe. In 1938 he married a Canadian, the now well-known crime novelist Margaret Millar. For over twenty years he lived in Santa Barbara and wrote mystery novels about the fascinating and changing society of his native state. He was a past president of the Mystery Writers of America. In 1964 his novel *The Chill* was given a Silver Dagger award by the Crime Writers' Association of Great Britain, which also named *The Far Side of the Dollar* as the best crime novel of 1965. In 1966, *The Moving Target* was made into the highly successful film, *Harper*, starring Paul Newman. Ross Macdonald died in 1983.

The Lew Archer Omnibus Volume 2

ROSS MACDONALD

a&b

This edition first published
in Great Britain in 1994 by
Allison & Busby
an imprint of Wilson & Day Ltd
5 The Lodge
Richmond Way
London W12 8LW

A catalogue record for this book is available from the British Library

ISBN 0 74900 201 8

Printed and bound in Great Britain by

THE MOVING TARGET

I

THE CAB TURNED off U.S. 101 in the direction of the sea. The road looped round the base of a brown hill into a canyon lined with scrub oak.

"This is Cabrillo Canyon," the driver said.

There weren't any houses in sight. "The people live in caves?"

"Not on your life. The estates are down by the ocean."

A minute later I started to smell the sea. We rounded another curve and entered its zone of coolness. A sign beside the road said: "Private Property: Permission to pass over revocable at any time."

The scrub oak gave place to ordered palms and Monterey cypress hedges. I caught glimpses of lawns effervescent with sprinklers, deep white porches, roofs of red tile and green copper. A Rolls with a doll at the wheel went by us like a gust of wind, and I felt unreal.

The light-blue haze in the lower canyon was like a thin smoke from slowly burning money. Even the sea looked precious through it, a solid wedge held in the canyon's mouth, bright blue and polished like a stone. Private property: colour guaranteed fast: will not shrink egos. I had never seen the Pacific look so small.

We turned up a drive between sentinel yews, cruised round in a private highway network for a while, and came out above the sea stretching deep and wide to Hawaii. The house stood part way down the shoulder of the bluff, with its back to the canyon. It was long and low. Its wings met at an obtuse angle pointed at the sea like a massive white arrowhead. Through screens of shrubbery I caught the white glare of tennis courts, the blue-green shimmer of a pool.

The driver turned on the fan-shaped drive and stopped beside the garages. "This is where the cavemen live. You want the service entrance?"

"I'm not proud."

"You want me to wait?"

"I guess so."

A heavy woman in a blue linen smock came out on the service porch and watched me climb out of the cab. "Mr Archer?"

"Yes. Mrs Sampson?"

"Mrs Kromberg. I'm the housekeeper." A smile passed over her lined face like sunlight on a ploughed field. "You can let your taxi go. Felix can drive you back to town when you're ready."

I paid off the driver and got my bag out of the back. I felt a little embarrassed with it in my hand. I didn't know whether the job would last an hour or a month.

"I'll put your bag in the storeroom," the housekeeper said. "I don't think you'll be needing it."

She led me through a chromium-and-porcelain kitchen, down a hall that was cool and vaulted like a cloister, into a cubicle that rose to the second floor when she pressed a button.

"All the modern conveniences," I said to her back.

"They had to put it in when Mrs Sampson hurt her legs. It cost seven thousand five hundred dollars."

If that was supposed to silence me, it did. She knocked on a door across the hall from the elevator. Nobody answered. After knocking again, she opened the door on a high white room too big and bare to be feminine. Above the massive bed there was a painting of a clock, a map, and a woman's hat arranged on a dressing-table. Time, space, and sex. It looked like a Kuniyoshi.

The bed was rumpled but empty. "Mrs Sampson!" the housekeeper called.

A cool voice answered her: "I'm on the sun deck. What do you want?"

"Mr Archer's here – the man you sent the wire to."

"Tell him to come out. And bring me some more coffee."

"You go out through the french windows," the housekeeper said, and went away.

Mrs Sampson looked up from her book when I stepped out. She was half lying on a chaise longue with her back to the late morning sun, a towel draped over her body. There was a wheelchair standing beside her, but she didn't look like an invalid. She was very lean and brown, tanned so dark that her flesh seemed hard. Her hair was bleached, curled tightly on her narrow head like blobs of whipped cream. Her age was as hard to tell as the age of a figure carved from mahogany.

She dropped the book on her stomach and offered me her hand. "I've heard about you. When Millicent Drew broke with Clyde, she said you were helpful. She didn't exactly say how."

"It's a long story," I said. "And a sordid one."

"Millicent and Clyde are dreadfully sordid, don't you think? These aesthetic men! I've always suspected his mistress wasn't a woman."

"I never think about my clients." With that I offered her my boyish grin, a little the worse for wear.

"Or talk about them?"

"Or talk about them. Even with my clients."

Her voice was clear and fresh, but the sickness was there in her laugh, a little clatter of bitterness under the trill. I looked down into her eyes, the eyes of something frightened and sick hiding in the fine brown body. She lowered the lids.

"Sit down, Mr Archer. You must be wondering why I sent for you. Or don't you wonder either?"

I sat on a deck chair beside the chaise. "I wonder. I even conjecture. Most of my work is divorce. I'm a jackal, you see."

"You slander yourself, Mr Archer. And you don't talk like a detective, do you? I'm glad you mentioned divorce. I want to make it clear at the start that divorce is not what I want. I want my marriage to last. You see, I intend to outlive my husband."

I said nothing, waiting for more. When I looked more closely, her brown skin was slightly roughened, slightly withered. The sun was hammering her copper legs, hammering down on my head. Her toenails and her fingernails were painted the same blood colour.

"It mayn't be survival of the fittest. You probably know I can't use my legs any more. But I'm twenty years younger than he is, and I'm going to survive him." The bitterness had come through into her voice, buzzing like a wasp.

She heard it and swallowed it at a gulp. "It's like a furnace out here, isn't it? It's not fair that men should have to wear coats. Please take yours off."

"No, thanks."

"You're very gentlemanly."

"I'm wearing a shoulder holster. And still wondering. You mentioned Albert Graves in your telegram."

"He recommended you. He's one of Ralph's lawyers. You can talk to him after lunch about your pay."

"He isn't D.A. any more?"

"Not since the war."

"I did some work for him in '40 and '41. I haven't seen him since."

"He told me. He told me you were good at finding people." She smiled a white smile, carnivorous and startling in her dark face. "Are you good at finding people, Mr Archer?"

"'Missing Persons' is better. Your husband's missing?"

"Not missing, exactly. Just gone off by himself, or in company. He'd be frantically angry if I went to the Missing Persons Bureau."

"I see. You want me to find him if possible and identify the company. And what then?"

"Just tell me where he is, and with whom. I'll do the rest myself." Sick as I am, said the little whining undertone, legless though I be.

"When did he go away?"

"Yesterday afternoon."

"Where?"

"Los Angeles. He was in Las Vegas – we have a desert place near there – but he flew to Los Angeles yesterday afternoon with Alan. Alan's his pilot. Ralph gave him the slip at the airport and went off by himself."

"Why?"

"I suppose because he was drunk." Her red mouth curved contemptuously. "Alan said he'd been drinking."

"You think he's gone off on a binge. Does he often?"

"Not often, but totally. He loses his inhibitions when he drinks."

"About sex?"

"All men do, don't they? But that isn't what concerns me. He loses his inhibitions about money. He tied one on a few months ago and gave away a mountain."

"A mountain?"

"Complete with hunting-lodge."

"Did he give it to a woman?"

"I almost wish he had. He gave it to a man, but it's not what you're thinking. A Los Angeles holy man with a long grey beard."

"He sounds like a soft touch."

"Ralph? He'd go stark staring mad if you called him that to his face. He started out as a wildcat oil operator. You know the type, half man, half alligator, half bear trap, with a piggy bank where his heart should be. That's when he's sober. But alcohol softens him up, at least it has the last few years. A few drinks, and he wants to be a little boy again. He goes looking for a mother type or a father type to blow his nose and dry away his tears and spank him when he's naughty. Do I sound cruel? I'm simply being objective."

"Yes," I said. "You want me to find him before he gives away another mountain." Dead or alive, I thought; but I wasn't her analyst.

"And if he's with a woman, naturally I'll be interested. I'll want to know all about her, because I couldn't afford to give away an advantage like that."

I wondered who her analyst was.

"Have you any particular woman in mind?"

"Ralph doesn't confide in me – he's much closer to Miranda than he is to me – and I'm not equipped to spy on him. That's why I'm hiring you."

"To put it bluntly," I said.

"I always put things bluntly."

II

A Filipino houseboy in a white jacket appeared at the open french window. "Your coffee, Mrs Sampson."

He set down the silver coffee service on a low table by the chaise. He was little and quick. The hair on his small round head was slick and black like a coating of grease.

"Thank you, Felix." She was gracious to her servants or making an impression on me. "Will you have some, Mr Archer?"

"No, thanks."

"Perhaps you'd like a drink."

"Not before lunch. I'm the new-type detective."

She smiled and sipped her coffee. I got up and walked to the seaward end of the sun deck. Below it the terraces descended in long green steps to the edge of the bluff, which fell sharply down to the shore.

I heard a splash around the corner of the house and leaned out over the railing. The pool was on the upper terrace, an oval of green water set in blue tile. A girl and a boy were playing tag, cutting the water like seals. The girl was chasing the boy. He let her catch him.

Then they were a man and a woman, and the moving scene froze in the sun. Only the water moved, and the girl's hands. She was standing behind him with her arms around his waist. Her fingers moved over his ribs gently as a harpist's, clenched in the tuft of hair in the centre of his chest. Her face was hidden against his back. His face held pride and anger like a blind bronze.

He pushed her hands down and stepped away. Her face was naked then, and terribly vulnerable. Her arms hung down as if they had lost their purpose. She sat down on the edge of the pool and dangled her feet in the water.

The dark young man did a flip and a half from the springboard. She didn't look. The drops fell off the tips of her hair like tears and ran down into her bosom.

Mrs Sampson called me by name. "You haven't had lunch?"

"No."

"Lunch for three in the patio, then, Felix. I'll eat up here as usual."

Felix bowed slightly and started away. She called him back. "Bring the photo of Mr Sampson from my dressing-room. You'll have to know what he looks like, won't you, Mr Archer?"

The face in the leather folder was fat, with thin grey hair and a troubled mouth. The thick nose tried to be bold and succeeded in being obstinate. The smile that folded the puffed eyelids and creased the sagging cheeks was fixed and forced. I'd seen such smiles in mortuaries on the false face of death. It reminded me that I was going to grow old and die.

"A poor thing, but mine own," said Mrs Sampson.

Felix let out a sound that could have been a snicker, grunt, or sigh. I couldn't think of anything to add to his comment.

He served lunch in the patio, a red-tiled triangle between the house and the hillside. Above the masonry retaining wall the slope was planted with ground cover, ageratum, and trailing lobelia in an unbreaking blue-green wave.

The dark young man was there when Felix led me out. He had laid away his anger and his pride, changed to a fresh light suit, and looked at ease. He was tall enough when he stood up to make me feel slightly undersized – six foot three or four. His grip was hard.

"Alan Taggert's my name. I pilot Sampson's plane."

"Lew Archer."

He rotated a small drink in his left hand. "What are you drinking?"

"Milk."

"No kidding? I thought you were a detective."

"Fermented mare's milk, that is."

He had a pleasant white smile. "Mine's gin and bitters. I picked up the habit at Port Moresby."

"Done a good deal of flying?"

"Fifty-five missions. And a couple of thousand hours."

"Where?"

"Mostly in the Carolines. I had a P-38."

He said it with loving nostalgia, like a girl's name.

The girl came out then, wearing a black-striped dress, narrow in the right places, full in the others. Her dark-red hair, brushed and dried, bubbled around her head. Her wide green eyes were dazzling and strange in her brown face, like light eyes in an Indian.

Taggert introduced her. She was Sampson's daughter Miranda. She seated us at a metal table under a canvas umbrella that grew out of the table's centre on an iron stem. I watched her over my salmon mayonnaise; a tall girl whose movements had a certain awkward charm, the kind who developed slowly and was worth waiting for. Puberty around fifteen, first marriage or affair at twenty or twenty-one. A few hard years outgrowing romance and changing from girl to woman; then the complete fine woman at twenty-eight or thirty. She was about twenty-one, a little too old to be Mrs Sampson's daughter.

"My stepmother" – she said, as if I'd been thinking aloud –

"my stepmother is always going to extremes."

"Do you mean me, Miss Sampson? I'm a very moderate type."

"Not you, especially. Everything she does is extreme. Other people fall off horses without being paralyzed from the waist down. But not Elaine. I think it's psychological. She isn't the raving beauty she used to be, so she retired from competition. Falling off the horse gave her a chance to do it. For all I know she deliberately fell off."

Taggert laughed shortly. "Come off it, Miranda. You've been reading a book."

She looked at him haughtily. "You'll never be accused of that."

"Is there a psychological explanation for my being here?" I said.

"I'm not exactly sure why you're here. Is it to track Ralph down, or something like that?"

"Something like that."

"I suppose she wants to get something on him. You have to admit it's pretty extreme to call in a detective because a man stays away overnight."

"I'm discreet, if that's what's worrying you."

"Nothing's worrying me," she said sweetly. "I merely made a psychological observation."

The Filipino servant moved unobtrusively across the patio. Felix's steady smile was a mask behind which his personality waited in isolation, peeping furtively from the depths of his bruised-looking black eyes. I had the feeling that his pointed ears heard everything I said, counted my breathing, and could pick up the beat of my heart on a clear day.

Taggert had been looking uncomfortable, and changed the subject abruptly. "I don't think I ever met a real-life detective before."

"I'd give you my autograph, only I sign it with an 'X'."

"Seriously, though, I'm interested in detectives. I thought I'd like to be one at one time – before I went up in a plane. I guess most kids dream about it."

"Most kids don't get stuck with the dream."

"Why? Don't you like your work?"

"It keeps me out of mischief. Let's see, you were with Mr Sampson when he dropped out of sight?"

"Right."

"How was he dressed?"

"Sports clothes. Harris tweed jacket, brown wool shirt, tan slacks, brogues. No hat."

"And when was this exactly?"

"About three-thirty – when we landed at Burbank yesterday afternoon. They had to move another crate before I could park the plane. I always put it away myself; it's got some special gadgets we wouldn't want stolen. Mr Sampson went to call the hotel to send out a limousine."

"What hotel?"

"The Valerio."

"The pueblo off Wilshire?"

"Ralph keeps a bungalow there," Miranda said. "He likes it because it's quiet."

"When I got out to the main entrance," Taggert continued, "Mr Sampson was gone. I didn't think much about it. He'd been drinking pretty hard, but that was nothing unusual, and he could still look after himself. It made me a little sore, though. There I was stranded in Burbank, simply because he couldn't wait five minutes. It's a three-dollar taxi ride to the Valerio, and I couldn't afford that."

He glanced at Miranda to see if he was saying too much. She looked amused.

"Anyway," he said, "I took a bus to the hotel. *Three* buses, about half an hour on each. And then he wasn't there. I waited around until nearly dark, and then I flew the plane home."

"Did he ever get to the Valerio?"

"No. He hasn't been there at all."

"What about his luggage?"

"He didn't carry luggage."

"Then he wasn't planning to stay overnight?"

"It doesn't follow," Miranda put in. "He kept whatever he needed in the bungalow at the Valerio."

"Maybe he's there now."

"No. Elaine's been phoning every hour on the hour."

I turned to Taggert. "Didn't he say anything about his plans?"

"He was going to spend the night at the Valerio."

"How long was he by himself when you were parking the

plane?"

"Fifteen minutes or so. Not more than twenty."

"The limousine from the Valerio would've had to get there pretty fast. He may never have called the hotel at all."

"Somebody might have met him at the airport," Miranda said.

"Did he have many friends in Los Angeles?"

"Business acquaintances mostly. Ralph's never been much of a mixer."

"Can you give me their names?"

She moved her hand in front of her face as if the names were insects. "You'd better ask Albert Graves. I'll call his office and tell him you're coming. Felix will drive you in. And then I suppose you'll be going back to Los Angeles."

"It looks like the logical place to start."

"Alan can fly you." She stood up and looked down at him with a flash of half-learned imperiousness. "You're not doing anything special this afternoon, are you, Alan?"

"Glad to," he said. "It'll keep me from getting bored."

She switch-tailed into the house, a pretty piece in a rage.

"Give her a break," I said.

He stood up and overshadowed me. "What do you mean?"

He had a trace of smugness, of high-school arrogance, and I needled it. "She needs a tall man. You'd make a handsome pair."

"Sure, sure." He wagged his head negatively from side to side. "More people jump to conclusions about me and Miranda."

"Including Miranda?"

"I happen to be interested in somebody else. Not that it's any of your business. Or that God damn eight ball's either."

He meant Felix, who was standing in the doorway that led to the kitchen. He suddenly disappeared.

"The bastard gets on my nerves." Taggert said. "He's always hanging around and listening in."

"Maybe he's just interested."

He snorted. "He's just one of the things that gripes me about this place. I eat with the family, yeah, but don't think I'm not a servant when the chips are down. A bloody flying chauffeur."

Not to Miranda, I thought, but didn't say it. "It's an easy

enough job, isn't it? Sampson can't be flying much of the time."

"The flying doesn't bother me. I like it. What I don't like is being the old guy's keeper."

"He needs a keeper?"

"He can be hell on wheels. I couldn't tell you about him in front of Miranda, but the last week in the desert you'd think he was trying to drink himself to death. A quart and a pint a day. When he drinks like that he gets delusions of grandeur, and I get sick of taking chicken from a lush. Then he goes sentimental. He wants to adopt me and buy an airline for me." His voice went harsh and loose, in satiric mimicry of a drunk old man's: "I'll look after you, Alan boy. You'll get your airline."

"Or a mountain?"

"I'm not kidding about the airline. He could do it, too. But he doesn't give anything away when he's sober. Not a thin dime."

"Strictly schizo," I said. "What makes him like that?"

"I wouldn't know for sure. The bitch upstairs would drive anybody crazy. Then he lost a son in the war. That's where I come in, I guess. He doesn't really need a full-time pilot. Bob Sampson was a flier, too. Shot down over Sakashima. Miranda thinks that that's what broke the old man up."

"How does Miranda get along with him?"

"Pretty well, but they've been feuding lately. Sampson's been trying to make her get married."

"To anybody in particular?"

"Albert Graves." He said it deadpan, neither pro nor con.

III

The highway entered Santa Teresa at the botton of the town near the sea. We drove through a mile of slums: collapsing shacks and storefront tabernacles, dirt paths where sidewalks should have been, black and brown children playing in the dust. Nearer the main street there were a few tourist hotels with neon signs like icing on a cardboard cake, red-painted chili houses, a series of shabby taverns where the rumdums were congregating. Half the men in the street had short Indian bodies and morocco faces. After Cabrillo Canyon I felt like a man from another planet. The Cadillac was a space ship skimming just above the ground.

Felix turned left at the main street, away from the sea. The street changed as we went higher. Men in coloured shirts and seersucker suits, women in slacks and midriff dresses displaying various grades of abdomen, moved in and out of California Spanish shops and office buildings. Nobody looked at the mountains standing above the town, but the mountains were there, making them all look silly.

Taggert had been sitting in silence, his handsome face a blank. "How do you like it?" he asked me.

"I don't have to like it. How about you?"

"It's pretty dead for my money. People come here to die, like elephants. But then they go on living – call it living."

"You should have seen it before the war. It's a hive of activity compared with what it was. There was nothing but the rich old ladies clipping coupons and pinching pennies and cutting the assistant gardener's wages."

"I didn't know you knew the town."

"I worked on a couple of cases with Bert Graves – when he was District Attorney."

Felix parked in front of a yellow stucco archway that led into the courtyard of an office building. He opened the glass partition. "Mr Graves's office is on the second floor. You can take the elevator."

"I'll wait out here," Taggert said.

Graves's office was a contrast to the grimy cubicle in the courthouse where he used to prepare his cases. The waiting-room was finished in cool green cloth and bleached wood. A blonde receptionist with cool green eyes completed the colour scheme and said:

"Do you have an appointment, sir?"

"Just tell Mr Graves it's Lew Archer."

"Mr Graves is busy at the moment."

"I'll wait."

I sat down in an overstuffed chair and thought about Sampson. The blonde's white fingers danced on her typewriter keys. I was restless and still feeling unreal, hired to look for a man I couldn't quite imagine. An oil tycoon who consorted with holy men and was drinking himself to death. I pulled his photograph out of my pocket and looked at it again. It looked back at me.

The inner door was opened, and an old lady backed out bobbing and chortling. Her hat was something she'd found washed up on the beach. There were diamonds in the watch that was pinned to her purple silk bosom.

Graves followed her out. She was telling him how clever he was, very clever and helpful. He was pretending to listen. I stood up. When he saw me he winked at me over the hat.

The hat went away, and he came back from the door. "It's good to see you, Lew."

He didn't slap backs, but his grip was as hard as ever. The years had changed him, though. His hairline was creeping back at the temples, his small grey eyes peered out from a network of little wrinkles. The heavy blue-shadowed jaw was drooping at the sides in the beginning of jowls. It was unpleasant to remember that he wasn't five years older than I was. But Graves had come up the hard way, and that was an ageing process.

I told him I was glad to see him. I was.

"It must be six or seven years," he said.

"All of that. You're not prosecuting any more."

"I couldn't afford to."

"Married?"

"Not yet. Inflation." He grinned. "How's Sue?"

"Ask her lawyer. She didn't like the company I kept."

"I'm sorry to hear it, Lew."

"Don't be." I changed the subject. "Doing much trial work?"

"Not since the war. It doesn't pay off in a town like this."

"Something must." I looked around the room. The cool blonde girl permitted herself to smile.

"This is just my front. I'm still a struggling attorney. But I'm learning to talk to the old ladies." His smile was wry. "Come inside, Lew."

The inner office was bigger, cooler, more heavily furnished. There were hunting prints on the two bare walls. The others were lined with books. He looked smaller behind his massive desk.

"What about politics?" I said. "You were going to be Governor, remember?"

"The party's gone to pieces in California. Anyway, I've had my fill of politics. I ran a town in Bavaria for two years. Military Government."

"Carpetbagger, eh? I was Intelligence. Now what about Ralph Sampson?"

"You talked to Mrs Sampson?"

"I did. It was quite an experience. But I don't quite get the point of this job. Do you?"

"I should. I talked her into it."

"Why?"

"Because Sampson might need protection. A man with five million dollars shouldn't take the chances he does. He's an alcoholic, Lew. He's been getting worse since his boy was killed, and sometimes I'm afraid he's losing his mind. Did she tell you about Claude, the character he gave the hunting-lodge to?"

"Yeah. The holy man."

"Claude seems to be harmless, but the next one might not be. I don't have to tell you about Los Angeles. It isn't safe for an elderly lush by himself."

"No," I said. "You don't have to tell me. But Mrs Sampson seemed to think he's off on a round of pleasures."

"I encouraged her to think that. She wouldn't spend money to protect him."

"But you would."

"*Her* money. I'm just his lawyer. Of course, I rather like the old guy."

And hope to be his son-in-law, I thought.

"How much is she good for?"

"Whatever you say. Fifty a day and expenses?"

"Make it seventy-five. I don't like the imponderables in this case."

"Sixty-five." He laughed. "I've got to protect my client."

"I won't argue. There may not even be a case. Sampson could be with friends."

"I've tried them. He didn't have many friends here. I'll give you a list of contacts, but I wouldn't waste time on it except as a last resort. His real friends are in Texas. That's where he made his money."

"Your'e taking this pretty seriously," I said. "Why don't you go one step further and take it to the police?"

"Trying to talk yourself out of a job?"

"Yes."

"It can't be done, Lew. If the police found him for me, he'd fire me in a minute. And I can't be sure he isn't with a woman. Last year I found him in a fifty-dollar house in San Francisco."

"What were you doing there?"

"Looking for him."

"This smells more and more like divorce," I said. "But Mrs Sampson insisted that isn't it. I still don't get it – or her."

"You can't expect to. I've known her for years and I don't understand her. But I can handle her, up to a point. If anything ticklish comes up, bring it to me. She has a few dominant motives, like greed and vanity. You can count on them when you're dealing with her. And she doesn't want a divorce. She'd rather wait and inherit all his money – or half of it. Miranda gets the other half."

"Were those always her dominant motives?"

"Ever since I've known her, since she married Sampson. She tried to have a career before that: dancing, painting, dress-designing. No talent. She was Sampson's mistress for a while, and finally she fell back on him, married him as a last resort. That was six years ago."

"And what happened to her legs?"

"She fell off a horse she was trying to train, and hit her head on a stone. She hasn't walked since."

"Miranda thinks she doesn't want to walk."

"Were you talking to Miranda?" His face lit up. "Isn't she a marvellous kid?"

"She certainly is." I stood up. "Congratulations."

He blushed and said nothing. I have never seen Graves blush before. I felt slightly embarrassed.

On the way down in the automatic elevator he asked me:

"Did she say anything about me?"

"Not a word. I plucked it out of the air."

"She's a marvellous kid," he repeated. At forty he was drunk on love.

He sobered up in a hurry when we reached the car. Miranda was in the back seat with Alan Taggert. "I followed you in. I decided to fly down to Los Angeles with you. Hello, Bert."

"Hello, Miranda."

He gave her a hurt look. She was looking at Taggert. Taggert was looking nowhere in particular. It was a triangle, but not an equilateral one.

IV

We rode into the offshore wind sweeping across the airport and climbed toward the southern break in the mountains. Santa Teresa was a coloured air map on the mountains' knees, the sailboats in the harbour white soap chips in a tub of bluing. The air was very clear. The peaks stood up so sharply that they looked like papier-mâché I could poke my finger through. Then we rose past them into chillier air and saw the wilderness of mountains stretching to the fifty-mile horizon.

The plane leaned gradually and turned out over the sea. It was a four-seater equipped for night flying. I was in the back seat. Miranda was in front on Taggert's right. She watched his right hand, careful on the stick. He seemed to take pride in holding the plane quiet and steady.

We hit a downdraft and fell a hundred feet. Her left hand grasped his knee. He let it stay there.

What was obvious to me must have been obvious to Albert Graves. Miranda was Taggert's if he wanted her, brain and body. Graves was wasting his time, building himself up to a very nasty letdown.

I knew enough about him to understand it. Miranda was everything he dreamed about – money, youth, bud-sharp breasts, beauty on the way. He'd set his mind on her and had to have her. All his life he'd been setting his mind on things – and getting them.

He was a farmer's son from Ohio. When he was fourteen or fifteen his father lost his farm and died soon after. Bert supported his mother by building tires in a rubber factory for six years. When she died he put himself through college and came out a Phi Beta Kappa. Before he was thirty he had taken his law degree at the University of Michigan. He spent one year in corporation law in Detroit and decided to come west. He settled in Santa Teresa because he had never seen mountains or swum in the sea. His father had always intended to retire in California, and Bert inherited the midwestern dream – which included the daughter of a Texas oil millionaire.

The dream was intact. He'd worked too hard to have any time for women. Deputy D.A., City Attorney, D.A. He prepared his cases as if he were laying the foundations of society. I knew, because I'd helped him. His courtroom work had been cited by a state-supreme-court judge as a model of forensic jurisprudence. And now at forty Graves had decided to beat his head against a wall.

But perhaps he could scale the wall, or the wall would fall down by itself. Taggert shook his leg like a horse frightening flies. The plane veered and returned to its course. Miranda removed her hand.

With a little angry flush spreading to his ears, Taggert pulled the stick and climbed – climbed as if he could leave her behind and be all alone in the heart of the sky. The thermometer in the roof sank below forty. At eight thousand feet I could see Catalina far down ahead to the right. After a few minutes we turned left toward the white smudge of Los Angeles.

I shouted over the roar: "Can you set her down at Burbank? I want to ask some questions."

"I'm going to."

The summer heat of the valley came up to meet us as we circled in. Heat lay like a fine ash on the rubbish lots and fields and half-built suburbs, slowing the tiny cars on the roads and boulevards, clogging the air. The impalpable white dust invaded my nostrils and dried my throat. Dryness of the throat went with the feeling I always had, even after half a day, when I came back to the city.

The taxi starter at the airport wore steel-wire armbands on the sleeves of his red-striped shirt. A yellow cap hung almost vertically from the back of his grey head. Seasons of sun and personal abuse had given him an angry red face and an air of great calm.

He remembered Sampson when I showed him the photograph.

"Yeah, he was here yesterday. I noticed him because he was a little under the weather. Not blotto, or I would of called a guard. Just a couple of drinks too many."

"Sure," I said. "Was anybody with him?"

"Not that I saw."

A woman wearing two foxes that looked as if they had died from the heat broke out of the line at the curb. "I have to get downtown right away."

"Sorry, madam. You got to wait your turn."

"I tell you this is urgent."

"You got to wait your turn," he said monotonously. "We got a cab shortage, see?"

He turned to me again. "Anything else, bud? This guy in trouble or something?"

"I wouldn't know. How did he leave?"

"By car – a black limousine. I noticed it because it didn't carry no sign. Maybe from one of the hotels."

"Was there anybody in it?"

"Just the driver."

"You know him?"

"Naw. I know some of the hotel drivers, but they're always changing. This was a little guy, I think, kind of pale."

"You don't remember the make or the licence number?"

"I keep my eyes open, bud, but I ain't a genius."

"Thanks." I gave him a dollar. "Neither am I."

I went upstairs to the cocktail bar, where Miranda and Taggert were sitting like strangers thrown together by accident.

"I called the Valerio," Taggert said. "The limousine should be here any minute."

The limousine, when it came, was driven by a pale little man in a shiny blue-serge suit like an umpire's, and a cloth cap. The taxi-starter said he wasn't the man who had picked up Sampson the day before.

I got into the front seat with him. He turned with nervous quickness, grey-faced, concave-chested, convex-eyed. "Yes, sir?" The question trailed off gently and obsequiously.

"We're going to the Valerio. Were you on duty yesterday afternoon?"

"Yes, sir." He shifted gears.

"Was anybody else?"

"No, sir. There's another fellow on the night shift, but he doesn't come on till six."

"Did you have any calls to the Burbank airport yesterday

afternoon?"

"No, sir." A worried expression was creeping into his eyes and seemed to suit them. "I don't believe I did."

"But you're not certain."

"Yes, sir. I'm certain. I didn't come out this way."

"You know Ralph Sampson?"

"At the Valerio? Yes, sir. Indeed I do, sir."

"Have you seen him lately?"

"No, sir. Not for several weeks."

"I see. Tell me, who takes the calls for you?"

"The switchboard operator. I do hope there's nothing wrong, sir. Is Mr Sampson a friend of yours?"

"No," I said. "I'm one of his employees."

All the rest of the way he drove in tight-mouthed silence, regretting the wasted sirs. When I got out I gave him a dollar to confuse him. Miranda paid the fare.

"I'd like to look at the bungalow," I told her in the lobby. "But first I want to talk to the switchboard operator."

"I'll get the key and wait for you."

The operator was a frozen virgin who dreamed about men at night and hated them in the daytime. "Yes?"

"Yesterday afternoon you had a call for a limousine from the Burbank airport."

"We do not answer questions of that nature."

"That wasn't a question. It was a statement."

"I'm very busy," she said. Her tone clicked like pennies; her eyes were small and hard and shiny like dimes.

I put a dollar bill on the desk by her elbow. She looked at it as if it was unclean. "I'll have to call the manager."

"All right. I work for Mr Sampson."

"Mr *Ralph* Sampson?" She lilted, she trilled.

"That's correct."

"But he was the one that made the call!"

"I know. What happened to it?"

"He cancelled it immediately, before I had an opportunity to tell the driver. Did he have a change of plan?"

"Apparently. You're sure it was him both times?"

"Oh yes," she said. "I know Mr Sampson well. He's been coming here for years."

She picked up the unclean dollar lest it contaminate her desk and tucked it into a cheap plastic handbag. Then she turned to the switchboard, which had three red lights on it.

Miranda stood up when I came back to the lobby. It was hushed and rich, deep-carpeted, deep-chaired, with mauve-coated bellboys at attention. She moved like a live young nymph in a museum. "Ralph hasn't been here for nearly a month. I asked the assistant manager."

"Did he give you the key?"

"Of course. Alan's gone to open the bungalow."

I followed her down a corridor that ended in a wrought-iron door. The grounds back of the main building were laid out in little avenues, with bungalows on either side, set among terraced lawns and flower beds. They covered a city block, enclosed by high stone walls like a prison. But the prisoners of those walls could lead a very full life. There were tennis courts, a swimming pool, a restaurant, a bar, a night club. All they needed was a full wallet or a blank cheque-book.

Sampson's bungalow was larger than most of the others and had more terrace. The door at the side was standing open. We passed through a hall cluttered with uncomfortable-looking Spanish chairs into a big room with a high oak-beamed ceiling.

On the chesterfield in front of the dead fireplace Taggert was hunched over a telephone directory. "I thought I'd call a buddy of mine." He looked up at Miranda with a half smile. "Since I have to hang around anyway."

"I thought you were going to stay with me." Her voice was high and uncertain.

"Did you?"

I looked around the room, which was mass-produced and impersonal like most hotel rooms. "Where does your father keep his private stuff?"

"In his room, I suppose. He doesn't keep much here. A few changes of clothes."

She showed me the door of the bedroom across the hall and switched on the light.

"What on earth has he done to it?" she said.

The room was twelve-sided and windowless. The indirect lights were red. The walls were covered with thick red stuff that hung in folds from the ceiling to the floor. A heavy armchair and the bed in the room's centre were covered with the same dark red. The crowning touch was a circular mirror in the ceiling which repeated the room upside down. My memory struggled in the red gloom and found the comparison it wanted: a Neapolitan-type bordello I'd visited in Mexico City – on a case.

"No wonder he took to drink, if he had to sleep in here."

"It didn't used to be like this," she said. "He must have had it redone."

I moved around the room. Each of the twelve panels was embroidered in gold with one of the twelve signs of the zodiac – the archer, the bull, the twins, and the nine others.

"Is your father interested in astrology?"

"Yes, he is." She said it shamefacedly. "I've tried to argue with him, but it doesn't do any good. He went off the deep end when Bob died. I had no idea he'd gone so far in it, though."

"Does he go to a particular astrologist? The woods are full of them."

"I wouldn't know."

I found the entrance to the closet behind a movable curtain. It was stuffed with suits and shirts and shoes, from golf clothes to evening dress. I went through the pockets systematically. In the breast pocket of a jacket I found a wallet. The wallet contained a mass of twenties and a single photograph.

I held it up to the bulb that lit the closet. It was a sibylline face, with dark and mournful eyes and a full drooping mouth. On either side the black hair fell straight to the high neckline of a black dress that merged into artistic shadows at the bottom of the picture. A feminine hand had written in white ink across the shadows: "To Ralph from Fay with Blessings."

It was a face I should know. I remembered the melancholy eyes but nothing else. I replaced the wallet in Sampson's jacket and added the picture to my photographic collection of one.

"Look," Miranda said, when I stepped back into the room. She was lying on the bed with her skirt above her knees. Her body in the rosy light seemed to be burning. She closed her eyes. "What does this mad room make you think of?"

Her hair was burning all around the edges. Her upturned face was closed and dead. And her slender body was burning up, like a sacrifice on an altar.

I crossed the room and put my hand on her shoulder. The ruddy light shone through my hand and reminded me that I contained a skeleton. "Open your eyes."

She opened them, smiling. "You saw it, didn't you? The sacrifice on the heathen altar – like Salammbô."

"You do read too many books," I said.

My hand was still on her shoulder, conscious of sunned flesh. She turned upward toward me and pulled me down. Her lips were hot on my face.

"What goes on?" Taggert asked, from the doorway. The red light on his face made him look choleric, but he was smiling his same half smile. The incident amused him.

I stood up and straightened my coat. I was not amused. Miranda was the freshest thing I'd touched in many a day. She made the blood run round in my veins like horses on a track.

"What's so hard in your coat pocket?" Miranda said distinctly.

"I'm wearing a gun."

I pulled out the dark woman's picture and showed it to both of them. "Did you ever see her before? She signs herself 'Fay'."

"I never did," said Taggert.

"No," said Miranda. She was smiling at him side-eyed and secretly, as if she had won a point.

She'd been using me to stir him up, and it made me angry. The red room made me angry. It was like the inside of a sick brain, with no eyes to see out of, nothing to look at but the upside-down reflection of itself. I got out.

V

I PRESSED THE BELL, and in a minute a rich female voice gurgled in the speaking-tube. "Who is it, please?"

"Lew Archer. Is Morris home?"

"Sure. Come on up." She sounded the buzzer that opened the inner door of the apartment lobby.

She was waiting when I reached the head of the stairs, a fat and fading blonde, happily married. "Long time no see." I winced, but she didn't notice. "Morris slept in this morning. He's still eating breakfast."

I glanced at my watch. It was three-thirty. Morris Cramm

was night legman for a columnist and worked from seven in the evening to five in the morning.

His wife led me through a living-room-bedroom combination crowded with papers and books and an unmade studio bed. Morris was at the kitchen table, in a bathrobe, staring down two fried eggs that were looking up at him. He was a dark little man with sharp black eyes behind thick spectacles. And behind the eyes was a card index brain that contained the vital statistics of Los Angeles.

"Morning, Lew," he said, without getting up.

I sat down opposite him. "It's late afternoon."

"It's morning to me. Time is a relative concept. In summer when I go to bed the yellow sun shines overhead – Robert Louis Stevenson. Which lobe of my brain do you want to pick this *morning*?"

He italicized the last word, and Mrs Cramm punctuated it by pouring me a cup of coffee. They half convinced me I had just got up after having a dream about the Sampsons. I wouldn't have minded being convinced that the Sampsons were a dream.

I showed him the picture signed "Fay." "Do you know the face? I have a hunch I've seen it before, and that could mean she's in pictures. She's a histrionic type."

He studied the piece of cardboard. "Superannuated vampire. Fortyish, but the picture's maybe ten years old. Fay Estabrook."

"You know her?"

He stabbed an egg and watched it bleed yellow on his plate. "I've seen her around. She was a star in the Pearl White era."

"What does she do for a living?"

"Nothing much. Lives quietly. She's been married once or twice." He overcame his reluctance and began to eat his eggs.

"Is she married now?"

"I wouldn't know. I don't think her last one took. She makes a little money doing bit parts. Sim Kuntz makes a place for her in his pictures. He was her director in the old days."

"She wouldn't be an astrologist on the side?"

"Could be." He jabbed at his second egg. It humiliated him not to know the answer to a question. "I got no file on her, Lew. She isn't that important any more. But she must have found some income. She makes a moderate splash. I've seen her at Chasen's."

"All by herself, no doubt."

He screwed up his small face, chewing sideways like a camel. "You're picking both lobes, you son of a gun. Do I get paid for wearying my lobes?"

"A fin," I said. "I'm on an expense account." Mrs Cramm hovered breastily over me and poured me another cup of coffee.

"I've seen her more than once with an English remittance-man type."

"Description?"

"White hair, premature, eyes blue or grey. Middle-sized and wiry. Well-dressed. Handsome if you like an ageing chorus boy."

"You know I do. Anybody else?" I couldn't show him Sampson's picture or mention Sampson's name. He was paid for collecting names in groups of two. Very badly paid.

"Once at least. She had late supper with a fat tourist-type dressed in ten-dollar bills. He was so squiffed he had to be helped to the door. That was several months ago. I haven't seen her since."

"And you don't know where she lives?"

"Somewhere out of town. It's off my beat. Anyway, I've given you a fin's worth."

"I won't deny it, but there's one more thing. Is Simeon Kuntz working now?"

"He's doing an independent on the Telepictures lot. She might be out there. I heard they're shooting."

I handed him his bill. He kissed it and pretended to use it to light a cigarette. His wife snatched it out of his hand. When I left they were chasing each other around the kitchen, laughing like a couple of amiable maniacs.

My taxi was waiting in front of the apartment house. I took it home and went to work on the telephone directories for Los Angeles and environs. There was no Fay Estabrook listed.

I called Telepictures in Universal City and asked for Fay Estabrook. The operator didn't know if she was on the lot; she'd have to make inquiries. On a small lot it meant that Fay was definately a has-been where pictures were concerned.

The operator came back to the telephone: "Miss Estabrook is here, but she's working just now. Is there a message?"

"I'll come out. What stage is she on?"

"Number three."

"Is Simeon Kuntz directing?"

"Yes. You have to have a pass, you know."

"I have," I lied.

Before I left I made the mistake of taking off my gun and hanging it away in the hall closet. Its harness was uncomfortable on a hot day, and I didn't expect to be using it. There was a bag of battered golf clubs in the closet. I took them out to the garage and slung them into the back of my car.

Universal City wore its stucco façades like yellowing paper collars. The Telepictures buildings were newer than the rest, but they didn't seem out of place among the rundown bars and seedy restaurants that lined the boulevard. Their plaster walls had a jerry-built look, as if they didn't expect to last.

I parked around the corner in a residential block and lugged my bag of clubs to the main entrance of the studio. There were ten or twelve people sitting on straight-backed chairs outside the casting-office, trying to look sought-after and complacent. A girl in a neat black suit brushed threadbare was taking off her gloves and putting them on. A grim-faced woman sat with a grim-faced little girl on her knee, dressed in pink silk and whining. The usual assortment of displaced actors – fat, thin, bearded, shaven, tuxedoed, sombreroed, sick, alcoholic, and senile – sat there with great dignity, waiting for nothing.

I tore myself away from all that glamour, and went down the dingy hall to the swinging gate. A middle-aged man with a chin like the butt end of a ham was sitting beside the gate in a blue guard's uniform, with a black visored cap on his head and a black holster on his hip. I stopped at the gate, hugging the golf bag as if it meant a great deal to me. The guard half opened his eyes and tried to place me.

Before he could ask anything that might arouse his suspicions, I said: "Mr Kuntz wants these right away."

The guards at the majors asked for passports and visas and did everything but probe the body cavities for concealed hand grenades. The independents were more lax, and I was taking a chance on that.

He pushed open the gate and waved me through. I emerged in a white-hot concrete alley like the entrance to a maze and lost myself among the anonymous buildings. I turned down a dirt road with a sign that said "Western Main Street," and went up to a couple of painters who were painting the weather-warped front of a saloon with a swinging door and no insides.

"Stage three?" I asked them.

"Turn right, then left at the first turn. You'll see the sign across the street from New York Tenement."

I turned right and passed London Street and Pioneer Log Cabin, then left in front of Continental Hotel. The false fronts looked so real from a distance, so ugly and thin close up, that they made me feel suspicious of my own reality. I felt like throwing away the golf bag and going into Continental Hotel for an imitation drink with the other ghosts. But ghosts had no glands, and I was sweating freely. I should have brought something lighter, like a badminton racquet.

When I reached stage three the red light was burning and the soundproof doors were shut. I set the golf bag down against the wall and waited. After a while the light went out. The door opened, and a herd of chorus girls in bunny costumes came out and wandered up the street. I held the door for the last pair and stepped inside.

The interior of the sound stage was a reproduction of a theatre, with red plush orchestra seats and boxes, and gilt rococo decorations. The orchestra pit was empty and the stage was bare, but there was a small audience grouped in the first few rows. A young man in shirt sleeves was adjusting an overhead baby spot. He called for lights, and the baby spot illuminated the head of a woman sitting in the centre of the first row facing a camera. I moved down the side aisle and recognized Fay before the light went out.

The light came on again, a buzzer sounded, and there was a heavy silence in the room. It was broken by the woman's deep voice:

"Isn't he marvellous?"

She turned to a grey-moustached man beside her and gently shook his arm. He smiled and nodded.

"Cut!" A tired-looking little man with a bald head, beautifully clothed in pale-blue gabardines, got up from behind the camera and leaned toward Fay Estabrook. "Look, Fay, you're his mother. He's up there on the stage singing his heart out for you. This is his first big chance; it's what you've hoped and prayed for all these years."

His emotional central European voice was so compelling that I glanced at the stage involuntarily. It was still empty.

"Isn't he marvellous?" the woman said strenuously.

"Better. Better. But remember the question is not a real question. It is a rhetorical question. The accent is on the 'marvellous.'"

"Isn't he marvellous!" the woman cried.

"More accent. More heart, my dear Fay. Pour out your mother love to your son singing so gloriously up there behind the footlight. Try again."

"Isn't he *marvellous*!" the woman yelped viciously.

"No! Sophistication is not the line. You must keep your intelligence out of this. Simplicity. Warm, loving simplicity. Do you get it, my dear Fay?"

She looked angry and distraught. Everyone in the room, from assistant director to prop man, was watching her expectantly. "Isn't he marvellous?" she said throatily.

"Much, much better," said the little man. He called for lights and camera.

"Isn't he marvellous?" she said again. The grey-moustached man smiled and nodded some more. He put his hand over hers, and they smiled into each other's eyes.

"Cut!"

The smiles faded into weary boredom. The lights went out. The little director called for number seventy-seven. "You may go, Fay. To-morrow at eight. And try to get a good night's sleep, darling." The way he said it sounded very unpleasant.

She didn't answer. While a new group of actors was forming in the wings of the theatre stage and a camera rolled toward them, she rose and walked up the central aisle. I followed her out of the gloomy warehouse-like building into the sun.

I stood in the doorway as she walked away, not quickly, with movements a little random and purposeless. In her dowdy costume – black hat with a widow's veil and plain black coat – her big, handsome body looked awkward and ungainly. It may have been the sun in my eyes or simple romanticism, but I had the feeling that the evil which hung in studio air like an odourless gas was concentrated in that heavy black figure wandering up the empty factitious street.

When she was out of sight around the Continental Hotel corner, I picked up the golf bag and followed her. I started to sweat again, and I felt like an ageing caddy, the kind that never quite became a pro.

She had joined a group of half a dozen women of all ages and shapes which was headed for the main entrance. Before they got there, they turned off into an alley. I trotted after them and saw them disappearing under a stucco arch labelled "Dressing Rooms."

I pushed open the swinging gate beside the guard and started out. He remembered me and the golf clubs:

"Didn't he want them?"

"He's going to play badminton instead."

VI

I WAS WAITING when she came out, parked with my motor idling at a yellow curb near the entrance. She turned up the sidewalk in the other direction. She had changed to a well-cut dark suit, a small slanted hat. Will or foundation garments had drawn her body erect. From the rear she looked ten years younger.

Half a block from me she stopped by a black sedan, unlocked it and got in. I eased out in the traffic and let her slide into the lane ahead of me. The sedan was a new Buick. I wasn't concerned about her noticing my car. Los Angeles County was crawling with blue convertibles, and the traffic on the boulevard was a kaleidoscope being shaken.

She added her personal touch to the pattern, cutting in and out of lanes, driving furiously and well. In the overpass I had to touch seventy to keep her in sight. I didn't think she was aware of me; she was doing it for fun. She went down Sunset at a steady fifty, headed for the sea. Fifty-five and sixty on the curves in Beverly Hills. Her heavy car was burning rubber. In my lighter car I was gambling at even odds with centrifugal force. My tyres screeched and shuddered.

On the long, looping final grade sloping down to Pacific Palisades I let her go away from me and almost lost her. I caught her again in the straightaway a minute before she turned off the boulevard to the right.

I followed her up a road marked "Woodlawn Lane", which wound along the hillside. A hundred yards ahead of me as I came out of a curve she swung wide and turned into a driveway. I stopped my car where I was and parked under a eucalyptus tree.

Through the japonica hedge that lined the sidewalk I saw her climb the steps to the door of a white house. She unlocked it and went in. The house was two-storied, set far back from the street among the trees, with an attached garage built into the side of the hill. It was a handsome house for a woman on her way out.

After a while I got tired of watching the unopening door. I took off my coat and tie, folded them over the back of the seat, and rolled up my sleeves. There was a long-spouted oil-can in the trunk, and I took it with me. I walked straight up the driveway past the Buick and into the open door of the garage.

The garage was enormous, big enough to hold a two-ton truck with space for the Buick to spare. The queer thing was that it looked as if a heavy truck had recently been there. There were wide tyre marks on the concrete floor, and thick oil drippings.

A small window high in the rear wall of the garage looked out on the back yard just above the level of the ground. A heavy-shouldered man in a scarlet silk sport shirt was sitting in a canvas deck chair with his back to me. His short hair looked thicker and blacker than Ralph Sampson's should have. I raised myself on my toes and pressed my face against the glass. Even through its dingy surface the scene was as vivid as paint: the broad, unconscious back of the man in the scarlet shirt, the brown bottle of beer and the bowl of salted peanuts in the grass beside him, the orange tree over his head hung with unripe oranges like dark-green golf balls.

He leaned sideways, the crooked fingers of his large hand groping for the bowl of peanuts. The hand missed the bowl and scrabbled in the grass like a crippled lobster. Then he turned his head, and I saw the side of his face. It wasn't Ralph Sampson's, and it wasn't the face the man in the scarlet shirt had started out with. It was a stone face hacked out by a primitive sculptor. It told a very common twentieth-century story:

too many fights, too many animal guts, not enough brains.

I returned to the tyre marks and went down on my knees to examine them. Too late to do anything but stay where I was, I heard shuffling footsteps on the driveway.

The man in the scarlet shirt said from the door: "What business you got messing around in here? You got no business messing around in here."

I inverted the oilcan and squirted a stream of oil at the wall. "Get out of my light, please."

"What's that?" he said laboriously. His upper lip was puffed thick as a mouth guard.

He was no taller than I was, and he wasn't as wide as the door, but he gave that impression. He made me nervous, the way you feel talking to a strange bulldog on his master's property. I stood up.

"Yes," I said. "You certainly got them, brother."

I didn't like the way he moved towards me. His left shoulder was forward and his chin in, as if every hour of his day was divided into twenty three-minute rounds.

"What do you mean, we got them? We ain't got nothing, but you get yourself some trouble you come selling your woof around here."

"Termites," I said rapidly. He was close enough to let me smell his breath. Beer and salted peanuts and bad teeth. "You tell Mrs Goldsmith she's got them for sure."

"Termites?" He was flat on his heels. I could have knocked him down, but he wouldn't have stayed down.

"The tiny animals that eat wood." I squirted more oil at the wall. "The little muckers."

"What you got in that there can? That there can."

"This here can?"

"Yeah." I'd established rapport.

"It's termite killer," I said. "They eat it and they die. You tell Mrs Goldsmith she's got them all right."

"I don't know no Mrs Goldsmith."

"The lady of the house. She called up headquarters for an inspection."

"Headquarters?" he said suspiciously. His scar-tissue-padded brows descended over his little empty eyes like shutters.

"Termite-control headquarters. Killabug is termite-control

headquarters for the Southern California area."

"Oh!" He was puzzling over the works. "Yeah. But we got no Mrs Goldsmith here."

"Isn't this Eucalyptus Lane?"

"Naw, this is Woodlawn Lane. You got the wrong address, bud."

"I'm awfully sorry," I said. "I thought this was Eucalyptus Lane."

"Naw, Woodlawn." He smiled widely at my ridiculous mistake.

"I better be going then. Mrs Goldsmith will be looking for me."

"Yeah. Only wait a minute."

His left hand came out fast and took me by the collar. He cocked his right. "Don't come messing around in here any more. You got no business messing around in here."

His face filled out with angry blood. His eyes were hot and wild. There was a bright seepage of saliva at the cracked and folded corners of his mouth. A punchy fighter was less predictable than a bulldog, and twice as dangerous.

"Look." I raised the can. "This stuff will blind you."

I squirted oil in his eyes. He let out a howl of imaginary agony. I jerked sideways. His right went by my ear and left it burning. My shirt collar ripped loose and dangled from his clenched hand. He spread his right hand over his oil-doused eyes and moaned like a baby. Blindness was the one thing he feared.

A door opened behind me when I was halfway down the drive, but I didn't show my face by looking back. I ducked around the corner of the hedge and kept running, away from my car. I circled the block on foot.

When I came back to the convertible the road was deserted. The garage doors were closed, but the Buick was still standing in the drive. The white house among its trees looked very peaceful and innocent in the early evening light.

It was nearly dark when the lady of the house came out in a spotted ocelot coat. I passed the entrance to the drive before the Buick backed out, and waited for it on Sunset Boulevard. She drove with greater fury and less accuracy all the way back to Hollywood, through Westwood, Bel-Air, Beverly Hills. I kept her in sight.

Near the corner of Hollywood and Vine, where everything ends and a great many things begin, she turned into a private parking lot and left her car. I double-parked in the street till I saw her enter Swift's, a gaudy figure walking like a slightly elated lady. Then I went home and changed my shirt.

The gun in my closet tempted me, but I didn't put it on. I compromised by taking it out of the holster and putting it in the glove compartment of my car.

VII

THE BACK ROOM of Swift's was panelled in black oak that glowed dimly under the polished brass chandeliers. It was lined on two sides with leather-cushioned booths. The rest of the floor space was covered with tables. All of the booths and most of the tables were crowded with highly dressed people eating or waiting to be fed. Most of the women were tight-skinned, starved too thin for their bones. Most of the men had the masculine Hollywood look, which was harder to describe. An insistent self-consciousness in their loud words and wide gestures, as if God had a million-dollar contract to keep an eye on them.

Fay Estabrook was in a back booth, with a blue flannel elbow on the table opposite her. The rest of her companion was hidden by the partition.

I went to the bar against the third wall and ordered a beer.

"Bass ale, Black Horse, Carta Blanca or Guinness stout? We don't serve domestic beer after six o'clock."

I ordered Bass, gave the bartender a dollar and told him to keep the change. There wasn't any change. He went away.

I leaned forward to look in the mirror behind the bar and caught a three-quarters view of Fay Estabrook's face. It was earnest and intense. The mouth was moving rapidly. Just then the man stood up.

He was the kind who was usually in the company of younger women, the neat and ageless kind who turned a dollar year after year at nobody knew what. He was the ageing chorus boy Cramm had described. His blue jacket fitted him too well. A white silk scarf at his throat set off his silver hair.

He was shaking hands with a red-haired man who was standing by the booth. I recognized the red-haired man when he turned and wandered back to his own table in the centre of the room. He was a contract writer for Metro named Russell Hunt.

The silver-haired man waved good-bye to Fay Estabrook and set his course for the door. I watched him in the mirror. He walked efficiently and neatly, looking straight ahead as if the place was deserted. As far as he was concerned it was deserted. Nobody lifted a hand or raised a lip over teeth. When he went out a few heads turned, a couple of eyebrows were elevated. Fay Estabrook was left in her booth by herself as if she had caught his infection and could communicate it.

I carried my glass to Russell Hunt's table. He was sitting with a fat man who had a round ugly nose turned up at the,tip and bright little agent's eyes.

"How's the word business, Russell?"

"Hello, Lew."

He wasn't glad to see me. I earned three hundred a week when I was working, and that made me one of the peasantry. He made fifteen hundred. An ex-reporter from Chicago who had sold his first novel to Metro and never written another, Hunt was turning from a hopeful kid to a nasty old man with the migraine and a swimming pool he couldn't use because he was afraid of water. I had helped him lose his second wife to make way for his third, who was no improvement.

"Sit down, sit down," he said, when I didn't go away. "Have a drink. It dissipates the megrims. I do not drink to dissipate myself. I dissipate the megrims."

"Hold it," said agent eyes. "If you're a creative artist you may sit down. Otherwise I can hardly be expected to waste my time with you."

"Timothy is my agent," Russell said. "I am the goose that lays his golden eggs. Observe his nervous fingers toying with the steak knife, his eyes fastened wistfully upon my rounded throat. Boding me no good, I ween."

"He weens," said Timothy. "Do you create?"

I slid into the patois and a chair. "I am a man of action. A sleuth hound, to wit."

"Lew's a detective," Russell said. "He unearths people's

guilty secrets and exposes them to the eyes of a scandalized world."

"Now, how low can you get?" asked Timothy cheerfully.

I didn't like the crack, but I'd come for information, not exercise. He saw the look on my face and turned to the waiter who was standing by his chair.

"Who was that you were shaking hands with?" I asked Russell.

"The elegant lad in the scarf? Fay said his name was Troy. They were married at one time, so she ought to know.

"What does he do?"

"I wouldn't know for sure. I've seen him around: Palm Springs, Las Vegas, Tia Juana."

"Las Vegas?"

"I think so. Fay says he's an importer, but if he's an importer I'm a monkey's uncle." He remembered his role. "Curiously enough, I am a monkey's uncle, though I must confess that no one was more suprised than I when my younger sister, the one with three breasts, gave birth last Whitsuntide to the cutest little chimpanzee you ever did see. She was Lady Greystoke by her first marriage, you know."

His patter ceased abruptly. His face became grim and miserable again. "Another drink," he said to the waiter. "A double Scotch. Make it the same all round."

"Just a minute, sir." The waiter was a wizened old man with black thumbtack eyes. "I'm taking this gentleman's order."

"He won't serve me." Russell flung out his arms in a burlesque gesture of despair. "I'm eighty-six again."

The waiter pretended to be absorbed in what Timothy was saying.

"But I don't want French fried potatoes. I want au gratin potatoes."

"We don't have au gratin, sir."

"You can make them, can't you?" Timothy said, his rettoussé nostrils flaring.

"Thirty-five or forty minutes, sir."

"O God!" Timothy said. "What kind of a beanery is this? Let's go to Chasen's, Russell. I got to have au gratin potatoes."

The waiter stood watching him as if from a great distance. I glanced around him and saw that Fay Estabrook was still at her table, working on a bottle of wine.

"They don't let me into Chasen's any more," Russell said. "On account of I am an agent of the Cominform. I wrote a movie with a Nazi for a villain, so I am an agent of the Cominform. That's where my money comes from, friends. It's tainted Moscow gold."

"Cut it out," I said. "Do you know Fay Estabrook?"

"A little. I passed her on the way up a few years ago. A few more years, and I'll pass her on the way down."

"Introduce me to her."

"Why?"

"I've always wanted to meet her."

"I don't get it, Lew. She's old enough to be your wife."

I said in a language he could understand: "I have a sentimental regard for her, stemming from the dear dead days beyond recall."

"Introduce him if he wants," said Timothy. "Sleuth hounds make me nervous. Then I can eat my au gratin potatoes in peace."

Russell got up laboriously, as if the top of his red head supported the ceiling.

"Good night," I said to Timothy. "Have fun with the hired help before they throw you out on your fat neck."

I picked up my drink and steered Russell across the room. "Don't tell her my business," I said in his ear.

"Who am I to wash your dirty linen in public? In private it's another matter. I'd love to wash your dirty linen in private. It's a fetish with me."

"I throw it away when it's dirty."

"But what a waste. Please save it for me in future. Just send it to me care of Krafft-Ebing at the clinic."

Mrs Estabrook looked up at us with eyes like dark searchlights.

"This is Lew Archer, Fay. The agent. Of the Communist International, that is. He's an old admirer of yours in his secret heart."

"How nice!" she said, in a voice that was wasted on mother roles. "Won't you sit down?"

"Thank you." I sat down in the leather seat opposite her.

"Excuse me," Russell said. "I have to look after Timothy.

He's waging a class war with the waiter. To-morrow night it's his turn to look after me. Oh goody!" He went away, lost in his private maze of words.

"It's nice to be remembered occasionally," the woman said. "Most of my friends are gone, and all of them are forgotten. Helene and Florence and Mae – all of them gone and forgotten."

Her winy sentimentality, half phony and half real, was a pleasant change in a way from Russell's desperate double-talk. I took my cue.

"*Sic transit gloria mundi.* Helene Chadwick was a great player in her day. But you're still carrying on."

"I try to keep my hand in, Archer. The life has gone out of the town, though. We used to care about picture-making – really care. I made three grand a week at my peak, but it wasn't the money we worked for."

"The play's the thing." It was less embarrassing to quote.

"The play *was* the thing. It isn't like that any more. The town has lost its sincerity. No life left in it. No life left in either it or me."

She poured the final ounce from her half bottle of sherry and drank it down in one long mournful swallow. I nursed my drink.

"You're doing all right." I let my glance slide down the heavy body half revealed by the open fur coat. It was good for her age, tight-waisted, high-bosomed, with amphora hips. And it was alive, with a subtly persistent female power, an animal pride like a cat's.

"I like you, Mr Archer. You're sympathetic. Tell me, when were you born?"

"What year, you mean?"

"The date."

"The second of June."

"Really? I didn't expect you to be Geminian. Geminis have no heart. They're double-souled like the Twins, and they lead a double life. Are you coldhearted, Archer?"

She leaned toward me with wide, unfocused eyes. I couldn't tell whether she was kidding me of herself.

"I'm everybody's friend," I said, to break the spell. "Children and dogs adore me. I raise flowers and have green thumbs."

"You're a cynic," she answered sulkily. "I thought you were going to by sympathetic, but you're in the Air triplicity and

I'm in the Water."

"We'd make a wonderful air-sea rescue team."

She smiled and said chidingly: "Don't you believe in the stars?"

"Do you?"

"Of course I do – in a purely scientific way. When you look at the evidence, you simply can't deny it. I'm Cancer, for example, and anybody can see that I'm the Cancer type. I'm sensitive and imaginative; I can't do without love. The people I love can twist me around their little finger, but I can be stubborn when I have to be. I've been unlucky in marriage, like so many other Cancerians. Are you married, Archer?"

"Not now."

"That means you were. You'll marry again. Gemini always does. And he often marries a woman older than himself, did you know that?"

"No." Her insistent voice was pushing me slighly off balance, threatening to dominate the conversation and me. "You're very convincing," I said.

"What I'm telling you is the truth."

"You should do it professionally. There's money in it for a smooth operator with a convincing spiel."

Her candid eyes narrowed to two dark slits like peepholes in a fort. She studied me through them, made a tactical decision, and opened them wide again. They were dark pools of innocence, like poisoned wells.

"Oh, no," she said. "I never do this professionally. It's a talent I have, a gift – Cancer is frequently psychic – and I feel it's my duty to use it. But not for money – only for my friends."

"You're lucky to have an independent income."

Her thin-stemmed glass twirled out of her fingers and broke in two pieces on the table. "That's Gemini for you," she said. "Always looking for facts."

I felt a slight twinge of doubt and shrugged it off. She'd fired at random and hit the target by accident. "I didn't mean to be curious," I said.

"Oh, I know that." She rose suddenly, and I felt the weight of her body standing over me. "Let's get out of here, Archer. I'm starting to drop things again. Let's go some place we can talk."

"Why not?"

She left an unbroken bill on the table and walked out with heavy dignity. I followed her, pleased with my startling success but feeling a little like a male spider about to be eaten by a female spider.

Russell was at his table with his head in his arms. Timothy was yelping at the captain of waiters like a terrier who has cornered some small defenceless animal. The captain of waiters was explaining that the au gratin potatoes would be ready in fifteen minutes.

VIII

IN THE HOLLYWOOD ROOSEVELT BAR she complained of the air and said she felt wretched and old. Nonsense, I told her, but we moved to the Zebra Room. She had shifted to Irish whiskey, which she drank straight. In the Zebra Room she accused a man at the next table of looking at her contemptuously. I suggested more air. She drove down Wilshire as if she was trying to break through into another dimension. I had to park the Buick for her at the Ambassador. I'd left my car at Swift's.

She quarrelled with the Ambassador doorman on the grounds that he laughed at her when he turned his back. I took her to the downstairs bar at the Huntoon Park, which wasn't often crowded. Wherever we went, there were people who recognized her, but nobody joined us or stood up. Not even the waiters made a fuss over her. She was on her way out.

Except for a couple leaning together at the other end of the bar, the Huntoon Park was deserted. The thickly carpeted, softly lighted basement was a funeral parlour where the evening we had killed was laid out. Mrs Estabrook was pale as a corpse, but she was vertical, able to see, talk, drink, and possibly even think.

I was steering her in the direction of the Valerio, hoping that she'd name it. A few more drinks, and I could take the risk of suggesting it myself. I was drinking with her, but not enough to affect me. I made inane conversation, and she didn't notice the difference. I was waiting. I wanted her far enough gone to say whatever came into her head. Archer the heavenly twin and midwife to oblivion.

I looked at my face in the mirror behind the bar and didn't like it too well. It was getting thin and predatory looking. My nose was too narrow, my ears were too close to my head. My eyelids were the kind that overlapped at the outside corners and made my eyes look triangular in a way that I usually liked. Tonight my eyes were like tiny stone wedges hammered between the lids.

She leaned forward over the bar with her chin in her hands, looking straight down into her half-empty liqueur glass. The pride that had kept her body erect and organized her face had seeped away. She was hunched there tasting the bitterness at the bottom of her life, droning out elegies:

"He never took care of himself, but he had the body of a wrestler and the head of an Indian chief. He was part Indian. Nothing mean about him, though. One sweet guy. Quiet and easy, never talked much. But passionate, and a real one-woman man, the last I ever seen. He got T.B. and went off in one summer. It broke me up. I never got over it since. He was the only man I ever loved."

"What did you say his name was?"

"Bill." She looked at me slyly. "I didn't say. He was my foreman. I had one of the first big places in the valley. We were together for a year, and then he died. That was twenty-five years ago, and I been feeling ever since I might as well be dead myself."

She raised her large tearless eyes and met my glance in the mirror. I wanted to respond to her melancholy look, but I didn't know what to do with my face.

I tried smiling to encourage myself. I was a good Joe after all. Consorter with roughnecks, tarts, hard cases and easy marks; private eye at the keyhole of illicit bedrooms; informer to jealousy, rat behind the walls, hired gun to anybody with fifty dollars a day; but a good Joe after all. The wrinkles formed at the corner of my eyes, the wings of my nose; the lips drew back from the teeth, but there was no smile. All I got was a lean famished look like a coyote's sneer. The face had seen too many bars, too many rundown hotels and crummy love nests, too many courtrooms and prisons, post-mortems and police lineups, too many nerve ends showing like tortured worms. If I found the face on a stranger, I wouldn't trust it. I caught myself wondering how it looked to Miranda Sampson.

"To hell with the three-day parties," Mrs Estabrook said. "To hell with the horses and the emeralds and the boats. One good friend is better than any of them, and I haven't got one good friend. Sim Kuntz said he was my friend, and he tells me I'm making my last picture. I lived my life twenty-five years ago, and I'm all washed up. You don't want to get mixed up with me, Archer."

She was right. Still, I was interested, apart from my job. She'd had a long journey down from a high place, and she knew what suffering was. Her voice had dropped its phony correctness and the other things she had learned from studio coaches. It was coarse and pleasantly harsh. It placed her childhood in Detroit or Chicago or Indianapolis, at the beginning of the century, on the wrong side of town.

She drained her glass and stood up. "Take me home, Archer."

I slid off my stool with gigolo alacrity and took her by the arm. "You can't go home like this. You need another drink to snap you back."

"You're nice." My skin was thin enough to feel the irony. "Only I can't take this place. It's a morgue. For Christ's sake," she yelled at the bartender, "where are all the merrymakers?"

"Aren't you a merrymaker, madam?

I pulled her away from the start of another quarrel, up the steps and out. There was a light fog in the air, blurring the neons. Above the tops of the buildings the starless sky was dull and low. She shivered, and I felt the tremor in her arm.

"There's a good bar next street up," I said.

"The Valerio?"

"I think that's it."

"All right. One more drink, then I got to go home."

I opened the door of her car and helped her in. Her breast leaned against my shoulder heavily. I moved back. I preferred a less complicated kind of pillow, stuffed with feathers, not memories and frustrations.

The waitress in the Valerio cantina called her by name, escorted us to a booth, emptied the empty ash tray. The bartender, a smooth-faced young Greek, came all the way around from behind the bar to say hello to her and to ask after Mr Sampson.

"He's still in Nevada," she said. I was watching her face, and she caught my look. "A very good friend of mine. He stops here when he's in town."

The two-block ride, or her welcome, had done her good. She was almost sprightly. Maybe I'd made a mistake.

"A great old guy," the bartender said. "We miss him around here."

"Ralph's a wonderful, wonderful man," said Mrs Estabrook. "One sweet guy."

The bartender took our order and went away.

"Have you cast his horoscope?" I said. "This friend of yours?"

"Now, how did you know? He's Capricorn. One sweet guy, but a very dominant type. He's had a tragedy in his life, though. His only boy was killed in the war. Ralph's sun was squared by Uranus, you see. You wouldn't know what that can mean to a Capricornian."

"No. Does it mean much to him?"

"Yes, it does. Ralph has been developing his spiritual side. Uranus is against him, but the other planets are with him. It's given him courage to know that." She leaned toward me confidentially. "I wish I could show you the room I redecorated for him. It's in one of the bungalows here, but they wouldn't let us in."

"Is he staying here now?"

"No, he's in Nevada. He has a very lovely home on the desert."

"Ever been there?"

"You ask so many questions." She smiled side-eyed in ghastly coquetry. "You wouldn't be getting jealous?"

"You told me you had no friends."

"Did I say that? I was forgetting Ralph."

The bartender brought our drinks, and I sipped mine. I was facing the back of the room. A door in the wall beside the silent grand piano opened into the Valerio lobby. Alan Taggert and Miranda came through the door together.

"Excuse me," I said to Mrs Estabrook.

Miranda saw me when I stood up, and started forward. I put a finger to my mouth and waved her back with the other hand. She moved away with a wide-mouthed, bewildered look.

Alan was quicker. He took her arm and hustled her out the door. I followed them. The bartender was mixing a drink. The waitress was serving a customer. Mrs Estabrook hadn't looked up. The door closed behind me.

Miranda turned on me. "I don't understand this. You're supposed to be looking for Ralph."

"I'm working on a contact. Go away, please."

"But I've been trying to get in touch with you." She was strained to the point of tears.

I said to Taggert: "Take her away before she spoils my night's work. Out of the city, if possible." Three hours of Fay had sharpened my temper.

"But Mrs Sampson's been phoning for you," he said.

A Filipino bellboy was standing against the wall hearing everything we said. I took them around the corner into the half-lit lobby. "What about?"

"She's heard from Ralph." Miranda's eyes glowed amber like a deer's. "A special-delivery letter. He wants her to send him money. Not send it exactly, but have it ready for him."

"How much money?"

"A hundred thousand dollars."

"Say that again."

"He wants her to cash a hundred thousand dollars' worth of bonds."

"Does she have that much?"

"*She* hasn't, but she can get it. Bert Graves has Ralph's power of attorney."

"What's she supposed to do with the money?"

"He said we'll hear from him again or he'll send a messenger for it."

"You're sure the letter's from him?"

"Elaine says it's in his writing."

"Does he say where he is?"

"No, but the letter's postmarked Santa Maria. He must have been there to-day."

"Not necessarily. What does Mrs Sampson want me to do?"

"She didn't say. I suppose she wants your advice."

"All right, this is it. Tell her to have the money ready, but not to hand it over to anybody without proof that your father's alive."

"You think he's dead?" Her hand plucked at the neckline of her dress.

"I can't afford to guess." I turned to Taggert. "Can you fly Miranda up to-night?"

"I just phoned Santa Teresa. The airport's fogged in. First thing in the morning, though."

"Then tell her over the phone. I have a possible lead and I'm following it up. Graves had better contact the police, quietly. The local police and the Los Angeles police. And the F.B.I."

"The F.B.I.?" Miranda whispered.

"Yes," I said. "Kidnapping is a federal offence."

IX

When I went back to the bar, a young Mexican in a tuxedo was leaning against the piano with a guitar. His small tenor, plaintive and remote, was singing a Spanish bullfighting song. His fingers marched thunderously in the strings. Mrs Estabrook was watching him and barely noticed me when I sat down.

She clapped loudly when the song was finished, and beckoned him to our booth. "*Bábalu.* Pretty please." She handed him a dollar.

He bowed and smiled and returned to his singing.

"It's Ralph's favourite song," she said. "Domingo sings it so well. He's got real Spanish blood in his veins."

"About this friend of yours, Ralph."

"What about him?"

"He wouldn't object to you being here with me?"

"Don't be silly. I want you to meet him some time. I know you'll like him."

"What does he do?"

"He's more or less retired. He's got money."

"Why don't you marry him?"

She laughed harshly. "Didn't I tell you I had a husband? But you don't have to worry about *him.* It's purely a business proposition."

"I didn't know you were in business."

"Did I say I was in business?" She laughed again, much too alertly, and changed the subject: "It's funny you suggested I should marry Ralph. We're both married to other people. Anyway, our friendship is on a different level. You know, more spiritual."

She was sobering up on me. I raised my glass. "To friendship. On a different level."

While she was still drinking, I held up two fingers to the waitress. The second drink fixed her.

Her face went to pieces as if by its own weight. Her eyes went dull and unblinking. Her mouth hung open in a fixed yawn, the scarlet lips contrasting with the pink-and-white interior. She brought it together numbly and whispered: "I don't feel so good."

"I'll take you home."

"You're nice."

I helped her to her feet. The waitress held the door open, with a condoning smile for Mrs Estabrook and a sharp glance at me. Mrs Estabrook stumbled across the sidewalk like an old woman leaning on a cane that wasn't there. I held her up on her anæsthetized legs, and we made it to the car.

Getting her in was like loading a sack of coal. Her head rolled into the corner between the door and the back of the seat. I started the car and headed for Pacific Palisades.

The motion of the car revived her after a while. "Got to get home," she said dully. "You know where I live?"

"You told me."

"Got to climb on the treadmill in the morning. Crap! I should weep if he throws me out of pictures. I got independent means."

"You look like a businesswoman," I said encouragingly.

"You're nice, Archer." The line was beginning to get me down. "Taking care of an old hag like me. You wouldn't like me if I told you where I got my money."

"Try me."

"But I'm not telling you." Her laugh was ugly and loose, in a low register. I thought I caught overtones of mockery in it, but they may have been in my head. "You're too nice a boy."

Yeah, I said to myself, a clean-cut American type. Always willing to lend a hand to help a lady fall flat in the gutter.

The lady passed out again. At least she said nothing more. It was a lonely drive down the midnight boulevard with her half-conscious body. In the spotted coat it was like a sleeping animal beside me in the seat, a leopard or a wildcat heavy with age. It wasn't really old – fifty at the most – but it was full of the years, full and fermenting with bad memories. She'd told me a number of things about herself, but not what I wanted to know, and I was too sick of her to probe deeper. The one sure thing I knew about her she hadn't had to tell me: she was bad company for Sampson or any incautious man. Her playmates were dangerous – one rough, one smooth. And if anything had happened to Sampson she'd know it or find out.

She was awake when I parked in front of her house. "Put the car in the drive. Would you, honey?"

I backed across the road and took the car up the driveway. She needed help to climb the steps to the door, and handed me the key to open it. "You come in. I been trying to think of something I want to drink."

"You're sure it's all right? Your husband?"

Laughter growled in her throat. "We haven't lived together for years."

I followed her into the hallway. It was thick with darkness and her two odours, musk and alcohol, half animal and half human. I felt slippery waxed floors under my feet and wondered if she'd fall. She moved in her own house with the blind accuracy of a sleepwalker. I felt my way after her into a room to the left, where she switched on a lamp.

The room it brought out of darkness was nothing like the insane red room she had made for Ralph Sampson. It was big and cheerful, even at night behind closed Venetian blinds. A solid middle-class room with post-Impressionist reproductions on the walls, built-in bookshelves, books on them, a radio-phonograph and a record cabinet, a glazed brick fireplace with a heavy sectional chesterfield curved in front of it. The only strangeness was in the pattern of the cloth that covered the chesterfield and the armchair under the lamp: brilliant green tropical plants against a white desert sky, with single eyes staring between the fronds. The pattern changed as I looked at it. The eyes disappeared and reappeared again. I sat down on a batch of them.

She was at the portable bar in the corner beside the fire place. "What are you drinking?"

"Whiskey and water."

She brought me my glass. Half of its contents slopped out en route, leaving a trail of dark splotches across the light-green carpet. She sat down beside me, depressing the cushioned seat. Her dark head swayed toward my shoulder and lodged there. I could see the few iron-grey strands the hairdresser had left in her hair so it wouldn't look dyed.

"I can't think of anything I want to drink," she whined. "Don't let me fall."

I put one arm around her shoulders, which were almost as wide as mine. She leaned hard against me. I felt the stir and swell of her breathing, gradually slowing down.

"Don't try to do anything to me, honey, I'm dead to-night. Some other night. . . ." Her voice was soft and somehow girlish, but blurred. Blurred like the submarine glints of youth in her eyes.

Her eyes closed. I could see the faint tremor of her heartbeat in the veins of her withering eyelids. Their fringe of curved dark lashes was a vestige of youth and beauty which made her ruin seem final and hard. It was easier to feel sorry for her when she was sleeping.

To make certain that she was, I gently raised one of her eyelids. The marbled eyeball stared whitely at nothing. I took away my arm and let her body subside on the cushions. Her breasts hung askew. Her stockings were twisted. She began to snore.

I went into the next room, closed the door behind me, and turned on the light. It shone down from the ceiling on a bleached mahogany refectory table with artificial flowers in the centre, a china cabinet at one side, a built-in buffet at the other, six heavy chairs ranged around the wall on their haunches. I turned the light off and went into the kitchen, which was neat and well equipped.

I wondered for an instant if I had misjudged the woman. There were honest astrologists – and plenty of harmless drunks. Her house was like a hundred thousand others in Los Angeles County, almost too typical to be true. Except for the huge garage and the bulldog that guarded it.

The bathroom had walls of pastel-blue tile and a square blue tub. The cabinet over the sink was stuffed and heaped with tonics and patent medicines, creams and paints and powders, luminol, nembutal, veronal. The hypochondriac bottles and boxes overflowed on the back of the sink, the laundry hamper, and the toilet top. The clothes in the hamper were female. There was only one toothbrush in the holder. A razor but no shaving cream, nor any other trace of a man.

The bedroom next to the bathroom was flowered and prettied in pink like a prewar sentimental hope. There was a book on the stars on the bedside table. The clothes in the closet were women's, and there were a great many of them, with Saks and Magnin labels. The undergarments and nightclothes in the chest of drawers were peach and baby blue and black lace.

I looked under the twisted mass of stockings in the second drawer and found the core of the strangeness in the house. It was a row of narrow packages held together with elastic bands. The packages contained money, all in bills, ones and fives and tens. Most of the bills were old and greasy. If all the packages assayed like the one I examined, the bottom of the drawer was lined with eight or ten thousand dollars.

I sat on my heels and looked at all that money. A bedroom drawer was hardly a good place to keep it. But it was safer than a bank for people who couldn't declare their income.

The burring ring of a telephone cut the silence like a dentist's drill. It struck a nerve, and I jumped. But I shut the drawer before I went into the hall where the telephone was. There was no sound from the woman in the living-room.

I muffled my voice with my tie. "Hello."

"Mr Troy?" It was a woman.

"Yes."

"Is Fay there?" Her speech was rapid and clipped. "This is Betty."

"No."

"Listen, Mr Troy. Fay was fried in the Valerio about an hour ago. The man she was with could be plain-clothes. He said he was taking her home. You wouldn't want him around when the truck goes through. And you know Fay when she's oiled."

"Yes," I said, and risked: "Where are you now?"

"The Piano, of course."

"Is Ralph Sampson there?"

Her answer was a hiccup of suprise. She was silent for a moment. At the other end of the line I could hear the murmur of people, the clatter of dishes. Probably a restaurant.

She recovered her voice: "Why ask me? I haven't seen him lately?"

"Where is he?"

"I don't know. Who is this talking? Mr Troy?"

"Yes. I'll attend to Fay." I hung up.

The knob on the front door rattled slightly behind me. I froze with my hand on the telephone and watched the cut-glass knob as it slowly rotated, sparkling in the light from the living-room. The door swung open suddenly, and a man in a light topcoat stood in the opening. His silver head was hatless. He stepped inside like an actor coming on stage, shutting the door neatly with his left hand. His right hand was in the pocket of the topcoat. The pocket was pointed at me.

I faced him. "Who are you?"

"I know it isn't polite to answer one question with another." His voice was softened by a trace of south-of-England accent a long way from home. "But who are you?"

"If this is a stickup. . ."

The weight in his pocket nodded at me dumbly. He became more peremptory. "I asked you a simple quesion, old chap. Give me a simple answer."

"The name is Archer," I said. "Do you use bluing when you wash your hair? I had an aunt who said it was very effective."

His face didn't change. He showed his anger by speaking more precisely. "I dislike superfluous violence. Please don't make it necessary."

I could look down on the top of his head, see the scalp shining through the carefully parted hair. "You terrify me," I said. "An Italiante Englishman is a devil incarnate."

But the gun in his pocket was a small intense refrigerating unit cooling off the hallway. His eyes had already turned to ice.

"And what do you do for a living, Mr Archer?"

"I sell insurance. My hobby is stooging for gunmen." I reached for my wallet to show him my "insurance of all descriptions" card.

"No, keep your hands where I can see them. And guard your

tongue, won't you?"

"Gladly. Don't expect me to sell you insurance. You're not a good risk, toting a gun in L.A."

The words went over his head and left it ruffled. "What are you doing here, Mr Archer?"

"I brought Fay home."

"Are you a friend of hers?"

"Apparently. Are you?"

"I'll ask the questions. What do you plan to do next?"

"I was just going to call a taxi and go home."

"Perhaps you had better do that now," he said.

I picked up the receiver and called a Yellow Cab. He moved toward me lightly. His left hand palpated my chest and armpits, moved down my flanks and hips. I was glad I'd left my gun in the car, but I hated to be touched by him. His hands were epicene.

He stepped back and showed me his gun, a nickel-plated revolver, .32 or .38 calibre. I was calculating my chances of kicking him off balance and taking it.

His body stiffened slightly, and the gun came into focus like an eye. "No," he said. "I'm a quick shot, Mr Archer. You'd stand no chance at all. Now turn around."

I turned. He jammed the gun into my back above the kidneys. "Into the bedroom."

He marched me into the lighted bedroom and turned me to face the door. I heard his quick feet cross the room, a drawer open and shut. The gun came back to my kidneys.

"What were you doing in here?"

"I wasn't in here. Fay turned on the light."

"Where is she now?"

"In the front room."

He walked me into the room where Mrs Estabrook was lying, hidden by the back of the chesterfield. She had sunk into a stuporous sleep that resembled death. Her mouth was open, but she was no longer snoring. One of her arms hung down to the floor like an overfed white snake.

He looked at her with contempt, the contempt that silver might feel for sodden flesh.

"She never could hold her liquor."

"We were pub-crawling," I said. "We had a wizard do."

He looked at me sharply. "Evidently. Now why should you be interested in a bag of worms like this?"

"You're talking about the woman I love."

"My wife." A slight twitch of his nostrils proved that his face could move.

"Really?"

"I'm not a jealous man, Mr Archer, but I must warn you to keep away from her. She has her own small circle of associates, and you simply wouldn't fit in. Fay's very tolerant, of course. I am less tolerant. Some of her associates aren't tolerant in the least."

"Are they all as wordy as you?"

He showed his small, regular teeth and subtly changed his posture. His torso leaned, and his head sideways with it, glinting in the light. He was an obscene shape, a vicious boy alert and eager behind an old man's mask. The gun twirled on his finger like a silver wheel and came to rest pointed at my heart. "They have other ways of expressing themselves. Do I make myself clear?"

"The idea is a simple one to grasp." The sweat was cold on my back.

A car honked in the street. He went to the door and held it open for me. It was warmer outside.

X

"I'M GLAD I CALLED in," the driver said. "Saves me a dry run. I had a long haul out to Malibu. Four pigs called out to a beach party. They'll never get near the water."

The back of the cab still had a hothouse odour.

"You should have heard those women talk." He slowed for the stop sign at Sunset. "Going back to town?"

"Wait a minute." He stopped.

"Do you know a place called the Piano?"

"The Wild Piano?" he said. "In West Hollywood. Sort of a bottle joint."

"Who runs it?"

"They never showed me their books," he said airily, shifting into gear. "You want to go there?"

"Why not?" I said. "The night is young." I was lying. The night was old and chilly, with a slow heartbeat. The tyres whined like starved cats on the fog-sprinkled black-top. The neons along the Strip glared with insomnia.

The night was no longer young at the Wild Piano, but her heartbeat was artificially stimulated. It was on a badly lit sidestreet among a row of duplexes shouldering each other across garbage-littered alleys. It had no sign, no plastic-and-plate-glass front. An arch of weather-browned stucco, peeling away like scabs, curved over the entrance. Above it a narrow balcony with a wrought-iron railing masked heavily curtained windows.

A negro doorman in uniform came out from under the arch and opened the door of the cab. I paid off the driver and followed him in. In the dim light from over the door I could see that the nap of his blue coat was worn down to the bare fibre. The brown leather door had been stained black around the handle by the pressure of many sweating hands. It opened into a deep, narrow room like a tunnel.

Another Negro in a waiter's jacket, a napkin over his arm, came to the door to meet me. His smile-stretched lips were indigo in the blue light that emanated from the walls. The walls were decorated with monochromatic blue nudes in various postures. There were white-clothed tables along them on either side, with an aisle between. A woman was playing a piano on a low platform at the far end of the room. She looked unreal through the smoke, a mechanical doll with clever hands and a rigid immovable back.

I handed my hat to the hat-check girl in a cubbyhole and asked for a table near the piano. The waiter skidded ahead of me down the aisle, his napkin fluttering like a pennon, trying to create the illusion that business was brisk. It wasn't. Two thirds of the tables were empty. The rest were occupied by couples. The men were a representative off-scouring of the better bars, putting off going home. Fat and thin, they were fish-faced in the blue acquarium light, fish-faced and oyster-eyed.

Most of their companions looked paid or willing to be paid. Two or three were blondes I had seen in chorus lines, with ingenue smiles fixed on their faces as if they could arrest the passage of time. Several were older women whose pneumatic bodies would keep them afloat for another year of two. These women were working hard with hands, with tongues, with eyes. If they slipped from the level of the Wild Piano, there were worse places to fall to.

A Mexican girl with a bored yellow face was sitting by herself at the table next to mine. Her eyes reached for me, turned away again.

"Scotch or bourbon, sir?" the waiter said.

"Bourbon and water. I'll mix it."

"Yes, sir. We have sandwiches."

I remembered that I was hungry. "Cheese."

"Very good, sir."

I looked at the piano, wondering if I was being too literal. The woman who called herself Betty had said she was at the piano. Its hoarse voice threaded the irregular laughter from the tables in melancholy counterpoint. The pianist's fingers moved in the keyboard mirror with a hurried fatality, as if the piano played itself and she had to keep up with it. Her tense bare shoulders were thin and shapely. Her hair poured down on them like tar and made them seem stark white. Her face was hidden.

"Hello, handsome. Buy me a drink."

The Mexican girl was standing by my chair. When I looked up she sat down. Her round-shouldered hipless body moved like a whip. Her low-cut gown was incongruous – clothes on a savage. She tried to smile, but her wooden face had never learned that art.

"I should buy you a pair of glasses."

She knew it was meant to be funny and that was all. "You are a funny boy. I like a funny boy." Her voice was guttural and forced, the voice you would expect from a wooden face.

"You wouldn't like me. But I'll buy you a drink."

She moved her eyes in order to express pleasure. They were solid and unchanging like lumps of resin. Her hands moved onto my arm and began to stroke it. "I like you, funny boy. Say something funny."

She didn't like me, and I didn't like her. She leaned forward to let me look down her dress. The breasts were little and tight, with pencil-sharp nipples. Her arms and upper lip were furred with black.

"On second thought I'll buy you hormones," I said.

"Is it something to eat? I am very hungry." She showed me her hungry white teeth by way of illustration.

"Why don't you take a bite of me?"

"You are kidding me," she said sulkily. But her hands continued working on my arm.

The waiter appeared and gave me a chance to break loose. He transferred from his tray to the table a small sandwich on a plate, a glass of water, a teacup with a half inch of whisky at the bottom, an empty teapot, and a glass of something he had telepathically brought along for the girl.

"That will be six dollars, sir."

"I beg your pardon."

"Two dollars per drink, sir. Two dollars for the sandwich."

I lifted the upper layer of the sandwich and looked at the slice of cheese it contained. It was as thin as a gold leaf and almost as expensive. I put down a ten-dollar bill and left the change on the table. My primitive companion drank her fruit juice, glanced at the four ones, and went back to work on my arm.

"You have very passionate hands," I said; "only I happen to be waiting for Betty."

"Betty?" She flung a disdainful black glance at the pianist's back. "But Betty is arteest. She will not –" A gesture finished the sentence.

"Betty is the one for me."

Her lips came together with a red tip of tongue protruding as if she was going to spit. I signalled a waiter and ordered a drink for the woman at the piano. When I turned back to the Mexican girl, she was gone.

The waiter pointed me out when he set down the drink on the piano, and the pianist turned to look. Her face was oval, so small and delicately modelled it looked pinched. Her eyes were indeterminate in colour and meaning. She made no effort to smile. I raised my chin by way of invitation. Her head jerked negatively and bent over the keyboard again.

I watched her white hands picking their way through the artificial boogie-woogie jungle. The music followed them like giant footsteps rustling in metallic undergrowth. You could see the shadow of the giant and hear his trip-hammer heartbeat.

She was hot.

Then she changed her tune. Her left hand still drummed and rolled in the bass, while her right hand elaborated a blues. She began to sing in a hard, sibilant voice, frayed at the edges but somehow moving:

> Brain's in my stomach,
> Heart's in my mouth,
> Want to go north –
> My feet point south.
> I got the psychosomatic blues,
> Doctor, doctor, doctor,
> Analyze my brian.
> Organize me, doctor.
> Doctor, ease my pain –
> I got the psychosomatic blues.

She phrased her song with decadent intelligence. I didn't like it, but it deserved a better audience than the chattering room behind me. I clapped when it ended and ordered her another drink.

She brought it to my table and sat down. She had a Tanagra figurine body, small and perfect, poised timelessly somewhere between twenty and thirty. "You like my music," she stated. She inclined her forehead and looked up at me from under it, the mannerism of a woman proud of her eyes. Their brown-flecked irises were centreless and disturbing.

"You should be on Fifty-second Street."

"Don't think I wasn't. But you haven't been there for a while, have you? The street has gone to the dogs."

"There's no percentage in this place. It's going to fold. Anybody can see the signs. Who runs it?"

"A man I know. Got a cigarette?"

When I lit it for her, she inhaled deeply. Her face unconsciously waited for the lift and dropped a little when it didn't come. She was a baby with an ageless face, sucking a dry bottle. The rims of her nostrils were bloodless, as white as snow, and that was no Freudian error.

"My name is Lew," I said. "I must have heard of you."

"I'm Betty Fraley." The statement had a margin of regret

like a thin black border on a card. The name didn't mean anything to me, but it did to her.

"I remember you," I lied more boldly. "You got a tough break, Betty." All snowbirds wore stigmata of bad luck.

"You can say it twice. Two years in a white cell, and no piano. The conspiracy rap was a hummer. All they could prove was I needed it myself. They took me for my own good, they said. Their own good! They wanted publicity, and my name was known. It isn't any more, and if I ever kick the habit, it won't be with the help of the feds." Her red mouth twisted over the wet red end of the cigarette. "Two years without a piano."

"You do nicely for a girl that's out of practice."

"You think so? You should have heard me in Chicago when I was at my peak. I draped the piano over the beams in the ceiling and swung from the keys. You heard my records, maybe?"

"Who hasn't?"

"Were they like I said?"

"Marvellous! I'm crazy about them."

But hot piano wasn't my dish, I'd picked the wrong words or overdone my praise.

The bitterness of her mouth spread to her eyes and voice. "I don't believe you. Name one."

"It's been a long time."

"Did you like my *Gin Mill Blues*?"

"I did," I said with relief. "You do it better than Sullivan."

"You're a liar, Lew. I never recorded that number. Why would you want to make me talk too much?"

"I like your music."

"Yeah. You're probably tone-deaf." She look intently into my face. The mutable eyes had hard, bright diamond centres. "You could be a cop, you know. You're not the type, but there's something about the way you look at things, wanting them but not liking things, You got cop's eyes – they want to see people hurt."

"Take it easy Betty. You're only half psychic. I don't like to see people hurt, but I'm a cop."

"Narcotics?" Her face was brushed by white terror.

"Nothing like that. A private cop. I don't want anything from you. I just happen to like your music."

"You lie." In spite of her hatred and fear she was still whispering. Her voice was a dry rustle. "You're the one that answered Fay's phone and said you were Troy. What do you think you're after?"

"A man called Sampson. Don't tell me you haven't heard of him. You have."

"I never heard of him."

"That's not what you said on the phone."

"All right. I've seen him in here like anybody else. Does that make me his nurse? Why come to me? He's just another barfly in my book."

"You came to me. Remember?"

She leaned toward me, projecting hatred like a magnetic field. "Get out of here and stay out."

"I'm staying."

"You think." She jerked a taut white hand at the waiter, who came running. "Call Puddler. This jerk's a private cop."

He looked at me with uncertainty tugging at his blue-black face.

"Take it easy," I said.

She stood up and went to the door behind the piano. "Puddler!" Every head in the room jerked up.

The door sprang open, and the man in the scarlet shirt came out. His small eyes moved from side to side, looking for trouble.

She pointed a finger at me. "Take him out and work him over. He's a peeper, trying to pump me."

I had time to run, but I lacked the inclination. Three run-outs were too many in one day. I went to meet him and took the sucker punch. The scarred head rolled away easily. I tried with my right. He caught it on the forearm and moved in.

His dull eyes shifted. I had the funny feeling that they didn't recognize me. One fist came into my stomach. I dropped my guard. The other came into my neck below the ear.

My legs were caught by the edge of the platform. I fell against the piano. Consciousness went out in jangling discord, swallowed by the giant shadow.

XI

AT THE BOTTOM of a black box a futile little man was sitting with his back against something hard. Something equally hard was hitting him in the face. First on one side of the jaw, then on the other. Every time this happened his head bounced once against the hard surface behind him. This distressing sequence – the blow followed by the bounce – continued with monotonous regularity for a considerable period of time. Each time the fist appraoched his jaw the futile man snapped at it futilely with his aching teeth. His arms, however, hung peacefully at his sides. His legs were remarkably inert and distant.

A tall shadow appeared at the mouth of the alley, stood one-legged like a stork for an instant, then limped grotesquely toward us. Puddler was too absorbed in his work to notice. The shadow straightened up behind him and swung one arm high in the air. The arm came down with a dark object swinging at the end of it. It made a cheerful sound, like cracking walnuts, on the back of Puddler's head. He knelt in front of me. I couldn't read his soul in his eyes because only the whites were showing. I pushed him over backward.

Alan Taggert put his shoe on and squatted beside me. "We better get out of here. I didn't hit him very hard."

"Let me know when you're going to hit him hard. I want to be present."

My lips felt puffed. My legs were like remote and rebellious colonies of my body. I established mandates over them and got to my feet. It was just as well I couldn't stand on one of them. I would have kicked the man on the pavement and regretted it later – several years later.

Taggert took hold of my arm and pulled me toward the mouth of the alley. A taxi with one door open was standing at the curb. Across the street the stucco entrance of the Wild Piano was deserted. He pushed me into the cab and got in after me.

"Where do you want to go?"

My brain was a vacuum for an instant. Then anger surged into the vaccum. "Home to bed, but I'm not going. Swift's on the Hollywood Boulevard."

"They're closed," the driver said.

"My car's in their parking lot." And my gun was in the car.

We were halfway there before my brain caught up with my tongue. "Where in hell did you come from?" I said to Taggert.

"Out of the everywhere into the here."

I snarled at him: "Don't double-talk. I'm not in the mood."

"Sorry," he said seriously. "I was looking for Sampson. There's a place back there called the Wild Piano. Sampson took me there once, and I thought I'd ask them about him."

"That's what I thought I'd do. You saw the answer they gave me."

"How did you happen to go there?"

I couldn't be bothered explaining. "I stumbled in. Then I stumbled out."

"I saw you coming out," he said.

"Did I walk out?"

"More or less. You had some help. I waited in the taxi to see what gave. When the bruiser took you into the alley I came in after you."

"I haven't thanked you," I said.

"Don't bother." He leaned toward me and said in an earnest whisper: "You really think Sampson's been kidnapped?"

"I'm not thinking so well just now. It's one idea I had when I was having ideas."

"Who would have kidnapped him?"

"There's a woman named Estabrook," I said, "a man named Troy. Ever met him?"

"No, but I've heard of the Estabrook woman. She was with Sampson in Nevada a couple of months ago."

"In what capacity?" My bruised face felt like leering. I let it leer.

"I wouldn't know for sure. She went there by car. The plane was out of commission, and I was in Los Angeles with it. I never got to see her, but Sampson mentioned her to me. As far as I could tell, they sat around in the sun talking about religion. I think she's a sidekick of this holy man Claude. The one Sampson gave the mountain to."

"You should have told me before. That was her picture I showed you."

"I didn't know that."

"It doesn't matter now. I spent the evening with her. She was the woman I was with in the Valerio."

"She was?" He seemed astonished. "Does she know where Sampson is?"

"It's possible she does, but she wasn't saying. I'm going to pay her another visit now. And I could use some help. Her household is a rather violent one."

"Good," said Taggert.

My reactions were still too slow, and I let him drive. He tended to bank on the turns, but all went well until we got to the Estabrook house. It was dark. The Buick was gone from the driveway, and the garage was empty. I knocked on the front door with the muzzle of my gun. No answer.

"She must have gotten suspicious," Taggert said.

"We'll break in."

But the door was bolted and too strong for our shoulders. We went around to the back. In the yard I stumbled over a smooth, round object that turned out to be a beer bottle.

"Steady there, old man," Taggert said in a Rover Boy way. He seemed to be enjoying himself.

He flung himself with youthful abandon against the kitchen door. When we pushed together it splintered at the lock and gave. We went through the kitchen into the dark hall.

"You're not carrying a gun?" I said.

"No."

"But you know how to use one?"

"Naturally. I prefer a machine gun," he bragged.

I handed him my automatic. "Make do with this." I went to the front door, pulled back the bolt, and opened it a crack. "If anybody comes let me know. Don't show yourself."

He took up his position with great solemnity, like a new sentry at Buckingham Palace. I went the rounds of the living-room, the dining-room, the kitchen, the bathroom, turning lights on and off. Those rooms were as I had seen them last. The bedroom was slightly different.

The difference was that the second drawer had nothing but stockings in it. And a used envelope, torn and empty, which was crumpled in a corner behind the stockings. The envelope was addressed to Mrs Estabrook at the address I was visiting.

Someone had scrawled some words and figures in pencil on the back:

> Avge. gross $2000. Avge. expense (Max) $500. Avge. net $1500. May – 1500 x 31 – 46,500 less 6,5001 (emerg.)
>
> $$-40{,}000 \ \frac{40{,}000}{2} = 20{,}000$$

It looked like a crude prospectus for a remarkably profitable business. One thing I knew for sure: the Wild Piano wasn't making that kind of money.

I turned the envelope over again. It was dated April 30, a week before, and postmarked Santa Maria. While that was sinking in, I heard a heavy motor growling in the road. I snapped off the light and moved into the hall.

A wave of light washed over the front of the house, poured in at the crack of the door where Taggert was standing. "Archer!" he whispered hoarsely.

Then he did a bold and foolish thing. He stepped out onto the porch, in the full white glare, and fired the gun in his hand.

"Hold it," I said, too late. The bullet rapped metal and whined away in ricochet. There was no answering shot.

I elbowed past him and plunged down the front steps. A truck with a closed van was backing out of the drive in a hurry. I sprinted across the lawn and caught the truck in the road before it could pick up speed. The window was open on the right side of the cab. I hooked my arm through it and braced one foot on the fender. A thin white cadaver's face turned toward me at the wheel, its small frightened eyes gleaming. The truck stopped as if it had struck a stone wall. I lost my grip and fell in the road.

The truck backed away, changed gears with a grinding clash, and came toward me while I was still on my knees. The bright lights hypnotized me for a second. The roaring wheels bore down on me. I saw their intention and flung myself sideways, rolled to the curb. The truck passed ponderously over the place in the road where I had been, and went on up the street, the roar of its motor mounting in pitch and volume. Its licence plate, if it had one, wasn't lighted. The back doors were windowless.

When I reached my car Taggert had started the engine. I

pushed him out of the driver's seat and followed the truck. It was out of sight when we reached Sunset. There was no way of knowing whether it had turned toward the mountains or toward the sea.

I turned to Taggert, who was sitting rather forlornly with the gun in his lap. "Hold your fire when I tell you to."

"It was too late when you told me. I aimed over the driver's head, anyway, to force him out of the cab."

"He tried to run me down. He wouldn't have got away if you could be trusted with firearms."

"I'm sorry," he said contritely. "I guess I was trigger happy." He handed me the gun, butt foremost.

"Forget it." I turned left toward the city. "Did you get a good look at the truck?"

"I think it was Army surplus, the kind they used for carrying personnel. Painted black, wasn't it?"

"Blue. What about the driver?"

"I couldn't make him out very well. He was wearing a peaked cap, that's all I could see."

"You didn't see his front plate?"

"I don't think there was any."

"That's too bad," I said. "It's barely possible Sampson was in that truck. Or had been."

"Really? Do you think we should go to the police?"

"I think we should. But first I'll have to talk to Mrs Sampson. Did you phone her?"

"I couldn't get her. She was out with sleeping pills when I called her back. She can't sleep without them."

"I'll see her in the morning, then."

"Are you going to fly up with us?"

"I'll drive up. There's something I want to do first."

"What's that?"

"A little private business," I said flatly.

He was silent after that. I didn't want to talk. It was getting on toward dawn. The murky red cloud over the city was turning pale at the edges. The late-night traffic of cabs and private cars had dwindled to almost nothing, and the early-morning trucks were beginning to roll. I watched for a blue Army surplus truck with a closed van and didn't see one.

I dropped Taggert at the Valerio and went home. A quart

of milk was waiting on my doorstep. I took it in for company. The electric clock in the kitchen said twenty after four. I found a box of frozen oysters in the freezing compartment of the refrigerator and made an oyster stew. My wife had never liked oysters. Now I could sit at my kitchen table at any hour of the day or night and eat oysters to my heart's content, building up my virility.

I undressed and got into bed without looking at the empty twin bed on the other side of the room. In a way it was a relief not to have to explain to anyone what I had been doing all day.

XII

IT WAS TEN IN THE MORNING before I got downtown. Peter Colton was at the flat-topped desk in his office. He had been my colonel in Intelligence. When I opened the ground-glass door he glanced up sharply from a pile of police reports, then lowered his eyes immediately to show that I wasn't welcome. He was a senior investigator in the D.A.'s office, a heavy middle-aged man with cropped fair hair and a violent nose like the prow of a speed-boat inverted. His office was a plaster cubicle with a single steel-framed window. I made myself uncomfortable on a hard-backed chair against the wall.

After a while he pointed his nose at me. "What happened to that which, for want of a better term, I choose to call your face?"

"I got into an argument."

"And you want me to arrest the neighbourhood bully." His smile dragged down the corners of his mouth, "You'll have to fight your own battles, my little man, unless of course there's something in it for me."

"A popsicle," I said sourly, "and three little sticks of bubble gum."

"You attempt to bribe the forces of the law with three sticks of bubble gum? Don't you realize that this is the atomic age, my friend? Three sticks of bubble gum contain enough primal energy to blow us all to bits."

"Forget it. The argument was with a wild piano."

"And you think I have nothing better to do with my time

than to go about pulling the arm on beserk pianos? Or putting on a vaudeville act with a run-down divorce detective? All right, spill it. You want something for nothing again."

"I'm giving you something. It could grow up to be the biggest thing in your life."

"And of course you want something in return."

"A little something," I admitted.

"Let's see the colour of your story. In twenty-five words."

"Your time isn't that valuable."

"Five," he said, leaning his nose on the ball of his thumb.

"My client's husband left Burbank Airport day before yesterday in a black limousine, ownership unknown. He hasn't been seen since."

"Twenty-five."

"Shut up. Yesterday she got a letter in his handwriting asking for a hundred grand in bills."

"There isn't that much money. Not in bills."

"There is. They have it. What does it suggest to you?"

He had taken a sheaf of mimeographed sheets from the upper left-hand drawer of his desk and was scanning them in quick succession. "Kidnapping?" he said absently.

"It smells like a snatch to me. Could be my nostrils are insensate. What does the hot sheet say?"

"No black limousines in the last seventy-two hours. People with limousines look after them. Day before yesterday, you say. What time?"

I gave him the details.

"Isn't your client a little slow on the uptake?"

"She has a passion for discretion."

"But not for her husband, I take it. It would help if you gave me her name."

"Wait a minute. I told you I want something. Two things. One, this isn't for publication. My client doesn't know I'm here. Besides, I want the guy back alive. Not dead."

"It's too big to sit on, Lew." He was up and walking, back and forth like a caged bear between the window and the door.

"You'll be getting it through official channels. Then it's out of my hands. In the meantime you can be doing something."

"For you?"

"For yourself. Start checking the car-rental agencies. That's number two. Number three is the Wild Piano –"

"That's enough." He flapped his hands in front of his face. "I'll wait for the official report, if there is any."

"Did I ever give you a bum lead?"

"Plenty, but we won't go into that. You could be doing a little exaggerating, you know."

"Why should I be pitching curves?"

"It's a cheap and easy way to get your leg work done." His eyes were narrowed to intelligent blue slits. "There's an awful lot of car rentals in the county."

"I'd do it myself but I have to go out of town. These people live in Santa Teresa."

"And their name?"

"Can I trust you?"

"Some. Further than you can see me."

"Sampson," I said. "Ralph Sampson."

"I've heard of him. And I see what you mean about the hundred grand."

"The trouble is we can't be sure what happened to him. We've got to wait."

"That's what you said." He swung on his heel to the window and spoke with his back to the room. "You also said something about the Wild Piano."

"That was before you said I was looking for cheap leg work."

"Don't tell me you've got feelings I can hurt."

"You merely disappoint me," I said. "I bring you a setup involving a hundred grand in cash and five million in capital assets. So you haggle over a day of your precious time."

"I don't work for myself, Lew." He turned on me suddenly. "Is Dwight Troy in this?"

"Who," I said, "is Dwight Troy?"

"Poison in a small package. He runs the Wild Piano."

"I thought there were laws against places like that. And people like him. Excuse my ignorance."

"You know who he is, then?"

"If he's a white-haired Englishman, yes." Colton nodded his head. "I met him once. He waved a gun at me for some reason. I left. It wasn't my job to take his gun away."

Colton moved his thick shoulders uncomfortably. "We've been trying to get him for years. He's smooth and versatile. He goes just so far in a racket, until his protection wears thin, then he shifts to something else. He rode high in the early thirties, running liquor from Baja California until that petered out. Since then he's had his ups and downs. He had a gambling pitch in Nevada for a while, but the syndicate forced him out. His pickings have been slender lately, I hear, but we're still waiting to take him."

"While you're waiting," I said, with heavy irony, "You could close the Wild Piano."

"We close it every six months," he snapped. "You should have seen it before the last raid, when it was the Rhinestone. They had a one-way window upstairs for voyeurs and masochists, a regular act of a woman whipping a man, and such stuff. We put an end to that."

"Who ran it then?"

"A woman by the name of Estabrook. And what happened to her? She wasn't even prosecuted." He snorted angrily. "I can't do anything about conditions like that. I'm not a politician."

"Neither is Troy," I said. "Do you know where he lives?"

"No. I asked you a question about him, Lew."

"So you did. The answer is I don't know. But he and Sampson have been moving in some of the same circles. You'd be smart to put a man on the Wild Piano."

"If we can spare one." He moved toward me unexpectedly and put a heavy hand on my shoulder. "If you meet Troy again, don't try to take his gun. It's been tried."

"Not by me."

"No," he said. "The men that tried it are dead."

XIII

IT WAS A TWO-HOUR DRIVE at sixty from Los Angeles to Santa Teresa. The sun was past its zenith when I reached the Sampson house, declining toward the sea through scattered clouds that made moving shadows on the terraces. Felix admitted me and led me through the house to the living-room.

It was so big the heavy furniture seemed sparse. The wall

that faced the sea was a single sheet of glass, with spun-glass curtains at each end like gathered lengths of light. Mrs Sampson was a life-size doll propped in a padded chair beside the giant window. She was fully dressed, in lime-coloured silk jersey. Her gold-shod feet rested on a footstool. Not a hair of her bleached head was out of place. The metal wheelchair was beside the door.

She was motionless and silent, making a deliberate tableau that verged on the ridiculous as the seconds passed. When the silence had twisted my arm for a quarter of a minute, "Very nice," I said. "You were trying to get in touch with me?"

"You've taken your time about coming." The voice of the still mahogany face was petulant.

"I can't apologize. I've been working hard on your case, and I relayed my advice to you. Have you taken it?"

"In part. Come closer, Mr Archer, and sit down. I'm perfectly harmless, really." She indicated an armchair facing her own. I moved across the room to it.

"Which part?"

"All of me," she said, with the carnivore smile. "My sting has been removed. But of course you mean the advice. Bert Graves is attending to the money now."

"Has he seen the police?"

"Not yet. I want to discuss that with you. But first you'd better read the letter."

She picked up an envelope from the coffee table beside her and tossed it to me. I took out the empty envelope I'd found in Mrs Estabrook's drawer and compared the two. They differed in size and quality and the handwriting of the address. The only similarity was in the Santa Maria postmark. Sampson's letter was addressed to Mrs Sampson and had been collected at four thirty the previous afternoon.

"What time did you get it?"

"About nine o'clock last night. It's special delivery, as you can see. Read it."

The letter was a single sheet of plain white typewriter paper covered on one side with a blue-ink scrawl:

Dear Elaine:

I am involved in a deal which came up suddenly, and I need some cash in a hurry. There are a number of bonds in our joint safety deposit box at the Bank of America. Albert Graves can identify those that are negotiable and arrange to have them cashed. I want you to cash bonds for me to the value of one hundred thousand dollars. I want no bills larger than fifties and hundreds. Do not permit the bank to mark them or record the numbers, since the deal I mentioned is confidential and highly important. Keep the money in my safe at home until you hear from me again, as you shortly will, or until I send a messenger bearing a letter of identification from me.

You will have to take Bert Graves into your confidence, of course, but it is of the outmost importance that you should not tell anyone else about this business. If you do, I stand to lose a very large profit and might even find myself on the wrong side of the law. It must be kept completely secret from everyone. That is why I am asking you to obtain the money for me, instead of going directly to my bank. I will be finished with this business within the week, and will see you soon.

My best love, and don't worry.

Ralph Sampson

"It's carefully done," I said, "but not convincing. The reason he gives for not going to the bank himself sounds pretty weak. What does Graves think of it?"

"He pointed that out, too. He thinks it's a put-up job. But, as he says, it's my decision."

"Are you absolutely certain this is your husband's writing?"

"There's no doubt about that. And did you notice the spelling of 'utmost'? It's one of his favourite words, and he always misspells it. He even pronounces it 'outmost.' Ralph isn't a cultivated man."

"The question is, is he a living one?"

Her level blue eyes turned to me with dislike. "Do you really think it's as serious as that, Mr Archer?"

"He doesn't normally do business like this, does he?"

"I know nothing about his ways of doing business. Actually

he retired from business when we were married. He bought and sold some ranches during the war, but he didn't confide the details of the transactions to me."

"Have any of his transactions been illegal?"

"I simply don't know. He's perfectly capable of it. It's one of the things that ties my hands."

"What are the others?"

"I don't trust him," she said thinly. "I have no way of knowing what he intends to do. With all that money he may be planning a trip around the world. Perhaps he intends to leave me. I don't know."

"I don't either, but this is my guess. Your husband is being held for ransom. He wrote this letter from dictation with a gun at his head. If it was really a business deal, he'd have no reason to write to you. Graves has his power of attorney, but kidnappers prefer to deal with the victim's wife. It makes things easier for them."

"What am I going to do?" she said, in a strained voice.

"Follow instructions to the letter, except that you should bring in the police. Not in an obvious or public way, but so they'll be standing by. You see, Mrs Sampson, the easy way for kidnappers to dispose of a victim, after the money's been collected, is to blow his brains out and leave him. He's got to be found before that happens, and I can't do it alone."

"You seem very sure he's been kidnapped. Have you found out anything you haven't told me?"

"Quite a few things. They add up to the fact that your husband's been keeping bad company."

"I knew it." Her face slipped out of control for an instant, sprang into curves of triumph. "He loves to pose as a family man and a good father, but he never fooled me."

"Very bad company," I said heavily. "As bad as there is in Los Angeles, and that's as bad as there is."

"He's always had a taste for low companions –" She broke off suddenly, raising her eyes to the door behind me.

Miranda was standing there. Wearing a grey gaberdine suit that emphasized her height, her copper hair swept up on top of her head, she looked like an older sister of the girl I'd met the day before. But her eyes were wide with fury, and her words came out in a rush.

"You dare to say that about my father! He may be dying, and all you care about is proving something against him."

"Is that all I care about, dear?" The brown face was impassive again. Only the pale eyes moved, and the carefully painted mouth.

"Don't 'dear' me." Miranda strode toward us. Even in anger her body had the grace of a young cat. She showed her claws. "All you really care about is yourself. If I ever saw a narcissist, you're one, Elaine. With your precious vanity, your primping, and your curling, and your special hairdresser, and your diet – it's all for your own benefit, isn't it? – so you can go on loving yourself. You surely don't expect anyone else to love you."

"Not you, certainly," the older woman said coolly. "The thought repels me. But what do you care about, my dear? Alan Taggert, perhaps? I believe you spent last night with him, Miranda."

"I didn't. You lie."

She was standing over her stepmother with her back to me. I was embarrassed, but I stayed where I was, balanced on the edge of my chair. I'd seen verbal cat fights end in violence more than once.

"Did Alan stand you up again? When is he going to marry you?"

"Never! I wouldn't have him." Miranda's voice was breaking. She was too young and vulnerable to stand the quarrel for long. "It's easy for you to make fun of me; you've never cared for anyone. You're frigid, that's what you are. My father wouldn't be God knows where if you'd given him any love. You made him come out here to California, away from all his friends, and now you've driven him away from his own house."

"Nonsense!" But Mrs Sampson too was showing the strain. "I want you to think that over, Miranda. You've hated me from the beginning and sided against me whether I was right or wrong. Your brother was fairer to me –"

"You leave Bob out of this. I know you had him under your thumb, but it's no credit to you. It pleased your vanity, didn't it, to have your stepson dancing attendance?"

"That's enough," Mrs Sampson said hoarsely. "Go away, you wretched girl."

Miranda didn't move, but she fell silent. I turned in my seat and looked out the window. Below the terraced lawn a stone walk led out to a pergola that stood on the edge of the bluff overlooking the sea. It was a small octagonal building with a conical roof, completely walled with glass. Through it and beyond it I could see the shifting colours of the ocean: green and white where the surf began, sage-honey-coloured in the kelp zone further out, then deep-water blue to the deep-sky-blue horizon.

My eye was caught by an unexpected movement beyond the belt of white water where the waves began to break. A little black disc skimmed out along the surface, skipped from wave to wave, and sank out of sight. Another followed it a moment later. The source of the skimming objects was too near shore to be seen, hidden by the steep fall of the cliff. When six or seven had skipped along the water and disappeared, there were no more. Unwillingly I turned to the silent room.

Miranda was still standing above the other woman's chair, but her posture had altered. Her body had come unstarched. One of her hands was lifted from her side toward her step-mother, not in anger. "I'm sorry, Elaine." I couldn't see her face.

Mrs Sampson's was visible. It was hard and clever. "You hurt me," she said. "You can't expect me to forgive you."

"You hurt me too," with a sobbing rhythm. "You mustn't throw Alan in my face."

"Then don't throw yourself at his head. No, I don't really mean that, and you know it. I think you ought to marry him. You want to, don't you?"

"Yes. But you know how Father feels about it. Not to mention Alan."

"You take care of Alan," Mrs Sampson said, almost gaily, "and I'll take care of your father."

"Will you really?"

"I give you my word. Now please go away, Miranda. I'm dreadfully tired." She glanced at me. "All this must have been very instructive to Mr Archer."

"I beg your pardon?" I said. "I was admiring your private view."

"Yes, lovely, isn't it?" She called to Miranda, who had started out of the room: "Stay if you wish, dear. I'm going upstairs."

She lifted a silver handbell that stood on the table beside her.

Its sudden peal was like the bell at the end of a round. Miranda completed the picture by sitting down, with her face averted, in a far corner of the room.

"You've seen us at our worst," Mrs Sampson said to me. "Please don't judge us by it. I've decided to do as you say."

"Shall I call the police?"

"Bert Graves will do it. He's familiar with all the Santa Teresa authorities. He should be here any minute."

Mrs Kromberg, the housekeeper, entered the room and wheeled the rubber-tyred chair across the carpet. Almost effortlessly she raised Mrs Sampson in her arms and placed her in the chair. They left the room in silence.

An electric motor murmured somewhere in the house as Mrs Sampson ascended toward heaven.

XIV

I SAT DOWN BESIDE MIRANDA on the divan in the corner of the room. She refused to look at me. "You must think we're terrible people," she said. "To fight like that in public."

"You seem to have something to fight about."

"I don't really know. Elaine can be so sweet at times, but she's always hated me, I think. Bob was her pet. He was my brother, you know."

"Killed in the war?"

"Yes. He was everything I'm not. Strong and controlled and good at everything he tried. They gave him the Navy Cross posthumously. Elaine worshipped the ground he walked on. I used to wonder if she was in love with him. But of course we all loved him. Our family's been quite different since he died and since we came out here. Father's gone to pieces, and Elaine's come up with this fake paralysis, and I'm all mixed up. But I'm talking too much, aren't I?" The turning of her half-averted head to me was a lovely gesture. Her mouth was soft and tremulous, her large eyes were blind with thought.

"I don't mind."

"Thank you." She smiled. "I have no one to talk to, you see. I used to think I was lucky, with all of Father's money behind me. I was an arrogant little bitch – maybe I still am. But I've learned that money can cut you off from people. We haven't got what it takes for the Santa Teresa social life, the international-Hollywood set, and we have no friends here. I suppose I shouldn't blame Elaine for that, but she was the one that insisted we come here to live during the war. My mistake was leaving school."

"Where did you go?"

"Radcliffe. I didn't fit in too well, but I had friends in Boston. They fired me for insubordination last year. I should have gone back. They would have taken me, but I was too proud to apologize. Too arrogant. I thought I could live with Father, and he tried to be good to me, but it didn't work out. He hasn't got along with Elaine for years. There's always tension in the house. And now something's happened to him."

"We'll get him back." I said. But I felt that I should hedge. "Anyway, you have other friends. Alan and Bert, for example."

"Alan doesn't really care for me. I thought he did once – no, I don't want to talk about him. And Bert Graves isn't my friend. He wants to marry me, and that's different. You can't relax with a man that wants to marry you."

"He loves you, by all the signs."

"I know he does." She raised her round, proud chin. "That's why I can't relax with him. And why he bores me."

"You're asking for a hell of a lot, Miranda." And I was talking a hell of a lot, talking like somebody out of *Miles Standish.* "Things never work out quite perfectly no matter how hard you push them. You're romantic, and an egotist. Some day you'll come down to earth so hard you'll probably break your neck. Or fracture your ego, anyway, I hope."

"I told you I was an arrogant bitch," she said, too lightly and easily. "Is there any charge for the diagnosis?"

"Don't go arrogant on me now. You already have once."

She opened her eyes very wide in demure parody. "Kissing you yesterday?"

"I won't pretend I didn't like it. I did. But it made me mad. I resent being used for other people's purposes."

"And what were my sinister purposes?"

"Not sinister. Sophomore stuff. You should be able to think of better ways to fascinate Taggert."

"Leave him out of this." Her tone was sharp, but then she softened it. "Did it make you very mad?"

"This mad."

I took hold of her shoulders with my hands, of her mouth with mine. Her mouth was half open and hot. Her body was cool and firm from breast to knee. She didn't struggle. Neither did she respond.

"Did you get any satisfaction out of that?" she said, when I released her.

I looked into her wide green eyes. They were candid and steady, but they had murky depths. I wondered what went on in those sea depths, and how long it had been going on.

"It salved my ego."

She laughed. "It salved your lips, at least. There's lipstick on them."

I wiped my mouth with my handkerchief. "How old are you?"

"Twenty. Old enough for your sinister purposes. Do you think I act like a child?"

"You're a woman." I looked at her body deliberately – round breasts, straight flanks, round hips, straight round legs – until she squirmed. "That involves certain responsibilities."

"I know." Her voice was harsh with self-reproach. "I shouldn't fling myself around. You've seen a lot of life, haven't you?"

It was a girlish question, but I answered her seriously. "Too much, of one kind. I make my living seeing a lot of life."

"I guess I haven't seen enough. I'm sorry for making you mad." She leaned toward me suddenly and kissed my cheek very lightly.

I felt a letdown, because it was the kind of kiss a niece might give to an uncle. Well, I had fifteen years on her. The letdown didn't last. Bert Graves had twenty.

There was the sound of a car in the drive, then movement in the house.

"That must be Bert now," she said.

We were standing well apart when he entered the room. But he gave me a single glance, veiled and questioning and hurt, before he found control of his face. Even then there were vertical lines of anxiety between his eyebrows. He looked as if he hadn't slept. But he moved with speed and decision, cat-footed for a heavy man. His body, at least, was glad to get into action. He said hello to Miranda and turned to me.

"What do you say, Lew?"

"Did you get the money?"

He took the calfskin briefcase from under his arm, unlocked it with a key, and dumped its contents on the coffee table – a dozen or more oblong packages wrapped in brown bank paper and tied together with red tape.

"One hundred thousand dollars," he said. "A thousand fifties and five hundred hundreds. God knows what we're going to do with it."

"Put it in the safe for now. There's one in the house, isn't there?"

"Yes," Miranda said. "In Father's study. The combination's in his desk."

"And another thing. You need protection for this money and the people in this house."

Graves turned to me with the brown packages in his hand. "What about you?"

"I'm not going to be here. Get one of the sheriff's deputies to come out. It's what they're for."

"Mrs Sampson wouldn't let me call them."

"She will now. She wants you to turn the whole thing over to the police."

"Good! She's getting some sense. I'll put this stuff away and get on the phone."

"See them in person, Bert."

"Why?"

"Because," I said, "this has some of the earmarks of an inside job. Somebody in the house could be interested in the conversation."

"You're ahead of me, but I see what you mean. The letter shows inside knowledge, which they might or might not have got from Sampson. Assuming there is a 'they,' and he has been kidnapped."

"We'll work on that assumption till another turns up. And for God's sake make the cops go easy. We can't afford to frighten them. Not if we want Sampson alive."

"I understand that. But where are you going to be?"

"This envelope is postmarked Santa Maria." I didn't bother

telling him about the other envelope in my pocket. "There's a chance he may be there on legitimate business. Or illegitimate business, for that matter. I'm going there."

"I've never heard of his doing any business there. Still, it might be worth looking into."

"Have you tried the ranch?" Miranda said to Graves.

"I called the superintendent this morning. They haven't heard from him."

"What ranch is that?" I said.

"Father has a ranch on the other side of Bakersfield. A vegetable ranch. He wouldn't be likely to go there now, though, on account of the trouble."

"The field-workers are out on strike," Graves said. "They've been out for a couple of months, and there's been some violence. It's a nasty situation."

"Could it have anything to do with this one?"

"I doubt it."

"You know," Miranda said, "he may be at the Temple. When he was there before, his letters came through Santa Maria."

"The Temple?" Once or twice before, I'd caught myself slipping off the edge of the case into fairy tale. It was one of the occupational hazards of working in California, but it irked me.

"The Temple in the Clouds, the place he gave to Claude. Father spent a couple of days there in the early spring. It's in the mountains near Santa Maria."

"And who," I said, "is Claude?"

"I told you about him," Graves said. "The holy man he gave the mountain to. He's made the lodge over into some kind of temple.

"Claude's a phony," Miranda put in. "He wears his hair long and never cuts his beard and talks like a bad imitation of Walt Whitman."

"Have you been up there?" I asked her.

"I drove Ralph up, but I left when Claude started to talk. I couldn't bear him. He's a dirty old goat with a foghorn voice and the nastiest eyes I ever looked into."

"How about taking me there now?"

"All right. I'll put on a sweater."

Graves's mouth moved as if he was going to protest. He watched her anxiously as she left the room.

"I'll bring her home safely," I said. I should have held my tongue.

He moved towards me with his head down like a bull's, a big man and still hard. His arms were stiff at his sides. The fists were clenched at the end of them.

"Listen to me, Archer," he said in a monotone. "Wipe the lipstick off your cheek or I'll wipe it off for you."

I tried to cover my embarrassment with a smile. "I'd take you, Bert. I've had a lot of practice of handling jealous males."

"That may be. But keep your hands off Miranda, or I'll spoil your good looks."

I rubbed my left cheek where Miranda had left her mark. "Don't get her wrong –"

"I suppose it was Mrs. Sampson you were playing kissing games with?" He uttered a small heartbroken laugh. "No soap!"

"It was Miranda, and it wasn't a game. She was feeling low and I talked to her and she kissed me once. It didn't mean a thing. Purely a filial kiss."

"I'd like to believe you," he said uncertainly. "You know how I feel about Miranda."

"She told me."

"What did she say?"

"That you were in love with her."

"I'm glad she knows that, anyway. I wish she'd talk to me when she's feeling low." He smiled bitterly. "How do you do it, Lew?"

"Don't come to me with your heart problems. I'll foul you up for sure. I have one little piece of advice, though."

"Shoot."

"Take it easy," I said. "Just take it easy. We've got a big job on our hands and we've got to pull together. I'm no threat to your love life and I wouldn't be if I could. And while I'm being blunt, I don't think Taggert is, either. He simply isn't interested."

"Thanks," he said in a harsh voice. He wasn't the kind of man who went in for intimate confessions. But he added miserably: "She's so much younger than I am. Taggert has youth and looks."

There was a soft plopping of feet in the hall outside the door, and Taggert appeared in the doorway as if on cue. "Did somebody take my name in vain?"

He was naked except for wet bathing trunks, wide-shouldered, narrow-waisted and long-legged. With the wet dark hair curling on his small skull, the lazy smile on his face, he could have posed for the Greeks as a youthful god. Bert Graves looked him over with dislike and said slowly:

"I was just telling Archer how handsome I thought you were."

The smile contracted slightly but stayed on his face. "That sounds like a left-handed compliment, but what the hell! Hello, Archer, anything new?"

"No," I said. "And I was telling Graves that you're not interested in Miranda."

"Right you are," he answered airily. "She's a nice girl but not for me. Now if you'll excuse me I'll put on some clothes."

"Gladly," Graves said.

But I called him back: "Wait a minute. Do you have a gun?"

"A pair of target pistols. .32's."

"Load one and keep it one you, eh? Stick around the house and keep your eyes open. Try not to be trigger happy."

"I learned my lesson," he said cheerfully. "Do you expect something to break?"

"No, but if something does, you'll want to be ready. Will you do what I said?"

"I sure will."

"He's not a bad kid," Graves said, when he was gone, "but I can't stand the sight of him. It's funny; I've never been jealous before."

"Ever been in love before?"

"Not until now." He stood with his shoulders bowed, burdened by fatality and exaltation and despair. He was in love for the first time and for keeps. I was sorry for him.

"Tell me," he said, "what was Miranda feeling low about? This business of her father?"

"Partly that. She feels the family's been going to pieces. She needs some sort of steady backing."

"I know she does. It's one reason I want to marry her. There are other reasons, of course; I don't have to tell you that."

"No," I said. I risked a candid question. "Is money one of them?"

He glanced at me sharply. "Miranda has no money of her

own."

"She will have, though?"

"She will have, naturally, when her father dies. I wrote his will for him, and she gets half. I don't object to the money –" he smiled wryly "– but I'm not a fortune hunter, if that's what you mean."

"It isn't. She might come into that money sooner than you think, though. The old man's been running in some fast and funny circles in L.A. Did he ever mention a Mrs Estabrook? Fay Estabrook? Or a man called Troy?"

"You know Troy? What sort of character is he, anyway?"

"A gunman," I said. "I've heard that he's done murders."

"I'm not surprised. I tried to tell Sampson to keep away from Troy, but Sampson thinks he's fine."

"Have you met Troy?"

"Sampson introduced me to him in Las Vegas a couple of months ago. The three of us went the rounds, and a lot of people seemed to know him. All the croupiers knew him, if that's a recommendation."

"It isn't. But he had his own place in Las Vegas at one time. He's done a lot of things. And I don't think kidnapping would be beneath his dignity. How did Troy happen to be with Sampson?"

"I got the impression that he worked for Sampson, but I couldn't be sure. He's a queer fish. He watched me and Sampson gamble, but he wouldn't himself. I dropped an even thousand that night. Sampson won four thousand. To him that hath shall be given." He smiled ruefully.

"Maybe Troy was making a good impression," I said.

"Maybe. The bastard gave me the creeps. Do you think he's mixed up in this?"

"I'm trying to find out," I said. "Does Sampson need money, Bert?"

"Hell, no! He's a millionaire."

"Why would he go into business with a jerk like Troy?"

"The time hangs heavy on his hands. The royalties roll in from Texas and Oklahoma, and he gets bored. Sampson's a natural money-maker the way I'm a natural money-loser. He's not happy unless he's making it; I'm not happy unless I'm losing it." He broke off short when Miranda entered the room.

"Ready? she said. "Don't worry about me, Bert."

She pressed his shoulder with her hand. Her light-brown coat fell open in front, and her small sweatered breasts, pointed like weapons, were half impatient promise, half gradual threat. She had let her hair down and brushed it behind her ears. Her bright face slanted toward him like a challenge.

He kissed her cheek lightly and tenderly. I still felt sorry for him. He was a strong, intelligent man, but he looked a little stuffy beside her in his blue pin-stripe business suit. A little weary and old to tame a filly like Miranda.

XV

THE PASS ROAD CLIMBED through sloping fields of dust-coloured chaparral and raw red cutbacks. By holding the accelerator to the floor I kept our speed at fifty. The road narrowed and twisted more abruptly as we went up. I caught quick glimpses of boulder-strewn slopes, mile-wide canyons lined with mountain oak and spanned by telephone cables. Once through a gap in the hills I saw the sea like a low blue cloud slanting away behind. Then the road looped round into landlocked mountain wilderness, grayed and chilled suddenly by the clouds in the pass.

The clouds looked heavy and dense from the outside. When we entered them they seemed to thin out, blowing across the road in whitish filaments. Barren and dim through the clouds, the mountainside shouldered us. In a 1946 car, with a late-model girl beside me, I could still imagine we were crossing the watershed between Colton's atomic age and the age of stone when men stood up on their hind legs and began to count time by the sun.

The fog grew denser, limiting my vision to twenty-five or thirty feet. I took the last hairpin curves in second. Then the road straightened out. At a definite point the labouring motor accelerated of its own accord, and we came out of the cloud. From the summit of the pass we could see the valley filled with sunlight like a bowl brimming with yellow butter, and the mountains clear and sharp on the other side.

"Isn't it glorious?" Miranda said. "No matter how cloudy it

is on the Santa Teresa side, it's nearly always sunny in the valley. In the rainy season I often drive over by myself just to feel the sun."

"I like the sun."

"Do you really? I didn't think you'd go in for simple things like sun. You're the neon type, aren't you?"

"If you say so."

She was silent for a while, watching the leaping road, the blue sky streaming backward. The road cut straight and flat through the green-and-yellow checkerboard valley. With no one in sight but the Mexican *braceros* in the fields, I floor-boarded. The speedometer needle stuck halfway between eighty-five and ninety.

"What are you running away from, Archer?" she said, in a mocking tone.

"Not a thing. Do you want a serious answer?"

"It would be nice for a change."

"I like a little danger. Tame danger, controlled by me. It gives me a sense of power, I guess, to take my life in my hands and know damn' well I'm not going to lose it."

"Unless we have a blowout."

"I've never had one."

"Tell me," she said, "is that why you do your kind of work? Because you like danger?"

"It's as good a reason as any. It wouldn't be true, though."

"Why, then?"

"I inherited the job from another man."

"Your father?"

"Myself when I was younger. I used to think the world was divided into good people and bad people, that you could pin responsibility for evil on certain definite people and punish the guilty. I'm still going through the motions. And talking too much."

"Don't stop."

"I'm fouled up. Why should I foul you up?"

"I am already. And I don't understand what you said."

"I'll take it from the beginning. When I went into police work in 1935. I believed that evil was a quality some people were born with, like a harelip. A cop's job was to find those people and put them away. But evil isn't so simple. Everybody has it in him, and whether it comes out in his actions depends on a number of things. Environment, opportunity, economic pressure, a piece of bad luck, a wrong friend. The trouble is a cop has to go on judging people by the rule of thumb, and acting on the judgment."

"Do you judge people?"

"Everybody I meet. The graduates of the police schools make a big thing of scientific detection, and that has its place. But most of my work is watching people, and judging them."

"And you find evil in everybody?"

"Just about. Either I'm getting sharper or people are getting worse. And that could be. War and inflation always raise a crop of stinkers, and a lot of them have settled in California."

"You wouldn't be talking about our family?" she said.

"Not especially."

"Anyway, you can't blame Ralph on the war – not entirely. He's always been a bit of a stinker, at least since I've known him."

"All your life?"

"All my life."

"I didn't know you felt that way about him."

"I've tried to understand him," she said. "Maybe he had his points when he was young. He started out with nothing, you know. His father was a tenant farmer who never had land of his own. I can understand why Ralph spent his life acquiring land. But you'd think he'd be more sympathetic to poor people, because he was poor himself. The strikers on the ranch, for instance. Their living conditions are awful and their wages aren't decent, but Ralph won't admit it. He's been doing everything he can to starve them out and break the strike. He can't seem to see that Mexican field-workers are people."

"It's a common enough illusion, and a useful one. It makes it easier to gouge people if you don't admit they're human – I'm developing into quite a moralist in early middle age."

"Are you judging me?" she asked, after a pause.

"Provisionally. The evidence isn't in. I'd say you have nearly everything, and could develop into nearly anything."

"Why 'nearly'? What's my big deficiency?"

"A tail on your kite. You can't speed up time. You have to pick up its beat and let it support you."

"You're a strange man," she said softly. "I didn't know you'd be able to say things like that. And do you judge yourself?"

"Not when I can help it, but I did last night. I was feeding alcohol to an alcoholic, and I saw my face in the mirror."

"What was the verdict?"

"The judge suspended sentence, but he gave me a tongue-lashing."

"And that's why you drive so fast?"

"Maybe it is."

"I do it for different reasons. I still think your reason is a kind of running away. Death wish."

"No jargon, please. Do you drive fast?"

"I've done a hundred and five on this road in the Caddie."

The rules of the game we were playing weren't clear yet, but I felt outplayed. "And what's your reason?"

"I do it when I'm bored. I pretend to myself I'm going to meet something – something utterly new. Something naked and bright, a moving target in the road."

My obscure resentment came out as fatherly advice, "You'll meet something new if you do it often. A smashed head and oblivion."

"Damn you!" she cried. "You said you liked danger, but you're as stuffy as Bert Graves."

"I'm sorry if I frightened you."

"Frightened me?" Her short laugh was thin and cracked like a sea bird's cry. "All you men still have the Victorian hangover. I suppose you think woman's place is in the home, too?"

"Not my home."

The road began to twist restlessly and rise toward the sky. I let the gradient brake the car. At fifty we had nothing to say to each other.

XVI

AT A HEIGHT THAT MADE ME conscious of my breathing we came to a high-backed road of new gravel, barred by a closed wooden gate. A metal mailbox on the gatepost bore the name "Claude" in stencilled white letters. I opened the gate, and Miranda drove the car through.

"It's another mile," she said. "Do you trust me?"

"No, but I want to look at the scenery. I've never been here before."

Apart from the road the country looked as if no one had ever been there. A valley dotted with boulders and mountain evergreen opened below us as we spiralled upwards. Far down among the trees I caught the slight brown shudder of a deer's movements and disappearance. Another deer went after it in a rocking-horse leap. The air was so clear and still I wouldn't have been surprised to hear the rustle of their hoofs. But there was no sound above the whine of the motor. Nothing to hear, and nothing to look at but light-saturated air and the bare stone face of the mountain opposite.

The car crawled over the rim of a saucer-shaped depression in the top of the mountain. Below us, in the centre of the mesa, the Temple in the Clouds stood, hidden from everyone but hawks and airmen. It was a square one-storied structure of white-painted stone and adobe, built around a central court. There were a few outbuildings inside the wire fence that formed a kind of stockade around it. From one of them a thin black smoke was trickling up the sky.

Then something moved on the flat roof of the main building, something that had been so still my eyes had taken it for granted. An old man was squatting there with his legs folded under him. He rose with majestic slowness, a huge leather brown figure. With the uncut tangles of his grey hair and beard standing out from his head, he looked like a rayed sun in an old map. He stooped deliberately to pick up a piece of cloth, which he wound around his naked middle. He raised one arm as if to tell us to be patient, and descended into the inner court.

Its ironbound door creaked open. He emerged and waddled to the gate, which he unlocked. I saw his eyes for the first time. They were milky blue, bland and conscienceless, like an animal's. In spite of his great sun-blacked shoulders and the heavy beard that fanned across his chest, he had a womanish air. His rich self-conscious voice was a subtle blend of baritone and contralto.

"Greetings, greetings, my friends. Any traveller who comes to my out-of-the-way doorstep is welcome to share my fare.

Hospitality stands high among the virtues, close to the supreme virtue of health itself."

"Thanks. Do we drive in?"

"Please leave the automobile outside the fence, my friend. Even the outer circle should not be sullied by the trappings of a mechanical civilization."

"I thought you knew him," I said to Miranda, as we got out of the car.

"I don't think he can see very well."

When we came nearer, his blue-white eyes peered at her face. He leaned toward her, and his straggling grey hair swung forward, brushing his shoulders.

"Hello, Claude," she said crisply.

"Why, Miss Sampson! I was not looking for a visit from youth and beauty to-day. Such youth! Such beauty!"

He breathed through his lips, which were very heavy and red. I looked at his feet to check his age. Shod in rope-soled sandals with thongs between the toes, they were gnarled and swollen: sixty-year-old feet.

"Thank you," she said unpleasantly. "I came to see Ralph, if he's here."

"But he isn't, Miss Sampson. I am alone here. I have sent my disciples away for the present." He smiled vaguely without uncovering his teeth. "I am an old eagle communing with the mountains and the sun."

"An old vulture!" Miranda said audibly. "Has Ralph been here recently?"

"Not for several months. He has promised me, but he has not yet come. Your father has spiritual potentialities, but he is still caged and confined by the material life. It is hard to draw him up into the azure world. It is painful for him to open his nature to the sun." He said it with a chanting rhythm, an almost liturgical beat.

"Do you mind if I look around?" I said. "To make sure he isn't here."

"I tell you I am alone." He turned to Miranda. "Who is this young man?"

"Mr Archer. He's helping me look for Ralph."

"I see. I'm afraid you must take my word that he is not here, Mr Archer. I cannot permit you to enter the inner circle, since you have not submitted to the rite of purification."

"I think I'll have a look around anyway."

"But that is not possible." He placed his hand on my shoulder. It was soft and thick and brown, like a fried fish. "You must not enter the temple. It would anger Mithras."

His breath was sour-sweet and foul in my nostrils. I picked his hand off my shoulder. "Have you been purified?"

He raised his innocent eyes to the sun. "You must not jest of these matters. I was a lost and sinful man, blind-hearted and sinful, till I entered the azure world. The sword of the sun slew the black bull of the flesh, and I was purified."

"And I'm the wild bull of the pampas," I said to myself.

Miranda stepped between us. "All this is nonsense. We're going in to look. I wouldn't take your word for anything, Claude."

He bowed his shaggy head and smiled a close-mouthed smile of sour benevolence that made my stomach queasy. "As you will, Miss Sampson. The sacrilege will rest upon your heads. I hope and trust that the wrath of Mithras will not be heavy."

She brushed past him disdainfully. I followed her through the arched doorway into the inner court. The red sun over the mountain to the west remained impassive. Without a look or another word Claude mounted the stone staircase inside the door and disappeared onto the roof.

The stone-paved court was empty. Its walls were lined with closed wooden doors. I pressed the latch of the nearest. It opened into an oak-raftered room that contained a built-in bed covered with dirty blankets, a scarred iron trunk, un-labelled, a cheap cardboard wardrobe, and the sour-sweet smell of Claude.

"The odour of sanctity," Miranda said, at my shoulder.

"Did your father actually stay here with Claude?"

"I'm afraid so." She wrinkled her nose. "He takes this sun-worshipping nonsense seriously. It's all tied up with astrology in his mind."

"And he actually gave this place to Claude?"

"I don't know if he deeded it to him. He handed it over for Claude to use as a temple. I suppose he'll take it back sometime, if he can. And if he ever gets over this religious lunacy of his."

"It's a queer sort of hunting-lodge," I said.

"It's not really a hunting-lodge. He built it as a kind of hideout."

"A hideout from what?"

"War. This dates from Ralph's last phase, the prereligious one. He was convinced that another war was just around the corner. This was to be his sanctuary if we were invaded. But he got over the fear last year, just before they started work on the bomb shelter. The plans for the shelter were all ready, too. He took refuge in astrology instead."

"I didn't use the word 'lunacy,'" I said. "You did. Were you serious?"

"Not really." She smiled a little bleakly. "Ralph doesn't seem so crazy if you understand him. He felt guilty, I think, because he made money out of the last war. And then there was Bob's death. Guilt can cause all sorts of irrational fears."

"You read another book," I said. "This time it was a psychology textbook."

Her reactions were surprising. "You make me sick, Archer. Don't you get bored with yourself playing the dumb detective?"

"Sure I get bored. I need something naked and bright. A moving target in the road."

"You!" She bit her lip, flushed, and turned away.

We went from room to room, opening and closing the doors. Most of the rooms had beds in them and very little else. In the big living-room at the end there were five or six straw pallets on the floor. It was narrow-windowed and thick-walled like a fortress, and the air smelled like the tank of a county jail.

"The disciples live well, whoever they are. Did you see any when you were here before?"

"No. But I didn't come inside."

"Some people are suckers for a pitch like Claude's. They'll hand over everything they own and get nothing in return but a starvation diet and the prospect of a nervous breakdown. But I've never heard of a sun-worshippers' monastery before. I wonder where the suckers are to-day."

We finished our circuit of the court without seeing anyone. I looked up at the roof. Claude was sitting with his face to the sun, his naked back to us. The flesh hung down in heavy folds from his flanks and hips. His head was moving jerkily back and forth, as if he was arguing with someone, but no sound came from him. Like a bearded woman who knew two sexual worlds, the great eunuch back and head outlined by the sun were strange and ridiculous and dreadful.

Miranda touched my arm. "Speaking of lunacy –"

"He's putting on an act," I said, and half believed it. "At least he was telling the truth about your father. Unless he's in one of the other buildings."

We crossed the gravel yard to the adobe with the smoking chimney. I looked in through the open door. A girl with a shawl over her head was sitting on her heels in front of a glowing fireplace stirring a bubbling pot. It was a five-gallon pot, and it was full of what looked like beans.

"It looks as if the disciples are coming for supper."

Without moving her shoulders the girl turned her head to look at us. The whites of her eyes shone like porcelain in the clay-coloured Indian face.

"Have you seen an old man?" I asked her in Spanish.

She shrugged one calico shoulder in the general direction of the temple.

"Not that old man. One who is beardless. Beardless, fat, and rich. His name is Señor Sampson."

She shrugged both shoulders and turned back to her steaming pot. Claude's sandals crunched in the gravel behind us.

"I am not wholly alone, as you can see. There is my handmaiden, but she is little better than an animal. If you have done with us, perhaps you will permit me to return to my meditation. Sunset is approaching, and I must pay my respects to the departing god."

Beside the adobe there was a galvanized iron shed with a padlocked door. "Before you go, open the shed."

Sighing, he took some keys from the folds of his body cloth. The shed contained a pile of bags and cartons, most of which were empty. There were several sacks of beans, a case of condensed milk, some overalls and work boots in a few of the cartons.

Claude stood in the doorway watching me. "My disciples sometimes work in the valley by the day. Such work in the vegetable fields is a form of worship."

He moved back to let me out. I noticed the imprint of a tyre in the clay at the edge of the gravel where his foot had been. It was a wide truck tyre. I'd seen the herringbone pattern of the tread before.

"I thought you didn't let mechanical trappings come inside the fence?"

He peered at the ground and came up smiling. "Only when necessary. A truck delivered some provisions the other day."

"I hope and trust it was purified?"

"The driver has been purified, yes."

"Good. I suppose that you'll be doing some housecleaning now that we've contaminated the place."

"It is between you and the god." With a backward glance at the declining sun he returned to his perch on the roof.

On the way back to the state highway I had memorized the route so that I could drive it blind at night if I had to.

XVII

BEFORE WE CROSSED THE VALLEY the red sun had plunged behind the clouds over the coastal range. The shadowed fields were empty. We passed a dozen truckloads of field-workers returnimg to their bunkhouses on the ranches. Crammed like cattle in the rattling vans of the trucks, they stood in patient silence, men, women, and children waiting for food and sleep and the next day's sunrise. I drove carefully, feeling a little depressed, stalled in the twilight period when day has run down and night hasn't picked up speed.

The clouds flowed in the pass like a torrent of milk and preceded us down the other side of the mountain, blending with the gradual night and the deepening cold. Once or twice on a curve Miranda leaned against me, trembling. I didn't ask her whether she was cold or afraid. I didn't want to force her to make a choice.

The clouds had rolled down the mountain all the way to U.S. 101. From far up the pass road I could see the headlights on the highway blurred enormous by the fog. While I was waiting at the stop sign for a break in the highway traffic, a pair of bright lights came up fast from the direction of Santa Teresa. They suddenly swung toward us like wild eyes. The speeding car was going to try to turn into the pass road. Its brakes screamed, its rubber skittered and snarled. It wasn't going to get past me.

"Head down," I said to Miranda, and tightened my grip on the wheel.

The other driver straightened out, roared into second gear at forty-five or fifty, spun in front of my bumper, and passed on my right in the seven-foot space between me and the stop sign. I caught a flashing glimpse of the driver's face, a thin, pale face jaundiced by my fog lights, under a peaked leather cap. His car was a dark limousine.

I backed and turned and started after it. The black-top was slick from the wet, and I was slow in getting under way. The red rear light hightailing up the road was swallowed by the fog. It was no use anyway. He could turn off on any one of the county roads that paralleled the highway. And perhaps the best thing I could do for Sampson was to let the limousine go. I stopped so fast that Miranda had to brace both hands on the dashboard. My reflexes were getting violent.

"What on earth's the matter? He didn't actually crash us, you know."

"I wish he had."

"He's reckless, but he drives very well."

"Yeah. He's a moving target I'd like to hit some time."

She looked at me curiously. Shadowed from below by the dashlights, her face was dark, with huge bright eyes. "You're looking grim, Archer. Have I made you angry again?"

"Not you," I said. "It's waiting for a break in this case. I prefer direct action."

"I see." She sounded disappointed. "Please take me home now. I'm cold and hungry."

I turned in the shallow ditch and drove back across the highway to Cabrillo Canyon. Beyond the plough of yellow light that the fog lamps pushed ahead of us the trees and hedges hung in the thick air, ash-grey emanations abandoned by the sun. The landscape matched the clouded pattern in my skull. My thoughts were blind and slow, groping for a lead to the place where Ralph Sampson was hidden.

The lead was waiting in the mailbox at the entrance to Sampson's drive, and it took no cunning to find it. Miranda noticed it first. "Stop the car."

When she opened the door, I saw the white envelope stuck in the slot of the mailbox. "Wait. Let me handle it."

My tone held her still with one foot on the ground, one hand reaching for the envelope. I took it by one corner and wrapped it in a clean handkerchief. "There may be fingerprints."

"How do you know it's from Father?"

"I don't. You drive up to the house."

I unwrapped the envelope in the kitchen. The fluorescent tube in the ceiling cast a white morgue glow on the white enamelled table. There was no name or address on the envelope. I slit one end and drew out the folded sheet it contained with my fingernails.

My heart dropped when I saw the printed letters pasted to the sheet of paper. The letters had been cut out individually and arranged in words, in the classic tradition of kidnapping. These were the words:

> Mr Sampson is well in good hands put one hundred thousand dollars in plain paper parsel ty with string put parsel on grass in middle of road at south end of highway division oposite Fryers Road one mile south of Santa Teresa limits do this at nine oclock tonite after you leave parsel drive away imediately you will be watched drive away north direction Santa Teresa do not attent pollice ambush if you value Sampsons life you will be watched he will come home tomorrow if no ambush no attent to chase no marked bills
>
> too bad for Sampson if you dont
>
> friend of the family

"You were right," Miranda said, in a half whisper.

I wanted to say something consoling. All I could think of was – too bad for Sampson.

"Go and see if Graves is around," I said. She went immediately.

I leaned over the sheet of paper without touching it, and examined the cut-out letters. They varied widely in size and type, and were printed on smooth paper, probably cut from the advertising pages of a big-circulation magazine. The spelling pointed at semi-literacy, but you couldn't always tell. Some pretty well-educated people were poor spellers. And it might have been faked.

I had memorized the letter when Graves came into the kitchen with Taggert and Miranda trailing behind. He came toward me on heavy piston-quick legs, with an iron gleam in his eyes.

I pointed to the table. "That was in the mailbox—"

"Miranda told me."

"It may have been dropped a few minutes ago by a car that passed me on the highway."

Graves leaned over the letter and read it aloud to himself. Taggert stayed by Miranda in the doorway, uncertain whether he was wanted but quite at ease. Though physically they could have been sibs, Miranda was his temperamental opposite. Ugly blue patches had blossomed under her eyes. Her wide lips drooped sullenly over her fine, prominent teeth. She leaned against the doorjamb in a jagged, disconsolate pose.

Graves raised his head. "This is it. I'll get the deputy."

"Here now?"

"Yes. In the study with the money. And I'll call the sheriff."

"Has he got a fingerprint man?"

"The D.A.'s is better."

"Call him too. They're probably too smart to leave fresh prints, but there may be latent ones. It's hard to do cut-outs with gloves on."

"Right. Now what was that about a car that passed you?"

"Keep it to yourself for now. I'll handle that end."

"I guess you know what you're doing."

"I know what I'm not doing. I'm not getting Sampson bumped if I can help it."

"That's what's worrying me," he said, and went through the door so fast that Taggert had to jump back out of his way.

I glanced at Miranda. She looked ready to drop. "Make her eat something, Taggert."

"If I can."

He crossed the kitchen to the refrigerator. Her eyes followed him. I hated her for an instant. She was like a dog, a bitch in the rutting season.

"I couldn't possibly eat," she said. "Do you think he's alive?"

"Yes. But I thought you barely liked him."

"This letter makes it so real. It wasn't real before."

"It's too damned real! Now go away. Go and lie down." She wandered out of the room.

The deputy sheriff came in. He was a heavy, dark man in his thirties, wearing brown store clothes that didn't quite fit his shoulders, a lopsided look of surprise that didn't quite fit his face. His right hand rested on the gun in his hip holster as if to remind him that he had authority.

He said with tentative belligerence: "What goes on out here?"

"Nothing much. Kidnapping and extortion."

"What's this?" He reached for the letter on the table. I had to take hold of his wrist to keep him from touching it.

His black eyes glared dully into my face. "Who do you think you are?"

"The name is Archer. Settle down, officer. You have an evidence case?"

"Yeah, in the car."

"Get it, eh? We'll hold this for the fingerprint men."

He went out and came back with a black metal box. I dropped the letter into it, and he locked it. It seemed to give him great satisfaction.

"Take good care of it," I said, as he left the room with the box under his arm. "Don't let it out of your little hands."

Taggert was standing by the open refrigerator with a half-eaten turkey drumstick in his fingers. "What do we do now?" he asked me, between bites.

"You stick around. You may see a little excitement. Got your gun?"

"Sure thing!" He patted the pocket of his jacket. "How do you think it was done? You think they grabbed Sampson when he left the airport at Burbank?"

"I wouldn't know. Where's a phone?"

"There's one in the butler's pantry. Right through here." He opened a door at the end of the kitchen and closed it after me.

It was a small room lined with cupboards, with a single window over the copper sink, a wall telephone by the door. I asked long distance for Los Angeles. Peter Colton would be off duty, but he might have left a message.

The operator gave me his office, and Colton answered the phone himself.

"Lew speaking. It's a snatch. We got the ransom note a few minutes ago. The letter from Sampson was a gimmick to loosen things up. You better talk to the D.A. It probably happened in your territory when Sampson left the Burbank airport day before yesterday."

"They're taking things slow for kidnappers."

They can afford to. They've got the operation blueprinted. Did you get anything on the black limousine?"

"Too much. There were twelve of them rented that day, but most of them look legit. All but two came back to the agencies the same day. The other two were taken for a week, paid in advance."

"Descriptions?"

"Number one – a Mrs Ruth Dickson, blonde dame, around forty, living at the Beverly Hills Hotel. We checked there, and she's registered but she wasn't in. Number two was a guy on his way to San Francisco. He hasn't turned in the car at that end; but it's only two days, and he has it for a week. Name of Lawrence Becker, a little thin guy not too well dressed—"

"That may be our man. Did you get the number?"

"Wait a minute. I have it here – 62 s 895. It's a 1940 Lincoln."

"Agency?"

"The Deluxe in Pasadena. I'll go out there myself."

"Get the best description you can, and spread the word."

"Natch! But why the sudden enthusiasm, Lew?"

"I saw a man on the highway here who could fit your description. He passed me in a long black car about the time the ransom note was dropped. And the same Joe or his brother tried to run me down with a blue truck in Pacific Palisades this morning. He wears a peaked leather cap."

"Why didn't you put the arm on him?"

"The same reason you're not going to. We don't know where Sampson is, and if we throw our weight around, we'll never find out. Put out the word for tailing purposes only."

"You telling me my business?"

"Apparently."

"All right. Any more helpful hints?"

"Plant a man in the Wild Piano when it opens. Just in case—"

"I've already assigned him. Is that all?"

"Have your office contact the Santa Teresa D.A. I'm turning

the ransom note over to them for fingerprinting. Goodnight and thanks."

"Uh-huh."

He hung up, and the operator broke the connection. I kept the receiver to my ear, listening to the dead line. In the middle of the conversation there had been a click and crackle on the wire. It could have been a momentary break in the connection, or it could have been a receiver being lifted on another extension.

A full minute passed before I heard the faint metallic rustle of a receiver's being replaced somewhere in the house.

XVIII

Mrs Kromberg was in the kitchen with the cook, a flustered white-haired woman with motherly hips. They both jumped when I opened the door of the pantry.

"I was using the phone," I said.

Mrs Kromberg managed a crumpled smile. "I didn't hear you in there."

"How many phones are there in the house?"

"Four or five. Five. Two upstairs, three down."

I gave up the idea of checking the phones. Too many people had access to them. "Where is everybody?"

"Mr Graves called the staff together in the front room. He wanted to know if anybody saw the car that left the note."

"Did anybody?"

"No. I heard a car a while back, but I didn't think anything about it. They're always coming down here and turning around in the drive. They don't know it's a dead end." She moved closer to me and whispered confidentially: "What was in the note, Mr Archer?'

"They want money," I said as I went out.

Three other servants passed me in the hallway, two young Mexicans in gardeners' clothes, walking in single file with their heads down, and Felix bringing up the rear. I raised a hand to him, but he didn't respond. His eyes were opaque and glittering like lumps of coal.

Graves was squatting in front of the fireplace in the living-room turning a charred log with a pair of tongs.

"What's the matter with the servants?" I asked him.

He stood up with a grunt and glanced at the door. "They seem to know they're under suspicion."

"I wish they didn't."

"I didn't say anything to give them the idea. They got it by osmosis. I simply asked them if they'd seen the car. What I really wanted, of course, was a look at their faces before they could close them up."

"You think it's an inside job, Bert?"

"Obviously it's not entirely one. But whoever put together that letter is too well posted. How did he know, for example, that the money would be ready for a nine-o'clock deadline?" He glanced at his watch. "Seventy minutes from now."

"Sheer blind faith, maybe ."

"Maybe."

"We won't argue. You're probably right that it's partly an inside job. Did anyone see the car?"

"Mrs Kromberg heard it. The others played dumb, or are."

"And nobody gave himself away?"

"No. These Mexicans and Filipinos are hard to read." He was careful to add: "Not that I've any reason to suspect the gardners, or Felix either."

"What about Sampson himself?"

He looked at me ironically. "Don't try to be brilliant, Lew. You never were too strong on intuition."

"It's merely a suggestion. If Sampson pays an eighty-per-cent income tax, he could make himself a quick eighty grand by staging this."

"I admit it could be done—"

"It has been."

"But in Sampson's case it's fantastic."

"Don't tell me he's honest."

He picked up the tongs and struck the burning log. The sparks flew up like a swarm of bright wasps. "Not by everybody's standards. But he hasn't got the kind of brain for that sort of setup. It's too risky. Besides, he doesn't need the money. His oil properties are valued around five million, but they're worth more like twenty-five in terms of income. A hundred thousand dollars is small change to Sampson. This kidnapping is the real thing, Lew. You can't get around it."

"I'd like to," I said. "So many kidnappings end up in a murder of convenience."

"This one doesn't have to," he said in a deep growling voice, "and, by God, it isn't going to! We'll pay them their money, and if they don't come through with Sampson we'll hunt them down."

"I'm with you." But it was easier said than done. "Who delivers the lettuce?"

"Why not you?"

"For one thing, they may know me. And I have something else to do. You do it, Bert. And you'd better take Taggert along."

"I don't like him."

"He's a sharp kid, and he's not afraid of a gun. If anything goes wrong, you may need help."

"Nothing is going to go wrong. But I'll take him if you say so."

"I say so."

Mrs Kromberg appeared in the hall doorway, nervously pulling at the front of her smock. "Mr Graves?"

"Well?"

"I wish you'd talk to Miranda, Mr Graves. I tried to take her something to eat, and she wouldn't unlock the door. She wouldn't even answer."

"She'll be all right. I'll talk to her later. Leave her alone for now."

"I don't like it when she acts this way. She's so emotional."

"Forget it. Ask Mr Taggert to meet me in the study, will you? And ask him to bring his pistols – loaded."

"Yes, sir." She was on the point of tears, but she compressed her heavy lips and went away.

When Graves turned from the door, I saw that she had communicated some of her anxiety to him. One of his cheeks was twitching slightly. His eyes were looking at something beyond the room.

"She's probably feeling guilty," he said, half to himself.

"Guilty about what?"

"Nothing tangible. I suppose it's basically because she hasn't been able to take her brother's place. She's watched the old man going downhill, and she probably feels he wouldn't have gone so far and so fast if she could have got closer to him."

"She isn't his wife," I said. "What's Mrs. Sampson's reactions? Have you seen her?"

"A few minutes ago. She's taking it very nicely. Reading a novel, in fact. How do you like that?"

"I don't. Maybe she's the one that should be feeling guilty."

"It wouldn't help Miranda if she did. Miranda's a funny girl. She's very sensitive, but I don't think she knows it. She's always sticking her neck out, living beyond her emotional resources."

"Are you going to marry her, Bert?"

"I will if I can." He smiled wryly. "I've asked her more than once. She hasn't said no."

"You could take good care of her. She's ripe for marriage."

He looked at me in silence for a moment. His lips continued to smile, but his eyes flashed a hands-off signal. "She said you had quite a talk on your drive this afternoon."

"I gave her some fatherly advice," I said. "About driving too fast."

"As long as you keep it on the paternal level." Abruptly he changed the subject. "What about this character, Claude? Could he be in on the kidnapping?"

"He could be in on anything. I wouldn't trust him with a burnt-out match. But I didn't get anything definite. He claimed he hadn't seen Sampson for months."

Straw-yellow fog lamps brushed the side of the house, and a moment later a car door slammed. "That must be the sheriff," Graves said. "It took him a hell of a long time."

The sheriff came in with a great show of haste, like a sprinter breasting the tape. He was a big man in a business suit, carrying a wide-brimmed rancher's hat. Like his clothes, his face was hybrid, half cop and half politician. The sternness of his jaw was denied by the softness of his mouth, a loosely folded mouth that liked women and drink and words.

He thrust out his hand to Graves. "I would have been here sooner, but you asked me to pick up Humphreys."

The other man, who had followed him quietly into the room, was wearing a tuxedo. "I was at a party," he said. "How are you, Bert?"

Graves introduced me. The sheriff's name was Spanner. Humphreys was the District Attorney. He was tall and balding, with the lean face and haunted eyes of an intellectual sharp shooter. He and Graves didn't shake hands. They were too close for that. Humphreys had been Deputy Prosecutor when Graves was District Attorney. I stood back and let Graves do the talking. He told them what they needed to know and left out what they didn't need to know."

When he had finished, the sheriff said: "The letter orders you to drive away in a northern direction. That means he'll be making his getaway in the other direction, towards Los Angeles."

"That's what it means," Graves said.

"Now if we set up a road block down the highway a piece, we should be able to catch him."

"We can't do that," I said in words of one syllable. "If we do, we can kiss good-bye to Sampson."

"But if we catch the kidnapper, we can make him talk—"

"Hold it, Joe," Humphreys put in. "We've got to assume that there are more than one. If we knock off one of them, the other or others will knock off Sampson. It's as clear as the nose on your face."

"And it's in the letter," I said. "Have you seen the letter?"

"Andrews has it," Humphreys said. "He's my fingerprint man."

"If he finds anything, you should check with the F.B.I. files." I sensed that I was making myself unpopular, but I had no time to be tactful and I didn't trust small-time cops to know their business. I turned to the sheriff: "Are you in touch with the L.A. County authorities?"

"Not yet. I felt I should assess the situation first."

"All right, this is the situation. Even if we obey instructions to the letter, there's a better than fifty-fifty chance that Sampson won't come out alive. He must be able to identify at least one of the gang – the one that picked him up in Burbank. That's bad for him. You'll make it worse if you try to trip the money pickup. You'll have a kidnapper in the county jail, and Sampson lying somewhere with his throat cut. The best thing you can do is get on the wires. Let Graves handle the business at this end."

Spanner's face was mottled with anger, his mouth half open to speak.

Humphreys cut him off. "That makes sense, Joe. It's not

good law enforcement, but we've got to compromise. The thing is to save Sampson's life. What say we get back to town now?

He stood up. The sheriff followed him out.

"Can we trust Spanner not to make his own arrangements?"

"I think so," Graves said slowly. "Humphreys will keep an eye on him."

"Humphreys sounds like a good head."

"The best. I worked with him for seven-odd years, and I never caught him in a bad mistake. I got him the appointment when I resigned." There was some regret in his voice.

"You should have stuck with the work," I said. "You got a lot of satisfaction out of it."

"And damned little money! I stuck with it for ten years, and I ended up in debt." He gave me a sly look. "Why did you quit the Long Beach force, Lew?"

"The money wasn't the main thing. I couldn't stand podex osculation. And I didn't like dirty politics. Anyway, I didn't quit, I was fired."

"All right, you win." He glanced at his watch again. It was nearly eight-thirty. "Time to get on our horse."

Alan Taggert was in the study, in a tan trench coat that bunched at the waist and made his shoulders look huge. He brought his hands out of his pockets with a gun in each fist. Graves took one, and Taggert kept the other. They were .32 target pistols with slender blue-steel snouts and prominent sights.

"Remember," I said, for Taggert's benefit, "no shooting unless you're shot at."

"Aren't you coming along?"

"No." I said to Graves: "You know the corner at Fryers Road?"

"Yes."

"There's no cover around?"

"Not a thing. The open beach on one side, and the cutbank on the other."

"There wouldn't be. You go ahead in your car. I'll tag along behind and park a mile or so down the highway."

"You're not going to try a fast one?"

"Not me. I just want to see him go by. I'll meet you at the filling station at the city limits afterward. The Last Chance."

"Right." Graves twirled the knobs of the wall safe.

From the city limits to Fryers Road the highway was four-lane, a mile-long shelf cut into the bluffs that stood along the shore. It was divided in the middle by a strip of turf between concrete curbs. At the intersection with Fryers Road the turf ended and the highway narrowed to three lanes. Graves's Studebaker made a quick U turn at the intersection and parked with its lights burning on the shoulder of the highway.

It was a good place for the purpose, a bare corner rimmed on the right by a line of white posts. The entrance to Fryers Road was a grey-black hole in the side of the bluff. There wasn't a house in sight, or a tree. The cars on the highway were few and far between.

It was ten minutes to nine by my dashboard clock. I waved to Taggert and Graves and drove on past them. It was seven tenths of a mile to the next side road. I checked it on my mileage. Two hundred yards beyond this side road a parking space for sightseers had been built up over the beach on the right side of the highway. I turned off and parked with the lights out and the nose of the car pointed south. It was seven minutes to nine. If everything went on schedule, the pay-off car should pass me in ten minutes.

The fog closed around the car when it stopped, rising from the shore like an impossible grey tide. A few pairs of headlights went north through the fog like the eyes of deep-sea fish. Below the guardrail the sea breathed and gargled in the darkness. At two minutes after nine the rushing headlights came around the curve from the direction of Fryers Road.

The plunging car wheeled sharply before it reached me and turned up the side road to the left. I couldn't see its colour or shape but I heard it losing rubber. The driver's technique seemed familiar.

Leaving my lights out, I drove across the highway and along its shoulder to the side road. Before I reached it I heard three sounds, remote and muffled by the fog. The banshee wail of brakes, the sound of a shot, the ascending roar of a motor picking up speed.

The trough of the side road was filled with diffused white lights. I stopped my car a few feet short of the intersection.

Another car came out of the side road and turned left in front of me toward Los Angeles. It was a long-nosed convertible painted light cream. I couldn't see the driver through the blurred side window, but I thought I saw a dark mass of woman's hair. I wasn't in a position to give chase, and I couldn't have anyway.

I switched on my fog lamps and turned up the road. A few hundred yards from the highway a car was standing with two of its wheels in the ditch. I parked behind it and got out with the gun in my hand. It was a black limousine, a pre-war Lincoln custom job. The engine was idling and the lights were on. The licence number was 62 s 895. I opened the front door with my left hand, my gun cocked in my right.

A little man leaned toward me, peering into the fog with intent dead eyes. I caught him before he fell out. I'd been feeling death in my bones for twenty-four hours.

XIX

He was still wearing his leather cap sharply tilted on the left side of his head. There was a small round hole in the cap above his left ear. The left side of his face was peppered with black powder burns. His head had been knocked askew by the force of the bullet, and rolled on his shoulder when I pushed him upright. His black-nailed hands slipped off the steering wheel and dangled at his sides.

Holding him up in the seat with one hand, I went through his pockets with the other. The side pockets of his leather windbreaker contained a windproof lighter smelling of gasoline, a cheap wooden case half full of cigarettes rolled in brown wheat-straw paper, and a four-inch spring-knife. There was a worn sharkskin wallet in the hip pocket of his levis, containing eighteen or twenty dollars in small bills and a California driver's licence recently issued to one Lawrence Becker. The address on the licence was a cheap Los Angeles hotel teetering on the edge of Skid Row. It wouldn't be his address, and Lawrence Becker wouldn't be his name.

The left side pocket of the levis held a dirty comb in a

leatherette case. The other pocket held a heavy bunch of car keys on a chain – keys for every make of car from Chevrolet to Cadillac – and a half-used book of matches labelled: "Souvenir of The Corner, Cocktails and Steaks, Highway 101 South of Buenavista." He had nothing on under his windbreaker but a T-shirt.

There were a few short marijuana butts in the dashboard ash tray, but the rest of the car was as clean as a whistle. Not even a registration card in the glove-compartment, nor a hundred thousand dollars in moderate-sized bills.

I put the things back in his pocket and propped him up in the seat, slamming the door to hold him. I looked back once before I got into my car. The lights of the Lincoln were still burning, the idling motor still sending out a steady trickle of vapour from the exhaust. The dead man hunched at the wheel looked ready to start on a long, fast trip to another part of the country.

Graves's Studebaker was parked by the pumps at the filling station. Graves and Taggert were standing beside it and came running when I drove up. Their faces were pale and sick with excitement.

"It was a black limousine," Graves said. "We drove away slow and saw him stop at the corner. I couldn't see his face, but he was wearing a cap and a leather windbreaker."

"He still is."

"Did you see him pass you?" Taggert's voice was so tense he whispered.

"He turned off before he got to me. He's sitting in his car on the next side road with a bullet in his head."

"Good Christ!" Graves cried. "You didn't shoot him, Lew?"

"Somebody else did. A cream convertible came out of the side road a minute after the shot. I think a woman was driving. She headed for L.A. Now, are you sure he got the money?"

"I saw him pick it up."

"He hasn't got it any more; so one of two things happened. It was a heist, or his partners double-crossed him. If he was hijacked, his partners don't get the hundred grand. If they double-crossed him, they'll double-cross us. Either way it's bad for Sampson."

"What do we do now?" Taggert said.

Graves answered him. "We take the wraps off the case. Give the police the go-ahead. Post a reward. I'll see Mrs. Sampson about it."

"One thing, Bert," I said. "We've got to keep this shooting quiet – out of the papers anyway. If hijackers did it, his partners will blame us, and that's the end of Sampson."

"The dirty bastards!" Graves's voice was heavy and grim. "We kept our side of the bargain. If I could get my hands on them—"

"You wouldn't know it. All we have is a dead man in a rented car. You better start with the sheriff; he won't do much, but it's a nice gesture. Then the highway patrol and the F.B.I. Get as many men on it as you can."

I released my emergency brake and let the car roll a few inches. Graves backed away from the window. "Where do you think you're going?"

"On a wild-goose chase. Things look so bad for Sampson I might as well."

It took me down the highway fifty miles to Buenavista. The highway doubled as the town's main street. It was lit by motel and tavern signs and three theatre fronts. Two of the three theatres advertised Mexican films. The Mexicans lived off the land when the canneries were closed. The rest of the townspeople lived off the Mexicans and the fishing fleet.

I stopped in the middle of the town, in front of an overgrown cigar store that sold guns, magazines, fishing tackle, draught beer, stationery, baseball gloves, contraceptives, and cigars. Two dozen Mexican boys with grease-slicked duck-tail haircuts were swarming in and out of the store, drawn two ways by the pinball machines in the back and the girls on the street. The girls went by in ribbons and paints, cutting the air with their bosoms. The boys whistled and postured or pretended to be uninterested.

I called one to the curb and asked where The Corner was. He conferred with another *pachuco*. Then they both pointed south.

"Straight ahead, about five miles, where the road goes down the White Beach."

"There's a big red sign," the other boy said, stretching out his arms enthusiastically. "You can't miss it. The Corner."

I thanked them. They bowed and smiled and nodded as if I had done them a favour.

The sign spelled out "The Corner" in red-neon script on the roof of a long, low building to the right of the highway. A black-and-white sign at the intersection beyond it pointed to White Beach. I parked in the asphalt parking-space beside the building. There were eight or ten other cars in the lot, and a trailer truck on the shoulder of the highway. Through the half-curtained windows I could see a few couples at tables, a few others dancing.

To the left as I went in was a long bar, totally empty. The dining-room and dance floor was to the right. I stood at the entrance as if I was looking for somebody. There weren't enough dancers to bring the room to life. Their music came from a jukebox. There was an empty orchestra stand at the back of the room. All that was left of the big war nights were the foot-grained floor, rows of unset rickety tables, odours like drunken memories in the walls, tattered decorations like drunken hopes.

The customers felt the depression in the room. Their faces groped for laughter and enjoyment and couldn't quite get hold of them. None of the faces meant anything to me.

The solitary waitress came up to me. She had dark eyes and a soft mouth, a good body going to seed at twenty. You could read her history in her face and body. She walked carefully as if she had sore feet.

"You want a table, sir?"

"Thanks, I'll sit in the bar. You may be able to help me, though. I'm looking for a man I met at a baseball game. I don't see him."

"What's his name?"

"That's the trouble – I don't know his name. I owe him money on a bet, and he said he'd meet me here. He's a little fellow, about thirty-five, wears a leather windbreaker and a leather cap. Blue eyes, sharp nose." And a hole in his head, sister, a hole in his head.

"I think I know who you mean. His name's Eddie something, or something. He comes in for a drink sometimes, but he hasn't been in to-night."

"He said he'd meet me here. What time does he usually come in?"

"Later than this – around midnight. He drives a truck, don't he?"

"Yeah, a blue truck."

"That's the one," she said. "I seen it in the parking lot. He was in a couple of nights ago, used our phone for a long-distance telephone call. Three nights ago, it was. The boss didn't like it – you never know how much to collect when it runs over three minutes – but Eddie said he'd reverse the charges, so the boss let him go ahead. How much do you owe him, anyway?"

"Plenty. You don't know where he was calling?"

"No, It's none of my business, anyway. Is it any of yours?"

"It's just that I want to get in touch with him. Then I could send him his money."

"You can leave it with the boss if you want to."

"Where's he?"

"Chico, behind the bar."

A man at one of the tables rapped with his glass, and she walked carefully away. I went to the bar.

The bartender's face, from receding hairline to slack jaw, was terribly long and thin. His night of presiding at an empty bar made it seem even longer. "What'll it be?"

"A beer."

His jaw dropped another notch. "Eastern or Western?"

"Eastern."

"That's thirty-five with the music." His jaw recovered the lost ground. "We provide the music."

"Can I get a sandwich?"

"Sure thing," he said almost cheerfully. "What kind?"

"Bacon and egg."

"O.K." He signalled the waitress through the open door.

"I'm looking for a guy called Eddie," I said. "The one that phoned me long-distance the other night."

"You from Las Vegas?"

"Just came from there."

"How's business in L.V.?"

"Pretty slow."

"That's too bad," he said happily. "What were you looking for him for?"

"I owe him some money. Does he live around here?"

"Yeah, I think he does. I don't know where, though. He come

in once or twice with a blonde dame. Probably his wife. He might come in to-night for all I know. Stick around."

"Thanks. I will."

I took my beer to a table beside the window, from which I could watch the parking lot and the main entrance. After a while the waitress brought my sandwich. She lingered even after I paid and tipped her.

"Going to leave the money with the boss?"

"I'm thinking about it. I want to be sure he gets it."

"You must be eaten up with honesty, eh?"

"You know what happens to bookies that don't pay off."

"I sort of thought you was a bookie." She leaned toward me with sudden urgency. "Listen, mister, I got a girl friend, she goes out with an exercise boy, she says he says Jinx is a cert in the third to-morrow. Would you bet it on the nose or across the board?"

"Save your money," I said. "You can't beat them."

"I only bet tip money. This boy, my girl friend's boy friend, he says Jinx is a cert."

"Save it."

Her mouth pursed sceptically. "You're a funny kind of bookie."

"All right." I handed her two ones. "Play Jinx to show."

She looked at me with a scowl of suprise. "Gee, thanks, mister – only I wasn't asking for money."

"It's better than losing your own money," I said.

I hadn't eaten for nearly twelve hours, and the sandwich tasted good. While I was eating it several cars arrived. A party of young people came in laughing and talking, and business picked up at the bar. Then a black sedan rolled into the parking lot, a black Ford sedan with a red police search-light sticking out like a sore thumb beside the windshield.

The man who got out wore plain clothes as obvious as a baseball umpire's suit, with gun wrinkles over the right hip. I saw his face when he came into the circle of light from the entrance. It was the deputy sheriff from Santa Teresa. I got up quickly and went through the door at the end of the bar into the men's lavatory, locking the door behind me. I lowered the top of the toilet seat and sat down to brood over my lack of foresight. I shouldn't have left the book matches in Eddie something's pocket.

I put in eight or ten minutes reading the inscriptions on the whitewashed walls. "John 'Rags' Latino, Winner 120 Hurdles, Dearborn High School, Dearborn, Mich., 1946." "Franklin P. Schneider, Osage County, Oklahoma, Deaf Mute, Thank you." The rest of them were the usual washroom *graffiti* interspersed with primitive line drawings.

The naked bulb in the ceiling shone in my eyes. My brain skipped a beat, and I went to sleep sitting up. The room was a whitewashed corridor slanting down into the bowels of the earth. I followed it down to the underground river of filth that ran under the city. There was no turning back. I had to wade the excremental river. Fortunately, I had my stilts with me. They carried me untainted, wrapped in cellophane, to the landing on the other side. I tossed my stilts away – they were also crutches – and mounted a chrome-plated escalator that gleamed like the jaws of death. Smoothly and surely it lifted me through all the zones of evil to a rose-embowered gate, which a maid in gingham opened for me, singing *Home, Sweet Home.*

I stepped out into a stone-paved square, and the gate clanged shut behind me. It was the central square of the city, but I was alone in it. It was very late. Not a streetcar was in sight. A single yellow light shone down on the foot-smoothed pavement. When I moved, my footsteps echoed lonesomely, and on all four sides the hunchbacked tenements muttered like a forest before a storm. The gate clanged shut again, and I opened my eyes.

Something metallic was pounding on the door.

"Open up," the deputy sheriff said. "I know you're in there."

I slipped the bolt and pulled the door wide open. "You in a hurry, officer?"

"So it's you. I thought maybe it was you." His black eyes and heavy lips were bulging with satisfaction. He had a gun in his hand.

"I knew damn' well it was you," I said. "I didn't think it was necessary to tell everybody in the place."

"Maybe you had a reason for keeping it quiet, eh? Maybe you had a reason for hiding in here when I come in? The sheriff thinks it's an inside job, and he'll want to know what you're doing here."

"This is the guy," the bartender said, at his shoulder. "He said Eddie phoned him in Las Vegas."

"What you got to say to that?" the deputy demanded. He waggled the gun in my face.

"Come in and close the door."

"Yeah? Then put your hands on your head."

"I don't think so."

"Put your hands on your head." The gun poked into my solar plexus. "You carrying a gun?" He started to frisk me with his other hand.

I stepped back out of his reach. "I'm carrying a gun. You can't have it."

He moved toward me again. The door swung closed behind him. "You know what you're doing, eh? Resisting an officer-inperformancehisduty. I got a good mind to put you under arrest."

"You got a good mind, period."

"No cracks from you, jerk. All I want to know is what you're doing here."

"Enjoying myself."

"So you won't talk, eh?" he said, like a comic-book cop. He raised his free hand to slap me.

"Hold it," I said. "Don't lay a finger on me."

"And why not?"

"Because I've never killed a cop. It would be a blot on my record."

Our glances met and deadlocked. His raised hand hung stiff in the air and gradually subsided.

"Now put your gun away," I said. "I don't like being threatened."

"Nobody asked you what you liked," he said, but his fire had gone out. His swarthy face was caught between conflicting emotions: anger and doubt, suspicion and bewilderment.

"I came here for the same reason you did – officer." The word came out hard, but I managed to get it out. "I found the book matches in Eddie's pocket—"

"How come you know his name?" he said alertly.

"The waitress told me."

"Yeah? The bartender said he phoned you in Las Vegas."

"I was trying to pump the bartender. Get it? It was a gag. I was trying to be subtle."

"Well, what did you find out?"

"The dead man's name is Eddie, and he drove a truck. He came in here for drinks sometimes. Three nights ago he phoned Las Vegas from here. Sampson was in Las Vegas three nights ago."

"No kidding?"

"I wouldn't kid you, officer, even if I could."

"Jesus," he said, "it all fits in, don't it?"

"I never thought of that," I said. "Thank you very much for pointing it out to me."

He gave me a queer look, before he put away his gun.

XX

I DROVE A HALF MILE down the highway, turned, drove back again, and parked at the intersection diagonally across from The Corner. The deputy's car was still in the parking lot.

The fog was lifting, dissolving into the sky like milk in water, and blowing out to sea. The expanding horizon only reminded me that Ralph Sampson could be a long way from there – anywhere at all. Starving to death in a mountain cabin, drowned at the bottom of the sea, or wearing a hole in the head like Eddie. The cars went by the roadhouse in both directions, headed for home or headed for brighter lights. In the rear-vision mirror my face was ghostly pale, as if I had caught a little death from Eddie. There were circles under my eyes, and I needed a shave.

A truck came up from the south and passed me slowly. It wheeled into the parking lot of The Corner. The truck was blue and had a closed van. A man jumped down from the cab and shuffled across the asphalt. I knew his rubber-kneed walk, and in the light from the entrance I knew his face. A savage sculptor had hacked it out of stone and smashed it with another stone.

He stopped with a jerk when he saw the black police car. Stopped and turned and ran back to the blue truck. It backed out with a grinding of gears, and turned down the road toward White Beach. When its tail light had dwindled to a red spark,

I followed it. The road changed from black-top to gravel, and finally to sand. For two miles I ate his dust.

Where the road came down to the beach between two bluffs, another road crossed it. The lights of the truck turned left and climbed the slope. When they were over the rise and out of sight, I followed them. The road was a single track cut into the side of the hill. From the crest I could see the ocean below to my right. There was a travelling moon in the clouds, which were drifting out to sea. Its light on the black water made a dull lead-foil shine.

The hill flattened out ahead, and the road straightened. I drove on slowly with my lights out. Before I knew it I was abreast of the truck. It was standing in the lane with no lights showing, fifty yards off the road. I kept going.

The road ended abruptly at the bottom of the hill a quarter mile farther on. A lane meandered off toward the ocean on the right, but its entrance was blocked by a wooden gate. I turned my car in the dead end and climbed the hill on foot.

A row of eucalyptus trees, ragged against the sky, edged the lane where the truck was standing. I left the road and kept them between me and the truck. The ground was uneven, dotted with clumps of coarse grass. I stumbled more than once. Then space fell open in front of me, and I nearly walked off the edge of the bluff. Far down below, the white surf stroked the beach. The sea looked close enough for a dive, but hard as metal.

Below me to the right there was a white square of light. I climbed and slid down the side of the hill, holding onto the grass to keep from falling. A small building took shape around the light, a white cottage held in a groin of the bluff.

The unblinded window gave me a full view of the single room. I felt the gun in my holster and approached the window on my hands and knees. There were two people in the room. Neither of them was Sampson.

Puddler was wedged in a chair cut out of a barrel, his broken profile toward me, a bottle of beer in his fist. He was facing a woman on an unmade studio bed against the wall. The gasoline lamp that hung from a rafter in the unplastered ceiling threw a hard white light on her streaked blonde hair and her face. It was a thin and harried face, with wide resentful nostrils and a parched mouth. Only the cold brown eyes were lively in it, darting and peering from the puckered skin of their sockets. I moved my head sideways, out of their range.

The room wasn't large, but it seemed to be terribly bare. The pine floor was carpetless, slick with grime. A wooden table piled with dirty dishes stood under the light. Beyond it against the far wall were a two burner oil stove, a sagging icebox, a rust-mottled sink with a tin pail under it to catch the drip.

The room was so still, the clapboard walls so thin, that I could hear the steady suspiration of the lamp. And Puddler's voice when he said:

"I can't wait here all night, can I? You can't expect me to wait here all night. I got a job to get back to. And I don't like that *pol*ice car setting up there at The Corner."

"That's what you said before. The car don't mean anything."

"I'm saying it again. I should of been back at the Piano already; you know that. Mr Troy was mad when Eddie didn't show."

"Let him get apoplexy." The woman's voice was sharp and thin like her face. "If he don't like the way Eddie does the job, he can stick it."

"You ain't in no position to talk like that." Puddler looked from side to side of the room. "You didn't talk like that when Eddie come sucking around for a job when he got out of the pen. When he got out of the pen and come sucking around for a job and Mr Troy give him one—"

"For God's sake! Can't you stop repeating yourself, dim brain?

His scarred face gathered in folds of hurt suprise. He drew in his head, and his thick neck wrinkled up like a turtle's neck. "That's no way to talk, Marcie."

"You shut your yap about Eddie and the pen." Her voice bit like a thin knife blade. "How many jails you seen the inside of, dim brain?"

His answer was a tormented bellow. "Lay off me, hear."

"All right then, lay off Eddie."

"Where the hell is Eddie, anyway?"

"I don't know where he is or why, but I know he's got a reason."

"It better be good when he talks to Mr Troy."

"*Mister* Troy, *Mister* Troy. He's got you hypnotized, hasn't he? Maybe Eddie won't be talking to Mr Troy."

His small eyes peered at her, trying to read her meaning in her face, and gave up. "Listen, Marcie," he said after a pause. "You can drive the truck."

"The hell you say! I want no part of that racket."

"It's good enough for me. It's good enough for Eddie. You're getting awful fancy-pants since he took you off the street—"

"Shut up, or you'll be sorry!" she said. "The trouble with you is you're yellow. You see a patrol car and you wet your pants. So you try to get a woman to take your rap, like any other pimp."

He stood up suddenly, brandishing the bottle. "Lay off me, hear. I don't take nothing from nobody. You was a man, I spoil your face for you, hear." The beer foamed out on the floor and over her knees.

She answered very coolly. "Yoy wouldn't say that in front of Eddie. He'd saw you to pieces, and you know it."

"That little monkey!"

"Yeah, that little monkey! Sit down, Puddler. Everybody knows you're a powerful battler. I'll get you another beer."

She got up and moved across the room, stepping lightly and furiously like a starved cat. Taking a towel from a nail beside the sink, she dabbed at her beer-stained bathrobe.

"You drive the truck?" Puddler said hopefully.

"Do I have to say everything twice, the same as you? I'm not driving the truck. If you're afraid, let one of them drive."

"Naw, I can't do that. They don't know the road; they get knocked off."

"You're wasting time, then, aren't you?"

"Yeah, I guess so." He moved toward her uncertainly, casting a huge shadow on the floor and wall. "How's about a little something before I go? A little party. Eddie's probably in the sack with somebody else. I got plenty what it takes."

She picked up a bread knife from the table, the kind with a wavy cutting edge. "Take it away with you, Puddler, or I'll love you up with this."

"Come on now, Marcie. We could get along." He stood still, keeping his distance.

She gulped to control her rising hysteria, but her voice came out as a scream. "Beat it!" The bread knife moved in the glaring light, pointed at his throat.

"O.K., Marcie. You don't have to get mad." He shrugged his shoulders and turned away with the hurt and helpless look of any rejected lover.

I left the window and started up the hill. Before I reached the top, a door swung open, projecting an oblong of light on the hillside. I froze on my hands and knees. I could see the shadow of my head on the dry grass in front of my face.

Then the door closed, drawing darkness over me. Puddler's shadow came out of the pool of shadows behind the house. He went up the steep lane, scuffing the dust with his feet, and disappeared behind the eucalyptus trees.

I had to choose between him and the blonde woman, Marcie. I chose Puddler. Marcie could wait. She'd wait forever before Eddie something came back.

XXI

A FEW MILES NORTH of Buenavista the blue truck left the highway, turning off to the right. I stopped to let it get well ahead. A sign at the intersection said "Lookout Road". Before I turned up after it, I switched to my fog lamps. The fog had blown out to sea, but I didn't want Puddler to see the same headlights behind him all the way.

All the way was close to seventy miles, two hours of rough driving through mountains. One five-mile stretch, along a ridge so high that my ears hurt, was as bad as any road I'd driven by daylight: two ruts along a black cliff edge, with dark eternity waiting below each curve. The truck highballed along as if it was safe on rails. I let it get out of sight, switched my lights again, and tried to feel like a new man driving a different car.

We came by a different route into the valley Miranda and I had crossed in the afternoon. On the straight valley road I turned out my car lights entirely and drove by the light of the moon, eked out by memory. I thought I knew where the truck was going. I had to be certain.

On the other side of the valley it climbed into the mountains, up the twisting black-top which led to the Temple in the Clouds.

I had to use my lights again to follow it. When I reached Claude's mailbox the wooden gate beside it had been closed. The truck was far above me, a glowworm crawling up the mountain. Higher still, above the jagged black horizon, the cleared sky was salted with stars. The unclouded moon was motionless among them, a round white hole in the night.

I was tired of waiting, of following people down dark roads and never seeing their faces. So far as I knew, there were only the two of them there, Puddler and Claude. I had a gun – and the advantage of surprise.

I opened the gate and drove through, up the winding lane to the rim of the mesa, and down toward the Temple. Above its white mass there was a faint glow from an interior light. The truck was standing inside the open wire gate, its back doors swinging wide. I parked at the gate and got out.

There was nothing inside the truck but crouched shadows, a wooden bench padded with burlap along each side, the pungent odour of men who have sweated and dried in their clothes.

The ironbound door of the Temple creaked open then. Claude came out, a moonlit caricature of a Roman senator. His sandals crunched in the gravel. "Who is that?" he said.

"Archer. Remember me?"

I moved from behind the truck and let him see me. He had an electric lantern in his hand. It shone on the gun in mine.

"What are you doing here?" His beard waggled, but his voice was steady.

"Still looking for Sampson," I said.

As I approached he backed toward the door. "You know he is not here. Was one sacrilege not enough for you?"

"Skip the mumbo jumbo, Claude. Did it ever fool anybody at all?"

"Come in if you must, then," he said. "And I see you must."

He held the door for me and closed it after me. Puddler was standing in the centre of the court.

"Get over there with Puddler," I said to Claude.

But Puddler came toward me in a shuffling run. I shot once at his feet. The bullet made a white scar in the stone in front of him and whined into the adobe wall on the other side of the court. Puddler stood still and looked at me.

Claude made a half-hearted try to knock down my gun. I

took him in the stomach with my elbow. He doubled up on the pavement.

"Come here," I said to Puddler. "I want to talk to you."

He stayed where he was. Claude sat up hugging his torso and cried out loudly in a Spanish dialect I didn't understand. A door sprang open as if it knew Spanish, on the other side of the court. A dozen men came out. They were small and brown, moving quickly toward me. Their teeth flashed in the moonlight. They came on silently, and I was afraid of them. Because of that, or something else, I held my fire. The brown men looked at the gun and came on anyway.

I clubbed the gun and waited. The first two got bloody scalps. Then they swarmed over me, hung on my arms, kicked my legs from under me, kicked consciousness out of my head. It slid like a disappearing tail light down the dark mountainside of the world.

I came fighting. My arms were pinned, my raw mouth kissing cement. I realized after a while that I was fighting myself. My arms were tied behind me, my legs bent up and tied to my waist. All I could do was rock a little and beat the side of my head against cement. I decided against this policy.

I tried yelling. My skull vibrated like live skin on a drumhead. I couldn't hear my voice above the roar. I gave up yelling. The roar went on in my head, rising higher and higher until it was out of my range, a silent screech. Then the real pain began, pounding my temples in syncopated rhythm like roustabouts driving stakes. I was grateful for any interruption, even Claude.

"The wrath of the god is heavy," he said, above and behind me. "You may not desecrate his temple with impunity."

"Stop gabbling," I said, to the cement. "You'll be up against two kidnapping raps instead of one."

"Bum raps, Mr Archer." He made a clucking sound, tongue against palate. By straining my neck I could see his gnarled sandaled feet on the floor near my head.

"You misunderstand the situation," he said, putting on his vocabulary like a garment. "You invaded our retreat by armed force, assaulted me, attacked my friends and disciples—"

I tried to laugh mirthlessly, and succeeded. "Is Puddler one of your disciples? He's a very spiritual type."

"Listen to me, Mr Archer. We might with perfect justification have killed you in self-defence. Your life is still our gift."

"Why don't you climb up the chimney and ride away?"

"You fail to understand the seriousness of this—"

"I understand that you're a smelly old crook." I tried to think of subtler insults, but my brain wasn't functioning properly.

He stamped with his heel in my side, just above the kidney. My mouth opened, and my teeth ground on the cement. No sound came out.

"Think about it," he said.

The light receded and a door slammed. The pain in my head and body pulsated like a star. Small and remote, then large and near, then dwindling down to a whirring point, the tip of a restless drill.

On the threshold of consciousness my mind swarmed with images from beyond the threshold; uglier faces than I'd seen in any street, eviler streets than I'd seen in any city. I came to the empty square in the city's heart. Death lurked behind the muttering windows, an old whore with sickness under her paint. A face looked down at me, changing by the second: Miranda's brown young face sprouting grey hair, Claude's mouth denuded to become Fay's smile, Fay shrinking down, all but the great dark eyes, to the Filipino's head, which was withered by rapid age to the silver head of Troy. Eddie's bright dead gaze came back again and again, and the Mexican faces repeated themselves, each one like the other, with flat black eyes and shining teeth curved downward in a smile of anger and fear. With my arms roped tight behind me, my heels pressed into my buttocks, I slid over the threshold into a bad sleep.

Light against my eyelids brought me back to a closed red world. I heard a voice above me and kept my eyes closed. The voice was Troy's soft purr.

"You've made a serious error, Claude. I know this chap, you see. Now why shouldn't you have told me about his earlier visit?"

"I didn't think it was important. He was looking for Sampson, that was all. Sampson's daughter was with him." Claude was speaking naturally for the first time. His voice had lost its orotundity and risen a full octave. He made sounds like a frightened woman.

"You didn't think it was important, eh? I'll tell you just how important it is for you. It means that your usefulness is ended. You can take your brown-skinned doxy and get out."

"This is my place! Sampson said I could live here. You can't order me out."

"I've already done so, Claude. You've bungled your piece of the line, and that means you're finished. Probably the whole thing is finished. We're clearing out of the Temple, and we're not leaving you behind to turn stool pigeon."

"But where can I go? What can I do?"

"Open another store-front church. Go back to Gower Gulch. What you do is no concern of mine."

"Fay won't like this," Claude said hesitantly.

"I don't propose to consult her. And we'll have no more argument, or I'll turn you over to Puddler to argue it out with him. I don't want to do that, because I have one more job for you."

"What is it?" Claude's voice tried to sound eager.

"You can complete the delivery of the current truckload. I'm not at all sure you're competent even for that, but I must risk it. The risk will be largely yours in any case. The ranch foreman will meet you at the southeast entrance to give them safe conduct. Do you know where the southeast entrance is?"

"Yes. Just off the highway."

"Very good. When you've unloaded, drive the truck back to Bakersfield and lose it. Don't try to sell it. Leave it in a parking lot and disappear. Can I trust you to do that?"

"Yes, Mr Troy. But I have no money."

"Here's a hundred."

"Only a hundred?"

"You're lucky to get that, Claude. You can start now. Tell Puddler I want him when he's finished eating."

"You're not going to let him hurt me, Mr Troy?"

"Don't be silly. I wouldn't let him disarrange a hair of your filthy head."

Claude's sandals scraped away. This time the light remained. Something pulled at the rope that held my wrists. My hands and forearms were numb, but I could feel the strain in my shoulders.

"Lay off!" The movement of my jaw set off a fit of chattering. I had to clench my teeth to stop it.

"You'll be perfectly all right in a jiffy," Troy said. "They've trussed you up like a fowl for market, haven't they?"

I heard a knife whisper through fibre. The tension in my arms and legs was released. They thudded on the cement like pieces of wood. A terrier chill took hold of the back of my neck and shook me.

"Do get up, old fellow."

"I like it here." Sense was returning to the nerves in my arms and legs, burning like a slow fire.

"You mustn't give way to the sulks, Mr Archer. I warned you once about my associates. If they've dealt with you rather violently, you must admit that you asked for it. And may I suggest that you sell insurance in a highly unusual way. On a mountaintop in the very early morning, with a gun in your hand. Among men whose life expectancy is considerably better than yours."

I moved my arms on the pavement and kicked my feet together. The blood was moving through them now, like coarse hot rope. Troy stepped back in two quick tapping movements.

"The gun in my hand is aimed at the back of your head, Mr Archer. You may get up slowly, however, if you feel quite able."

I gathered my arms and legs under me and forced my body off the pavement. The room spun and lurched to rest. It was one of the bare cells off the court of the Temple. An electric lantern stood on a bench against one wall. Troy was beside it, as dapper and well groomed as ever, with the same nickel-plated gun.

"I gave you the benefit of the doubt last night," he said. "You've rather disappointed me."

"I'm doing my job."

"It seems to conflict with mine." He moved the gun in his hand as if to punctuate the sentence. "Just what exactly is your job, old man?"

"I'm looking for Sampson."

"Is Sampson missing?"

I looked into his impassive face, trying to judge how much he knew. His face didn't say.

"Rhetorical questions bore me, Troy. The point is that you won't gain anything by pulling a second snatch on top of the first. It will pay you to let me go."

"Are you offering me a deal, my dear fellow? You're rather low on bargaining power, aren't you?"

"I'm not working alone," I said. "The cops are in the Piano to-night. They're watching Fay's. Miranda Sampson will be bringing them here today. No matter what you do to me, your racket is finished. Shoot me, and you're finished."

"Perhaps you overestimate your importance." He smiled carefully. "You wouldn't be considering a percentage of tonight's gross?"

"Wouldn't I?" I was trying to think my way around the gun in his hand. My mind was a little vague. I was putting too much effort into standing up.

"Consider my position," Troy said. "A small-time private eye blunders into my business, not once, but twice in rapid succession. I grin and bear it. Instead of killing you, I offer you a one-third cut of tonight's gross. Seven hundred dollars, Mr Archer."

"A one-third cut of tonight's gross is thirty-three grand."

"What?" He was startled, and his face showed it.

"You want me to spell it out for you?"

He recovered his poise immediately. "You mentioned thirty-three thousand. That's a rather grandiose estimate."

"One third of a hundred thousand is thirty-three thousand three hundred and thirty three dollars and thirty three cents."

"What kind of shakedown are you trying to pull?" His voice was anxious and harsh. I didn't like all that tension covering the gun hand.

"Forget it," I said. "I wouldn't touch your money."

"But I don't understand," he said earnestly. "And you mustn't talk in riddles. It makes me jumpy. It makes my hands nervous." The gun moved in illustration.

"Don't you know what goes on, Troy? I thought you knew the angles."

"Assume that I don't know anything. And talk fast."

"Read it in the papers."

"I said talk fast." He raised the gun and let me look into its eye. "Tell me about Sampson and a hundred grand."

"Why should I tell you your business? You kidnapped Sampson two days ago."

"Go on."

"Your driver picked up the hundred grand last night. Wasn't it enough?"

"Puddler did that?" His impassivity had gone for good. A new expression had taken charge of his face, a killer's expression, cruel and intent.

He went to the door and opened it, holding the gun between us. "Puddler!" His voice rose high and cracked.

"The other driver," I said. "Eddie."

"You're lying, Archer."

"All right. Wait for the cops to come and tell you in person. They know by now who Eddie was working for."

"Eddie hasn't the brains."

"Enough brains for a fall guy."

"What do you mean?"

"Eddie's in the morgue."

"Who killed him? Coppers?"

"Maybe you did," I said slowly. "A hundred grand is a lot of money to a small-timer."

He let it pass. "What happened to the money?"

"Somebody shot Eddie and took it away. Somebody in a cream-coloured convertible."

Those three words hit him behind the eyes and turned them blank for an instant. I moved to my right and swatted his gun with the palm of my left hand. It spun to the floor without discharging, and slid to the open door.

Puddler was in at the door and on the gun before me. I backed away.

"Do I let him have it, Mr Troy?"

Troy was shaking his injured hand. It fluttered like a white moth in the circle of light from the lantern.

"Not now," he said. "We've got to clear out of here, and we don't want to leave a mess behind us. Take him to the pier on the Rincon. Use his car. Hold him there until I send word. You follow me?"

"I get it, Mr Troy. Where are you going to be?"

"I don't quite know, Is Betty at the Piano to-night?"

"Not when I left."

"Do you know where she lives?"

"Naw – she moved the last couple of weeks. Somebody lent her a cabin somewheres, I don't know where–"

"Is she driving the same car?"

"The convertible? Yeah. She was last night, anyway."

"I see," said Troy. "I'm surrounded by fools and knaves as usual. They can't keep their heads out of trouble, can they? We'll show them trouble, Puddler."

"Yessir."

"Move," Troy said to me.

XXII

THEY MARCHED ME OUT to my car. Troy's Buick was standing beside it. The truck was gone. Claude and the brown men were gone. It was still black night, with the moon at its lower edge now.

Puddler brought a coil of rope from the shack beside the adobe.

"Put your hands behind you," Troy said to me.

I kept my hands at my sides.

"Put your hands behind you."

"So far I've been doing my job," I said. "If you push me around some more, I'll have a grudge against you."

"You talk a great fight," Troy said. "Quiet him, Puddler."

I turned to face Puddler, not fast enough. His fist struck the nape of my neck. Pain whistled through my body like splintered glass, and the night fell on me solidly again. Then I was on the road. The road was crowded with traffic. I was responsible for the occupants of every car. I had to write a report on each, giving age, occupation, hobby, religion, bank balance, sexual proclivities, politics, crimes, and favourite eating places. The passengers changed cars frequently, like people playing musical chairs. The cars changed numbers and colour. My pen ran out of ink. A blue truck picked me up and changed to funeral black. Eddie was at the wheel, and I let him drive. I was planning to kill a man.

The plan was half complete, when I came to. I was wedged on the floor of my car between the front and back seats. The floor was vibrating with motion, and the pain in my head kept time. My hands were bound behind me again. Puddler's wide back was in the front seat, outlined by the reflection of the headlights. I couldn't get to my feet, and I couldn't reach him.

I tried to work my hands loose from the rope, twisting and pulling until my wrists were raw and my clothes were wet. The rope held out better than I did. I threw my plan away and started another.

By dark untravelled roads we came down out of the mountains and back to the sea. He parked the car under a tarpaulin stretched on poles. As soon as the engine died I could hear the waves below us beating on the sand. He lifted me out by my coat collar and set me on my feet. I noticed that he pocketed my ignition key.

"Don't make no noise," he said, "unless you want it again."

"You've got a lot of guts," I said. "It takes a lot of guts to hit a man from behind while somebody else holds a gun on him."

"You shut up." He spread his fingers across my face and hooked them downward. They tasted of sweat, as rank as a horse's.

"It takes a lot of guts," I said, "to push a man in the face when his hands are tied behind him."

"You shut up," he said. "I shut you up for good."

"Mr Troy wouldn't like that."

"You shut up. Get moving." He put his hands on my shoulders, turned me, and pushed me out from under the tarpaulin.

I was at the shore end of a long pier that was built out over the water on piles. There were oil derricks on the skyline behind me, but no lights. No movement but the sea's, and the systole and diastole of an oil pump at the end of the pier. The planks of the footwalk were warped and badly put together. Black water gleamed in the cracks.

When we were about a hundred yards from shore I made out the pump at the end of the pier, rising and falling like a mechanical teeter-totter. There was a tool shed beside it, nothing but ocean beyond.

Puddler unlocked the door of the shed, lifted a lantern off a nail, and lit it.

"Sit down, mug." He swung the lantern toward a heavy bench that stood against the wall. There was a vice at one end of the bench and a few tools scattered along it: pincers, wrenches of various sizes, a rusty file.

I sat down on a clear space. Puddler shut the door and set the lantern on an oil drum. Lit from below by the yellow flaring light, his face was barely human. It was low-browed and prognathous like a Neanderthal man's, heavy and forlorn, without thought. It wasn't fair to blame him for what he did. He was a savage accidentally dropped in the steel-and-concrete jungle, a trained beast of burden, a fighting machine. But I blamed him. I had to. I had to take what he'd handed me or find a way to hand it back to him.

"You're in a rather unusual position," I said.

He didn't hear me, or refused to answer. He leaned against the door, a thick stump of a man blocking my way, I listened to the thump and creak of the pump outside, the water lapping below against the piling. And I thought over the things I knew about Puddler.

"You're in a rather unusual position," I said again.

"Button your lip."

"Acting as jailer, I mean. It's usually the other way around, isn't it. You sit in the cell while somebody else watches you."

"I said button your lip."

"How many jails you seen the inside of, dim brain?"

"Fa Christ sake!" he yelled. "I warned you." He slouched toward me.

"It takes a lot of guts," I said, "To threaten a man when his hands are tied behind him."

His open hand stung my face.

"The trouble with you is you're yellow," I said. "Just like Marcie said. You're even afraid of Marcie, aren't you, Puddler?"

He stood there blinking, overshadowing me. "I kill you, hear, you talk like that to me. I kill you, hear." The words came out disjointed, moving too fast for his labouring mouth. A bubble of saliva formed at one corner.

"But Mr Troy wouldn't like that. He told you to keep me safe, remember? There's nothing you can do to me, Puddler."

"Beat your ears off," he said. "I beat your ears off."

"Not if my hands were free, you poor palooka."

"Who you calling palooka?" He drew back his hand again.

"You fifth-rate bum," I said. "You has-been. Down-and-outer. Hit a man when he's tied – it's all you're good for."

He didn't hit me. He took a clasp knife out of his pocket and opened it. His little eyes were red and shining. His whole mouth was wet with saliva now.

"Stand up," he said. "I show you who's a bum."

I turned my back to him. He cut the ropes on my wrists and snapped the knife shut. Then he whirled me toward him and met me, with a quick right cross that took away the feeling from my face. I knew I was no match for him. I kicked him in the stomach, and he went to the other side of the room.

While he was coming back I picked up the file from the bench. Its point was blunt, but it would do. I clinched with him. Holding the file near the point in my right hand, I cut him across the forehead with it from temple to temple. He backed away from me. "You cut me," he said incredulously.

"Pretty soon you won't be able to see, Puddler." A Finnish sailor on the San Pedro had taught me how Baltic knife-fighters blind their opponents.

"I kill you yet." He came at me like a bull.

I went to the floor and came up under him, jabbing with the file where it would hurt him. He bellowed and went down. I made for the door. He came after me and caught me in the opening. We staggered the width of the pier and fell into space. I took a quick breath before we struck. We went down together. Puddler fought me violently, but his blows were cushioned by the water. I hooked my fingers in his belt and held on.

He threshed and kicked like a terrified animal. I saw his air come out, and silver bubbles rising through the black water to the surface. I held on to him. My lungs were straining for air, my chest was collapsing. The contents of my head were slowing and thickening. And Puddler wasn't struggling any more.

I had to let go of him to reach the surface in time. One deep breath, and I went down after him. My clothes hampered me, and the shoes were heavy on my feet. I went down through strata of increasing cold until my ears were aching with the pressure of the water. Puddler was out of reach and out of sight. I tried six times before I gave him up. The key to my car was in his trousers pocket.

When I swam to shore my legs wouldn't hold me up. I had to crawl out of reach to the surf. It was partly physical exhaustion and partly fear. I was afraid of what was behind me in the cold water.

I lay in the sand until my heartbeat slowed. When I got to my feet the derricks on the horizon were sharply outlined against a lightening sky. I climbed the bank to the shelter where my car was and turned on the lights.

There was a piece of copper wire attached to one of the poles that held the tarpaulin. I pulled it loose and wired my ignition terminals under the dash. The engine started on the first try.

XXIII

THE SUN WAS OVER the mountains when I reached Santa Teresa. It put an edge on everything, each leaf and stone and blade of grass. From the canyon road the Sampson house looked like a toy villa built of sugar cubes. Closer up I could feel its massive silence, which dominated the place when I stopped the car. I had to unwire the ignition to cut the motor.

Felix came to the service entrance when I knocked. "Mr Archer?"

"Is there any doubt about it?"

"You were in an accident, Mr Archer?"

"Apparently. Is my bag still in the storeroom?" I had fresh clothes in, it and a duplicate set of car keys.

"Yes, sir. There are contusions on your face, Mr Archer. Should I call a doctor?"

"Don't bother. I could do with a shower, though, if there's one handy."

"Yes, sir. I have a shower over the garage."

He led me to his quarters and brought my bag. I showered and shaved in the dinky bathroom, and changed my sea-sodden clothes. It was all I could do not to stretch out on the unmade bed in his neat little cell of a room and let the case go hang.

When I returned to the kitchen he was setting a tray with a silver breakfast set. "Do you want something to eat, sir?"

"Bacon and eggs, if possible."

He bobbed his round head. "As soon as I have finished with this, sir."

"Who's the tray for?"

"Miss Sampson, sir."

"So early?"

"She will breakfast in her room."

"Is she all right?"

"I do not know, sir. She had a very little sleep. It was past midnight when she came home."

"From where?"

"I do not know, sir. She left at the same time as you and Mr Graves."

"Driving herself?"

"Yes, sir."

"What car?"

"The Packard convertible."

"Let's see, that's the cream one, isn't it?"

"No, sir. It is red. Bright scarlet. She drove over two hundred miles in the time she was gone."

"You keep a pretty close watch on the family, don't you, Felix?"

He smiled blandly. "It is one of my duties to check the cars for gas and oil, sir, since we have no regular chauffeur."

"But you don't like Miss Sampson very well?"

"I am devoted to her, sir." His opaque black eyes were their own mask.

"Do they give you a rough time, Felix?"

"No, sir. But my family is well known on Samar. I have come to the United States to attend the California Polytechnic College when I am able to do this. I resent Mr Graves's assumption that I am suspect because of the colour of my skin. The gardeners also resent it for themselves."

"You're talking about last night?"

"Yes, sir."

"I don't think he meant it that way."

Felix smiled blandly.

"Is Mr Graves here now?"

"No, sir. He is at the sheriff's office, I think. If you will excuse me, sir?" He hoisted the tray to his shoulder.

"You know the number? And do you have to say 'sir' every second word?"

"No, sir," he said with mild irony. "23665."

I dialled the number from the butler's pantry and asked for

Graves. A sleepy deputy called him.

"Graves speaking." His voice was hoarse and tired.

"This is Archer."

"Where in God's name have you been?"

"I'll tell you later. Any trace of Sampson?"

"Not yet, but we've made some progress. I'm working with a major case squad from the F.B.I. We wired the classification of the dead man's prints to Washington, and we got an answer about an hour ago. He's in the F.B.I. files with a long record. Name's Eddie Lassiter."

"I'll be over as soon as I eat. I'm at the Sampson place."

"Perhaps you'd better not." He lowered his voice. "The sheriff's peeved at you for running out last night. I'll come there." He hung up, and I opened the door to the kitchen.

Bacon was making cheerful noises in a pan. Felix transferred it to a warming-dish, inserted bread in the toaster beside the stove, broke the eggs in the hot grease, poured me a cup of coffee from a steaming Silex maker.

I sat down at the kitchen table and gulped the scalding coffee. "Are all the phones in the house on the same line?"

"No, sir. The phones in the front of the house are on a different line from the servants' phones. Do you wish your eggs turned over, Mr Archer?"

"I'll take them the way they are. Which ones are connected with the phone in the pantry?"

"The one in the linen closet and the one in the guest cottage above the house. Mr Taggert's cottage."

Between mouthfuls I asked him: "Is Mr Taggert there now?"

"I do not know, sir. I think I heard him drive in during the night."

"Go and make sure, will you?"

"Yes, sir." He left the kitchen by the back door.

A car drove up a minute later, and Graves came in. He had lost some of his momentum, but he still moved quickly. His eyes were red-rimmed.

"You look like hell, Lew."

"I just came from there. Did you bring the dope on Lassiter?"

"Yeah."

He took a teletype flimsy out of his inside pocket and handed it to me. My eye skipped down the closely printed sheet.

Brought before Children's Court, New York, March 29, 1923, father's complaint, truancy. Committed to New York Catholic Protectory, April 4, 1923. Released August 5, 1925. . . . Brooklyn Special Sessions Court, January 9, 1928, charged with bicycle theft. Received suspended sentence and placed on probation. Discharged from probation November 12, 1929. . . . Arrested May 17, 1932, and charged with possession of a stolen money order. Case dismissed for lack of evidence on recommendation U.S. Attorney. . . . Arrested for car theft October 5, 1936, sentenced to 3 years in Sing Sing. . . . Arrested with sister Betty Lassiter by agents of the U.S. Narcotics Bureau, April 23, 1943. Convicted of selling one ounce of cocaine, May 2, 1943, sentenced to year and a day in Leavenworth. . . . Arrested August 3, 1944, for participating in holdup of General Electric payroll truck. Pleaded guilty, sentenced to 5 to 10 years in Sing Sing. Released on parole September 18, 1947. Broke parole and disappeared, December 1947.

Those were the high points in Eddie's record, the dots in the dotted line that marked his course from a delinquent childhood to a violent death. Now it was just as if he had never been born.

Felix said at my shoulder: "Mr Taggert is in his cottage, sir."

"Is he up?"

"Yes, he is dressing."

"How about some breakfast?" Graves said.

"Yes, sir."

Graves turned to me. "Is there anything useful in it?"

"Just one thing, and it isn't nailed down. Lassiter had a sister named Betty who was arrested with him on a narcotics charge. There's a woman named Betty in Los Angeles with narcotics in her record, a pianist in Troy's clipjoint. She calls herself Betty Fraley."

"Betty Fraley!" Felix said from the stove.

"This doesn't concern you," Graves told him unpleasantly.

"Wait a minute," I said. "What about Betty Fraley, Felix? Do you know her?"

"I do not know her, no, but I have seen her records, in Mr Taggert's cottage. I have noticed the name when I dusted there."

"Are you telling the truth?" Graves said.

"Why should I lie, sir?"

"We'll see what Taggert has to say about that." Graves got to his feet.

"Wait a minute, Bert." I put my hand on his arm, which was hard with tension. "Bulldozing won't get us anywhere. Even if Taggert has the woman's records, it doesn't have to mean anything. We're not even certain she's Lassiter's sister. And maybe he's a collector."

"He has quite a large collection," Felix said.

Graves was stubborn. "I think we should take a look at it."

"Not now. Taggert may be as guilty as hell, but we won't get Sampson back by being blunt about it. Wait until Taggert isn't there. Then I'll look over his records."

Graves let me pull him back into his seat. He stroked his closed eyelids with his fingertips. "This case is the wildest mess I've ever seen or heard of," he said.

"It is." Graves only knew the half of it. "Is the general alarm out for Sampson?"

He opened his eyes. "Since ten o'clock last night. We've alerted the highway patrol and the F.B.I., and every single police department and county sheriff between here and San Diego."

"You'd better get on the phone," I said, "and put out another state-wide alarm. This time for Betty Fraley. Take in the whole Southwest."

He smiled ironically, with his heavy jaw thrust out. "Doesn't that fall under the category of bluntness?"

"In this case I think it's necessary. If we don't get to Betty fast there'll be somebody there ahead of us. Dwight Troy is gunning for her."

He gave me a curious look. "Where do you get your information, Lew?"

"I got that the hard way. I talked to Troy himself last night."

"He is mixed up in this, then?"

"He is now. I think he wants the hundred grand for himself and I think he knows who has it."

"Betty Fraley?" He took a notebook out of his pocket.

"That's my guess. Black hair, green eyes, regular features,

five foot two or three, between twenty-five and thirty, probably cocaine addict, thin, but well stacked, and pretty if you like to play with reptiles. Wanted on suspicion of the murder of Eddie Lassiter."

He glanced up sharply from his writing. "Is that another guess, Lew?"

"Call it that. Will you put it on the wires?"

"Right away." He started across the room to the butler's pantry.

"Not that phone, Bert. It's connected with the one in Taggert's cottage."

He stopped and turned to me with a shadow of grief on his face. "You seem pretty sure that Taggert's our man."

"Would it break your heart if he was?"

"Not mine," he said, and turned away. "I'll use the phone in the study."

XXIV

I WAITED IN THE HALL at the front of the house until Felix came to tell me that Taggert was eating breakfast in the kitchen. He led me around the back of the garages, up a path that became a series of low stone steps climbing the side of the hill. When we came within sight of the guest cottage, he left me.

It was a one-storey white frame house perched among trees with its back to the hillside. I opened the unlocked door and went in. The living-room was panelled in yellow pine and furnished with easy chairs, a radio-phonograph, a large refectory table covered with magazines and piles of records. The view through the big western window took in the whole estate and the sea to the horizon.

The magazines on the table were *Jazz Record* and *Downbeat*. I went through the records and albums one by one, Decca and Bluebird and Asch, twelve-inch Commodores and Blue Notes. There were many names I had heard of: Fats Waller, Red Nichols, Lux Lewis, Mary Lou Williams – and titles I never had heard of: *Numb Fumblin'* and *Viper's Drag, Night Life, Denapas Parade*. But no Betty Fraley.

I was at the door on my way to talk to Felix when I remembered the black discs skipping out to sea the day before. A few minutes after I saw them, Taggert had come through the house in bathing trunks.

Avoiding the house, I headed for the shore. From the glassed-in pergola on the edge of the bluff a long flight of concrete steps descended the cliff diagonally to the beach. There was a bath house with a screened veranda at the foot of the steps, and I went in. I found a rubber-and-plate-glass diving mask hanging on a nail in one of the bathhouse cubicles. I stripped to my shorts and adjusted the mask to my head.

A fresh offshore breeze was driving in the waves and blowing off their crests in spray before they broke. The morning sun was hot on my back, the dry sand warm against the soles of my feet. I stood for a minute in the zone of wet brown sand just above the reach of the waves and looked at them. The waves were blue and sparkling, curved as gracefully as women, but I was afraid of them. The sea was cold and dangerous. It held dead men.

I waded in slowly, pulled the mask down over my face, and pushed off. About fifty yards from shore, beyond the surf, I turned on my back and breathed deeply through my mouth. The rise and fall of the swells, and the extra oxygen, made me a little dizzy. Through the misted glass the blue sky seemed to be spinning over my head. I ducked under water to clear the glass, surface-dived, and breast-stroked to the bottom.

It was pure white sand broken by long brown ribs of stone. The sand was roiled a little by the movement of the water, but not enough to spoil the visibility. I zigzagged forty or fifty feet along the bottom and found nothing but a couple of undersized abalones clinging to a rock. I kicked off and went to the surface for air.

When I raised the mask I saw that a man was watching me from the cliff. He ducked down behind the wild-cherry windbreak by the pergola, but not before I had recognized Taggert. I took several deep breaths and dived again. When I came up, Taggert had disappeared.

On the third dive I found what I was looking for, an unbroken black disc half buried in the sand of the bottom. Holding the record against my chest, I turned on my back and kicked myself to shore. I took it into the shower and washed and dried it with tender care, like a mother with an infant.

Taggert was on the veranda when I came out of the dressing-rooms. He was sitting in a canvas chair with his back to the screen door. In flannel slacks and a white T-shirt, he looked very young and brown. The black hair on his small head was carefully brushed.

He gave me a boyish grin that didn't touch his eyes. "Hello there, Archer. Have a nice swim?"

"Not bad. The water's a little cold."

"You should have used the pool. It's always warmer."

"I prefer the ocean. You never know what you're going to find. I found this."

He looked at the record in my hands as if he were noticing it for the first time. "What is it?"

"A record. Somebody seems to have scraped the labels off and thrown it in the sea. I wonder why."

He took a step toward me, long and noiseless on the grass rug. "Let me see."

"Don't touch it. You might break it."

"I won't break it."

He reached for it. I jerked it out of his reach. His hand grasped air.

"Stand back," I said.

"Give it to me, Archer."

"I don't think so."

"I'll take it away from you."

"Don't do that," I said. "I think I can break you in two."

He stood and looked at me for ten long seconds. Then he turned on the grin again. The boyish charm was very slow in coming. "I was just kidding, man. But I'd still like to know what's on the bloody thing."

"So would I."

"Let's play it then. There's a portable player here." He moved around me to the table in the centre of the veranda and opened a square fibre box.

"I'll play it," I said.

"That's right – you're afraid I'll break it." He went back to his chair and sat down, stretching his legs in front of him.

I cranked the machine and placed the record on the turntable.

Taggert was smiling expectantly. I stood and watched him, waiting for a sign, a wrong move. The handsome boy didn't fit into the system of fears I had. He didn't fit into any pattern I knew.

The record was scratched and tired. A single piano began to beat, half drowned in surface noise. Three or four hackneyed boogie chords were laid down and repeated. Then the right hand wove through them, twisting them alive. The first chords multiplied and built themselves around the room. The place they made was half jungle, half machine. The right hand moved across it and back again like something being chased. Chased through an artificial jungle by the shadow of a giant.

"You like it?" Taggert said.

"Within limits. If the piano was a percussion-instrument it would be first-rate."

"But that's just the point. It is a percussion instrument if you want to use it that way."

The record ended, and I turned off. "You seem to be interested in boogie-woogie. You wouldn't know who made this record?"

"I wouldn't, no. The style could be Lux Lewis."

"I doubt it. It sounds more like a woman's playing."

He frowned in elaborate concentration. His eyes were small in his head. "I don't know of any woman who can play like that."

"I know one. I heard her in the Wild Piano night before last. Betty Fraley."

"I never heard of her," he said.

"Come off it, Taggert. This is one of her records."

"Is it?"

"You should know. You tossed it in the sea. Now why would you do that?"

"The question doesn't arise, because I didn't do it. I wouldn't dream of throwing good records away."

"I think you dream a great deal, Taggert. I think you've been dreaming about a hundred thousand dollars."

He shifted slightly in his chair. His stretched-out pose had stiffened and lost its air of casualness. If someone had lifted him by the nape of the neck, his legs would have stayed as they were, straight out before him in the air.

"Are you suggesting that I kidnapped Sampson?"

"Not personally. I'm suggesting that you conspired to do it – with Betty Fraley and her brother Eddie Lassiter."

"I never heard of them, either of them." He drew a deep breath.

"You will. You'll meet one of them in court, and hear about the other."

"Now just a minute," he said. "You're going too fast for me. Is this because I threw those records away?"

"This is your record, then?"

"Sure." His voice was vibrantly frank. "I admit I had some of Betty Fraley's recrods. I got rid of them last night when I heard you talking to the police about the Wild Piano."

"You also listen to other people's telephone conversations?"

"It was purely accidental. I overheard you when I was trying to make a phone call of my own."

"To Betty Fraley?"

"I told you I don't know her."

"Excuse me," I said. "I thought perhaps you phoned her last night to give her the green light on the murder."

"The murder?"

"The murder of Eddie Lassiter. You don't have to act so surprised, Taggert."

"But I don't know anything about these people."

"You knew enough to throw away Betty's records."

"I'd heard of her, that's all. I knew she played in the place, I got rid of her records. You know how unreasonable they can be about circumstantial evidence."

"Don't try to kid me the way you've kidded yourself," I said. "An innocent man would never have thought of throwing those records away. People all over the country have them, haven't they?"

"That's just my point. There's nothing incriminating about them."

"But you thought there was, Taggert. You'd have no reason to think of them as evidence against you, if you really weren't in this thing with Betty Fraley. And it happens that you threw them in the sea a good many hours before you heard my phone call – before Betty was ever mentioned in connection with this case."

"Maybe I did," he said. "But you're going to have a time

hanging anything on me on the basis of those records."

"I'm not going to try to. They put me on to you and served their purpose. So let's forget about the records and talk about something important." I sat down in a wicker chair across the veranda from him.

"What do you want to talk about?" He still had perfect control. His puzzled smile was natural, and his voice was easy. Only his muscles gave him away, bunched at the shoulders, quivering in the thighs.

"Kidnapping," I said. "We'll leave the murder till later. Kidnapping is just about as serious in this state. I'll give you my version of the kidnapping, and then I'll listen to yours. A great many people will be eager to listen to yours."

"Too bad. I haven't any version."

"I have. I'd have seen it sooner if I hadn't happened to like you. You had more opportunity than anyone, and more motive. You resented Sampson's treatment of you. You resented all that money he had. You hadn't much yourself—"

"Still haven't," he said.

"You should be well fixed for the present. Half of the hundred thousand is fifty thousand. The very temporary present."

He spread his hands humorously. "Am I carrying it with me?"

"You're not that dull," I said. "But you're dull enough. You've acted like a rube, Taggert. The city slickers sucked you in and used you. You'll probably never see your half of the hundred grand."

"You promised me a story," he said smoothly. He was going to be hard to break down.

I showed him my best card. "Eddie Lassiter phoned you the night before you flew Sampson out of Las Vegas."

"Don't tell me you're psychic, Archer. You said the man was dead." But there was a new white line around Taggert's mouth.

"I'm psychic enough to tell you what you said to Eddie. You told him you'd by flying into Burbank about three o'clock the next day. You told him to rent a black limousine and wait for your phone call from the Burbank airport. When Sampson phoned the Valerio for a limousine, you cancelled the call and sent for Eddie instead. The operator at the Valerio thought it was Sampson calling back. You do a pretty good imitation of him, don't you?"

"Go on," he said. "I've always been fond of fantasy."

"When Eddie turned up at the front of the airport in the rented car, Sampson got in as a matter of course. He had no reason to suspect anything. You had him so drunk he wouldn't have noticed the difference in drivers – so drunk that even a little guy like Eddie could handle him when they got to a private place. What did Eddie use on him, Taggert? Chloroform?"

"This is supposed to be your story," he said. "Is your imagination getting tired?"

"The story belongs to both of us. That cancelled telephone call was important, Taggert. It was the thing that tied you into the story in the first place. Nobody else could have known that Sampson was going to phone the Valerio. Nobody else knew when Sampson was going to fly in from Nevada. Nobody else could have made all the arrangements and run them off on schedule."

"I never denied I was at the airport with Sampson. There were a few hundred other people there at the same time. You're hipped on circumstantial evidence, like any other cop. And this business of the records isn't even circumstantial evidence. It's circular argument. You haven't got anything on Betty Fraley, and you haven't proved any connection between us. Hundreds of collectors have her records."

His voice was still cool and clear, bright with candour, but he was worried. His body was hunched and tense, as if I had forced him into a narrow space. And his mouth was turning ugly.

"It shouldn't be hard to prove a connection," I said. "You must have been seen together at one time or another. And wasn't it you that called her the other night when you saw me in the Valerio with Fay Estabrook? You weren't really looking for Sampson at the Wild Piano, were you? You were going to see Betty Fraley. You put me off when you pulled Puddler out of my hair. I thought you were on my side. So much so that I put it down to stupidity when you fired at the blue truck. You were warning Eddie off, weren't you, Taggert? I'd call you a smart boy if you hadn't dirtied your hands with kidnapping and murder. Stupidity like that cancels out the smartness."

"If you're through calling me names," he said, "we'll get down to business."

He was still sitting quietly in the canvas chair, but his hand came up from beside him with a gun. It was the .32 target pistol I had seen before, a light gun but heavy enough to make my stomach crawl.

"Keep your hands on your knees," he said.

"I didn't think you'd give up so easily."

"I haven't given up. I'm simply guaranteeing my freedom of action."

"Shooting me won't guarantee it. It'll guarantee something else. Death by gas. Put your gun away and we'll talk this over."

"There's nothing to talk over."

"You're wrong, as usual. What do you think I'm trying to do in this case?"

He didn't answer. Now that the gun was in his hand, ready for violence, his face was smooth and relaxed. It was the face of a new kind of man, calm and unfrightened, because he laid no special value on human life. Boyish and rather innocent, because he could do evil almost without knowing it. He was the kind of man who had grown up and found himself in war.

"I'm trying to find Sampson," I said. "If I can get him back, nothing else counts."

"You've gone about it the wrong way, Archer. You forgot what you said last night: if anything happens to the people that kidnapped Sampson, it's the end of him."

"Nothing has happened to you – yet."

"Nothing has happened to Sampson."

"Where is he?"

"Where he won't be found until I want him to be."

"You have your money. Let him go."

"I intend to, Archer. I was going to turn him loose today. But that will have to be postponed – indefinitely. If anything happens to me, it's good-bye Sampson."

"We can reach an understanding."

"No," he said. "I couldn't trust you. We have to get clear away. Don't you see that you've spoilt it? You have the power to spoil things, but you haven't the power to guarantee that we'll get clear. There's nothing I can do with you but this."

He glanced down at the gun, which was pointed at the middle of my body, then casually back at me. Any second he could shoot, without preparation, without anger. All he had to do was pull the trigger.

"Wait," I said. My throat was tight. My skin felt desiccated, and I wanted to sweat. My hands were clutching my knees.

"We don't want to stretch this out." He stood up and moved toward me.

I shifted the weight of my body in the chair. One shot wouldn't kill me, unless my luck was bad. Between the first and the second I could reach him. As I drew back my feet I talked rapidly.

"If you give me Sampson, I can guarantee that I won't try to hold you and I won't talk. You'll have to take your chances with the others. Kidnapping is like other business enterprises: you have to take your chances."

"I'm taking them," he said, "but not on you."

His rigid arm came up with the gun at the end like a hollow blue finger. I looked sideways, away from the direction I was going to move in. I was halfway out of the chair when the gun went off. Taggert was listless when I got to him. The gun slid out of his hand.

Another gun had spoken. Albert Graves was in the doorway with the twin of Taggert's pistol in his hand. He poked the end of his little finger through a round hole in the screen.

"Too bad," he said, "but it had to be done."

The water ran down my face.

XXV

I CAUGHT TAGGERT'S LIMBER BODY as it fell, and laid it out on the grass rug. The dark eyes were open and glistening. They didn't react to the touch of my fingertips. The round hole in the right temple was bloodless. A death mark like a little red birthmark, and Taggert was thirty dollars' worth of organic chemicals shaped like a man.

Graves was standing over me. "He's dead?"

"He didn't fall down in a fit. You did a quick, neat job."

"It was you or Taggert."

"I know," I said. "I don't like to quibble. But I wish you'd shot the gun out of his hand or smashed the elbow of his gun arm."

"I couldn't trust myself to do that kind of shooting any more. I got out of practice in the Army." His mouth twisted wryly, and one of his eyebrows went up. "You're a carping son of a bitch, Lew. I save your life, and you criticize the method."

"Did you hear what he said?"

"Enough. He kidnapped Sampson."

"But he wasn't alone. His friends aren't going to like this. They'll take it out on Sampson."

"Sampson is alive, then?

"According to Taggert he is."

"Who are these others?"

"Eddie Lassiter was one. Betty Fraley is another. There may be more. You'll be calling the police about this shooting?"

"Naturally."

"Tell them to keep it quiet."

"I'm not ashamed of it, Lew," he told me sharply, "though you seem to think I should be. It had to be done, and you know the law on it as well as I do."

"Look at it from Betty Fraley's point of view. It won't be the legal one. When she hears what you've done to her sidekick she'll beeline for Sampson and make a hole in *his* head. Why should she bother keeping him alive? She's got the money—"

"You're right," he said. "We've got to keep it out of the papers and off the radio."

"And we've got to find her before she gets to Sampson. Watch yourself, too, Bert. She's dangerous, and I have an idea that she was gone on Taggert."

"Her, too?" he said, and after a pause: "I wonder how Miranda's going to take it."

"Pretty hard. She liked him, didn't she?"

"She had a crush on him. She's a romantic, you know, and awfully young. Taggert had the things she thought she wanted, youth and good looks and a hell of a combat record. This thing is going to shock her."

"I don't shock easily," I said, "but it took me by surprise. I thought he was a pretty sound kid, a little self-centred but solid."

"You don't know the type like I do," Graves said. "I've seen this same thing happen to other boys, not to such an extreme degree, of course, but the same thing. They went out of high school into the Army or the Air Corps and made good in a big way. They were officers and gentlemen with high pay, an even higher opinion of themselves, and all the success they needed to keep it blown up. War was their element, and when the war was finished, they were finished. They had to go back to boys' jobs and take orders from middle-aged civilians. Handling pens and adding machines instead of flight sticks and machine guns. Some of them couldn't take it and went bad. They thought the world was their oyster and couldn't understand why it had been snatched away from them. They wanted to snatch it back. They wanted to be free and happy and successful without laying any foundation for freedom or happiness or success. And there's the hangover."

He looked down at the new corpse on the floor. Its eyes were still open, gazing through the roof at the empty sky. I bent down and closed them.

"We're becoming very elegiac," I said. "Let's get out of here."

"In a minute." He laid his hand on my arm. "I want you to do me a favour, Lew."

"What is it?"

He spoke with diffidence. "I'm afraid if I tell Miranda about this, she won't see it the way it happened. You know what I mean – she might blame me."

"You want me to tell her?"

"I know it's not your baby, but I'd appreciate it."

"I can do that," I said. "I suppose you did save my life."

Mrs Kromberg was running a vacuum cleaner in the big front room. She glanced up when I entered, and switched it off. "Mr Graves find you all right?"

"He found me."

Her face sharpened. "Anything wrong?"

"It's over now. Do you know where Miranda is?"

"She was in the morning-room a few minutes ago."

She led me through the house and left me at the door of a sun-filled room. Miranda was at a window that overlooked the patio. She had daffodils in her hands and was arranging them in a bowl. The yellow flowers clashed with her sombre clothes. The only colour on her body was a scarlet bow at the neck of her black wool suit. Her small sharp breasts pressed angrily against the cloth.

"Good morning," she said. "I am expressing a wish, not making a statement."

"I understand that." The flesh around her eyes was swollen and faintly blue. "But I have some moderately good news for you."

"Moderately?" She raised her round chin, but her mouth remained doleful.

"We have some reason to think that your father is alive."

"Where is he?"

"I don't know."

"Then how do you know he's alive?"

"I didn't say I knew. I said I thought. I talked to one of his kidnappers."

She came at me headlong, clutching at my arm. "What did he say?"

"That your father is alive."

Her hand released my arm and took hold of her other hand. Her brown fingers interlocked and strained against each other. The daffodils fell to the floor with broken stems. "But you can't trust what they say? They'd naturally claim he's alive. What did they want? Did they phone you?"

"It was just one of them I talked to. Face to face."

"You saw him and let him go?"

"I didn't let him go. He's dead. His name is Alan Taggert."

"But that's impossible. I –" Her lower lip went slack and showed her lower row of teeth.

"Why is it impossible?" I said.

"He couldn't do it. He was decent. He was always honest with me – with us."

"Until the big chance came. Then he wanted money more than anything else. He was ready to murder to get it."

A question formed in her eyes. "You said Ralph was alive?"

"Taggert didn't murder your father. He tried to murder me."

"No," she said. "He wasn't like that. That woman twisted him. I knew she'd ruin him if he went with her."

"Did Taggert tell you about her?"

"Of course he told me. He told me everything."

"And you still loved him?"

"Did I say I loved him?" Her mouth was firm again and curved with pride.

"I understood you did."

"That stupid gawk! I used him for a while. He served the purpose."

"Stop it," I said violently. "You can't fool me, and you can't fool yourself. You'll tear yourself to pieces."

Yet her hands were motionless in each other, her tall body was still. Still as a tree bent out of line and held there by a continuous wind. The wind pushed her against me. Her feet trampled the daffodils. Her mouth closed over mine. Her body held me close from breast to knee, too long and not enough.

"Thank you for killing him, Archer." Her voice was anguished and soft, the kind of voice a wound would have if it could speak.

I took her by the shoulders and held her off. "You're wrong. I didn't kill him."

"You said he was dead, that he tried to murder you."

"Albert Graves shot him."

"Albert?" Her giggle passed back and forth like a quick spark between laughter and hysteria. "Albert did that?"

"He's a dead shot – we used to do a lot of target-shooting together," I said. "If he wasn't, I wouldn't be here with you now."

"Do you like being here with me now?"

"It makes me a little sick. You're trying to swallow these things without going to pieces, and you can't get them down."

Her glance travelled down my body, and she grinned as much like a monkey as a pretty girl could. "Did it make you sick when I kissed you?"

"You could tell it didn't. But it's confusing to be in a room with five or six competing personalities."

"Sick-making, you mean," she said with her monkey grin.

"You'll be the sick one if you don't settle down. Find out what you feel about this business, and have a good cry, or you'll end up schizo."

"I always was a schizoid type," she said. "But why should I cry, *Herr Doktor*?"

"To see if you can."

"You don't take me seriously, do you, Archer?"

"I can't afford to put my hand in a cleft tree."

"My God," she said. "I'm sick-making, I'm schizo, I'm split

wood. What do you really think of me?"

"I wouldn't know. I'd have a better idea if you'll tell me where you went last night."

"Last night? Nowhere."

"I understand you did a lot of driving in the red Packard convertible last night."

"I did, but I didn't go anywhere. I was just driving. I wanted to be by myself to make up my mind."

"About what?"

"About what I'm going to do. Do you know what I'm going to do, Archer?"

"No. Do you?"

"I want to see Albert," she said. "Where is he?"

"In the bathhouse, where it happened. Taggert's there, too."

"Take me to Albert."

We found him on the screened veranda sitting over the dead man. The sheriff and the District Attorney were looking at Taggert's face, which was still uncovered, and listening to Graves's story. All three stood up for Miranda.

She had to step over Taggert in order to reach Albert Graves. She did this without a downward glance at the uncovered face. She took one of Graves's hands between hers and raised it to her lips. It was his right hand she kissed, the one that had fired the gun.

"I'll marry you now," she said.

Whether Graves knew it or not, he'd had his reason for shooting Alan Taggert through the head.

XXVI

For half a minute nobody spoke. The lovers stood together above the body. The others stood and watched them.

"We'd better get out of here, Miranda," Graves said finally. He glanced at the District Attorney. "If you'll excuse us? Mrs Sampson will have to be told about this."

"Go ahead, Bert," Humphreys said.

While a man from his office took notes, and another photographed the body on the floor, Humphreys questioned me. His questions covered the ground quickly and thoroughly. I told him who Taggert was, how he died, and why he had to die. Sheriff Spanner listened restlessly, biting a cigar to shreds.

"There will have to be an inquest," Humphreys said. "You and Bert are in the clear, of course. Taggert had a deadly weapon in his hand and was obviously intending to use it. Unfortunately this shooting leaves us worse off than before. We have practically no leads."

"You're forgetting Betty Fraley."

"I'm not forgetting her. But we haven't caught her, and even if we do, we can't be certain that she knows where Sampson is. The problem hasn't changed, and we're no nearer to its solution than we were yesterday. The problem is to find Sampson."

"And the hundred thousand dollars," Spanner said.

Humphreys looked up impatiently. "The money is secondary, I think."

"Secondary, yes, but a hundred thousand in cash is always important." He tugged at his elastic lower lip. His grey eyes shifted to me. "If you're finished with Archer here, I want to have a talk with him."

"Take him," Humphreys said coldly. "I've got to get back to town." He took the body with him.

When we were alone the sheriff got up heavily and stood over me.

"Well?" I said. "What's the trouble, Sheriff?"

"Maybe you can tell me." He folded his thick arms across his chest.

"I've told you what I know."

"Maybe so. You didn't tell me everything you should of last night. I heard from your friend Colton this morning. He told me about the limousine this Lassiter was driving: it came from a car-rental in Pasadena, and you knew it." He raised his voice suddenly, as if he hoped to startle me into a confession. "You didn't tell me you saw it before, when the ransom note was delivered."

"I saw one like it. I didn't know it was the same car."

"But you guessed it was. You told Colton it was. You gave the information to an officer that couldn't use it because he's got no jurisdiction in this county. But you didn't tell me, did you? If you had, we could have taken him in. We could have stopped the shooting and saved the money—"

"But not Sampson," I said.

"You're not the judge of that." His face was bursting at the seams with angry blood. "You took things in your own hands and interfered with my duty. You withheld information. Right after Lassiter got shot, you disappeared. You were the only witness, and you disappeared. A hundred thousand dollars disappeared at the same time."

"I don't like the implication." I stood up. He was a big man, and our eyes were level.

"*You* don't like it. How do you think I like it? I'm not saying you took the money – that remains to be seen. I want your gun, and I want to know what you were doing when my deputy caught up with you down south. And I want to know what you were doing after that."

"I was looking for Sampson."

"You were looking for Sampson," he said, with heavy irony. "You expect me to take your word for that."

"You don't have to take my word. I'm not working for you."

He leaned toward me with his hands on his hips. "If I wanted to be ugly, I could put you away this minute."

My patience broke. "Don't look now," I said, "but you are ugly."

"Do you know who you're talking to?"

"A sheriff. A sheriff with a tough case on his hands, and no ideas. So you're looking for a goat."

The blood went out of his face, leaving it haggard with rage. "They'll hear about this in Sacramento," he stuttered. "When your licence comes up—"

"I've heard that one before. I'm still in business, and I'll tell you why. I've got a clean record, and I don't push people around until they start to push me."

"So you're threatening me!" His right hand fumbled for the holster on his hip. "You're under arrest, Archer!"

I sat down and crossed my legs. "Take it easy, Sheriff. Sit down and relax. We've got some things to talk over."

"I'll talk to you at the courthouse."

"No," I said. "Here. Unless you want to take me to the immigrant inspector."

"What's he got to do with it?" He wrinkled up his eyelids in an effort to look shrewd, and succeeded in looking puzzled. "You're not an alien?"

"I'm a native son," I said. "Is there an immigrant inspector in town?"

"Not in Santa Teresa. The nearest ones are at the federal office in Ventura. Why?"

"Do you do much work with them?"

"A fair amount. When I pick up an illegal alien I turn him over. You trying to kid me, Archer?"

"Sit down," I said again. "I didn't find what I was looking for last night, but I found something else. It should make you and the inspectors very happy. I'm offering it to you as a free gift, no strings."

He lowered his haunches into the canvas chair. His anger had passed off suddenly, and curiosity had taken its place. "What is it? It better be good."

I told him about the closed blue truck, the brown men at the Temple, Troy and Eddie and Claude. "Troy is the head of the gang, I'm pretty sure. The others work for him. They've been running an underground railway on a regular schedule between the Mexican border and the Bakersfield area. The southern end is probably at Calexico."

"Yeah," Spanner said. "That's an easy place to cross the border. I took a trip down there with the border guard a couple of months ago. All they got to do is crawl through a wire fence from one road to the other."

"And Troy's truck would be waiting to pick them up. They used the Temple in the Clouds as a receiving station for illegal immigrants. God knows how many have passed through there. There were twelve or more last night."

"Are they still there?"

"They're in Bakersfield by now, but they shouldn't be hard to round up. If you get hold of Claude I'm pretty sure he'll talk."

"Jesus!" Spanner siad. "If they brought over twelve a night, that's three hundred and sixty a month. Do you know how much they pay to get smuggled in?"

"No."

"A hundred bucks apiece. This Troy has been making big money."

"Dirty money," I said. "Trucking in a bunch of poor Indians, taking their savings away, and turning them loose to be migrant labourers."

He looked at me a little queerly. "They're breaking the law, too, don't forget. We don't prosecute, though, unless they got criminal records. We just ship them back to the border and let them go. But Troy and his gang are another matter. What they been doing is good for thirty years."

"That's fine," I said.

"You don't know where he hangs out in Los Angeles?"

"He runs a place called the Wild Piano, but he won't be showing there. I've told you what I know." With two exceptions: the man I had killed, and the blonde woman who would still be waiting for Eddie.

"You seem to be on the level," the sheriff said slowly. "You can forget what I said about arrest. But if this turns out to be a song-and-dance you gave me, I'll remember it again."

I hadn't expected to be thanked, and I wasn't disappointed.

XXVII

I PARKED IN THE LANE under the eucalyptus trees. The marks of the truck tyres were still visible in the dust. Further down the lane a green A-model sedan, acned with rust, was backed against a fence post. On the registration card strapped to the steering gear I read the name, "Mrs Marcella Finch."

The moonlight had been kind to the white cottage. It was ugly and mean and dilapidated in the noon sun, a dingy blot against the blue field of the sea. Nothing in sight lived or moved, except the sea itself and a few weak puffs of wind in the withered grass on the hillside. I felt for my gun butt. The dry dust muffled my footsteps.

The door creaked partly open when I knocked.

A woman's voice said dully: "Who's that?"

I stood aside and waited, in case she had a gun. She raised her voice. "Is somebody there?"

"Eddie," I whispered. Eddie had no further use for his name, but it was a hard thing to say.

"Eddie?" A hushed and wondering word.

I waited. Her sibilant feet crossed the floor. Before I could see her face in the dim interior, her right hand grasped the edge of the door. Under the peeling scarlet polish, her fingernails were dirty. I took hold of her hand.

"Eddie!" The face that looked around the door was blind with the sun and a desperate hopefulness. Then she blinked and saw I wasn't Eddie.

She had aged rapidly in twelve hours. She was puffed around the eyes, drawn at the mouth, drooping at the chin. Waiting for Eddie had drained away her life. A kind of galvanic fury took its place.

Her nails bit into my hand like parrot's claws. She squawked like a parrot: "Dirty liar!"

The name hit me hard, but not as hard as a bullet. I caught her other wrist and forced her back into the house, slamming the door with my heel. She tried to knee me, then to bite my neck. I pushed her down on the bed.

"I don't want to hurt you, Marcie."

From a round open mouth she screamed up into my face. The scream broke down in a dry hiccupping. She flung herself sideways, burrowing under the covers. Her body moved in a rhythmic orgasm of grief. I stood above her and listened to the dry hiccupping.

Filtered through dirty windows, reflected from rain-stained walls and shabby furniture, the light in the room was grey. On top of an old battery radio beside the bed there were a handful of matches and a pack of cigarettes. She sat up after a while and lit a brown cigarette, dragging deep. Her bathrobe gaped open as if her slack breasts didn't matter any more.

The voice that came out with the smoke was contemptuous and flat. "I should stage a crying jag to give a copper his kicks."

"I'm no copper."

"You know my name. I been waiting all morning to hear from the law." She looked at me with cold interest. "How low can you bastards get? You blow Eddie down when he ain't even heeled. Then you come and tell me you're Eddie at the door. For a minute you make me think the newscast was wrong or you bastards was bluffing me. Can you get any lower than that?"

"Not much," I said. "I thought you might answer the door with a gun."

"I got no gun. I never carried a gun, nor Eddie neither. You wouldn't be walking around if Eddie was heeled last night. Jumping for you on his grave." The flat voice broke again. "Maybe I'll waltz on yours, copper."

"Be quiet for a minute. Listen to me."

"Gladly, gladly." The voice recaptured its tinny quality. "You'll be doing all the talking from now on. You can lock me up and throw away the key, You won't get nothing out of me."

"Douse the muggles, Marcie. I want you to talk some sense."

She laughed and blew smoke in my face. I took the half-burned cigarette from her fingers and ground it under my heel. The scarlet claws reached for my face. I stepped back, and she lapsed onto the bed.

"You must have been in on it, Marcie. You knew what Eddie was doing?"

"I deny everything. He had a job driving a truck. He trucked beans from the Imperial Valley." She stood up suddenly and threw off her bathrobe. "Take me down to headquarters and get it over. I'll deny everything formal."

"I don't belong to headquarters."

When she raised her arms to pull a dress over her head, her body drew itself up, the breasts erect, the belly taut and white. The hair on her body was black.

"Like it?" she said. She pulled the dress down with a vicious gesture and fumbled with the buttons at the neck. Her streaked blonde hair was down around her face.

"Sit down," I said. "We're not going anywhere. I came here to tell you a thing."

"Aren't you a copper?"

"You repeat yourself like Puddler. Listen to me. I want Sampson. I'm a private cop hired to find him. He's all I want – do you understand? If you can give him to me, I'll keep you in the clear."

"You're a dirty liar," she said. "I wouldn't trust a cop, private or any other kind. Anyway, I don't know where Sampson is."

I looked hard into her bird-brown eyes. They were shallow and meaningless. I couldn't tell from them if she was lying.

"You don't know where Sampson is –"

"I said I didn't."

"But you know who does."

She sat down on the bed. "I don't know a damn' thing. I told you that."

"Eddie didn't do it by himself. He must have had a partner."

"He did it by himself. If he didn't – would you take me for a squealer? Do I go to work for the cops after what they done to Eddie?"

I sat down in the barrel chair and lit a cigarette. "I'll tell you a funny thing. I was there when Eddie was shot. There wasn't a cop within two miles, unless you count me."

"You killed him?" she said thinly.

"I did not. He stopped on a side road to pass the money to another car. It was a cream-coloured convertible. It had a woman in it. She shot him. Where would that woman be now?"

Her eyes were glistening like wet brown pebbles. The red tip of her tongue moved across her upper lip and shifted to her lower lip. "Ever since she was on the white stuff," she said to herself. "They allus hate us vipers."

"Are you going to sit and take it, Marcie? Where is she?"

"I don't know who you're talking about."

"Betty Fraley," I said.

After a long silence she repeated. "I don't know who you're taking about."

I left her sitting on the bed and drove back to The Corner. I parked in the parking lot and lowered the sun screen over the windshield. She knew my face but not my car.

For half an hour the road from White Beach was empty. Then a cloud of dust appeared in the distance, towed by a green A-model sedan. Before the car turned south toward Los Angeles I caught a glimpse of a highly painted face, a swirl of grey fur, an aggressively tilted hat with a bright-blue feather. Clothes and cosmetics and half an hour alone had done a lot for Marcie.

Two or three other cars went by before I turned into the highway. The A-model's top driving speed was under fifty, and it was easy to keep in sight. Driving slow on a hot day, down a highway I knew too well, the only trouble I had was staying awake. I narrowed the distance between us as we approached Los Angeles and the traffic increased.

The A-model left the highway at Sunset Boulevard and went through Pacific Palisades without a pause. It laboured and trailed dark-blue oil smoke on the hills below the Santa Monica

Mountains. On the edge of Beverly Hills it left the boulevard suddenly and disappeared.

I followed it up a winding road lined on both sides with hedges. The A-model was parked behind a laurel hedge in the entrance to a gravel drive. In the instant of passing I saw Marcie crossing the lawn toward a deep brick porch screened with oleanders. She seemed to be thrust forward and hustled along by a deadly energy.

XXVIII

I TURNED AT THE NEXT DRIVE and parked on the shoulder of the road, waiting for a signal to break the suburban peace. The seconds piled up precariously like a tower of poker chips.

I had the car door open and one foot in the road when the Ford engine coughed. I drew in my leg and crouched down behind the wheel. The Ford engine roared and went into gear, then died away. A deeper sound took its place, and the black Buick backed out of the drive. A man I didn't know was at the wheel. The eyes in his fleshy face were like raisins stuck in unbaked dough. Marcie was beside him in the front seat. Grey hearse-like curtains were drawn over the rear windows.

At the boulevard the Buick turned back toward the sea. I followed as closely as I dared. Between Brentwood and Pacific Palisades it went off to the right, up a climbing road that led into a canyon. I had the feeling that there wasn't much mileage left in the Sampson case. We were coming into a narrow place for the end.

The road was cut in the western wall of the canyon. Below its unfenced edge was a tangle of underbrush. Above the road to my left a scattering of houses stood in roughly cleared patches. The houses were new and raw-looking. The opposite slope was scrub-oak wilderness.

From the top of a rise I caught a glimpse of the Buick climbing over the crest of the next hill. I accelerated on the downhill grade, crossed a narrow stone bridge that spanned a dry *barranca,* and climbed the hill after it. I was moving slowly down the other side, like a heavy black beetle feeling its way in unfamiliar territory. A rutted lane branched off to the right. The beetle paused and followed it.

I parked behind a tree, which half hid my car from below, and watched the Buick diminish down the lane. When it was no larger than an actual beetle, it stopped in front of a yellow matchbox house. A matchstick woman with a black head came out of the house. Two men and two women got out of the car and surrounded her. All five went into the house like a single insect body with many legs.

I left my car and climbed down through the underbrush to the dry river bed at the bottom of the canyon. It wound among boulders from which small lizards scampered as I came near. The gnarled trees along the bank hid me from the yellow house until I was directly behind it. It was an unpainted wooden shack with its rear end resting on short fieldstone columns.

Inside it a woman screamed, very loudly, again and again. The screams raked at my nerves, but I was grateful for them. They covered the noises I made climbing the bank and crawling under the house. The screaming died away after a while. I lay flat and listened to scrabbling movements on the floor above me. The silence under the house seemed to be crouched and waiting for another scream. I smelled new pine, damp earth, my own sour sweat.

A soft voice began to talk over my head. "You don't quite understand the circumstances. You seem to feel that our motive is pure sadism or simple revenge. Certainly if we were inclined to harbour vengeful motives, we might feel that your conduct had justified them."

"Tie a can to it, for Christ's sake!" said Mrs Estabrook's voice. "This isn't getting us anywhere."

"I'll make my point if you don't mind. My point is, Betty, that you've acted very badly. Without consulting me, you went into business for yourself, a thing I seldom approve in my employees. To make matters worse, you made an incautious choice of enterprise and failed in it. The police are looking for you now, and for me and Fay and Luis as well. Furthermore, you chose a valuable associate of mine as the victim of your wretched little plot. And to cap the climax you showed yourself devoid, not only of *esprit de corps,* but of sisterly affection. You shot and killed your brother Eddie Lassiter."

"We know you swallowed the dictionary," Fay Estabrook said. "Get on with it, Troy."

"I didn't kill him." The whine of a hurt cat.

"You're a liar," yapped Marcie.

Troy raised his voice. "Be quiet, all of you. We're going to let bygones be bygones, Betty—"

"I'm going to kill her if you don't," Marcie said.

"Nonsense, Marcie. You'll do exactly as I say. We have a chance to recoup, and we won't allow our more primitive passions to destroy it. Which brings us to the occasion of this pleasant little party, doesn't it, Betty? I don't know where the money is, but of course I am going to. And when I do, you'll have bought your absolution, so to speak."

"She ain't fit to live," Marcie said. "I swear I'll kill her if you don't."

Fay laughed contemptuously. "You haven't got the guts, dearie. You wouldn't have called us in if you had the guts to tackle her yourself."

"Hold your tongue, both of you." Troy lowered his voice to a gentle monologue again. "You know I can handle Marcie, don't you, Betty? I think you know by now I can handle even you. You might just as well come clean, I think. Otherwise you'll suffer rather terribly. You may never walk again, in fact. I think I can promise you that you never shall."

"I'm not talking," she said.

"But if you decide to co-operate," Troy went on smoothly, "to put the welfare of the group ahead of your selfish interest, I'm sure the group will be glad to help you in turn. We'll take you out of the country tonight, in fact. You know that Luis and I can do that for you."

"You wouldn't do it," she said. "I know you, Troy."

"More intimately by the moment, dear. Take off her other shoe, Luis."

Her body squirmed on the floor. I could hear its breathing. A dropped shoe rapped the floorboards. I calculated my chances of ending it there. But there were four of them too many for one gun. And Betty Fraley had to come out alive.

Troy said: "We'll test the plantar reflex, I think it's called."

"I don't like this," Fay said.

"Neither do I, my dear. I quite abhor it. But Betty is being most dreadfully obdurate."

A moment of silence stretched out like membrane on the point of tearing. The screaming began again. When it ended I found that I had closed my teeth in the earth.

"Your plantar reaction is very fine," Troy said. "It's a pity that your tongue doesn't work so well."

"Will you let me go if I give it to you?"

"You have my word."

"Your word!" She sighed horribly,

"I do wish you'd take it, Betty. I don't enjoy hurting you, and you can't possibly enjoy being hurt."

"Let me up, then. Let me sit up."

"Of course, my dear."

"It's in a locker in the bus station in Buenavista. The key is in my bag."

As soon as I was out of sight of the house I began to run. When I reached my car the Buick was still standing at the end of the lane below me. I backed down the hill to the stone bridge and halfway up the grade on the other side. I waited for the Buick with one foot on the clutch and the other on the brake.

After a long while I heard its motor whining up the other side of the hill. I went into gear and moved ahead in low. Its chromium flashed in the sun at the top of the hill. I held the middle of the road and met it on the bridge. Brakes screeched above the bellow of the horn. The big car came to a stop five feet from my bumper. I was out of my seat before it stopped rolling.

The man called Luis glared at me over the wheel, his fat face twisted and shiny with anger. I opened the door on his side and showed him my gun. Beside him Fay Estabrook cried out in fury.

"Out!" I said. Luis put one foot down and reached for me. I moved back. "Be careful. Hands on your head."

He raised his hands and stepped into the road. An emerald ring flashed green on one of his fingers. His wide hips swayed under his cream gabardine suit.

"You too, Fay. This side."

She came out, teetering on her high heels.

"Now turn around."

They rotated cautiously, watching me over their shoulders.

I clubbed the gun and swung it to the base of Luis's skull. He went down on his knees and collapsed softly on his face. Fay cowered away with her arms protecting her head. Her hat slipped forward dowdily over one eye. On the road her long shadow mocked her movements.

"Put him in the back seat," I said.

"You dirty little sneak!" she said. Then she said other things. The rouge stood out on her cheekbones.

"Hurry."

"I can't lift him."

"You have to." I took a step toward her.

She stooped awkwardly over the fallen man. He was inert, and heavy. With her hands in his armpits she raised the upper part of his body and dragged him to the car. I opened the door, and together we slung him into the back seat.

She stood up gasping for breath, the colours running in her face. The rustic stillness of the sun-filled canyon made a queer setting for what we were doing. I could see the two of us as if from a height, tiny foreshortened figures alone in the sun, with blood and money on our minds.

"Now give me the key."

"The key?" She overdid her puzzled frown, making her face a caricature. "What key?"

"The key to the locker, Fay. Hurry."

"I haven't got any key." But her gaze had flickered almost imperceptibly toward the front seat of the Buick.

There was a black suede purse on the seat. The key was in it. I transferred it to my wallet.

"Get in," I said. "No, on the driver's side. You're going to do the driving."

She did as I said, and I got in behind her. Luis was slumped in the far corner of the back seat. His eyes were partly open, but the pupils were turned up out of sight. His face looked more than ever like dough.

"I can't get past your car," Fay said petulantly.

"You're backing up the hill."

She went into reverse gear with a jerk.

"Not so fast," I said. "If we have an accident you won't survive it."

She cursed me, but she also slowed down. She backed cautiously up the hill and down the other side. At the entrance to the lane I told her to turn and drive down to the cottage.

"Slow and careful, Fay. No leaning on the horn. You wouldn't be any good without a spinal column, and Geminis have no heart."

I touched the back of her neck with the muzzle of my gun. She winced, and the car leaped forward. I rested my weight on Luis and lowered the rear window on the right side. The lane opened out in a small level clearing in front of the cottage.

"Turn left," I said, "and stop in front of the door. Then set the emergency."

The door of the cottage began to open inward. I ducked my head. When I raised it again, Troy was in the doorway, with his right hand, knuckles out, resting on the edge of the frame. I sighted and fired. At twenty feet I could see the mark the bullet had made, like a fat red insect alighting, between the first and second knuckles of his right hand.

Before his left hand could move across his body for his gun he was immobile for an instant. Long enough for me to reach him and use the gun butt again. He sat down on the doorstep, with his silver head hanging between his knees.

The motor of the Buick roared behind me. I went after Fay, caught the car before she could turn it, and pulled her out by the shoulders. She tried to spit at me and slobbered on her chin.

"We'll go inside," I said. "You first."

She walked almost drunkenly, stumbling on her heels. Troy had rolled out of the doorway and was curled on the shallow porch, perfectly still. We stepped over him.

The odour of burned flesh was still in the room. Betty Fraley was on the floor with Marcie at her throat, worrying her like a terrier. I pulled Marcie off. She hissed at me and drummed her heels on the floor, but she didn't try to get up. I motioned to Fay with the gun to stand in the corner beside her.

Betty Fraley sat up, her breath whistling in her throat. Across one side of her face, from hairline to jawbone, four parallel scratches dipped blood. The other side of her face was yellowish white.

"You're a pretty picture," I said.

"Who are you?" Her voice was a flat caw. Her eyes were fixed.

"It doesn't matter. Let's get out of here before I have to kill these people."

"That would be pleasant work," she said. She tried to stand up and fell forward on hands and knees. "I can't walk."

I lifted her. Her body was light and hard as a dry stick. Her head hung loosely across my arm. I had the feeling that I was holding an evil child. Marcie and Fay were watching me from the corner. It seemed to me then that evil was a female quality, a poison that women secreted and transmitted to men like disease.

I carried Betty out to the car and sat her down in the front seat. I opened the back door, laid Luis out on the ground. There were suds on his thick blue lips, blown in and out by his shallow breathing.

"Thank you," her tiny caw said, as I climbed behind the wheel. "You saved my life, if that's worth anything."

"It isn't worth much, but you're going to pay me for it. The price is a hundred thousand – and Ralph Sampson."

XXIX

I PARKED THE BUICK in the road at the entrance to the bridge and kept the ignition key. As I lifted Betty Fraley out of the seat her right arm slipped around my shoulders. I could feel her small fingers on the nape of my neck.

"You're very strong," she said. "You're Archer, aren't you?" She looked up at me with a sly and feline innocence. She didn't know about the blood on her face.

"It's time you remembered me. Take your hands off me, or I'll drop you."

She lowered her eyelids. When I started to back my car she cried out suddenly:

"What about them?"

"We don't have room for them."

"You're going to let them go?"

"What do you want me to hold them for? Mayhem?" I found a wide place in the road and turned the car toward Sunset Boulevard.

Her fingers pinched my arm. "We've got to go back."

"I told you to keep your hands off me. I don't like what you did to Eddie any more than they do."

"But they've got something of mine!"

"No," I said. "I have it, and it isn't yours any more."

"The key?"

"The key."

She slumped down in the seat as if her spine had melted. "You can't let them go," she said sullenly. "After what they did to me. You let Troy run loose, and he'll get you for today."

"I don't think so," I said. "Forget about them and start worrying for yourself."

"I haven't got a future to worry about. Have I?"

"I want to see Sampson first. Then I'll decide."

"I'll take you to him."

"Where is he?"

"Not very far from home. He's in a place on the beach, about forty miles from Santa Teresa"

"This is straight?"

"The straight stuff, Archer. But you won't let me go. You won't take money, will you?"

"Not from you."

"Why should you?" she said nastily. "You've got my hundred grand."

"I'm working for the Sampsons. They'll get it back."

"They don't need the money. Why don't you get smart, Archer. There's another person in this with me. This other person had nothing to do with Eddie. Why don't you keep the money and split it with this other person?"

"Who is he?"

"I didn't say it was a man." Her voice had recovered from the pressure of Marcie's fingers, and she modulated it girlishly.

"You couldn't work with a woman. Who's the man?" She didn't know that Taggert was dead, and it wasn't time to tell her.

"Forget it. I thought for a minute maybe I could trust you. I must be going soft in the head."

"Maybe you are. You haven't told me where Sampson is. The longer it takes you to tell me, the less I'll feel like doing anything for you."

"He's in a place on the beach about ten miles north of

Buenavista. It used to be the dressing-room of a beach club that folded during the war."

"And he's alive?"

"He was yesterday. The first day he was sick from the chloroform, but he's all right now."

"He was yesterday, you mean. Is he tied up?"

"I haven't seen him. Eddie was the one."

"I suppose you left him there to starve to death."

"I couldn't go there. He knew me by sight. Eddie was the one he didn't know."

"And Eddie died by an act of God."

"No, I killed him." She said it almost smugly. "You'll never be able to prove it, though. I wasn't thinking of Sampson when I shot Eddie."

"You were thinking of the money, weren't you? A two-way cut instead of a three-way cut."

"I admit it was partly that, but only partly. Eddie pushed me around all the time I was a kid. When I finally got on my feet and was heading places, he sang me into the pen. I was using the stuff, but he was selling it. He helped the feds to hang conspiracy on me, and got off with a light sentence himself. He didn't know I knew that, but I promised myself to get him. I got him when he thought he was riding high. Maybe he wasn't so surprised. He told Marcie where to find me if anything went wrong."

"It always does," I said. "Kidnappings don't come off. Especially when the kidnappers start murdering each other."

I turned onto the boulevard and stopped at the first gas station I came to. She watched me remove the ignition key.

"What are you going to do?"

"Phone help for Sampson. He may be dying, and it's going to take us an hour and a half to get there. Has the place got a name?"

"It used to be the Sunland Beach Club. It's a long green building. You can see if from the highway, out near the end of a little point."

For the first time I was sure she was telling the truth. I called Santa Teresa from the station's pay telephone while the attendant filled the tank of my car. I could watch Betty Fraley through the window.

Felix answered the phone. "This is the Sampson residence."

"Archer speaking. Is Mr Graves there?"

"Yes, sir. I will call him."

Graves came to the phone. "Where the hell are you?"

"Los Angeles. Sampson is alive, or at least he was yesterday. He's locked up in the dressing-room of a beach club called the Sunland. Know it?"

"I used to. It's been out of business for years. I know where it is, north of Buenavista on the highway."

"See how fast you can get there with first aid and food. And you better bring a doctor and the sheriff."

"Is he in bad shape?"

"I don't know. He's been alone since yesterday. I'll be there as soon as I can."

I hung up on Graves and called Peter Colton. He was still on duty.

"I've got something for you," I said. "Partly for you and partly for the Department of Justice."

"Another migraine headache, no doubt." He didn't sound glad to hear from me. "This Sampson case is the mess of the century."

"It was. I'm closing it today."

His voice dropped a full octave. "Say again, please."

"I know where Sampson is, and I've got the last of the kidnap gang with me now."

"Don't be coy, for Christ's sake! Spill it. Where is he?"

"Out of your territory, in Santa Teresa County. The Santa Teresa sheriff is on his way to him now."

"So you called up to brag, you poor narcissistic bastard. I thought you had something for me and the Department of Justice."

"I have, but not the kidnapping. Sampson wasn't carried across the state line, so the F.B.I. is out. The case has by-products, though. There's a canyon feeding into Sunset between Brentwood and the Palisades. The road that leads into it is Hopkins Lane. About five miles in, there's a black Buick sedan in the road, past that a lane leading down to an unpainted pine cottage. There are four people in the cottage. One of them is Troy. Whether it knows it or not, the Department of Justice wants them."

"What for?"

"Smuggling illegal immigrants. I'm in a hurry. Have I said enough?"

"For the present," he said. "Hopkins Lane."

Betty Fraley looked at me blankly when I went back to the car. Meaning returned to her eyes like a snake coming out of its hole. "Little man, what now?" she said.

"I did you a favour. I called the police to pick up Troy and the others."

"And me?"

"I'm saving you." I headed down Sunset towards U.S. 101.

"I'll turn state's evidence against him," she said.

"You don't have to. I can pin it on him myself."

"The smuggling rap?"

"Right. Troy disappointed me. Trucking in Mexicans is a pretty low-grade racket for a gentleman crook. He should be selling in Hollywood Bowl to visiting firemen."

"It paid him well. He made it pay off double. He took the poor creeps' money for the ride, then turned them over to the ranches at so much a head. The Mexicans didn't know it, but they were being used as strike breakers. That way Troy got protection from some of the local cops. Luis greased the Mexican federals at the other end."

"Was Sampson buying strikebreakers from Troy?"

"He was, but you'd never prove it. Sampson was very careful to keep himself in the clear."

"He wasn't careful enough," I said. She was silent after that.

As I turned north on the highway I noticed that her face was ugly with pain. "There's a pint of whisky in the glove compartment. You can use it to clean your burns and the scratches on your face. Or you can drink it."

She followed both suggestions and offered me the open bottle.

"Not for me."

"Because I drank from it first? All my diseases are mental."

"Put it away."

"You don't like me, do you?"

"Poison isn't my drink. Not that you don't have your points. You seem to have some brains, on a low level."

"Thanks for nothing, my intellectual friend."

"And you've been around."

"I'm not a virgin, if you're talking about that. I haven't been since I was eleven. Eddie saw a chance to turn a dollar. But I never did my living below the belt. The music saved me from that."

"It's too bad it didn't save you from this."

"I took my chance. It didn't work out. What makes you think I care one way or the other?"

"You care about this other person. You want him to have the money, no matter what happens to you."

"I told you to forget that." After a pause she said: "You could let me go and keep the money yourself. You'll never have another crack at a hundred grand."

"Neither will you, Betty. Neither will Alan Taggert."

She uttered a groan of surprise and shock. When she recovered her voice she said in a hostile tone: "You've been kidding me. What do you know about Taggert?"

"What he told me."

"I don't believe you. He never told you a thing."

She corrected herself. "He doesn't know anything to tell."

"He did."

"Did something happen to him?"

"Death happened to him. He's got a hole in the head like Eddie."

She started to say something, but the words were broken up by a rush of crying, a high drawn-out whimper giving place to steady dry sobs. After a long time she whispered:

"Why didn't you tell me he was dead?"

"You didn't ask me. Were you crazy about him?"

"Yes," she said. "We were crazy about each other."

"If you were so crazy about him, why did you drag him into a thing like this?"

"I didn't drag him in. He wanted to do it. We were going to go away together."

"And live happily ever after."

"Keep your cheap cracks to yourself."

"I won't buy love's young dream from you, Betty. He was a boy, and you're an old woman, as experience goes. I think you sucked him in. You needed a finger man, and he looked easy."

"That's not the way it was." Her voice was surprisingly gentle. "We've been together for half a year. He came into the

Piano with Sampson the week after I opened. I fell, and it was the same with him. But neither of us had anything. We had to have money to make a clean break."

"And Sampson was the obvious source. Kidnapping was the obvious method."

"You don't have to waste your sympathy on Sampson. But we had other ideas at first. Alan was going to marry the girl, Sampson's daughter, and get Sampson to buy him off. Sampson spoilt that himself. He lent Alan his bungalow at the Valerio one night. In the middle of the night we caught Sampson behind the curtains in the bedroom peeping at us. After that Sampson told the girl that if she married Alan he'd cut her off. He was going to fire Alan too, only we knew too much about him."

"Why didn't you blackmail him? That would be more your line."

"We thought of that, but he was too big for us to handle and he has the best lawyers in the state. We knew plenty about him, but he would be hard to pin down. This Temple in the Clouds, for example. How could we prove that Sampson knew what Troy and Claude and Fay were using it for?"

"If you know so much about Sampson," I said, "what makes him tick?"

"That's a hard one. I used to think maybe he had some faggot blood, but I don't know. He's getting old, and I guess he felt washed up. He was looking for anything that would make him feel like a man again: astrology or funny kinds of sex, anything at all. The only thing he cares about is his daughter. I think he caught on that she was struck on Alan, and never forgave Alan."

"Taggert should have stuck to her," I said.

"You think so?" Her voice cracked. It was humble and small when she spoke again. "I didn't do him any good. I know that, you don't have to tell me. I couldn't help myself, and neither could he. How did he die, Archer?"

"He got into a tight corner and tried to push out with a gun. Somebody else shot first. A man called Graves."

"I'd like to meet that man. You said before that Alan talked. He didn't do that?"

"Not about you."

"I'm glad of that," she said. "Where is he now?"

"In the morgue in Santa Teresa."

"I wish I could see him – once more."

The words came softly out of a dark dream. In the silence that followed, the dream spread beyond her mind and cast a shadow as long as the shadows thrown by the setting sun.

XXX

When I slowed down for Buenavista, twilight was softening the ugliness of the buildings, and the lights were going on along the main street. I noticed the neon greyhound at the bus station but didn't stop. A few miles beyond the town the highway converged with the shoreline again, winding along the bluffs above the uninhabited beaches. The last grey shreds of daylight clung to the surface of the sea and were slowly absorbed.

"This is it," Betty Fraley said. She had been so still I'd almost forgotten she was in the seat beside me.

I stopped on the asphalt shoulder of the highway, just short of a crossroads. On the ocean side of the road slanted down to the beach. A weather-faded sign at the corner advertised a desirable beach development, but there were no houses in sight. I could see the old beach club, though, a mass of buildings two hundred yards below the highway, long and low and neutral-coloured against the glimmering whiteness of the surf.

"You can't drive down," she said. "The road's washed out at the bottom."

"I thought you hadn't been down there."

"Not since last week. I looked it over with Eddie when he found it. Sampson's in one of the little rooms on the men's side of the dressing-rooms."

"He better be."

I took the ignition key and left her in the car. As I went down, the road narrowed to a humped clay pathway with deeply eroded ditches on both sides. The wooden platform in front of the first building was warped, and I could feel the clumps of grass growing up through the cracks under my feet. The windows were high under the eaves, and dark.

I turned my flashlight on the twin doors in the middle, and saw the stencilled signs: "Gentlemen" on one, "Ladies" on the other. The one on the right for "Gentlemen", was hanging partly open. I pulled it wide, but not very hopefully. The place seemed empty and dead. Except for the restless water there was no sign of life in it or around it.

No sign of Sampson, and no sign of Graves. I looked at my watch, which said a quarter to seven. It was well over an hour since I'd called Graves. He'd had plenty of time to drive the forty-five miles from Cabrillo Canyon. I wondered what had happened to him and the sheriff.

I shot my flashlight beam across the floor, which was covered with blown sand and the detritus of years. Opposite me was a row of closed doors in a plywood partition. I took a step toward the row of doors. The movement behind me was so lizard-quick I had no time to turn. "Ambush" was the last word that flashed across my consciousness before it faded out.

"Sucker" was the first word when consciousness returned. The cyclops eye of an electric lantern stared down at me like the ghastly eye of conscience. My impulse was to get up and fight. The deep voice of Albert Graves inhibited the impulse:

"What happened to you?"

"Turn the lantern away." Its light went through my eye sockets like swords and out at the back of my skull.

He set the lantern down and kneeled beside me. "Can you get up, Lew?"

"I can get up." But I stayed where I was on the floor. "You're late."

"I had some trouble finding the place in the dark."

"Where's the sheriff? Couldn't you find him either?"

"He was out on a case, committing a paranoiac to the county hospital. I left word for him to follow me down and bring a doctor. I didn't want to waste time."

"It looks to me as if you've wasted a lot of time."

"I thought I knew the place, but I must have missed it. I drove on nearly to Buenavista before I realized it. Then when I came back I couldn't find it."

"Didn't you see my car?"

"Where?"

I sat up. A swaying sickness moved back and forth like a pendulum in my head. "At the corner just above here."

"That's where I parked. I didn't see your car."

I felt for my car keys. They were in my pocket. "You're sure? They didn't take my car keys."

"Your car isn't there, Lew. Who are they?"

"Betty Fraley and whoever sapped me. There must have been a fourth member of the gang guarding Sampson." I told him how I had come there.

"It wasn't smart to leave her in the car." he said.

"Three sappings in two days are making Jack a dull boy."

I got to my feet and found that my legs were weak. He offered his shoulder for me to lean on. I leaned against the wall.

He raised the lantern. "Let me look at your head." The broad planes of his face in the moving light were furrowed by anxiety. He looked heavy and old.

"Later," I said.

I picked up my flashlight and crossed to the row of doors. Sampson was waiting behind the second one, a fat old man slumped on a bench against the rear wall of the cubicle. His open eyes were suffused with blood.

Graves crowded in behind me and said: "God!"

I handed him the flashlight and bent over Sampson. His hands and ankles were bound together with quarter-inch rope, one end of which was strung through a staple in the wall. The other end of the rope was sunk in Sampson's neck and tied under his left ear in a hard knot. I reached behind the body for one of the bound wrists. It wasn't cold, but the pulse was gone. The pupils of the red eyeballs were asymmetric. There was something pathetic about the bright plaid socks, yellow and red and green, on thick dead ankles.

Graves breath came out. "Is he dead?"

"Yes." I felt a terrific letdown, which was followed by inertia. "He must have been alive when I got here. How long was I out?"

"It's a quarter after seven now."

"I got here about a quarter to. They've had a half-hour's start. We've got to move."

"And leave Sampson here?"

"Yes. The police will want him this way."

We left him in the dark. I drew on my last reserve to get up the hill. My car was gone. Graves's Studebaker was parked at the other side of the intersection.

"Which way?" he said, as he climbed behind the wheel.

"Buenavista. We'll go to the highway patrol."

I looked in my wallet, expecting the locker key to be gone. But it was there, tucked in the card compartment. Whoever sapped me hadn't had a chance to compare notes with Betty Fraley. Or they decided to make their getaway and let the money go. Somehow that didn't seem likely.

I said to Graves, as we passed the town limits: "Drop me at the bus station."

"Why?"

I told him why, and added: "If the money's there, they may be back for it. If it isn't, it probably means they came this way and broke open the locker. You go to the highway patrol and pick me up later."

He let me out at the red curb in front of the bus station. I stood outside the glass door and looked into the big square waiting-room. Three or four men in overalls were slouched on the scarred benches reading newspapers. A few old men, ancient-looking in the fluorescent lights, were leaning against the poster-papered walls and talking among themselves. A Mexican family in one corner, father and mother and several children, formed a solid unit like a six-man football team. The ticket booth under the clock at the back of the room was occupied by a pimply youth in a flowered Hawaiian shirt. There was a doughnut counter to the left, a fat blonde woman in uniform behind it. The bank of green metal lockers was against the wall to the right.

None of the people in the room showed the tension I was looking for. They were waiting for ordinary things: supper, a bus, Saturday night, a pension cheque, or a natural death in bed.

I pushed the glass door open and crossed the butt-strewn floor to the lockers. The number I wanted was stamped on the key: twenty-eight. As I pushed the key into the lock I glanced around the room. The doughnut woman's boiled blue eyes were watching me incuriously. Nobody else seemed interested.

There was a red canvas beach bag in the locker. When I pulled it out I could hear the rattling paper inside. I sat down on the nearest empty bench and opened the bag. The brown paper package it contained was torn open at one end. I felt the edges of the stiff new bills with my fingers.

I tucked the bag under my arm, went to the doughnut

counter, and ordered coffee.

"Did you know you got blood on your shirt?" the blonde woman said.

"I know it. I wear it that way."

She looked me over as if she doubted my ability to pay. I restrained the impulse I had to give her a hundred-dollar bill, and slapped a dime on the counter. She gave me coffee in a thick white cup.

I watched the door as I drank it, holding the cup in my left hand, with my right hand ready to take out my gun. The electric clock above the ticket booth took little bites of time. A bus arrived and departed, shuffling the occupants of the room. The clock chewed very slowly, masticating each minute sixty times. By ten to eight it was too late to hope for them. They had by-passed the money or gone the other way.

Graves appeared in the doorway gesticulating violently. I set down my cup and followed him out. His car was double-parked across the street.

"They just wrecked your car," he told me, on the sidewalk. "About fifteen miles north of here."

"Did they get away?"

"Apparently one of them did. The Fraley woman's dead."

"What happened to the other?"

"The H.P. don't know yet. All they had was the first radio report."

We covered the fifteen miles in less than fifteen minutes. The place was marked by a line of standing cars, a crowd of human figures like animated black cut-outs in the headlights. Graves pulled up short of a policeman who was trying to wave us on with a red-beamed flashlight.

Jumping out of the Studebaker, I could see beyond the line of cars to the edge of the swathe of light. My car was there, its nose crumpled into the bank. I took off at a run and elbowed my way through the crowd around the wreck.

A highway patrolman with a seamed brown face put his hand on my arm. I shook it off. "This is my car."

His eyes narrowed, and the sun wrinkles fanned back to his ears. "You sure? What's your name?"

"Archer."

"It's all right. That's who she's registered to." He called out to a young patrolman who was standing uneasily by his motorcycle: "Come here, Ollie! It's this guy's car."

The crowd began to re-form, focusing on me. When they broke their tight circle around the smashed car, I could see the blanket-covered figure on the ground beside it. I pushed between a pair of women whose eyes were drinking it in, and lifted one end of the blanket. The object underneath wasn't recognizably human, but I knew it by its clothes.

Two of them in an hour was too much for me, and my stomach revolted. Empty of everything but the coffee I had drunk, it brought up bitterness. The two patrolmen waited until I was able to talk.

"This woman steal your car?" the older one said.

"Yes. Her name is Betty Fraley."

"The office said they had a bulletin on her–"

"That's right. But what happened to the other one?"

"What other one?"

"There was a man with her."

"Not when she wrecked the car," the young patrolman said.

"You can't be sure."

"I am sure, though. I saw it happen. I was responsible in a way."

"Naw, naw, Ollie." The older man put his hand on Ollie's shoulder. "You did exactly the right thing. Nobody's going to blame you."

"Anyway," Ollie blurted, "I'm glad the car was hot."

That irritated me. The convertible was insured, but it would be hard to replace. Besides, I had a feeling for it, the kind of feeling a rider has for his horse.

"What did happen?" I asked him sharply.

"I was tooling along about fifty a few miles south of here, heading north. This dame in the convertible passed me as if I was standing still, and I gave chase. I was travelling around ninety before I started to pull up on her. Even when I was abreast of her, she went right on gunning down the road. She didn't pay any attention when I signalled to pull over, so I cut in ahead. She swerved and tried to pass me on the right and lost control of the car. It skidded a couple of hundred feet and piled up in the bank. When I pulled her out of it she was dead."

His face was wet when he finished. The older man shook him

gently by the shoulder. "Don't let it worry you, kid. You got to enforce the law."

"You're absolutely sure," I asked, "there was nobody else in the car?"

"Unless they went up in smoke – it's a funny thing," he added in a high, nervous voice, "there was no fire, but the soles of her feet were blistered. And I couldn't find her shoes. She was in her bare feet."

"That is funny," I said. "Extremely funny."

Albert Graves had forced his way through the crowd. "They must have had another car."

"Then why would she bother with mine?" I reached inside the wreck, under the warped and bloody dashboard, and felt the ignition wires. The terminals had been reconnected with the copper wire I had left there in the morning. "She had to rewire my ignition to start the engine."

"That's more like a man's work, isn't it?"

"Not necessarily. She could have picked it up from her brother. Every car thief knows the trick."

"Maybe they decided to split up for the getaway."

"Maybe, but I don't see it. She was smart enough to know my car would identify her."

"I got to fill out a report," the older patrolman said. "Can you spare a few minutes?"

While I was answering the last of the questions, Sheriff Spanner arrived in a radio car driven by a deputy. The two of them got out and trotted toward us. Spanner's heavy chest bounced almost like a woman's as he ran.

"What's been happening?" He looked from me to Graves with moist, suspicious eyes.

I let Graves tell him. When he had heard what had happened to Sampson and Betty Fraley, Spanner turned back to me.

"You see what's come of your meddling, Archer. I warned you to work under my supervision."

I wasn't in the mood to take it quietly. "Supervision, hell! If you'd got to Sampson soon enough, he might be alive now."

"You knew where he was, and you didn't tell me about it," he yammered. "You're going to suffer for that, Archer."

"Yeah, I know. When my licence comes up for renewal. You said that before. But what are you going to tell Sacramento about your own imcompetence? You're out at the county hospital committing a loony when the case is breaking wide open."

"I haven't been out at the hospital since yesterday," he said. "What are you talking about?"

"Didn't you get my message about Sampson? A couple of hours ago?"

"There was no message. You can't cover yourself that way."

I looked at Graves. His eyes avoided mine. I held my tongue.

An ambulance with its siren whooping came down the highway from the direction of Santa Teresa.

"They take their time," I said to the patrolman.

"They knew she was dead. No hurry."

"Where will they take her?"

"The morgue in Santa Teresa, unless she's claimed."

"She won't be. It's a good place for her."

Alan Taggert and Eddie, her lover and her brother, were there already.

XXXI

GRAVES DROVE VERY SLOWLY, as if the sight of the wreck had had an effect on him. It took us nearly an hour to get back to Santa Teresa. I spent it thinking – about Albert Graves and then about Miranda. My thoughts were poor company.

He looked at me curiously as we entered the city. "I wouldn't give up hope, Lew. The police have a good chance to catch him."

"Who do you mean?"

"The murderer, of course. The other man."

"I'm not sure there was another man."

His hands tightened on the wheel. I could see the knuckles stand out. "But somebody killed Sampson."

"Yes," I said. "Somebody did."

I watched his eyes as they turned slowly to meet mine. He looked at me coldly for a long moment.

"Watch your driving, Graves. Watch everything."

He turned his face to the road again, but not before I had caught its look of shame.

Where the highway crossed the main street of Santa Teresa,

he stopped for a red light. "Where do we go from here?"

"Where do you want to go?"

"It doesn't matter to me."

"We'll go to the Sampson place," I said. "I want to talk to Mrs Sampson."

"Do you have to do it now?"

"I'm working for her. I owe her a report."

The light changed. Nothing more was said until we turned up the drive to the Sampson house. Its dark mass was pierced by a few lights.

"I don't want to see Miranda if it can be helped," he said. "We were married this afternoon."

"Didn't you jump the gun a little?"

"What do you mean by that? I've been carrying the licence for months."

"You might have waited until her father was home. Or decently laid away."

"She wanted it done to-day," he said. "We were married in the courthouse."

"You'll probably be spending your wedding night there. The jail's in the same building, isn't it?"

He didn't answer. When he stopped the car by the garages, I leaned forward to look into his face. He had swallowed the shame. Nothing was left but a gambler's resignation.

"It's an ironic thing," he said. "This is our wedding night, the night that I've been waiting for for years. And now I don't want to see her."

"Do you expect me to leave you out here by yourself?"

"Why not?"

"I can't trust you. You were the one man I thought I could trust –" I couldn't find the words to end the sentence.

"You can trust me, Lew."

"We'll make it Mr Archer from now on."

"Mr Archer, then. I've got a gun in my pocket. But I'm not going to use it. I've had enough of violence. Do you understand that? I'm sick of it."

"You should be sick," I said, "with two murders on your stomach. You've had your fill of violence for a while."

"Why did you say two murders, Lew?"

"Mr Archer," I said.

"You don't have to take a high moral tone. I didn't plan it this way."

"Not many do. You shot Taggert on the spur of the moment, and you've improvised ever since. Toward the end you've been getting pretty careless. You might have known I'd find out you didn't call the sheriff to-night."

"You can't prove you told me to."

"I don't have to. But it was enough to let me know what you were up to. You wanted to be alone with Sampson in the shack for a little while. You had to finish the job that Taggert's partners had failed to do for you."

"Do you seriously think I had anything to do with the kidnapping?"

"I know damn' well you didn't. But the kidnapping has something to do with you. It made a murderer out of you by giving you a reason to kill Taggert."

"I shot Taggert in good faith," he said. "I admit I wasn't sorry to have him out of the way. Miranda liked him too well. But the reason I shot him was to save you."

"I don't believe you." I sat there in cold anger. The stars clung like snow crystals in the black sky, pouring cold down on my head.

"I didn't plan it," he said. "I had no time to plan it. Taggert was going to shoot you, and I shot him instead. It was as simple as that."

"Killing is never simple, not when it's done by a man with your brains. You're a dead shot, Graves. You didn't have to kill him."

He answered me harshly. "Taggert deserved to die. He got what was coming to him."

"But not at the right time. I've been wondering how much you heard of what he said to me. You must have heard enough to know he was one of the kidnappers. Probably enough to be pretty sure that if Taggert died, his partners would kill Sampson."

"I heard very little. I saw he was going to shoot you, and I shot him instead." The iron returned to his voice. "Evidently I made a mistake."

"You made several mistakes. The first was killing Taggert – that's what started it all, isn't it? It wasn't really Taggert you wanted dead. It was Sampson himself. You never wanted Sampson to come home alive, and you thought that by killing Taggert you'd arranged that. But Taggert had only one surviving partner, and she was hiding out. She didn't even know Taggert was dead until I told her, and she had no chance to kill Sampson, though she probably would have if she'd had the chance. So you had to murder Sampson for yourself."

Shame, and what looked like uncertainty, pulled at his face again. He shook them off. "I'm a realist, Archer. So are you. Sampson's no loss to anybody."

His voice had changed, become suddenly shallow and flat. The whole man was shifting and fencing, trying out attitudes, looking for one that would sustain him.

"You're taking murder more lightly than you used to," I said. "You've sent men to the gas chamber for murder. Has it occurred to you that that's where you're probably headed?"

He managed to smile. The smile made deep and ugly lines around his mouth and betweem his eyes. "You have no proof against me. Not a scrap."

"I have moral certainty and your own implicit confession—"

"But no record of it. You haven't even enough to bring me to trial."

"It isn't my job to do that. You know where you stand, better than I do. I don't know why you had to murder Sampson."

He was silent for some time. When he spoke, his voice had changed again. It was candid and somehow young, the voice of the man I had known in bull sessions years ago. "It's strange that you should say that I had to, Lew. That was how I felt. I had to do it. I hadn't made up my mind until I found Sampson there by himself in the dressing-room. I didn't even speak to him. I saw what could be done, and once I'd seen it, I had to do it whether I liked it or not."

"I think you liked it."

"Yes," he said. "I liked killing him. Now I can't bear to think of it."

"Aren't you being a little easy on yourself? I'm no analyst, but I know you had other motives. More obvious and not so interesting. You got married this afternoon to a girl who was potentially very rich. If her father was dead she was actually very rich. Don't tell me you're not aware that you and your bride have been worth five million dollars for the last couple of hours."

"I know it well enough," he said. "But it's not five million. Mrs Sampson gets half."

"I forgot about her. Why didn't you kill her too?"

"You're bearing down pretty hard."

"You bore down harder on Sampson, for a paltry million and a quarter. Half of one half of his money. Weren't you being a piker, Graves? Or were you planning to murder Mrs Sampson and Miranda later on?"

"You know that isn't true," he said tonelessly. "What do you think I am?"

"I haven't made up my mind. You're a man who married a girl and killed her father the same day to convert her into an heiress. What was the matter, Graves? Didn't you want her without a million-dollar dowry? I thought you were in love with her."

"Lay off." His voice was tormented. "Leave Miranda out of it."

"I can't. If it wasn't for Miranda, we might have something more to talk about."

"No," he said. "There's nothing more to talk about."

I left him sitting in the car, smiling his stony gambler's smile. My back was to him as I crossed the gravel drive to the house, and he had a gun in his pocket, but I didn't look back. I believed him when he said he was sick of violence.

The lights were on in the kitchen, but nobody answered my knock. I went through the house to the elevator. Mrs Kromberg was in the upstairs hall when I stepped out.

"Where are you going?"

"I have to see Mrs Sampson."

"You can't. She's been awful nervous to-day. She took three grains of nembutal about an hour ago."

"This is important."

"How important?"

"The thing she's been waiting to hear."

Comprehension flickered in her eyes, but she was too good a servant to question me. "I'll see if she's asleep." She went to the closed door of Mrs Sampson's room and opened it quietly.

A frightened whisper came from inside the room. "Who's

that?"

"Kromberg. Mr Archer says he has to see you. He says it's very important."

"Very well," the whisper said. A light switched on. Mrs Kromberg stood back to let me enter.

Mrs Sampson leaned on her elbows, blinking in the light. Her brown face was drugged and sodden with sleep or the hope of sleep. The round dark tips of her breasts stared through the silk pyjamas like dull eyes.

I shut the door behind me. "Your husband is dead."

"Dead," she repeated after me.

"You don't seem surprised."

"Should I be surprised? You don't know the dreams I've been having. It's terrible when you can't quiet your mind, when you're far enough gone to see the faces but you can't quite go to sleep. The faces have been so vivid to-night. I saw his face all bloated by the sea, threatening to devour me."

"Did you hear what I said, Mrs Sampson? Your husband is dead. He was murdered two hours ago."

"I heard you. I knew I was going to outlive him."

"Is that all it means to you?"

"What more should it mean?" Her voice was blurred and empty of feeling, a wandering sibilance adrift in the deep channel between sleep and waking. "I was widowed before, and I felt it then. When Bob was killed I cried for days. I'm not going to grieve for his father. I wanted him to die."

"You have your wish, then."

"Not all of my wish. He died too soon, or not soon enough. Everybody died too soon. If Miranda had married the other one, Ralph would have changed his will and I'd have it all for myself." She looked up at me slyly. "I know what you must be thinking, Archer. That I'm an evil woman. But I'm not evil really. I have so little, don't you see? I have to look after the little I have."

"Half of five million dollars," I said.

"It's not the money. It's the power it gives you. I needed it so badly. Now Miranda will go away and leave me all alone. Come and sit beside me for a minute. I have such terrible fears before I go to sleep. Do you think I'll have to see his face every night before I go to sleep?"

"I don't know, Mrs Sampson." I felt pity for her, but the other feelings were stronger. I went to the door and shut it on her.

Mrs Kromberg was still in the hall. "I heard you say that Mr Sampson is dead."

"He is. Mrs Sampson is too far gone to talk. Do you know where Miranda is?"

"Some place downstairs, I think."

I found her in the living-room, hugging her legs on a hassock beside the fireplace. The lights were out, and through the great central window I could see the dark sea and the silverpoint horizon.

She looked up when I entered the room, but she didn't rise to greet me. "Is that you, Archer?"

"Yes. I have something to tell you."

"Have you found him?" A glowing log in the fireplace lit up her head and neck with a fitful rosiness. Her eyes were a wide and steady black.

"Yes. He's dead."

"I knew that he'd be dead. He's been dead from the beginning, hasn't he?"

"I wish I could tell you that he had."

"What do you mean?"

I put off explaining what I meant. "I recovered the money."

"The money?"

"This." I tossed the bag at her feet. "The hundred thousand."

"I don't care about it. Where did you find him?"

"Listen to me, Miranda. You're on your own."

"Not entirely," she said. "I married Albert this afternoon."

"I know. He told me. But you've got to get out of this house and look after yourself. The first thing you've got to do is put that money away. I went to a lot of trouble to get it back, and you may be needing part of it."

"I'm sorry. Where shall I put it?"

"The safe in the study, until you can get to a bank."

"All right." She rose with a sudden decisiveness and led the way into the study. Her arms were stiff and her shoulders high, as if they were resisting a downward pressure.

While she was opening the safe I heard a car go down the drive. She turned to me with an awkward movement more appealing than grace. "Who was that?"

"Albert Graves. He drove me out here."

"Why on earth didn't he come in?"

I gathered the remnants of my courage together, and told her: "He murdered your father tonight."

Her mouth moved breathlessly and then forced out words. "You're joking, aren't you? He couldn't have."

"He did." I took refuge in facts. "I found out this afternoon where your father was being held. I phoned Graves from Los Angeles and told him to get there as soon as he could, with the sheriff. Graves got there ahead of me, without the sheriff. When I arrived, there was no sign of him. He'd parked his car somewhere out of sight and was still inside the building with your father. When I went inside, he hit me from behind and knocked me out. When I came to, he pretended he'd just arrived. Your father was dead. His body was still warm."

"I can't believe Albert did it."

"You do believe it, though."

"Have you proof?"

"It will have to be technical proof. I had no time to look for it. It's up to the police to find the proof."

She sat down limply in a leather armchair. "So many people have died. Father, and Alan–"

"Graves killed them both."

"But he killed Alan to save you. You told me—"

"It was a complex killing," I said, "a justifiable homicide and something more. He didn't have to kill Taggert. He's a good shot. He could have wounded him. But he wanted Taggert dead. He had his reasons."

"What possible reasons?"

"I think you know of one."

She raised her face in the light. It seemed to me that she had made a choice between a number of different things and settled on boldness. "Yes, I do. I was in love with Alan."

"But you were planning to marry Graves."

"I hadn't made my mind up until last night. I was going to marry someone, and he seemed to be the one. 'It is better to marry than to burn.'"

"He gambled on you, and won. But the other thing he had gambled on didn't happen. Taggert's partner failed to kill your father. So Graves strangled your father himself."

She spread one hand over her eyes and forehead. The blue veins in her temples were young and delicate. "It's incredibly ugly," she said. "I can't understand how he did it."

"He did it for money."

"But he's never cared for money. It's one of the things I admired in him." She removed he hand from her face, and I saw that she was smiling bitterly. "I haven't been wise in my admirations."

"There may have been a time when Graves didn't care about money. There may be places where he could have stayed that way. Santa Teresa isn't one of them. Money is lifeblood in this town. If you don't have it, you're only half alive. It must have galled him to work for millionaires and handle their money and have nothing of his own. Suddenly he saw his chance to be a millionaire himself. He realized that he wanted money more than anything else on earth."

"Do you know what I wish at this moment?" she said. "I wish I had no money and no sex. They're both more trouble than they're worth to me."

"You can't blame money for what it does to people. The evil is in people, and money is the peg they hang it on. They go wild for money when they've lost their other values."

"I wonder what happened to Albert Graves."

"Nobody knows. He doesn't know himself. The important thing now is what is going to happen to him."

"Do you have to tell the police?"

"I'm going to tell them. It will make it easier for me if you agree. Easier for you in the long run, too."

"You're asking me to share the responsibility, but you don't really care what I think. You're going to tell them anyway. Yet you admit you haven't any proof." She moved restlessly in the chair.

"He won't deny it if he is accused. You know him better than I do."

"I thought I knew him well. Now I'm uncertain – about everything."

"That's why you should let me go ahead. You have doubts to resolve, and you can't resolve them by doing nothing. You can't go on living with uncertainty, either."

"I'm not sure I have to go on living."

"Don't go romantic on me," I said harshly. "Self-pity isn't your way out. You've had terrible luck with two men. I think you're a strong enough girl to take it. I told you before that you've got a life to make. You're on your own."

She inclined toward me. Her breasts leaned out from her body, vulnerable and soft. Her mouth was soft. "I don't know how to begin. What shall I do?"

"Come with me."

"With you. You want me to go with you?"

"Don't try to shift your weight to me, Miranda. You're a lovely girl, and I like you very much, but you're not my baby. Come with me, and we'll talk to the D.A. We'll let him decide."

"Very well. We'll go to Humphreys. He's always been close to Albert."

She drove me up a winding road to the mesa that overlooked the city. When she stopped in front of Humphreys's redwood bungalow, another car was standing in the drive.

"That's Albert's car," she said. "Please go in alone. I don't want to see him."

I left her in the car and climbed the stone steps to the terrace. Humphreys opened the door before I could reach the knocker. His face was more than ever like a skull's.

He stepped out on the terrace and closed the door behind him. "Graves is here," he said. "He came a few minutes ago. He told me he murdered Sampson."

"What are you going to do?"

"I've called the sheriff. He's on his way over." He ran his fingers through his thinning hair. His gestures like his voice, were light and distant, as if reality had moved back out of his reach. "This is a tragic thing. I believed that Albert Graves was a good man."

"Crime often spreads out like that," I said. "It's an epidemic. You've seen it happen before."

"Not to one of my friends." He was silent for a moment. "Bert was talking about Kierkegaard just a minute ago. He quoted something about innocence, that it's like standing on the edge of a deep gulf. You can't look down into the gulf without losing your innocence. Once you've looked, you're guilty. Bert said that he looked down, that he was guilty before he murdered

Sampson."

"He's still being easy on himself," I said. "He wasn't looking down; he was looking up. Up to the houses in the hills where the big money lives. He was going to be big himself for a change, with a quarter of Sampson's millions."

Humphreys answered slowly: "I don't know. He never cared for money very much. He still doesn't, I don't think. But something happened to him. He hated Sampson, but so did lots of others. Sampson made anyone who worked for him feel like a valet. But it was something deeper than that in Graves. He'd worked hard all his life, and the whole thing suddenly went sour. It lost meaning for him. There was no more virtue or justice, in him or in the world. That's why he gave up prosecuting, you know."

"I didn't know."

"Finally he struck out blindly at the world and killed a man."

"Not blindly. Very shrewdly."

"Very blindly," Humphreys said. "I've never seen a man so miserable as Bert Graves is now."

I went back to Miranda. "Graves is here. You weren't entirely wrong about him. He decided to do the right thing."

"Confessed?"

"He was too honest to bluff it through. If nobody had suspected him, he might have. Anyone's honesty has its conditions. But he knew that I knew. He went to Humpreys and told his story."

"I'm glad he did." She denied this a moment later by the sounds she made. Deep shaking sobs bowed her over the wheel.

I lifted her over, and drove myself. As we rolled down the hill, I could see all the lights of the city. They didn't seem quite real. The stars and the house lights were firefly gleams, sparks of cold fire suspended in the black void. The real thing in my world was the girl beside me, warm and shuddering and lost.

I could have put my arms around her and taken her over. She was that lost, that vulnerable. But if I had, she'd have hated me in a week. In six months I might have hated Miranda. I kept my hands to myself and let her lick her wounds. She used my shoulder to cry on as she would have used anyone's.

Her crying was settling down to a steady rhythm, rocking itself to sleep. The sheriff's radio car passed us at the foot of the hill and turned up toward the house where Graves was waiting.

THE BARBAROUS COAST

For
Stanley Tenny

I

THE CHANNEL CLUB lay on a shelf of rock overlooking the sea, toward the southern end of the beach called Malibu. Above its long brown buildings, terraced gardens climbed like a richly carpeted stairway to the highway. The grounds were surrounded by a high wire fence topped with three barbed strands and masked with oleanders.

I stopped in front of the gate and sounded my horn. A man wearing a blue uniform and an official-looking peaked cap came out of the stone gatehouse. His hair was black and bushy below the cap, sprinkled with gray like iron filings. In spite of his frayed ears and hammered-in nose, his head had the combination of softness and strength you see in old Indian faces. His skin was dark.

'I seen you coming,' he said amiably. 'You didden have to honk, it hurts the ears.'

'Sorry.'

'It's all right.' He shuffled forward, his belly overhanging the belt that supported his holster, and leaned a confidential arm on the car door. 'What's your business, mister?'

'Mr Basset called me. He didn't state his business. The name is Archer.'

'Yah, sure, he is expecting you. You can drive right on down. He's in his office.'

He turned to the reinforced wire gate, jangling his keyring. A man came out of the oleanders and ran past my car. He was a big young man in a blue suit, hatless, with flying pink hair. He ran almost noiselessly on his toes toward the opening gate.

The guard moved quickly for a man of his age. He whirled and got an arm around the young man's middle. The young man struggled in his grip, forcing the guard back against the gatepost. He said something guttural and inarticulate. His shoulder jerked, and he knocked the guard's cap off.

The guard leaned against the gatepost and fumbled for his gun. His eyes were small and dirty like the eyes of a potato. Blood began to drip from the end of his nose and spotted his blue shirt where it curved out over his belly. His revolver came up in his hand. I got out of my car.

The young man stood where he was, his head turned sideways, halfway through the gate. His profile was like something chopped out of raw planking, with a glaring blue eye set in its corner. He said:

'I'm going to see Bassett. You can't stop me.'

'A slug in the guts will stop you,' the guard said in a reasonable way. 'You move, I shoot. This is private property.'

'Tell Bassett I want to see him.'

'I already told him. He don't want to see you.' The guard shuffled forward, his left shoulder leading, the gun riding steady in his right hand. 'Now pick up my hat and hand it to me and git.'

The young man stood still for a while. Then he stopped and picked up the cap and brushed at it ineffectually before he handed it back.

'I'm sorry. I didn't mean to hit you. I've nothing against you.'

'I got something against you, boy.' The guard snatched the cap out of his hands. 'Now beat it before I knock your block off.'

I touched the young man's shoulder, which was broad and packed with muscle. 'You better do what he says.'

He turned to me, running his hand along the side of his jaw. His jaw was heavy and pugnacious. In spite of this, his light eyebrows and uncertain mouth made his face seem formless. He sneered at me very youngly:

'Are you another one of Bassett's muscle boys?'

'I don't know Bassett.'

'I heard you ask for him.'

'I do know this. Run around calling people names and pushing in where you're not wanted, and you'll end up with a flat profile. Or worse.'

He closed his right fist and looked from it to my face. I shifted my weight a little, ready to block and counter.

'Is that supposed to be a threat?' he said.

'It's a friendly warning. I don't know what's eating you. My advice is go away and forget it—'

'Not without seeing Bassett.'

'And, for God's sake, keep your hands off old men.'

'I apologized for that.' But he flushed guiltily.

The guard came up behind him and poked him with the revolver. 'Apology not accepted. I used to could handle two like you with one arm tied behind me. Now are you going to git or do I have to show you?'

'I'll go,' the young man said over his shoulder. 'Only, you can't keep me off the public highway. And sooner or later he has to come out.'

'What's your beef with Bassett?' I said.

'I don't care to discuss it with a stranger. I'll discuss it with him.' He looked at me for a long moment, biting his lower lip. 'Would *you* tell him I've got to see him? That it's very important to me?'

'I guess I can tell him that. Who do I say the message is from?'

'George Wall. I'm from Toronto.' He paused. 'It's about my wife. Tell him I won't leave until he sees me.'

'That's what you think,' the guard said. 'March now, take a walk.'

George Wall retreated up the road, moving slowly to show his independence. He dragged his long morning shadow around a curve and out of sight. The guard put his gun away and wiped his bloody nose with the back of his hand. Then he licked his hand, as though he couldn't afford to waste the protein.

'The guy's a cycle-path what they call them,' he said. 'Mr Bassett don't know him, even.'

'Is he what Bassett wants to see me about?'

'Maybe, I dunno.' His arms and shoulders moved in a sinuous shrug.

'How long has he been hanging around?'

'Ever since I come onto the gate. For all I know, he spent the night in the bushes. I ought to have him picked up, but Mr Bassett says no. Mr Bassett is too softhearted for his own good.

Handle him yourself, he says, we don't want trouble with law.'

'You handled him.'

'You bet you. Time was, I could take on two like him, like I said.' He flexed the muscle in his right arm and palpated it admiringly. He gave me a gentle smile. 'I was a fighter one time—pretty good fighter. Tony Torres? You ever hear my name? The Fresno Gamecock?'

'I've heard it. You went six with Armstrong.'

'Yes.' He nodded solemnly. 'I was an old man already, thirty-five, thirty-six. My legs was gone. He cut my legs off from under me or I could of lasted ten. I felt fine, only my legs. You know that? You saw the fight?'

'I heard it on the radio. I was a kid in school, I couldn't make the price.'

'What do you know?' he said with dreamy pleasure. 'You heard it on the radio.'

II

I LEFT MY car on the asphalt parking-lot in front of the main building. A Christmas tree painted brilliant red hung upside-down over the entrance. It was a flat-roofed structure of fieldstone and wood. Its Neutraesque low lines and simplicity of design kept me from seeing how big it was until I was inside. Through the inner glass door of the vestibule I could see the fifty-yard swimming-pool contained in its U-shaped wings. The ocean end opened on bright blue space.

The door was locked. The only human being in sight was a black boy bisected by narrow white trunks. He was sweeping the floor of the pool with a long-handled underwater vacuum. I tapped on the door with a coin.

After a while he heard me and came trotting. His dark, intelligent eyes surveying me through the glass seemed to divide the world into two groups: the rich, and the not so rich. I qualified for the second group, it seemed. He said when he opened the door:

'If you're selling, mister, the timing could be better. This is the off-season, anyway, and Mr Bassett's in a rotten mood. He just got through chopping *me* out. It isn't my fault they threw the tropical fish in the swimming-pool.'

'Who did?'

'The people last night. The chlorine water killed them, poor little beggars, so I got to suck them out.'

'The people?'

'The tropical fish. They scooped 'em out of the aquarium and chunked 'em in the pool. People go out on a party and get drunk, they forget all the ordinary decencies of life. So Mr Bassett takes it out on me.'

'Don't hold it against him. My clients are always in a rotten mood when they call me in.'

'You an undertaker or something?'

'Something.'

'I just wondered.' A white smile lit his face. 'I got an aunt in the undertaking business. I can't see it myself. Too creepy. But she enjoys it.'

'Good. Is Bassett the owner here?'

'Naw, just the manager. The way he talks, you'd think he owns it, but it belongs to the members.'

I followed his wedge-shaped lifeguard's back along the gallery, through shifting green lights reflected from the pool. He knocked on a gray door with a MANAGER sign. A high voice answered the knock. It creaked along my spine like chalk on a damp blackboard:

'Who is it, please?'

'Archer,' I said to the lifeguard.

'Mr Archer to see you, sir.'

'Very well. One moment.'

The lifeguard winked at me and trotted away, his feet slapping the tiles. The lock snicked, and the door was opened slightly. A face appeared in the crack, just below the level of my own. Its eyes were pale and set too wide apart; they bulged a little like the eyes of a fish. The thin, spinsterly mouth emitted a sigh:

'I *am* glad to see you. Do come in.'

He relocked the door behind me and waved me to a chair in front of his desk. The gesture was exaggerated by nerves. He sat down at the desk, opened a pigskin pouch, and began to stuff a big-pot briar with dark flakes of English tobacco. This and his Harris tweed jacket, his Oxford slacks, his thick-soled brown brogues, his Eastern-seaboard accent, were all of a piece. In spite of the neat dye job on his brown hair, and the unnatural youth which high color lent his face, I placed his age close to sixty.

I looked around the office. It was windowless, lit by hidden fluorescence and ventilated by an air-conditioning system. The furniture was dark and heavy. The walls were hung with photographs of yachts under full sail, divers in the air, tennis-players congratulating each other with forced smiles on their faces. There were several books on the desk, held upright between elephant bookends made of polished black stone.

Bassett applied a jet lighter to his pipe and laid down a blue smoke screen, though which he said:

'I understand, Mr Archer, that you're a qualified bodyguard.'

'I suppose I'm qualified. I don't often take on that kind of work.'

'But I understood—Why not?'

'It means living at close quarters with some of the damnedest jerks. They usually want a bodyguard because they can't get anybody to talk to them. Or else they have delusions.'

He smiled crookedly. 'I can hardly take that as a compliment. Or perhaps I wasn't intended to?'

'You're in the market for a bodyguard?'

'I hardly know.' He added carefully: 'Until the situation shapes up more clearly, I really can't say what I need. Or why.'

'Who gave you my name?'

'One of our members mentioned you to me some time ago. Joshua Severn, the television producer. You'll be interested to know that he considers you quite a fireball.'

'Uh-huh.' The trouble with flattery was that people expected to be paid for it in kind. 'Why do you need a detective, Mr Bassett?'

'I'll tell you. A certain young chap has threatened my—threatened my safety. You should have heard him on the telephone.'

'You've talked to him?'

'Just for a minute, last night. I was in the midst of a party—our annual post-Christmas party—and he called from Los Angeles. He said he was going to come over here and assault me unless I gave him certain information. It jarred me frightfully.'

'What kind of information?'

'Information which I simply don't possess. I believe he's outside now, lying in wait for me. The party didn't break up until very late and I spent the night here, what remained of it. This morning the gateman telephoned down that he had a young man there who wished to see me. I told him to keep the fellow out. Shortly after that, when I'd gathered my wits together, I telephoned you.'

'And what do you want to do, exactly?'

'Get rid of him. You must have ways and means. I don't want any violence, of course, unless it should prove to be absolutely necessary.' His eyes gleamed palely between new strata of smoke. 'It may be necessary. Do you have a gun?'

'In my car. It's not for hire.'

'Of course not. You misinterpret my meaning, old boy. Perhaps I didn't express myself quite clearly. I yield to no man in my abhorrence of violence. I merely meant that you might have use for a pistol as an—ah—instrument of persuasion. Couldn't you simply escort him to the station, or the airfield, and put him aboard a plane?'

'No.' I stood up.

He followed me to the door and took hold of my arm. I disliked the coziness, and shook him off.

'Look here, Archer, I'm not a wealthy man, but I do have some savings. I'm willing to pay you three hundred dollars to dispose of this fellow for me.'

'Dispose of him?'

'Without violence, of course.'

'Sorry, no sale.'

'Five hundred dollars.'

'It can't be done. What you want me to do is merely kidnapping under California law.'

'Good *Lord*, I didn't mean *that*.' He was genuinely shocked.

'Think about it. For a man in your position, you're pretty dim about law. Let the police take care of him, why don't you? You say he threatened you.'

'Yes. As a matter of fact, he mentioned horse-whipping. But you can't go to the police with that sort of thing.'

'Sure you can.'

'Not I. It's so ridiculously old-fashioned. I'd be the laughing-stock of the entire Southland. You don't seem to grasp the personal aspects, old boy. I'm manager and secretary of a very, very exclusive club. The finest people on the coast confide their children, their young daughters, to my trust. I have to be clear of any breath of scandal—Calpurnia, you know.'

'Where does the scandal come in?'

Calpurnia took his pipe out of his mouth and blew a wobbly smoke-ring. 'I'd hoped to avoid going into it. I certainly didn't expect to be cross-questioned on the subject. However. Something has to be done, before the situation deteriorates irreparably.'

His choice of words annoyed me, and I let the annoyance show. He gave me an appealing look, which fell with a thud between us:

'Can I trust you, *really* trust you?'

'So long as it's legal.'

'Oh, heavens, it's legal. I am in a bit of a jam, though, through no fault of my own. It's not what I've done, but what people might think I've done. You see, there's a woman involved.'

'George Wall's wife?'

His face came apart at the seams. He tried to put it together again around the fixed point of the pipe, which he jammed into his mouth. But he couldn't control the grimace tugging like hooks at the end of his lips.

'You know her? Does everybody know?'

'Everybody soon will if George Wall keeps hanging around. I

ran into him on my way in—'

'Good God, he is on the grounds, then.'

Bassett crossed the room in awkward flight. He opened a drawer of his desk and took out a medium-caliber automatic.

'Put that thing away,' I said. 'If you're worried about your reputation, gunfire can really blow it to hell. Wall was outside the gate, trying to get in. He didn't make it. He did give me a message for you: he won't leave until you see him. Over.'

'Damn it, man, why didn't you say so? Here we've been wasting time.'

'You have.'

'All *right*. We won't quarrel. We've got to get him away from here before any members come.'

He glanced at the chronometer strapped to his right wrist, and accidentally pointed the automatic at me.

'Put the gun down, Bassett. You're too upset to be handling a gun.'

He laid it on the embossed blotter in front of him and gave me a shamefaced smile. 'Sorry. I am a bit nervy. I'm not accustomed to these alarums and excursions.'

'What's all the excitement about?'

'Young Wall seems to have some melodramatic notion that I stole his wife from him.'

'Did you?'

'Don't be absurd. The girl is young enough to be my daughter.' His eyes were wet with embarrassment. 'My relations with her have always been perfectly proper.'

'You do know her, then?'

'Of course. I've known her for years—much longer than George Wall has. She's been using the pool for diving practice ever since she was in her teens. She's not far out of her teens now, as a matter of fact. She can't be more than twenty-one or two.'

'Who is she?'

'Hester Campbell, the diver. You may have heard of her. She came close to winning the national championship a couple of years ago. Then she dropped out of sight. Her family moved away from here and she gave up amateur competition. I had no idea that she was married, until she turned up here again.'

'When was this?'

'Five or six months ago. *Six* months ago, in June. She seemed to have had quite a bad time of it. She'd toured with an aquacade for a while, lost her job and been stranded in Toronto. Met this young Canadian sportswriter and married him in desperation. Apparently the marriage didn't work out. She left him after less than a year together, and came back here. She was on her uppers, and rather beaten, spiritually. Naturally I did what I could for her. I persuaded the board to let her use the pool for diving instruction, on a commission basis. She did rather well at that while the summer season lasted. And when she lost her pupils, I'm frank to say I helped her out financially for a bit.' He spread his hands limply. 'If that's a crime, then I'm a criminal.'

'If that's all there is to it, I don't see what you're afraid of.'

'You don't understand—you don't understand the position I'm in, the enmities and intrigues I have to contend with here. There's a faction among the membership who would like to see me discharged. If George Wall made it appear that I was using my place to procure young women—'

'How could he do that?'

'I mean if he brought court action, as he threatened to. An unprincipled lawyer could make some kind of case against me. The girl told me that she planned a divorce, and I suppose I wasn't thoroughly discreet. I was seen in her company more than once. As a matter of fact, I cooked several dinners for her.' His color rose slightly. 'Cooking is one of my hobby-horses. I realize now it wasn't wise to invite her into my home.'

'He can't do anything with that. This isn't the Victorian age.'

'It is in certain circles. You just don't grasp how precarious my position is. I'm afraid the accusation would be enough.'

'Aren't you exaggerating?'

'I hope I am. I don't feel it.'

'My advice to you is, level with Wall. Tell him the facts.'

'I tried to, on the telephone last night. He refused to listen. The man's insane with jealousy. You'd think I had his wife hidden somewhere.'

'You haven't, though?'

'Of course not. I haven't seen her since the early part of September. She left here suddenly without a good-by or a thank-you. She didn't even leave a forwarding address.'

'Run off with a man?'

'It's more than likely,' he said.

'Tell Wall that. In person.'

'Oh, no. I couldn't possibly. The man's a raving maniac, he'd assault me.'

Bassett ran tense fingers through his hair. It was soaked at the temples, and little rivulets ran down in front of his ears. He took the folded handkerchief out of his jacket pocket and wiped his face with it. I began to feel a little sorry for him. Physical cowardice hurts like nothing else.

'I can handle him,' I said. 'Call the gate. If he's still up there, I'll go and bring him down.'

'Here?'

'Unless you can think of a better place.'

After a nervous moment, he said: 'I suppose I have to see him. I can't leave him rampaging around in public. There are several members due for their morning dip at any moment.'

His voice took on a religious coloring whenever he mentioned the members. They might have belonged to a higher race, supermen or avenging angels. And Bassett himself had a slipping toehold on the edge of the earthly paradise. Reluctantly, he picked up the intramural phone:

'Tony? Mr Bassett. Is that young maniac still rampaging around? . . . Are you certain? Absolutely certain? . . . Well, fine. Let me know if he shows up again.' He replaced the receiver.

'Gone?'

'It seems so.' He inhaled deeply through his open mouth. 'Torres says he took off on foot some time ago. I'd appreciate it, though, if you stayed around for a bit, just in case.'

'All right. This trip is costing you twenty-five dollars, anyway.'

He took the hint and paid me in cash from a drawer. Then he got an electric razor and a mirror out of another drawer. I sat and watched him shave his face and neck. He clipped the hairs in his nostrils with a tiny pair of scissors, and plucked a few hairs out of his eyebrows. It was the sort of occasion that made me hate the job of guarding bodies.

I looked over the books on the desk. There were a Dun and Bradstreet, a Southern California Blue Book, a motion-picture almanac for the previous year, and a thick volume bound in worn green cloth and entitled, surprisingly, *The Bassett Family.* I opened this to the title page, which stated that the book was an account of the genealogy and achievements of the descendants of William Bassett, who landed in Massachusetts in 1634; down to the outbreak of the World War in 1914. By Clarence Bassett.

'I don't suppose you'd be interested,' Bassett said, 'but it's quite an interesting story to a member of the family. My father wrote that book: he occupied his declining years with it. We really did have a native aristocracy in New England, you know—governors, professors, divines, men of affairs.'

'I've heard rumors to that effect.'

'Sorry, I don't mean to bore you,' he said in a lighter tone, almost self-mocking. 'Curiously enough, I'm the last of my branch of the family who bears the name of Bassett. It's the one sole reason I have for regretting my not having married. But then I've never been the philoprogenitive type.'

Leaning forward toward the mirror, he began to squeeze a blackhead out of one of the twin grooves that ran from the base of his nose. I got up and roamed along the walls, examining the photographs. I was stopped by one of three divers, a man and two girls, taking off in unison from the high tower. Their bodies hung clear of the tower against a light summer sky, arched in identical swan dives, caught at the height of their parabolas before gravity took hold and snatched them back to earth.

'That's Hester on the left,' Bassett said behind me.

Her body was like an arrow. Her bright hair was combed back by the wind from the oval blur of her face. The girl on the right was a dark brunette, equally striking in her full-breasted way. The man in the middle was dark, too, with curly black hair and muscles that looked hammered out of bronze.

'It's one of my favorite photographs,' Bassett said. 'It was taken a couple of years ago, when Hester was in training for the nationals.'

'Taken here?'

'Yes. We let her use our tower for practicing, as I said.'

'Who are her friends in the picture?'

'The boy used to be our lifeguard. The girl was a young friend of Hester's. She worked in the snack bar here, but Hester was grooming her for competitive diving.'

'Is she still around?'

'I'm afraid not.' His face lengthened. 'Gabrielle was killed.'

'In a diving accident?'

'Hardly. She was shot.'

'Murdered?'

He nodded solemnly.

'Who did it to her?'

'The crime was never solved. I doubt that it ever will be now. It happened nearly two years ago, in March of last year.'

'What did you say her name was?'

'Gabrielle. Gabrielle Torres.'

'Any relation to Tony?'

'She was his daughter.'

III

THERE WAS A heavy knock on the door. Bassett shied like a frightened horse.

'Who is it?'

The knock was repeated. I went to the door. Bassett neighed at me:

'Don't open it.'

I turned the key in the lock and opened the door a few inches against my foot and shoulder. George Wall was outside. His face was greenish-gray in the reflected light. The torn white meat of his leg showed through a rip in his trousers. He breathed hard into my face:

'Is he in here?'

'How did you get in?'

'I came over the fence. Is Bassett in here?'

I looked at Bassett. He was crouched behind the desk, with only his white eyes showing, and his black gun. 'Don't let him come in. Don't let him touch me.'

'He's not going to touch you. Put that down.'

'I will not. I'll defend myself if I have to.'

I turned my back on his trigger-happy terror. 'You heard him, Wall. He has a gun.'

'I don't care what he has. I've got to talk to him. Is Hester here?'

'You're on the wrong track. He hasn't seen her for months.'

'Naturally he says that.'

'I'm saying it, too. She worked here during the summer, and left some time in September.'

His puzzled blue look deepened. His tongue moved like a slow red snail across his upper lip. 'Why wouldn't he see me before, if she's not with him?'

'You mentioned horsewhipping, remember? It wasn't exactly the approach diplomatic.'

'I don't have time for diplomacy. I have to fly home tomorrow.'

'Good.'

His shoulder leaned into the opening. I felt his weight on the door. Basset's voice rose an octave:

'Keep him away from me!'

Bassett was close behind me. I turned with my back against the door and wrenched the gun out of his hand and put it in my pocket. He was too angry and scared to say a word. I turned back to Wall, who was still pressing in but not with all his force. He looked confused. I spread one hand on his chest and pushed him upright and held him. His weight was stubborn and inert, like a stone statue's.

A short, broad-shouldered man came down the steps from the

vestibule. He walked toward us fussily, almost goosestepping, glancing out over the pool and at the sea beyond it as if they were his personal possessions. The wind ruffled his crest of silver hair. Self-importance and fat swelled under his beautifully tailored blue flannel jacket. He was paying no attention to the woman trailing along a few paces behind him.

'Good Lord,' Bassett said in my ear, 'it's Mr and Mrs Graff. We can't have a disturbance in front of Mr Graff. Let Wall come in. Quickly, man!'

I let him in. Bassett was at the door, bowing and smiling, when the silver-haired man came up. He paused and chopped the air with his nose. His face was brown and burnished-looking.

'Bassett? You've got the extra help lined up for tonight? Orchestra? Food?'

'Yes, Mr Graff.'

'About drinks. We'll use the regular bar bourbon, not my private stock. They're all barbarians, anyway—none of them knows the difference.'

'Yes, Mr Graff. Enjoy your swim.'

'I always enjoy my swim.'

The woman came up behind him, moving a little dazedly, as though the sunlight distressed her. Her black hair was pulled back severely from a broad, flat brow, to which her Greek nose was joined without indentation. Her face was pale and dead, except for the dark searchlights of her eyes, which seemed to contain all her energy and feeling. She was dressed in black jersey, without ornament, like a widow.

Bassett bade her good-morning. She answered with sudden animation that it was a lovely day for December. Her husband strode away toward the *cabañas*. She followed like a detached shadow. Bassett sighed with relief.

'Is he the Graff in Helio-Graff?' I said.

'Yes.'

He edged past Wall to his desk, rested a haunch on one corner, and fumbled with his pipe and tobacco pouch. His hands were shaking. Wall hadn't moved from the door. His face was red in patches, and I didn't like the glacial stare of his eyes. I kept my bulk between the two men, watching them in turn like a tennis referee.

Wall said throatily: 'You can't lie out of it, you must know where she is. You paid for her dancing lessons.'

'Dancing lessons? I?' Bassett's surprise sounded real.

'At the Anton School of Ballet. I spoke to Anton yesterday afternoon. He told me she took some dancing lessons from him, and paid for them with your check.'

'So that's what she did with the money I lent her.'

Wall's lip curled to one side. 'You've got an answer for everything, haven't you? Why would you lend her money?'

'I like her.'

'I bet you do. Where is she now?'

'Frankly, I don't know. She left here in September. I haven't set eyes on Miss Campbell since.'

'The name is Mrs Wall, Mrs George Wall. She's my wife.'

'I'm beginning to suspect that, old boy. But she used her maiden name when she was with us. She was planning to divorce you, I understood.'

'Who talked her into that?'

Bassett gave him a long-suffering look. 'If you want the truth, I tried to talk her out of it. I advised her to go back to Canada, to you. But she had other plans.'

'What other plans?'

'She wanted a career,' Bassett said with a trace of irony. 'She was brought up in the Southland here, you know, and she had the movie fever in her blood. And of course her diving gave her a taste for the limelight. I honestly did my best to talk her out of it. But I'm afraid I made no impression on her. She was determined to find an outlet for her talent—I suppose that explains the dancing lessons.'

'Does she have talent?' I said.

Wall answered: 'She thinks she has.'

'Come now,' Bassett said with a weary smile. 'Let's give the lady her due. She's a lovely child, and she could develop—'

'So you paid for her dancing lessons.'

'I lent her money. I don't know how she spent it. She took off from here very suddenly, as I was telling Archer. One day she was living quietly in Malibu, working at her diving, making good contacts here. And the next day she'd dropped out of sight.'

'What sort of contacts?' I said.

'A good many of our members are in the industry.'

'Could she have gone off with one of them?'

Bassett frowned at the idea. 'Certainly not to my knowledge. You understand, I made no attempt to trace her. If she chose to leave, I had no right to interfere.'

'I have a right.' Wall's voice was low and choked, 'I think you're lying about it. You know where she is, and you're trying to put me off.'

His lower lip and jaw stuck out, changing the shape of his face into something unformed and ugly. His shoulders leaned outward from the door. I watched his fists clench, white around the knuckles.

'Act your age,' I said.

'I've got to find out where she is, what happened to her.'

'Wait a minute, George.' Bassett pointed his pipe like a token gun, a wisp of smoke at the stem.

'Don't call me George. My friends call me George.'

'I'm not your enemy, old boy.'

'And don't call me old boy.'

'*Young boy*, then, if you wish. I was going to say, I'm sorry this ever came up between us. Truly sorry. I've done you no harm, believe me, and I wish you well.'

'Why don't you help me, then? Tell me the truth: is Hester alive?'

Bassett looked at him in dismay.

I said: 'What makes you think she isn't?'

'Because she was afraid. She was afraid of being killed.'

'When was this?'

'The night before last. Christmas night. She phoned long-distance to the flat in Toronto. She was terribly upset, crying into the telephone.'

'What about?'

'Someone had threatened to kill her, she didn't say who. She wanted to get out of California. She asked me if I was willing to take her back. I was, and I told her so. But before we could make any arrangements, the call was cut off. Suddenly she wasn't there, there was nobody there on the end of the line.'

'Where was she calling from?'

'Anton's Ballet School on Sunset Boulevard. She had the charges reversed, so I was able to trace the call. I flew out here as soon as I could get away, and saw Anton yesterday. He didn't know about the telephone call, or he said he didn't. He'd been throwing some kind of a party for his students that night, and things were pretty confused.'

'Your wife is still taking lessons from him?'

'I don't know. I believe so.'

'He should have her address, then.'

'He says not. The only address she gave him was the Channel Club here.' He threw a suspicious look in Bassett's direction. 'Are you certain she doesn't live here?'

'Don't be ridiculous. She never did. I invite you to check on that. She rented a cottage in Malibu—I'll look up the address for you. The landlady lives next door, I believe, and you can talk to her. She's Mrs Sarah Lamb—an old friend and employee of mine. Just mention my name to her.'

'So she can lie for you?' Wall said.

Bassett rose and moved toward him, tentatively. 'Won't you listen to reason, old boy? I befriended your wife. It's rather hard, don't you think, that I should have to suffer for my good deeds. I can't spend the whole day arguing with you. I've an important party to prepare for tonight.'

'That's no concern of mine.'

'No, and your affairs are no concern of mine. But I do have a suggestion. Mr Archer is a private detective. I'm willing to pay him, out of my pocket, to help you find your wife. On condition that you stop badgering me. Now, is that a fair proposal or isn't it?'

'You're a detective?' Wall said.

I nodded.

He looked at me doubtfully. 'If I could be sure this isn't a put-up job—Are you a friend of Bassett's?'

'Never saw him until this morning. Incidentally, I haven't been consulted about this deal.'

'It's right down your alley, isn't it?' Bassett said smoothly. 'What's your objection?'

I had none, except that there was trouble in the air and it was the end of a rough year and I was a little tired. I looked at George Wall's pink, rebellious head. He was a natural-born trouble-maker, dangerous to himself and probably to other people. Perhaps if I tagged along with him, I could head off the trouble he was looking for. I was a dreamer.

'How about it, Wall?'

'I'd like to have your help,' he answered slowly. 'I'd rather pay you myself, though.'

'Absolutely not!' Bassett said. 'You must let me do something—I'm interested in Hester's welfare, too.'

'So I gather.' Wall's voice was surly.

I said: 'We'll toss for it. Heads Bassett pays, tails Wall.'

I flipped a quarter and slapped it down on the desk. Tails. I was George Wall's boy. Or he was mine.

IV

GRAFF WAS FLOATING on his back in the pool when George Wall and I went outside. His brown belly swelled above its surface like the humpback of a Galápagos tortoise. Mrs Graff, fully clothed, was sitting by herself in a sunny corner. Her black dress and black hair and black eyes seemed to annul the sunlight. Her face and body had the distinction that takes the place of beauty in people who have suffered long and hard.

She interested me, but I didn't interest her. She didn't even raise her eyes when we passed.

I led Wall out to my car. 'You better duck down in the seat when we get up to the gate. Tony might take a pot shot at you.'

'Not really?'

'He might. Some of these old fighters can get very upset very quickly, especially when you take a poke at them.'

'I didn't mean to do that. It was a rotten thing to do.'

'It wasn't smart. Twice this morning you nearly got yourself shot. Bassett was scared enough to do it, and Tony was mad enough. I don't know how it is in Canada, but you can't throw your weight around too much in these parts. A lot of harmless-looking souls have guns in their drawers.'

His head sank lower. 'I'm sorry.'

He sounded more than ever like an adolescent who hadn't caught up with his growth. I liked him pretty well, in spite of that. He had the makings, if he lived long enough for them to jell.

'Don't apologize to me. The life you save may be your own.'

'But I'm really sorry. The thought of Hester with that old sissy—I guess I lost my head.'

'Find it again. And for God's sake, forget about Bassett. He's hardly what you'd call a wolf.'

'He gave her money. He admitted it.'

'The point is, he did admit it. Probably somebody else is paying her bills now.'

He said in a low, growling voice: 'Whoever it is, I'll kill him.'

'No, you won't.'

He sat in stubborn silence as we drove up to the gate. The gate was open. From the door of the gatehouse, Tony waved to me and made a face at Wall.

'Wait,' George said. 'I want to apologize to him.'

'No. You stay in the car.'

I made a left turn onto the coast highway. It followed the contour of the brown bluffs, then gradually descended toward the sea. The beach cottages began, passing like an endless and dilapidated freight train.

'I know how terrible I look to you,' George blurted. 'I'm not usually like this. I don't go around flexing my muscles and threatening people.'

'That's good.'

'Really,' he said. 'It's just—well, I've had a bad year.'

He told me about his bad year. It started at the Canadian

National Exhibition, in August of the previous year. He was a sportswriter on the Toronto *Star*, and he was assigned to cover the aquacade. Hester was one of the featured tower divers. He'd never cared much about diving—football was his sport—but there was something special about Hester, a shine about her, a kind of phosphorescence. He went back to see her on his own time, and took her out after the show.

The third night, she came out of a two-and-a-half too soon, struck the water flat, and was pulled out unconscious. They took her away before he could get to her. She didn't appear for her act the following night. He found her eventually in a hotel on lower Yonge Street. Both her eyes were black and bloodshot. She said she was through with diving. She'd lost her nerve.

She cried on his shoulder for some time. He didn't know what to do to comfort her.

It was his first experience with a woman, except for a couple of times that didn't count, in Montreal, with some of his football buddies. He asked her to marry him in the course of the night. She accepted his proposal in the morning. They were married three days later.

Perhaps he hadn't been as frank with Hester as he should have been. She'd assumed, from the way he spent money, that he had plenty of it. Maybe he'd let on that he was a fairly important figure in Toronto newspaper circles. He wasn't. He was a cub, just one year out of college, at fifty-five dollars a week.

Hester had a hard time adjusting to life in a two-room flat on Spadina Avenue. One trouble was her eyes, which were a long time clearing. For weeks she wouldn't leave the flat. She gave up grooming her hair, making up, even washing her face. She refused to cook for him. She said she'd lost her looks, lost her career, lost everything that made her life worth living.

'I'll never forget last winter,' George Wall said.

There was such intensity in his voice, I turned to look at him. He didn't meet my eyes. With a dreaming expression on his face, he was staring past me at the blue Pacific. Winter sunlight crumpled like foil on its surface.

'It was a cold winter,' he said. 'The snow creaked under your feet and the hair froze in your nostrils. The frost grew thick on the windows. The oil furnace in the basement kept going out. Hester got quite chummy with the custodian of the building, a woman named Mrs Bean who lived in the next flat. She started going to church with Mrs Bean—some freakish little church that carried on in an old house on Bloor. I'd get home from work and hear them in the bedroom talking about redemption and reincarnation, stuff like that.

'One night after Mrs Bean left, Hester told me that she was being punished for her sins. That was why she missed her dive and got stuck in Toronto with me. She said she had to purify herself so her next incarnation would be on a higher level. For about a month after that, I slept on the chesterfield. Jesus, it was cold.

'On Christmas Eve she woke me up in the middle of the night and announced that she was purified. Christ had appeared in her sleep and forgiven all her sins. I didn't take her seriously at first—how could I? I tried to kid her out of it, laugh it off. So she told me what she meant, about her sins.'

He didn't go on.

'What did she mean?' I said.

'I'd just as soon not say.'

His voice was choked. I looked at him out of the corner of my eyes. Blood burned in his half-averted cheek and reddened his ear.

'Anyway,' he continued, 'we had a kind of reconciliation. Hester dropped the phony-religious kick. Instead, she developed a sudden craze for dancing. Dance all night and sleep all day. I couldn't stand the pace. I had to go to work and drum up the old enthusiasm for basketball and hockey and other childish pastimes. She got into the habit of going out by herself, down into the Village.'

'I thought you said you were living in Toronto.'

'Toronto has its own Village. It's very much like the original in New York—on a smaller scale, of course. Hester got in with a gang of ballet buffs. She went overboard for dancing lessons, with a teacher by the name of Padraic Dane. She had her hair clipped short, and her ears pierced for earrings. She took to wearing white silk shirts and matador pants around the flat. She was always doing entrechats or whatever you call 'em. She'd ask me for things in French—not that she knew French—and when I didn't catch on, she'd give me the silent treatment.

'She'd sit and stare at me without blinking for fifteen or twenty minutes at a time. You'd think I was a piece of furniture that she was trying to think of a better place for. Or maybe by that time I didn't exist at all for her. You know?'

I knew. I'd had a wife and lost her in those silences. I didn't tell George Wall, though. He went on talking, pouring out the words as though they'd been frozen in him for a long time and finally been thawed by the California sun. He probably would have spilled his soul that day to an iron post or a wooden Indian.

'I know now what she was doing,' he said. 'She was getting her confidence back, in a crazy, unreal way, pulling herself together to make a break with me. The crowd she was playing with, Paddy Dane and his gang of pixies, were encouraging her to do it. I should have seen it coming.

'They put on some kind of a dance play late in the spring, in a little theater that used to be a church. Hester played the boy lead. I went to see it, couldn't make head nor tail of it. It was something about a split personality falling in love with itself. I heard them afterwards filling her up with nonsense about herself. They told her she was wasting herself in Toronto, married to a slob like me. She owed it to herself to go to New York, or back to Hollywood.

'We had a battle when she finally came home that night. I laid it on the line for her: she had to give up those people and their ideas. I told her she was going to drop her dancing lessons and her acting and stay home and wear ordinary women's clothes and look after the flat and cook a few decent meals.'

He laughed unpleasantly. It sounded like broken edges rubbing together inside him.

'I'm a great master of feminine psychology,' he said. 'In the morning after I left for work she went to the bank and drew out the money I'd saved towards a house and got on a plane for

Chicago. I found that out by inquiring at the airport. She didn't even leave me a note—I guess she was punishing me for *my* sins. I didn't know where she'd gone. I looked up some of her rum friends in the Village, but they didn't know, either. She dropped them just as flat as she dropped me.

'I don't know how I got through the next six months. We hadn't been married long, and we hadn't been close to each other, the way married people should be. But I was in love with her, I still am. I used to walk the streets half the night and every time I saw a girl with blond hair I'd get an electric shock. Whenever the telephone rang, I'd *know* that it was Hester. And then one night it was.

'It was Christmas night, the night before last. I was sitting in the flat by myself, trying not to think about her. I felt like a nervous breakdown getting ready to happen. Wherever I looked, I kept seeing her face on the wall. And then the telephone rang, and it was Hester. I told you what she said, that she was afraid of being killed and wanted to get out of California. You can imagine how I felt when she was cut off. I thought of calling the Los Angeles police, but there wasn't much to go on. So I had the call traced, and caught the first plane I could get out of Toronto.'

'Why didn't you do that six months ago?'

'I didn't know where she was—she never wrote me.'

'You must have had some idea.'

'Yes, I thought she'd probably come back here. But I didn't have the heart to track her down. I wasn't making much sense there for a while. I pretty well convinced myself she was better off without me.' He added after a silence: 'Maybe she is, at that.'

'All you can do is ask her. But first we have to find her.'

V

WE ENTERED A dead-end street between the highway and the beach. The tires shuddered on the pitted asphalt. The cottages that lined the street were run-down and disreputable-looking, but the cars that stood in front of them were nearly all late models. When I turned off my engine, the only sound I could hear was the rumble and gasp of the sea below the cottages. Above them a few gulls circled, tattletale gray.

The one that Hester had lived in was a board-and-batten box which had an unused look, like a discarded container. Its walls had been scoured bare and grained by blowing sands. The cottage beside it was larger and better kept, but it was losing its paint, too.

'This is practically a slum,' George said. 'I thought that Malibu was a famous resort.'

'Part of it is. This is the other part.'

We climbed the steps to Mrs Lamb's back porch, and I knocked on the rusty screen door. A heavy-bodied old woman in a wrapper opened the inside door. She had a pleasantly ugly bulldog face and a hennaed head, brash orange in the sun. An anti-wrinkle patch between her eyebrows gave her an air of calm eccentricity.

'Mrs Lamb?'

She nodded. She held a cup of coffee in her hand, and she was chewing.

'I understand you rent the cottage next door.'

She swallowed whatever was in her mouth. I watched its passage down her withered throat. 'I may as well tell you right off, I don't rent stag. Now if you're married, that's another matter.' She paused expectantly and took a second swallow, leaving a red half-moon on the rim of the cup.

'I'm not married.'

That was as far as I got.

'Too bad,' she said. Her nasal Kansas voice hummed on like a wire in a rushing wind: 'I'm all for marriage myself, went out with four men in my lifetime and married two of them. The first one lasted thirty-three years, I guess I made him happy. He didn't bother *me* with his Copenhagen snuff and his dirt around the house. It takes more than that to bother *me*. So when he died I married again, and that one wasn't so bad. Could have been better, could have been worse. It was kind of a relief, though, when *he* died. He didn't do a lick of work in seven years. Luckily I had the strength to support him.'

Her sharp eyes, ringed with concentric wrinkles, flicked from me to George Wall and back again. 'You're both nice-appearing young men, you ought to be able to find a girl willing to take a chance with you.' She smiled fiercely, swirled her remaining coffee around in the cup, and drank it down.

'I had a wife,' George Wall said heavily. 'I'm looking for her now.'

'You don't say. Why didn't you say so?'

'I've been trying to.'

'Don't get mad. I like a little sociability, don't you? What's her name?'

'Hester.'

Her eyes flattened. 'Hester Campbell?'

'Hester Campbell Wall.'

'Well, I'll be darned. I didn't know she was married. What happened, did she run away?'

He nodded solemnly. 'Last June.'

'What do you know? She's got less sense than I thought she had, running away from a nice young fellow like you.' She inspected his face intently through the screen, clucking in decrescendo. ' 'Course I never did give her credit for too much sense. She was always full of razzmatazz, ever since she was a kid.'

'Have you known her long?' I said.

'You bet I have. Her and her sister and her mother both. She was a hoity-toity one, her mother, always putting on airs.'

'Do you know where her mother is now?'

'Haven't seen her for years, or the sister either.'

I looked at George Wall.

He shook his head. 'I didn't even know she had a mother. She never talked about her family. I thought she was an orphan.'

'She had one,' the old woman said. 'Her and her sister, Rina, they were both well supplied with a mother. Mrs Campbell was bound to make something out of those girls if it killed them. I don't know how she afforded all those lessons she gave them—

music lessons and dancing lessons and swimming lessons.'

'No husband?'

'Not when I knew her. She was clerking in the liquor store during the war, which is how we became acquainted, through my second. Mrs Campbell was always bragging about her girls, but she didn't really have their welfare at heart. She was what they call a movie-mother, I guess, trying to get her little girls to support her.'

'Does she still live here?'

'Not to my knowledge. She dropped out of sight years ago. Which didn't break my heart.'

'And you don't know where Hester is, either?'

'I haven't laid eyes on the girl since September. She moved out, and that was that. We have some turnover in Malibu, I can tell you.'

'Where did she move to?' George said.

'That's what I'd like to know.' Her gaze shifted to me: 'Are you a relative, too?'

'No, I'm a private detective.'

She showed no surprise. 'All right, I'll talk to you, then. Come inside and have a cup of coffee. Your friend can wait outside.'

Wall didn't argue; he merely looked disgruntled. Mrs Lamb unhooked her screen door, and I followed her into the tiny white kitchen. The red plaid of the tablecloth was repeated in the curtains over the sink. Coffee was bubbling on an electric plate.

Mrs Lamb poured some of it for me in a cup which didn't match hers, and then some more for herself. She sat at the table, motioned to me to sit opposite.

'I couldn't exist without coffee. I developed the habit when I ran the snack bar. Twenty-five cups a day, silly old woman.' But she sounded very tolerant of herself. 'I do believe if I cut myself I'd bleed coffee. Mr Finney—he's my adviser at the Spiritualist Church—says I should switch to tea, but I say no. Mr Finney, I told him, the day I have to give up my favorite vice, I'd just as soon lay down and fold my hands around a lily and pass on into another life.'

'Good for you,' I said. 'You were going to tell me something about Hester.'

'Yes, I was. I hated to say it right out in front of the husband. I had to evict her.'

'What for?'

'Carrying on,' she said vaguely. 'The girl's a fool about men. Doesn't he know that?'

'It seems to be at the back of his mind. Any particular men?'

'One particular man.'

'Not Clarence Bassett?'

'Mr Bassett? Heavens, no. I've known Mr Bassett going on ten years—I ran the snack bar at the club until my legs give out—and you can take my word for it, he ain't the carrying-on *type*. Mr Bassett was more like a father to her. I guess he did his best to keep her out of trouble, but his best wasn't good enough. Mine, either.'

'What kind of trouble did she get into?'

'Man trouble, like I said. Nothing that you could put your finger on, maybe, but I could see she was heading for disaster. One of the men she brought here to her house was a regular gangster type. I *told* Hester if she was going to have bums like him visiting her, spending the night, she'd have to find another house to do it in. I felt I had a right to speak out, knowing her from childhood and all. But she took it the wrong way, said she would look after her affairs and I could look after mine. I told her what she did on my property *was* my affair. She said, all right, if that's the way you feel about it she'd get out, said I was an interfering old bag. Which maybe I am, at that, but I don't take talk like that from any flibberty-gibbet who plays around with gunmen.'

She paused for breath. An ancient refrigerator throbbed emotionally in the corner of the kitchen. I took a sip of my coffee and looked out the window which overlooked the street. George Wall was sitting in the front seat of my car with a rejected expression on his face. I turned back to Mrs Lamb:

'Who was he, do you know?'

'I never did learn his name. Hester wouldn't tell me his name.

When I took the matter up with her, she said he was her boyfriend's manager.'

'Her boyfriend?'

'The Torres boy. Lance Torres, he calls himself. He was a fairly decent boy at one time, least he put up a nice front when he had his lifeguard job.'

'Was he a lifeguard at the club?'

'Used to be, for a couple of summers. His Uncle Tony got him the job. But lifeguard was too slow for Lance, he had to be a big shot. I heard he was a boxer for a while and then he got into some trouble, I think they put him in jail for it last year.'

'What kind of trouble?'

'I don't know, there's too many good people in the world to make it worth my while to keep track of bums. You could of knocked me over with a brick when Lance turned up here with his gunman friend, sucking around Hester. I thought he had more self-respect.'

'How do you know he was a gunman?'

'I saw him shooting, that's how. I woke up one morning and heard this popping noise down on the beach. It sounded like gunfire. It was. This fellow was out there shooting at beer bottles with a nasty black gun he had. That was the day I said to myself, either she stops messing around with bums or good-by Hester.'

'Who was he?'

'I never did learn his name. That nasty snub-nosed gun and the way he handled it was all I needed to know about him. Hester said he was Lance's manager.'

'What did he look like?'

'Looked like death to me. Those glassy brown eyes he had, and kind of a flattened-out face, fishbelly color. But I talked right up to him, told him he ought to be ashamed of himself shooting up bottles where people could cut themselves. He didn't even look at me, just stuck another clip in his gun and went on shooting at the bottles. He'd probably just as soon been shooting at me, least that was how he acted.'

Remembered anger heightened her color. 'I don't like being brushed off like that—it ain't *human*. And I'm touchy about shooting, specially since a friend of mine was shot last year. Right on this very beach, a few miles south of where you're sitting.'

'You don't mean Gabrielle Torres?'

'I should say I do. You heard about Gabrielle, eh?'

'A little. So she was a friend of yours.'

'Sure, she was. Some people would have a prejudice, her being part Mex, but I say if a person is good enough to work with you, a person is good enough to be your friend.' Her monolithic bosom rose and fell under the flowered-cotton wrapper.

'Nobody knows who shot her, I hear.'

'Somebody knows. The one that did it.'

'Do you have any ideas, Mrs Lamb?'

Her face was as still as stone for a long moment. She shook her head finally.

'Her cousin Lance, maybe, or his manager?'

'I wouldn't put it past them. But what reason could they have?'

'You've thought about it, then.'

'How could I help it, with them going in and out of the cottage next door, shooting off guns on the beach? I told Hester the day she left, she should learn a lesson from what happened to her friend.'

'But she went off with them anyway?'

'I guess she did. I didn't see her leave. I don't know where she went, or who with. That day I made a point of going to visit my married daughter in San Berdoo.'

VI

I RELAYED AS little as possible of this to George Wall, who showed signs of developing into a nuisance. On the way to Los Angeles, I turned into the drive of the Channel Club. He gave a wild look around, as though I was taking him into an ambush.

'Why are we coming back here?'

'I want to talk to the guard. He may be able to give me a lead to your wife. If not, I'll try Anton.'

'I don't see the point of that. I talked to Anton yesterday, I told you all he said.'

'I may be able to squeeze out some more. I know Anton, did a piece of work for him once.'

'You think he was holding out on me?'

'Could be. He hates to give anything away, including information. Now you sit here and see that nobody swipes the hubcaps. I want to get Tony talking, and you have bad associations for him.'

'What's the use of my being here at all?' he said sulkily. 'I might as well go back to the hotel and get some sleep.'

'That's an idea, too.'

I left him in the car out of sight of the gate, and walked down the curving drive between thick rows of oleanders. Tony heard me coming. He shuffled out of the gatehouse, gold gleaming in the crannies of his smile.

'What happened to your loco friend? You lose him?'

'No such luck. You have a nephew, Tony.'

'Got a lot of nephews.' He spread his arms. 'Five-six nephews.'

'The one that calls himself Lance.'

He grunted. Nothing changed in his face, except that he wasn't smiling any more. 'What about him?'

'Can you tell me his legal name?'

'Manuel,' he said. 'Manuel Purificación Torres. The name my brother give him wasn't good enough for him. He had to go and change it.'

'Where is he living now, do you know?'

'No, sir, I don't know. I don't have nothing to do with that one no more. He was close to me like a son one time. No more.' He wagged his head from side to side, slowly. The motion shook a question loose: 'Is Manuel in trouble again?'

'I couldn't say for sure. Who's his manager, Tony?'

'He don't got no manager. They don't let him fight no more. I was his manager couple years ago, trained him and managed him both. Brought him along slow and easy, gave him a left and taught him the combinations. Kept him living clean, right in my own house: up at six in the morning, skip-the-rope, light and heavy bag, run five miles on the beach. Legs like iron, beautiful. So he had to ruinate it.'

'How?'

'Same old story,' Tony said. 'I seen it too many times. He wins a couple-three fights, two four-rounders and a six-rounder in San Diego. Right away he's a bigshot, he *thinks* he's a bigshot. Uncle Tony, poor old Uncle Tony, he's too dumb in the head to tell him his business. Uncle Tony don't know from nothing, says lay off muscadoodle, lay off dames and reefers, sell your noisy, stinky motorcycle before you break your neck, you got a future. Only he wants it now. The whole world, right now.'

'Then something come up between us. He done something I don't like, I don't like it at all. I says, you been wanting out from me, now you can get out. We didden have no contract, nothing between us any more, I guess. He clumb on his motorcycle and tooted away, back to Los Angeles. There he was, a Main Street bum, and he wasn't twenty-one years old yet.

'My sister Desideria blamed me, I should go after him on my hands and knees.' Tony shook his head. 'No, I says, Desideria, I been around a long time. So have you, only you're a woman and don't see things. A boy gets ants in his pants, you can't hire no exterminator for that. Let him do it the hard way, we can't live his life.

'So one of these crooks he wants to be like—this crook sees Manny working out in the gym. He asks him for a contract and Manny gives it to him. He wins some fights and throws some, makes some dirty money, spends it on dirty things. They caught him with some caps in his car last year, and put him in jail. When he gets out, he's suspended, no more fights—back where he started in the starvation army.'

Tony spat dry. 'Long ago, I tried to tell him, my father, his grandfather, was *bracero*. Manny's father and me, we was born in a chickenhouse in Fresno, nowhere, from nothing. We got two strikes on us already, I says, we got to keep our nose clean. But would he listen to me? No, he got to stick his neck under the chopper.'

'How much time did he serve?'

'I guess he was in all last year. I dunno for sure. I got troubles of my own then.'

His shoulders moved as if they felt the entire weight of the sky. I wanted to ask him about his daughter's death, but the grief in his face tied my tongue. The scars around his eyes, sharp and deep in the sun, had been left there by crueller things than fists. I asked a different question:

'Do you know the name of the man that held his contract?'

'Stern, his last name is.'

'Carl Stern?'

'Yeah.' Squinting at my face, he saw the effect of the name on me. 'You know him?'

'I've seen him in nightclubs, and heard some stories about him. If ten per cent of them are true, he's a dangerous character. Is your nephew still with him, Tony?'

'I dunno. I bet you he is in trouble. I think you know it, only you won't tell me.'

'What makes you think that?'

'Because I seen him last week. He was all dressed up like a movie star and driving one of those sporty cars.' He made a low sweeping motion with his hands. 'Where would he get the money? He don't work, and he can't fight no more.'

'Why didn't you ask him?'

'Don't make me laugh, ask him. He wooden say hello to his Uncle Tony. He is too busy riding around with blondes in speedy cars.'

'He was with a blonde girl?'

'Sure.'

'Anybody you know?'

'Sure. She used to work here last summer. Hester Campbell, her name is. I thought she had more brains, to run around with my nephew Manny.'

'How long has she been running with him?'

'I wooden know. I got no crystal ball.'

'Where did you see them?'

'Venice Speedway.'

'Wasn't the Campbell girl a friend of your daughter's?'

His face set hard and dark. 'Maybe. What is this all about, mister? First you ask for my nephew, now it's my daughter.'

'I just heard about your daughter this morning. She was a friend of the Campbell girl, and I'm interested in the Campbell girl.'

'I'm not, and I don't know nothing. It's no use asking me. What do I know?' His mood had swung heavily downward. He made an idiot face. 'I'm a punchy bum. My brains don't think straight. My daughter is dead. My nephew is a crooked *pachuco*. People come and punch me in the nose.'

VII

ANTON'S WINDOWS OVERLOOKED the boulevard from the second floor of a stucco building in West Hollywood. The building was fairly new, but it had been painted and scraped and repainted in blotches of color, pink and white and blue, to make it look like something from the left bank of the Seine. You entered it through a court which contained several small arty shops and had a terrazzo fountain in the center. A concrete nymph stood with her feet in its shallow water, covering her pudenda with one hand and beckoning with the other.

I climbed the outside stairs to the second-floor balcony. Through an open door, I saw a half-dozen girls in leotards stretching their ligaments on barres along the wall. A woman with flat breasts and massive haunches called out orders in a drill-sergeant's voice:

'*Grand battement, s'il vous plaît. Non, non*, grand *battement*.'

I walked on to the end of the balcony, trailed by the salt-sweet odor of young sweat. Anton was in his office, short and wide behind the desk in a gabardine suit the color of lemon ice cream. His face was sunlamp brown. He rose very lightly, to demonstrate his agelessness. The hand he extended had rings on two of the fingers, a seal ring and a diamond to go with the diamond in his foulard tie. His grip was like a bull lobster's.

'Mr Archer.'

Anton had been in Hollywood longer than I had, but he still pronounced my name 'Mester Arshair.' The accent was probably part of his business front. I liked him in spite of it.

'I'm surprised you remember my name.'

'I think of you with gratitude,' he said. 'Frequently.'

'What wife are you on now?'

'Please, you are very vulgar.' He raised his hands in a fastidious gesture, and while he was at it, examined his manicure. 'Number five. We are very happy. You are not needed.'

'Yet.'

'But you didn't come to discuss my marital problems. Why do you come?'

'Missing girl.'

'Hester Campbell again?'

'Uh-huh.'

'Are you employed by that big *naïf* of a husband?'

'You're psychic.'

'He is a fool. Any man of his age and weight who runs after a woman in this city is a fool. Why doesn't he stand still, and they'll come swarming?'

'He's only interested in the one. Now what about her?'

'What about her?' he repeated, offering his hands palms up to show how clean they were. 'She has had some ballet lessons from me, three or four months of lessons. The young ladies come and go. I am not responsible for their private lives.'

'What do you know about her private life?'

'Nothing. I wish to know nothing. My friend Paddy Dane in Toronto did me no favor when he sent her here. There is a young lady very much on the make. I could see trouble in her.'

'If you could see all that, why turn her husband loose on Clarence Bassett?'

His shoulders rose. '*I* turned him loose on Bassett? I merely answered his questions.'

'You made him believe that she was living with Bassett.

Bassett hasn't seen her for nearly four months.'

'What would I know about that?'

'Don't kid me, Anton. Did you know Bassett before this?'

'*Pas trop.* He would not remember, probably.'

He moved to the window and cranked the louvers wider. The sound of traffic rose from the Boulevard. Under it, his voice was sibilant:

'But I do not forget. Five years ago, I applied for membership in the Channel Club. They refused me, with no reason given. I heard through my sponsor that Bassett never presented my name to the membership committee. He wanted no dancing-masters in his club.'

'So you thought you'd make trouble for him.'

'Perhaps.' He looked at me over his shoulder, his eye bright and empty as a bird's. 'Did I succeed?'

'I stopped it before it happened. But you could have triggered a murder.'

'Nonsense.' He turned and came toward me, stepping with feline softness on the carpet. 'The husband is a nothing, a hysterical boy. There is no danger in him.'

'I wonder. He's big and strong, and crazy about his wife.'

'Is he rich?'

'Hardly.'

'Then tell him to forget her. I have seen many like her, in love with themselves. They think they aspire to an art, acting or dancing or music. But all they really aspire to is money and clothes. A man comes along who can give them these things, and there is the end of aspiration.' His hands went through the motions of liberating a bird and throwing it a good-by kiss.

'Did one come along for Hester?'

'Possibly. She seemed remarkably prosperous at my Christmas party. She had a new mink stole. I complimented her on it, and she informed me that she was under personal contract to a movie producer.'

'Which one?'

'She did not say, and it does not matter. She was lying. It was a little fantasy for my benefit.'

'How do you know?'

'I know women.'

I was ready to believe him. The wall behind his desk was papered with inscribed photographs of young women.

'Besides,' he said, 'no producer in his right mind would give that girl a contract. There is something lacking in her—essential talent, feeling. She became cynical so young, and she makes no attempt to hide it.'

'How did she act the other night?'

'I did not observe her for very long. I had over a hundred guests.'

'She made a telephone call from here. Did you know?'

'Not until yesterday. The husband told me she was frightened of something. Perhaps she drank too much. There was nothing at my party to frighten anyone—a lot of nice young people amusing themselves.'

'Who was she with?'

'A boy, a good-looking boy.' He snapped his fingers. 'She introduced him to me, but I forget his name.'

'Lance Torres?'

His eyelids crinkled. 'Possibly. He was quite dark, Spanish-looking. A very well-built boy—one of those new young types with the *apache* air. Perhaps Miss Seeley can identify him for you. I saw them talking together.' He pushed his right cuff back and looked at his wristwatch. 'Miss Seeley is out for coffee, but she should be back very soon.'

'While we're waiting, you could give me Hester's address. Her real address.'

'Why should I make things easy for you?' Anton said with his edged smile. 'I don't like the fellow you are working for. He is too aggressive. Also, I am old and he is young. Also my father was a streetcar conductor in Montreal. Why should I help an Anglo from Toronto?'

'So you won't let him find his wife?'

'Oh, you can have the address. I simply wished to express my emotions on the subject. She lives at the Windsor Hotel in Santa Monica.'

'You know it by heart, eh?'

'I happen to remember. I had a request for her address from another detective last week.'

'Police detective?'

'Private. He claimed to be a lawyer with money for her, a bequest, but his story was very clumsy and I am not stupid.' He glanced at his wristwatch again. 'If you'll excuse me, now, I have to dress for a class. You can wait here for Miss Seeley if you wish.'

Before I could ask him any more questions, he went out through an inner door and closed it behind him. I sat down at his desk and looked up the Windsor Hotel in the telephone directory. The desk clerk told me that Miss Hester Campbell didn't stay there any more. She'd moved out two weeks ago, leaving no forwarding address.

I was masticating this fact when Miss Seeley came in. I remembered her from the period when Anton divorced his third wife, with my assistance. She was a little older, a little thinner. Her tailored pinstriped suit emphasized the boniness of her figure. But she still wore hopeful white ruffles at her wrists and throat.

'Why, Mr Archer.' The implications of my presence struck her. 'We're not having wife trouble again?'

'Wife trouble, yes, but nothing to do with the boss. He says you may be able to give me some information.'

'My telephone number, by any chance?' Her smile was warm and easygoing behind her lipstick mask.

'That I could do with, too.'

'You flatter me. Go right ahead. I can stand a smattering of flattering for a change. You don't meet many eligible males in this business.'

We exchanged some further pleasantries, and I asked her if she remembered seeing Hester at the party. She remembered.

'And her escort?'

She nodded. 'Dreamy. A real cute thing. That is, if you like the Latin type. I don't go for the Latin type myself, but we got along just fine. Until he showed his true colors.'

'You talked to him?'

'For a while. He was kind of shy with all the people, so I took him under my wing. He told me about his career and all. He's an actor. Helio-Graff Studios have him under long-term contract.'

'What's his name?'

'Lance Leonard. It's kind of a cute name, don't you think? He told me he chose it himself.'

'He didn't tell you his real name?'

'No.'

'And he's under contract to Helio-Graff?'

'That's what he said. He's certainly got the looks for it. *And* the artistic temperament.'

'You mean he made a pass at you?'

'Oh, no. Not that I'd permit it. He's stuck on Hester anyway, I could see that. They were at the bar after, drinking out of the same glass, just as close as close.' Her voice was wistful. She added by way of consolation to herself: 'But then he showed his true colors.'

'How did he do that?'

'It was awful,' she said with relish. 'Hester came in here to put in a telephone call. I let her have the key. It must have been to another man, because he followed her in and made a scene. These Latins are so emotional.'

'You were here?'

'I heard him yelling at her. I had things to do in my own office, and I couldn't *help* overhearing. He called her some awful names: b-i-t-c-h and other words I won't repeat.' She tried to blush, and failed.

'Did he threaten her in any way?'

'You bet he did. He said she wouldn't last a week unless she played along with the operation. She was in it deeper than anybody, and she wasn't going to ruin his big chance.' Miss Seeley was a fairly decent woman, but she couldn't quite restrain the glee fluttering at the corners of her mouth.

'Did he say what the operation was?'

'Not that I heard.'

'Or threaten to kill her?'

'He didn't say that *he* was going to do anything to her. What he said—' She looked up at the ceiling and tapped her chin. 'He said if she didn't stay in line, he'd get this friend of his after her. Somebody called Carl.'

'Carl Stern?'

'Maybe. He didn't mention the last name. He just kept saying that Carl would fix her wagon.'

'What happened after that?'

'Nothing. They came out and left together. She looked pretty subdued, I mean it.'

VIII

THERE WAS AN outdoor telephone booth in the court, and I immured myself with the local directories. Lance Leonard wasn't in them. Neither was Lance Torres, or Hester Campbell, or Carl Stern. I made a telephone call to Peter Colton, who had recently retired as senior investigator in the DA's office.

Carl Stern, he told me, had also retired recently. That is, he'd moved to Vegas and gone legit, if you could call Vegas legit. Stern had invested his money in a big new hotel-and-casino which was under construction. Personally Colton hoped he'd lose his dirty gold-plated shirt.

'Where did the gold come from, Peter?'

'Various sources. He was a Syndicate boy. When Siegel broke with the Syndicate and died of it, Stern was one of the heirs. He made his heavy money out of the wire service. When the Crime Commission broke that up, he financed a narcotics ring for a while.'

'So you put him away, no doubt.'

'You know the situation as well as I do, Lew.' Colton sounded angry and apologetic at the same time. 'Our operation is essentially a prosecuting agency. We work with what the cops bring into us. Carl Stern was using cops for bodyguards. The politicians that hire and fire the cops went on fishing trips with him to Acapulco.'

'Is that how he wangled himself a gambling license in Nevada?'

'He didn't get a license in Nevada. With his reputation, they couldn't give him one. He had to get himself a front.'

'Do you know who his front man would be?'

'Simon Graff,' Colton said. 'You must have heard of him. They're going to call their place Simon Graff's Casbah.'

That stopped me for a minute. 'I thought Helio-Graff was making money.'

'Maybe Graff saw his chance to make some more money. I'd tell you what I think of that, but it wouldn't be good for my blood pressure.' He went ahead and told me anyway, in a voice that was choked with passion: 'They've got no decency, they've got no sense of public responsibility—these goddam lousy big Hollywood names that go to Vegas and decoy for thieves and pander for mobsters and front for murderers.'

'Is Stern a murderer?'

'Ten times over,' Colton said. 'You want his record in detail?'

'Not just now. Thanks, Peter. Take it easy.'

I knew a man at Helio-Graff, a writer named Sammy Swift. The studio switchboard put me on to his secretary, and she called Sammy to the phone.

'Lew? How's the Sherlock kick?'

'It keeps me in beer and skittles. By the way, what are skittles? You're a writer, you're supposed to know these things.'

'I let the research department know them for me. Division of labor. Will you cut it short now, boy? Any other time. I'm fighting script, and the mimeographers are hounding me.' His voice was hurried, in time with a rapid metronome clicking inside his head.

'What's the project?'

'I'm flying to Italy with a production unit next week. Graff's doing a personal on the Carthage story.'

'The Carthage story?'

'*Salambô*, the Flaubert historical. Where you been?'

'In geography class. Carthage is in Africa.'

'It was, not any more. The Man is building it in Italy.'

'I hear he's doing some building in Vegas, too.'

'The Casbah, you mean? Yeah.'

'Isn't it kind of unusual for a big independent producer to put his money in a slot-machine shop?'

'Everything the Man does is unusual. And moderate your language, Lew.'

'You bugged?'

'Don't be silly,' he said uncertainly. 'Now, what's your problem? If you think you're broke, I'm broker, ask my broker.'

'No problem. I want to get in touch with a new actor you have. Lance Leonard?'

'Yeah, I've seen him around. Why?'

I improvised. 'A friend of mine, newspaperman from the east, wants an interview.'

'About the Carthage story?'

'Why, is Leonard in it?'

'Minor role, his first. Don't you read the columns?'

'Not when I can help it. I'm illiterate.'

'So are the columns. So's Leonard, but don't let your friend print that. The kid should do all right as a North African barbarian. He's got prettier muscles than Brando, used to be a fighter.'

'How did he get into pictures?'

'The Man discovered him personally.'

'And where does he board his pretty muscles?'

'Coldwater Canyon, I think. My secretary can get you the address. Don't let on you got it from me, though. The kid is afraid of the press. But he can use the publicity.' Sammy caught his breath. He liked to talk. He liked anything that interrupted his work. 'I hope this isn't one of your fast ones, Lew.'

'You know better than that. I lost my fast one years ago. I'm down to my slider.'

'So are we all, boy. With bursitis yet. See you.'

I got the address in Coldwater Canyon, and went out to the street. The sun shimmered on the car roof. George Wall was slumped in the front seat with his head thrown back. His face was flushed and wet. His eyes were closed. The interior was oven-hot.

The starting engine woke him. He sat up, rubbing his eyes. 'Where are we going?'

'Not we. I'll drop you off at your hotel. Which one?'

'But I don't want to be dropped off.' He took hold of my right arm. 'You found out where she is, haven't you? You don't want me to see her.'

I didn't answer. He tugged at my arm, causing the car to swerve. 'That's the idea, isn't it?'

I pushed him away, into the far corner of the seat. 'For God's sake, George, relax. Take a sedative when you get back to the hotel. Now, where is it?'

'I'm not going back to the hotel. You can't force me.'

'All right, all right. If you promise to stay in the car. I have a lead that may pan out and it may not. It won't for sure, if you come barging it.'

'I won't. I promise.' After a while he said: 'You don't understand how I feel. I dreamed of Hester just now when I was asleep. I tried to talk to her. She wouldn't answer, and then I saw she was dead. I touched her. She was as cold as snow—'

'Tell it to your head-shrinker,' I said unpleasantly. His self-pity was getting on my nerves.

He withdrew into hurt silence, which lasted all the way to the Canyon. Lance Leonard lived near the summit, in a raw new redwood house suspended on cantilevers over a steep drop. I parked above the house and looked around. Leonard had no close neighbours, though several other houses dotted the further slopes. The hills fell away from the ridge in folds like heavy drapery trailing in the horizontal sea.

I nailed George in place with one of my masterful looks, and went down the slanting asphalt drive to the house. The trees in the front yard, lemons and avocados, were recently planted: I could see the yellow burlap around their roots. The garage contained a dusty gray Jaguar two-door and a light racing motorcycle. I pressed the button beside the front door, and heard chimes in the house softly dividing the silence.

A young man opened the door. He was combing his hair with a sequined comb. His hair was black, curly on top and straight at the sides. The height of the doorstep brought his head level with mine. His face was darkly handsome, if you overlooked the spoiled mouth and slightly muddy eyes. He had on blue nylon pajamas, and his brown feet were bare. He was the central diver in Bassett's photograph.

'Mr Torres?'

'Leonard,' he corrected me. Having arranged the curls low on his forehead to his satisfaction, he dropped the comb in his pajama pocket. He smiled with conscious charm. 'Got a new name to go with my new career. What's the mission, cap?'

'I'd like to see Mrs Wall.'

'Never heard of her. You got the wrong address.'

'Her maiden name was Campbell. Hester Campbell.'

He stiffened. 'Hester? She ain't married—isn't married.'

'She's married. Didn't she tell you?'

He glanced over his shoulder into the house, and back at me. His movements were lizard-quick. He took hold of the knob and started to shut the door. 'Never heard of her. Sorry.'

'Who does the comb belong to? Or do you merely adore bright things?'

He paused in indecision, long enough for me to get my foot in the door. I could see past him through the house to the sliding glass wall at the rear of the living-space, and through it the outside terrace which overhung the canyon. A girl was lying on a metal chaise in the sun. Her back was brown and long, with a breathtaking narrow waist from which the white hip arched up. Her hair was like ruffled silver feathers.

Leonard stepped outside, forcing me back onto the flagstone walk, and shut the front door behind him. 'Drag 'em back into their sockets, cousin. No free shows today. And get this, I don't know any Hester what's-her-name.'

'You did a minute ago.'

'Maybe I heard the name once. I heard a lot of names. What's yours, for instance?'

'Archer.'

'What's your business?'

'I'm a detective.'

His mouth went ugly, and his eyes blank. He'd come up fast out of a place where cops were hated and feared: the hatred was still in him like a chronic disease. 'What you want with me, cop?'

'Not you. Hester.'

'Is she in a jam?'

'She probably is if she's shacked up with you.'

'Naw, naw. She gave me the brush-off, frankly.' He brushed his nylon flanks illustratively. 'I haven't seen the chick for a long time.'

'Have you tried looking on your terrace?'

His hands paused and tightened on his hips. He leaned forward from the waist, his mouth working like a red bivalve: 'You keep calling me a liar. I got a public position to keep up, so I stand here and take it like a little gentleman. But you better get off my property or I'll clobber you, cop or no cop.'

'That would go good in the columns. The whole set-up would.'

'What set-up? What do you mean?'

'You tell me.'

He squinted anxiously up toward the road where my car was parked. George's face hung at the window like an ominous pink moon.

'Who's your sidekick?'

'Her husband.'

Leonard's eyes blurred with thought. 'What is this, a shake-down? Let's see your buzzer.'

'No buzzer. I'm a private detective.'

'Dig him,' he said to an imaginary confidant on his left.

At the same time, his right shoulder dropped. The hooked arm swinging from it drove a fist into my middle below the rib-cage. It came too fast to block. I sat down on the flagstones and discovered that I couldn't get up right away. My head was cool and clear, like an aquarium, but the bright ideas and noble intentions that swam around in it had no useful connection with my legs.

Leonard stood with his fists ready, waiting for me to get up. His hair had fallen forward over his eyes, blue-black and shining like steel shavings. His bare feet danced a little on the stone. I reached for them and clutched air. Leonard smiled down at me, dancing:

'Come on, get up. I can use a workout.'

'You'll get it, sucker-puncher,' I said between difficult breaths.

'Not from you, old man.'

The door opened behind him, and featherhead looked out. She wore dark harlequin glasses whose sequined rims matched the comb. Oil glistened on her face. A terrycloth towel held under her armpits clung to the bulbs and narrows of her body.

'What's the trouble, hon?'

'No trouble. Get inside.'

'Who is this character? Did you hit him?'

'What do you think?'

'I think you're crazy, taking the chances you take.'

'*Me* take chances? Who shot off her mouth on the telephone? You *brought* the bastard here.'

'All right, so I wanted out. So I changed my mind.'

'Shut it off.' He threatened her with a movement of his shoulders. 'I said inside.'

Running footsteps clattered on the driveway. George Wall called out: 'Hester! I'm here!'

What I could see of her face didn't change expression. Leonard spread a hand on her terrycloth breast and pushed her in and shut the door on her. He turned as George charged in on him, met him with a stiff left to the face. George stopped dead. Leonard waited, his face smooth and intent like a man's listening to music.

I got my legs under me and stood up and watched them fight. George had been wanting a fight: he had the advantage of height and weight and reach: I didn't interfere. It was like watching a man get caught in a machine. Leonard stepped inside of a looping swing, rested his chin on the big man's chest, and hammered his stomach. His elbows worked like pistons in oiled grooves close to his body. When he stepped back, George doubled over. He went to his knees and got up again, very pale.

The instant his hands left the flagstone, Leonard brought up his right hand into George's face, his back uncoiling behind it. George walked backward onto the tender new lawn. He looked at the sky in a disappointed way, as if it had dropped something on him. Then he shook his head and started back toward Leonard. He tripped on a garden hose and almost fell.

I stepped between them, facing Leonard. 'He's had it. Knock it off, eh?'

George shouldered me aside. I grabbed his arms.

'Let me at the little runt,' he said through bloody lips.

'You don't want to get hurt, boy.'

'Worry about him.'

He was stronger than I was. He broke loose and spun me away. Threw another wild one which split the back of his suit coat and accomplished nothing else. Leonard inclined his head two or three inches from the vertical and watched the fist go by. George staggered off balance. Leonard hit him between the eyes with his right hand, hit him again with his left as he went down. George's head made a dull noise on the flagstone. He lay still.

Leonard polished the knuckles of his right fist with his left hand, as though it were a bronze object of art.

'You shouldn't use it on amateurs.'

He answered reasonably: 'I don't unless I have to. Only sometimes I get damn browned off, big slobs thinkin' they can push me around. I been pushed around plenty, I don't have to take it no more.' He balanced himself on one foot and touched George's outflung arm with the tip of his big toe. 'Maybe you better take him to a doctor.'

'Maybe I better.'

'I hit him pretty hard.'

He showed me the knuckles of his right hand. They were swelling and turning blue. Otherwise, the fight had done him good. He was cheerful and relaxed, and he pranced a little when he moved, like a stallion. Featherhead was watching him from the window. She had on a linen dress now. She saw me looking at her, and moved back out of sight.

Leonard turned on the hose and ran cold water over George's

head. George opened his eyes and tried to sit up. Leonard turned off the hose.

'He'll be all right. They don't come out of it that fast when they're bad hurt. Anyway, I hit him in self-defense, you're a witness to that. If there's any beef about it, you can take it up with Leroy Frost at Helio.'

'Leroy Frost is your fixer, eh?'

He gave me a faintly anxious smile. 'You know Leroy?'

'A little.'

'Maybe we won't bother him about it, eh? Leroy, he's got a lot of troubles. How much you make in a day?'

'Fifty when I'm working.'

'Okay, how's about I slip you fifty and you take care of the carcass?' He turned on all his neon charm. 'Incidentally, I should apologize. I kind of lost my head there for a minute. I shouldn't ought to of took the sucker punch on you. You can pay me back some time.'

'Maybe I will at that.'

'Sure you will, and I'll let you. How's the breadbasket, cap?'

'Feels like a broken tennis racquet.'

'But no hard feelings, eh?'

'No hard feelings.'

'Swell, swell.'

He offered me his hand. I set myself on my heels and hit him in the jaw. It wasn't the smartest thing in the world to do. My legs were middle-aging, and still wobbly. If I missed the nerve, he could run circles around me and cut me to ribbons with his left alone. But the connection was good.

I left him lying. The front door was unlocked, and I went in. The girl wasn't in the living-room or on the terrace. Her terrycloth towel was crumpled on the bedroom floor. A sun-hat woven of plaited straw lay on the floor beside it. The leather band inside the hat was stamped with the legend: 'Handmade in Mexico for the Taos Shop.'

A motor coughed and roared behind the wall. I found the side door which opened from the utility room into the garage. She was at the wheel of the Jaguar, looking at me with her mouth wide open. She locked the door on her side before I got hold of the handle. Then it was torn from my fist.

The Jaguar screeched in the turnaround, laying down black spoor, and leaped up the driveway to the road. I let it go. I couldn't leave George with Leonard.

They were sitting up in front of the house, exchanging dim looks of hatred across the flagstone walk. George was bleeding from the mouth. The flesh around one of his eyes was changing color. Leonard was unmarked, but I saw when he got to his feet that there was a change in him.

He had a hangdog air, a little furtive, as if I'd jarred him back into his past. He kept running his fingers over his nose and mouth.

'Don't worry,' I said, 'you're still gorgeous.'

'Funny boy. You think it's funny? I kill you, it wasn't for this.' He displayed his swollen right hand.

'You offered me a sucker punch, remember. Now we're even. Where did she go?'

'*You* can go to hell.'

'What's her address?'

'Go to hell.'

'You might as well give me her address. I got her license number. I can trace her.'

'Go right ahead.' He gave me a superior look, which probably meant that the Jaguar was his.

'What did she change her mind about? Why did she want out?'

'I can't read minds. I dunno nothin' about her. I service plenty of women, see? They ask me for it, I give 'em a bang sometimes. Does that mean I'm responsible?'

I reached for him. He backed away, his face sallow and pinched. 'Keep your hands off me. And drag your butt off of my property. I'm warning you, I got a loaded shotgun in the house.'

He went as far as the door, and turned to watch us. George was on his hands and knees now. I got one of his arms draped over my shoulders and heaved him up to his feet. He walked like a man trying to balance himself on a spring mattress.

When I turned for a last look at the house, Leonard was on the doorstep, combing his hair.

IX

I DROVE DOWN the long grade to Beverly Hills, slowly, because I was feeling accident-prone. There were days when you could put your finger on the point of stress and everything fell into rational patterns around you. And there were the other days.

George bothered me. He sat hunched over with his head in his hands, groaning from time to time. He had a fine instinct, even better than mine, for pushing his face in at the wrong door and getting it bloodied. He needed a keeper: I seemed to be elected.

I took him to my own doctor, a GP named Wolfson who had his office on Santa Monica Boulevard. Wolfson laid him out on a padded metal table in a cubicle, went over his face and skull with thick, deft fingers, flashed a small light in his eyes, and performed other rituals.

'How did it happen?'

'He fell down and hit his head on a flagstone walk.'

'Who pushed him? You?'

'A mutual friend. We won't go into that. Is he all right?'

'Might be a slight concussion. You ever hurt your head before?'

'Playing football, I have,' George said.

'Hurt it bad?'

'I suppose so. I've blacked out a couple of times.'

'I don't like it,' Wolfson said to me. 'You ought to take him to the hospital. He should spend a couple of days in bed, at least.'

'No!' George sat up, forcing the doctor backward. His eyes rolled heavily in their swollen sockets. 'A couple of days is all I've got. I have to see her.'

Wolfson raised his eyebrows. 'See who?'

'His wife. She left him.'

'So what? It happens every day. It happened to you. He's still got to go to bed.'

George swung his legs off the table and stood up shakily. His face was the color of newly poured cement. 'I refuse to go to the hospital.'

'You're making a serious decision,' Wolfson said coldly. He was a fat doctor who loved only medicine and music.

'I can put him to bed at my house. Will that do?'

Wolfson looked at me dubiously. 'Could you keep him down?'

'I think so.'

'Very well,' George stated solemnly, 'I accept the compromise.'

Wolfson shrugged. 'If that's the best we can do. I'll give him a shot to relax him, and I'll want to see him later.'

'You know where I live,' I said.

In a two-bedroom stucco cottage on a fifty-foot lot off Olympic. For a while the second bedroom hadn't been used. Then for a while it had been. When it was vacated finally, I sold the bed to a secondhand-furniture dealer and converted the room into a study. Which for some reason I hated to use.

I put George in my bed. My cleaning woman had been there that morning, and the sheets were fresh. Hanging his torn clothes on a chair, I asked myself what I thought I was doing and why. I looked across the hall at the door of the bedless bedroom where nobody slept any more. An onion taste of grief rose at the back of my throat. It seemed very important to me that George should get together with his wife and take her away from Los Angeles. And live happily ever after.

His head rolled on the pillow. He was part way out by now, under the influence of paraldehyde and Leonard's sedative fists:

'Listen to me, Archer. You're a good friend to me.'

'Am I?'

'The only friend I have within two thousand miles. You've got to find her for me.'

'I did find her. What good did it do?'

'I know, I shouldn't have come tearing down to the house like that. I frightened her. I always do the wrong thing. Christ, I wouldn't hurt a hair of her head. You've got to tell her that for me. Promise you will.'

'All right. Now go to sleep.'

But there was something else he had to say: 'At least she's alive, isn't she?'

'If she's a corpse, she's a lively one.'

'Who are these people she's mixed up with? Who was the little twerp in the pajamas?'

'Boy named Torres. He used to be a boxer, if that's any comfort to you.'

'Is he the one who threatened her?'

'Apparently.'

George raised himself on his elbows. 'I've heard that name Torres. Hester used to have a friend named Gabrielle Torres.'

'She told you about Gabrielle, did she?'

'Yes. She told me that night she—confessed her sins to me.' His gaze moved dully around the room and settled in a corner, fixed on something invisible. His dry lips moved, trying to name the thing he saw:

'Her friend was shot and killed, in the spring of last year. Hester left California right after.'

'Why would she do that?'

'I don't know. She seemed to blame herself for the other girl's death. And she was afraid of being called as a witness, if the case ever came to trial.'

'It never did.'

He was silent, his eyes on the thing in the empty corner.

'What else did she tell you, George?'

'About the men she'd slept with, from the time that she was hardly in her teens.'

'That Hester had slept with?'

'Yes. It bothered me more than the other, even. I don't know what that makes me.'

Human, I thought.

George closed his eyes. I turned the venetian blinds down and went into the other room to telephone. The call was to CHP headquarters, where a friend of mine named Mercero worked as a dispatcher. Fortunately he was on the daytime shift. No, he wasn't busy but he could be any minute, accidents always came in pairs and triples to foul him up. He'd try to give me a quick report on the Jaguar's license number.

I sat beside the telephone and lit a cigarette and tried to have a brilliant intuition, like all the detectives in books and some in real life. The only one that occurred to me was that the Jaguar belonged to Lance Leonard and would simply lead me around in a circle.

Cigarette smoke rumbling in my stomach reminded me that I was hungry. I went out to the kitchen and made myself a ham-and-cheese sandwich on rye and opened a bottle of beer. My cleaning woman had left a note on the kitchen table:

> Dear Mr Archer, Arrived nine left twelve noon, I need the money for today will drive by and pick it up this aft, please leave $3.75 in mailbox if your out. Yours truly, Beatrice M. Jackson.
>
> P.S.—There is mouse dirt in the cooler, you buy a trap Ill set it out, mouse dirt is not sanitary.
>
> Yours truly, Beatrice M. Jackson.

I sealed four dollars in an envelope, wrote her name across the face, and took it out to the front porch. A pair of house wrens chitchatting under the eaves made several snide references to me. The mailbox was full of mail: four early bills, two requests for money from charitable organizations, a multigraphed letter from my Congressman which stated that he was alert to the threat, a brochure describing a book on the Secrets of Connubial Bliss marked down to $2.98 and sold only to doctors, clergymen, social-service workers, and other interested parties; and a New Year's card from a girl who had passed out on me at a pre-Christmas party. This was signed 'Mona' and carried a lyric message:

True friendship is a happy thing
Which makes both men and angels sing.

As the year begins, and another ends,
Resolved: that we shall still be friends.

I sat down at the hall table with my beer and tried to draft an answer. It was hard. Mona passed out at parties because she had lost a husband in Korea and a small son at Children's Hospital. I began to remember that I had no son, either. A man got lonely in the stucco wilderness, pushing forty with no chick, no child. Mona was pretty enough, and bright enough, and all she wanted was another child. What was I waiting for? A well-heeled virgin with her name in the Blue Book?

I decided to call Mona. The telephone rang under my hand. 'Mercero?' I said.

But it was Bassett's voice, breathy in my ear: 'I tried to get you earlier.'

'I've been here for the last half-hour.'

'Does that mean you've found her, or given up?'

'Found her and lost her again.' I explained how, to the accompaniment of oh's and ah's and tut-tut's from the other end of the line. 'This hasn't been one of my days so far. My biggest mistake was taking Wall along.'

'I hope he's not badly hurt?' There was a vein of malice in Bassett's solicitude.

'He's a hardhead, he'll survive.'

'Why do you suppose she ran away from him this time?'

'Simple panic, maybe. Maybe not. There seems to be more to this than a lost-wife case. Gabrielle Torres keeps cropping up.'

'It's odd you should mention her. I've been thinking about her off and on all morning—ever since you commented on her picture.'

'So have I. There are three of them in the picture: Gabrielle and Hester and Lance. Gabrielle was murdered, the murderer hasn't been caught. The other two were very close to her. Lance was her cousin. Hester was her best friend.'

'You're not suggesting that Lance, or Hester—?' His voice was hushed, but buzzing with implications.

'I'm only speculating. I don't think Hester killed her friend. I do think she knows something about the murder that nobody else knows.'

'Did she say so?'

'Not to me. To her husband. It's all pretty vague. Except that nearly two years later she turns up in Coldwater Canyon. She's suddenly prosperous, and so is her little friend with the big fists.'

'It does give one to think, doesn't it?' He tittered nervously. 'What do *you* have in mind?'

'Blackmail is most obvious, and I never rule out the obvious. Lance spread the word that he's under contract at Helio-Graff, and it seems to be legit. The question is, how did he latch on to a contract with a big independent? He's a good-looking boy, but it takes more than that these days. You knew him when he was a lifeguard at the Club?'

'Naturally. Frankly, I wouldn't have hired him if his uncle hadn't been extremely persistent. We generally use college boys in the summer.'

'Did he have acting ambitions?'

'Not to my knowledge. He was training to be a pugilist.' Bassett's voice was contemptuous.

'He's an actor now. It could be he's an untutored genius—stranger things have happened—but I doubt it. On top of that, Hester claims to have a contract, too.'

'With Helio-Graff?'

'I don't know. I intend to find out.'

'You'll probably find it's with Helio-Graff.' His voice had become sharper and more definite. 'I've hesitated to tell you this, though it's what I called you about. In my position, one acquires the habit of silence. However, I was talking to a certain person this morning, and Hester's name came up. So did the name of Simon Graff. They were seen together in rather compromising circumstances.'

'Where?'

'In a hotel in Santa Monica—the Windsor, I believe.'

'It fits. She used to live there. When was this?'

'A few weeks ago. My informant saw them coming out of a room on one of the upper floors. At least, Mr Graff came out.

Hester only came as far as the door.'

'Who is your informant?'

'I couldn't possibly tell you that, old man. It was one of our members.'

'So is Simon Graff.'

'Don't think I'm not aware of it. Mr Graff is the most powerful single member of the Club.'

'Aren't you sticking your neck out, telling me this?'

'Yes. I am. I hope my confidence in you—in your discretion—hasn't been misplaced.'

'Relax. I'm a clam. But what about your switchboard?'

'I'm on the switchboard myself,' he said.

'Is Graff still out there?'

'No. He left hours ago.'

'Where can I find him?'

'I have no idea. He's having a party here tonight, but you mustn't approach him. You're not on any account to approach him.'

'All right.' But I made a mental reservation. 'This secret informant of yours—it wouldn't be Mrs Graff?'

'Of course not.' His voice was fading. Either he was lying, or the decision to tell me about the Windsor Hotel episode had drained his energy. 'You mustn't even consider such a thought.'

'All right,' I said, considering it.

I called the Highway Patrol number and got Mercero.

'Sorry, Lew, no can do. Three accidents since you called, and I've been hopping.' He hung up on me.

It didn't matter. A pattern was forming in the case, like a motif in discordant, angry music. I had the slimmest of leads, a sun-hat from a shop in Santa Monica. I also had the queer tumescent feeling you get when something is going to break.

I looked in on George before I left the house. He was snoring. I shouldn't have left him.

X

THE TAOS SHOP was a little tourist trap on the Coast Highway. It sold Navajo blankets and thunderbird necklaces and baskets and hats and pottery in an atmosphere of disordered artiness. A mouse blonde in a brown Indian blouse clicked her wampum at me languidly and asked me what I desired, a gift for my wife perhaps? I told her I was looking for another man's wife. She had romantic plum-colored eyes, and it seemed like the right approach. She said:

'How fascinating. Are you a detective?'

I said I was.

'How fascinating.'

But when I told her about the hat, she shook her head regretfully. 'I'm sorry. I'm sure it's one of ours, all right—we import them ourselves from Mexico. But we sell so many of them, I couldn't possibly—' She waved a willowy arm toward a tray piled with hats at the far end of the counter. 'Perhaps if you described her?'

I described her. She shook her head dolefully. 'I never could tell one Hollywood blonde from another.'

'Neither could I.'

'Ninety-nine and forty-four one-hundredths of them are blonde out of a bottle, anyway. I could be a blonde if I wanted to, just with a rinse now and then. Only I've got too much personal pride.' She leaned toward me, and her wampum swung invitingly over the counter. 'I'm sorry I can't help you.'

'Thanks for trying. It was an off-chance anyway.' I started out, and turned. 'Her name is Hester Wall, by the way. That doesn't ring a bell?'

'Hester? I know of a Hester, but her last name isn't Wall. Her mother used to work here.'

'What is her last name?'

'Campbell.'

'She's the one. Campbell's her maiden name.'

'Now, isn't that fascinating?' She smiled in dimpled glee, and her large eyes glowed. 'The most exciting things happen to *people*, don't you think? I suppose you're looking for her about her inheritance?'

'Inheritance?'

'Yes. It's why Mrs Campbell quit her job, on account of her daughter's inheritance. Don't tell me she's come into another fortune!'

'Who did she inherit the first one from?'

'Her husband, her late husband.' She paused, and her soft mouth quivered. 'It's sort of sad, when you realize, nobody inherits anything unless somebody else dies.'

'That's true. And you say her husband died?'

'Yes. She married a wealthy husband in Canada, and he died.'

'Is that what Hester told you?'

'No. Mrs Campbell told me. I don't know Hester myself.' Her face went blank suddenly. 'I certainly hope it's not a false alarm. We were all so thrilled when Mrs Campbell got the news. She's a dear, really, such a cute little duck for her age, and she used to have money, you know. Nobody begrudges her good fortune.'

'When did she find out about it?'

'A couple of weeks ago. She only quit the beginning of this week. She's moving in with her daughter.'

'Then she can tell me where her daughter is. If you'll tell me where *she* lives.'

'I have her address someplace.'

'Doesn't she have a phone?'

'No, she uses a neighbour's phone. Teeny Campbell's had hard sledding these last few years.' She paused, and gave me a liquid look. 'I'm not going to give you her address if it means trouble for her. Why are you looking for Hester?'

'One of her Canadian relatives wants to get in touch with her.'

'One of her husband's relatives?'

'Yes.'

'Cross your heart and hope to die.'

'Cross my heart,' I said. It felt like the kind of lie that would bring me bad luck. It was. 'And hope to die.'

Mrs Campbell lived on a poor street of stucco and frame cottages half hidden by large, ancient oak trees. In their sun-flecked shadows, pre-school children played their killing games: Bang bang, you're dead; I'm not dead; you are so dead. A garbage truck on its rounds started a chorus of dogs barking in resentment at the theft of their masters' garbage.

Mrs Campbell's cottage stood behind a flaked stucco wall in which a rusty gate stood permanently open. There was a new cardboard FOR SALE sign wired to the gate. In the courtyard, red geraniums had thrust up through a couple of stunted lime trees and converted them into red-flowering bushes which seemed to be burning in the sun. The thorned and brighter fire of a bougainvillæa vine surged up the front porch and the roof.

I stepped in under its cool shade and knocked on the screen door, which was tufted with cotton to ward off flies. A tiny barred window was set in the inner door. Its shutter snapped open, and an eye looked out at me. It was a blue eye, a little faded, surrounded with curled lashes and equipped with a voice like the sparrows' in the oak trees:

'Good morning, are you from Mr Gregory?'

I mumbled something indistinguishable which might have been, yes, I was.

'Goodie, I've been expecting you.' She unlocked the door and opened it wide. 'Come in, Mr—?'

'Archer,' I said.

'I'm absotively delighted to see you, Mr Archer.'

She was a small, straight-bodied woman in a blue cotton dress too short and frilly for her age. This would be about fifty, though everything about her conspired to deny it. For an instant in the dim little box of a hallway, her bird voice and quick graces created the illusion that she was an adolescent blonde.

In the sunlit living-room, the illusion died. The dry cracks of experience showed around her eyes and mouth, and she couldn't smile them away. Her ash-blond boyish bob was fading into gray, and her neck was withering. I kind of liked her, though. She saw that. She wasn't stupid.

She ankled around the small living-room, lifting clean ashtrays and setting them down again. 'Do have a chair, or would you prefer to stand up and look around? How nice of you to be interested in my little nest. Please notice the sea view, which is one of the little luxuries I have. Isn't it lovely?'

She posed her trim, small body, extended her arm toward the window and held it stiff and still, slightly bent up at the elbow, fingers apart. There was a view of the sea: a meager blue ribbon, tangled among the oak-tree branches.

'Very nice.' But I was wondering what ghostly audience or dead daddy she was playing to. And how long she would go on taking me for a prospective buyer.

The room was crammed with dark old furniture made for a larger room, and for larger people: a carved refectory table flanked by high-backed Spanish chairs, an overstuffed red plush divan, thick red drapes on either side of the window. These made a cheerless contrast with the plaster walls and ceiling, which were dark green and mottled with stains from old leaks in the roof.

She caught me looking at the waterstains. 'It won't happen again, I can guarantee you that. I had the roof repaired last fall, and, as a matter of fact, I've been saving up to redecorate this room. When all of a sudden my big move came up. I've had the most wondrous good luck, you know, or should I say my daughter has.' She paused in a dramatic listening attitude, as if she were receiving a brief message in code on her back fillings. 'But let me tell you over coffee. Poor man, you look quite peaked. I know what house-hunting is.'

Her generosity disturbed me. I hated to accept anything from her under false pretenses. But before I could frame an answer she'd danced away through a swinging door to the kitchen. She came back with a breakfast tray on which a silver coffee set shone proudly, laid it on the table, and hovered over it. It was a pleasure to watch her pour. I complimented the coffeepot.

'Thank you very mooch, kind sir. It was one of my wedding presents, I've kept it all these years. I've held on to a lot of things, and now I'm glad I did, now that I'm moving back into the big house.' She touched her lips with her fingertips and chuckled musically. 'But of course you can't know what I'm talking about, unless Mr Gregory told you.'

'Mr Gregory?'

'Mr Gregory the realtor.' She perched on the divan beside me, confidentially. 'It's why I'm willing to sell without a cent of profit, as long as I get my equity out of this place. I'm moving out the first of the week, to go and live with my daughter. You see, my daughter is flying to Italy for a month or so, and she wants me to be in the big house, to look after it while she's gone. Which I'll be very happy to do, I can tell you.'

'You're moving into a larger house?'

'Yes indeedy I am. I'm moving back into my own house, the one my girls were born in. You might not think it to look around you, unless you have an eye for good furniture, but I used to live in a grand big house in Beverly Hills.' She nodded her head vigorously, as though I'd contradicted her. 'I lost it—we lost it way back before the war when my husband left us. But now that clever daughter of mine has bought it back! And she's asked me to live with her!' She hugged her thin chest. 'How she must love her little mother! Eh? Eh?'

'She certainly must,' I said. 'It sounds as if she's come into some money.'

'Yes.' She plucked at my sleeve. 'I *told* her it would happen, if she kept faith and worked hard and made herself agreeable to people. I told the girls the very day we moved out that someday we'd move back. And, sure enough, it's happened. Hester's come in to all this uranium money.'

'She found uranium?'

'Mr Wallingford did. He was a Canadian mining tycoon. Hester married an older man, just as I did in my time. Unfortunately the poor man died before they'd been married a year. I never met him.'

'What was his name?'

'George Wallingford,' she said. 'Hester draws a substantial monthly income from the estate. And then she's got her movie money, too. Everything seems to have broken for her at once.'

I watched her closely, but could see no sign that she was lying consciously.

'What does she do in the movies?'

'Many things,' she said with a wavy flip of her hand. 'She dances and swims and dives—she was a professional diver—and of course she acts. Her *father* was an actor, back in the good old days. You've heard of Raymond Campbell?'

I nodded. The name belonged to a swashbuckling silent-movie star who had tried to make the transition to the talkies and been tripped by advancing years and a tenor voice. I could remember a time in the early twenties when Campbell's serials filled the Long Beach movie houses on Saturday afternoons. Me they had filled with inspiration: his Inspector Fate of Limehouse series had helped to make me a cop, for good or ill. And when the cops went sour, the memory of Inspector Fate had helped to pull me out of the Long Beach force.

She said: 'You do remember Raymond, don't you? Did you know him personally?'

'Just on the screen. It's been a long time. What ever happened to him?'

'He died,' she said, 'he died of a broken heart, way back in the depression. He hadn't had a picture for years, his friends turned against him, he was terribly in debt. And so he died.' Her eyes became glazed with tears, but she smiled bravely through them like one of Raymond Campbell's leading ladies. 'I carried on the faith, however. I was an actress myself, before I subordinated my life to Raymond's, and I brought up my girls to follow in his footsteps, just as he would have wished. One of them, at least, has made the most of it.'

'What does your other daughter do?'

'Rina? She's a psychiatric nurse, can you imagine? It's always been a wonder to me that two girls so close in age and looks could differ so in temperament. Rina actually doesn't *have* any temperament. With all the artistic training I gave her, she grew up just as cold and hard and practical as they come. Why, I'd drop dead with shock if Rina ever offered me a home. No!' she cried melodramatically. 'Rina would rather spend her time with crazy people. Why would a pretty girl do a thing like that?'

'Maybe she wants to help them.'

Mrs Campbell looked blank. 'She could have found a more feminine way. Hester brings real joy to others without demeaning herself.'

A funny look must have crossed my face. She regarded me shrewdly, then snapped her eyelids wide and turned on her brights. 'But I mustn't bore you with my family affairs. You came to look at the house. It's got just the three rooms, but it's *most* convenient, especially the kitchen.'

'Don't bother with that, Mrs Campbell. I've been imposing on your hospitality.'

'Why, no you haven't. Not at all.'

'I have, though. I'm a detective.'

'A detective?' Her tiny fingers clawed at my arm and took hold. She said in a new voice, a full octave lower than her bird tones: 'Has something happened to Hester?'

'Not that I know of. I'm simply looking for her.'

'Is she in trouble?'

'She may be.'

'I knew it. I've been so afraid that something would go wrong. Things never work out for us. Something goes wrong, always.' She touched her face with her fingertips: it was like crumpled paper. 'I'm in a damned hole,' she said hoarsely. 'I gave up my job on the strength of this, and I owe half the people in town. If Hester falls down on me now, I don't know what I'll do.' She dropped her hands, and raised her chin. 'Well, let's have the bad news. Is it all a bunch of lies?'

'Is what a bunch of lies?'

'What I've been telling you, what she told me. About the movie contract and the trip to Italy and the rich husband who died. I had my doubts about it, you know—I'm not that much of a fool.'

'Part of it may be true. Part of it isn't. Her husband isn't dead. He isn't old, and he isn't rich, and he wants her back. Which is where I come in.'

'Is that all there is to it? No.' Her eyes regarded me with hard suspicion. The shock had precipitated a second personality in her, and I wondered how much of the hardness belonged to her, and how much to hysteria. 'You're holding out on me. You admitted she's in trouble.'

'I said she may be. What makes you so sure?'

'You're a hard man to get information out of.' She stood up in front of me, planting her fists on her insignificant hips and leaning forward like a bantam fighter. 'Now don't try to give me the runaround, though God knows I'm used to it after thirty years in this town. Is she or isn't she in trouble?'

'I can't answer that, Mrs Campbell. So far as I know, there's nothing against her. All I want to do is talk to her.'

'On what subject?'

'The subject of going back to her husband.'

'Why doesn't he talk to her himself?'

'He intends to. At the moment he's a little under the weather. And we've had a lot of trouble locating her.'

'Who is he?'

'A young newspaperman from Toronto. Name's George Wall.'

'George Wall,' she said. 'George Wallingford.'

'Yes,' I said, 'it figures.'

'What sort of a man is this George Wall?'

'I think he's a good one, or he will be when he grows up.'

'Is he in love with her?'

'Very much. Maybe too much.'

'And what you want from me is her address?'

'If you know it.'

'I ought to know it. I lived there for nearly ten years. 14 Manor Crest Drive, Beverly Hills. But if that's all you wanted, why didn't you say so? You let me beat my gums and make a fool of myself. Why do that to me?'

'I'm sorry. It wasn't very nice. But this may be more than a runaway-wife case. You suggested yourself that Hester's in trouble.'

'Trouble is what the word detective means to me.'

'Has she been in trouble before?'

'We won't go into that.'

'Have you been seeing much of her this winter?'

'Very little. I spent one weekend with her—the weekend before last.'

'In the Beverly Hills house?'

'Yes. She'd just moved in, and she wanted my advice about redecorating some of the rooms. The people who had it before Hester didn't keep it up—not like the days when we had our Japanese couple.' Her blue gaze strained across the decades, and returned to the present. 'Anyway, we had a good time together, Hester and I. A wonderful weekend all by our lonesomes, chatting and tending to her clothes and pretending it was old times. And it ended up with Hester inviting me to move in the first of the year.'

'That was nice of her.'

'Wasn't it? I was so surprised and pleased. We hadn't been close at all for several years. I'd hardly seen her, as a matter of fact. And then, out of the blue, she asked me to come and live with her.'

'Why do you think she did?'

The question seemed to appeal to her realistic side. She sat on the edge of her chair, in thinking position, her fingertips to her temple. 'It's hard to say. Certainly not on account of my beautiful blue eyes. Of course, she's going to be away and she needs someone to stay in the house and look after it. I think she's been lonely, too.'

'And frightened?'

'She didn't act frightened. Maybe she was. She wouldn't tell me if she was. My girls don't tell me anything.' She inserted the knuckle of her right thumb between her teeth, and wrinkled her face like a baby monkey. 'Will I still be able to move the first of the year? Do you think I will?'

'I wouldn't count on it.'

'But the house must belong to her. She wouldn't spend all that money on redecorating. Mr Archer—is that your name? Archer?—where is all the money coming from?'

'I have no idea,' I said, though I had several.

XI

MANOR CREST DRIVE was one of those quiet palm-lined avenues which had been laid out just before the twenties went into their final convulsions. The houses weren't huge and fantastic like some of the rococo palaces in the surrounding hills, but they had pretensions. Some were baronial pseudo-Tudor with faked half-timbered façades. Others were imitation Mizener Spanish, thick-walled and narrow-windowed like stucco fortresses built to resist imaginary Moors. The street was good, but a little disappointed-looking, as though maybe the Moors had already been and gone.

Number 14 was one of the two-story Spanish fortresses. It sat well back from the street behind a Monterey cypress hedge. Water from a sprinkling system danced in the air above the hedge, rainbowed for an instant as I passed. A dusty gray Jaguar was parked in the driveway.

I left my car in front of one of the neighbouring houses, walked back, and strolled down the driveway to the Jaguar. According to the white slip on the steering-post, it was registered to Lance Leonard.

I turned and surveyed the front of the house. Tiny gusts from the sprinkler wet my face. It was the only sign of life around. The black oak door was closed, the windows heavily draped. The pink tile roof pressed down on the house like a lid.

I mounted the stoop and pressed the bellpush and heard the electric buzzer sound deep inside the building. I thought I heard footsteps approaching the ironbound door. Then I thought I heard breathing. I knocked on the door and waited. The breathing on the other side of the door, if it was breathing, went away or ceased.

I knocked a few more times and waited some more, in vain. Walking back toward the driveway, I caught a movement from the corner of my eye. The drape in the end window twitched at the edge. When I looked directly at it, it had fallen back in place. I reached across a spiky pyracantha and tapped on the window, just for kicks. Kicks were all I got.

I returned to my car, U-turned at the next intersection, drove back past the pink-roofed house, and parked where I could watch its front in my rear-view mirror. The street was very quiet. Along both sides of it, the fronds of the palms hung in the air like static green explosions caught by a camera. In the middle distance, the tower of the Beverly Hills City Hall stood flat white against the flat blue sky. Nothing happened to mark the passage of time, except that the hands of my wristwatch bracketed two o'clock and moved on past.

About two ten, a car rolled into sight from the direction of the City Hall. It was an old black Lincoln, long and heavy as a hearse, with gray curtains over the rear windows completing the resemblance. A man in a black felt hat was at the wheel. He was doing about fifty in a twenty-five-mile zone. As he entered the block I was in, he started to slow down.

I reached for a yesterday's newspaper in the back seat and propped it up on the wheel to hide my face. Its headlines read like ancient history. The Lincoln seemed to take a long time to pass me. Then it did. Small-eyed, saddle-nosed, rubber-mouthed, its driver's face was unforgettable. Unforgettably ugly.

He turned into the driveway of Number 14, entering my rear-view mirror, and parked beside the Jaguar and got out. He moved quickly and softly, without swinging his arms. In a long charcoal-gray raglan topcoat, his slope-shouldered body looked like a torpedo sliding on its base.

The door opened before he knocked. I couldn't see who opened it. The door closed for a while, two or three long minutes, and then opened again.

Lance Leonard came out of the house. In a queer little hustling run, like a puppet jerked by wires, he descended the steps and crossed the lawn to the Jaguar, not noticing the sprinkler, though it wet his white silk open-necked shirt and spotted his light-beige slacks.

The Jaguar backed roaring into the street. As it raced past on squealing tires I caught a glimpse of Lance Leonard's face. His face was a blank, dead yellow. The nose and chin were drawn sharp. The eyes blazed black. They didn't see me.

The Jaguar plunged away into silence. I got out the ·38 Special which I kept in the dash compartment and crossed the street. The Lincoln was registered to a Theodore Marfeld who lived at a Coast Highway address in South Malibu. Its black leather interior was shabby and smelt of cat. The back seat and floor were covered with sheets of heavy wrapping paper. The dashboard clock had stopped at eleven twenty.

I went to the door of the house and lifted my fist to knock and saw that the door was standing slightly ajar. I pushed it wider, stepped into a dim hall with a round Moorish ceiling. Ahead to my left a flight of red tile steps rose cumbrously through the ceiling. To the right, an inner door threw a bent fan of brightness across the floor and up the blank plaster side of the staircase.

A hatted shadow moved into the brightness and blotted most of it out. The head and shoulder of Saddlenose leaned from the doorway.

'Mr Marfeld?' I said.

'Yeah. Who the hell are you? You got no right barging into a private residence. Get the hell out.'

'I'd like to speak to Miss Campbell.'

'What about? Who sent you?' he said mouthily.

'Her mother sent me, as a matter of fact. I'm a friend of the family. Are you a friend of the family?'

'Yeah. A friend of the family.'

Marfeld raised his right hand to his face. His left hand was out of sight behind the door frame. I was holding the gun in my pocket with my finger on the trigger. Marfeld seemed puzzled. He took hold of the entire lower part of his face and pulled it sideways. There was a red smear on the ball of his thumb. It left a red thumbprint on the side of his indented nose.

'Cut yourself?'

He turned his hand around and looked at this thumb and closed his fist over it. 'Yeah, I cut myself.'

'I'm an expert at First Aid. If you're in pain, I have some monoacetic acid ester of salicylic acid in the car. I also have some five-per-cent tincture of iodine to offset the risk of blood-poisoning or other serious infection.'

His right hand pushed the words away from his face. Neurosis cheeped surprisingly in his voice. 'Shut up, God damn you, I can't stand doubletalk.' He got himself under control and returned to his lower-register personality. 'You heard me tell you to get out of here. What are you waiting for?'

'That's no way for a friend of the family to talk to another friend of the family.'

He leaned round-shouldered out of the doorway, a metal rod glittering in his left hand. It was a brass poker. He shifted it to his right hand and lunged toward me, so close I could smell his breath. His breath was sour with trouble. 'God-damn double-mouth.'

I could have shot him through my pocket. Maybe I should have. The trouble was, I didn't know him well enough to shoot him. And I trusted the speed of my reflexes, forgetting Leonard's knockdown punch and the residence of languor in my legs.

Marfeld raised the poker. A dark drop flew from its hooked point and spattered the plaster wall like a splash of wet red paint. My eye stayed on it a millisecond too long. The poker seared and chilled the side of my head. It was a glancing blow, or I would have gone all the way out. As it was, the floor upended and rapped my knees and elbows and my forehead. The gun went skittering through a hole in the broken light.

I crawled up the steep floor toward it. Marfeld stamped at my fingers. I got my hands on one of his feet, my shoulder against his knee, and threw him over backward. He went down hard and lay whooping for breath.

I groped for the gun among jagged shards of light. The bright room beyond the doorway flashed on my angled vision with a hallucination's vividness. It was white and black and red. The blonde girl in the linen dress lay on a white rug in front of a raised black fireplace. Her face was turned away. An inkblot of red darkness spread around it.

Then there were footsteps behind me, and as I turned, the front end of the Sunset Limited hit the side of my head and knocked me off the rails into deep red darkness.

I came to, conscious of motion and a rumbling noise in my stomach which gradually detached itself from me and became the sound of a car engine. I was sitting propped up in the middle of the front seat. Shoulders were jammed against me on both sides. I opened my eyes and recognized the dashboard clock which had stopped at eleven twenty.

'People are dying to get in there,' Marfeld said across me from the right.

My eyeballs moved grittily in their sockets. Marfeld had my gun on his knee. The driver, on my left, said:

'Brother, you kill me. You pull the same old gag out of the file every time you pass the place.'

We were passing Forest Lawn. Its Elysian fields were distorted by moving curves, heat waves in the air or behind my eyes. I felt a craving nostalgia for peace. I thought how nice it would be to lie down in the beautiful cemetery and listen to organ music. Then I noticed the driver's hands on the wheel. They were large, dirty hands, with large, dirty fingernails, and they made me mad.

I reached for the gun on Marfeld's knee. Marfeld pulled it away like somebody taking candy from a baby. My reactions were so feeble and dull it scared me. He rapped my knuckles with the gun muzzle.

'How about that? The sleeper awakes.'

My wooden tongue clacked around in my desiccated mouth and produced some words: 'You jokers know the penalty for kidnapping?'

'Kidnapping?' The driver had a twisted little face which sprouted queerly out of a massive body. He gave me a corkscrew look. 'I didn't hear of any kidnapping lately. You must of been dreaming.'

'Yeah,' Marfeld said. 'Don't try to kid me, peeper. I was on the county cops for fifteen years. I know the law and what you can do and what you can't do. You can't go bulling into a private house with a deadly weapon. You was way out of line and I had a right to stop you. Christ, I could of killed you, they wouldn't even booked me.'

'Count your blessings,' the driver said. 'You peepers, some of you, act like you think you can get away with murder.'

'Somebody does.'

Marfeld turned violently in the seat and pushed the gun muzzle into the side of my stomach. 'What's that? Say that again. I didn't catch it.'

My wits were still widely scattered around Los Angeles County. I had just enough of them with me to entertain a couple of ideas. They couldn't be sure, unless I told them, that I had seen the girl in the bright room. If she was dead and they knew I knew, I'd be well along on my way to a closed-coffin funeral.

'What was that about murder?'

Marfeld leaned hard on the gun. I tensed my stomach muscles against its pressure. The taste of the little seeds they put in rye bread rose in my throat. I concentrated on holding it down.

Marfeld got tired of prodding me after a while, and sat back with the gun on his knee. 'Okay. You can do your talking to Mr Frost.'

He made it sound as if nothing worse could ever happen to me.

XII

LEROY FROST WAS not only the head of Helio-Graff's private police force. He had other duties, both important and obscure. In certain areas, he could fix a drunk-driving or narcotics rap. He knew how to bring pressure to settle a divorce suit or a statutory-rape charge out of court. Barbiturate suicides changed, in his supple hands, to accidental overdoses. Having served for a time as deputy security chief of a Washington agency, he advised the editorial department on the purchase of scripts and the casting department on hiring and firing. I knew him slightly, about as well as I wanted to.

The studio occupied a country block surrounded by a high

white concrete wall on the far side of San Fernando. Twistyface parked the Lincoln in the semicircular drive. The white-columned colonial façade of the administration building grinned emptily into the sun. Marfeld got out and put my gun in his coat pocket and pointed the pocket at me.

'March.'

I marched. Inside in the vestibule a blue-uniformed guard sat in a glass cage. A second uniformed guard came out of the white oak woodwork. He led us up a curved ramp, along a windowless corridor with a cork floor and a glass roof, past rows of bigger-than-life-size photographs: the heads that Graff and, before him, Heliopoulos had blown up huge on the movie screens of the world.

The guard unlocked a door with a polished brass sign: SECURITY. The room beyond was large and barely furnished with filing cabinets and typewriter desks, one of which was occupied by a man in earphones typing away like mad. We passed into an anteroom, with a single desk, unoccupied, and Marfeld disappeared through a further door which had Leroy Frost's name on it.

The guard stayed with me, his right hand near the gun on his hip. His face was heavy and blank and content to be heavy and blank. Its lower half stuck out like the butt end of a ham, in which his mouth was a small, meaningless slit. He stood with his chest pushed out and his stomach held in, wearing his unofficial uniform as though it was very important to him.

I sat on a straight chair against the wall and didn't try to make conversation. The dingy little room had the atmosphere of an unsuccessful dentist's waiting-room. Marfeld came out of Frost's office looking as if the dentist had told him he'd have to have all his teeth pulled. The uniform that walked like a man waved me in.

I'd never seen Leroy Frost's office. It was impressively large, at least the size of a non-producing director's on long-term contract. The furniture was heavy but heterogeneous, probably inherited from various other rooms at various times: leather chairs and a camel-backed English settee and a bulging rosewood Empire desk which was big enough for table tennis.

Frost sat behind the desk, holding a telephone receiver to his head. 'Right now,' he said into it. 'I want you to contact her right now.'

He laid the receiver in its cradle and looked up, but not at me. I had to be made to realize how unimportant I was. He leaned back in his swivel chair, unbuttoned his waistcoat, buttoned it up again. It had mother-of-pearl buttons. There were crossed cavalry sabers on the wall behind him, and the signed photographs of several politicians.

In spite of all this backing, and the word on the outer door, Frost looked insecure. The authority that thick brown eyebrows lent his face was false. Under them, his eyes were glum and yellowish. He had lost weight, and the skin below his eyes and jaw was loose and quilted like a half-sloughed snakeskin. His youthful crewcut only emphasized the fact that he was sick and prematurely aging.

'All right, Lashman,' he said to the guard. 'You can wait outside. Lew Archer and me, we're buddy-buddy from way back.'

His tone was ironic, but he also meant that I had eaten lunch at Musso's with him once and made the mistake of letting him pick up the tab because he had been on an expense account and I hadn't. He didn't invite me to sit down. I sat down anyway, on the arm of one of the leather chairs.

'I don't like this, Frost.'

'*You* don't like it. How do you think I feel? Here I thought we were buddy-buddy like I said, I thought there was a basis of mutual live-and-let-live there. My God, Lew, people got to be able to have faith and confidence in each other, or the whole fabric comes to pieces.'

'You mean the dirty linen you're washing in public?'

'Now what kind of talk is that? I want you to take me seriously, Lew, it offends my sense of fitness when you don't. Not that *I* matter personally. I'm just another joe working my way through life—a little cog in a big machine.' He lowered his eyes in humility. 'A *very* big machine. Do you know what our investment is, in plant and contracts and unreleased film and all?'

He paused rhetorically. Through the window to my right, I could see hangarlike sound stages and a series of open sets: Brownstone Front, Midwestern Town, South Sea Village, and the Western Street where dozens of celluloid heroes had take the death walk. The studio seemed to be shut down, and the sets were deserted, dream scenes abandoned by the minds that had dreamed them.

'Close to fifteen million,' Frost said in the tone of a priest revealing a mystery. 'A huge investment. And you know what its safety depends on?'

'Sun spots?'

'It isn't sun spots,' he said gently. 'The subject isn't funny, fifteen million dollars isn't funny. I'll tell you what it depends on. You know it, but I'll tell you anyway.' His fingers formed a Gothic arch a few inches in front of his nose. 'Number one is glamour, and number two is goodwill. The two things are interdependent and interrelated. Some people think the public will swallow anything since the war—any stinking crud—but I know different. I'm a student of the problem. They swallow just so much, and then we lose them. Especially these days, when the industry's under attack from all sides. We got to keep our glamour dry for the public. We got to hold on to our strategic goodwill. It's psychological warfare, Lew, and I'm on the firing line.'

'So you send your troopers out to push citizens around. You want a testimonial from me?'

'You're not just any old ordinary citizen, Lew. You get around so fast and you make so many mistakes. You go bucketing up to Lance Leonard's house and invade his privacy and throw your weight around. I was on the phone to Lance just now. It wasn't smart what you did, and it wasn't ethical, and nobody's going to forget it.'

'It wasn't smart,' I admitted.

'But it was brilliant compared with the rest of it. Merciful God, Lew, I thought you had some feeling for situations. When we get to the payoff—you trying to force you way into the house of a lady who shall be nameless—' He spread his arms wide and dropped them, unable to span the extent of my infamy.

'What goes on in that house?' I said.

He munched the inside corner of his mouth, watching my face. 'If you were smart, as smart as I used to think, you wouldn't ask that question. You'd let it lie. But you're so interested in facts, I'll tell you the one big fact. The less you know, the better for you. The more you know, the worse for you. You got a reputation for discretion. Use it.'

'I thought I was.'

'Uh-uh, you're not that stupid, kiddo. Nobody is. Your neck's out a mile, and you know it. You follow the thought, or do I have to spell it out in words of one syllable?'

'Spell it out.'

He got up from behind the desk. His sick yellow glance avoided mine as he moved around me. He leaned on the back of my chair. His allusive little whisper was scented with some spicy odor from his hair or mouth:

'A nice fellow like you that percolates around where he isn't wanted—he could stop percolating period.'

I stood up facing him. 'I was waiting for that one, Frost. I wondered when we were getting down to threats.'

'Call me Leroy. Hell, I wouldn't threaten you.' He repudiated the thought with movements of his shoulders and hands. 'I'm not a man of violence, you know that. Mr Graff doesn't like violence, and I don't like it. That is, when I can prevent it. The trouble with a high-powered operation like this one, sometimes it runs over people by accident when they keep getting in the way. It's our business to make friends, see, and we got friends all over, Vegas, Chicago, all over. Some of them are kind of rough, and they might get an idea in their little pointed heads—you know how it is.'

'No. I'm very slow on the uptake. Tell me more.'

He smiled with his mouth; his eyes were dull yellow flint. 'The point is, I like you, Lew. I get a kick out of knowing that you're in town, in good health and all. I wouldn't want your name to be bandied about on the long-distance telephone.'

'It's happened before. I'm still walking around, and feeling pretty good.'

'Let's keep it that way. I owe it to you to be frank, as one old friend to another. There's a certain gun that would blast you in a minute if he knew what you been up to. For his own reasons he'd do it, in his own good time. And it could be he knows now. That's a friendly warning.'

'I've heard friendlier. Does he have a name?'

'You'd know it, but we won't go into that.' Frost leaned forward across the back of the chair, his fingers digging deep into the leather. 'Get wise to yourself, Lew. You trying to get yourself killed and drag us down with you, or what?'

'What's all the melodrama about? I was looking for a woman. I found her.'

'You found her? You mean you saw her—you talked to her?'

'I didn't get to talk to her. Your goon stopped me at the door.'

'So you didn't actually see her?'

'No,' I lied.

'You know who she is?'

'I know her name. Hester Campbell.'

'Who hired you to find her? Who's behind this?'

'I have a client.'

'Come on now, don't go fifth-amendment on me. Who hired you, Lew?'

I didn't answer.

'Isobel Graff? Did she sick you onto the girl?'

'You're way off in left field.'

'I used to play left field. Let me tell you something, just in case it's her. She's nothing but trouble—schizzy from way back. I could tell you things about Isobel you wouldn't believe.'

'Try me.'

'Is she the one?'

'I don't know the lady.'

'Scout's honor?'

'Eagle Scout's honor.'

'Then where's the trouble coming from? I got to know, Lew. It's my job to know. I got to protect the Man and the organization.'

'What do you have to protect them against?' I said experimentally. 'A murder rap?'

The experiment got results. Fear crossed Leroy Frost's face like a shadow chased by shadows. He said very mildly and reasonably: 'Nobody said a word about murder, Lew. Why bring up imaginary trouble? We got enough real ones. The trouble I'm featuring just this minute is a Hollywood peeper name of Archer who is half smart and half stupid and who has been getting too big for his goddam breeches.' While he spoke, his fear was changing to malice. 'You going to answer my question, Lew? I asked you who's your principal and why.'

'Sorry.'

'You'll be sorrier.'

He came around the chair and looked me up and down and across like a tailor measuring me for a suit of clothes. Then he turned his back on me, and flipped the switch on his intercom.

'Lashman! Come in here.'

I looked at the door. Nothing happened. Frost spoke into the intercom again, on a rising note:

'Lashman! Marfeld!'

No answer. Frost looked at me, his yellow eyes dilating.

'I wouldn't slug a sick old man,' I said.

He said something in a guttural voice which I didn't catch. Outside the window, like his echo vastly amplified, men began to shout. I caught some words:

'He's comin' your way.' And further off: 'I see him.'

A pink-haired man in a dark suit ran under the window, chasing his frenzied shadow across the naked ground. It was George Wall. He was running poorly, floundering from side to side and almost falling. Close behind him, like a second bulkier shadow struggling to make contact with his heels, Marfeld ran. He had a gun in his hand.

Frost said: 'What goes on?'

He cranked open the casement window and shouted the same question. Neither man heard him. They ran on in the dust, up Western Street, through the fake tranquillity of Midwestern Town. George's legs were pumping weakly, and Marfeld was closing up the distance between them. Ahead of George, in South Sea Village, Lashman jumped into sight around the corner of a palm-thatched hut.

George saw him and tried to swerve. His legs gave under him. He got up, swaying in indecision as Lashman and Marfeld converged on him. Marfeld's shoulder took him in the side, and he went down again. Lashman dragged him up to his feet, and Marfeld's dark bulk blotted out his face.

Frost was leaning on the window sill, watching the distant figures. Marfeld's shoulder, leaning over George, moved in a jerky rhythm from side to side. I pushed Frost out of the way—he was light as straw—and went out through the window and across the lot.

Marfeld and Lashman were fascinated and oblivious. Marfeld was pistol-whipping George while Lashman held him up. Blood streaked his blind face and spotted his charcoal-gray suit. I noticed the irrelevant fact that the suit belonged to me: I'd last seen it hanging in my bedroom closet. I moved on them in ice-cold anger, got one hand on Marfeld's collar and the other on the slippery barrel of the gun. I heaved. The man and the gun came apart. The man went down backward. The gun stayed in my hand. It belonged to me, anyway. I reversed it and held it on Lashman:

'Turn him loose. Let him down easy.'

The little, cruel mouth in his big jaw opened and closed. The fever left his eyes. He laid George out on the white imported sand. The boy was out, with the whites of his eyes glaring.

I took the revolver off Lashman's hip, stepped back and included Marfeld in the double line of fire. 'What are you cookies up to, or you just do this for fun?'

Marfeld got to his feet, but he remained silent. Lashman answered the guns in my hands politely:

'The guy's a crackpot. He bust into Mr Graff's office, threatened to kill him.'

'Why would he do that?'

'It was something about his wife.'

'Button it down,' Marfeld growled. 'You talk too much, Lashman.'

There were muffled footsteps in the dust behind me. I circled Marfeld and Lashman, and backed against the bamboo wall of a hut. Frost and the guard from the vestibule were crossing the lot towards us. This guard had a carbine on his arm. He stopped, and raised it into firing position.

'Drop it,' I said. 'Tell him to drop it, Frost.'

'Drop it,' he said to the guard.

The carbine thudded on the ground and sent up a little dust cloud. The situation was mine. I didn't want it.

'What goes on?' Frost said in a querulous tone. 'Who is he?'

'Hester Campbell's husband. Kick him around some more if you really want bad publicity.'

'Jesus Christ!'

'You better get him to a doctor.'

Nobody moved. Frost slid his hand up under his waistcoat and fingered his rib-cage to see if his heart had stopped. He said faintly:

'You brought him here?'

'You know better than that.'

'The guy tried to kill Mr Graff,' Lashman said virtuously. 'He was chasing Mr Graff around the office.'

'Is Graff all right?'

'Yeah, sure. I heard the guy yelling and run him out of there before he did any damage.'

Frost turned to the guard who had dropped the carbine: 'How did he get in?'

The man looked confused, then sullen. He broke his lips apart with difficulty:

'He had a press card. Said he had an appointment with Mr Graff.'

'You didn't clear it with me.'

'You were busy, you said not to disturb—'

'Don't tell me what I said. Get out of here. You're finished here. Who hired you?'

'You did, Mr Frost.'

'I ought to be shot for that. Now get out of my sight.' His voice was very mild. 'Tell anybody about this, anybody at all, and you might as well leave town, it'll save you hospital bills.'

The man's face had turned a grainy white, the color of rice pudding. He opened and closed his mouth several times without speaking, turned on his heel, and trudged toward the gate.

Frost looked down at the bloody man in the sand. He whined with pity, all of it for himself:

'What am I going to do with him?'

'Move your butt and get him an ambulance.'

Frost turned his measuring look on me. Over it, he tried on a Santa Claus smile that didn't fit. A fluttering tic in one eyelid gave him the air of having a secret understanding with me:

'I talked a little rough back there in the office. Forget it, Lew. I like you. As a matter of fact, I like you very much.'

'Get him an ambulance,' I said, 'or you'll be needing one for yourself.'

'Sure, in a minute.' He rolled his eyes toward the sky like a producer having an inspiration. 'I been thinking for some time, long before this came up, we can use you in the organization, Lew. How would you like to go to Italy, all expenses paid? No real work, you'll have men under you. It'll be a free vacation.'

I looked at his sick, intelligent face and the cruel, stupid faces of the two men beside him. They went with the unreal buildings which stood around like the cruel, sick pretense of a city.

'I wouldn't let you pay my way to Pismo Beach. Now turn around and walk, Frost. You too, Marfeld, Lashman. Stay close together. We're going to a telephone and call the Receiving Hospital. We've wasted enough time.'

I had very little hope of getting out of there and taking George out with me. I merely had to try. What hope I had died a sudden death. Two men appeared ahead of us in Midwestern Town, running stooped over behind a clean white picket fence. One was the guard Frost had fired. Both of them had Thompson guns at the ready.

They saw me and ducked behind a deep front porch with an old-fashioned glider on it. Frost and his goons stopped walking.

I said to Frost's back:

'You're going to have to handle this with care. You'll be the first one drilled. Tell them to come out into the middle of the street and put their tommyguns down.'

Frost turned to face me, shaking his head. Out of the tail of my left eye, I saw a third man running and crouching toward me, hugging the walls of the South Sea huts. He had a riot gun. I felt like a major strike was being broken. Frost made a mock-lugubrious face which fitted all his wrinkles.

'You'd never get out alive.' He raised his voice. 'Drop 'em, Lew. I'll count to three.'

The man in the tail of my left eye was on his elbows and knees, crawling. He lay still and aimed as Frost began to count. I dropped the guns on the count of two. Marfeld and Lashman turned at the sound.

Frost nodded. 'Now you're being smart.'

Marfeld scooped up the guns. Lashman took a step forward. He had a black leather sap in his right hand. The man with the riot gun was on his feet now, trotting. The commandos behind the front porch came out from behind it, cautiously at first and then more quickly. The one Frost had fired had a silly, sickly grin on his face. He was ashamed of what he was doing, but couldn't stop doing it.

Away off on the other side of the lot, Simon Graff stood in a doorway and watched Lashman swing his sap.

XIII

TIME BEGAN TO tick again, in fits and starts. Pain glowed in my mind like lightning in a cloud, expanding and contracting with my heartbeat. I lay on my back on a hard surface. Somewhere above me, Lance Leonard said through flutter and wow:

'This is a neat layout Carlie's got himself here. I been out here plenty of times. He gives me the run of the place. I get the use of it any time he's away. It's swell for dames.'

'Be quiet.' It was Frost.

'I was just explaining.' Leonard's voice was aggrieved. 'I know this place like I know the back of my hand. Anything you want, any kind of booze or wine, I can get it for you.'

'I don't drink.'

'Neither do I. You on drugs?'

'Yah, I'm on drugs,' Frost said bitterly. 'Now shut it off. I'm trying to think.'

Leonard subsided. I lay in the unblessed silence for a while. Sunlight was hot on my skin and red through my eyelids. When I raised my eyelids slightly, scalpels of light probed the inside of my head.

'His eyelids just fluttered,' Leonard said.

'Better take a look at him.'

Boots scraped concrete. I felt a toe in my side. Leonard squatted and pulled open one of my eyelids. I had turned up my eyes.

'He's still out.'

'Throw some water on him. There's a hose on the other side of the pool.'

I waited, and felt its stream gush into my face, hot from the sun, then lukewarm. I let a little of the water run into my dry mouth.

'Still out,' Leonard said glumly. 'What if he don't wake up? What do we do then?'

'That's your friend Stern's problem. He will, though. He's a hardhead, bone all the way through. I almost wish he wouldn't.'

'Carlie ought to been here long ago. You think his plane crashed?'

'Yah, I think his plane crashed. Which makes you a goddam orphan.' There was a rattlesnake buzz in Frost's voice.

'You're stringing me, ain't you? Aren't you?' Leonard was dismayed.

Frost failed to answer him. There was another silence. I kept my eyes shut, and sent a couple of messages down the red-lit avenues behind them. The first one took a long time getting here, but when it arrived it flexed the fingers of my right hand. I willed my toes to wiggle, and they wiggled. It was very encouraging.

A telephone rang behind a wall.

'I bet that's Carlie now,' Leonard said brightly.

'Don't answer it. We'll sit here and guess who it is.'

'You don't have to get sarcastic. Flake can answer it. He's in there watching television.'

The telephone hadn't rung again. A sliding wall hissed in its grooves and bumped. Twistyface's voice said:

'It's Stern. He's in Victorville, wants to be picked up.'

'Is he still on the line?' Leonard asked.

'Yeah, he wants to talk to you.'

'Go and talk to him,' Frost said. 'Put him out of his misery.'

Footsteps receded. I opened my eyes, looked up into glaring blue sky in which the declining sun hung like an inverted hot-plate. I raised my pulsating head, a little at a time. A winking oval pool was surrounded on three sides by a blue Fiberglas fence, on the fourth side by the glass wall of an adobe-colored desert house. Between me and the pool, Frost sat lax in a long aluminum chair under a blue patio umbrella. He was half-turned away from me, listening to a murmur of words from the house. An automatic hung from his limp right hand.

I sat up slowly, leaning my weight on my arms. My vision had a tendency to blur. I focused on Frost's neck. It looked like a scrawny plucked rooster's, easy to wring. I gathered my legs under me. They were hard to control, and one shoe scraped the concrete.

Frost heard the little sound it made. His eyes swiveled toward me. His gun came up. I crawled toward him anyway, dripping reddish water. He scrambled out of the long chair and backed toward the house.

'Flake! Come out here.'

Twistyface appeared in the opening of the wall. I wasn't thinking well, and my movements were sluggish. I got up, made a staggering lunge for Frost, and fell short, onto my knees. He aimed a kick at my head, which I was too slow to avoid. The sky broke up in lights. Something else hit me, and the sky turned black.

I swung in black space, supported by some kind of sky hook above the bright scene. I could look down and see everything very clearly. Frost and Leonard and Twistyface stood over a prostrate man, palavering in doubletalk. At least, it sounded like doubletalk to me. I was occupied with deep thoughts of my own. They flashed on my wind like brilliant lantern slides: Hollywood started as a meaningless dream, invented for money. But its colors ran, out through the holes in people's heads, spread across the landscape and solidified. North and south along the coast, east across the desert, across the continent. Now we were stuck with the dream without a meaning. It had become the nightmare that we lived in. Deep thoughts.

I realized with some embarrassment that the body on the deck belonged to me. I climbed air down to it and crawled back in, a rat who lived in a scarecrow. It was familiar, even cozy, except for the leaks. But something had happened to me. I was hallucinating a little bit, and self-pity opened up in front of me like a blue, inviting pool where a man could drown. I dove in. I swam to the other side, though. There were barracuda in the pool, hungry for my manhood. I climbed out.

Came to my senses and saw I hadn't moved. Frost and Leonard had gone away. Twistyface sat in the aluminum chair and watched me sit up. He was naked to the waist. Black fur made tufted patterns on his torso. He had breasts like a female gorilla. The inevitable gun was in his paw.

'That's better,' he said. 'I don't know about you, but ole Flake feels like going in and watching some TV. It's hotter than the hinges out here.'

It was like walking on stilts, but I made it inside, across a large, low room, into a smaller room. This was paneled in dark wood and dominated by the great blind eye of a television set. Flake pointed with his gun at the leather armchair beside it.

'You sit there. Get me a Western movie.'

'What if I can't?'

'There's always a Western movie at this time of day.'

He was right. I sat for what seemed a long time and listened to the clop-clop and bang-bang. Flake sat close up in front of the screen, fascinated by simple virtue conquering simple evil with fists and guns and rustic philosophy. The old plot repeated itself like a moron's recurrent wish-fulfillment dream. The pitchman in the intervals worked hard to build up new little mechanical wishes. Colonel Risko says buy Bloaties, they're yum-yum delicious, yum-yum nutritious. Get your super-secret badge of membership. You'll ell-oh-vee-ee Bloaties.

I flexed my arms and legs from time to time and tried to generate willpower. There was a brass lamp on top of the television set. It had a thick base, and looked heavy enough to be used as a weapon. If I could find the will to use it, and if Flake would forget his gun for two consecutive seconds.

The movie ended in a chaste embrace which brought tears to Flake's eyes. Or else his eyes were watering from eyestrain. The gun sagged between his spread knees. I rose and got hold of the lamp. It wasn't as heavy as it looked. I hit him on the head with it anyway.

Flake merely looked surprised. He fired in reflex. The pitchman on the television screen exploded in the middle of a deathless sentence. In a hail of glass I kicked at the gun in Flake's hand. It hopped through the air, struck the wall, and went off again. Flake lowered his little dented head and charged me.

I sidestepped. His wild fist cracked a panel in the wall. Before he recovered his balance, I got a half-nelson on him and then a full nelson.

He was a hard man to bend. I bent him, and rapped his head on the edge of the television box. He lunged sideways, dragging me across the room. I retained my hold, clenched hands at the back of his neck. I rapped his head on the steel corner of an air-conditioning unit set in the window. He went soft, and I dropped him.

I got down on my knees and found the gun and had a hard time getting up again. I was weak and trembling. Flake was worse off, snoring through a broken nose.

I found my way to the kitchen and had a drink of water and went outside. It was already evening. There were no cars in the carport, just a flat-tired English bicycle and a motor scooter that couldn't start. Not for me it wouldn't. I thought of waiting there for Frost and Leonard and Stern, but all I could think of to do with them was shoot them. I was sick and tired of violence. One more piece of violence and they could reserve my room at Camarillo, in one of the back wards. Or such was my opinion at the time.

I started down the dusty private road. It descended a low rise toward the bed of a dry stream in the middle of a wide, flat valley. There were mountain ranges on two sides of the valley, high in the south and medium high in the west. On the slopes of the southern range, drifts of snow gleamed impossibly white between the deep-blue forests. The western range was jagged black against a sky where the last light was breaking up into all its colors.

I walked toward the western range. Pasadena was on the other side of it. On my side of it, in the middle of the valley, tiny cars raced along a straight road. One of them turned toward me, its headlights swinging up and down on the bumps. I lay down in the sage beside the road.

It was Leonard's Jaguar, and he was driving it. I caught a glimpse of the face in the seat beside him: a pale, flat oval like a dish on which flat eyes were painted, a pointed chin resting on a spotted bow tie. I'd seen that old-young face before, in the papers after Siegel died, on television during the Kefauver hearings, once or twice at nightclub tables flanked by bodyguards. Carl Stern.

I stayed off the road, cutting at an angle across the high desert toward the highway. The air was turning chilly. In the darkness rising from the earth and spreading across the sky, the evening star hung alone. I was a bit lightheaded, and from time to time I thought that the star was something I had lost, a woman or an ideal or a dream.

Self-pity stalked me, snuffing at my spoor. He was invisible, but I could smell him, a catty smell. Once or twice he fawned on the backs of my legs, and once I kicked at him. The joshua trees waved their arms at me and tittered.

XIV

THE FOURTH CAR I thumbed stopped for me. It was a cut-down jalopy with a pair of skis strapped to the top, driven by a college boy on his way back to Westwood. I told him I'd turned my car over on a back road. He was young enough to accept my story without too many questions, and decent enough to let me go to sleep in the back seat.

He took me to the ambulance entrance of St John's Hospital. A resident surgeon put some stitches in my scalp, gave me quiet hell, and told me to go to bed for a couple of days. I took a taxi home. Traffic was sparse and rapid on the boulevard. I sat back in the seat and watched the lights go by, flashing like thrown knives. There were nights when I hated the city.

My house looked shabby and small. I turned on all the lights. George Wall's dark suit lay like a crumpled man on the bedroom floor. To hell with him, I thought, and repeated the thought aloud. I took a bath and turned off all the lights and went to bed.

It didn't do any good. A nightmare world sprang up around the room, a world of changing faces which wouldn't hold still. Hester's face was there, refracted through George Wall's mind. It changed and died and came alive and died again smiling, staring with loveless eyes out of the red darkness. I thrashed around for a while and gave up. Got up and dressed and went out to my garage.

It hit me then, and not until then, that I was minus a car. If the Beverly Hills cops hadn't hauled it away, my car was parked on Manor Crest Drive, across the street from Hester's house. I called another taxi and asked to be let off on a corner half a block from the house. My car was where I had left it, with a parking ticket under the windshield-wiper.

I crossed the street for a closer look at the house. There was no car in the drive, no light behind the windows. I climbed the front steps and leaned on the bellpush. Inside, the electric bell chirred like a cricket on an abandoned hearth. The nobody-home sound, the empty-house girl-gone one-note blues.

I tried the door. It was locked. I glanced up and down the street. Lights shone at the intersections and from the quiet houses. The people were all inside. They had given up night walks back in the cold war.

Call me trouble looking for a place to happen. I went around to the side of the house, through a creaking wooden gate into a walled patio. The flagstone paving was uneven under my feet. Crab grass grew rank in the spaces between the stones. I made my way among wrought-iron tables and disemboweled chaises to a pair of French doors set into the wall.

My flashlight beam fell through dirty glass into a lanai full of obscene shadows. They were cast by rubber plants and cacti growing in earthenware pots. I reversed the light and used its butt to punch out one of the panes, drew back a reluctant bolt, and forced the door open.

The house was mostly front, like the buildings on Graff's sets. Its rear had been given over to ghosts and spiders. Spiders had rigged the lanai's bamboo furniture and black oak rafters with loops and hammocks and wheels of dusty webbing. I felt like an archaeologist breaking into a tomb.

The door at the end of the lanai was unlocked. I passed through a storeroom full of once-expensive junk: high, unsittable Spanish chairs, a grand piano with grinning yellow keys, brownish oil paintings framed in gilt: through another door, into the central hallway of the house. I crossed to the door of the living-room.

White walls and a half-beamed ceiling rose in front of me, supported by the upward beam from my light. I lowered it to the floor, which was covered with ivory carpeting. White and black sectional furniture, low-slung and cubistic, was grouped in angular patterns around the room. The fireplace was faced with black tile and flanked by a square white leather hassock. On the other side of the fireplace, a faint dark patch showed in the carpet.

I got down on my knees and examined it. It was a wet spot the size of a large dinner plate, of no particular color. Through the odor of detergent, and under the other odors in the room, perfume and cigarette smoke and sweet mixed drinks, I could smell blood. The odor of blood was persistent, no matter how you scrubbed.

Still on my knees, I turned my attention to the raised fireplace. It was equipped with a set of brass fire tools in a rack: brush, shovel, a pair of leather bellows with brass handles. The set was new, and looked as if it had never been used or even touched. Except that the poker was missing.

Beyond the fireplace there was a doorless arch which probably opened into the dining-room. Most of the houses of this style and period had similar floor plans, and I had been in a lot of them. I moved to the arch, intending to go over the rest of the downstairs, then the upstairs.

A motor droned in the street. Light washed the draped front windows and swept past. I went to the end window and looked out through the narrow space between the drape and the window frame. The old black Lincoln was standing in the driveway. Marfeld was at the wheel, his face grotesquely shadowed by the reflection of the headlights. He switched them off and climbed out.

Leroy Frost got out on the far side. I knew him by his hurrying feeble walk. The two men passed within three or four feet of me, headed for the front door. Frost was carrying a glinting metal rod which he used as a walking-stick.

I went through the archway into the next room. In its center a polished table reflected the wan light filtered through lace-curtained double windows. A tall buffet stood against the wall inside the arch, a chair in the corner behind it. I sat down in the deep shadow, with my flashlight in one hand and my gun in the other.

I heard a key turn in the front door, then Leroy Frost's voice, jerking with strain:

'I'll take the key. What happened to the other key?'

'Lance give it to the pig.'

'That was a sloppy way to handle it.'

'It was your idea, chief. You told me not to talk to her myself.'

'All right, as long as she got it.' Frost mumbled something indistinguishable. I heard him shuffling in the entrance to the living-room. Suddenly he exploded: 'Where is the goddam light? You been in and out of this house, you expect me to grope around in the dark all night?'

The lights went on in the living-room. Footsteps crossed it. Frost said:

'You didn't do a very good job on the rug.'

'I did the best I could in the time. Nobody's gonna go over it with a fine-tooth comb, anyway.'

'You hope. You better bring that hassock over here, cover it up until it dries. We don't want her to see it.'

Marfeld grunted with effort. I heard the hassock being dragged across the carpet.

'Fine,' Frost said. 'Now wipe my prints off the poker and put it where it belongs.'

There was the sound of metal coming in contact with metal.

'You sure you got it clean, chief?'

'Don't be a birdbrain, it isn't the same poker. I found a match for it in the prop warehouse.'

'I be damned, you think of everything.' Marfeld's voice was moist with admiration. 'Where did you ditch the other one?'

'Where nobody's going to find it. Not even you.'

'Me? What would I want with it?'

'Skip it.'

'Hell, don't you *trust* me, chief?'

'I trust nobody. I barely trust myself. Now let's get out of here.'

'What about the pig? Don't we wait for her?'

'No, she won't be here for a while. And the less she sees of us, the better. Lance told her what she's supposed to do, and we don't want her asking us questions.'

'I guess you're right.'

'I don't need you to tell me I'm right. I know more about heading off blackmail than any other two men in this town. Bear it in mind in case you develop any ideas.'

'I don't get it, chief. What kind of ideas you mean?' Marfeld's voice was full of injured innocence.

'Ideas of retiring, maybe, with a nice fat pension.'

'No, sir. Not me, Mr Frost.'

'I guess you know better, at that. You try to put the bite on me or any friend of mine—it's the quickest way to get a hole in the head to go with the hole in the head you already got.'

'I know that, Mr Frost. Christ amighty, I'm *loyal.* Didn't I prove it to you?'

'Maybe. Are you sure you saw what you said you saw?'

'When was that, chief?'

'This afternoon. Here.'

'Christ, yes.' Marfeld's plodding mind caught the implication and was stung by it. 'Christ, Mr Frost, I wouldn't lie to you.'

'You would if you did it yourself. That would be quite a trick, to do a murder and con the organization into covering for you.'

'Aw now, chief, you wouldn't accuse me. Why would I kill anybody?'

'For kicks. You'd do it for kicks, any time you thought you could get away with it. Or to make yourself into a hero, if you had a few more brains.'

Marfeld whined adenoidally: 'Make myself into a hero?'

'Yah, Marfeld to the rescue, saving the company's cookies for it again. It's kind of a coincidence that you been in on both killings, Johnny-on-the-spot. Or don't you think so?'

'That's crazy, chief, honest to God.' Marfeld's voice throbbed with sincerity. It ran down, and began on a new note: 'I been loyal all my life, first to the sheriff and then to you. I never asked for anything for myself.'

'Except a cash bonus now and then, eh?' Frost laughed. Now that Marfeld was jittery, too, Frost was willing to forgive him. His laughter rustled like a Santa Ana searching among dry leaves. 'Okay, you'll get your bonus, if I can get it past the comptroller.'

'Thank you, chief. I mean it very sincerely.'

'Sure you do.'

The light went out. The front door closed behind them. I waited until the Lincoln was out of hearing, and went upstairs. The front bedroom was the only room in use. It had quilted pink walls and a silk-canopied bed, like something out of a girl's adolescent dream. The contents of the dressing-table and closet told me that the girl had been spending a lot of money on clothes and cosmetics, and hadn't taken any of it with her.

XV

I LEFT THE house the way I had entered, and drove up into the Canyon. A few sparse stars peered between the streamers of cloud drifting along the ridge. Houselights on the slopes islanded the darkness through which the road ran white under my headlight beam. Rounding a high curve, I could see the glow of the beach cities far below to my left, phosphorescence washed up on the shore.

Lance Leonard's house was dark. I parked on the gravel shoulder a hundred yards short of the entrance to his driveway. Its steep grade was slippery with fog. The front door was locked, and nobody answered my knock.

I tried the garage door. It opened easily when I lifted the handle. The Jaguar had returned to the fold, and the motorcycle was standing in its place. I moved between them to the side entrance. This door wasn't locked.

The concentric ovals of light from my flash slid ahead of me across the floor of the utility room, the checkerboard linoleum in the kitchen, the polished oak in the living-room, up along the glass walls on which the gray night pressed heavily, around and over the fieldstone-faced fireplace, where a smoking log was disintegrating into talc-like ash and dulled flakes of fire. The mantel held a rack of pipes and a tobacco jar, an Atmos clock which showed that it was three minutes to eleven, a silver-framed glamour shot of Lance Leonard smiling with all his tomcat charm.

Lance himself was just inside the front door. He wore a plaid evening jacket and midnight-blue trousers and dull-blue dancing-pumps, but he wasn't going anywhere. He lay on his back with his toes pointing at opposite corners of the ceiling. One asphalt eye looked into the light, unblinking. The other had been broken by a bullet.

I put on gloves and got down on my knees and saw the second bullet wound in the left temple. It was bloodless. The hair around it was singed, the skin peppered with powder marks. I covered the floor on my hands and knees. Pushing aside one of the stiff legs, I found a used copper shellcase, medium caliber. Apparently it had rebounded from the wall or from the murderer's clothes and rolled across the floor where Leonard fell on it.

It took me a long time to find the second shell. I opened the front door, finally, and saw it glinting in the crack between the lintel and the concrete stoop. I squatted in the doorway with my back to the dead man and tried to reconstruct his murder. It looked simple enough. Someone had knocked on the door, waited with a gun for Lance to open it, shot him in the eye, shot him again after he fell to make certain, and gone away, closing the door behind him. The door had a self-locking mechanism.

I left the shells where they were, and shook down the rest of the house. The living-room was almost as impersonal as a hotel room. Even the pipes on the mantel had been bought by the set, and only one of them had ever been smoked. The tobacco in the jar was bone dry. These was nothing but tobacco in the jar, nothing but wood in the woodbox. The portable bar in one corner was well stocked with bottles, most of which were unopened.

I went into the bedroom. The blond oak chests of drawers were stuffed with loot from the Miracle Mile haberdasheries: stacks of shirts custom-made out of English broadcloth and wool gabardine and Madras, hand-painted ties, Argyle socks, silk scarves, a rainbow of cashmere sweaters. A handkerchief drawer contained gold cufflinks and monogrammed tie-bars; a gold identification bracelet engraved with the name Lance Leonard; a tarnished medal awarded to Manuel Torres (it said on the back) for the Intermediate Track and Field Championships, Serena Junior High School, 1945; five expensive wristwatches and a stopwatch. The boy had been running against time.

I looked into the closet. A wooden shoe-rack held a dozen pairs of shoes to go with the dozen suits and jackets hanging above them. A double-barreled shotgun stood in a corner beside a two-foot pile of comic books and crime magazines. I leafed through some of the top ones: Fear, Lust, Horror, Murder, Passion.

On the shelves at the head of the bed there were some other books of a different kind. A morocco-bound catechism inscribed in a woman's hand: 'Manuel Purificación Torres, 1943,' An old life of Jack Dempsey, read to pieces, whose flyleaf bore the legend: 'Manny "Terrible" Torres, 1734 West Nopal Street, Los Angeles, California, The United States, The Western Hemisfear, the World, The Universe.' A manual of spoken English whose first few pages were heavily underscored in pencil. The name on the flyleaf of this one was Lance Leonard.

The fourth and final book was a stamped-leather album of clippings. The newspaper picture on the first page showed a boyish Lance leaning wide-shouldered and wasp-waisted into the camera. The caption stated that Manny Torres was being trained by his Uncle Tony, veteran club-fighter, and experts conceded him an excellent chance of capturing the lightweight division of the Golden Gloves. There was no follow-up to this. The second entry was a short account of Lance Torres' professional debut; he had knocked out another welterweight in two minutes of the second round. And so on for twenty fights, through six-rounders up to twelve. None of the clippings mentioned his arrest and suspension.

I replaced the album on the shelf and went back to the dead man. His breast pocket contained an alligator billfold thick with money, a matching address book filled with girls' names and telephone numbers scattered from National City to Ojai. Two of the names were Hester Campbell and Rina Campbell. I wrote down their Los Angeles telephone numbers.

There was a gold cigarette case full of reefers in the side pocket of his dinner jacket. In the same pocket, I found an engraved invitation in an envelope addressed to Lance Leonard, Esq., at the Coldwater Canyon address. Mr and Mrs Simon Graff requested his presence at a Roman Saturnalia to be held at the Channel Club tonight.

I put everything back and stood up to leave, turned at the door for a final look at the boy. He lay exhausted by his incredible leap from nowhere into the sun. His face was old-ivory in the flashlight beam. I switched it off and let the darkness take him.

'Lance Manuel Purificación Torres Leonard,' I said out loud by way of epitaph.

Outside, a wisp of cloud dampened my face like cold and meager tears. I climbed on heavy legs to my car. Before I started the motor, I heard another motor whining up the grade from the direction of Ventura Boulevard. Headlights climbed the hanging cloud. I left my own lights off.

The headlights swerved around the final curve, projected by a dark sedan with a massive chrome cowcatcher. Without hesitating, they entered Leonard's driveway and lit up the front of his house. A man got out of the driver's seat and waded through the flowing light to the front door. He wore a dark raincoat belted tight at the waist, and he stepped lightly, with precision. All I could see of his head was the short, dark crewcut that surmounted it.

Having knocked and got no answer, he pulled out a flashing keyring and opened the door. The lights came on in the house. A minute later, half muffled by its redwood walls, a man's voice rose in a scream which sounded like a crow cawing. The lights went out again. The cawing continued for some time in the dark interior of the house.

There was an interval of silence before the door was opened. The man stepped out into the glare of his own headlights. He was Carl Stern. In spite of the crewcut and the neat bow tie, his face resembled an old woman's who had been bereaved.

He turned his sedan rather erratically and passed my car without appearing to notice it. I had to start and turn my car, but I caught him before he reached the foot of the hill. He went through boulevard stops as if he had a motorcycle escort. So did I. I had him.

Then we were on Manor Crest Drive, and I was completing the circuit of the roller-coaster. There was a difference, though. Hester's house was lighted upstairs and down. On the second floor, a woman's shadow moved across a blind. She moved like a young woman, with an eager rhythm.

Stern left his sedan in the driveway with the motor running, knocked and was admitted, came out again before I'd decided what to do. He got in and drove away. I didn't follow him. It was beginning to look as though Hester was home again.

XVI

I WENT IN by the broken lanai door and through to the front. Feet were busy on the floor over my head. I heard quick, clacking heels and a girl's tuneless humming. I climbed the stairs, leaning part of my weight on the banister. At the end of the upstairs hallway, light spilled from the doorway of the front bedroom. I moved along the wall to a point from which I could see into the room.

The girl was standing by the canopied bed with her back to me. She was very simply dressed in a tweed skirt and a short-sleeved white blouse. Her bright hair was brushed slick around the curve of her skull. A white leather suitcase with a blue silk lining lay open on the bed. She was folding some kind of black dress into it, tenderly.

She straightened and went to the far-side of the room, her hips swinging from a flexible small waist. She opened the mirror door of a closet and entered its lighted interior. When she came out, with more clothes in her arms, I was in the room.

Her body went stiff. The bright-coloured dresses fell to the floor. She stepped backward against the mirrored door, which closed with a snap.

'Hello, Hester. I thought you were dead.'

Her teeth showed, and she pressed her knuckles against them. She said behind the knuckles: 'Who are you?'

'The name is Archer. Don't you remember me from this morning?'

'Are you the detective—the one that Lance had a fight with?'

I nodded.

'What do you want with me?'

'A little talk.'

'You get out of here.' She glanced at the ivory telephone on the bedside table, and said uncertainly: 'I'll call the police.'

'I doubt that very much.'

She took her hand away from her mouth and laid it against her side below the swell of her breast, as though she felt a pain there. Anger and anxiety wrenched at her face, but she was one of those girls who couldn't look ugly. There was a sculptured beauty built into her bones, and she held herself with a sense that her beauty would look after her.

'I warn you,' she said, 'some friends of mine are coming here, any minute now.'

'Fine. I'd like to meet them.'

'You think so?'

'I think so.'

'Stick around if you like, then,' she said. 'Do you mind if I go on with my packing?'

'Go right ahead, Hester. You are Hester Campbell, aren't you?'

She didn't answer me or look at me. She picked up the fallen dresses, carried the rustling sheaf to the bed, and began to pack.

'Where are you going at this time of night?' I said.

'It's no concern of yours.'

'Cops might be interested.'

'Might they? Go and tell them, why don't you? Do anything you like.'

'That's kind of reckless talk for a girl on the lam.'

'I'm not on the lam, as you put it, and you don't frighten me.'

'You're just going away for a weekend in the country.'

'Why not?'

'I heard you tell Lance this morning that you wanted out.'

She didn't react to the name as I'd half suspected she would.

Her deft hands went on folding the last of the dresses. I liked her courage, and distrusted it. There could be a gun in the suitcase. But when she finally turned she was empty-handed.

'Wanted out of what?' I said.

'I don't know what you're talking about, and I couldn't care less.' But she cared.

'These friends of yours who are coming here—is Lance Leonard one of them?'

'Yes, and you better get out before he does come.'

'You're sure he's coming?'

'You'll see.'

'It ought to be something to see. Who's going to carry the basket?'

'The basket?' she said in a high little voice.

'Lance isn't getting around much any more. They have to carry him in a basket.'

Her hand went to her side again. The pain had risen higher. Her body moved angrily, hips and shoulders, trying to pass through the narrow space between the bed and me. I blocked her way.

'When did you see him last?'

'Tonight.'

'What time tonight?'

'I don't know. Several hours ago. Does it matter?'

'It matters to you. How was he when you left him?'

'He was fine. Why, has something happened to him?'

'You tell me, Hester. You leave a trail of destruction like Sherman marching through Georgia.'

'What happened? Is he hurt?'

'Badly hurt.'

'Where is he?'

'At home. He'll soon be in the morgue.'

'He's dying?'

'He's dead. Didn't Carl Stern tell you?'

She shook her head. It was more of a convulsion than a denial. 'Lance couldn't be dead. You're crazy.'

'Sometimes I think I'm the only one who isn't.'

She sat down on the edge of the bed. A row of tiny droplets stood along her peaked hairline. She brushed at them with her hand, and her right breast rose with the movement of her arm. She looked up at me, her eyes sleepy with shock. She was a very good actress, if she was acting.

I didn't think she was. 'Your good friend is dead,' I said. 'Somebody shot him.'

'You're lying.'

'Maybe I should have brought along the body. Shall I tell you where he took the slugs? One in the temple, one in the eye. Or do you know all this? I don't want to bore you to death.'

Her forehead crinkled. Her mouth stretched in the tragic rectangle.

'You're horrible. You're making all this up, trying to make me tell you things. You said the same thing about—about me—that I was dead.' Tears started in her eyes. 'You'd say anything to make me talk.'

'What kind of things could you tell me if you did?'

'I don't have to answer your questions, any of them.'

'Give it a little thought, and you might want to. It looks as though they're using you for a patsy.'

She gave me a bewildered look.

'You're kind of naïve, aren't you, in view of the company you keep? Nice company. They're setting you up for a murder rap. They saw a chance to kill two birds with one stone, to knock off Lance and fix you at the same time.'

I was playing by ear, but it was a familiar tune to me, and she was listening hard. She said in a hushed voice:

'Who would do such a thing?'

'Whoever talked you into taking a trip.'

'Nobody talked me into it. I wanted to.'

'Whose idea was it? Leroy Frost's?'

Her gaze flickered and dimmed.

'What did Frost tell you to do? Where did he tell you to go?'

'It wasn't Mr Frost. It was Lance who contacted me. So what you say can't be true. He wouldn't plan his own murder.'

'Not if he knew what the plan was. Obviously he didn't. They conned him into it the same way they conned you.'

'Nobody conned me,' she said stubbornly. 'Why would anybody try to con me?'

'Come off it, Hester, you're no ingenue. You know better than I do what you've been doing.'

'I haven't done anything wrong.'

'People have different standards, don't they? Some of us think that blackmail is the dirtiest game in the world.'

'Blackmail?'

'Look around you, and stop pretending. Don't tell me Graff's been giving you things because he likes the way you do your hair. I've seen a lot of blackmail in this town, it's got so I can smell it on people. And you're in it up to your neck.'

She fingered her neck. Her resistance to suggestion was wearing thin. She looked around at the pink walls and slowly turned their color. It was an authentic girlish blush, the first I had seen for some time, and it made me doubtful. She said:

'You're inventing all this.'

'I have to. You won't tell me anything. I go by what I see and hear. A girl leaves her husband, takes up with a washed-up fighter who runs with mobsters. In no time at all, you're in the chips. Lance has a movie contract, you have your nice big house in Beverly Hills. And Simon Graff turns out to be your fairy godmother. Why?'

She didn't answer. She looked down at her hands twisting in her lap.

'What have you been selling him?' I said. 'And what has Gabrielle Torres got to do with it?'

The color had drained out of her face, leaving it wan, blue-shadowed around the eyes. Her gaze turned inward on an image in her mind. The image seemed to appall her.

'I think you know who killed her,' I said. 'If you do, you'd better tell me. It's time to break these things out into the open, before more people are killed. Because you'll be next, Hester.'

Her lips flew open like a dummy's controlled by a ventriloquist: 'I'm not—' Her will took over, biting the sentence off.

She shook her head fiercely, dislodging tears from her eyes.

She covered her streaked face with her hands and flung herself sideways on the bed. Fear ran through her, silent and rigorous as an electric current, shaking her entire body. Something that felt like pity rose from the center of mine. The trouble with pity was that it always changed to something else—repulsion or desire. She lay still now, one hip arching up in a desolate slope.

'Are you going to tell me about Gabrielle?'

'I don't know anything to tell you.' Her voice was small and muffled.

'Do you know who shot Lance?'

'No. Leave me alone.'

'What did Carl Stern say to you?'

'Nothing. We had a date. He wanted to postpone it, that's all.'

'What kind of a date?'

'It's none of your business.'

'Is he going to take you for a ride?'

'Perhaps.' She seemed to miss the implication.

'A one-way ride?'

This time she caught it, and sat up almost screaming: 'Get away from me, you sadist. I know your kind. I've seen police detectives, and the way they torment helpless people. If you're a man at all, you'll get out of here.'

Her torso was twisted sideways, her breasts sharp under the white blouse. Her red lips curled, and her eyes sparked blue. She was an extraordinarily good-looking girl, but there was more to her than that. She sounded like a straight one.

I caught myself doubting my premises, doubting that she could be any kind of hustler. Besides, there was just enough truth in her accusation, enough cruelty in my will to justice, enough desire in my pity, to make the room uncomfortable for me. I said good-night and left it.

The problem was to love people, try to serve them, without wanting anything from them. I was a long way from solving that one.

XVII

THERE WAS NO guard on duty when I got to the Channel Club. The gate was open, though, and the party was still going on. Music and light spilled from one wing of the building. Several dozen cars stood in the parking-lot. I left mine between a black Porsche and a lavender Cadillac convertible with wine-colored leather upholstery and gold trim; and went in under the inverted red Christmas tree. It seemed to be symbolic of something, but I couldn't figure out what.

I knocked on Bassett's office door and got no answer. The pool was a slab of green brilliance, lit from below by underwater floodlights and spotlit from above. People were gathered at the far end under the aluminum-painted diving tower. I went down a shallow flight of steps and along the tiled edge toward the people.

Most of them were Hollywood fillies, sleek and self-conscious in strapless evening gowns or bathing suits not intended for the water. Among the men, I recognized Simon Graff and Sammy Swift and the Negro lifeguard I had talked to in the morning. Their faces were turned up toward a girl who stood absolutely still on the ten-meter platform.

She ran and took off into the light-crossed air. Her body bowed and turned in a smooth flip-and-a-half, changed from a bird to a fish as it entered the water. The spectators applauded. One of them, an agile youth in a dinner jacket and his middle forties, took a flashbulb picture as she came dripping up the ladder. She shook the water out of her short black hair contemptuously, and retired to a corner to dry herself. I followed her.

'Nice dive.'

'You think so?' She turned up her taut brown face and I saw that she wasn't a girl and hadn't been for years. 'I wouldn't give myself a score of three. My timing was way off. I can do it with a twist when I'm in shape. But thank you anyway.'

She toweled one long brown leg, and then the other, with a kind of impersonal affection, like somebody grooming a racehorse.

'You dive competitively?'

'I did at one time. Why?'

'I was just wondering what makes a woman do it. That tower's high.'

'A person has to be good at something, and I'm not pretty.' Her smile was thin and agonized. 'Dr Frey—he's a psychiatrist friend of mine—says the tower is a phallic symbol. Anyway, you know what the swimmers say— a diver is a swimmer with her brains knocked out.'

'I thought a diver was a swimmer with guts.'

'That's what the *divers* say. Do you know many divers?'

'No, but I'd like to. Would Hester Campbell be a friend of yours?'

Her face became inert. 'I know Hester,' she said cautiously. 'I wouldn't call her a friend.'

'Why not?'

'It's a long story, and I'm cold.' She turned brusquely and trotted away toward the dressing-room. Her hips didn't bounce.

'Quiet, everyone,' a loud voice said. 'You are about to witness the wonder of the century, brought to you at fabulous expense.'

It came from a gray-haired man on the five-meter platform of the tower. His legs were scrawny, his chest pendulous, his belly a brown leather ball distending his shorts. I looked again and saw it was Simon Graff.

'Ladies and gentlemen.' Graff shaded his eyes with a hand and looked around facetiously. 'Are there any ladies present? Any gentlemen?'

The women tittered. The men guffawed. Sammy Swift, who was standing near me, looked more than ever like a ghost who had seen a goblin.

'Watch it, boys and girls,' Graff shouted in a high, unnatural voice. 'The Great Graffissimo, in his unique and death-defying leap.'

He took a flat-footed little run and launched himself with his arms at his sides in what boys used to call a dead-soldier dive. His people waited until he came to the surface and then began to applaud, clapping and whistling.

Sammy Swift noticed my silence and moved toward me. He didn't recognize me until I called him by name. I could have set fire to his breath.

'Lew Archer, by damn. What are you doing in this *galère*?'

'Slumming.'

'Yah, I bet. Speaking of slumming, did you get to see Lance Leonard?'

'No. My friend got sick and we gave up on the interview.'

'Too bad, the boy's had quite a career. He'd make a story.'

'Fill me in.'

'Uh-uh.' He wagged his head. 'You tell your friend to take it up with Publicity. There's an official version and an unofficial version, I hear.'

'What do you hear in detail?'

'I didn't know you did leg work for newspapers, Lew. What's the pitch, you trying to get something on Leonard?'

His fogged eyes had cleared and narrowed. He wasn't as drunk as I'd thought, and the subject was touchy. I backed away from it:

'Just trying to give a friend a lift.'

'You looking for Leonard now? I haven't seen him here tonight.'

Graff raised his voice again:

'*Achtung*, everyone. Time for lifesaving practice.' His eyes were empty and his mouth was slack. He stepped toward the twittering line of girls and pointed at one who was wearing a silver gown. His forefinger dented her shoulder. 'You! What is your name?'

'Martha Matthews.' She smiled in an agony of delight. The lightning was striking her.

'You're a cute little girl, Martha.'

'Thank you.' She towered over him. 'Thank you very much, Mr Graff.'

'Would you like me to save your life, Martha?'

'I'd simply adore it.'

'Go ahead, then. Jump in.'

'But what about my dress?'

'You can take it off, Martha.'

Her smile became slightly dazed. 'I can?'

'I just said so.'

She pulled the dress off over her head and handed it to one of the other girls. Graff pushed her backward into the pool. The agile photographer took a shot of the action. Graff went in after her and towed her to the ladder, his veined hand clutching her flesh. She smiled and smiled. The lifeguard watched them with no expression at all on his black face.

I felt like slugging somebody. There wasn't anybody big enough around. I walked away, and Sammy Swift tagged along. At the shallow end of the pool, we leaned against a raised planter lush with begonia, and lit cigarettes. Sammy's face was thin and pale in the half-light.

'You know Simon Graff pretty well,' I stated.

His light eyes flickered. 'You got to know him well to feel the way I do about him. I been making a worm's-eye study of the Man for just about five years. What I don't know about him isn't worth knowing. What I do know about him isn't worth knowing, either. It's interesting, though. You know why he pulls his lifesaving stunt, for instance? He does it every party, just like clockwork, but I bet I'm the only one around who's got it figured out. I bet Sime doesn't even know, himself.'

'Tell me.'

Sammy assumed an air of wisdom. He said in the jargon of the parlor analyst:

'Sime's got a compulsion neurosis, he has to do it. He's fixated on this girl that got herself killed last year.'

'What girl would that be?' I said, trying to keep the excitement out of my voice.

'The girl they found on the beach with the bullets in her. It happened just below here.' He gestured toward the ocean, which lay invisible beyond the margin of the light. 'Sime was stuck on her.'

'Interesting if true.'

'Hell, you can take my word for it. I was with Sime that morning when he got the news. He's got a ticker in his office—he always wants to be the first to know—and when he saw her name on the tape he turned as white as a sheet, to coin a simile. Shut himself up in his private bathroom and didn't come out for an hour. When he finally did come out, he passed it off as a hangover. Hangover is the word. He hasn't been the same since the girl died. What was her name?' He tried to snap his fingers, unsuccessfully. 'Gabrielle something.'

'I seem to remember something about the case. Wasn't she a little young for him?'

'Hell, he's at the age when they really go for the young ones. Not that Sime's so old. It's only the last year his hair turned gray, and it was the girl's death that did it to him.'

'You're sure about this?'

'Sure, I'm sure. I saw them together a couple of times that spring, and I got X-ray eyes, boy, it's one thing being a writer does for you.'

'Where did you see them?'

'Around, and once in Vegas. They were lying beside the pool of one of the big hotels, smoking the same cigarette.' He looked down at the glowing butt of his own cigarette, and threw it spinning into the water. 'Maybe I shouldn't be telling tales out of school, but you won't quote me, and it's all in the past, anyway. Except that he keeps going through these crazy lifesaving motions. He's re-enacting her death, see, trying to save her from it. Only please note that he does it in a heated pool.'

'This is your own idea, no doubt.'

'Yeah, but it makes sense,' he said with some fanaticism. 'I been watching him for years, like you watch the flies on the wall, and I *know* him. I can read him like a book.'

'Who wrote the book? Freud?'

Sammy didn't seem to hear me. His gaze had roved to the far end of the pool, where Graff was posing for more pictures with some of the girls. I wondered why picture people never got tired of having their pictures taken. Sammy said:

'Call me Œdipus if you want to. I really hate that bastard.'

What did he do to you?'

'It's what he does to Flaubert. I'm writing the Carthage script, version number six, and Sime Graff keeps breathing down my neck.' His voice changed; he mimicked Graff's accent: 'Matho's our juvenile lead, we can't let him die on us. We got to keep him alive for the girl, that's basic. I got it. I got it. She nurses him back to health after he gets chopped up, how about that? We lose nothing by the gimmick, and we gain heart, the quality of heart. Salammbô rehabilitates him, see? The boy was kind of a revolutionary type before, but he is saved from himself by the influence of a good woman. He cleans up on the barbarians for her. The girl watches from the fifty-yard line. They clinch. They marry.' Sammy resumed his own voice: 'You ever read *Salammbô?*'

'A long time ago, in translation. I don't remember the story.'

'Then you wouldn't see what I'm talking about. *Salammbô* is a tragedy, its theme is dissolution. So Sime Graff tells me to tack a happy ending onto it. And I write it that way. Jesus,' he said in a tone of surprise, 'this is the way I've written it. What makes me do it to myself and Flaubert? I used to worship Flaubert.'

'Money?' I said.

'Yeah, Money. Money.' He repeated the word several times, with varying inflections. He seemed to be finding new shades of meaning in it, subtle drunken personal meanings which brought the tears into his voice. But he was too chancy and brittle to hold the emotion. He slapped himself across the eyes, and giggled. 'Well, no use crying over spilled blood. How about a drink, Lew? How about a drink of Danziger Goldwasser, in fact?'

'In a minute. Do you know a girl called Hester Campbell?'

'I've seen her around.'

'Lately?'

'No, not lately.'

'What's her relation to Graff, do you know?'

'No, I wouldn't know,' he answered sharply. The subject disturbed him, and he took refuge in clowning: 'Nobody tells me anything, I'm just an intellectual errand boy around here. An ineffectual intellectual errand boy. Song.' He began to sing in a muffled tenor to an improvised tune: 'He's so reprehensible yet so indispensable he maks things comprehensible he's my joy. That intellectual—ineffectual—but oh so sexual—intellectual errand boy. Whom nothing can alloy. . . . Dig that elegant whom.'

'I dug it.'

'It's the hallmark of genius, boy. Did I ever tell you I was a genius? I had an IQ of 183 when I was in high school in Galena, Illinois.' His forehead crinkled. 'What ever happened to me? Wha' happen? I used to like people, by damn, I used to have talent. I didn't know what it was worth. I came out here for the kicks, going along with the gag—seven fifty a week for playing word games. Then it turns out that it isn't a gag. It's for keeps, it's your life, the only one you've got. And Sime Graff has got you by the short hairs and you're not inner-directed any more. You're not yourself.'

'Who are you, Sam?'

'That's my problem.' He laughed, and almost choked. 'I had a vision of myself last week, I could see it as plain as a picture. Dirty word, picture, but let it pass. I was a rabbit running across a desert. Rear view.' He laughed and coughed again. 'A goddam white-tailed bunny rabbit going lickety-split across the great American desert.'

'Who was chasing you?'

'I don't know,' he said with a lopsided grin. 'I was afraid to look.'

XVIII

GRAFF CAME STRUTTING toward us along the poolside, trailed by his twittering harem and their eunuchs. I wasn't ready to talk to him, and turned my back until he'd passed. Sammy was yawning with hostility.

'I really need a drink,' he said. 'My eyes are focusing. How's about joining me in the bar?'

'Later, maybe.'

'See you. Don't quote me on anything.'

I promised that I wouldn't, and Sammy went away toward the lights and the music. At the moment the pool was deserted except for the Negro lifeguard, who was moving around under the diving tower. He trotted in my direction with a double armful of soiled towels, took them into a lighted room at the end of the row of *cabañas*.

I went over and tapped on the open door. The lifeguard turned from a canvas bin where he had dumped the towels. He had on gray sweat-clothes with CHANNEL CLUB stenciled across the chest.

'Can I get you something, sir?'

'No, thanks. How are the tropical fish?'

He gave me a quick grin of recognition. 'No tropical-fish trouble tonight. People trouble is all. There's always people trouble. Why they want to go swimming on a night like this! I guess it's the drinking they do. The way they pour it down is a revelation.'

'Speaking of pouring it down, your boss is pretty good at it.'

'Mr Bassett? Yeah, he's been drinking like a fish lately, ever since his mother died. A tropical fish. Mr Bassett was very devoted to his mother.' The black face was smooth and bland, but the eyes were sardonic. 'He told me she was the only woman he ever loved.'

'Good for him. Do you know where Bassett is now?'

'Circulating.' He stirred the air with his finger. 'He circulates around at all the parties. You want me to find him for you?'

'Not just now, thanks. You know Tony Torres?'

'Know him well. We worked together for years.'

'And his daughter?'

'Some,' he said guardedly. 'She worked here, too.'

'Would Tony still be around? He isn't on the gate.'

'No, he goes off at night, party or no party. His fill-in didn't show up tonight. Maybe Mr Bassett forgot to call him.'

Where does Tony live, do you know?'

'I ought to. He lives under my feet, practically. He's got a place next to the boiler room, he moved in there last year. He used to get so cold at night, he told me.'

'Show me, will you?'

He didn't move, except to look at his wristwatch. 'It's half past one. You wouldn't want to wake him up in the middle of the night.'

'Yes,' I said. 'I would.'

He shrugged and took me along a corridor filled with a soapy shower-room odor, down a flight of concrete steps into hothouse air, through a drying-room where bathing suits hung like sloughed snakeskins on wooden racks, between the two great boilers which heated the pool and the buildings. Behind them, a room-within-a-room had been built out of two-by-fours and plywood.

'Tony lives here because he wants to,' the lifeguard said rather defensively. 'He won't live in his house on the beach any more, he rents it out. I wish you wouldn't wake him up. Tony's an old man, he needs his rest.'

But Tony was already awake. His bare feet slithered on the floor. Light came on, blazing through all the cracks in the plywood walls and framing the door. Tony opened it and blinked at us, a big-bellied little old man in long underwear with a religious locket hanging around his neck.

'Sorry to get you out of bed. I'd like to talk to you.'

'What about? What's the trouble?' He scratched at his tousled, graying hair.

'No trouble.' Just two murders in his family, one of which I wasn't supposed to know about. 'May I come in?'

'Sure thing. Matter 'fact, I been thinking I'd like to talk to you.'

He pushed the door wide and stepped back with a gesture that was almost courtly. 'You comin' in, Joe?'

'I got to get back upstairs,' the lifeguard said.

I thanked him and went in. The room was hot and small, lit by a naked bulb on an extension cord. I'd never seen a monk's cell, but the room could probably have served as one. A blistered oak-veneer bureau, an iron cot, a kitchen chair, a doorless cardboard wardrobe containing a blue serge suit, a horsehide windbreaker, and a clean uniform. Faded blue flannelette sheets covered the cot, and an old brass-fitted suitcase protruded from underneath it. Two pictures shared the wall above the head of the bed. One was a hand-tinted studio photograph of a pretty dark-eyed girl in a white dress that looked like a high-school graduation dress. The other was a Virgin in four colors, holding a blazing heart in her extended hand.

Tony indicated the kitchen chair for me, and sat on the bed himself. Scratching his head again, he looked down at the floor, his eyes impassive as anthracite. The big knuckles of his right hand were jammed and swollen.

'Yeah, I been thinkin',' he repeated, 'All day and half of the night. You're a detective, Mr Bassett says.'

'A private one.'

'Yeah, private. That's for me. These country cops, who can trust 'em? They run around in their fancy auto*mo*biles and arrest people for no-taillight or throw-a-beer-can-in-the-highway-ditch. Something real bad happens, they ain't there.'

'They're usually there, Tony.'

'Maybe. I seen some funny things in my time. Like what happened last year, right in my own family.' His head turned slowly to the left, under intangible but irresistible pressure, until he was looking at the girl in the white dress. 'I guess you heard about Gabrielle, my daughter.'

'Yes. I heard.'

'Shot on the beach, I found her. March twenty-first, last year. She was gone all night supposed to be with a girl friend. I found her in the morning, eighteen years old, my only daughter.'

'I'm sorry.'

His black glance probed my face, gauging the depth of my sympathy. His wide mouth was wrenched by the pain of truth-telling: 'I ain't no bleeding heart. It was my fault, I seen it coming. How could I bring her up myself? A girl without a mother? A pretty young girl?' His gaze rotated in a quarter-circle again, and returned to me. 'What could I tell her what to do?'

'What happened to your wife, Tony?'

'My wife?' The question surprised him. He had to think for a minute. 'She run out on me, many years now. Run away with a man, last I heard she's in Seattle, she's always crazy for men. My Gabrielle took after her, I think. I went to Catholic Welfare, ask them what I should do, my girl is running out of control like a loco mare in heat—I didden say that to the Father, not them words.

'The Father says, put her in a convent school, but it was too much money. Too much money to save my daughter's life. All right, I saved the money, I got the money in the bank, nobody to spend it for.' He turned and said to the Virgin: 'I am a dirty old fool.'

'You can't live their life for them, Tony.'

'No. What I could do, I coulda kept her locked up with good people looking after her. I coulda kept Manuel out of my house.'

'Did he have something to do with her death?'

'Manuel is in jail when it happens. But he was the one started her running wild. I didden catch on for a long time, he taught her to lie to me. It was high-school basketball, or swimming team, or spend-the-night-with-a-friend. Alla time she was riding around on the back of motorcycles from Oxnard, learning to be a dirty—' His mouth clamped down on an unspoken word.

After a pause, he went on more calmly: 'That girl I seen with Manuel on the Venice Speedway in the low-top car. Hester Campbell. She's the one Gabrielle's supposed to spend the night with, the night that she got killed. Then you come here this morning asking about Manuel. It started me thinking, about who done it to her. Manuel and the blondie girl, why do they get together, can you tell me?'

'Later on I may be able to. Tell me, Tony, is thinking all you've been doing?'

'Huh?'

'Did you leave the Club today or tonight? Did you see your nephew Manuel?'

'No. No to both questions.'

'How many guns do you have?'

'Just the one.'

'What caliber?'

'Forty-five Colt revolver.' His mind was one-track and too preoccupied to catch the inference. 'Here.'

He reached behind the mashed pillow and handed me his revolver. Its chambers were full, and it showed no signs of having been fired recently. In any case, the shells I had found beside his nephew's body were medium-caliber, probably thirty-two's.

I hefted the Colt. 'Nice gun.'

'Yeah. It belongs to the Club. I got a permit to carry it.'

I gave it back to him. He pointed it at the door, sighting along the barrel. He spoke in a very old voice, dry, sexless, dreadful:

'If I ever know who killed her, this is what he gets. I don't wait for crooked cops to do my business.' He leaned forward and tapped my arm with the barrel, very lightly: 'You're a detective, mister, find me who killed my girl, you can have all I got. Money in the bank, over a thousand dollars, I *save* my money these days. Piece of rented property onna beach, mortgage all paid off.'

'Keep it that way. And put the gun away, Tony.'

'I was a gunner's mate in the World War Number One. I know how to handle guns.'

'Prove it. Too many people would get a boot out of it if I got myself drilled in a shooting accident.'

He slipped the revolver under the pillow and stood up. 'It's too late, huh? Nearly two years, a long time. You are not interested in wild-duck cases, you got other business.'

'I'm very much interested. In fact, this is why I wanted to talk to you.'

'It's what you call a coincidence, eh?' He was proud of the word.

'I don't believe much in coincidences. If you trace them back far enough, they usually have a meaning. I'm pretty sure this one has.'

'You mean,' he said slowly, 'Gabrielle and Manuel and Manuel's blondie?'

'And you, and other things. They all fit together.'

'Other things?'

'We won't go into them now. What did the cops tell you last March?'

'No evidence, they said. They poked around here a few days and closed down the case. They said some robber, but I dunno. What robber shoots a girl for seventy-five cents?'

'Was she raped?'

Something like dust gathered on the surface of his anthracite eyes. The muscles stood out in his face like walnuts of various sizes in a leather bag, altering its shape. I caught a glimpse of the gamecock passion that had held him up for six rounds against Armstrong in the old age of his legs.

'No rape,' he said with difficulty. 'Doctor at the autopsy says a man was with her some time in the night. I don't wanna talk about it. Here.'

He stooped and dragged the suitcase out from under the bed, flung it open, rummaged under a tangle of shirts. Stood up breathing audibly with a dog-eared magazine in his hand.

'Here,' he said violently. 'Read it.'

It was a lurid-covered true-crime book which fell open to an article near the middle entitled 'The Murder of the Violated Virgin.' This was an account of the murder of Gabrielle Torres, illustrated with photographs of her and her father, one of which was a smudgy reproduction of the photograph on the wall. Tony was shown in conversation with a sheriff's plainclothesman identified in the caption as Deputy Theodore Marfeld. Marfeld had aged since March of the previous year. The account began:

> It was a balmy Spring night at Malibu Beach, gay playground of the movie capital. But the warm tropical wind that whipped the waves shoreward seemed somehow threatening to Tony Torres, onetime lightweight boxer and now watchman at the exclusive Channel Club. He was not easily upset after many years in the squared circle, but tonight Tony was desperately worried about his gay young teen-aged daughter, Gabrielle.
>
> What could be keeping her? Tony asked himself again and again. She had promised to be in by midnight at the latest. Now it was three o'clock in the morning, now it was four

o'clock, and still no Gabrielle. Tony's inexpensive alarm clock ticked remorselessly on. The waves that thundered on the beach below his modest seaside cottage seemed to echo in his ears like the very voice of doom itself. . . .'

I lost patience with the clichés and the excess verbiage, which indicated that the writer had nothing much to say. He hadn't. The rest of the story, which I scanned in a hurry, leered a great deal under a veil of pseudo-poetic prose, on the strength of a few facts:

Gabrielle had a bad reputation. There had been men in her life, unnamed. Her body had been found to contain male seed and two bullets. The first bullet had inflicted a superficial wound in her thigh. This had bled considerably. The implication was that several minutes at least had elapsed between the firing of the first bullet and the firing of the second. The second had entered her back, found its way through the ribs, and stopped her heart.

Both slugs were twenty-two long, and had been fired from the same long-barreled revolver, location unknown. That is what the police ballistics experts said. Theodore Marfeld said—the quotation ended the article: 'Our daughters must be protected. I am going to solve this hideous crime if it takes me the rest of my life. At the moment I have no definite clues.'

I looked up at Tony. 'Nice fellow, Marfeld.'

'Yah.' He heard the irony. 'You know him, huh?'

'I know him.'

I stood up. Tony took the magazine from my hand, tossed it into the suitcase, kicked the suitcase under the bed. He reached for the string that controlled the light, and jerked the grief-stricken room downward into darkness.

XIX

I WENT UPSTAIRS and along the gallery to Bassett's office. He still wasn't in it. I went in search of a drink. Under the half-retracted roof of a great inner court, dancers were sliding around on the waxed tiles to the music of a decimated orchestra. JEREMY CRANE AND HIS JOY BOYS was the legend on the drum. Their sad musicians' eyes looked down their noses at the merrymaking squares. They were playing lilting melancholy Gershwin: 'Someone to Watch Over Me.'

My diving friend whose hips didn't bounce was dancing with the perennial-bachelor type who loved taking pictures. Her diamonds glittered on his willowy right shoulder. He didn't like it when I cut in, but he departed gracefully.

She had on a tiger-striped gown with a slashed neckline and a flaring skirt which didn't become her. Her dancing was rather tigerish. She plunged around as if she was used to leading. Our dance was politely intense, like an amateur wrestling match, with no breath wasted on words. I said when it ended:

'Lew Archer is my name. May I talk to you?'

'Why not?'

We sat at one of several marble-topped tables separated by a glass windscreen from the pool. I said:

'Let me get you a drink.'

'Thank you, I don't drink. You're not a member, and you're not one of Sime Graff's regulars. Let me guess.' She fingered her pointed chin, and her diamonds flashed. 'Reporter?'

'Guess again.'

'Policeman?'

'You're very acute, or am I very obvious?'

She studied me from between narrowed eyelids, and smiled narrowly. 'No, I wouldn't say you're obvious. It's just you asked me something about Hester Campbell before. And it kind of made me wonder if you were a policeman.'

'I don't follow your line of reasoning.'

'Don't you? Then how does it happen that you're interested in her?'

'I'm afraid I can't tell you that. My lips are sealed.'

'Mine aren't,' she said. 'Tell me, what is she wanted for? Theft?'

'I didn't say she was wanted.'

'Then she ought to be. She's a thief, you know.' Her smile had a biting edge. 'She stole from me. I left my wallet in the dressing-room in my *cabaña* one day last summer. It was early in the morning, no one was around except the staff, so I didn't bother locking up the place. I did a few dives and showered, and when I went to dress, my wallet was gone.'

'How do you know she took it?'

'There's no doubt whatever that she did. I saw her slinking down the shower-room corridor just before I found it missing. She had something wrapped in a towel in her hand, and a guilty smirk on her face. She didn't fool me for a minute. I went to her afterwards and asked her point-blank if she had it. Of course she denied it, but I could see the deceitful look in her eyes.'

'A deceitful look is hardly evidence.'

'Oh, it wasn't only that. Other members have suffered losses, too, and they always coincided with Miss Campbell's being around. I know I sound prejudiced, but I'm not, really. I'd done my best to help the girl, you see. I considered her almost a protégée at one time. So it rather hurt when I caught her stealing from me. There was over a hundred dollars in the wallet, and my driver's license and keys, which had to be replaced.'

'You say you caught her.'

'Morally speaking, I did. Of course she wouldn't admit a thing. She'd cached the wallet somewhere in the meantime.'

'Did you report the theft?' My voice was sharper than I intended.

She drummed on the tabletop with blunt fingertips. 'I must say, I hardly expected to be cross-questioned like this. I'm voluntarily giving you information, and I'm doing so completely without malice. You don't understand, I *liked* Hester. She had bad breaks when she was a kid, and I felt sorry for her.'

'So you didn't report it.'

'No, I didn't, not to the authorities. I did take it up with Mr Bassett, which did no good at all. She had him thoroughly hoodwinked. He simply couldn't believe that she'd do wrong—until it happened to him.'

'What happened to him?'

'Hester stole from him, too,' she said with a certain complacency. 'That is, I can't swear that she did, but I'm morally certain of it. Miss Hamblin, his secretary, is a friend of mine, and I hear things. Mr Bassett was dreadfully upset the day she left.' She leaned toward me across the table: I could see the barred rib-cage between her breasts. 'And Miss Hamblin said he changed the combination of his safe that very day.'

'All this is pretty tenuous. Did he report a theft?'

'Of course he didn't. He never said a word to anybody. He was too ashamed of being taken in by her.'

'And you've never said a word to anybody, either?'

'Until now.'

'Why bring it all out now?'

She was silent, except for her drumming fingers. The lower part of her face set in a dull, thick expression. She had turned her head away from the source of light, and I couldn't see her eyes. 'You asked me.'

'I didn't ask you anything specific.'

'You talk as if you were a friend of hers. Are you?'

'Are *you*?'

She covered her mouth with her hand, so that her whole face was hidden, and mumbled behind it: 'I thought she was my friend. I could have forgiven her the wallet, even. But I saw her last week in Myrin's. I walked right up to her, prepared to let bygones be bygones, and she snubbed me. She pretended not to know me.' Her voice became deep and harsh, and the hand in front of her mouth became a fist. 'So I thought, if she's suddenly loaded, able to buy clothes at Myrin's, the least she can do is repay me my hundred dollars.'

'You need the money, do you?'

Her fist repelled the suggestion, fiercely, as if I'd accused her of having a moral weakness, or a physical disease. 'Of course I don't need the money. It's the principle of the thing.' After a thinking pause she said: 'You don't like me the least little bit, do you?'

I hadn't expected the question, and I didn't have an answer ready. She had the peculiar combination of force and meanness you often find in rich, unmarried women. 'You're loaded,' I said, 'and I'm not, and I keep remembering the difference. Does it matter?'

'Yes, it matters. You don't understand.' Her eyes emerged from shadow, and her meager breast leaned hard against the table edge. 'It isn't the money, so much. Only I thought Hester *liked* me. I thought she was a true friend. I used to coach her diving, I let her use Father's pool. I even gave a party for her once—a birthday party.'

'How old was she?'

'It was her eighteenth birthday. She was the prettiest girl in the world then, and the nicest. I can't understand—what happened to all her niceness?'

'It's happening to a lot of people.'

'Is that a crack at me?'

'At me,' I said. 'At all of us. Maybe it's atomic fallout or something.'

Needing a drink more than ever, I thanked her and excused myself and found my way to the drinking-room. A curved mahogany bar took up one end of it. The other walls were decorated with Hollywood-Fauvist murals. The large room contained several dozen assorted couples hurling late-night insults at each other and orders at the Filipino bar-tenders. There were actresses with that numb and varnished look, and would-be actresses with that waiting look; junior-executive types hacking diligently at each other with their profiles; their wives watching each other through smiles; and others.

I sat at the bar between strangers, wheedled a whisky-and-water out of one of the white-coated Filipinos, and listened to the people. These were movie people, but a great deal of their talk was about television. They talked about communications media and the black list and the hook and payment for second showings and who had money for pilot films and what their agents said. Under their noise, they gave out a feeling of suspense. Some of them seemed to be listening hard for the rustle of a dropping option. Some of their eyes were knowing previews of that gray, shaking hangover dawn when all the mortgage payments came due at once and the options fell like snow.

The man on my immediate right looked like an old actor and sounded like a director. Maybe he was an actor turned director. He was explaining something to a frog-voiced whisky blonde: 'It means it's happening to you, you see. You're the one in love with the girl, or the boy, as the case may be. It's not the girl on the screen he's making a play for, it's you.'

'Empathy-schwempathy,' she croaked pleasantly. 'Why not just call it sex?'

'It isn't sex. It includes sex.'

'Then I'm for it. Anything that includes sex, I'm for it. That's my personal philosophy of life.'

'And a fine philosophy it is,' another man said, 'Sex and television are the opium of the people.'

'I thought marijuana was the opium of the people.'

'Marijuana is the *marijuana* of the people.'

There was a girl on my left. I caught a glimpse of her profile, young and pretty and smooth as glass. She was talking earnestly to the man beside her, an aging clown I'd seen in twenty movies.

'You said you'd catch me if I fell,' she said.

'I was feeling stronger then.'

'You said you'd marry me if it ever happened.'

'You got more sense than to take me seriously. I'm two years behind on alimony now.'

'You're very romantic, aren't you?'

'That's putting it mildly, sweetheart. I got some sense of responsibility, though. I'll do what I can for you, give you a telephone number. And you can tell him to send the bill to me.'

'I don't want your dirty telephone number. I don't want your dirty money.'

'Be reasonable. Think of it like it was a tumor or something—that is, if it really exists. Another drink?'

'Make mine prussic acid,' she said dully.

'On the rocks?'

I left half my drink standing. It was air I needed. At one of the marble-topped tables in the court, under the saw-toothed shadow of a banana tree, Simon Graff was sitting with his wife. His gray hair was still dark and slick from the shower. He wore a dinner jacket with a pink shirt and a red cummerbund. She wore a blue mink coat over a black gown figured with gold which was out of style. His face was brown and pointed, talking at her. I couldn't see her face. She was looking out through the windscreen at the pool.

I had a contact mike in my car, and I went out to the parking-lot to get it. There were fewer cars than there had been, and one additional one: Carl Stern's sedan. It had Drive-Yourself registration. I didn't take time to go over it.

Graff was still talking when I got back to the poolside. The pool was abandoned now, but wavelets still washed the sides, shining in the underwater light. Hidden from Graff by the banana tree, I moved a rope chair up against the windscreen and pressed the mike to the plate glass. The trick had worked before, and it worked again. He was saying:

'Oh yes, certainly, everything is my fault, I am your personal *bête noire*, and I apologize deeply.'

'Please, Simon.'

'Simon who? There is no Simon here. I am Mephisto Bête Noire, the famous hell husband. No!' His voice rose sharply on the word. 'Think a minute, Isobel, if you have any mind left to think with. Think of what I have done for you, what I have endured and continue to endure. Think where you would be if it weren't for my support.'

'This is support?'

'We won't argue. I know what you want. I know your purpose in attacking me.' His voice was smooth as butter salted with tears. 'You have suffered, and you want me to suffer. I refuse to suffer. You cannot make me suffer.'

'God damn you,' she said in a rustling whisper.

'God damn me, eh? How many drinks have you had?'

'Five or ten or twelve. Does it signify?'

'You know you cannot drink, that alcohol is death for you. Must I call Dr Frey and have you locked up again?'

'No!' She was frightened. 'I'm not drunk.'

'Of course not. You are sobriety personified. You are the girl ideal of the Women's Christian Temperance Union, *mens sana in corpore sano*. But let me tell you one thing, Mrs Sobriety. You are not going to ruin my party, no matter what. If you cannot or will not act as hostess, you will take yourself off, Toko will drive you.'

'Get *her* to be your hostess, why don't you?'

'Who? Who are you talking about?'

'Hester Campbell,' she said. 'Don't tell me you're not seeing her.'

'For business purposes. I have seen her for business purposes. If you have hired detectives, you will regret it.'

'I don't need detectives, I have my sources. Did you give her the house for business purposes? Did you buy her those clothes for business purposes?'

'What do you know about that house? Have you been in that house?'

'It's none of your business.'

'Yes.' The word hissed like steam escaping from an overloaded pressure system. 'I make it my business. Were you in that house today.'

'Maybe.'

'Answer me, crazy woman.'

'You can't talk to me like that.' She began to call him names in a low, husky voice. It sounded like something tearing inside of her, permitting the birth of a more violent personality.

She rose suddenly, and I saw her walking across the patio in a straight line, moving among the dancers as though they were phantoms, figments of her mind. Her hip bumped the door frame as she went into the bar.

She came right out again, by another door. I caught a glimpse of her face in the light from the pool. It was white and frightened-looking. Perhaps the people frightened her. She skirted the shallow end of the pool, clicking along on high heels, and entered a *canbaña* on the far side.

I strolled toward the other end of the pool. The diving tower rose gleaming against a bank of fog that hid the sea. The ocean end was surrounded by a heavy wire fence. From a locked gate in the fence, a flight of concrete steps led down to the beach. High tides had gnawed and crumbled the lower steps.

I leaned on the gatepost and lit a cigarette. I had to cup the match against the stream of cold air which flowed upward from the water. This and the heavy sky overhead created the illusion that I was on the bow of a slow ship, and the ship was headed into foggy darkness.

XX

SOMEWHERE BEHIND ME, a woman's voice rose sharp. A man's voice answered it and drowned it out. I turned and looked around the bright, deserted pool. The two were standing close together at the wavering margin of the light, so close they might have been a single dark and featureless body. They were at the far end of the gallery, maybe forty yards away from me, but their voices came quite clearly across the water.

'No!' she repeated. 'You're crazy. I did not.'

I crossed to the gallery and walked toward them, keeping in its shadow.

'I'm not the one who is crazy,' the man was saying. 'We know who's crazy, sweetheart.'

'Leave me alone. Don't touch me.'

I knew the woman's voice. It belonged to Isobel Graff. I couldn't place the man's. He was saying:

'You bitch. You dirty bitch. Why did you do it? What did he do to you?'

'I didn't. Leave me alone, you filth.' She called him other names which reflected on his ancestry and her vocabulary.

He answered her in a low, blurred voice I didn't catch. There were Lower East Side marbles in his mouth. I was close enough to recognize him now. Carl Stern.

He let out a feline sound, a mewling growl, and slapped her face, twice, very hard. She reached for his face with hooked fingers. He caught her by the wrists. Her mink coat slid from her shoulders and lay on the concrete like a large blue animal without a head. I started to run on my toes.

Stern flung her away from him. She thudded against the door of a *cabaña* and sat down in front of it. He stood over her, dapper and broad in his dark raincoat. The greenish light from the pool lent his head a cruel bronze patina.

'Why did you kill him?'

She opened her mouth and closed it and opened it, but no sound came. Her upturned face was like a cratered moon. He leaned over her in silent fury, so intent on her that he didn't know I was there until I hit him.

I hit him with my shoulder, pinned his arms, palmed his flanks for a gun. He was clean, in that respect. He bucked and snorted like a horse, trying to shake me off. He was almost as strong as a horse. His muscles cracked in my grip. He kicked at my shins and stamped my toes and tried to bite my arm.

I released him and, when he turned, chopped at the side of his jaw with my right fist. I didn't like men who bit. He spun and went down with his back to me. His hand dove up under his trouser-leg. He rose and turned in a single movement. His eyes were black nailheads on which his face hung haggard. A white line surrounded his mouth and marked the edges of his black nostrils, which glared at me like secondary eyes. Protruding from the fist he held at the center of his body was the four-inch blade of the knife he carried on his leg.

'Put it away, Stern.'

'I'll carve your guts.' His voice was high and rasping like the sound of metal being machined.

I didn't wait for him to move. I threw a sneak right hand which crashed into his face and rocked him hard. His jaw turned to meet the left hook that completed the combination and finished Stern. He swayed on his feet for a few seconds, then collapsed on himself. The knife clattered and flashed on the concrete. I picked it up and closed it.

Footsteps came trotting along the gallery. It was Clarence Bassett, breathing rapidly under his boiled shirt. 'What on earth?'

'Cat fight. Nothing serious.'

He helped Mrs Graff to her feet. She leaned on the wall and

straightened her twisted stockings. He picked up her coat, brushing it carefully with his hands, as though the mink and the woman were equally important.

Carl Stern got up groggily. He gave me a dull-eyed look of hatred. 'Who are you?'

'The name is Archer.'

'You're the eye, uh?'

'I'm the eye who doesn't think that women should be hit.'

'Chivalrous, eh? You're going to hate yourself for this Archer.'

'I don't think so.'

'I think so. I got a lot of friends. I got connections. You're through in LA, you know that? All finished.'

'Put it in writing, will you? I've been wanting to get out of the smog.'

'Speaking of connections,' Bassett said quietly to Stern, 'you're not a member of this club.'

'I'm a guest of a member. And you're going to get crucified, too.'

'Oh, my, yes. What fun. Whose guest would you happen to be?'

'Simon Graff's. I want to see him. Where is he?'

'We won't bother Mr Graff just now. And may I make a suggestion? It's getting latish, more for some than for others. Don't you think you'd better leave?'

'I don't take orders from servants.'

'Don't you indeed?' Bassett's smile was a toothy mask which left his eyes sad. He turned to me.

I said: 'You want to be hit again, Stern? It would be a pleasure.'

Stern glared at me for a long moment, red lights dancing on his shallow eyes. The lights went out. He said:

'All right. I'll leave. Give me back my knife.'

'If you promise to cut your throat with it.'

He tried to go into another fury, but lacked the energy. He looked sick. I tossed him the closed knife. He caught it and put it in the pocket of his coat, turned and walked away toward the entrance. He stumbled several times. Bassett marched behind him, at a distance, like a watchful policeman.

Mrs Graff was fumbling with a key at the door of the *cabaña.* Her hands were shaking, out of control. I turned the key for her and switched on the light. It was indirect, and shone from four sides on a bellying brown fishnet ceiling. The room was done in primitive Pacific style, with split-bamboo screens at the windows, grass matting on the floor, rattan armchairs and chaise longues. Even the bar in one corner was rattan. Beside it, at the rear of the room, two louvered doors opened into the dressing-rooms. The walls were hung with tapa cloths and Douanier Rousseau reproductions, bamboo-framed.

The only discordant note was a Matisse travel poster lithographed in brilliant colors and advertising Nice. Mrs Graff paused in front of it, and said to no one in particular:

'We have a villa near Nice. Father gave it to us as a wedding present. Simon was all for it in those days. All for me, and all for one.' She laughed, for no good reason. 'He won't even take me to Europe with him any more. He says I always make trouble for him when we go away together, any more. It isn't true, I'm as quiet as a quilt. He flies away on his trans-polar flights and leaves me here to rot in the heat and cold.'

She clasped her head with both hands, tightly, for a long moment. Her hair stuck up between her fingers like black untidy feathers. The silent pain she was fighting to control was louder than a scream.

'Are you all right, Mrs Graff?'

I touched her blue mink back. She sidestepped away from my touch, whirled the coat off, and flung it on a studio bed. Her back and shoulders were dazzling, and her breast over-flowed the front of her strapless dress like whipped cream. She held her body with a kind of awkward pride mixed with shame, like a young girl suddenly conscious of her flesh.

'Do you like my dress? It isn't new. I haven't been to a party for years and years and years. Simon doesn't take me any more.'

'Nasty old Simon,' I said. 'Are you all right, Mrs Graff?'

She answered me with a bright actress's smile which didn't go with the stiffness of the upper part of her face, the despair in her eyes:

'I'm wonderful. Wonderful.'

She did a brief dance-step to prove it, snapping her fingers at the end of rigid arms. Bruises were coming out on her white forearms, the size and color of Concord grapes. Her dancing was mechanical. She stumbled and lost a gold slipper. Instead of putting it on again, she kicked off the other slipper. She sat on one of the bar stools, wriggling her stockinged feet, clasping and rubbing them together. They looked like blind, flesh-colored animals making furtive love under the hem of her skirt:

'Incidentally,' she said, 'and accidentally, I haven't thanked you. I thank you.'

'What for?'

'For saving me from a fate worse than life. That wretched little drug-peddler might have killed me. He's terribly strong, isn't he?' She added resentfully: 'They're not supposed to be strong.'

'Who aren't? Drug-peddlers?'

'Pansies. All pansies are supposed to be weak. Like all bullies are cowards, and all Greeks run restaurants. That isn't a good example, though. My father was a Greek, at least he was a Cypriot, and, by God, he ran a restaurant in Newark, New Jersey. Great oaks from little acorns grow. Miracles of modern science. From a greasy spoon in Newark to wealth and decadence in one easy generation. It's the new accelerated pace, with automation.'

She looked around the alien room. 'He might as well have stayed in Cyprus, for God's sake. What good did it do me? I ended up in a therapy room making pottery and weaving rugs like a God-damn cottage industry. Except that *I* pay them. I always do the paying.'

Her contact seemed to be better, which encouraged me to say: 'Do you always do the talking, too?'

'Am I talking too much?' She gave me her brilliant, disorganized smile again, as if her mouth could hardly contain her teeth. 'Am I making any sense, for God's sake.'

'From time to time you are, for God's sake.'

Her smile became slightly less intense and more real. 'I'm sorry, I get on a talking jag sometimes and the words come out wrong and they don't mean what I want them to. Like in James Joyce, only to me it just *hap*pens. Did you know his daughter was schizzy?' She didn't wait for an answer. 'So sometimes I'm a wit and sometimes I'm a nit-wit, so they tell me.' She extended her bruise-mottled arm: 'Sit down and have a drink and tell me who *you* are.'

'Archer,' she repeated thoughtfully, but she wasn't interested in me. Memory flared and smoked inside of her like a fire in changing winds: 'I'm nobody in particular, either. I used to think I was. My father was Peter Heliopoulos, at least that's what he called himself, his real name was longer than that and much more complicated. And I was much more complicated, too. I was the crown princess, my father *called* me Princess. So now—' her voice jangled harshly off-key—'so now a cheap Hollywood drug-peddler can push me around and get away with it. In my father's day they would have flayed him alive. So what does my husband do? He goes into business with him. They're palsy-walsies, cerebral palsy-walsies.'

'Do you mean Carl Stern, Mrs Graff?'

'Who else?'

'What kind of business are they in?'

'Whatever people do in Las Vegas, gambling and helling around. I never go there myself, never go anywhere.'

'How do you know he's a drug-peddler?'

'I bought drugs from him myself when I ran out of doctors—yellow jackets and demerol and the little kind with the red stripe. I'm off drugs now, however. Back on liquor again. It's one thing Dr Frey did for me.' Her eyes focused on my face, and she said impatiently: 'You haven't made yourself a drink. Go ahead and make yourself a drink, and make one for me, too.'

'Do you think that's a good idea, Isobel?'

'*Don't* talk to me as though I were a child. I'm not drunk. I can hold my liquor.' The bright smile gashed her face. 'The only trouble with me is that I am somewhat crazy. But not at the moment. I was upset there for a moment, but you're very soothing and smoothing, aren't you? Kind of kind of kind.' She was mimicking herself.

'Any more,' I said.

'Any more. But you won't make fun of me, will you? I get so mad sometimes—angry-mad, I mean—when people mock my dignity. I may be going into wind-up, I don't know, but I haven't taken off yet. On my trans-polar flight,' she added wryly, 'into the wild black yonder.'

'Good for you.'

She nodded in self-congratulation. 'That was one of the wit ones, wasn't it? It isn't really true, though. When it happens, it isn't like flying or any sort of arrival or departure. The *feel* of things changes, that's all, and I can't tell the difference between me and other things. Like when Father died and I saw him in the coffin and had my first breakdown. I thought *I* was in the coffin. I felt dead, my flesh was cold. There was embalming fluid in my veins, and I could smell myself. At the same time I was lying dead in the coffin and sitting in the pew in the Orthodox Church, mourning for my own death. And when they buried him, the earth—I could hear the earth dropping on the coffin and then it smothered me and I was the earth.'

She took hold of my hand and held it, trembling. 'Don't let me talk so much. It does me harm. I almost *went*, just then.'

'Where did you go?' I said.

'Into my dressing-room.' She dropped her hand and gestured toward one of the louvered doors. 'For a second I was in there, watching us through the door and listening to myself. *Please* pour me a drink. It does me good, honestly. Scotch on the rocks.'

I moved around behind the bar and got ice cubes out of the small beige refrigerator and opened a bottle of Johnnie Walker and made a couple of drinks, medium strength. I felt more comfortable on the wrong side of the bar. The woman disturbed me basically, the way you can be disturbed by starvation in a child, or a wounded bird, or a distempered cat running in yellow circles. She seemed to be teetering on the verge of a psychotic episode. Also, she seemed to know it. I was afraid to say anything that might push her over the edge.

She raised her glass. The steady tremor in her hand made the brown liquor slosh around among the ice cubes. As if to demonstrate her self-control, she barely sipped at it. I sipped at mine, leaned on my elbow across the formica counter in the attitude of a bartender with a willing ear.

'What was the trouble, Isobel?'

'Trouble? You mean with Carl Stern?'

'Yes. He got pretty rough.'

'He hurt me,' she said, without self-pity. A taste of whisky had changed her mood, as a touch of acid will change the color of blue litmus paper. 'Interesting medical facts. I bruise very easily.' She exhibited her arms. 'I bet my entire body is covered with bruises.'

'Why would Stern do it to you?'

'People like him are sadists, at least a lot of them are.'

'You know a lot of them?'

'I've known my share. I attract them, apparently, I don't know why. Or maybe I do know why. Women like me, we don't expect too much. I don't expect *any*thing.'

'Lance Leonard one of them?'

'How should I know? I guess so. I hardly knew—I hardly knew the little mackerel.'

'He used to be a lifeguard here.'

'I don't mess with lifeguards,' she said harshly. 'What is this? I thought we were going to be friends, I thought we were going to have fun. I never have any *fun*.'

'Any more.'

She didn't think it was funny. 'They lock me up and punish me, it isn't fair,' she said. 'I did one terrible thing in my life, and now they blame me for everything that happens. Stern's a filthy liar. I never touched his lover-boy, I didn't even know that he was dead. Why would I shoot him? I have enough on my conscious—on my conscience.'

'Such as?'

She peered at my face. Hers was as stiff as a board. 'Such as, you're trying to pump me, aren't you, such as? Trying to dig things out of me?'

'Yes, I am. What terrible thing did you do?'

Something peculiar happened to her face. One of her eyes became narrow and sly, one became hard and wide. On the sly side, her upper lip lifted and her white teeth gleamed under it. She said: 'I'm a naughty, naughty, naughty girl. I watched them doing it. I stood behind the door and watched them doing it. Miracles of modern science. And I was in the room and behind the door.'

'What did you do?'

'I killed my mother.'

'How?'

'By wishing,' she said slyly. 'I wished my mother to death. Does that take care of your question, Mr Questionnaire? Are you a psychiatrist? Did Simon hire you?'

'The answer is no and no.'

'I killed my father, too. I broke his heart. Shall I tell you my other crimes? It's quite a decalogue. Envy and malice and pride and lust and rage. I'd sit at home and plan his death, by hanging, burning, shooting, drowning, poison. I'd sit at home and imagine him with them, all the young girls with their bodies and waving white legs. I sat at home and tried to have men friends. It never seemed to work out. They were exhausted by the heat and cold or else I frightened them. One of them told me I frightened him, the lousy little nance. They'd drink up my liquor and never come back.' She sipped from her glass. 'Go ahead,' she said. 'Drink up your liquor.'

'Drink up yours, Isobel. I'll take you home. Where do you live?'

'Quite near here, on the beach. But I'm not going home. You won't make me go home, will you? I haven't been to a party for so long. Why don't we go and dance? I am very ugly to look at, but I am a good dancer.'

'You are very beautiful, but I am lousy dancer.'

'I'm ugly,' she said. 'You mustn't mock me. I know how ugly I am. I was born ugly through and through, and nobody ever loved me.'

The door opened behind her, swinging wide. Simon Graff

appeared in the opening. His face was stony.

'Isobel! What kind of *Walpurgisnacht* is this? What are you doing here?'

Her reaction was slow, almost measured. She turned and rose from the stool. Her body was tense and insolent. The drink was shaking in her hand.

'What am I doing? I'm telling my secrets. I'm telling all my dirty little secrets to my dear friend.'

'You fool. Come home with me.'

He took several steps toward her. She threw her glass at his head. It missed him and dented the wall beside the door. Some of the liquid spattered his face.

'Crazy woman,' he said. 'You come home now with me. I will call Dr Frey.'

'I don't have to go with you. You're not my father.' She turned to me, the look of lopsided cunning still on her face. 'Do I have to go with him?'

'I don't know. Is he your legal guardian?'

Graff answered: 'Yes, I am. You will keep out of this.' He said to her: 'There is nothing but grief for you, for all of us, if you try to break loose from me. You would be really lost.' There was a new quality in his voice, a largeness and a darkness and an emptiness.

'I'm lost now. How lost can a woman get?'

'You will find out, Isobel. Unless you come with me and do as I say.'

'Svengali,' I said. 'Very old-hat.'

'Keep out of this, I warn you.' I felt his glance like an icicle parting my hair. 'This woman is my wife.'

'Lucky her.'

'Who are you?'

I told him.

'What are you doing in this club, at this party?'

'Watching the animals.'

'I expect a specific answer.'

'Try using a different tone, and you might get one.' I came around the end of the bar and stood beside Isobel Graff. 'You've been spoiled by all those yes-men in your life. I happen to be a no-man.'

He looked at me in genuine shock. Maybe he hadn't been contradicted for years. Then he remembered to be angry, and turned on his wife:

'Did he come here with you?'

'No.' She sounded intimidated. 'I thought he was one of your guests.'

'What is he doing in this *cabaña*?'

'I offered him a drink. He helped me. A man hit me.' Her voice was monotonous, threaded by a whine of complaint.

'What man hit you?'

'Your friend Carl Stern,' I said. 'He slapped her around and pushed her down. Bassett and I threw him out.'

'You threw him out?' Graff's alarm turned to anger, which he directed against his wife again: 'You permitted this, Isobel?'

She hung her head and assumed an awkward, ugly posture, standing on one leg like a schoolgirl.

'Didn't you hear me, Graff? Or don't you object to thugs pushing your wife around?'

'I will look after my wife in my own way. She is mentally disturbed, sometimes she requires to be firmly handled. You are not needed. Get out.'

'I'll finish my drink first, thank you.' I added conversationally: 'What did you do with George Wall?'

'George Wall? I know no George Wall.'

'Your strong-arm boys do—Frost and Marfeld and Lashman.'

The names piqued his interest. 'Who is this George Wall?'

'Hester's husband.'

'I am not acquainted with any Hester.'

His wife gave him a swift, dark look, but said nothing. I fixed him with my steeliest glance and tried to stare him down. It didn't work. His eyes were like holes in a wall; you looked through them into a great, dim, empty place.

'You're a liar, Graff.'

His face turned purple and white. He went to the door and called Bassett in a loud, trembling voice. When Bassett appeared, Graff said: 'I want this man thrown out. I don't permit party-crashers—'

'Mr Archer is not exactly a party-crasher,' Bassett said coolly.

'Is he a friend of yours?'

'I think of him as a friend, yes. A friend of brief standing, shall we say. Mr Archer is a detective, a private detective I hired for personal reasons.'

'What reasons?'

'A crackpot threatened me last night. I hired Mr Archer to investigate the matter.'

'Instruct him, then, to leave my friends alone. Carl Stern is an associate of mine. I want him treated with respect.'

Bassett's eyes gleamed wetly, but he stood up to Graff. 'I am manager of this club. As long as I am, I'll set the standards for the behavior of the guests. No matter whose friends they are.'

Isobel Graff laughed tinnily. She had sat down on her coat, and was plucking at the fur.

Graff clenched his fists at his sides and began to shake. 'Get out of here, both of you.'

'Come along, Archer. We'll give Mr Graff a chance to recover his manners.'

Bassett was white and scared, but he carried it off. I didn't know he had it in him.

XXI

WE WENT ALONG the gallery to his office. His walk was a stiff-backed, high-shouldered march step. His movements seemed to be controlled by a system of outside pressures that fitted him like a corset.

He brought glasses out of his portable bar and poured me a stiff slug of whisky, a stiffer one for himself. The bottle was a different bottle from the one I had seen in the morning, and it was nearly empty. Yet the long day's drinking, like a passage of years, had improved Bassett in some ways. He'd lost his jaunty self-consciousness, and he wasn't pretending to be younger than he was. The sharp skull pressed like a death mask behind the thin flesh of his face.

'That was quite a performance,' I said. 'I thought you were a little afraid of Graff.'

'I am, when I'm totally sober. He's on the board of trustees, and you might say he controls my job. But there are limits to what a man can put up with. It's rather wonderful not to feel frightened, for a change.'

'I hope I didn't get you into trouble.'

'Don't worry about me. I'm old enough to look after myself.' He waved me into a chair and sat behind his desk with the half-glass of neat whisky in his hand. He drank from it and regarded me over the rim. 'What brings you here, old man? Has something happened?'

'Plenty has happened. I saw Hester tonight.'

He looked at me as though I'd said that I had seen a ghost. 'You saw her? Where?'

'In her house in Beverly Hills. We had some conversation, which got us nowhere—'

'Tonight?'

'Around midnight, yes.'

'Then she's alive!'

'Unless she was wired for sound. Did you think she was dead?'

It took him a while to answer. His eyes were wet and glassy. Behind them, something obscure happened to him. I guessed he was immensely relieved. 'I was mortally afraid that she was dead. I've been afraid all day that George Wall was going to kill her.'

'That's nonsense. Wall has disappeared himself. He may be in a bad way. Graff's people may have killed him.'

Bassett wasn't interested in Wall. He came around the desk and laid a tense hand on my shoulder. 'You're not lying to me? You're certain that Hester's all right?'

'She was all right, physically, a couple of hours ago. I don't know what to make of her. She looks and talks like a nice girl, but she's involved with the crummiest crew in the Southwest. Carl

Stern, for instance. What do you make of her, Bassett?'

'I don't know what to make of her. I never have.'

He leaned on the desk, pressed his hand to his forehead, and stroked his long horse face. His eyelids lifted slowly. I could see the dull pain peering out from under them.

'You're fond of her, aren't you?'

'Very fond of her. I wonder if you can understand my feeling for the girl. It's what you might call an avuncular feeling. There's nothing—nothing fleshly about it at all. I've known Hester since she was an infant, her and her sister, too. Her father was one of our members, one of my dearest friends.'

'You've been here a long time.'

'Twenty-five years as manager. I was a charter member of the Club. There were twenty-five of us originally. Each of us put up forty thousand dollars.'

'You put up forty thousand?'

'I did. Mother and I were fairly well fixed at one time, until the crash of '29 wiped us out. When that happened, my friends in the Club offered me the post of manager. This is the first and only job I've ever had.'

'What happened to Campbell?'

'He drank himself to death. As I am doing, on a somewhat retarded schedule.' Grinning sardonically, he reached for his glass and drained it. 'His wife was a silly woman, completely impractical. Lived up Topanga Canyon after Raymond's death. I did what I could for the fatherless babes.'

'You didn't tell me all this yesterday morning.'

'No. I was brought up not to boast of my philanthropies.'

His speech was very formal, and slightly blurred. The whisky was getting to him. He looked from me to the bottle, his eyes swiveling heavily. I shook my head. He poured another quadruple shot for himself, and sipped at it. If he drank enough of it down, there would be no more pain behind his eyelids. Or the pain would take strange forms. That was the trouble with alcohol as a sedative. It floated you off reality for a while, but it brought you back by a route that meandered through the ash-dumps of hell.

I threw out a question, a random harpoon before he floated all the way down to Lethe: 'Did Hester doublecross you?'

He looked startled, but he handled his alcohol-saturated words with care: 'What in heaven's name are you talking about?'

'It was suggested to me that Hester stole something from you when she left here.'

'Stole from me? Nonsense.'

'She didn't rob your safe?'

'Good Lord, no. Hester wouldn't do a thing like that. Not that I have anything worth stealing. We handle no cash at the club, you know, all our business is done by chit—'

'I'm not interested in that. All I want is your word that Hester didn't rob your safe in September.'

'Of course she didn't. I can't imagine where you got such a notion. People have such poisonous tongues.' He leaned toward me, swaying slightly. 'Who was it?'

'It doesn't matter.'

'I say it does matter. You should check your sources, old man. It's character-assassination. What kind of a girl do you think Hester is?'

'It's what I'm trying to find out. You knew her as well as anyone, and you say she isn't capable of theft.'

'Certainly not from me.'

'From anyone?'

'I don't know what she's capable of.'

'Is she capable of blackmail?'

'You ask the weirdest questions— weirder and weirder.'

'Earlier in the day, you didn't think blackmail was so far-fetched. You might as well be frank with me. Is Simon Graff being blackmailed?'

He wagged his head solemnly. 'What could Mr Graff be blackmailed for?'

I glanced at the photograph of the three divers. 'Gabrielle Torres. I've heard that there was a connection between her and Graff.'

'What kind of connection?'

'Don't pretend to be stupid, Clarence. You're not. You knew

the girl—she worked for you. If there was a thing between her and Graff, you'd probably know it.'

'If there was,' he said stolidly, 'it never came to my knowledge.' He meditated for a while, swaying on his feet. 'Good Lord, man, you're not suggesting he *killed* her?'

'He could have. But Mrs Graff was the one I had in mind.'

Bassett gave me a stunned and murky look. 'What a perfectly dreadful notion.'

'That's what you'd say if you were covering for them.'

'But thish ish utterly—' He grimaced and started over: 'This is utterly absurd and ridiculous—'

'Why? Isobel is crazy enough to kill. She had a motive.'

'She isn't crazy. She was—she did have serious emotional problems at one time.'

'Ever been committed?'

'Not committed, I don't believe. She's been in a private sanitorium from time to time. Dr Frey's in Santa Monica.'

'When was she in last?'

'Last year.'

'What part of last year?'

'All of it. So you shee—' He waved his hand in front of his face, as if a buzzing fly had invaded his mouth. 'You see, it's quite impossible. Isobel was incarcerated at the time the girl was shot. Absolutely imposhible.'

'Do you know this for a fact?'

'Shertainly I do. I visited her regularly.'

'Isobel is another old friend of yours?'

'Shertainly is. Very dear old friend.'

'Old enough and dear enough to lie for?'

'Don't be silly. Ishobel wouldn't harm a living creashur.'

His eyes were clouding up, as well as his voice, but the glass in his hand was steady. He raised it to his mouth and drained it, then sat down rather abruptly on the edge of his desk. He swayed gently from side to side, gripping the empty glass in both hands as though it was his only firm support.

'Very dear old friend,' he repeated sentimentally. 'Poor Ishbel, hers is a tragic story. Her mother died young, her father gave her everything but love. She needed sympathy, someone to talk to. I tried to be that shomeone.'

'You did?'

He gave me a shrewd, sad look. The jolt of whisky had partly and temporarily sobered him, but he had reached the point of diminishing returns. His face was the color of boiled meat, and his thin hair hung lank at the temples. He detached one hand from its glass anchor and pushed his hair back.

'I know it sounds unlikely. Remember, this was twenty years ago. I wasn't always an old man. At any rate, Isobel liked older men. She was devoted to her father, but he couldn't give her the understanding she needed. She'd just flunked out of college, for the third or fourth time. She was terribly withdrawn. She used to spend her days here, alone on the beach. Gradually she discovered that she could talk to me. We talked all one summer and into the fall. She wouldn't go back to school. She wouldn't leave me. She was in love with me.'

'You're kidding.'

I was deliberately needling him, and he reacted with alcoholic emotionalism. Angry color seeped into his capillaries, stippling his gray cheeks with red:

'It's true, she loved me. I'd had emotional problems of my own, and I was the only one who understood her. And she respected me! I am a Harvard man, did you know that? I spent three years in France in the first war. I was a stretcher-bearer.'

That would make him about sixty, I thought. And twenty years ago he would have been forty to Isobel's twenty, say.

'How did you feel about her?' I said. 'Avuncular?'

'I loved her. She and my mother were the only two women I ever loved. And I'd have married her, too, if her father hadn't stood in the way. Peter Heliopoulos disapproved of me.'

'So he married her off to Simon Graff.'

'To Simon Graff, yah.' He shuddered with the passion of a weak and timid man who seldom lets his feelings show. 'To a climber and a pusher and a whoremonger and a cheat. I knew Simon Graff when he was an immigrant nobody, a nothing in this town. Assistant director on quickie Westerns with one decent suit to his name. I liked him, he pretended to like me. I lent him money, I got him a guest membership in the Club, I introduced him to people. I introduced him to Heliopoulos, by heaven. Within two years he was producing for Helio, and married to Isobel. Everything he has, everything he's done, has come out of that marriage. And he hasn't the common decency to treat her decently!'

He stood up and made a wide swashbuckling gesture which carried him sideways all the way to the wall. Dropping the glass, he spread the fingers of both hands against the wall to steady himself. The wall leaned toward him, anyway. His forehead struck the plaster. He jackknifed at the hips and sat down with a thud on the carpeted floor.

He looked up at me, chuckling foolishly. One of his boiled blue eyes was straight, and one had turned outward. It gave him the appearance of mild, ridiculous lunacy.

'There's a seavy hea running,' he said.

'We'll hatten down the batches.'

I took him by the arms and set him on his feet and walked him to his chair. He collapsed in it, hands and jaw hanging down. His divided glance came together on the bottle. He reached for it. Five or six ounces of whisky swished around in the bottom. I was afraid that another drink might knock him out, or maybe even kill him. I lifted the bottle out of his hands, corked it, and put it away. The key of the portable bar was in the lock. I turned it and put it in my pocket.

'By what warrant do you sequester the grog?' Working his mouth elaborately around the words, Bassett looked like a camel chewing. 'This is illegal—false seizure. I demand a writ of habeas corpus.'

He leaned forward and reached for my glass. I snatched it away. 'You've had enough, Clarence.'

'Make those decisions myself. Man of decision. Man of distinction. Bottle-a-day, by God. Drink you under table.'

'I don't doubt it. Getting back to Simon Graff, you don't like him much?'

'Hate him,' he said. 'Lez be frank. He stole away only woman

I ever loved. 'Cept Mother. Stole my maître dee, too. Best maître dee in Southland, Stefan. They offered him double shallery, spirited him away to Las Vegas.'

'Who did?'

'Graff and Stern. Wanted him for their slo-called club.'

'Speaking of Graff and Stern, why would Graff be fronting for a mobster?'

'Sixty-four-dollar question, *I* don't know the ansher. Wouldn't tell *you* if did know. *You* don't like me.'

'Buck up, Clarence. I like you fine.'

'Liar. Cruel and inhuman.' Two tears detached themselves from the corners of his eyes and crawled down his grooved cheeks like little silver slugs. 'Won't give me a drink. Trying to make me talk, withholding my grog. 'Snot fair, 'snot humane.'

'Sorry. No more grog tonight. You don't want to kill yourself.'

'Why not? All alone in the world. Nobody loves me.' He wept suddenly and copiously, so that his whole face was wet. Transparent liquid streamed from his nose and mouth. Great sobs shook him like waves breaking in his body.

It wasn't a pretty sight. I started out.

'Don't leave me,' he said between sobs. 'Don't leave me alone.'

He came around the desk, buckled at the knees as if he'd struck an invisible wire, and lay full-length on the carpet, blind and deaf and dumb. I turned his head sideways so that he wouldn't smother and went outside.

XXII

THE AIR WAS turning chilly. Laughter and other party sounds still overflowed the bar, but the music in the court had ceased. A car toiled up the drive to the highway, and then another. The party was breaking up.

There was light in the lifeguard's room at the end of the row of *cabañas*. I looked in. The young Negro was sitting inside, reading a book. He closed it when he saw me, and stood up. The name of the book was *Elements of Sociology.*

'You're a late reader.'

'Better late than never.'

'What do you do with Bassett when he passes out?'

'Is he passed out again?'

'On the floor of his office. Does he have a bed around?'

'Yeah, in the back room.' He made a resigned face. 'Guess I better put him in it, eh?'

'Need any help?'

'No, thanks, I can handle him myself, I had plenty of practice.' He smiled at me, less automatically than before. 'You a friend of Mr Bassett's?'

'Not exactly.'

'He give you some kind of a job?'

'You could say that.'

'Working around the Club here?'

'Partly.'

He was too polite to ask what my duties were. 'Tell you what, I'll pour Mr Bassett in bed, you stick around, I'll make you a cup of coffee.'

'I could use a cup of coffee. The name is Lew Archer, by the way.'

'Joseph Tobias.' His grip was the kind that bends horse-shoes. 'Kind of an unusual name, isn't it? You can wait here, if you like.'

He trotted away. The storeroom was jammed with folded beach umbrellas, piled deckchairs, deflated plastic floats and beach balls. I set up one of the deckchairs for myself and stretched out on it. Tiredness hit me like pentothal. Almost immediately, I went to sleep.

When I woke up, Tobias was standing beside me. He had opened a black iron switchbox on the wall. He pulled a series of switches, and the glimmering night beyond the open door turned charcoal gray. He turned and saw that I was awake.

'Didn't like to wake you up. You look tired.'

'Don't you ever get tired?'

'Nope. For some reason I never do. Only time in my life I got tired was in Korea. There I got bone-tired, pushing a jeep through that deep mud they have. You want your coffee now?'

'Lead me to it.'

He led me to a brightly lighted white-walled room with SNACK BAR over the door. Behind the counter, water was bubbling in a glass coffee-maker. An electric clock on the wall was taking spasmodic little bites of time. It was a quarter to four.

I sat on one of the padded stools at the counter. Tobias vaulted over the counter and landed facing me with a dead-pan expression.

'Cuchulain the Hound of Ulster,' he said surprisingly. 'When Cuchulain was weary and exhausted from fighting battles, he'd go down by the riverside and exercise. That was his way of resting. I turned the fire on under the grill in case we wanted eggs. I could use a couple of eggs or three, personally.'

'Me, too.'

'Three?'

'Three.'

'How's about some tomato juice to start out with? It clarifies the palate.'

'Fine.'

He opened a large can and poured two glasses of tomato juice. I picked up my glass and looked at it. The juice was thick and dark red in the fluorescent light. I put the glass down again.

'Something the matter with the juice?'

'It looks all right to me,' I said unconvincingly.

He was appalled by this flaw in his hospitality. 'What is it—dirt in the juice?' He leaned across the counter, his forehead wrinkled with solicitude. 'I just opened the can, so if there's something in it, it must be the cannery. Some of these big corporations think that they can get away with murder, especially now that we have a businessmen's administration. I'll open another can.'

'Don't bother.'

I drank the red stuff down. It tasted like tomato juice.

'Was it all right?'

'It was very good.'

'I was afraid there for a minute that there was something the matter with it.'

'Nothing the matter with it. The matter was with me.'

He took six eggs out of the refrigerator and broke them onto the grill. They sputtered cozily, turning white at the edges. Tobias said over his shoulder:

'It doesn't alter what I said about the big corporations. Mass production and mass marketing do make for some social benefits, but sheer size tends to militate against the human element. We've reached the point where we should count the human cost. How do you like your eggs?'

'Over easy.'

'Over easy it is.' He flipped the six eggs with a spatula, and inserted bread in the four-hole toaster. 'You want to butter your own toast, or you want me to butter it for you? I have a butter brush. Personally, I prefer that, myself.'

'You butter it for me.'

'Will do. Now how do you like your coffee?'

'At this time in the morning, black. This is a very fine service you have here.'

'We endeavor to please. I used to be a snack-bar bus boy before I switched over to lifeguard. Lifeguard doesn't pay any better, but it gives me more time to study.'

'You're a student, are you?'

'Yes, I am.' He dished up our eggs and poured our coffee. 'I bet you're surprised at the facility with which I express myself.'

'You took the words right out of my mouth.'

He beamed with pleasure, and took a bite of toast. When he had chewed and swallowed it, he said: 'I don't generally let the language flow around here. People, the richer they get, the more they dislike to hear a Negro express himself in well-chosen words. I guess they feel there's no point in being rich unless you can feel superior to somebody. I study English on the college level, but if I talked that way I'd lose my job. People are very sensitive.'

'You go to UCLA?'

'Junior College. I'm working up to UCLA. Heck,' he said, 'I'm only twenty-five, I've got plenty of time. 'Course I'd be way ahead of where I am now if I'd of caught on sooner. It took a hitch in the Army to jolt me out of my unthinking complacency.' He rolled the phrase lovingly on his tongue. 'I woke up one night on a cold hill on the way back from the Yalu. And suddenly it hit me—wham!—I didn't know what it was all about.'

'The war?'

'Everything. War and peace. Values in life.' He inserted a forkful of egg into his mouth and munched at me earnestly. 'I realized I didn't know who *I* was. I wore this kind of mask, you know, over my face and over my mind, this kind of blackface mask, and it got so I didn't know who I was. I decided I had to find out who I was and be a man. If I could make it. Does that sound like a foolish thing for a person like me to decide?'

'It sounds sensible to me.'

'I thought so at the time. I still do. Another coffee?'

'Not for me, thanks. You have another.'

'No, I'm a one-cup man, too. I share your addiction for moderation.' He smiled at the sound of the words.

'What do you plan to do in the long run?'

'Teach school. Teach and coach.'

'It's a good life.'

'You bet it is. I'm looking forward to it.' He paused, taking time out to look forward to it. 'I love to tell people important things. Especially kids. I love to communicate values, ideas. What do you do, Mr Archer?'

'I'm a private detective.'

Tobias looked a little disappointed in me. 'Isn't that kind of a dull life? I mean, it doesn't bring you into contact with ideas very much. Not,' he added quickly, for fear he had hurt my feelings, 'not that I place *ideas* above other values. Emotions. Action. Honorable action.'

'It's a rough life,' I said. 'You see people at their worst. How's Bassett, by the way?'

'Dead to the world. I put him to bed. He sleeps it off without any trouble, and *I* don't mind putting him to bed. He treats me pretty well.'

'How long have you worked here?'

'Over three years. I started out in the snack bar here, and shifted over to lifeguard summer before last.'

'You knew Gabrielle here, then.'

He answered perfunctorily: 'I knew her. I told you that.'

'At the time that she was murdered?'

His face closed up entirely. The brightness left his eyes like something quick and timid retreating into its hole. 'I don't know what you're getting at.'

'Nothing to do with you. Don't run out on me, Joseph, just because I asked you a couple of questions.'

'I'm not running out.' But his voice was dull and sing-song. 'I already answered all the questions there are.'

'What do you mean?'

'You know what I mean, if you're a detective. When Gabrielle—when Miss Torres was killed, I was the very first one that they arrested. They took me down to the sheriff's station and questioned me in relays, all day and half the night.'

He hung his head under the weight of the memory. I hated to see him lose his fine *élan.*

'Why did they pick on you?'

'For no good reason.' He raised his hand and turned it before his eyes. It was burnished black in the fluorescent light.

'Didn't they question anybody else?'

'Sure, when I proved to them I was at home all night. They picked up some winoes and sex deviates that live around Malibu and up the canyons, and some hoboes passing through. And they asked Miss Campbell some questions.'

'Hester Campbell?'

'Yes. She was the one that Gabrielle was supposed to be spending the evening with.'

'How do you know?'

'Tony said so.'

'Where did she really spend the evening?'

'How would I know that?'

'I thought you might have some idea.'

'You thought wrong, then.' His gaze, which had been avoiding mine, returned slowly to my face. 'Are you reopening that murder case? Is that what Mr Bassett hired you to do?'

'Not exactly. I started out investigating something else, but it keeps leading me back to Gabrielle. How well did you know her, Joseph?'

He answered carefully: 'We worked together. Weekends, she took orders for sandwiches and drinks around the pool and in the *cabañas*. She was too young to serve the drinks herself, so I did that. Miss Torres was a very nice young lady to work with. I hated to see the thing that happened to her.'

'You saw what happened to her?'

'I don't mean that. I didn't see what happened to her when it happened. But I was right here in this room when Tony came up from the beach. Somebody shot her, I guess you know that, shot her and left her lying just below the Club. Tony lived down the shore a piece from here. He expected Gabrielle home by midnight. When she didn't come home, he phoned the Campbell's house. They said they hadn't seen her, so he went out looking for her. He found her in the morning with bulletholes in her, the waves splashing up around her. She was supposed to be helping Mrs Lamb that day, and Tony came up here first thing to tell Mrs Lamb about it.'

Tobias licked his dry lips. His eyes looked through me at the past. 'He stood right there in front of the counter. For a long time he couldn't say a word. He couldn't open his mouth to tell Mrs Lamb that Gabrielle was dead. She could see that he needed comfort, though. She walked around the end of the counter and put her arms around him and held him for a while like he was a child. Then he told her. Mrs Lamb sent me to call the police.'

'You called them yourself?'

'I was going to. But Mr Bassett was in his office. He called them. I went down to the end of the pool and peeked down through the fence. She was lying there in the sand, looking up at the sky. Tony had pulled her up out of the surf. I could see sand in her eyes. I wanted to go down and wipe the sand out of her eyes, but I was afraid to go down there.'

'Why?'

'She had no clothes on. She looked so *white*. I was afraid they'd come and catch me down there and get a crazy idea about me. They went ahead and got their ideas anyway. They arrested me right that very morning. I was half expecting it.'

'You were?'

'People have to blame somebody. They've been blaming us for three hundred years now. I guess I had it coming. I shouldn't have let myself get—friendly with her. And then, to make it worse, I had this earring belonging to her in my pocket.'

'What earring was that?'

'A little round earring she had, made of mother-of-pearl. It was shaped like a lifesaving belt, with a hole in the middle, and USS Malibu printed on it. The heck of it was, she was still—the other earring that matched it was still on her ear.'

'How did you happen to have the earring?'

'I just picked it up,' he said, 'and I was going to give it back to her. I found it alongside the pool,' he added after a moment.

'That morning?'

'Yes. Before I knew she was dead. That Marfeld and the other cops made a big deal about it. I guess they thought they had it made, until I proved out my alibi.' He made a sound which was half snort and half groan. 'As if I'd lay a hand on Gabrielle to hurt her.'

'Were you in love with her, Joseph?'

'I didn't say that.'

'It's true, though, isn't it?'

He rested his elbow on the counter and his chin on his hand, as though to steady his thinking. 'I could have been,' he admitted, 'if I'd had a chance with her. Only there was no mileage in it. She was only half Spanish-American, and she never really saw me as a human being.'

'That could be a motive for murder.'

I watched his face. It lengthened, but it showed no other sign of emotion. The planes of his cheeks, his broad lips, had the look of a carved and polished mask balanced on his palm.

'You didn't kill her yourself, Joseph?'

He winced, but not with surprise, as though I'd pressed on the scar of an old wound. He shook his head sadly. 'I wouldn't hurt a hair on her head, and you know it.'

'All right. Let it pass.'

'I won't let it pass. You can take it back or get out of here.'

'All right. I take it back.'

'You shouldn't have said it in the first place. She was my friend. I thought you were my friend.'

'I'm sorry, Joseph. I have to ask these questions.'

'Why do you have to? Who makes you? You should be careful what you say about who did what around here. Do you know what Tony Torres would do if he thought I killed his girl?'

'Kill you.'

'That's right. He threatened to kill me when the police turned me loose. It was all I could do to talk him out of it. He gets these fixed ideas in his head, and they stick there like a bur. And he's got a lot of violence in him yet.'

'So do we all.'

'I know it, Mr Archer. I know it in myself. Tony's got more than most. He killed a man with his fists once, when he was young.'

'In the ring?'

'Not in the ring, and it wasn't an accident. It was over a woman, and he meant to do it. He asked me down to his room one night and got drunk on muscatel and told me all about it.'

'When was this?'

'A couple of months ago. I guess it was really eating him up. Gabrielle's mother was the woman, you see. He killed the man that she was running with, and she left him. The other man had a knife, so the judge in Fresno called it self-defense, but Tony blamed himself. He connected it up with Gabrielle, said that what happened to her was God's punishment on him. Tony's very superstitious.'

'You know his nephew Lance?'

'I know him.' Joseph's tone defined his attitude. It was negative. 'He used to have the job I have a few years back, when I started in the snack bar. I heard he's a big wheel now, it's hard to believe. He was so bone lazy he couldn't even hold a lifeguard job without his uncle filling in for him. Tony used to do his clean-up work while Lance practiced fancy diving.'

'How does Tony feel about him now?'

Joseph scratched his tight hair. 'He finally caught on to him. I'd say he almost hates him.'

'Enough to kill him?'

'What's all this talk about killing, Mr Archer? Did somebody get killed?'

'I'll tell you, if you can keep a secret.'

'I can keep a secret.'

'See that you do. Your friend Lance was shot last night.'

He didn't lift his eyes from the counter. 'He was no friend of mine. He was nothing in my life.'

'He was in Tony's.'

He shook his head slowly from side to side. 'I shouldn't have told you what I did about Tony. He did something once when he was young and crazy. He wouldn't do a thing like that again. He wouldn't hurt a flea, unless it was biting him.'

'You can't have it both ways at once, Joseph. You said he hated Lance.'

'I said almost.'

'Why did he hate him?'

'He had good reason.'

'Tell me.'

'Not if you're going to turn it against Tony. That Lance isn't fit to tie his shoelaces for him.'

'You think yourself that Tony may have shot him.'

'I'm not saying what I think, I don't think anything.'

'You said he had good reason. What was the reason?'

'Gabrielle,' he said to the floor. 'Lance was the first one she went with, back when she was just a kid in high school. She told me that. He started her drinking, he taught her all the ways of doing it. If Tony shot that *pachuco*, he did a good service to the world.'

'Maybe, but not to himself. You say Gabrielle told you all these things?'

He nodded, and his black, despondent shadow nodded with him.

'Were you intimate with her?'

'I never was, not if you mean what I think you mean. She treated me like I had no human feelings. She used to torture me with these things she told me—the things he taught her to do.' His voice was choked. 'I guess she didn't know she was torturing me. She just didn't know I had feelings.'

'You've got too many feelings.'

'Yes, I have. They break me up inside sometimes. Like when she told me what he wanted her to do. He wanted her to go to LA with him and live in a hotel, and he would get her dates with men. I blew my top on that one, and went to Tony with it. That was when he broke off with Lance, got him fired from here and kicked him out of the house.'

'Did Gabrielle go with him?'

'No, she didn't. I thought with him out of the way, maybe she'd straighten out. But it turned out to be too late for her. She was already gone.'

'What happened to her after that?'

'Listen, Mr Archer,' he said in a tight voice. 'You could get me in trouble. Spying on the members is no part of my job.'

'What's a job?'

'It isn't the job. I could get another job. I mean really bad trouble.'

'Sorry. I didn't mean to frighten you. I thought you wanted to be serviceable.'

XXIII

HE LOOKED UP at the light. His face was smooth. No moral strain showed. But I could feel the cracking tension in him.

'Gabrielle is dead,' he said to the unblinking light. 'What service can I do her by talking about her?'

'There are other girls, and it could happen to them.'

His silence stretched out. Finally he said:

'I'm not as much of a coward as you think. I tried to tell the policemen, when they were asking me questions about the earring. But they weren't interested in hearing about it.'

'Hearing about what?'

'If I've got to say it, I'll say it. Gabrielle used to go in one of the *cabañas* practically every day and stay there for an hour or more.'

'All by herself?'

'You know I don't mean that.'

'Who was with her, Joseph?'

I was almost certain what his answer would be.

'Mr Graff used to be with her.'

'You're sure of that?'

'I'm sure. You don't understand about Gabrielle. She was young and silly, proud that a man like Mr Graff would take an interest in her. Besides, she wanted me to cover for her by taking orders in the other *cabañas* when she was—otherwise occupied. She wasn't ashamed for me to know,' he added bitterly. 'She was just ashamed for Mrs Lamb to know.'

'Did they ever meet here at night?' I said. 'Graff and Gabrielle?'

'Maybe they did. I don't know. I never worked at night in those days.'

'She was in the Club the night she was killed,' I said. 'We know that.'

'How do we know that? Tony found her on the beach.'

'The earring you found. Where was it you found it?'

'On the gallery in front of the *cabañas*. But she could have dropped it there any time.'

'Not if she was still wearing the other one. Do you know for a fact that she was, or is this just what they told you?'

'I know it for a fact. I saw it myself. When they were asking me questions, they took me down to where she was. They opened up the drawer and made me look at her. I saw the little white earring on her ear.'

Tears started in his eyes, the color of blue-black ink. Memory had given him a sudden stab. I said:

'Then she must have been in the Club shortly before she was killed. When a girl loses one earring, she doesn't go on wearing the other one. Which means that Gabrielle didn't have time to notice the loss. It's possible that she lost it at the precise time that she was being killed. I want you to show me where you found it, Joseph.'

Outside, first light was washing the eastern slopes of the sky. The sparse stars were melting in it like grains of snow on stone. Under the dawn wind, the pool was gray and restless like a coffined piece of the sea.

Tobias led me along the gallery, about half the length of the pool. We passed the closed doors of half-a-dozen *cabañas*, including Graff's. I noticed that the spring had gone out of his walk. His sneakered feet slapped the concrete disconsolately. He stopped and turned to me:

'It was right about here, caught in this little grid.' A circular wire grating masking a drain was set into a shallow depression in the concrete. 'Somebody'd hosed down the gallery and washed it into the drain. I just happened to see it shine.'

'How do you know somebody hosed the gallery?'

'It was still wet in patches.'

'Who did it, do you know?'

'Could have been anybody, anybody that worked around the pool. Or any of the members. You never can tell what the members are going to do.'

'Who worked around the pool at that time?'

'Me and Gabrielle, mostly, and Tony and the lifeguard. . . . No, there wasn't any lifeguard just then—not until I took over in the summer. Miss Campbell was filling in as lifeguard.'

'Was she there that morning?'

'I guess she was. Yes, I remember she was. What are you trying to get at, Mr Archer?'

'Who killed Gabrielle, and why and where and how.'

He leaned against the wall, his shoulders high. His eyes and mouth gleamed in his black basalt face. 'For God's sake, Mr Archer, you're not pointing the finger at me again?'

'No. I'd like your opinion. I think that Gabrielle was killed in the Club, maybe right on this spot. The murderer dragged her down to the beach, or else she crawled there under her own power. She left a trail of blood, which had to be washed away. And she dropped an earring, which didn't get washed away.'

'A little earring isn't much to go on.'

'No,' I said, 'It isn't.'

'You think Miss Campbell did all this?'

'It's what I want your opinion about. Did she have any reason, any motive?'

'Could be she had.' He licked his lips. 'She made a play for Mr Graff herself, only he didn't go for her.'

'Gabrielle told you this?'

'She told me Miss Campbell was jealous of her. She didn't have to tell me. I can see things for myself.'

'What did you see?'

'The dirty looks between them, all that spring. They were still friends in a way, you know how girls can be, but they didn't like each other the way they used to. Then, right after it happened, right after the inquest, Miss Campbell took off for parts unknown.'

'But she came back.'

'More than a year later she came back, after it all died down. She was still very interested in the case, though. She asked me a lot of questions this last summer. She gave me a story that her and her sister Rina were going to write it up for a magazine, but I don't think that was her interest.'

'What kind of questions did they ask?'

'I don't know,' he said wearily. 'Some of the ones you asked me, I guess. You've asked me about a million of them now.'

'Did you tell her about the earring?'

'Maybe I did. I don't remember. Does it matter?' He pushed himself away from the wall, shuffled across the gallery, and looked up at the whitening sky. 'I got to go home and get some sleep, Mr Archer. I go back on duty at nine o'clock.'

'I thought you never got tired.'

'I get depressed. You stirred up a lot of things I want to forget. In fact, you've been giving me kind of a hard time.'

'I'm sorry. I'm tired too. It'll be worth it, though, if we can solve this murder.'

'Will it? Say you do, then what will happen?' His face was grim in the gray light, and his voice drew on old reserves of bitterness. 'The same thing will happen that happened before. The cops will take over your case and seal it off and nothing will happen, nobody get arrested.'

'Is that what happened before?'

'I'm telling you it did. When Marfeld saw he couldn't railroad me, he suddenly lost interest in the case. Well, I lost interest, too.'

'I can go higher than Marfeld if I have to.'

'What if you do? It's too late for Gabrielle, too late for me. It was always too late for me.'

He turned on his heel and walked away. I said after him:

'Can I drop you someplace?'

'I have my own car.'

XXIV

I SHOULD HAVE handled it better. I walked to the end of the pool, the last man at the party, feeling that early-morning ebb of heart when the blood runs sluggish and cold. The fog had begun to blow out to sea. It foamed and poured in a slow cataract toward the obscure west. Black-marble patches of ocean showed through here and there.

I must have seen it and known what it was before I was conscious of it. It was a piece of black driftwood with a twist of root at one end, floating low in the water near the shore. It rode in slowly and discontinuously, pushed by a series of breaking waves. Its branches were very flexible for a log. A wave lodged it on the wet brown sand. It was a man in a dark, belted overcoat, lying face-down.

The gate in the fence was padlocked. I picked up a DO NOT RUN sign with a heavy concrete base and swung it at the padlock. The gate burst open. I went down the concrete steps and turned Carl Stern over onto his back. His forehead was deeply ridged where it had struck or been struck by a hard object. The wound in his throat gaped like a toothless mouth shouting silently.

I went to my car, remembering from my bottom-scratching days that there was a southward current along this shore, about a mile an hour. Just under three miles north of the Channel Club, a paved view-point for sightseers blistered out from the highway to the fenced edge of a bluff which overhung the sea. Stern's rented sedan was parked with its heavy chrome front against the cable fence. Blood spotted the windshield and dashboard and the front seat. Blood stained the blade of the knife which lay on the floormat. It looked like Stern's own knife.

I didn't mess with any of it. I wanted no part of Stern's death. I drove home on automatic pilot and went to bed. I dreamed about a man who lived by himself in a landscape of crumbling stones. He spent a great deal of his time, without much success, trying to reconstruct in his mind the monuments and the buildings of which the scattered stones were the only vestiges. He vaguely remembered some kind of oral tradition to the effect that a city had stood there once. And a still vaguer tradition: or perhaps it was a dream inside of the dream: that the people who had built the city, or their descendants, were coming back eventually to rebuild it. He wanted to be around when the work was done.

XXV

MY ANSWERING SERVICE woke me at seven thirty. 'Rise and shine, Mr Archer!'

'Do I have to shine? I'm feeling kind of dim. I got to bed about an hour ago.'

'I haven't been to bed yet. And, after all, you could have cancelled your standing order.'

'I hereby cancel it, forever.' I was in one of those drained and chancy moods when everything seems either laughable or weepworthy, depending on the positions you hold your head in. 'Now hang the hell up and let me get back to sleep.

This is cruel and unusual punishment.'

'My, but we're in splendid spirits this morning!' Her secretarial instinct took over: 'Wait now, don't hang up. Couple of long-distance calls for you, both from Las Vegas. First at one forty, young lady, seemed very anxious to talk to you, but wouldn't leave her name. She said she'd call back, but she never did. Got that? Second at three fifteen, Dr Anthony Reeves, intern at the Memorial Hospital, said he was calling on behalf of a patient named George Wall, picked up at the airport with head injuries.'

'The Vegas airport?'

'Yes. Does that mean anything to you?'

It meant a surge of relief, followed by the realization that I was going to have to drag myself out to International Airport and crawl aboard a plane. 'Make me a reservation, will you, Vera?'

'First plane to Vegas?'

'Right.'

'One other call, yesterday afternoon. Man named Mercero from the CHP, said the Jag was registered to Lance Leonard. Is that the actor that got himself shot last night?'

'It's in the morning papers, eh?'

'Probably. I heard it on the radio.'

'What else did you hear?'

'That was all. It was just a flash bulletin.'

'No,' I said. 'It wasn't the same one. What did you say the name was again?'

'I forget.' She was a jewel among women.

Shortly before ten o'clock I was talking to Dr Anthony Reeves in his room in the Southern Nevada Hospital. He'd had the night duty on Emergency, and had given George Wall a preliminary examination when George was brought in by the Sheriff's men. They had found him wandering around McCarran Airfield in a confused condition. He had a fractured cheekbone, probably a brain concussion, and perhaps a fractured skull. George had to have absolute quiet for at least a week, and would probably be laid up for a month. He couldn't see anyone.

It was no use arguing with young Dr Reeves. Butter wouldn't

melt in his mouth. I went in search of a susceptible nurse, and eventually found a plump little redhead in an LA General cap who was impressed by an old Special Deputy badge I carried. On the strength of it, she led me to a semi-private room with a NO VISITORS sign on the door. George was the only occupant, and he was sleeping. I promised not to wake him.

The window shades were tightly drawn, and there was no light on in the room. It was so dim that I could barely make out George's white-bandaged head against the pillow. I sat in an armchair between his bed and the empty one, and listened to the susurrus of his breathing. It was slow and steady. After a while I almost went to sleep myself.

I was startled out of it by a cry of pain. I thought at first it was George, but it was a man on the other side of the wall. He cried loudly again.

George stirred and groaned and sat up, raising both hands to his half-mummified face. He swayed and threatened to fall out of bed. I held him by the shoulders.

'Take it easy, boy.'

'Let me go. Who are you?'

'Archer,' I said. 'The indigent's Florence Nightingale.'

'What happened to me? Why can't I see?'

'You've pulled the bandages down over your eyes. Also, it's dark in here.'

'Where is here? Jail? Am I in jail?'

'You're in the hospital. Don't you remember asking Dr Reeves to phone me long-distance?'

'I'm afraid I don't remember. What time is it?'

'It's Saturday morning, getting along towards noon.'

The information hit him hard. He lay back quietly for a while, then said in a puzzled tone:

'I seem to have lost a day.'

'Relax. You wouldn't want it back.'

'Did I do something wrong?'

'I don't know what you did. You ask too many questions, George.'

'You're just letting me down easy, aren't you?' Embarrassment thickened in his throat like phlegm. 'I suppose I made a complete ass of myself.'

'Most of us do from time to time. But hold the thought.'

He groped for the light-switch at the head of the bed, found the cord, and pulled it. Fingering the bandages on his face, he peered at me through narrow slits in them. Below the bandages, his puffed lips were dry and cracking. He said with a kind of awe in his voice:

'That little pug in the pajamas—did he do this to me?'

'Part of it. When did you see him last, George?'

'You ought to know, you were with me. What do you mean, part of it?'

'He had some help.'

'Whose help?'

'Don't you remember?'

'I remember something.' He sounded childishly uncertain. Physical and moral shock had cut his ego down small. 'It must have been just a nightmare. It was like a jumble of old movies running through my head. Only I was in it. A man with a gun was after me. The scene kept changing—it couldn't have been real.'

'It was real. You got into a hassle with the company guards at Simon Graff's studio. Does the name Simon Graff mean anything to you?'

'Yes, it does. I was in bed in some wretched little house in Los Angeles, and someone talking on the telephone said that name. I got up and called a taxicab and asked the driver to take me to see Simon Graff.'

'It was me on the telephone, George. In my house.'

'Have I ever been in your house?'

'Yesterday.' His memory seemed to be functioning very conveniently. I didn't doubt his sincerity, but I was irritated. 'You also lifted a wretched little old charcoal-gray suit of mine which cost me one-two-five.'

'Did I? I'm sorry.'

'You'll be sorrier when you get the bill. But skip it. How did you get from the Graff studio to Vegas? And what have you been doing between then and now?'

The mind behind his blood-suffused eyes groped dully in limbo. 'I think I came on a plane. Does that make any sense?'

'As much as anything does. Public or private plane?'

After a long pause, he said: 'It must have been private. There were just the two of us, me and another fellow. I think it was the same one who chased me with the gun. He told me that Hester was in danger and needed my help. I blacked out, or something. Then I was walking down a street with a lot of signs flashing in my eyes. I went into this hotel where she was supposed to be, but she had gone, and the desk clerk wouldn't tell me where.'

'Which hotel?'

'I'm not sure. The sign was in the shape of a wineglass. Or a martini glass. The Dry Martini? Does that sound possible?'

'There is one in town. When were you there?'

'Some time in the course of the night. I'd lost all track of time. I must have spent the rest of the night looking for her. I saw a number of girls who resembled her, but they always turned out to be someone different. I kept blacking out and coming to in another place. It was awful, with those lights in my eyes and the people milling about. They thought I was drunk. Even the policeman thought I was drunk.'

'Forget it, George. It's over now.'

'I won't forget it. Hester is in danger. Isn't that so?'

'She may be, I don't know. Forget about her, too, why don't you? Fall in love with the nurse or something. With your win-and-loss record, you ought to marry a nurse anyway. And, incidentally, you better lie down or the nurse will be reaming both of us.'

Instead of lying down, he sat up straighter, his shoulders arching under the hospital shirt. Between the bandages, his red eyes were fixed on my face. 'Something has happened to Hester. You're trying to keep me from knowing.'

'Don't be crazy, kid. Relax. You've sparked enough trouble.'

He said: 'If you won't help me, I'm getting up and walking out of here now. Somebody has to do something.'

'You wouldn't get far.'

Claimed I knew where she was. I had a hell of a time getting rid of him.'

I looked at my watch. 'She could be in trouble, at that. She's been gone eleven hours.'

'Think nothing of it. They stay on the town for twenty-four, thirty-six hours at a time, some of them. Maybe she hit a winning streak and's riding it out. Or maybe she had a date. Somebody must've clobbered the husband. He *is* her husband, isn't he?'

'He is, and several people clobbered him. He has a way of leading with his chin. Right now he's in the hospital, and I'm trying to find her for him.'

'Private dick?'

I nodded. 'Do you have any idea where she went?'

'I can find out, maybe, if it's important.' He looked me over, estimating the value of my clothes and the contents of my wallet. 'It's going to cost me something.'

'How much?'

'Twenty.' It was a question.

'Hey, I'm not buying you outright.'

'All right, ten,' he said quickly. 'It's better than getting poked in the eye with a carrot.'

He took the bill and waddled into a back room, where I heard him talking on the telephone to somebody named Rudy. He came back looking pleased with himself:

'I called her a taxi last night, was just talking to the dispatcher. He's sending over the driver that took the call.'

'How much is he going to cost me?'

'That's between you and him.'

I waited inside the glass front door, watching the noon traffic. It came from every state in the Union, but most of the license plates belonged to Southern California. This carney town was actually Los Angeles's most farflung suburb.

A shabby yellow cab detached itself from the westbound stream and pulled up at the curb. The driver got out and started across the sidewalk. He wasn't old, but he had a drooping face and posture like a hound that had been fed too long on scraps. I stepped outside.

For answer, he threw off the covers, swung his legs over th edge of the high bed, reached for the floor with his bare feet, and stood up tottering. Then he fell forward onto his knees, his head swinging loose, slack as a killed buck. I hoisted him back onto the bed. He lay inert, breathing rapidly and lightly.

I pressed the nurse's signal, and passed her on my way out.

XXVI

THE DRY MARTINI was a small hotel on the edge of the older downtown gambling district. Two old ladies were playing Canasta for money in the boxlike knotty-pine lobby. The desk clerk was a fat man in a rayon jacket. His red face was set in the permanently jovial expression which people expect of fat men.

'What can I do for you, sir?'

'I have an appointment with Miss Campbell.'

'I'm very much afraid Miss Campbell hasn't come in yet.'

'What time did she go out?'

He clasped his hands across his belly and twiddled his thumbs. 'Let's see, I came on at midnight, she checked in about an hour after that, stayed long enough to change her dress, and away she went again. Couldn't've been much later than one.'

'You notice things.'

'A sexburger like her I notice.' The tip of his tongue protruded between his teeth, which were a good grade of plastic.

'Was anybody with her, going or coming?'

'Nope. She came and went by herself. You're a friend of hers, eh?'

'Yeah.'

'Know her husband? Big guy with light-reddish hair?'

'I know him.'

'What goes with him? He came in here in the middle of the night looking like the wrath of God. Big welts on his face, blood in his hair, yackety-yacking like a psycho. He had some idea in his head that his wife was in trouble and I was mixed up in it.

'You the gentleman interested in the blondie?'

'I'm the one.'

'We're not supposed to give out information about our fares. Unless it's official—'

'A sawbuck official enough?'

He stood at attention and parodied a salute. 'What was it you wanted to know, bud?'

'You picked her up what time?'

'One fifteen. I checked it on my sheet.'

'And dropped her where?'

He gave me a yellow-toothed grin and pushed his peaked cap back. It hung almost vertically on the peaked rear of his skull. 'Don't rush me, bud. Let's see the color of your money first.'

I paid him.

'I set her out on the street,' he said. 'I didn't like to do it that time of night, but I guess she knew what she was doing.'

'Where was this?'

'It's out past the Strip a piece. I can show you if you want. It's a two-dollar fare.'

He opened the back door of his cab, and I got in. According to his identification card, his name was Charles Meyer. He told me about his troubles as we drove out past the Disney-Modern fronts where Hollywood and Times Square names decoyed for anonymous millionaires. Charles Meyer had many troubles. Drink had been his downfall. Women had wrecked his life. Gambling had ruined him. He told me in his singsong insistent whine:

'Three months I been hacking in this goddam burg trying to get together a stake to buy some clothes and a crate, get out of here. Last week I thought I had it made, two hundred and thirty bucks and all my debts paid off. So I went into the drugstore to get my insulin and they give me my change in silver, two dollars and a four-bits piece, and just for kicks I fed them in the machines and that was going to be that.' He clucked. 'There went two thirty. It took me a little over three hours to drop it. I'm a fast worker.'

'You could buy a bus ticket.'

'No, sir. I'm sticking here until I get a car, a postwar like the one I lost, and a suit of decent clothes. I'm not dragging my tail back to Dago looking like a bum.'

We passed several buildings under construction, identified by signs as additional club-hotels with fancy names. One of them was Simon Graff's Casbah. Their girders rose on the edge of the desert like armatures for people to build their glad bad dreams on.

The Strip degenerated into a long line of motels clinging to the fringes of glamour. Charles Meyer U-turned and stopped in front of one of them, the Fiesta Motor Court. He draped his hound face over the seat back:

'This is where I set her off.'

'Did anybody meet her?'

'Not that I saw. She was all by herself on the street when I pulled away.'

'But there was traffic?'

'Sure, there's always some traffic.'

'Did she seem to be looking for anybody?'

'How could I tell? She wasn't making much sense, she was in a kind of a tizzy.'

'What kind of a tizzy?'

'You know. Upset. Hysterical-like. I didn't like to leave her alone like that, but she says beat it. I beat it.'

'What was she wearing?'

'Red dress, dark cloth coat, no hat. One thing, she had on real high heels. I thought at the time, she wouldn't walk far with them on.'

'Which way did she walk?'

'No way, she just stood there on the curb, long as I could see her. You want to go back to the Martini now?'

'Stick around for a few minutes.'

'Okay, but I keep my meter running.'

The proprietor of the Fiesta Motor Court was sitting at an umbrella table in the small patio beside his office. He was smoking a waterpipe and fanning himself with a frayed palm-leaf fan. He looked like a happy Macedonian or a disappointed

Armenian. In the background several dark-eyed girls who could have been his daughters were pushing linen carts in and out of the tiny cottages.

No, he hadn't seen the young lady in the red dress. He hadn't seen anything after eleven thirty, got his NO VACANCY up at eleven twenty-five and went straight to bed. As I moved away he barked commands at one of the dark-eyed girls, as if to teach me by example how to keep my females out of trouble.

The Colonial Inn, next door, had a neat little office presided over by a neat little man with a clipped mustache and a north-by-northeast accent with asthmatic overtones. No, he certainly had not noticed the young lady in question, having better things to do with his time. He also had better things to do than answer questions about other people's wives.

Moving toward town and the unlit neon silo of the Flamingo, I tried the Bar-X Tourist Ranch and the Welcome Traveller and the Oasis. I got three different answers, all negative. Charles Meyer trailed me in his taxi, with many grins and nods.

The Rancho Eldorado was a double row of pastel chicken coops festooned with neon tubing. There was no one in the office. I rang until I got an answer, because it was close to the street and on a corner. A woman opened the door and looked at me down her nose, which was long and pitted with ancient acne craters. Her eyes were black and small, and her hair was up in pincurls. She was so homely that I felt sorry for her. It was practically an insult to offer her a description of a beautiful blonde in a red dress.

'Yes,' she said. 'I saw her.' Her black eyes glinted with malice. 'She stood on the corner for ten or twelve minutes last night. I don't set myself up as a judge of other people, but it made me mad to see her out there flaunting herself, deliberately trying to get herself picked up. I can tell when a girl's trying to get herself picked up. But it didn't work!' Her voice twanged triumphantly. 'Men aren't as easily taken in as they used to be, and nobody stopped for her.'

'What did she do to you?'

'Nothing, I just didn't like the way she flaunted herself under the light on my corner. That sort of thing is bad for business. This is a family motel. So I finally stepped outside and told her to move along. I was perfectly nice about it. I simply told her in a quiet way to peddle her papers elsewhere.' Her mouth closed, lengthening in a horizontal line with right angles at the corners. 'She's a friend of yours, I suppose?'

'No. I'm a detective.'

Her face brightened. 'I see. Well, I saw her go into the Dewdrop Inn, that's the second place down from here. It's about time somebody cleaned out that den of iniquity. Are you after her for some *crime*?'

'Third-degree pulchritude.'

She chewed on this like a camel, then shut the door in my face. The Dewdrop Inn was a rundown stucco ell with sagging shutters and doors that needed paint. Its office door was opened by a woman who was holding a soiled bathrobe tight around her waist. She had frizzled red hair. Her skin had been seared by blowtorch suns, except where her careless breast gleamed white in the V of her robe. She caught and returned my dipping glance, letting the V and the door both open wider.

'I'm looking for a woman.'

'What a lucky coincidence. I'm looking for a man. It's just it's just a leetle early for me. I'm still a teensy bit drunky from last night.'

Yawning, she cocked one fist and stretched the other arm straight up over her head. Her breath was a blend of gin and fermenting womanhood. Her bare feet were dirty white.

'Come on in, I won't bite you.'

I stepped up into the office. She held herself in the doorway so that I brushed against her from shoulder to knee. She wasn't really interested, just keeping in practice. The room was dirty and disordered, with a couple of lipsticky glasses on the registration desk, confession magazines scattered on the floor.

'Big night last night?' I said.

'Oh, sure. Big night. Drink cocktails until four and wake up at six and you can't get back to sleep. This divorce kick—well, it isn't all it's cracked up to be.'

I braced myself for another life-story. Something about my face, maybe a gullible look, invited them. But she spared me:

'Okay, Joe, we won't beat around the bush. You want the girlie in the red dress.'

'You catch on very quick.'

'Yeah. Well, she isn't here. I don't know where she is. You a mobster or what?'

'That's a funny question.'

'Yeah, sure, uproarious. You got a hand gun in your armpit, and you're not Davy Crockett.'

'You shatter my illusions.'

She gave me a hard and murky look. Her eyes resembled mineral specimens, malachite or copper sulphate, which had been gathering dust on somebody's back shelf. 'Come on, now, what's it all about? The kid said there was mobsters after her. You're no mobster, are you?'

'I'm a private dick. Her husband hired me to find her.' I realized suddenly that I was back where I'd started, twenty-eight hours later and in another state. It felt more like twenty-eight days.

The woman was saying: 'You find her for him, what's he plan to do with her? Beat her up?'

'Look after her. She needs it.'

'That could be. Was it all malarkey about the mobsters? I mean, was she stringing me?'

'I don't think so. Did she mention any names?'

She nodded. 'One. Carl Stern.'

'You know that name?'

'Yeah. The *Sun* dug into his record and spread it on the front page last fall when he put in for a gambling license. *He* wouldn't be her husband?'

'Her husband's a nice boy from Toronto. George Wall. Some of Stern's friends put him in the hospital. I want to get to his wife before they do it to her.'

'No kidding?'

'I mean it.'

'What did she do to Stern?'

'It's a question I want to ask her. Where is she now?'

She gave me the mineral look again. 'Let's see your license. Not that a license means much. The guy that got me my divorce was a licensed private detective, and he was a prime stinker if I ever saw one.'

'I'm not,' I said with the necessary smile, and showed her my photostat.

She looked up sharply. 'Your name is Archer?'

'Yes.'

'Is this a funny coincidence or what? She tried to phone you last night, person to person. Knocked on the door along towards two o'clock, looking pretty white and shaky, and asked to use my phone. I asked her what the trouble was. She broke down and told me that there were mobsters after her, or there soon would be. She wanted to call the airport, catch a plane out right away quick. I put in a call for her, but I couldn't get her on a flight till morning. So then she tried to call you.'

'What for?'

'She didn't tell me. If you're a friend of hers, why didn't you say so? *Are* you a friend of Rina Campbell's?'

'Who?' I said.

'Rina Campbell. The girl we're talking about.'

I made a not very smooth recovery. 'I think I am. Is she still here?'

'I gave her a nembutal and put her to bed myself. I haven't heard a peep out of her. She's probably still sleeping, poor dearie.'

'I want to see her.'

'Yeah, you made that clear. Only, this is a free country, and if she don't want to see you there's no way you can make her.'

'I'm not planning to push her around.'

'You better not, brother. Try anything with the kid, and I'll shoot you personally.'

'You like her, do you?'

'Why not? She's a real good girl, as good as they come. I don't care what she's done.'

'You're doing all right yourself.'

'Am I? That I doubt. I had it once, when I was Rina's age. I tried to save a little of it for an emergency. If you can't pass on a little loving-kindness in this world, you might as well be a gopher in a hole.'

'What did you say your name was?'

'I didn't say. My name is Carol, Mrs Carol Busch.' She offered me a red, unlovely hand. 'Remember, if she changed her mind about wanting to see you, you amscray.'

She opened an inner door, and shut it firmly behind her. I went outside where I could watch the exits. Charles Meyer was waiting in his cab.

'Hiyah. Any luck?'

'No luck. I'm quitting. How much do I owe you?'

He leaned sideways to look at the meter. 'Three seventy-five. Don't you want a ride downtown? I'll let you have it for half-price.'

'I'll walk. I need the exercise.'

His look was sad and canine. He knew that I was lying, and he knew the reason: I didn't trust him. Mrs Carol Busch called me from the doorway of the unit adjoining the office. 'Okay, she's up, she wants to talk to you.'

XXVII

MRS BUSCH STAYED outside and let me go in alone. The room was dim and cool. Blackout blinds and heavy drapes kept the sunlight out. A shaded bedside lamp was the only source of light. The girl sat on the foot of the unmade Hollywood bed with her face turned away from the lamp.

I saw the reason for this when she forgot her pose and looked up at me. Nembutal or tears had swollen her eyelids. Her bright hair was carelessly groomed. She wore her red wool dress as if it were burlap. Overnight, she seemed to have lost her assurance that her beauty would look after her. Her voice was small and high:

'Hello.'

'Hello, Rina.'

'You know who I am,' she said dully.

'I do now. I should have guessed it was a sister act. Where is your sister, Rina?'

'Hester's in trouble. She had to leave the country.'

'You're sure about that?'

'I'm not sure about anything since I found out Lance is dead.'

'How did you find out? You didn't believe me when I told you last night.'

'I have to believe you now. I picked up a Los Angeles paper at the hotel, and there was a headline about him—about his murder.' Her eyelids lifted heavily. Her dark-blue eyes had changed subtly in thirteen hours: they saw more and liked it less. 'Did my sister—did Hester kill him?'

'She may have, but I doubt it. Which way did they say she went—Mexico or Canada or Hawaii?'

'They didn't say. Carl Stern said it would be better if I didn't know.'

'What are you supposed to be doing here? Giving her an alibi?'

'I guess so. That was the idea.' She looked up again. 'Please don't stand over me. I'm willing to tell you what I know, but please don't cross-question me. I've had a terrible night.'

Her fingers dabbed at her forehead and came away wet. There was a box of Kleenex on the bedside table. I handed her a leaf of it, which she used to wipe her forehead and blow her nose. She said surprisingly, in a voice as thin as a flute:

'Are you a good man?'

'I like to think so,' but her candor stopped me. 'No,' I said, 'I'm not. I keep trying, when I remember to, but it keeps getting tougher every year. Like trying to chin yourself with one hand. You can practice off and on all your life, and never make it.'

She tried to smile. The gentle corners of her mouth wouldn't lift. 'You talk like a decent man. Why did you come to my sister's house last night? How did you get in?'

'I broke in.'

'Why? Have you got something against her?'

'Nothing personal. Her husband asked me to find her. I've been trying to.'

'She has no husband. I mean, Hester's husband is dead.'

'She told you he was dead, eh?'

'Isn't it true?'

'She doesn't tell the truth when a lie will do.'

'I know.' She added in an unsentimental tone: 'But Hester is my sister and I love her. I've always done what I could for her, I always will.'

'And that's why you're here.'

'That's why I'm here. Lance and Carl Stern told me that I could save Hester a lot of grief, maybe a penitentiary term. All I had to do was fly here under her name, and register in a hotel, then disappear. I was supposed to take a taxi out to the edge of the desert, past the airport, and Carl Stern was supposed to pick me up. I didn't meet him, though. I came back here instead. I lost my nerve.'

'Is that why you tried to phone me?'

'Yes. I got to thinking, when I saw the piece about Lance in the paper. You'd told me the truth about that, perhaps you'd told me the truth about everything. And I remembered something you said last night—the very first thing you said when you saw me in Hester's room. You said—' her voice was careful, like a child's repeating a lesson by rote—'you thought I was Hester, and you said you thought I was dead— that *she* was dead.'

'I said that, yes.'

'Is it true?'

I hesitated. She got to her feet, swaying a little. Her hand pressed hard on my arm:

'Is Hester dead? Don't be afraid to tell me if she is. I can take it.'

'Sorry, I don't know the answer.'

'What do you think?'

'I think she is. I think she was killed in the Beverly Hills house yesterday afternoon. And the alibi they're trying to set up isn't for Hester. It's for whoever killed her.'

'I'm sorry. I don't follow.'

'Say she was killed yesterday. You assumed her identity, flew here, registered, disappeared. They wouldn't be asking questions about her in LA.'

'*I* would.'

'If you got back alive.'

It took her a second to grasp the idea, another to apply it to her present situation. She blinked, and the shock wave hit her. Her eyes were like cracked blue Easter eggs.

'What do you think I should do?'

'Fade. Disappear, until I get this thing settled. But first I want your story. You haven't explained why you let them use you for a patsy. Or how much you knew about your sister's activities. Did she tell you what she was doing?'

'She didn't intend to, but I guessed. I'm willing to talk, Mr Archer. In a way, I'm as guilty as Hester. I feel responsible for the whole thing.'

She paused, and looked around the yellow plaster walls. She seemed to be dismayed by the ugliness of the room. Her gaze stopped at the door behind me, and hardened. The door sprang open as I turned. Harsh sunlight slapped me across the eyes, and glinted on three guns. Frost held one of them. Lashman and Marfeld flanked him. Behind them Mrs Busch crawled in the gravel. In the street Charles Meyer's shabby yellow taxi rolled away toward town. He didn't look back.

I saw all this while I reached for my left armpit. I didn't complete the motion. The day and the night and the day again had dulled me, and I wasn't reacting well, but I knew that a gun in my hand was all they needed. I stood with my right hand frozen on my chest.

Frost smiled like a death's-head against the aching blue sky. He had on a multicolored shot-silk shirt, a Panama hat with a matching colored band, and the kind of white flannels worn by tennis pro's. The gun in his hand was a German machine pistol. He pressed its muzzle into my solar plexus and took my gun.

'Hands on your head. This is a real lovely surprise.'

I put my hands on my head. 'I like it, too.'

'Now turn around.'

Mrs Busch had got to her feet. She cried out: 'Dirty bullying bastards!' and flung herself on the back of the nearest gunman. This happened to be Marfeld. He pivoted and slapped her face with the barrel of his gun. She fell turning and lay still on her face, her hair splashing out like fire. I said:

'I'm going to kill you, Marfeld.'

He turned to me, his eyes joyous, if Marfeld could feel joy. 'You and who else, boysie? You won't be doing any pitching. You're the catcher, see?'

He slapped the side of my head with the gun. The sky swayed like a blue balloon on a string.

Frost spoke sharply to Marfeld. 'Lay off. And, for God's sakes, lay off the woman.' He spoke to me more gently: 'Keep your hands on your head and turn around.'

I did these things, tickled by worms of blood crawling through my hair and down the side of my face. Rina was sitting on the bed against the wall. Her legs were drawn up under her, and she was shivering.

'You disappoint me, doll,' Frost said. 'You do too, Lew.'

'I disappoint myself.'

'Yeah, after all the trouble I went to, giving you good advice, and our years of friendly relationship.'

'You move me deeply. I haven't been so deeply moved since I heard a hyena howl.'

Frost pushed the gun muzzle hard into my right kidney. Marfeld moved around me, swinging his shoulders busily. 'That's no way to talk to Mr Frost.'

He swung the edge of his hand toward my throat. I pulled in my chin to protect my larynx and caught the blow on the mouth. I made a noise that sounded like *gar* and reached for him. Lashman locked my right arm and hung his weight on it. Marfeld's right shoulder dropped. At the end of his hooked right arm, his fist swung into my belly. It doubled me over. I straightened, gulping down bitter regurgitated coffee.

'That's enough of that,' Frost said. 'Hold a gun on him, Lash.'

Frost moved past me to the bed. He walked slackly with his shoulders drooping. His voice was dry and tired:

'You ready to go now, baby?'

'Where is my sister?'

'You know she had to leave the country. You want to do what's right for her, don't you?' He leaned toward her in a parody of wheedling charm.

She hissed at him, grinning with all her teeth: 'I wouldn't cross the street with you. You smell! I want my sister.'

'You're coming if you have to be carried. So, on your horse.'

'No. Let me out of here. You killed my sister.'

She scrambled off the bed and ran for the door. Marfeld caught her around the waist and wrestled with her, grinning, his belly pressed to her hip. She slashed his cheek with her nails. He caught her by the hand and bent her fingers backward, struck savagely at her head with the flat of his hand. She stood submissive against the ghastly wall.

The gun at my back had lost contact, leaving a cold vacuum. I whirled. Lashman had been watching the girl being hurt with a voyeur's hot, dreamy eyes. I forced his gun down before he fired. I got the gun away from him and swung it at the left front corner of his skull. He crumpled in the doorway.

Marfeld was on my back. He was heavy and strong, with an innate sense of leverage. His arm looped around my neck and tightened. I swung him against the door frame. He almost pulled my head off, but he fell on top of Lashman, his face upturned. With the butt of the gun, I struck him between the eyes.

I turned toward Frost in the instant that he fired, and flung myself sideways. His slugs whanged into the wall wide of my head. I shot him in the right arm. His gun clanked on the floor. I got my free hand on it and stood up and backed to the wall and surveyed the room.

The air-conditioner thumped and whirred like a wounded bird in the wall behind my head. The girl leaned white-faced and still on the opposite wall. Frost sat on the floor between us, holding his right arm with his left hand. Blood laced his fingers. He looked from them to me. The fear of death which never left his eyes had taken over the rest of his face. In the doorway, Marfeld lay with his head on Lashman's chest. His veined eyeballs were turned up and in toward the deep blue dent in his forehead. Except for his hoarse breathing and the noise of the air-conditioner, the room was very tranquil.

Mrs Busch appeared in the doorway, weaving slightly. One of her eyes was swollen and black, and her smiling mouth was bloody. She held a ·45 automatic in both hands. Frost looked into its roving eye and tried to crawl under the bed. It was too low to receive him. He lay beside it, whimpering:

'Please. I'm a sick man. Don't shoot.'

The redheaded woman laughed. 'Look at him crawl. Listen to him whine.'

'Don't kill him,' I said. 'Strange as it may seem, I have a use for him.'

XXVIII

RINA DROVE FROST'S Cadillac. I rode in the back seat with Frost. She had made a pressure bandage and a sling for his arm out of several Dewdrop Inn bath towels. He sat and nursed his arm, refusing to talk, except to give directions.

Beyond the airport, we turned right toward mountains which lay naked and wrinkled under the sun. The road climbed toward the sun, and as it climbed it dwindled, changing to gravel. We came over the first low hump and overlooked a white-floored valley where nothing grew.

Near the crest of the inner slope, a concrete building with a rounded roof was set into the side of the hill. Squat and windowless, it resembled a military strongpoint. It was actually a disused ammunition dump.

Frost said: 'She's in there.'

Rina looked over her shoulder. Her nervous foot on the power brakes jolted the car to a stop. We slipped out under the brilliant sky. A jet track crossed it like a long white scar. I told Rina to stay in the car.

'You can put your gun away,' Frost said. 'There's nobody

in there but her.'

I made him climb ahead of me, up the slope to the single door of the building. Sheathed with rusting steel, the door swung half open. A broken padlock hung from its hasp. I pulled the door wide, holding my gun on Frost. A puff of warm air came from the interior. It smelled like an oven where meat had been scorched.

Frost hung back. I forced him to enter ahead of me. We stood on a narrow platform, peering down into dimness. The concrete floor of the dump was about six feet below the level of the entrance. Framed in light, our shadows fell across it. I pushed Frost out of the rectangle of light, and saw what lay on the floor: a wizened thing like a mummy, blackened and consumed by fire instead of by time.

'You did this to her?'

Frost said without conviction: 'Hell, no, it was her husband. You should be talking to him. He followed her here from LA, did you know that? Knocked her off and set fire to the body.'

'You'll have to do better than that, Frost. I've been talking to the husband. You flew him here in Stern's plane to frame him for the killing. You probably brought the body on the same flight. The frame didn't take, though, and it's not going to. None of your dirty little plans is working out.'

He was silent for a period of time which was divided into shorter periods by the tic twitching at his eyelid. 'It wasn't my idea, it was Stern's. And the gasoline was his idea. He said to put her to the torch, so that when they found the body they couldn't establish when she died. The girl was dead already, see, all we did was cremate her.'

He looked down at the body. It was the image of the thing he feared, and it imposed silence on him. He reached out suddenly with his good arm, clawed at my shoulder and caught hold. 'Can't we get out of here, Lew? I'm a sick man, I can't stand it in here.'

I shook him off. 'When you've told me who killed the girl.'

There was another breathing silence. 'Isobel Graff killed her,' he said finally.

'How do you know?'

'Marfeld saw her. Marfeld saw her come tearing out of the house with the fantods. He went in, and there was Hester in the living-room. She had her head beaten in with a poker. The poker was lying across her. We couldn't leave her there. The cops would trace the Graff connection in no time—'

'What was Hester's connection with Graff?'

'Isobel thought they were shacked up, let's leave it at that. Anyway, it was up to me to do something with the body. I wanted to chuck it in the ocean, but Graff said no—he has a house on the ocean at Malibu. Then Lance Leonard got this other idea.'

'How did Leonard get into the act?'

'He was a friend of Hester's. She borrowed his car, he came by to pick it up. Leonard had a key to her house, and he walked in on Marfeld and the body. He had his own reasons for wanting to cover it up, so he suggested getting her sister to help. The two sisters are look-alikes, almost like twins, and Leonard knew both of them. He talked the sister into flying here.'

'What was going to happen to her?'

'That was Carl Stern's problem. But it looks as though Stern ran out on the whole deal. I don't see how he can afford to do that.'

'You're kind of out of touch,' I said. 'You used to be an operator. When did you start letting goons and gunsills do your thinking for you?'

Frost grimaced and hung his head. 'I'm not myself. I been full of demerol for the last three months.'

'You're on a demerol kick?'

'I'm a dying man, Lew. My insides are being eaten away. I'm in terrible pain right at this moment. I shouldn't be walking around.'

'You won't be walking around. You'll be sitting in a cell.'

'You're a hard man, Lew.'

'You keep calling me Lew. Don't do it. I ought to leave you here to find your own way back.'

'You wouldn't do that to me?' He caught at me again, chattering. 'Listen to me, Lew—Mr Archer. About that Italy deal. I can get you five hundred a week for twenty-six weeks. No duties, nothing to do. A free holiday—'

'Save it. I wouldn't touch a nickel of yours with rubber gloves on.'

'But you wouldn't leave me here?'

'Why not? You left her.'

'You don't understand. I only did what I had to. We were caught. The girl fixed it herself so that we were caught. She had something on the Man and his wife, evidence against them, and she turned it over to Carl Stern. He forced the deal on us, in a way. I would have handled it differently.'

'So everything you did was Stern's fault.'

'I don't say that, but he was calling the signals. We had to co-operate with him. We've had to now for months. Stern even forced the Man to lend his name to his big new operation.'

'What evidence does Stern hold against the Graffs?'

'Would I be likely to tell you?'

'You're going to tell me. Now. I'm getting sick of you, Frost.'

He backed away from me against the doorpost. The light fell on one side of his face and made his profile look as pale and thin as paper. As if corruption had eaten him away till he was only a surface laid on darkness.

'A gun,' he said. 'A target pistol belonging to Mr Graff. Isobel used it to kill a girl with, a couple of years ago.'

'Where does Stern keep the gun?'

'In a safe-deposit box. I found out that much, but I couldn't get to it. He was carrying it with him last night, though, in the car. He showed it to me.' His dull eyes brightened yellowly. 'You know, Lew, I'm authorized to pay a hundred grand for that little gun. You're a strong, smart boy. Can you get it away from Stern?'

'Somebody already has. Stern got his throat cut in the course of the night. Or maybe you know that, Frost.'

'No. I didn't know it. If it's true, it changes things.'

'Not for you.'

We went outside. Below, the valley floor shimmered in its own white heat. The jet trail which slashed the sky was blurring out.

In this anti-human place, the Cadillac on the road looked as irrelevant as a space-ship stalled on the mountains of the moon. Rina stood at the foot of the slope, her face upturned and blank. It was heavy news I carried down to her.

XXIX

MUCH LATER, ON the sunset plane, we were able to talk about it. Leroy Frost, denying and protesting and calling for lawyers and doctors, had been deposited with Marfeld and Lashman in the security ward of the hospital. The remains of Hester Campbell were in the basement of the same building, awaiting autopsy. I told the sheriff and the district attorney enough to have Frost and his men held for possible extradition on suspicion of murder. I didn't expect it to stick. The final moves in the case would have to be made in California.

The DC-6 left the runway and climbed the blue ramp of air. There were only a dozen other passengers, and Rina and I had the front end of the plane to ourselves. When the NO SMOKING sign went out, she crossed her legs and lit a cigarette. Without looking at me directly, she said in a brittle voice:

'I suppose I owe you my life, as they say in books. I don't know what I can do to repay you. No doubt I should offer to go to bed with you. Would you like that?'

'Don't,' I said. 'You've had a rough time and made a mistake, and I've been involved in it. But you don't have to take it out on me.'

'I didn't mean to be snide,' she said, a little snidely. 'I was making a serious offer of my body. Having nothing better to offer.'

'Rina, come off it.'

'I'm not attractive enough, is that what you mean?'

'You're talking nonsense. I don't blame you. You've had a bad scare.'

She sulked for a while, looking down at the Chinese Wall of

mountains we were crossing. Finally she said in a chastened tone:

'You're perfectly right. I was scared, really scared, for the first time in my life. It does funny things to a girl. It made me feel—well, almost like a whore—as though I wasn't worth anything to myself.'

'That's the way the jerks want you to feel. If everybody felt like a zombie, we'd all be on the same level. And the jerks could get away with the things jerks want to get away with. They're not, though. Jerkiness isn't as respectable as it used to be, not even in LA. Which is why they had to build Vegas.'

She didn't smile. 'Is it such a terrible place?'

'It depends on who you pick for your playmates. You picked the worst ones you could find.'

'I didn't pick them, and they're not my playmates. They never were. I despise them. I warned Hester years ago that Lance was poison for her. And I told Carl Stern what I thought of him to his face.'

'When was this? Last night?'

'Several weeks ago. I went out on a double date with Lance and Hester. Perhaps it was a foolish thing to do, but I wanted to find out what was going on. Hester brought Carl Stern for me, can you imagine? He's supposed to be a millionaire, and Hester always believed that money was the important thing. She couldn't see, even at that late date, why I wouldn't play up to Stern.

'Not that it would have done me any good,' she added wryly. 'He was no more interested in me than I was in him. He spent the evening in various nightclubs playing footsie with Lance under the table. Hester didn't notice, or maybe she didn't care. She could be very dense about certain things. I cared, though, for her sake. Finally I told them off and walked out on the three of them.'

'What did you say to them?'

'Just the plain, unvarnished truth. That Carl Stern was a pederast and probably much worse, and Hester was crazy to fool around with him and his pretty-boy.'

'Did you mention blackmail?'

'Yes. I told them I suspected it.'

'That was a dangerous thing to do. It gave Stern a reason to want you dead. I'm pretty sure he meant to kill you last night. Lucky for you he died first.'

'Really? I can't believe—' But she believed it. Her dry throat refused to function. She sat swallowing. 'Just because I—because I suspected something?'

'Suspected him of blackmail, and called him a fag. Killing always came easy to Stern. I went over his rap sheet this afternoon—the Nevada authorities have a full file on him. No wonder he couldn't get a gambling license in his own name. Back in the thirties he was one of Anastasia's boys, suspected of implication in over thirty killings.'

'Why wasn't he arrested?'

'He was, but they couldn't convict him. Don't ask me why. Ask the politicians that ran the cops in New York and Jersey and Cleveland and the other places. Ask the people that voted for the politicians. Stern ended up in Vegas, but he belonged to the whole country. He worked for Lepke, for Game Boy Miller in Cleveland, for Lefty Clark in Detroit, for the Trans America gang in LA. He finished his apprenticeship under Siegel, and after Siegel got it he went into business for himself.'

'What sort of business?'

'Wire service for bookies, narcotics, prostitution, anything with a fast and dirty buck in it. He was a millionaire, all right, several times over. He sank a million in the Casbah alone.'

'I don't understand why he would go in for blackmail. He didn't need the money.'

'He was Syndicate-trained, and blackmail's been one of their main sources of power ever since Maffia days. No, it wasn't money he needed. It was status. Simon Graff's name gave him his chance to go legit, to really build himself into the countryside.'

'And I helped him.' The bones had come out in her face so that it was almost ugly. 'I made it possible. I could bite my tongue out.'

'Before you do, I wish you'd explain what you mean.'

She drew in her breath sharply. 'Well, in the first place, I'm a psychiatric nurse.'

She fell silent. It was hard for her to get started.

'So your mother told me,' I said.

She gave me a sidelong glance. 'When did you run into Mother?'

'Yesterday.'

'What did you think of her?'

'I liked her.'

'Really?'

'I like women in general, and I'm not hypercritical.'

'I am,' Rina said. 'I've always been suspicious of Mother and her little airs and graces and her big ideas. And it was mutual. Hester was her favorite, her little pal. Or she was Hester's little pal. She spoiled my sister rotten, at the same time made terrible demands on her: all she wanted was for Hester to be great.

'I sat on the side lines for fifteen years and watched the two girls play emotional ping-pong. Or pong-ping. I was the not-so-innocent bystander, the third one that made the crowd, the one that wasn't simpatico.' It sounded like a speech she'd rehearsed to herself many times. There was bitterness in her voice, tempered with resignation. 'I broke it up as soon as Mother would let me, as soon as I finished high school. I went into nurse's training in Santa Barbara, and took my PG work at Camarillo.'

Talking about her profession, or talking out her feelings about her family, had given her back some of her self-assurance. She held her shoulders straighter, and her breasts were bold.

'Mother thought I was crazy. We had a knockdown dragout quarrel the first year, and I haven't seen much of Mother since. It just happens I like doing things for sick people, especially working with disturbed people. Need to be needed, I guess. My main interest now is occupational therapy. It's mainly what I'm doing with Dr Frey.'

'This is the Dr Frey who runs the sanitarium in Santa Monica?'

She nodded. 'I've worked there for over two years.'

'So you know Isobel Graff.'

'Do I ever. She was admitted to the san not long after I started there. She'd been in before, more than once. The doctor said she was worse than usual. She's schizophrenic, you know, has been for twenty years, and when it's acute she develops paranoid delusions. The doctor said they used to be directed against her father when he was alive. This time they were directed against Mr Graff. She believed that he was plotting against her, and she was going to get him first.

'Dr Frey thought Mr Graff should have her locked up for his own protection. Every now and then a paranoid delusion erupts into action. I've seen it happen. Dr Frey gave her a series of metrazol treatments, and she gradually came out of the acute phase and quieted down. But she was still quite remote when this thing happened. I still wouldn't turn my back on her. But Dr Frey said she wasn't dangerous, and he knew her better than I did and, after all, he was the doctor.

'In the middle of March, he gave her the run of the grounds. I shouldn't second guess a doctor, but that's where he made his mistake. She wasn't ready for freedom. The first little thing that happened set her off.'

'What did happen?'

'I don't know exactly. Perhaps someone made a thoughtless remark, or simply looked at her in the wrong tone of voice. Paranoid people are like that, almost like radio receivers. They pick a tiny signal out of the air and build it up with their own power until they can't hear anything else. Whatever happened, Isobel took off, and she was gone all night.

'When she came back, she was *really* in a bad way. With that terrible glazed look on her face, like a fish with a hook in its mouth. She was right back where she started in January—worse.'

'What night was she gone?'

'March 21, the first day of spring. I'm not likely to forget the date. A girl I used to know in Malibu, a girl named Gabrielle Torres, was killed that same night. I didn't connect the two events at the time.'

'But you do now?'

She inclined her head somberly. 'Hester made the connection for me. You see, she knew something I hadn't known, that Simon

Graff and Gabrielle were—lovers.'

'When did this come out?'

'One day last summer when we had lunch together. Hester was practically on her uppers then, I used to buy her lunch whenever I could. We were gossiping about this and that, and she brought up the case. It seemed to be on her mind: she was back at the Channel Club at the time, giving diving lessons. She told me about the love affair; apparently Gabrielle had confided in her. Without thinking what I was doing, I told her Isobel Graff had escaped that night. Hester reacted like a Geiger counter, and started asking me questions. I thought her only interest was in tracking down the person who killed her friend. I let down my back hair and told her all I knew, about Isobel and her runout and her mental condition when she came back.

'I had the early-morning duty that day, and I was the one who looked after her until Dr Frey got there. Isobel dragged herself in some time around dawn. She was in bad shape, and not just mentally. She was physically exhausted. I think now she must have walked and run and crawled along the shore all the way from Malibu. The surf must have caught her, too, because her clothes were wet and matted with sand. I gave her a hot bath first thing.'

'Did she tell you where she'd been?'

'No, she didn't say a thing. Actually, she didn't speak for days. Dr Frey was worried for a while that she might be going into catatonia. Even when she did come out of it and started to talk again, she never mentioned that night—at least, not in words. I saw her in the crafts room, though, later in the spring. I saw some of the objects she made out of clay. I shouldn't have been shocked after what I've seen in mental wards, but I was shocked by some of those objects.' She closed her eyees as if to shut out the sight of them, and went on in a hushed voice:

'She used to make these girl dolls and pinch their heads off and destroy them part by part, like some sort of jungle witch. And horrible little men dolls with huge—organs. Animals with human faces, coupling. Guns and—parts of the human body, all mixed up.'

'Not nice,' I said, 'but it wouldn't necessarily mean anything, would it? Did she ever discuss these things with you?'

'Not with me, no. Dr Frey doesn't encourage the nurses to practice psychiatry.'

She turned in the seat and her knee nudged mine, withdrawing quickly. Her dark-blue gaze came up to my face. It was strange that a girl who had seen so much should have such innocent eyes.

'Will you be seeing Dr Frey?' she said.

'Probably I will.'

'Please don't tell him about me, will you?'

'There's no reason why I should.'

'It's a terrible breach of ethics, you know, for a nurse to talk about her patients. I've worried myself sick these last few months since I spilled out everything to Hester. I was such a fool. I believed that she was sincere for once in her life, that all she wanted was the truth about Gabrielle's death. I should never have trusted her with dangerous information. It's obvious what she wanted it for. She wanted to use it to blackmail Mrs Graff.'

'How long have you known that, Rina?'

Her voice, or her candor, failed her for a time. I waited for her to go on. Her eyes were almost black with thought. She said:

'It's hard to say. You can know a thing and not know it. When you love a person, it takes so long to face the facts about them. I've really suspected the whole thing practically from the beginning. Ever since Hester left the Club and started living without any visible income. It came to a head on that horrible double date I told you about. Carl Stern got tight and started to boast about his new place in Vegas, and how he had Simon Graff under his thumb. And Hester sat there drinking it in, with stars in her eyes. I got a queer idea that she wanted me there to see how well she was doing. What a success she'd made of her life, after all. That was when I blew my top.'

'What was their reaction?'

'I didn't wait for any reaction. I walked out of the place—we were in the Bar of Dixie—and went home in a taxi by myself. I never saw Hester again. I didn't see any of them again, until yesterday when Lance called me.'

'To ask you to fly to Vegas under her name?'

She nodded.

'Why did you agree to do it?'

'You know why. I was supposed to be giving her an alibi.'

'It doesn't explain why you wanted to.'

'Do I have to explain? I simply wanted to.' She added after a time: 'I felt I owed it to Hester. In a way I'm as guilty as she is. This awful business would never have started if it hadn't been for me. I'd got her into it, I felt it was up to me to get her out. But Hester was dead already, wasn't she?'

A fit of shivering took hold of her, shaking her so that her teeth knocked together. I put my arm around her until the spasm passed. 'Don't blame yourself too much.'

'I have to. Don't you see, if Isobel Graff killed Hester, I'm to blame?'

'I don't see it. People are responsible for what they do themselves. Anyway, there's some doubt in my mind that Isobel killed your sister. I'm not even certain that she shot Gabrielle Torres. I won't be until I get hold of firm evidence; a confession, or an eyewitness, or the gun she used.'

'You're just saying that.'

'No, I'm not just saying it. I jumped to certain conclusions too early in this case.'

She didn't ask me what I meant, and that was just as well. I still had no final answers.

'Listen to me, Rina. You're a girl with a lot of conscience, and you've taken some hard blows. You have a tendency to blame yourself for things. You were probably brought up to blame yourself for everything.'

She sat stiff in the circle of my arm. 'It's true. Hester was young and always getting into trouble, and Mother blamed me. Only, how did you know that? You have a great deal of insight.'

'Too bad it mostly takes the form of hindsight. Anyway, there's one thing I'm sure of. You're not responsible for what happened to Hester, and you didn't do anything very wrong.'

'Do you really believe that?' She sounded astonished.

'Naturally I believe it.'

She was a good girl, as Mrs Busch had said. She was also a very tired girl, and a sad and nervous girl. We sat in uneasy silence for a while. The hum of the engines had changed. The plane had passed the zenith of its flight and begun the long descent toward Los Angeles and the red sun. Before the plane touched earth, Rina had cried a little on my shoulder. Then she slept a little.

XXX

MY CAR WAS in the parking-lot at International Airport. Rina asked me to drop her off at her mother's house in Santa Monica. I did so, without going in myself, and drove up Wilshire and out San Vicente to Dr Frey's sanitarium. It occupied walled grounds which had once belonged to a large private estate in the open country between Sawtelle and Brentwood. A male attendant in a business suit opened the automatic gate and told me that Dr Frey was probably at dinner.

The central building was a white Edwardian mansion, with more recent additions, which stood on a terraced hillside. Dr Frey lived in a guesthouse to one side of it. People who looked like anybody else were promenading on the terraces. Like anybody else, except that there was a wall around their lives. From Dr Frey's veranda, I could see over the wall, as far as the ocean. Fog and darkness were gathering on its convex surface. Below the horizon the lost sun smoldered like a great plane that had crashed and burned.

I talked to a costumed maid, to a gray-haired housekeeper, finally to Dr Frey himself. He was a stoop-shouldered old man in dinner clothes, with a highball glass in his hand. Intelligence and doubt had deeply lined his face. The lines deepened when I told him that I suspected Isobel Graff of murder. He set his glass on the mantelpiece and stood in front of it, rather belligerently, as though I had threatened the center of his house.

'Am I to understand that you are a policeman?'

'A private detective. Later I'll be taking this to the police. I came to you first.'

'I hardly feel favored,' he said. 'You can't seriously expect me to discuss such a matter, such an accusation, with a stranger. I know nothing about you.'

'You know quite a bit about Isobel Graff.'

He spread his long gray hands. 'I know that I am a doctor and that she is my patient. What do you expect me to say?'

'You could tell me there's nothing in it.'

'Very well, I do so. There is nothing in it. Now if you'll excuse me, I have guests for dinner.'

'Is Mrs Graff here now?'

He countered with a question of his own: 'May I ask, what is your purpose in making these inquiries?'

'Four people have been killed, three of them in the last two days.'

He showed no surprise. 'These people were friends of yours?'

'Hardly. Members of the human race, though.'

He said with the bitter irony of age: 'So you are an altruist, are you? A Hollywood culture-hero in a sports coat? You propose to cleanse the Augean stables single-handed?'

'I'm not that ambitious. And I'm not your problem, doctor. Isobel Graff is. If she killed four people, or one, she ought to be put away where she can't kill any more. Don't you agree?'

He didn't answer me for a minute. Then he said: 'I signed voluntary commitment papers for her this morning.'

'Does that mean she's on her way to the state hospital?'

'It should, but I'm afraid it doesn't.' It was the third time in three minutes that he'd been afraid. 'Before the papers could be—ah—implemented, Mrs Graff escaped. She was very determined, much more so than we bargained for. I confess error. I should have had her placed in maximum security. As it was, she broke a reinforced window with a chair and made good her escape in the back of a laundry truck.'

'When was this?'

'This morning, shortly before the lunch hour. She hasn't been found as yet.'

'How hard is she being looked for?'

'You'll have to ask her husband. His private police are searching. He forbade—' Dr Frey compressed his lips and reached for his drink. When he had sipped it: 'I'm afraid I can't submit to further interrogation. If you were an official—' He shrugged, and the ice tinkled in his glass.

'You want me to call the police in?'

'If you have evidence.'

'I'm asking you for evidence. Did Mrs Graff kill Gabrielle Torres?'

'I have no way of knowing.'

'What about the others?'

'I can't say.'

'You've seen her and talked to her?'

'Of course. Many times. Most recently this morning.'

'Was her mental condition consistent with homicide?'

He smiled wearily. 'This is not a courtroom, sir. Next you'll be framing a hypothetical question. Which I would refuse to answer.'

'The question isn't hypothetical. Did she shoot Gabrielle Torres on the night of March 21 last year?'

'It may not be hypothetical, but the question is certainly academic. Mrs Graff is mentally ill now, and she was ill on March 21 of last year. She couldn't possibly be convicted of murder, or any other crime. So you are wasting both our times, don't you think?'

'It's only time, and I seem to be getting somewhere. You've practically admitted that she did that shooting.'

'Have I? I don't think so. You are a very pertinacious young man, and you are making a nuisance of yourself.'

'I'm used to that.'

'I am not.' He moved to the door and opened it. Male laughter came from the other side of the house. 'Now if you will transport your rather shopworn charm to another location, it will save me the trouble of having you thrown out.'

'One more question, doctor. Why did she pick that day in March to run away? Did she have a visitor that day, or the day before?'

'Visitor?' I had succeeded in surprising him. 'I know nothing of any visitors.'

'I understand Clarence Bassett visited her regularly here.'

He looked at me, eyes veiled like an old bird's. 'Do you have a paid spy among my employees?'

'It's simpler than that. I've talked to Bassett. As a matter of fact, he brought me into this case.'

'Why didn't you say so? I know Bassett very well.' He closed the door and took a step toward me. 'He hired you to investigate these deaths?'

'It started out as a missing-girl case and turned into a murder case before I found her. The girl's name was Hester Campbell.'

'Why, I know Hester Campbell. I've known her for years at the Club. I gave her sister a job.' He paused, and the slight excitement ran through him and drained away. The only trace it left was a tremor in the hand that held his glass. He sipped from the glass to conceal its clinking. 'Is Hester Campbell one of the victims?'

'She was beaten to death with a poker yesterday afternoon.'

'And you have reason to believe that Mrs Graff killed her?'

'Isobel Graff is involved, I don't know how deeply. She was at the scene of the crime, apparently. Her husband seems to accept her guilt. But that's not conclusive. Isobel may have been framed. Another possibility is this, that she has been used as a cat's-paw in these killings. I mean that she committed them, physically, but was incited to do it by somebody else. Would she be open to that kind of suggestion?'

'The more I know of the human mind, the less I know.' He tried to smile, and failed miserably. 'I predicted that you would be asking hypothetical questions.'

'I keep trying not to, doctor. You seem to attract them. And you haven't answered my question about Bassett's visits here.'

'Why, there was nothing unusual in them. He visited Mrs Graff every week, I believe, sometimes more frequently when she asked for him. They were very close—indeed, they'd been engaged to be married at one time, many years ago, before her present marriage. I sometimes think she should have married

Clarence instead of the man she did marry. He has an almost feminine quality of understanding, which she was badly in need of. Neither of them is adequate to stand alone. Together, if marriage had been possible for them, they might have made a functioning unit.' His tone was elegiac.

'What do you mean when you say that neither of them is adequate?'

'It should be obvious in the case of Mrs Graff. She has been subject to schizophrenic episodes since her middle teens. She has remained, in a sense, a teen-aged girl inside of a middle-aged body—unable to cope with the demands of adult life.' He added with a trace of bitterness: 'She has received little help from Simon Graff.'

'Do you know what caused her illness?'

'The etiology of this disease is still mysterious, but I think I know something of this particular case. She lost her mother young, and Peter Heliopoulos was not a wise father. He pushed her towards maturity, at the same time deprived her of true human contact. She became in a social sense his second wife before she even reached puberty. Great demands were made on her as his little hostess, as the spearhead of his social ambition. The very vulnerable spearhead. These demands were too great for one who was perhaps predisposed from birth to schizophrenia.'

'What about Clarence Bassett? Is he mentally ill?'

'I have no reason to think so. He is the manager of my club, not my patient.'

'You said he was inadequate.'

'I meant in the social and sexual sense. Clarence is the perennial bachelor, the giver of the other people's parties, the man who is content to dwell on the sidelines of life. His interest in women is limited to young girls, and to flawed women like Isobel who have failed to outlive their childhood. All this is typical, and part of his adjustment.'

'His adjustment to what?'

'To his own nature. His weakness requires him to avoid the storm centers of life. Unfortunately, his adjustment was badly shaken, several years ago, by his mother's death. Since then he has been drinking heavily. I would hazard the guess that his alcoholism is essentially a suicidal gesture. He is literally drowning his sorrows. I suspect he would be glad to join his beloved mother in the grave.'

'You don't regard him as potentially dangerous?'

The doctor answered after a thinking pause: 'Perhaps he could be. The death-wish is powerfully ambivalent. It can be turned against the self or against others. Inadequate men have been known to try to complete themselves in violence. A Jack the Ripper, for instance, is probably a man with a strong female component who is trying to annul it in himself by destroying actual females.'

The abstract words fluttered and swerved like bats in the twilit room. 'Are you suggesting that Clarence Bassett could be a mass murderer?'

'By no means. I have been speaking most generally.'

'Why go to all the trouble?'

He gave me a complex look. There was sympathy in it, and tragic knowledge, and weariness. He had worn himself out in the Augean stables, and despaired of human action.

'I am an old man,' he said. 'I lie awake in the night watches and speculate on human possibility. Are you familiar with the newer interpersonal theories of psychiatry? With the concept of *folie à deux*?'

I said I wasn't.

'Madness for two, it might be translated. A madness, a violence may arise out of a relationship even though the parties of the relationship may be individually harmless. My nocturnal speculations have included Clarence Bassett and Isobel. Twenty years ago their relationship might have made a marriage. Such a relationship may also sour and deteriorate and make something infinitely worse. I am not saying that this is so. But it is a possibility worth considering, a possibility which arises when two persons have the same unconscious and forbidden desire. The same death-wish.'

'Did Bassett visit Mrs Graff before her escape in March last year?'

'I believe he did. I would have to check the records.'

'Don't bother, I'll ask him personally. Tell me this, Dr Frey: do you have anything more to go on than speculation?'

'Perhaps I have. If I had, I would not and could not tell you.' He raised his hand before his face in a faltering gesture of defense. 'You deluge me with questions, sir, and there is no end to them. I am an old man, as I said. This is, or was, my dinner hour.'

He opened the door a second time. I thanked him and went out. He slammed the heavy front door behind me. The people on the twilit terraces turned pale, startled, purgatorial faces toward the source of the noise.

XXXI

IT WAS FULL night when I got to Malibu. A single car stood in the Channel Club parking-lot, a beat-up prewar Dodge with Tony's name on the steering-post. Inside the club, around the pool, there was nobody in sight. I knocked on the door of Clarence Bassett's office and got no answer.

I walked along the gallery and down the steps to the poolside. The water shivered under a slow, cold offshore wind. The place seemed very desolate. I was the last man at the party for sure.

I took advantage of this circumstance by breaking into Simon Graff's *cabaña*. The door had a Yale-type lock which was easy to jimmy. I stepped in and turned on the light, half expecting to find someone in the room. But it was empty, its furnishings undisturbed, its pictures bright and still on the walls, caught out of time.

Time was running through me, harsh on my nerve-ends, hot in my arteries, impalpable as breath in my mouth. I had the sleepless feeling you sometimes get in the final hours of a bad case, that you can see around corners, if you want to, and down into the darkness in human beings.

I opened the twin doors of the dressing-rooms. Each had a back door opening into a corridor which led to the showers. The one on the right contained a gray steel locker and an assortment of men's beach clothes: robes and swimming trunks, Bermuda shorts and sport shirts and tennis shoes. The one on the left, which must have been Mrs Graff's, was completely bare except for a wooden bench and an empty locker.

I switched on the light in the ceiling, uncertain what I was looking for. It was something vague yet specific: a sure sense of what had happened on that spring night when Isobel Graff had been running loose and the first young girl had died. *For a second,* Isobel had said, *I was in there, watching us through the door, and listening to myself. Please pour me a drink.*

I closed the door of her dressing-room. The louvers were set high in it, fairly wide apart, and loose, so that the windowless cubicle could air itself. By getting up on my toes, I could look down between the crosspieces into the outer room. Isobel Graff would have had to stand on the bench.

I dragged the bench over to the door and stood on it. Six inches below by eye-level, in the edge of one of the louvers, there was a series of indentations which looked like toothmarks, around them a faint red lipstick crescent, dark with age. I examined the underside of the soft wooden strip and found similar markings. Pain jerked through my mind like a knotted string, pulling an image after it. It was pain for the woman who had stood on this bench in the dark, watching the outer room through the cracks between the louvers and biting down on the wood in agony.

I turned out the light and crossed the outer room and stood in front of Matisse's Blue Coast lithograph. I had a fierce nostalgia for that brilliant, orderly world which had never quite existed. A world where nobody lived or died, held in the eye of a never-sinking sun.

Behind me someone cleared his throat delicately. I turned and saw Tony in the doorway, squinting against the light. His hand was on his gun butt.

'Mr Archer, you broke the door?'

'I broke it.'

He shook his head at me in a monitory way, and stopped to look at the damage I had done. A bright scratch crossed the setting of the lock, and the edge of the wood was slightly dented. Tony's blunt brown forefinger traced the scratch and the dent.

'Mr Graff won't like this, he is crazy about his *cabaña*, he furnished it all himself, not like the others.'

'When did he do that?'

'Last year, before the start of the summer season. He brought in his own decorators and cleaned it out like a whistle and put in all new stuff.' His gaze was serious, black, unwavering. He removed his peaked cap and scratched his gray-flecked head. 'You the one that bust the lock on the fence gate, too?'

'I'm the one. I seem to be in a destructive mood today. Is it important?'

'Cops thought so. Captain Spero was asking me back and forth who bust the gate. They found another dead one on the bench, you know that, Mr Archer?'

'Carl Stern.'

'Yah, Carl Stern. He was my nephew's manager, one time. Captain Spero said it was one of these gang killings, but I dunno. What do you think?'

'I doubt it.'

Tony squatted on his heels just inside the open door. It seemed to make him nervous to be inside the Graffs' *cabaña*. He scratched his head again, and ran thumb and finger down the grooves that bracketed his mouth. 'Mr Archer. What happened to my nephew Manuel?'

'He was shot and killed last night.'

'I know that. Captain Spero told me he was dead, shot in the eye.' Tony touched the lid of his left eye with his right forefinger. His upturned face resembled a cracked clay death mask.

'What else did Spero say?'

'I dunno. Said it was maybe another gang killing, but I dunno. He asked me, did Manuel have enemies? I told him, yah, he had one big enemy, name of Manuel Torres. What did I know about his life, his friends? He bust up from me long ago and went on his own road, straight down to hell in a low-top car.' Through the stoic Indian mask, his eyes shone with black, living grief. 'I dunno, I coulden tear that boy loose from my heart. He was like my own son to me, one time.'

His bowed shoulders moved with his breathing. He said: 'I'm gonna get out of this place, it's bad luck for me and my family. I still got friends in Fresno. I ought to stayed in Fresno, never left it. I made the same mistake that Manuel made, thought I could come and take what I wanted. They wooden let me take it. They leave me with nothing, no wife, no daughter, no Manuel.'

He balled his fist and struck himself on the cheekbone and looked around the room in confused awe, as though it was the lair of gods which he had offended. The room reminded him of his duty to it:

'What you doing in here, Mr Archer? You got no right in here.'

'I'm looking for Mrs Graff.'

'Why didden you say so? You didden have to break the door down. Mrs Graff was here a few minutes ago. She wanted Mr Bassett, only he ain't here.'

'Where is Mrs Graff now?'

'She went down on the beach. I tried to stop her, she ain't in very good shape. She wooden come with me, though. You think I ought to telephone Mr Graff?'

'If you can get in touch with him. Where's Bassett?'

'I dunno, he was packing his stuff before. He's going away on his vacation, maybe. He always goes to Mexico, for a month in the off-season. Used to show me colored pictures—'

I left him talking to the empty room and went to the end of the pool. The gate in the fence was open. Twenty feet below it, the beach sloped away to the water, delimited by the wavering line of white foam. The sight of the ocean gave me a queasy feeling: it reminded me of Carl Stern doing the dead man's float.

Waves rose like apparitions at the surf-line and fell like masonry. Beyond them a padded wall of fog was sliding shoreward. I went down the concrete steps, met by a snatch of sound which blew up to me between the thumpings of the surf. It was Isobel Graff talking to the ocean in a voice like a gull's screek. She dared it to come and get her. She sat hunched over her knees, just beyond its reach, and shook her fist at the muttering water.

'Dirty old cesspool, I'm not afraid of you.'

Her profile was thrust forward, gleaming white with a gleaming dark eye in it. She heard me moving toward her and cowered away, one arm thrown over her face.

'Leave me alone. I won't go back. I'll die first.'

'Where have you been all day?'

Her wet black eyes peered up from under her arm. 'It's none of your business. Go away.'

'I think I'll stay with you.'

I sat beside her on the impacted sand, so close that our shoulders touched. She drew away from the contact, but made no other move. Her dark and unkempt bird's-head twisted toward me suddenly. She said in her own voice:

'Hello.'

'Hello, Isobel. Where have you been all day?'

'On the beach, mostly. I felt like a nice long walk. A little girl gave me an ice-cream cone, she cried when I took it away from her, I am an old horror. But it was all I had to eat all day. I promised to send her a check, only I'm afraid to go home. That dirty old man might be there.'

'What dirty old man?'

'The one that made a pass at me when I took the sleeping-pills. I saw him when I passed out. He had a rotten breath like Father's when he died. And he had worms that were his eyes.' Her voice was singsong.

'Who had?'

'Old Father Deathmas with the long white dirty beard.' Her mood was ugly and ambiguous. She wasn't too far gone to know what she was saying, just far enough gone to say it. 'He made a pass at me, only I was too tired, and there I was in the morning back at the old stand with the same hot and cold running people. What am I going to do? I'm afraid of the water. I can't stand the thought of the violent ways, and sleeping-pills don't work. They simply pump you out and walk you up and down and feed you coffee and there you are back at the old stand.'

'When did you try sleeping-pills?'

'Oh, a long time ago, when Father made me marry Simon.

I was in love with another man.'

'Clarence?'

'He was the only one I ever. Clare was so sweet to me.'

The wall of fog had crossed the foam-line and was almost on top of us. The surf pounded behind it like a despondent visitor. I didn't know whether to laugh or cry. I looked down at her face, which slanted close to mine: a pale ghost of a face with two dark eye-holes and a mouth-hole in it. She was tainted by disease and far from young, but in the foggy night she looked more like a child than a woman. A disordered child who had lost her way and met death on the detour.

Her head leaned on my shoulder. 'I'm caught,' she said. 'I've been trying all day to get up the nerve to walk into the water. What am I going to do? I can't endure forever in a room.'

'In the church you were brought up in, suicide is a sin.'

'I've committed worse.'

I waited. The fog was all around us now, an element composed of air and water and a fishy chill. It made a kind of limbo, out of this world, where anything could be said. Isobel Graff said:

'I committed the worst sin of all. They were together in the light and I was alone in the darkness. Then the light was like broken glass in my eyes, but I could see to shoot. I shot her in the groin and she died.'

'This happened in your *cabaña*?'

She nodded faintly. I felt the movement rather than saw it. 'I caught her there with Simon. She crawled out here and died on the beach. The waves came up and took her. I wish that they would take me.'

'What happened to Simon that night?'

'Nothing. He ran away. To do it again another day and do it and do it and do it. He was terrified when I came out of the back room with the gun in my hand. He was the one I really intended to kill, but he scuttled out the door.'

'Where did you get the gun?'

'It was Simon's target pistol. He kept it in his locker. He taught me to fire it himself, on this very beach.' She stirred in the crook of my arm. 'What do you think of me now?'

I didn't have to answer her. There was a moving voice in the fog above our heads. It was calling her name, Isobel.

'Who is it? Don't let them take me.' She turned on her knees and clutched my hand. Hers was fish-cold.

Footsteps and light were descending the concrete steps. I got up and went to meet them. The beam of light wavered toward me. Graff's dim and nimbused figure was behind it. The long, thin nose of a target pistol protruded from his other hand. My gun was already in mine.

'You're covered, Graff. Drop it directly in front of you.'

His pistol thudded softly in the sand. I stooped and picked it up. It was an early-model German Walther, ·22 caliber, with a custom-made walnut grip too small to fit my hand. The gun was loaded. Distrusting its hair-trigger action, I set the safety and shoved it down under my belt.

'I'll take the light, too.'

He handed me his flashlight. I turned its beam upward on his face and saw it naked for an instant. His mouth was soft and twisted, his eyes were frightened.

'I heard my wife. Where is she?'

I swung the flash-beam along the beach. Its cone of brilliance filled with swirling fog. Isobel Graff ran away from it. Black and huge on the gray air, her shadow ran ahead of her. She seemed to be driving off a fury which dwarfed her and tormented her and mimicked all her movements.

Graff called her name again and ran after her. I followed along behind and saw her fall and get up and fall again. Graff helped her to her feet. They walked back toward me, slowly and clumsily. She dragged her feet and hung her head, turning her face away from the light. Graff's arm around her waist propelled her forward.

I took the target pistol out of my belt and showed it to her. 'Is this the gun you used to shoot Gabrielle Torres?'

She glanced at it and nodded mutely.

'No,' Graff said. 'Admit nothing, Isobel.'

'She's already confessed,' I said.

'My wife is mentally incompetent. Her confession is not valid evidence.'

'The gun is. The sheriff's ballistics department will have the matching slugs. The gun and the slugs together will be unshakable evidence. Where did you get the gun, Graff?'

'Carl Walther made it for me, in Germany, many years ago.'

'I'm talking about the last twenty-four hours. Where did you get it this time?'

He answered carefully: 'I have had it in my possession continuously for over twenty years.'

'The hell you have. Stern had it last night before he was killed. Did you kill him for it?'

'That is ridiculous.'

'Did you have him killed?'

'I did not.'

'Somebody knocked off Stern to get hold of this gun. You must know who it was, and you might as well tell me. Everything's going to come out now. Not even your kind of money can stop it.'

'Is money what you want from me? You can have money.' His voice dragged with contempt—for me, and perhaps for himself.

'I'm not for sale like Marfeld,' I said: 'Your boss thug tried to buy me. He's in the Vegas clink with a body to explain.'

'I know that,' Graff said. 'But I am talking about a very great deal of money. A hundred thousand dollars in cash. Now. Tonight.'

'Where would you get that much in cash tonight?'

'From Clarence Bassett. He has it in his office safe. I paid it to him this evening. It was the price he set on the pistol. Take it away from him, and you can have it.'

XXXII

THERE WAS LIGHT in Bassett's office. I knocked so hard that I bruised my knuckles. He came to the door in shirt sleeves. His face was putty-colored, with blue hollows under the eyes. His eyes had a Lazarus look, and hardly seemed to recognize me.

'Archer? What's the trouble, man?'

'You're the trouble, Clarence.'

'Oh, I *hope* not.' He noticed the couple behind me, and did a big take. 'You've found her, Mr Graff. I'm so glad.'

'Are you?' Graff said glumly. 'Isobel has confessed everything to this man. I want my money back.'

Bassett's face underwent a process of change. The end product of the process was a bright, nervous grin which resembled the rictus of a dead horse.

'Am I to understand this? I return the money, and we drop the whole matter? Nothing more will be said?'

'Plenty more will be said. Give him his money, Clarence.'

He stood tense in the doorway, blocking my way. Visions of possible action flitted behind his pale-blue eyes and died. 'It's not here.'

'Open the safe and we'll see for ourselves.'

'You have no warrant.'

'I don't need one. You're willing to co-operate. Aren't you?'

He reached up and plucked at his neck above the open collar of his button-down shirt, stretching the loose skin and letting it pull itself back into place. 'This has been a bit of a shock. As a matter of fact, I am willing to co-operate. I have nothing to hide.'

He turned abruptly, crossed the room, and took down the photograph of the three divers. A cylindrical safe was set in the wall behind it. I covered him with the target pistol as he spun the bright chrome dials. The gun he had used on Leonard was probably at the bottom of the sea, but there could be another gun in the safe. All the safe contained was money, though—bundles of money done up in brown bank paper.

'Take it,' Graff said. 'It is yours.'

'It would only make a bum out of me. Besides, I couldn't afford to pay the tax on it.'

'You are joking. You must want money. You work for money, don't you?'

'I want it very badly,' I said. 'But I can't take this money. It wouldn't belong to me, I would belong to it. It would expect me to do things, and I would have to do them. Sit on the lid of this mess of yours, the way Marfeld did, until dry rot set in.'

'It would be easy to cover up,' Graff said.

He turned a basilisk eye on Clarence Bassett. Bassett flattened himself against the wall. The fear of death invaded his face and galvanized his body. He swatted the gun out of my hand, went down on his hands and knees, and got a grip on the butt. I snaked it away from him before he could consolidate his grip, lifted him by the collar, and set him in the chair at the end of his desk.

Isobel Graff had collapsed in the chair behind the desk. Her head was thrown back, and her undone hair poured like black oil over the back of the chair. Bassett avoided looking at her. He sat hunched far over to one side away from her, trembling and breathing hard.

'I've done nothing that I'm ashamed of. I shielded an old friend from the consequences of her actions. Her husband saw fit to reward me.'

'That's the gentlest description of blackmail I ever heard. Not that blackmail covers what you've done. Are you going to tell me you knocked off Leonard and Stern to protect Isobel Graff?'

'I have no idea what you're talking about.'

'When you tried to frame Isobel for the murder of Hester Campbell, was that part of your protection service?'

'I did nothing of the sort.'

The woman echoed him: 'Clare did nothing of the sort.'

I turned to her. 'You went to her house in Beverly Hills yesterday afternoon?'

She nodded.

'Why did you go there?'

'Clare told me she was Simon's latest chippie. He's the only one who tells me things, the only one who cares what happens to me. Clare said if I caught them together, I could force Simon to give me a divorce. Only she was already dead. I walked into the house, and she was already dead.' She spoke resentfully, as though Hester Campbell had deliberately stood her up.

'How did you know where she lived?'

'Clare told me.' She smiled at him in bright acknowledgment.

'Yesterday morning when Simon was having his dip.'

'All this is utter nonsense,' Bassett said. 'Mrs Graff is imagining it. I didn't even *know* where she lived, you can bear witness to that.'

'You wanted me to believe you didn't but you knew, all right. You'd had her traced, and you'd been threatening her. You couldn't afford to let George Wall get to her while she was still alive. But you wanted him to get to her eventually. Which is where I came in. You needed someone to lead him to her and help pin the frame on him. Just in case it didn't take, you sent Mrs Graff to the house to give you double insurance. The second frame was the one that worked—at least, it worked for Graff and his brilliant cohorts. They gave you a lot of free assistance in covering up that killing.'

'I had nothing to do with it,' Graff said behind me. 'I'm not responsible for Frost's and Marfeld's stupidity. They acted without consulting me.' He was standing by himself, just inside the door, as if to avoid any part in the proceedings.

'They were your agents,' I told him, 'and you're responsible for what they did. They're accessory after the fact of murder. You should be handcuffed to them.'

Bassett was encouraged by our split. 'You're simply fishing,' he said. 'I was fond of Hester Campbell, as you know. I had nothing against the girl. I had no reason to harm her.'

'I don't doubt you were fond of her, in some peculiar way of your own. You were probably in love with her. She wasn't in love with you, though. She was out to take you if she could. She ran out on you in September, and took along your most valuable possession.'

'I'm a poor man. I have no valuable possessions.'

'I mean this gun.' I held the Walther pistol out of his reach. 'I don't know exactly how you got it the first time. I think I know how you got it the second time. It's been passed around quite a bit in the last four months, since Hester Campbell stole it from your safe. She turned it over to her friend Lance Leonard. He wasn't up to handling the shakedown himself, so he co-opted Stern, who had experience in these matters. Stern also had connections which put him beyond the reach of Graff's strong-arm boys. But not beyond your reach.

'I'll give you credit for one thing. Clarence. It took guts to tackle Stern, even if I did soften him up for you. More guts than Graff and his private army had.'

'I didn't kill him,' Bassett said. 'You know I didn't kill him. You saw him leave.'

'You followed him out, though, didn't you? And you didn't come back for a while. You had time to slug him in the parking-lot, bundle him into his car, and drive it up the bluff where you could slit his throat and push him into the sea. That was quite an effort for a man your age. You must have wanted this gun back very badly. Were you so hungry for a hundred grand?'

Bassett looked up past me at the open safe. 'Money had nothing to do with it.' It was his first real admission. 'I didn't know he had that gun in his car until he tried to pull it on me. I hit him with a tire-iron and knocked him out. It was kill or be killed. I killed him in self-defense.'

'You didn't cut his throat in self-defense.'

'He was an evil man, a criminal, meddling in matters he didn't understand. I destroyed him as you would destroy a dangerous animal.' He was proud of killing Stern. The pride shone in his face. It made him foolish. 'A gangster and drug-peddler—is he more important than I? I'm a civilized man, I come from a good family.'

'So you cut Stern's throat. You shot Lance Leonard's eye out. You beat in Hester Campbell's skull with a poker. There are better ways to prove you're civilized.'

'They deserved it.'

'You admit you killed them?'

'I admit nothing. You have no right to bullyrag me. You can't prove a thing against me.'

'The police will be able to. They'll trace your movements, turn up witnesses to pin you down, find the gun you used on Leonard.'

'Will they really?' He had enough style left to be sardonic.

'Sure they will. You'll show them where you ditched it.

You've started to tattle on yourself already. You're no hard-faced pro, Clarence, and you shouldn't try to act like one. Last night when it was over and the three of them were dead, you had to knock yourself out with a bottle. You couldn't face the thought of what you had done. How long do you think you can hold out sitting in a cell without a bottle?'

'You hate me,' Bassett said. 'You hate me and despise me, don't you?'

'I don't think I'll answer that question. Answer one of mine. You're the only one who can. What sort of man would use a sick woman as his cat's-paw? What sort of man would cut a young girl like Gabrielle off from the light so he could collect a bounty on her death?'

Bassett made an abrupt squirming gesture of denial. The movement involved the entire upper half of his body, and resembled a convulsion. He said through rigid jaws:

'You've got it all wrong.'

'Then straighten me out.'

'What's the use? You would never understand.'

'I understand more than you think. I understand that you spied on Graff when his wife was in the sanitarium. You saw him using his *cabaña* for meetings with Gabrielle. You undoubtedly knew about the gun in his locker. Everything you knew or learned, you passed on to Isobel Graff. Probably you helped her to run away from the sanitarium, and provided her with the necessary pass-keys. It all adds up to remote-control murder. That much I understand. I don't understand what you had against Gabrielle. Did you try for her yourself and lose her to Graff? Or was it just that she was young and you were getting old, and you couldn't stand to see her living in the world?'

He stammered: 'I had nothing to do with her death.' But he turned in his chair as if a powerful hand had him by the nape of the neck. He looked at Isobel Graff for the first time, quickly and guiltily.

She was sitting upright now, as still as a statue. A statue of a blind and schizophrenic Justice, stonily returning Bassett's look:

'You did so, Clarence.'

'No, I mean I didn't plan it that way. I had no idea of blackmail. I didn't want to see her killed.'

'Who did you want to see killed?'

'Simon,' Isobel Graff said. 'Simon was to be the one. But I spoiled everything, didn't I, Clare? It was my fault it all went wrong.'

'Be quiet, Belle.' It was the first time that Bassett had spoken to her directly. 'Don't say anything more.'

'You intended to shoot your husband, Mrs Graff?'

'Yes. Clare and I were going to be married.'

Graff let out a snort, half angry and half derisive. She turned on him:

'Don't you dare laugh at me. You locked me up and stole my property. You treated me like a chattel-beast.' Her voice rose. 'I'm *sorry* I didn't kill you.'

'So you and your moth-eaten fortune-hunter could live happily ever after?'

'We could have been happy,' she said. 'Couldn't we, Clare? You love me, don't you, Clare? You've loved me all these years.'

'All these years,' he said. But his voice was empty of feeling, his eyes were dead. 'Now if you love me, you'll be quiet, Belle.' His tone, brusque and unfriendly, denied his words.

He had rebuffed her, and she had a deep, erratic intuition. Her mood swung violently. 'I know you,' she said in a hoarse monotone. 'You want to blame me for everything. You want them to put me in the forever room and throw the key away. But you're to blame, too. You said I could never be convicted of any crime. You said if I killed Simon *in fragrante—in flagrante*—the most they could do was lock me up for a while. Didn't you say that, Clare? Didn't you?'

He wouldn't answer her or look at her. Hatred blurred his features like a tight rubber mask. She turned to me:

'So you see, it was Simon I meant to kill. His chippie was just an animal he used—a little fork-legged animal. I wouldn't kill a pretty little animal.'

She paused, and said in queer surprise: 'But I did kill her. I shot her and smashed the connections. It came to me in the dark behind the door. It came to me like a picture of sin that she was the source of the evil. And she was the one the dirty old man was making passes at. So I smashed the connections. Clare was angry with me. He didn't see the wicked things she did.'

'Wasn't he with you?'

'Afterwards he was. I was trying to wipe up the blood—she bled on my nice clean floor. I was trying to wipe up the blood when Clare came in. He must have been waiting outside, and seen the chippie crawling out the door. She crawled away like a little white dog and died. And Clare was angry with me. He bawled me out.'

'How many times did you shoot her, Isobel?'

'Just once.'

'In what part of the body?'

She hung her head in ghastly modesty. 'I don't like to say, in public. I told you before.

'Gabrielle Torres was shot twice, first in the upper thigh, then in the back. The first wound wasn't fatal, it wasn't even serious. The second wound pierced her heart. It was the second shot that killed her.'

'I only shot her once.'

'Didn't you follow her down to the beach and shoot her again in the back?'

'No.' She looked at Bassett. 'Tell him, Clare. You know I couldn't have done that.'

Bassett glared at her without speaking. His eyes bulged like tiny pale balloons inflated by a pressure inside his skull.

'How would he know, Mrs Graff?'

'Because he took the gun. I dropped it on the *cabaña* floor. He picked it up and went out after her.'

The pressure forced words from Bassett's mouth. 'Don't listen to her. She's crazy—hallucinating. I wasn't within ten miles—'

'You were so, Clare,' she said quietly.

At the same time, she leaned across the desk and struck him a savage blow on the mouth. He took it stoically. It was the woman who began to cry. She said through tears:

'You had the gun when you went out after her. Then you came

back and told me she was dead, that I had killed her. But you would keep my secret because you loved me.'

Bassett looked from her to me. A line of blood lengthened from one corner of his mouth like a red crack in his livid mask. The blind worm of his tongue came out and nuzzled at the blood.

'I could use a drink, old man. I'll talk, if you'll only let me have a drink first.'

'In a minute. Did you shoot her, Clarence?'

'I had to.' He had lowered his voice to a barely audible whisper, as though a recording angel had bugged the room.

Isobel Graff said: 'Liar, pretending to be my friend! You let me live in hell.'

'I kept you out of worse hell, Belle. She was on her way to her father's house. She would have blabbed out everything.'

'So you did it all for me, you filthy liar! Young Lochinvar did it for Honeydew Heliopoulos, the girl of the golden west!' Her feelings had caught up with her. She wasn't crying now. Her voice was savage.

'For himself,' I said. 'He missed the jackpot when you failed to kill your husband. He saw his chance for a consolation prize if he could convince your husband that you murdered Gabrielle. It was a perfect set-up for a frame, so perfect that he even convinced you.'

The convulsion of denial went through Bassett again, leaving his mouth wrenched to one side. 'It wasn't that way at all. I never thought of money.'

'What's that we found in your safe?'

'It was the only money I got, or asked for. I needed it to go away, I planned to go to Mexico and live. I never thought of blackmail until Hester stole the gun and betrayed me to those criminals. They forced me to kill them, don't you see, with their greed and their indiscretion. Sooner or later the case would be reopened and the whole truth would come out.'

I looked to Graff for confirmation, but he had left the room. The empty doorway opened on darkness. I said to Bassett:

'Nobody forced you to kill Gabrielle. Why couldn't you let her go?'

'I simply couldn't,' he said. 'She was crawling home along the beach. I'd started the whole affair, I had to finish it. I could never bear to seen an animal hurt, not even a little insect or spider.'

'So you're a mercy killer?'

'No, I can't seem to make you understand. There we were, just the two of us in the dark. The surf was pounding in, and she was moaning and dragging her body along in the sand. Naked and bleeding, a girl I'd known for years, when she was an innocent child. The situation was so dreadfully horrible. Don't you see, I had to put an end to it somehow. I had to make her stop crawling.'

'And you had to kill Hester Campbell yesterday?'

'She was another one. She pretended to be innocent and wormed her way into my good graces. She called me Uncle Clarence, she pretended to like me, when all she wanted was the gun in my safe. I gave her money, I treated her like a daughter, and she betrayed me. It's a tragic thing when the young girls grow up and become gross and deceitful and lascivious.'

'So you see that they don't grow up, is that it?'

'They're better dead.'

I looked down into his face. It wasn't an unusual face. It was quite ordinary, homely and aging, given a touch of caricature by the long teeth and bulging eyes. Not the kind of face that people think of as evil. Yet it was the face of evil, drawn by a vague and passionate yearning toward the deed of darkness it abhorred.

Bassett looked up at me as if I were a long way off, communicating with him by thought-transference. He looked down at his clasped hands. The hands pulled apart from each other, and stretched and curled on his narrow thighs. The hands seemed remote from him, too, cut off by some unreported disaster from his intentions and desires.

I picked up the telephone on the desk and called the county police. They had routines for handling this sort of thing. I wanted it out of my hands.

Bassett leaned forward as I laid the receiver down. 'Look here, old fellow,' he said civilly, 'you promised me a drink. I could use a drink in the worst way.'

I went to the portable bar at the other end of the desk and got a bottle out. But Bassett received a more powerful sedative. Tony Torres came in through the open door. He slouched and shuffled forward, carrying his heavy Colt revolver. His eyes were dusty black. The flame from his gun was pale and brief, but its roar was very loud. Bassett's head was jerked to one side. It remained in that position, resting on his shoulder.

Isobel Graff looked at him in dull surprise. She rose and hooked her fingers in the neck of her denim blouse. Tore the blouse apart and offered her breast to the gun. 'Kill me. Kill me, too.'

Tony shook his head solemnly. 'Mr Graff said Mr Bassett was the one.'

He thrust the revolver into its holster. Graff entered behind him, diffidently. Stepping softly like an undertaker, Graff crossed the room to the desk where Bassett sat. His hand reached out and touched the dead man's shoulder. The body toppled, letting out a sound as it struck the floor. It was a mewling sound, like the faint and distant cry of a child for its mother.

Graff jumped back in alarm, as if his electric touch had knocked the life out of Bassett. In a sense, it had.

'Why drag Tony into this?' I said.

'It seemed the best way. The results are the same in the long run. I was doing Bassett a favor.'

'You weren't doing Tony one.'

'Don't worry about me,' Tony said. 'Two years now, two years in March, this is all I been living for, to get the guy that done it to her. I don't care if I never get back to Fresno or not.' He wiped his wet forehead with the back of his hand, and shook the sweat off his hand. He said politely: 'Is it okay with you gentlemen I step outside? It's hot in here. I'll stick around.'

'It's all right with me,' I told him.

Graff watched him go out, and turned to me with renewed assurance: 'I noticed that you didn't try to stop him. You had a gun, you could have prevented that shooting.'

'Could I?'

'At least we can keep the worst of it out of the papers now.'

'You mean the fact that you seduced a teen-aged girl and ran out on her in the clutch?'

He shushed me and looked around nervously, but Tony was out of hearing.

'I'm not thinking of myself only.'

He glanced significantly toward his wife. She was sitting on the floor in the darkest corner of the room. Her knees were drawn up to her chin. Her eyes were shut, and she was as still and silent as Bassett was.

'It's a little late to be thinking about Isobel.'

'No, you are wrong. She has great recuperative powers. I have seen her in worse condition than this. But you could not force her to face a public courtroom, you are not so inhuman.'

'She won't have to. Psychiatric Court can be held in a private hospital room. You're the one who has to face the public rap.'

'Why? Why should I have to suffer more? I have been victimized by an Iago. You don't know what I have endured in this marriage. I am a creative personality, I needed a little sweetness and gentleness in my life. I made love to a young woman, that is my only crime.'

'You lit the match that set the whole thing off. Lighting a match can be a crime if it sets fire to a building.'

'But I did nothing wrong, nothing out of the ordinary. A few tumbles in the hay, what do they amount to? You wouldn't ruin me for such a little thing? Is it fair to make me a public scapegoat, wreck my career? Is it just?'

His earnest eloquence lacked conviction. Graff had lived too long among actors. He was a citizen of the unreal city, a false front leaning on scantlings.

'Don't talk to me about justice, Graff. You've been covering up murder for nearly two years.'

'I have suffered terribly for those two years. I have suffered enough, and paid enough. It has cost me tremendous sums.'

'I wonder. You used your name to pay off Stern. You used your corporation to pay off Leonard and the Campbell girl. It's a nice trick if you can work it, letting Internal Revenue help you pay your blackmail.'

My guess must have been accurate. Graff wouldn't try to argue with it. He looked down at the valuable gun in my hand. It was the single piece of physical evidence that would force his name into the case. He said urgently:

'Give me my gun.'

'So you can put me down with it?'

Somewhere on the highway, above the rooftop, a siren whooped.

'Hurry up,' he said. 'The police are coming. Remove the shells and give me the gun. Take the money in the safe.'

'Sorry, Graff, I have a use for the gun. It's Tony's justifiable-homicide plea.'

He looked at me as if I was a fool. I don't know how I looked at Graff, but it made him drop his eyes and turn away. I closed the safe and spun the dials and rehung the photograph of the three young divers. Caught in unchanging flight, the two girls and the boy soared between the sea and the sky's bright desolation.

The siren's whoop was nearer and louder, like an animal on the roof. Before the sheriff's men walked in, I laid the Walther pistol on the floor near Bassett's outflung hand. Their ballistics experts would do the rest.

The Far Side of the Dollar

To Alfred

I

IT WAS AUGUST, and it shouldn't have been raining. Perhaps rain was too strong a word for the drizzle that blurred the landscape and kept my windshield wipers going. I was driving south, about halfway between Los Angeles and San Diego.

The school lay off the highway to my right, in large grounds of its own which stretched along the seashore. Toward the sea I caught the dull sheen of the slough that gave the place its name, Laguna Perdida. A blue heron, tiny in the distance, stood like a figurine at the edge of the ruffled water.

I entered the grounds through automatic gates which lifted when my car passed over a treadle. A gray-headed man in a blue serge uniform came out of a kiosk and limped in my direction.

'You got a pass?'

'Dr Sponti wants to see me. My name is Archer.'

'That's right, I got your name here.' He took a typewritten list out of the inside breast pocket of his jacket and brandished it as if he was proud of his literacy. 'You can park in the lot in front of the administration building. Sponti's office is right inside.' He gestured toward a stucco building a hundred yards down the road.

I thanked him. He started to limp back to his kiosk, then paused and turned and struck himself on the leg. 'Bad knee. World War I.'

'You don't look that old.'

'I'm not. I was fifteen when I enlisted, told them I was eighteen. Some of the boys in here,' he said with a sudden flashing look around him, 'could do with a taste of fire.'

There were no boys anywhere in sight. The buildings of the school, widely distributed among bare fields and dripping eucalyptus groves, lay under the gray sky like scattered components of an unbuilt city.

'Do you know the Hillman boy?' I said to the guard.

'I heard about him. He's a troublemaker. He had East Hall all stirred up before he took off. Patch was fit to be tied.'

'Who's Patch?'

'Mr Patch,' he said without affection, 'is the supervisor for East Hall. He lives in with the boys, and it plays hell with his nerves.'

'What did the Hillman boy do?'

'Tried to start a rebellion, according to Patch. Said the boys in the school had civil rights like anybody else. Which ain't so. They're all minors, and most of them are crazy in the head, besides. You wouldn't believe some of the things I've seen in my fourteen years on this gate.'

'Did Tommy Hillman go out through the gate?'

'Naw. He went over the fence. Cut a screen in the boys' dorm and sneaked out in the middle of the night.'

'Night before last?'

'That's right. He's probably home by now.'

He wasn't or I wouldn't have been there.

Dr Sponti must have seen me parking my car. He was waiting for me in the secretary's enclosure outside the door of his office. He had a glass of buttermilk in his left hand and a dietetic wafer in his right. He popped the wafer into his mouth and shook my hand, munching, 'I'm glad to see you.'

He was dark and florid and stout, with the slightly desperate look of a man who had to lose weight. I guessed that he was an emotional man—he had that liquid tremor of the eye—but one who had learned to keep his feelings under control. He was expensively and conservatively dressed in a dark-pinstripe suit which hung on him a little loosely. His hand was soft and chilly.

Dr Sponti reminded me of undertakers I had known. Even his office, with its dark mahogany furniture and the gray light at the window, had a funereal look, as if the school and its director were in continuous mourning for its students.

'Sit down,' he said with a melancholy flourish. 'We have a little problem, as I told you on the long-distance telephone. Ordinarily we don't employ private detectives to—ah—persuade our lost boys to come home. But this is a rather special case, I'm afraid.'

'What makes it special?'

Sponti sipped his buttermilk, and licked his upper lip with the tip of his tongue. 'Forgive me. Can I offer you some lunch?'

'No thanks.'

'I don't mean this.' Irritably, he jiggled the sluggish liquid in his glass. 'I can have something hot sent over from dining commons. Veal scallopini is on the menu today.'

'No thanks. I'd rather you gave me the information I need and let me get to work. Why did you call me in to pick up a runaway? You must have a lot of runaways.'

'Not as many as you might think. Most of our boys become quite school-centered in time. We have a rich and varied program for them. But Thomas Hillman had been here less than a week, and he showed very little promise of becoming group-oriented. He's quite a difficult young man.'

'And that's what makes him special?'

'I'll be frank with you, Mr Archer,' he said, and hesitated. 'This is rather a prickly situation for the school. I accepted Tom Hillman against my better judgment, actually without full knowledge of his history, simply because his father insisted upon it. And now Ralph Hillman blames us for his son's esca—that is, his surreptitious leavetaking. Hillman has threatened to sue if any harm comes to the boy. The suit wouldn't stand up in court—we've had such lawsuits before—but it could do us a great deal of public harm.' He added, almost to himself: 'Patch really was at fault.'

'What did Patch do?'

'I'm afraid he was unnecessarily violent. Not that I blame him as man to man. But you'd better talk to Mr Patch yourself. He can give you all the details of Tom's—ah—departure.'

'Later, I'd like to talk to him. But you can tell me more about the boy's background.'

'Not as much as I'd like. We ask the families, or their doctors, to give us a detailed history of our entering students. Mr Hillman promised to write one, but he hasn't as yet. And I've had great difficulty in getting any facts out of him. He's a very proud and very angry man.'

'And a wealthy one?'

'I don't know his Dun and Bradstreet rating. Most of our

parents are comfortably fixed,' he added with a quick little smug smile.

'I'd like to see Hillman. Does he live in town?'

'Yes, but please don't try to see him, at least not today. He's just been on the phone to me again, and it would only stir him up further.'

Sponti rose from his desk and moved to the window that overlooked the parking lot. I followed him. The fine rain outside hung like a visible depression in the air.

'I still need a detailed description of the boy, and everything I can find out about his habits.'

'Patch can give you that, better than I. He's been in daily contact with him. And you can talk to his housemother, Mrs Mallow. She's a trained observer.'

'Let's hope somebody is.' I was getting impatient with Sponti. He seemed to feel that the less he told me about the missing boy, the less real his disappearance was. 'How old is he, or is that classified material?'

Sponti's eyes crossed slightly, and his rather pendulous cheeks became faintly mottled. 'I object to your tone.'

'That's your privilege. How old is Tom Hillman?'

'Seventeen.'

'Do you have a picture of him?'

'None was provided by the family, though we ask for one as a matter of routine. I can tell you briefly what he looks like. He's quite a decent-looking young chap, if you overlook the sullen expression he wears habitually. He's quite big, around six feet, he looks older than his age.'

'Eyes?'

'Dark blue, I think. His hair is dark blond. He has what might be called aquiline features, like his father.'

'Identifying marks?'

He shrugged his shoulders. 'I know of none.'

'Why was he brought here?'

'For treatment, of course. But he didn't stay long enough to benefit.'

'Exactly what's the matter with him? You said he was difficult, but that's a pretty general description.'

'It was meant to be. It's hard to tell what ails these boys in adolescent storm. Often we help them without knowing how or why. I'm not a medical doctor, in any case.'

'I thought you were.'

'No. We have medical doctors associated with our staff, of course, both physicians and psychiatrists. There wouldn't be much point in talking to them. I doubt if Tom was here long enough even to meet his therapist. But there's no doubt he was high.'

'High?'

'Emotionally high, running out of control. He was in a bad way when his father brought him here. We gave him tranquillizers, but they don't always work in the same way on different subjects.'

'Did he cause you a lot of trouble?'

'He did indeed. Frankly, I doubt if we'll readmit him even if he does come back.'

'But you're hiring me to find him.'

'I have no choice.'

We discussed money matters, and he gave me a check. Then I walked down the road to East Hall. Before I went in to see Mr Patch, I turned and looked at the mountains on the far side of the valley. They loomed like half-forgotten faces through the overcast. The lonely blue heron rose from the edge of the slough and sailed toward them.

II

EAST HALL WAS a sprawling one-story stucco building which somehow didn't belong on that expansive landscape. Its mean and unprepossessing air had something to do with the high little windows, all of them heavily screened. Or with the related fact that it was a kind of prison which pretended not to be. The spiky pyracantha shrubs bordering the lawn in front of the building were more like barriers than ornaments. The grass looked dispirited even in the rain.

So did the line of boys who were marching in the front door as I came up. Boys of all ages from twelve to twenty, boys of all shapes and sizes, with only one thing in common: they marched like members of a defeated army. They reminded me of the very young soldiers we captured on the Rhine in the last stages of the last war.

Two students leaders kept them in some sort of line. I followed them, into a big lounge furnished with rather dilapidated furniture. The two leaders went straight to a ping-pong table that stood in one corner, picked up paddles, and began to play a rapid intense game with a ball that one of them produced from his windbreaker pocket. Six or seven boys began to watch them. Four or five settled down with comic books. Most of the rest of them stood around and watched me.

A hairy-faced young fellow who ought to have started to shave came up to me smiling. His smile was brilliant, but it faded like an optical illusion. He came so close that his shoulder nudged my arm. Some dogs will nudge you like that, to test your friendliness.

'Are you the new supervisor?'

'No. I thought Mr Patch was the supervisor.'

'He won't last.' A few of the younger boys giggled. The hairy one responded like a successful comedian. 'This is the violent ward. They never last.'

'It doesn't look so violent to me. Where is Mr Patch?'

'Over at dining commons. He'll be here in a minute. Then we have organized fun.'

'You sound pretty cynical for your age. How old are you?'

'Ninety-nine.' His audience murmured encouragingly. 'Mr Patch is only forty-nine. It makes it hard for him to be my father-image.'

'Maybe I could talk to Mrs Mallow.'

'She's in her room drinking her lunch. Mrs Mallow always drinks her lunch.' The bright malice in his eyes alternated with a darker feeling. 'Are you a father?'

'No.'

In the background the ping-pong ball was clicking back and forth like mindless conversation.

A member of the audience spoke up. 'He's not a father.'

'Maybe he's a mother,' said the hairy boy. 'Are you a mother?'

'He doesn't look like a mother. He has no bosoms.'

'My mother has no bosoms,' said a third one. 'That's why I feel rejected.'

'Come off it, boys.' The hell of it was, they wished I was a father, or even a mother, one of theirs, and the wish stood in their eyes. 'You don't want me to feel rejected, do you?'

Nobody answered. The hairy boy smiled up at me. It lasted a little longer than his first smile. 'What's your name? I'm Frederick Tyndal the Third.'

'I'm Lew Archer the First.'

I drew the boy away from his audience. He pulled back from my touch, but he came along and sat down with me on a cracked leather couch. Some of the younger boys had put an overplayed record on a player. Two of them began to dance together to the raucous self-parodying song. 'Surfin' ain't no sin,' was the refrain.

'Did you know Tom Hillman, Fred?'

'A little. Are you his father?'

'No. I said I wasn't a father.'

'Adults don't necessarily tell you the truth.' He plucked at the hairs on his chin as if he hated the signs of growing up. 'My father said he was sending me away to military school. He's a big shot in the government,' he added flatly, without pride, and then, in a different tone: 'Tom Hillman didn't get along with his father, either. So he got railroaded here. The Monorail to the Magic Kingdom.' He produced a fierce ecstatic hopeless grin.

'Did Tom talk to you about it?'

'A little. He wasn't here long. Five days. Six. He came in Sunday night and took off Saturday night.' He squirmed uneasily on the creaking leather. 'Are you a cop?'

'No.'

'I just wondered. You ask questions like a cop.'

'Did Tom do something that would interest the cops?'

'We all do, don't we?' His hot and cold running glance went around the room, pausing on the forlorn antics of the dancing boys. 'You don't qualify for East Hall unless you're a juvie. I was a criminal mastermind myself. I forged the big shot's name on a fifty-dollar check and went to San Francisco for the weekend.'

'What did Tom do?'

'Stole a car, I guess. It was a first offense, he said, and he would of got probation easy. But his father didn't want the publicity, so he put him in here. Also, I guess Tom had a fight with his father.'

'I see.'

'Why are you so fascinated in Tom?'

'I'm supposed to find him, Fred.'

'And bring him back here?'

'I doubt that they'll readmit him.'

'He's lucky.' More or less unconsciously, he moved against me again. I could smell the untended odor of his hair and body, and sense his desolation. 'I'd break out of here myself if I had a place to go. But the big shot would turn me over to the Youth Authority. It would save him money, besides.'

'Did Tom have a place to go?'

He jerked upright and looked at my eyes from the corners of his. 'I didn't say that.'

'I'm asking you.'

'He wouldn't tell me if he had.'

'Who was closest to him in the school?'

'He wasn't close to anybody. He was so upset when he came in, they put him in a room by himself. I went in and talked to him one night, but he didn't say much to me.'

'Nothing about where he planned to go?'

'He didn't *plan* anything. He tried to start a riot Saturday night but the rest of us were chicken. So he took off. He seemed to be very excited.'

'Was he emotionally disturbed?'

'Aren't we all?' He tapped his own temple and made an insane face. 'You ought to see my Rorschach.'

'Some other time.'

'Be my guest.'

'This is important, Fred. Tom is very young, and excited, as you said. He's been missing for two nights now, and he could get into very serious trouble.'

'Worse than this?'

'You know it, or you'd be over the fence yourself. Did Tom say anything about where he was going?'

The boy didn't answer.

'Then I assume he did tell you something?'

'No.' But he wouldn't meet my eyes.

Mr Patch came into the room and changed its carefree atmosphere. The dancing boys pretended to be wrestling. Comic books disappeared like bundles of hot money. The ping-pong players put away their ball.

Patch was a middle-aged man with thinning hair and thickening jowls. His double-breasted tan gabardine suit was creased across his rather corpulent front. His face was creased, too, into a sneer of power which didn't go with his sensitive small mouth. As he looked around the room, I could see that the whites of his eyes were tinted with red.

He strode to the record player and turned it off, insinuating his voice into the silence:

'Lunch time isn't music time, boys. Music time is after dinner, from seven to seven-thirty.' He addressed one of the ping-pong players: 'Bear that in mind, Deering. No music in the daytime. I'll hold you responsible.'

'Yessir.'

'And weren't you playing ping-pong?'

'We were just rallying, sir.'

'Where did you get the ball? I understood the balls were locked up in my desk.'

'They are, sir.'

'Where did you get the one you were playing with?'

'I don't know, sir.' Deering fumbled at his windbreaker. He was a gawky youth with an Adam's apple that looked like a hidden ping-pong ball. 'I think I must of found it.'

'Where did you find it? In my desk?'

'No sir. On the grounds, I think it was.'

Mr Patch walked toward him with a kind of melodramatic stealth. As he moved across the room, the boys behind him made faces, waved their arms, did bumps and grinds. One boy, one of the dancers, fell silently to the floor with a throat-slitting gesture, held the pose of a dying gladiator for a single frozen second, then got back onto his feet.

Patch was saying in a long-suffering tone: 'You bought it, didn't you, Deering? You know that regulations forbid you fellows to bring in private ping-pong balls of your own. You know that, don't you? You're president of the East Hall Legislative Assembly, you helped to frame those regulations yourself. Didn't you?'

'Yessir.'

'Then give it to me, Deering.'

The boy handed Patch the ball. Patch stooped to place it on the floor—while a boy behind him pretended to kick him—and squashed it under his heel. He gave Deering the misshapen ball.

'I'm sorry, Deering. I have to obey the regulations just as you do.' He turned to the roomful of boys, who snapped into conformity under his eyes, and said mildly: 'Well, fellows, what's on the agenda—?'

'I think I am,' I said, getting up from the couch. I gave him my name and asked if I could talk to him in private.

'I suppose so,' he said with a worried smile, as if I might in fact be his successor. 'Come into my office, such as it is. Deering and Bronson, I'm leaving you in charge.'

His office was a windowless cubicle containing a cluttered desk and two straight chairs. He closed the door on the noise that drifted down the corridor from the lounge, turned on a desk lamp, and sat down sighing.

'You've got to stay on top of them.' He sounded like a man saying his prayers. 'You wanted to discuss one of my boys?'

'Tom Hillman.'

The name depressed him. 'You represent his father?'

'No. Dr Sponti sent me to talk to you. I'm a private detective.'

'I see.' He pushed out his lips in a kind of pout. 'I suppose Sponti's been blaming me, as usual.'

'He did say something about unnecessary violence.'

'That's nonsense!' He pounded the desk between us with his clenched fist. His face became congested with blood. Then it went starkly pale, like a raw photograph. Only the reddish whites of his eyes held their color. 'Sponti doesn't work down here with the animals. I ought to know when physical discipline is necessary. I've been in juvenile work for twenty-five years.'

'It seems to be getting you down.'

With an effort that crumpled up his face, he brought himself under control. 'Oh no, I love the work, I really do. Anyway, it's the only thing I'm trained for. I love the boys. And they love me.'

'I could see that.'

He wasn't listening for my irony. 'I'd have been pals with Tom Hillman if he'd lasted.'

'Why didn't he?'

'He ran away. You know that. He stole a pair of shears from the gardener and used it to cut the screen on his bedroom window.'

'Exactly when was this?'

'Sometime Saturday night, between my eleven-o'clock bed-check and my early-morning one.'

'And what happened before that?'

'Saturday night, you mean? He was stirring up the other boys, inciting them to attack the resident staff. I'd left the common room after dinner, and I heard him from in here, making a speech. He was trying to convince the boys that they had been deprived of their rights and should fight for them. Some of the more excitable ones were affected. But when I ordered Hillman to shut up, he was the only one who rushed me.'

'Did he hit you?'

'I hit him first,' Patch said. 'I'm not ashamed of it. I had to preserve my authority with the others.' He rubbed his fist. 'I knocked him cold. You have to make a show of manliness. When I hit them, they go down for the count. You have to give them an image to respect.'

I said to stop him: 'What happened after that?'

'I helped him to his room, and then I reported the incident to Sponti. I thought the boy should be put in the padded room. But Sponti countermanded my advice. Hillman would never have broken out if Sponti had let me put him in the padded room. Just between you and me, it's Sponti's fault.' He brought himself up short and said in a smaller voice: 'Don't quote me to him.'

'All right.'

I was beginning to despair of getting anything useful out of

Patch. He was a little dilapidated, like the furniture in the common room. The noise coming from that direction was becoming louder. Patch rose wearily to his feet.

'I'd better get back there before they tear the place down.'

'I just wanted to ask you, do you have any thoughts on where Tom Hillman went after he left here?'

Patch considered my question. He seemed to be having difficulty in imagining the outside world into which the boy had vanished. 'LA,' he said finally. 'They usually head for LA Or else they head south for San Diego and the border.'

'Or east?'

'If their parents live east, they sometimes go that way.'

'Or west across the ocean?' I was baiting him.

'That's true. One boy stole a thirty-foot launch and headed for the islands.'

'You seem to have a lot of runaways.'

'Over the years, we have quite a turnover. Sponti's opposed to strict security measures, like we used to have at Juvenile Hall. With all the breakouts we've had, I'm surprised he wants to make such a production out of this one. The boy'll turn up, they nearly always do.'

Patch sounded as if he wasn't looking forward to the prospect.

Somebody tapped at the door behind me. 'Mr Patch?' a woman said through the panels.

'Yes, Mrs Mallow.'

'The boys are getting out of hand. They won't listen to me. What are you doing in there?'

'Conferring. Dr Sponti sent a man.'

'Good. We need a man.'

'Is that so?' He brushed past me and opened the door. 'Keep your cracks to yourself, please, Mrs Mallow. I know one or two things that Dr Sponti would dearly love to know.'

'So do I,' the woman said.

She was heavily rouged, with dyed red hair arranged in bangs on her forehead. She had on a dark formal dress, about ten years out of fashion, and several loops of imitation pearls. Her face was pleasant enough, in spite of eyes that had been bleared by horrors inner and outer.

She brightened up when she saw me. 'Hello.'

'My name is Archer,' I said. 'Dr Sponti brought me in to look into Tom Hillman's disappearance.'

'He's a nice-looking boy,' she said. 'At least he was until our local Marquis de Sade gave him a working-over.'

'I acted in self-defense,' Patch cried. 'I don't enjoy hurting people. I'm the authority figure in East Hall, and when I'm attacked it's just like killing their father.'

'You better go and make with the authority, Father. But if you hurt anybody this week I'll carve the living heart out of your body.'

Patch looked at her as if he believed she might do it. Then he turned on his heel and strode away toward the roaring room. The roaring subsided abruptly, as if he had closed a soundproof door behind him.

'Poor old Patch,' said Mrs Mallow. 'He's been around too long. Poor old all of us. Too many years of contact with the adolescent mind, if mind is the word, and eventually we all go blah.'

'Why stay?'

'We get so we can't live in the outside world. Like old convicts. That's the real hell of it.'

'People around here are extraordinarily ready to spill their problems—'

'It's the psychiatric atmosphere.'

'But,' I went on, 'they don't tell me much I want to know. Can *you* give me a clear impression of Tom Hillman?'

'I can give you my own impression.'

She had a little difficulty with the word, and it seemed to affect her balance. She walked into Patch's office and leaned on his desk facing me. Her face, half-shadowed in the upward light from the lamp, reminded me of a sibyl's.

'Tom Hillman is a pretty nice boy. He didn't belong here. He found that out in a hurry. And so he left.'

'Why didn't he belong here?'

'You want me to go into detail? East Hall is essentially a place for boys with personality and character problems, or with a sociopathic tendency. We keep the more disturbed youngsters, boys and girls, in West Hall.'

'And Tom belonged there?'

'Hardly. He shouldn't have been sent to Laguna Perdida at all. This is just my opinion, but it ought to be worth something. I used to be a pretty good clinical psychologist.' She looked down into the light.

'Dr Sponti seems to think Tom was disturbed.'

'Dr Sponti never thinks otherwise, about any prospect. Do you know what these kids' parents pay? A thousand dollars a month, plus extras. Music lessons. Group therapy.' She laughed harshly. 'When half the time it's the parents who should be here. Or in some worse place.

'A thousand dollars a month,' she repeated. 'So Dr Sponti so-called can draw his twenty-five thousand a year. Which is more than six times what he pays me for holding the kids' hands.'

She was a woman with a grievance. Sometimes grievances made for truth-telling, but not always. 'What do you mean, Dr Sponti so-called?'

'He's not a medical doctor, or any other kind of real doctor. He took his degree in educational administration, at one of the diploma mills down south. Do you know what he wrote his dissertation on? The kitchen logistics of the medium-sized boarding school.'

'Getting back to Tom,' I said, 'why would his father bring him here if he didn't need psychiatric treatment?'

'I don't know. I don't know his father. Probably because he wanted him out of his sight.'

'Why?' I insisted.

'The boy was in some kind of trouble.'

'Did Tom tell you that?'

'He wouldn't talk about it. But I can read the signs.'

'Have you heard the story that he stole a car?'

'No, but it would help to explain him. He's a very unhappy young man, and a guilty one. He isn't one of your hardened j.d.'s. Not that any of them *really* are.'

'You seem to have liked Tom Hillman.'

'What little I saw of him. He didn't want to talk last week, and I try never to force myself on the boys. Except for class hours, he spent most of the time in his room. I think he was trying to work something out.'

'Like a plan for revolution?'

Her eyes glinted with amusement. 'You heard about that, did you? The boy had more gumption than I gave him credit for. Don't look so surprised. I'm on the boys' side. Why else would I be here?'

I was beginning to like Mrs Mallow. Sensing this, she moved toward me and touched my arm. 'I hope that you are, too. On Tom's side, I mean.'

'I'll wait until I know him. It isn't important, anyway.'

'Yes it is. It's always important.'

'Just what happened between Tom and Mr Patch Saturday night?'

'I wouldn't know, really. Saturday night is my night off. You can make a note of that if you like, Mr Archer.'

She smiled, and I caught a glimpse of her life's meaning. She cared for other people. Nobody cared for her.

III

SHE LET ME out through a side door which had to be unlocked. The rain was just heavy enough to wet my face. Dense-looking clouds were gathering over the mountains, which probably meant that the rain was going to persist.

I started back toward the administration building. Sponti was going to have to be told that I must see Tom Hillman's parents, whether he approved or not. The varying accounts of Tom I'd had, from people who liked or disliked him, gave me no distinct impression of his habits or personality. He could be a persecuted teen-ager, or a psychopath who knew how to appeal to older women, or something in between, like Fred the Third.

I wasn't looking where I was going, and a yellow cab almost ran me down in the parking lot. A man in tweeds got out of the back seat. I thought he was going to apologize to me, but he didn't appear to see me.

He was a tall, silver-haired man, well fed, well cared for, probably good-looking under normal conditions. At the moment he looked haggard. He ran into the administration building. I walked in after him, and found him arguing with Sponti's secretary.

'I'm very sorry, Mr Hillman,' she intoned. 'Dr Sponti is in conference. I can't possibly interrupt him.'

'I think you'd better,' Hillman said in a rough voice.

'I'm sorry. You'll have to wait.'

'But I can't wait. My son is in the hands of criminals. They're trying to extort money from me.'

'Is that true?' Her voice was unprofessional and sharp.

'I'm not in the habit of lying.'

The girl excused herself and went into Sponti's office, closing the door carefully behind her. I spoke to Hillman, telling him my name and occupation:

'Dr Sponti called me in to look for your son. I've been wanting to talk to you. It seems to be time I did.'

'Yes. By all means.'

He took my hand. He was a large, impressive-looking man. His face had the kind of patrician bony structure that doesn't necessarily imply brains or ability, or even decency, but that generally goes with money. He was deep in the chest and heavy in the shoulders. But there was no force in his grasp. He was trembling all over, like a frightened dog.

'You said something about criminals and extortion.'

'Yes.' But his steel-gray eyes kept shifting away to the door of Sponti's office. He wanted to talk to somebody he could blame. 'What are they doing in there?' he said a little wildly.

'It hardly matters. If your son's been kidnapped, Sponti can't help you much. It's a matter for the police.'

'No! The police stay out. I've been instructed to keep them out.' His eyes focused on me for the first time, hard with suspicion. 'You're not a policeman, are you?'

'I told you I was a private detective. I just came down from Los Angeles an hour ago. How did you find out about Tom, and who gave you your instructions?'

'One of the gang. He telephoned my house when we were just

sitting down to lunch. He warned me to keep the matter quiet. Otherwise Tom will never come back.'

'Did he say that?'

'Yes.'

'What else did he say?'

'They want to sell me information about Tom's whereabouts. It was just a euphemism for ransom money.'

'How much?'

'Twenty-five thousand dollars.'

'Do you have it?'

'I'll have it by the middle of the afternoon. I'm selling some stock. I went into town to my broker's before I came here.'

'You move fast, Mr Hillman.' He needed some mark of respect. 'But I don't quite understand why you came out here.'

'I don't trust these people,' he said in a lowered voice. Apparently he had forgotten, or hadn't heard, that I was working for Sponti. 'I believe that Tom was lured away from here, perhaps with inside help, and they're covering up.'

'I doubt that very much. I've talked to the staff member involved. He and Tom had a fight Saturday night, and later Tom cut a screen and went over the fence. One of the students confirmed this, more or less.'

'A student would be afraid to deny the official story.'

'Not this student, Mr Hillman. If your son's been kidnapped, it happened after he left here. Tell me this, did he have any criminal connections?'

'Tom? You must be out of your mind.'

'I heard he stole a car.'

'Did Sponti tell you that? He had no right to.'

'I got it from other sources. Boys don't usually steal cars unless they've had some experience outside the law, perhaps with a juvenile gang—'

'He didn't steal it.' Hillman's eyes were evasive. 'He borrowed it from a neighbor. The fact that he wrecked it was pure accident. He was emotionally upset—'

Hillman was, too. He ran out of breath and words. He opened and closed his mouth like a big handsome fish hooked by circumstance and yanked into alien air. I said:

'What are you supposed to do with the twenty-five thousand? Hold it for further instructions?'

Hillman nodded, and sat down despondently in a chair. Dr Sponti's door had opened, and he had been listening, I didn't know for how long. He came out into the anteroom now, flanked by his secretary and followed by a man with a long cadaverous face.

'What's this about kidnapping?' Sponti said in a high voice. He forced his voice down into a more soothing register: 'I'm sorry, Mr Hillman.'

Hillman's sitting position changed to a kind of crouch. 'You're going to be sorrier. I want to know who took my son out of here, and under what circumstances, and with whose connivance.'

'Your son left here of his own free will, Mr Hillman.'

'And you wash your hands of him, do you?'

'We never do that with any of our charges, however short their stay. I've hired Ar Archer here to help you out. And I've just been talking to Mr Squerry here, our comptroller.'

The cadaverous man bowed solemnly. Black stripes of hair were pasted flat across the crown of his almost naked head. He said in a precise voice:

'Dr Sponti and I have decided to refund in full the money you paid us last week. We've just written out a check, and here it is.'

He handed over a slip of yellow paper. Hillman crumpled it into a ball and threw it back at Mr Squerry. It bounced off his thin chest and fell to the floor. I picked it up. It was for two thousand dollars.

Hillman ran out of the room. I walked out after him, before Sponti could terminate my services, and caught Hillman as he was getting into the cab.

'Where are you going?'

'Home. My wife's in poor shape.'

'Let me drive you.'

'Not if you're Sponti's man.'

'I'm nobody's man but my own. Sponti hired me to find your son. I'm going to do that if it's humanly possible. But I'll need some cooperation from you and Mrs Hillman.'

'What can we do?' He spread his large helpless hands.

'Tell me what kind of a boy he is, who his friends are, where he hangs out—'

'What's the point of all that? He's in the hands of gangsters. They want money. I'm willing to pay them.'

The cab driver, who had got out of his seat to open the door for Hillman, stood listening with widening mouth and eyes.

'It may not be as simple as that,' I said. 'But we won't talk about it here.'

'You can trust me,' the driver said huskily. 'I got a brother-in-law on the Highway Patrol. Besides, I never blab about my fares.'

'You better not,' Hillman said.

He paid the man, and came along with me to my car.

'Speaking of money,' I said when we were together in the front seat, 'you didn't really want to throw away two thousand dollars, did you?' I smoothed out the yellow check and handed it to him.

There's no way to tell what will make a man break down. A long silence, or a telephone ringing, or the wrong note in a woman's voice. In Hillman's case, it was a check for two thousand dollars. He put it away in his alligator wallet, and then he groaned loudly. He covered his eyes with his hands and leaned his forehead on the dash. Cawing sounds came out of his mouth as if an angry crow was tearing at his vitals.

After a while he said: 'I should never have put him in this place.' His voice was more human than it had been, as if he had broken through into a deeper level of self-knowledge.

'Don't cry over spilt milk.'

He straightened up. 'I wasn't crying.' It was true his eyes were dry.

'We won't argue, Mr Hillman. Where do you live?'

'In El Rancho. It's between here and the city. I'll tell you how to get there by the shortest route.'

The guard limped out of his kiosk, and we exchanged half-salutes. He activated the gates. Following Hillman's instructions, I drove out along a road which passed through a reedy wasteland where blackbirds were chittering, then through a suburban wasteland jammed with new apartments, and around the perimeter of a college campus. We passed an airport, where a plane was taking off. Hillman looked as if he wished he were on it.

'Why did you put your son in Laguna Perdida School?'

His answer came slowly, in bits and snatches. 'I was afraid. He seemed to be headed for trouble. I felt I had to prevent it somehow. I was hoping they could straighten him out so that he could go back to regular school next month. He's supposed to be starting his senior year in high school.'

'Would you mind being specific about the trouble he was in? Do you mean car theft?'

'That was one of the things. But it wasn't a true case of theft, as I explained.'

'You didn't explain, though.'

'It was Rhea Carlson's automobile he took. Rhea and Jay Carlson are our next-door neighbors. When you leave a new Dart in an open carport all night with the key in the ignition, it's practically an invitation to a joyride. I told them that. Jay would've admitted it, too, if he hadn't had a bit of a down on Tom. Or if Tom hadn't wrecked the car. It was fully covered, by my insurance as well as theirs, but they had to take the emotional approach.'

'The car was wrecked?'

'It's a total loss. I don't know how he managed to turn it over, but he did. Fortunately he came out of it without a scratch.'

'Where was he going?'

'He was on his way home. The accident happened practically at our door. I'll show you the place.'

'Then where had he been?'

'He wouldn't say. He'd been gone all night, but he wouldn't tell me anything about it.'

'What night was that?'

'Saturday night. A week ago Saturday night. The police brought him home about six o'clock in the morning, and told me I better have our doctor go over him, which I did. He wasn't hurt physically, but his mind seemed to be affected. He went into a rage when I tried to ask him where he had spent the night. I'd never seen him like that before. He'd always been a quiet-spoken boy. He said I had no right to know about him, that I wasn't really his father, and so on and so forth. I'm afraid I lost my temper and slapped him when he said that. Then he turned his back on me and wouldn't talk at all, about anything.'

'Had he been drinking?'

'I don't think so. No. I would have smelled it on him.'

'What about drugs?'

I could see his face turn toward me, large and vague in my side vision. 'That's out of the question.'

'I hope so. Dr Sponti told me your son had a peculiar reaction to tranquillizers. That sometimes happens with habitual users.'

'My son was not a drug user.'

'A lot of young people are, nowadays, and their parents are the last to know about it.'

'No. It wasn't anything like that,' he said urgently. 'The shock of the accident affected his mind.'

'Did the doctor think so?'

'Dr Shanley is an orthopedic surgeon. He wouldn't know about psychiatric disturbance. Anyway, he didn't know what happened that morning, when I went to the judge's house to arrange for bail. I haven't told anyone about it.'

I waited, and listened to the windshield wipers. A green and white sign on the shoulder of the road announced: 'El Rancho.' Hillman said, as if he was glad to have something neutral to say:

'You turn off in another quarter mile.'

I slowed down. 'You were going to tell me what happened that Sunday morning.'

'No. I don't believe I will. It has no bearing on the present situation.'

'How do we know that?'

He didn't answer me. Perhaps the thought of home and neighbors had silenced him.

'Did you say the Carlsons had a down on Tom?'

'I said that, and it's true.'

'Do you know the reason for it?'

'They have a daughter, Stella. Tom and Stella Carlson were very close. Jay and Rhea disapproved, at least Rhea did. So did Elaine, my wife, for that matter.'

I turned off the main road. The access road passed between

tall stone gateposts and became the palm-lined central road bisecting El Rancho. It was one of those rich developments whose inhabitants couldn't possibly have troubles. Their big houses sat far back behind enormous lawns. Their private golf course lay across the road we were travelling on. The diving tower of their beach club gleamed with fresh aluminum paint in the wet distance.

But like the drizzle, troubles fall in or out of season on everybody.

The road bent around one corner of the golf course. Hillman pointed ahead to a deep gouge in the bank, where the earth was still raw. Above it a pine tree with a damaged trunk was turning brown in places.

'This is where he turned the car over.'

I stopped the car. 'Did he explain how the accident happened?'

Hillman pretended not to hear me. We got out of the car. There was no traffic in sight, except for a foursome of die-hard golfers approaching in two carts along the fairway.

'I don't see any brake- or skid-marks,' I said. 'Was your son an experienced driver?'

'Yes. I taught him to drive myself. I spent a great deal of time with him. In fact, I deliberately reduced my work load at the firm several years ago, partly so that I could enjoy Tom's growing up.'

His phrasing was a little strange, as if growing up was something a boy did for his parents' entertainment. It made me wonder. If Hillman had been really close to Tom, why had he clapped him into Laguna Perdida School at the first sign of delinquency? Or had there been earlier signs which he was suppressing?

One of the golfers waved from his cart as he went by. Hillman gave him a cold flick of the hand and got into my car. He seemed embarrassed to be found at the scene of the accident.

'I'll be frank with you,' I said as we drove away. 'I wish you'd be frank with me. Laguna Perdida is a school for disturbed and delinquent minors. I can't get it clear why Tom deserved, or needed, to be put there.'

'I did it for his own protection. Good-neighbor Carlson was threatening to prosecute him for car theft.'

'That's nothing so terrible. He'd have rated probation, if this was a first offense. Was it?'

'Of course it was.'

'Then what were you afraid of?'

'I wasn't—' he started to say. But he was too honest, or too completely conscious of his fear, to finish the sentence.

'What did he do Sunday morning, when you went to see the judge?'

'He didn't do anything, really. Nothing happened.'

'But that nothing hit you so hard you won't discuss it.'

'That's correct. I won't discuss it, with you or anyone. Whatever happened last Sunday, or might have happened, has been completely outdated by recent events. My son has been kidnapped. He's a passive victim, don't you understand?'

I wondered about that, too. Twenty-five thousand dollars was a lot of money in my book, but it didn't seem to be in Hillman's. If Tom was really in the hands of professional criminals, they would be asking for all that the traffic would bear.

'How much money could you raise if you had to, Mr Hillman?'

He gave me a swift look. 'I don't see the point.'

'Kidnappers usually go the limit in their demands. I'm trying to find out if they have in this case. I gather you could raise a good deal more than twenty-five thousand.'

'I could, with my wife's help.'

'Let's hope it won't be necessary.'

IV

THE HILLMANS' PRIVATE drive meandered up an oak-covered rise and circled around in a lawn in front of their house. It was a big old Spanish mansion, with white stucco walls, wrought-iron ornamentation at the windows, red tile roof gleaming dully in the wet. A bright black Cadillac was parked in the circle ahead of us.

'I meant to drive myself this morning,' Hillman said. 'But then I didn't trust myself to drive. Thanks for the lift.'

It sounded like a dismissal. He started up the front steps, and I felt a keen disappointment. I swallowed it and went after him, slipping inside the front door before he closed it.

It was his wife he was preoccupied with. She was waiting for him in the reception hall, bowed forward in a high-backed Spanish chair which made her look tinier than she was. Her snakeskin shoes hung clear of the polished tile floor. She was a beautifully made thin blonde woman in her forties. An aura of desolation hung about her, a sense of uselessness, as if she was in fact the faded doll she resembled. Her green dress went poorly with her almost greenish pallor.

'Elaine?'

She had been sitting perfectly still, with her knees and fists together. She looked up at her husband, and then over his head at the huge Spanish chandelier suspended on a chain from the beamed ceiling two stories up. Its bulbs protruded like dubious fruit from clusters of wrought-iron leaves.

'Don't stand under it,' she said. 'I'm always afraid it's going to fall. I wish you'd have it taken down, Ralph.'

'It was your idea to bring it back and put it there.'

'That was a long time ago,' she said. 'I thought the space needed filling.'

'It still does, and it's still perfectly safe.' He moved toward her and touched her head. 'You're wet. You shouldn't have gone out in your condition.'

'I just walked down the drive to see if you were coming. You were gone a long time.'

'I couldn't help it.'

She took his hand as it slid away from her head, and held it against her breast. 'Did you hear anything?'

'We can't expect to hear anything yet for a while. I made arrangements for the money. Dick Leandro will bring it out later this afternoon. In the meantime we wait for a phone call.'

'It's hideous, waiting.'

'I know. You should try to think about something else.'

'What else is there?'

'Lots of things.' I think he tried to name one, and gave up. 'Anyway, it isn't good for you to be sitting out here in the cold hall. You'll give yourself pneumonia again.'

'People don't give it to *themselves*, Ralph.'

'We won't argue. Come into the sitting room and I'll make you a drink.'

He remembered me and included me in the invitation, but he didn't introduce me to his wife. Perhaps he considered me unworthy, or perhaps he wanted to discourage communication between us. Feeling rather left out, I followed them up three tile steps into a smaller room where a fire was burning. Elaine Hillman stood with her back to it. Her husband went to the bar, which was in an alcove decorated with Spanish bullfight posters.

She held out her hand to me. It was ice cold. 'I don't mean to monopolize the heat. Are you a policeman? I thought we weren't to use them.'

'I'm a private detective. Lew Archer is my name.'

Her husband called from the alcove: 'What will you drink, darling?'

'Absinthe.'

'Is that such a good idea?'

'It has wormwood in it, which suits my mood. But I'll settle for a short Scotch.'

'What about you, Mr Archer?'

I asked for the same. I needed it. While I rather liked both of the Hillmans, they were getting on my nerves. Their joint handling of their anxiety was almost professional, as if they were actors improvising a tragedy before an audience of one. I don't mean the anxiety wasn't sincere. They were close to dying of it.

Hillman came back across the room with three lowball glasses on a tray. He set it down on a long table in front of the fireplace and handed each of us a glass. Then he shook up the wood fire with a poker. Flames hissed up the chimney. Their reflection changed his face for a moment to a red savage mask.

His wife's face hung like a dead moon over her drink. 'Our son is very dear to us, Mr Archer. Can you help us get him back?'

'I can try. I'm not sure it's wise to keep the police out of this. I'm only one man, and this isn't my normal stomping ground.'

'Does that make a difference?'

'I have no informers here.'

'Do you hear him, Ralph?' she said to her crouching husband. 'Mr Archer thinks we should have the police in.'

'I hear him. But it isn't possible.' He straightened up with a sigh, as if the whole weight of the house was on his shoulders. 'I'm not going to endanger Tom's life by anything I do.'

'I feel the same way,' she said. 'I'm willing to pay through the nose to get him back. What use is money without a son to spend it on?'

That was another phrase that was faintly strange. I was getting the impression that Tom was the center of the household, but a fairly unknown center, like a god they made sacrifices to and expected benefits from, and maybe punishments, too. I was beginning to sympathize with Tom.

'Tell me about him, Mrs Hillman.'

Some life came up into her dead face. But before she could open her mouth Hillman said: 'No. You're not going to put Elaine through that now.'

'But Tom's a pretty shadowy figure to me. I'm trying to get some idea of where he might have gone yesterday, how he got tangled up with extortionists.'

'*I* don't know where he went,' the woman said.

'Neither do I. If I had,' Hillman said, 'I'd have gone to him yesterday.'

'Then I'm going to have to go out and do some legwork. You can let me have a picture, I suppose.'

Hillman went into an adjoining room, twilit behind pulled drapes, where the open top of a grand piano leaned up out of the shadows. He came back with a silver-framed studio photograph of a boy whose features resembled his own. The boy's dark eyes were rebellious, unless I was projecting my own sense of the household into them. They were also intelligent and imaginative. His mouth was spoiled.

'Can I take this out of the frame? Or if you have a smaller one, it would be better to show around.'

'To show around?'

'That's what I said, Mr Hillman. It's not for my memory book.'

Elaine Hillman said: 'I have a smaller one upstairs on my dressing table. I'll get it.'

'Why don't I go up with you? It might help if I went through his room.'

'You can look at his room,' Hillman said, 'but I don't want you searching it.'

'Why?'

'I just don't like the idea. Tom has the right to some privacy, even now.'

The three of us went upstairs, keeping an eye on each other. I wondered what Hillman was afraid I might find, but I hesitated to ask him. While everything seemed to be under control, Hillman could flare up at any moment and order me out of his house.

He stood at the door while I gave the room a quick once-over. It was a front bedroom, very large, furnished with plain chests of drawers and chairs and a table and a bed which all looked hand-finished and expensive. A bright red telephone sat on the bedside table. There were engravings of sailing ships and Audubon prints hung with geometric precision around the walls, Navajo rugs on the floor, and a wool bedspread matching one of them.

I turned to Hillman. 'Was he interested in boats and sailing?'

'Not particularly. He used to come out and crew for me occasionally, on the sloop, when I couldn't get anyone else. Does it matter?'

'I was just wondering if he hung around the harbor much.'

'No. He didn't.'

'Was he interested in birds?'

'I don't think so.'

'Who chose the pictures?'

'I did,' Elaine Hillman said from the hallway. 'I decorated the room for Tom. He liked it, didn't he, Ralph?'

Hillman mumbled something. I crossed the room to the deeply set front windows, which overlooked the semicircular driveway. I could see down the wooded slope, across the golf course, all the way to the highway, where cars rolled back and forth like children's toys out of reach. I could imagine Tom sitting here in the alcove and watching the highway lights at night.

A thick volume of music lay open on the leather seat. I looked at the cover. It was a well-used copy of *The Well-Tempered Clavier*.

'Did Tom play the piano, Mr Hillman?'

'Very well. He had ten years of lessons. But then he wanted—'

His wife made a small dismayed sound at his shoulder. 'Why go into all that?'

'All what?' I said. 'Trying to get information out of you people is like getting blood out of a stone.'

'I *feel* like a bloodless stone,' she said with a little grimace. 'This hardly seems the time to rake up old family quarrels.'

'We didn't quarrel,' her husband said. 'It was the one thing Tom and I ever disagreed on. And he went along with me on it. End of subject.'

'All right. Where did he spend his time away from home?'

The Hillmans looked at each other, as if the secret of Tom's whereabouts was somehow hidden in each other's faces. The red telephone interrupted their dumb communion, like a loud thought. Elaine Hillman gasped. The photograph in her hand fell to the floor. She wilted against her husband.

He held her up. 'It wouldn't be for us. That's Tom's private telephone.'

'You want me to take it?' I said through the second ring.

'Please do.'

I sat on the bed and picked up the receiver. 'Hello.'

'Tom?' said a high, girlish voice. 'Is that you, Tommy?'

'Who is this calling?' I tried to sound like a boy.

The girl said something like 'Augh' and hung up on me. I set down the receiver: 'It was a girl or a young woman. She wanted Tom.'

The woman spoke with a touch of malice that seemed to renew her strength: 'That's nothing unusual. I'm sure it was Stella Carlson. She's been calling all week.'

'Does she always hang up like that?'

'No. I talked to her yesterday. She was full of questions, which of course I refused to answer. But I wanted to make sure that she hadn't seen Tom. She hadn't.'

'Does she know anything about what's happened?'

'I hope not,' Hillman said. 'We've got to keep it in the family. The more people know, the worse—' He left another sentence dangling in the air.

I moved away from the telephone and picked up the fallen photograph. In a kind of staggering march step, Elaine Hillman went to the bed and straightened out the bedspread where I had been sitting. Everything had to be perfect in the room, I thought, or the god would not be appeased and would never return to them. When she had finished smoothing the bed, she flung herself face down on it and lay still.

Hillman and I withdrew quietly and went downstairs to wait for the call that mattered. There was a phone in the bar alcove off the sitting room, and another in the butler's pantry, which I could use to listen in. To get to the butler's pantry we had to go through the music room, where the grand piano loomed, and across a formal dining room which had a dismal air, like a reconstructed room in a museum.

The past was very strong here, like an odor you couldn't quite place. It seemed to be built into the very shape of the house, with its heavy dark beams and thick walls and deep windows; it would almost force the owner of the house to feel like a feudal lord. But the role of hidalgo hung loosely on Hillman, like something borrowed for a costume party. He and his wife must have rattled around in the great house, even when the boy was there.

Back in the sitting room, in front of the uncertain fire, I had a chance to ask Hillman some more questions. The Hillmans had two servants, a Spanish couple named Perez who had looked after Tom from infancy. Mrs Perez was probably out in the kitchen. Her husband was in Mexico, visiting his family.

'You *know* he's in Mexico?'

'Well,' Hillman said, 'his wife has had a card from Sinaloa. Anyway, the Perezes are devoted to us, and to Tom. We've had them with us ever since we moved here and bought this house.'

'How long ago was that?'

'Over sixteen years. We moved here, the three of us, after I was separated from the Navy. Another engineer and I founded our own firm here, Technological Enterprises. We've had very gratifying success, supplying components to the military and then NASA. I was able to go into semiretirement not long ago.'

'You're young to retire, Mr Hillman.'

'Perhaps.' He looked around a little restlessly, as if he disliked talking about himself. 'I'm still the chairman of the board, of course. I go down to the office several mornings a week. I play a lot of golf, do a lot of hunting and sailing.' He sounded weary of his life. 'This summer I've been teaching Tom calculus. It isn't available in his high school. I thought it would come in handy if he made it to Cal Tech or MIT I went to MIT myself. Elaine was a student at Radcliffe. She was born on Beacon Street, you know.'

We're prosperous and educated people, he seemed to be saying, first-class citizens: how can the world have aimed such a dirty blow at us? He leaned his large face forward until his hands supported it again.

The telephone rang in the alcove. I heard it ring a second time as I skidded around the end of the dining-room table. At the door of the butler's pantry I almost knocked down a small round woman who was wiping her hands on her apron. Her emotional dark eyes recoiled from my face.

'*I* was going to answer it,' she said.

'I will, Mrs Perez.'

She retreated into the kitchen and I closed the door after her. The only light in the pantry came through the semicircular hatch to the dining room. The telephone was on the counter inside it, no longer ringing. Gently I raised the receiver.

'What was that?' a man's voice said. 'You got the FBI on the line or something?' The voice was a western drawl with a faint whine in it.

'Certainly not. I've followed your instructions to the letter.'

'I hope I can believe you, Mr Hillman. If I thought you were having this call traced I'd hang up and goodbye Tom.' The threat came easily, with a kind of flourish, as if the man enjoyed this kind of work.

'Don't hang up.' Hillman's voice was both pleading and loathing. 'I have the money for you, at least I'll have it here in a very short while. I'll be ready to deliver it whenever you say.'

'Twenty-five thousand in small bills?'

'There will be nothing larger than a twenty.'

'All unmarked?'

'I told you I've obeyed you to the letter. My son's safety is all I care about.'

'I'm glad you get the picture, Mr Hillman. You pick up fast, and I like that. Matter of fact, I hate to do this to you. And I'd certainly hate to do anything to this fine boy of yours.'

'Is Tom with you now?' Hillman said.

'More or less. He's nearby.'

'Could I possibly talk to him?'

'No.'

'How do I know he's alive?'

The man was silent for a long moment. 'You don't trust me, Mr Hillman. I don't like that.'

'How can I trust—?' Hillman bit the sentence in half.

'I know what you were going to say. How can you trust a lousy creep like me? That isn't our problem, Hillman. Our problem is can I trust a creep like you. I know more about you than you think I do, Hillman.'

Silence, in which breath wheezed.

'Well, can I?'

'Can you what?' Hillman said in near-despair.

'Can I trust you, Hillman?'

'You can trust me.'

Wheezing silence. The wheeze was in the man's voice when he spoke again: 'I guess I'll have to take your word for it, Hillman. Okay. You'd probably like to talk all day about what a creep I am, but it's time to get down to brass tacks. I want my money, and this isn't ransom money, get that straight. Your son wasn't kidnapped, he came to us of his own free will—'

'I don't—' Hillman strangled the words in his throat.

'You don't believe me? Ask him, if you ever have a chance. You're throwing away your chances, you realize that? I'm trying to help you pay me the money—the information money, that's all it is—but you keep calling me names, liar and creep and God knows what else.'

'No. There's nothing personal.'

'That's what you think.'

'Look here,' Hillman said. 'You said it's time to get down to brass tacks. Simply tell me where and when you want the money delivered. It will be delivered. I guarantee it.'

Hillman's voice was sharp. The man at the other end of the line reacted to the sharpness perversely:

'Don't be in such a hurry. I'm calling the shots, you better not forget it.'

'Then call them,' Hillman said.

'In my own good time. I think I better give you a chance to think this over, Hillman. Get down off your high horse and down on your knees. That's where you belong.' He hung up.

Hillman was standing in the alcove with the receiver still in his hand when I got back to the sitting room. Absently he replaced it on its brackets and came toward me, shaking his silver head.

'He wouldn't give me any guarantees about Tom.'

'I heard him. They never do. You have to depend on his mercy.'

'His *mercy!* He was talking like a maniac. He seemed to revel in the—in the pain.'

'I agree, he was getting his kicks. Let's hope he's satisfied with the kicks he's already got, and the money.'

Hillman's head went down. 'You think Tom is in danger, don't you?'

'Yes. I don't think you're dealing with an outright maniac, but the man didn't sound too well-balanced. I think he's an amateur, or possibly a petty thief who saw his chance to move in on the heavy stuff. More likely a gifted amateur. Is he the same man who called this morning?'

'Yes.'

'He may be working alone. Is there any chance that you could recognize his voice? There was some hint of a personal connection, maybe a grievance. Could he be a former employee of yours, for example?'

'I very much doubt it. We only employ skilled workers. This

fellow sounded practically subhuman.' His face became gaunter. 'And you tell me I'm at his mercy.'

'Your son is. Could there be any truth in what he said about Tom going to him voluntarily?'

'Of course not. Tom is a good boy.'

'How is his judgment?'

Hillman didn't answer me, except by implication. He went to the bar, poured himself a stiff drink out of a bourbon bottle, and knocked it back. I followed him to the bar.

'Is there any possible chance that Tom cooked up this extortion deal himself, with the help of one of his buddies, or maybe with hired help?'

He hefted the glass in his hand, as if he was thinking of throwing it at my head. I caught a glimpse of his red angry mask before he turned away. 'It's quite impossible. Why do you have to torment me with these ideas?'

'I don't know your son. You ought to.'

'He'd never do a thing like that to me.'

'You put him in Laguna Perdida School.'

'I had to.'

'Why?'

He turned on me furiously. 'You keep hammering away at the same stupid question. What has it got to do with anything?'

'I'm trying to find out just how far gone Tom is. If there was reason to think that he kidnapped himself, to punish you or raise money, we'd want to turn the police loose—'

'You're crazy!'

'Is Tom?'

'Of course not. Frankly, Mr Archer, I'm getting sick of you and your questions. If you want to stay in my house, it's got to be on my terms.'

I was tempted to walk out, but something held me. The case was getting its hooks into my mind.

Hillman filled his glass with whisky and drank half of it down.

'If I were you, I'd lay off the sauce,' I said. 'You have decisions to make. This could be the most important day of your life.'

He nodded slowly. 'You're right.' He reached across the bar and poured the rest of his whisky into the metal sink. Then he excused himself, and went upstairs to see to his wife.

V

I LET MYSELF out the front door, quietly, got a hat and raincoat out of the trunk of my car, and walked down the winding driveway. In the dead leaves under the oak trees the drip made rustling noises, releasing smells and memories. When I was seventeen I spent a summer working on a dude ranch in the foothills of the Sierra. Toward the end of August, when the air was beginning to sharpen, I found a girl, and before the summer was over we met in the woods. Everything since had been slightly anticlimactic.

Growing up seemed to be getting harder. The young people were certainly getting harder to figure out. Maybe Stella Carlson, if I could get to her, could help me understand Tom.

The Carlsons' mailbox was a couple of hundred yards down the road. It was a miniature replica, complete with shutters, of their green-shuttered white colonial house, and it rubbed me the wrong way, like a tasteless advertisement. I went up the drive to the brick stoop and knocked on the door.

A handsome redheaded woman in a linen dress opened the door and gave me a cool green look. 'Yes?'

I didn't think I could get past her without lying. 'I'm in the insurance—'

'Soliciting is not allowed in El Rancho.'

'I'm not selling, Mrs Carlson, I'm a claims adjuster.' I got an old card out of my wallet which supported the statement. I had worked for insurance companies in my time.

'If it's about my wrecked car,' she said, 'I thought that was all settled last week.'

'We're interested in the cause of the accident. We keep statistics, you know.'

'I'm not particularly interested in becoming a statistic.'

'Your car already is. I understand it was stolen.'

She hesitated, and glanced behind her, as if there was a witness in the hallway. 'Yes,' she said finally. 'It was stolen.'

'By some young punk in the neighborhood, is that right?'

She flushed in response to my incitement. 'Yes, and I doubt very much that it was an accident. He took my car and wrecked it out of sheer spite.' The words boiled out as if they had been simmering in her mind for days.

'That's an interesting hypothesis, Mrs Carlson. May I come in and talk it over with you?'

'I suppose so.'

She let me into the hallway. I sat at a telephone table and took out my black notebook. She stood over me with one hand on the newel post at the foot of the stairs.

'Do you have anything to support that hypothesis?' I said with my pencil poised.

'You mean that he wrecked the car deliberately?'

'Yes.'

Her white teeth closed on her full red lower lip, and left a brief dent in it. 'It's something you couldn't make a statistic out of. The boy—his name is Tom Hillman—was interested in our daughter. He used to be a much nicer boy than he is now. As a matter of fact, he used to spend most of his free time over here. We treated him as if he were our own son. But the relationship went sour. Very sour.' She sounded both angry and regretful.

'What soured it?'

She made a violent sideways gesture. 'I prefer not to discuss it. It's something an insurance company doesn't have to know. Or anybody else.'

'Perhaps I could talk to the boy. He lives next door, doesn't he?'

'His parents do, the Hillmans. I believe they've sent him away somewhere. We no longer speak to the Hillmans,' she said stiffly. 'They're decent enough people, I suppose, but they've made awful fools of themselves over that boy.'

'Where did they send him?'

'To some kind of reform school, probably. He needed it. He was running out of control.'

'In what way?'

'Every way. He smashed up my car, which probably means he was drinking. I know he was spending time in the bars on lower Main Street.'

'The night before he wrecked your car?'

'All summer. He even tried to teach his bad habits to Stella. That's what soured the relationship, if you want to know.'

I made a note. 'Could you be a little more specific, Mrs Carlson? We're interested in the whole social background of these accidents.'

'Well, he actually dragged Stella with him to one of those awful dives. Can you imagine, taking an innocent sixteen-year-old girl to a wino joint on lower Main? That was the end of Tom Hillman, as far as we were concerned.'

'What about Stella?'

'She's a sensible girl.' She glanced up toward the head of the stairs. 'Her father and I made her see that it wasn't a profitable relationship.'

'So she wasn't involved in the borrowing of your car?'

'Certainly not.'

A small clear voice said from the head of the stairs: 'That isn't true, Mother, and you know it. I told you—'

'Be quiet, Stella. Go back to bed. If you're ill enough to stay home from camp, you're ill enough to stay in bed.'

As she was talking, Mrs Carlson surged halfway up the stairs. She had very good calves, a trifle muscular. Her daughter came down toward her, a slender girl with lovely eyes that seemed to take up most of her face below the forehead. Her brown hair was pulled back tight. She had on slacks and a high-necked blue wool sweater which revealed the bud-sharp outlines of her breasts.

'I'm feeling better, thank you,' she said with adolescent iciness. 'At least I was, until I heard you lying about Tommy.'

'How dare you? Go to your room.'

'I will if you'll stop telling lies about Tommy.'

'You shut up.'

Mrs Carlson ran up the three or four steps that separated them, grabbed Stella by the shoulders, turned her forcibly, and marched her up out of sight. Stella kept repeating the word

'Liar,' until a door slammed on her thin clear voice.

Five minutes later Mrs Carlson came down wearing fresh makeup, a green hat with a feather in it, a plaid coat, and gloves. She walked straight to the door and opened it wide.

'I'm afraid I have to rush now. My hairdresser gets very angry with me when I'm late. We were getting pretty far afield from what you wanted, anyway.'

'On the contrary. I was very interested in your daughter's remarks.'

She smiled with fierce politeness. 'Pay no attention to Stella. She's feverish and hysterical. The poor child's been upset ever since the accident.'

'Because she was involved in it?'

'Don't be silly.' She rattled the doorknob. 'I really have to go now.'

I stepped outside. She followed, and slammed the door hard behind me. She'd probably had a lot of practice slamming doors.

'Where's your car?' she called after me.

'I parachuted in.'

She stood and watched me until I reached the foot of the driveway. Then she went back into her house. I plodded back to the Hillmans' mailbox and turned up their private lane. The rustlings in the woods were getting louder. I thought it was a towhee scratching in the undergrowth. But it was Stella.

She appeared suddenly beside the trunk of a tree, wearing a blue ski jacket with the hood pulled up over her head and tied under her chin. She looked about twelve. She beckoned me with the dignity of a full-grown woman, ending the motion with her finger at her lips.

'I better stay out of sight. Mother will be looking for me.'

'I thought she had an appointment with the hairdresser.'

'That was just another lie,' she said crisply. 'She's always lying these days.'

'Why?'

'I guess people get in the habit of it or something. Mother always used to be a very straight talker. So did Dad. But this business about Tommy has sort of thrown them. It's thrown me, too,' she added, and coughed into her hand.

'You shouldn't be out in the wet,' I said. 'You're sick.'

'No, really, I mean not physically. I just don't feel like facing the kids at camp and having to answer their questions.'

'About Tommy?'

She nodded. 'I don't even know where he is. Do you?'

'No, I don't.'

'Are you a policeman, or what?'

'I used to be a policeman. Now I'm a what.'

She wrinkled her nose and let out a little giggle. Then she tensed in a listening attitude, like a yearling fawn. She threw off her hood.

'Do you hear her? That's Mother calling me.'

Far off through the trees I heard a voice calling : 'Stella.'

'She'll kill me,' the girl said. 'But somebody has to tell the truth some time. *I* know. Tommy has a tree house up the slope, I mean he used to have when he was younger. We can talk there.'

I followed her up a half-overgrown foot trail. A little redwood shack with a tar-paper roof sat on a low platform among the spreading branches of an oak. A homemade ladder, weathered gray like the tree house, slanted up to the platform. Stella climbed up first and went inside. A red-capped woodpecker flew out of an unglazed window into the next tree, where he sat and harangued us. Mrs Carlson's voice floated up from the foot of the slope. She had a powerful voice, but it was getting hoarse.

'Swiss Family Robinson,' Stella said when I went in. She was sitting on the edge of a built-in cot which had a mattress but no blankets. 'Tommy and I used to spend whole days up here, when we were children.' At sixteen, there was nostalgia in her voice. 'Of course when we reached puberty it had to stop. It wouldn't have been proper.'

'You're fond of Tommy.'

'Yes. I love him. We're going to be married. But don't get the wrong idea about us. We're not even *go*ing steady. We're not making out and we're not soldered.' She wrinkled her nose, as if she didn't like the smell of the words. 'We'll be married when the time is right, when Tommy's through college or at least has a good start. We won't have any money problems, you see.'

I thought she was using me to comfort herself a little with a story, a simple story with a happy ending. 'How is that?'

'Tommy's parents have lots of money.'

'What about your parents? Will they let you marry him?'

'They won't be able to stop me.'

I believed her, if Tommy survived. She must have seen the 'if' cross my eyes like a shadow. She was a perceptive girl.

'Is Tommy all right?' she said in a different tone.

'I hope so.'

She reached up and plucked at my sleeve. 'Where is he, Mister—?'

'I don't know, Stella. My name is Lew Archer. I'm a private detective working on Tommy's side. And you were going to tell me the truth about the accident.'

'Yes. It was my fault. Mother and Dad seem to think they have to cover up for me, but it only makes things worse for Tommy. I was the one responsible, really.' Her direct upward look, her earnest candor, reminded me of a child saying her prayers.

'Were you driving the car?'

'No. I don't mean I was with him. But I told him he could take it and I got the key for him out of Mother's room. It's really my car, too—I mean, to use.'

'She knows this?'

'Yes. I told her and Dad on Sunday. But they had already talked to the police, and after that they wouldn't change their story, or let me. They said it didn't alter the fact that he took it.'

'Why did you let him take it?'

'I admit it wasn't such a good idea. But he had to go someplace to see somebody and his father wouldn't let him use one of their cars. He was grounded. Mother and Dad were gone for the evening, and Tommy said he'd be back in a couple of hours. It was only about eight o'clock, and I thought it would be okay. I didn't know he was going to be out all night.' She closed her eyes and hugged herself. 'I was awake all night, listening for him.'

'Where did he go?'

'I don't know.'

'What was he after?'

'I don't know that, either. He said it was the most important thing in his life.'

'Could he have been talking about alcohol?'

'Tommy doesn't drink. It was somebody he had to see, somebody very important.'

'Like a drug pusher?'

She opened her wonderful eyes. 'You're twisting meanings, the way Dad does when he's mad at me. Are you mad at me, Mr Archer?'

'No. I'm grateful to you for being honest.'

'Then why do you keep dragging in crummy meanings?'

'I'm used to questioning crummy people, I guess. And sometimes an addict's own mother, or own girl, doesn't know he's using drugs.'

'I'm sure Tommy wasn't. He was dead against it. He knew what it had done to some—' She covered her mouth with her hand. Her nails were bitten.

'You were going to say?'

'Nothing.'

Our rapport was breaking down. I did my best to save it. 'Listen to me, Stella, I'm not digging dirt for the fun of it. Tommy's in real danger. If he had contacts with drug users, you should tell me.'

'They were just some of his musician friends,' she mumbled. 'They wouldn't do anything to hurt him.'

'They may have friends who would. Who are these people?'

'Just some people he played the piano with this summer, till his father made him quit. Tommy used to sit in on their jam sessions on Sunday afternoon at The Barroom Floor.'

'Is that one of the dives your mother mentioned?'

'It isn't a dive. He didn't take me to dives. It was merely a place where they could get together and play their instruments. He wanted me to hear them play.'

'And Tommy played with them?'

She nodded brightly. 'He's a very good pianist, good enough to make his living at it. They even offered him a weekend job.'

'Who did?'

'The combo at The Barroom Floor. His father wouldn't let him take it, naturally.'

'Tell me about the people in the combo.'

'Sam Jackman is the only one I know. He used to be a locker boy at the beach club. He plays the trombone. Then there was a saxophonist and a trumpeter and a drummer. I don't remember their names.'

'What did you think of them?'

'I didn't think they were very good. But Tommy said they were planning to make an album.'

'Every combo is. I mean, what kind of people were they?'

'They were just musicians. Tommy seemed to like them.'

'How much time had he been spending with them?'

'Just Sunday afternoons. He called it his other life.'

'His other life?'

'Uh-huh. *You* know, at home he had to hit the books and make his parents feel good and all that stuff. The same way I have to do when I'm at home. But it hasn't been working too well since the accident. Nobody feels good.'

She shivered. A cold wet wind was blowing through the windows of the tree house. Mrs Carlson's voice could no longer be heard. I felt uneasy about keeping the girl away from her mother. But I didn't want to let her go until she had told me everything she could.

I squatted on my heels in front of her. 'Stella, do you think Tommy's appointment that Saturday night had to do with his musician friends?'

'No. He would have told me if it had. It was more of a secret than that.'

'Did he say so?'

'He didn't have to. It was something secret and terribly important. He was terribly excited.'

'In a good way or a bad way?'

'I don't know how you tell the difference. He wasn't afraid, if that's what you mean.'

'I'm trying to ask you if he was sick.'

'Sick?'

'Emotionally sick.'

'No. I—That's foolish.'

'Then why did his father have him put away?'

'You mean, put away in a mental hospital?' She leaned

toward me, so close I could feel her breath on my face.

'Something like that—Laguna Perdida School. I didn't mean to tell you, and I'm going to ask you not to tell your parents.'

'Don't worry, I'll never tell them anything. So that's where he is! Those hypocrites!' Her eyes were fixed and wet. 'You said he was in danger. Are they trying to cut out his frontal lobe like in Tennessee Williams?'

'No. He was in no danger where he was. But he escaped from the place, the night before last, and fell into the hands of thieves. Now, I'm not going to load your mind with any more of this. I'm sorry it came out.'

'Don't be.' She gave me a second glimpse of the woman she was on her way to becoming. 'If it's happening to Tommy, it's just like it was happening to me.' Her forefinger tapped through nylon at the bone between her little breasts. 'You said he fell into the hands of thieves. Who are they?'

'I'm trying to answer that question, in a hurry. Could they be his friends from The Barroom Floor?'

She shook her head. 'Are they holding him prisoner or something?'

'Yes. I'm trying to get to them before they do something worse. If you know of any other contacts he had in his other life, particularly underworld contacts—'

'No. He didn't have any. He didn't have another life, really. It was just talk, talk and music.'

Her lips were turning blue. I had a sudden evil image of myself: a heavy hunched figure seen from above in the act of tormenting a child who was already tormented. A sense went through me of the appalling ease with which the things you do in a good cause can slip over into bad.

'You'd better go home, Stella.'

She folded her arms. 'Not until you tell me everything. I'm not a child.'

'But this is confidential information. I didn't intend to let any of it out. If it got to the wrong people, it would only make things worse.'

She said with some scorn: 'You keep beating around the bush, like Dad. Is Tommy being held for ransom?'

'Yes, but I'm pretty sure it's no ordinary kidnapping. He's supposed to have gone to these people of his own free will.'

'Who said so?'

'One of them.'

Her clear brow puckered. 'Then why would Tommy be in any danger from them?'

'If he knows them,' I said, 'they're not likely to let him come home. He could identify them.'

'I see.' Her eyes were enormous, taking in all at once the horror of the world and growing dark with it. 'I was *afraid* he was in some awful jam. His mother wouldn't tell me anything. I thought maybe he'd killed himself and they were keeping it quiet.'

'What made you think that?'

'Tommy did. He called me up and I met him here in the tree house the morning after the accident. I wasn't supposed to tell anyone. But you've been honest with me. He wanted to see me one more time—just as friends, you know—and say goodbye forever. I asked him if he was going away, or what he planned to do. He wouldn't tell me.'

'Was he suicidal?'

'I don't know. I was afraid that that was what it all meant. Not hearing from him since, I got more and more worried. I'm not as worried now as I was before you told me all those things.' She did a mental double take on one of them. 'But why would he deliberately go and stay with criminals?'

'It isn't clear. He may not have known they were criminals. If you can think of anyone—'

'I'm trying.' She screwed up her face, and finally shook her head again. 'I can't, unless they were the same people he had to see that other Saturday night. When he borrowed our car.'

'Did he tell you anything at all about those people?'

'Just that he was terribly keen about seeing them.'

'Were they men or women?'

'I don't even know that.'

'What about the Sunday morning, when you met him here? Did he tell you anything at all about the night before?'

'No. He was feeling really low, after the accident and all, and the terrible row with his parents. I didn't ask him any questions. I guess I should have, shouldn't I? I always do the wrong thing, either by commission or omission.'

'I think you do the right thing more often than most.'

'Mother doesn't think so. Neither does Dad.'

'Parents can be mistaken.'

'Are you a parent?' The question reminded me of the sad boys in Laguna Perdida School.

'No, I never have been. My hands are clean.'

'You're making fun of me,' she said with a glum face.

'Never. Hardly ever.'

She gave me a quick smile. 'Gilbert and Sullivan. I didn't know detectives were like you.'

'Neither do most of the other detectives.' Our rapport, which came and went, was flourishing again. 'There's one other thing I've been meaning to ask you, Stella. Your mother seems to believe that Tommy wrecked her car on purpose.'

'I know she does.'

'Could there be any truth in it?'

She considered the question. 'I don't see how. He wouldn't do it to me, *or* her, unless—' She looked up in dark surmise.

'Go on.'

'Unless he was trying to kill himself, and didn't care about anything any more.'

'Was he?'

'He may have been. He didn't want to come home, he told me that much. But he didn't tell me why.'

'I might learn something from examining the car. Do you know where it is?'

'It's down in Ringo's wrecking yard. Mother went to see it the other day.'

'Why?'

'It helps her to stay mad, I guess. Mother's really crazy about Tommy, at least she used to be, and so was Dad. This business has been terribly hard on them. And I'm not making it any easier staying away from home now.' She got to her feet, stamping them rapidly. 'Mother will be calling out the gendarmes. Also she'll kill me.'

'No she won't.'

'Yes she will.' But she wasn't basically afraid for herself. 'If you find out anything about Tommy, will you let me know?'

'That might be a little tough to do, in view of your mother's attitude. Why don't you get in touch with me when you can? This number will aways get me, through my answering service.' I gave her a card.

She climbed down the ladder and flitted away through the trees, one of those youngsters who make you feel like apologizing for the world.

VI

I MADE MY way back to the Hillmans' house. It resembled a grim white fortress under the lowering sky. I didn't feel like going in just now and grappling with the heavy, smothering fear that hung in the rooms. Anyway, I finally had a lead. Which Hillman could have given me if he'd wanted to.

Before I got into my car I looked up at the front window of Tom's room. The Hillmans were sitting close together in the niche of the window, looking out. Hillman shook his head curtly: no phone call.

I drove into town and turned right off the highway onto the main street. The stucco and frame buildings in this segment of town, between the highway and the railroad tracks, had been here a long time and been allowed to deteriorate. There were tamale parlors and pool halls and rummage stores and bars. The wet pavements were almost empty of people, as they always were when it rained in California.

I parked and locked my car in front of a surplus and sporting goods store and asked the proprietor where The Barroom Floor was. He pointed west, toward the ocean:

'I don't think they're open, in the daytime. There's lots of other places open.'

'What about Ringo's auto yard?'

'Three blocks south on Sanger Street, that's the first

stop-light below the railroad tracks.'

I thanked him.

'You're welcome, I'm sure.' He was a middle-aged man with a sandy moustache, cheerfully carrying a burden of unsuccess. 'I can sell you a rainproof cover for your hat.'

'How much?'

'Ninety-eight cents. A dollar-two with tax.'

I bought one. He put it on my hat. 'It doesn't do much for the appearance, but—'

'Beauty is functional.'

He smiled and nodded. 'You took the words out of my mouth. I figured you were a smart man. My name's Botkin, by the way, Joseph Botkin.'

'Lew Archer.' We shook hands.

'My pleasure, Mr Archer. If I'm not getting too personal, why would a man like you want to do your drinking at The Barroom Floor?'

'What's the matter with The Barroom Floor?'

'I don't like the way they handle their business, that's all. It lowers the whole neighborhood. Which is low enough already, God knows.'

'How do they handle their business?'

'They let young kids hang out there, for one thing—I'm not saying they serve them liquor. But they shouldn't let them in at all.'

'What do they do for another thing?'

'I'm talking too much.' He squinted at me shrewdly. 'And you ask a lot of questions. You wouldn't be from the Board of Equalization by any chance?'

'No, but I probably wouldn't tell you if I was. Is The Barroom Floor under investigation?'

'I wouldn't be surprised. I heard there was a complaint put in on them.'

'From a man named Hillman?'

'Yeah. You are from the Board of Equalization, eh? If you want to look the place over for yourself, it opens at five.'

It was twenty past four. I wandered along the street, looking through the windows of pawnshops at the loot of wrecked lives.

The Barroom Floor was closed all right. It looked as if it was never going to reopen. Over the red-checked half-curtains at the windows, I peered into the dim interior. Red-checked tables and chairs were grouped around a dime-size dance floor; and farther back in the shadows was a bandstand decorated with gaudy paper. It looked so deserted you'd have thought all the members of the band had hocked their instruments and left town years ago.

I went back to my car and drove down Sanger Street to Ringo's yard. It was surrounded by a high board fence on which his name was painted in six-foot white letters. I pushed in through the gate. A black German shepherd glided out of the open door of a shack and delicately grasped my right wrist between his large yellow teeth. He didn't growl or anything. He merely held me, looking up brightly at my face.

A wide fat man, with a medicine ball of stomach badly concealed under his plaid shirt, came to the door of the shack.

'That's all right, Lion.'

The dog let go of me and went to the fat man.

'His teeth are dirty,' I said. 'You should give him bones to chew. I don't mean wristbones.'

'Sorry. We weren't expecting any customers. But he won't hurt you, will you, Lion?'

Lion rolled his eyes and let his tongue hang out about a foot.

'Go ahead, pet him.'

'I'm a dog lover,' I said, 'but is he a man lover?'

'Sure. Go ahead and pet him.'

I went ahead and petted him. Lion lay down on his back with his feet in the air, grinning up at me with his fangs.

'What can I do you for, mister?' Ringo said.

'I want to look at a car.'

He waved his hand toward the yard. 'I got hundreds of them. But there isn't a one of them you could drive away. You want one to cannibalize?'

'This is a particular car I want to examine.' I produced my adjuster's card. 'It's a fairly new Dodge, I think, belonged to a Mrs Carlson, wrecked a week or so ago.'

'Yeah. I'll show it to you.'

He put on a black rubber raincoat. Lion and I followed him down a narrow aisle between two lines of wrecked cars. With their crumpled grilles and hoods, shattered windshields, torn fenders, collapsed roofs, disemboweled seats, and blown-out tires, they made me think of some ultimate freeway disaster. Somebody with an eye for detail should make a study of automobile graveyards, I thought, the way they study the ruins and potsherds of vanished civilizations. It could provide a clue as to why our civilization is vanishing.

'All the ones in this line are totaled out,' Ringo said. 'This is the Carlson job, second from the end. That Pontiac came in since. Head-on collision, two dead.' He shuddered. 'I never go on the highway when I can help it.'

'What caused the accident to the Carlson car?'

'It was taken for a joy ride by one of the neighbors' kids, a boy name of Hillman. You know how these young squirts are—if it isn't theirs, they don't care what happens to it. According to the traffic detail, he missed a curve and went off the road and probably turned it over trying to get back on. He must of rolled over several times and ended up against a tree.'

I walked around the end of the line and looked over the Dart from all sides. There were deep dents in the roof and hood and all four fenders, as if it had been hit with random sledgehammers. The windshield was gone. The doors were sprung.

Leaning in through the left-hand door, I noticed an oval piece of white plastic, stamped with printing, protruding from the space between the driver's seat and the back. I reached in and pulled it out. It was a brass door key. The printing on the plastic tab said: DACK'S AUTO COURT 7.

'Watch the glass in there,' Ringo said behind me. 'What are you looking for?'

I put the key in my pocket before I turned around. 'I can't figure out why the boy didn't get hurt.'

'He had the wheel to hang on to, remember. Lucky for him it didn't break.'

'Is there any chance he wrecked the car on purpose?'

'Naw. He'd have to be off his rocker to do that. Course you can't put anything past these kids nowadays. Can you, Lion?' He stooped to touch the dog's head and went on talking, either to it or to me. 'My own son that I brought up in the business went off to college and now he don't even come home for Christmas some years. I got nobody to take over the business.' He straightened up and looked around at his wrecks with stern affection, like the emperor of a wasteland.

'Could there have been anybody with him in the car?'

'Naw. They would of been really banged up, with no seat belts and nothing to hang on to.' He looked at the sky, and added impatiently: 'I don't mind standing around answering your questions, mister. But if you really want the dope on the accident, talk to the traffic detail. I'm closing up.'

It was ten minutes to five. I made my way back to The Barroom Floor. Somebody had turned on a few lights inside. The front door was still locked. I went back to my car and waited. I took out the Dack's Auto Court key and looked at it, wondering if it meant anything. It could have meant, among other farfetched possibilities, that the handsome Mrs Carlson was unfaithful to her husband.

Shortly after five a short dark man in a red jacket unlocked the front door of The Barroom Floor and took up his position behind the bar. I went in and sat down on a stool opposite him. He seemed much taller behind the bar. I looked over it and saw that he was standing on a wooden platform about a foot off the floor.

'Yeah,' he said 'it keeps me on the level. Without it I can barely see over the bar.' He grinned. 'My wife, now, is five foot six and built in proportion. She ought to be here now,' he added in a disciplinary tone, and looked at the wristwatch on his miniature wrist. 'What will you have?'

'Whisky sour. You own this place?'

'Me and the wife, we have an interest in it.'

'Nice place,' I said, though it wasn't particularly nice. It was no cleaner and no more cheerful than the average bar and grill with cabaret pretensions. The old waiter leaning against the wall beside the kitchen door seemed to be sleeping on his feet.

'Thank you. We have plans for it.' As he talked, he made my drink with expert fingers. 'You haven't been in before. I don't remember your face.'

'I'm from Hollywood. I hear you have a pretty fair jazz combo.'

'Yeah.'

'Will they be playing tonight?'

'They only play Friday and Saturday nights. We don't get the weekday trade to justify 'em.'

'What about the Sunday jam sessions? Are they still on?'

'Yeah. We had one yesterday. The boys were in great form. Too bad you missed them.' He slid my drink across the bar. 'You in the music business?'

'I represent musicians from time to time. I have an office on the Strip.'

'Sam would want to talk to you. He's the leader.'

'Where can I get in touch with him?'

'I have his address somewhere. Just a minute, please.'

A couple of young men in business suits with rain-sprinkled shoulders had taken seats at the far end of the bar. They were talking in carrying voices about a million-dollar real-estate deal. Apparently it was somebody else's deal, not theirs, but they seemed to enjoy talking about it.

The small man served them short whiskies without being asked. A lavishly built young woman came in and struggled out of a transparent raincoat which she rolled up and tossed under the bar. She had a Sicilian nose. Her neck was hung with jewelry like a bandit princess's.

The small man looked at her sternly. 'You're late. I can't operate without a hostess.'

'I'm sorry, Tony. Rachel was late again.'

'Hire another baby sitter.'

'But she's so good with the baby. You wouldn't want just anybody feeding him.'

'We won't talk about it now. You know where you're supposed to be.'

'Yes, Mr Napoleon.'

With a rebellious swing of the hip, she took up her post by the door. Customers were beginning to drift in by twos and fours. Most of them were young or young middle-aged. They looked respectable enough. Talking and laughing vivaciously, clinking her jewelry, the hostess guided them to the red-checked tables.

Her husband remembered me after a while. 'Here's Sam Jackman's address. He has no phone, but it isn't far from here.'

He handed me a sheet from a memo pad on which he had written in pencil: '169 Mimosa, apt. 2.'

It was near the railroad tracks, an old frame house with Victorian gingerbread on the facade half chewed away by time. The heavy carved front door was standing open, and I went into the hallway, feeling warped parquetry under my feet. On a closed door to my right, a number 2 stamped from metal hung upside down by a single nail. It rattled when I knocked.

A yellow-faced man in shirt sleeves looked out. 'Who is it you want?'

'Sam Jackman.'

'That's me.' He seemed surprised that anybody should want him. 'Is it about a job?' He asked the question with a kind of hollow hopefulness that answered itself in the negative.

'No, but I want to talk to you about something important, Mr Jackman.'

He caught the 'mister' and inclined his head in acknowledgement. 'All right.'

'May I come in? My name is Lew Archer. I'm a private detective.'

'I dunno, the place is a mess. With the wife working all day—but come on in.'

He backed into his apartment, as if he was afraid to expose his flank. It consisted of one large room which might once have been the drawing room of the house. It still had its fine proportions, but the lofty ceiling was scabbed and watermarked, the windows hung with torn curtains. A cardboard wardrobe, a gas plate behind a screen, stood against the inner wall. Run-down furniture, including an unmade double bed in one corner, cluttered the bare wooden floor. On a table beside the bed, a small television set was reeling off the disasters of the day in crisp elocutionary sentences.

Jackman switched it off, picked up a smoking cigarette from the lid of a coffee can on the table, and sat on the edge of the bed. It wasn't a marihuana cigarette. He was completely still and silent, waiting for me to explain myself. I sat down facing him.

'I'm looking for Tom Hillman.'

He gave me a swift glance that had fear in it, then busied himself putting out his cigarette. He dropped the butt into the pocket of his shirt.

'I didn't know he was missing.'

'He is.'

'That's too bad. What would make you think that he was here?' He looked around the room with wide unblinking eyes. 'Did Mr Hillman send you?'

'No.'

He didn't believe me. 'I just wondered. My Hillman has been on my back.'

'Why?'

'I interested myself in his boy,' he said carefully.

'In what way?'

'Personally.' He turned his hands palms upward on his knees. 'I heard him doodling on the piano at the beach club. That was one day last spring. I did a little doodling of my own. Piano isn't my instrument, but he got interested in some chords I showed him. That made me a bad influence.'

'Were you?'

'Mr Hillman thought so. He got me fired from the beach club. He didn't want his precious boy messing with the likes of me.' His upturned hands lay like helpless pink-bellied animals on their backs. 'If Mr Hillman didn't send you, who did?'

'A man named Dr Sponti.'

I thought the name would mean nothing to him, but he gave me another of his quick fearful looks. 'Sponti? You mean—?' He fell silent.

'Go on, Mr Jackman. Tell me what I mean.'

He huddled down into himself, like a man slumping into sudden old age. He let his speech deteriorate: 'I wouldn't know nothin' about nothin', mister.' He opened his mouth in an idiotic smile that showed no teeth.

'I think you know a good deal. I think I'll sit here until you tell me some of it.'

'That's your privilege,' he said, although it wasn't.

He took the butt out of his shirt pocket and lit it with a kitchen match. He dropped the distorted black match-end into the coffee lid. We looked at each other through smoke that drifted like ectoplasm from his mouth.

'You know Dr Sponti, do you?'

'I've heard the name,' Jackman said.

'Have you seen Tom Hillman in the last two days?'

He shook his head, but his eyes stayed on my face in a certain way, as if he was expecting to be challenged.

'Where have you heard Sponti's name?'

'A relative of mine. She used to work in the kitchen at L P S' He said with irony: 'That makes me an accessory, I guess.'

'Accessory to what?'

'Any crime in the book. I wouldn't even have to know what happened, would I?' He doused his butt in a carefully restricted show of anger.

'That sort of talk gets us nowhere.'

'Where does your sort of talk get us? Anything I tell you is evidence against me, isn't it?'

'You talk like a man with a record.'

'I've had my troubles.' He added after a long silence: 'I'm sorry Tommy Hillman is having his.'

'You seem to be fond of him.'

'We took to each other.' He threw the line away.

'I wish you'd tell me more about him. That's really what I came here for.'

My words sounded slightly false. I was suspicious of Jackman, and he knew it. He was a watcher and a subtle listener.

'Now I got a different idea,' he said. 'I got the idea you're after Tommy to put him back in the L P School. Correct me if I'm wrong.'

'You're wrong.'

'I don't believe you.' He was watching my hands to see if I might hit him. There were marks on his face where he had been hit before. 'No offense, but I don't believe you, mister—'

I repeated my name. 'Do you know where Tommy is?'

'No. I do know this. If Mr Hillman put him in the L P

School, he's better off on the loose than going home. His father had no right to do it to him.'

'So I've been told.'

'Who told you?'

'One of the women on the staff there. She said Tom wasn't disturbed in her opinion, and didn't belong in the school. Tom seemed to agree with her. He broke out Saturday night.'

'Good.'

'Not so good. At least he was safe there.'

'He's safe,' Jackman said, and quickly regretted saying it. He opened his mouth in its senseless toothless smile, a tragic mask pretending to be comic.

'Where is he then?'

Jackman shrugged his thin shoulders. 'I told you before and I'll tell you again, I don't know.'

'How did you know that he was on the loose?'

'Sponti wouldn't send you to me otherwise.'

'You're quick on the uptake.'

'I have to pick up what I can,' he said. 'You talk a lot without saying much.'

'You say even less. But you'll talk, Sam.'

He rose in a quick jerky movement and went to the door. I thought he was going to tell me to leave, but he didn't. He stood against the closed door in the attitude of a man facing a rifle squad.

'What do you expect me to do?' he cried. 'Put my neck in the noose so Hillman can hang me?'

I walked toward him.

'Stay away from me!' The fear in his eyes was burning brightly, feeding on a long fuse of experience. He lifted one crooked arm to shield his head. 'Don't touch me!'

'Calm down. That's hysterical talk, about a noose.'

'It's a hysterical world. I lost my job for teaching his kid some music. Now Hillman is raising the ante. What's the rap this time?'

'There is no rap if the boy is safe. You said he was. Didn't you?'

No answer, but he looked at me under his arm. He had tears in his eyes.

'For God's sake, Sam, we ought to be able to get together on this. You like the boy, you don't want anything bad to happen to him. That's all I have in mind.'

'There's bad and bad.' But he lowered his defensive arm and kept on studying my face.

'I know there's bad and bad,' I said. 'The line between them isn't straight and narrow. The difference between them isn't black and white. I know you favor Tom against his father. You don't want him cut off from you or your kind of music. And you think I want to drag him back to a school where he doesn't belong.'

'Aren't you?'

'I'm trying to save his life. I think you can help me.'

'How?'

'Let's sit down again and talk quietly the way we were. Come on. And stop seeing Hillman when you look at me.'

Jackman returned to the bed and I sat near him.

'Well, Sam, have you seen him in the last two days?'

'See who? Mr Hillman?'

'Don't go into the idiot act again. You're an intelligent man. Just answer my question.'

'Before I do, will you answer one of mine?'

'If I possibly can.'

'When you say you're trying to save his life, you mean save him from bad influences, don't you, put him back in Squaresville with all the other squares?'

'Worse things can happen to a boy.'

'You didn't answer my question.'

'You could have asked a better one. I mean save him from death. He's in the hands of people who may or may not decide to kill him, depending on how the impulse takes them. Am I telling you anything you don't know?'

'You sure are, man.' His voice was sincere, and his eyes filled up with compunction. But he and I could talk for a year, and he would still be holding something back. Among the things he was holding back was the fact that he didn't believe me.

'Why don't you believe me, Sam?'

'I didn't say that.'

'You don't have to. You're acting it out, by sitting on the information you have.'

'I ain't sitting' on nothin', 'ceptin' this here old raunchy bed,' he said in broad angry parody.

'Now I know you are. I've got an ear for certain things, the way you've got an ear for music. You play the trombone, don't you?'

'Yeah.' He looked surpised.

'I hear you blow well.'

'Don't flatter me. I ain't no J.C. Higginbotham.'

'And I ain't no Sherlock Holmes. But sooner or later you're going to tell me when you saw Tommy Hillman last. You're not going to sit on your raunchy ole bed and wait for the television to inform you that they found Tommy's body in a ditch.'

'Did they?'

'Not yet. It could happen tonight. When did you see him?'

He drew a deep breath. 'Yesterday. He was okay.'

'Did he come here?'

'No sir. He never has. He stopped in at The Barroom Floor yesterday afternoon. He came in the back way and only stayed five minutes.'

'What was he wearing?'

'Slacks and a black sweater. He told me once his mother knitted that sweater for him.'

'Did you talk to him yesterday afternoon?'

'I played him a special riff and he came up and thanked me. That was all. I didn't know he was on the run. Shucks, he even had his girl friend with him.'

'Stella?'

'The other one. The older one.'

'What's her name?'

'He never told me. I only seen her once or twice before that. Tommy knew I wouldn't approve of him squiring her around. She's practically old enough to be his mother.'

'Can you describe her?'

'She's a bottle blonde, with a lot of hair, you know how they're wearing it now.' He swept his hand up from his wrinkled forehead. 'Blue eyes, with a lot of eye shadow. It's hard to tell what she looks like under all that makeup.'

I got out my notebook and made some notes. 'What's her background?'

'Show business, maybe. Like I say, I never talked to her. But she has the looks.'

'I gather she's attractive.'

'She appears to be to Tom. I guess she's his first. A lot of young boys start out with an older woman. But,' he added under his breath, 'he could do better than that.'

'How old is she?'

'Thirty, anyway. She didn't show me her birth certificate. She dresses younger—skirts up over her knees. She isn't a big girl, and maybe in some lights she can get away with the youth act.'

'What was she wearing yesterday?'

'A dark dress, blue satin or something like that, with sequins on it, a neckline down to here.' He touched his solar plexus. 'It grieved me to see Tom with his arm around her.'

'How did she seem to feel about him?'

'You're asking me more than I can answer. He's a good-looking boy, and she makes a show of affection. But I don't need X-ray eyes to know what is in her mind.'

'Would she be a hustler?'

'Could be.'

'Did you ever see her with any other man?'

'I never did. I only saw her once or twice with Tom.'

'Once, or twice?'

He ruminated. 'Twice before yesterday. The first time was two weeks ago yesterday. That was a Sunday, he brought her to our jam session that afternoon. The woman had been drinking and first she wanted to sing and then she wanted to dance. We don't allow dancing at these sessions, you have to pay cabaret tax. Somebody told her that and she got mad and towed the boy away.'

'Who told her not to dance?'

'I disremember. One of the cats sitting around, I guess, they object to dancing. The music we play Sundays isn't to dance to, anyway. It's more to the glory of God,' he said surprisingly.

'What about the second time you saw her?'

He hesitated, thinking. 'That was ten nights ago, on a Friday. They came in around midnight and had a sandwich. I drifted by their table, at the break, but Tom didn't introduce me or ask me to sit down. Which was all right with me. They seemed to have things to talk about.'

'Did you overhear any part of their conversation?'

'I did.' His face hardened. 'She needed money, she was telling him, money to get away from her husband.'

'You're sure you heard that?'

'Sure as I'm sitting here.'

'What was Tom's attitude?'

'Looked to me like he was fascinated.'

'Had he been drinking?'

'*She* was. He didn't drink. They don't serve drinks to minors at the Floor. No sir. She had him hyped on something worse than drink.'

'Drugs?'

'You know what I mean.' His hands moulded a woman's figure in the air.

'You used the word "hyped." '

'It was just a manner of speaking,' he said nervously, rubbing his upper arm through the shirt sleeve.

'Are you on the needle?'

'No sir. I'm on the TV,' he said with a sudden downward smile.

'Show me your arms.'

'I don't have to. You got no right.'

'I want to test your veracity. Okay?'

He unbuttoned his cuffs and pushed his sleeves up his thin yellow arms. The pitted scars in them were old and dry.

'I got out of Lexington seven years ago,' he said, 'and I haven't fallen since, I thank the good Lord.'

He touched his scars with a kind of reverence. They were like tiny extinct volcanoes in his flesh. He covered them up.

'You're doing all right, Mr Jackman. With your background, you'd probably know if Tom was on drugs.'

'I probably would. He wasn't. More than once I lectured him

on the subject. Musicians have their temptations. But he took my lectures to heart.' He shifted his hand to the region of his heart. 'I ought to of lectured him on the subject of women.'

'I never heard that it did much good. Did you ever see Tom and the blonde with anyone else?'

'No.'

'Did he introduce her to anyone?'

'I doubt it. He was keeping her to himself. Showing her off, but keeping her to himself.'

'You don't have any idea what her name is?'

'No. I don't.'

I got up and thanked him. 'I'm sorry if I gave you a rough time.'

'I've had rougher.'

VII

DACK'S AUTO COURT was on the edge of the city, in a rather rundown suburb named Ocean View. The twelve or fifteen cottages of the court lay on the flat top of a bluff, below the highway and above the sea. They were made of concrete block and painted an unnatural green. Three or four cars, none of them recent models, were parked on the muddy gravel.

The rain had let up and fresh yellow light slanted in from a hole in the west, as if to provide a special revelation of the ugliness of Dack's Auto Court. Above the hutch marked 'Office', a single ragged palm tree leaned against the light. I parked beside it and went in.

A hand-painted card taped to the counter instructed me to 'Ring for Proprietor.' I punched the handbell beside it. It didn't work.

Leaning across the counter, I noticed on the shelf below it a telephone and a metal filing box divided into fifteen numbered sections. The registration card for number seven was dated three weeks before, and indicated that 'Mr and Mrs Robt. Brown' were paying sixteen dollars a week for that cottage. The spaces provided on the card for home address and license number were empty.

The screen door creaked behind me. A big old man with a naked condor head came flapping into the office. He snatched the card from my fingers and looked at me with hot eyes. 'What do you think you're doing?'

'I was only checking.'

'Checking what?'

'To see if some people I know are here. Bob Brown and his wife.'

He held the card up to the light and read it, moving his lips laboriously around the easy words. 'They're here,' he said without joy. 'Leastways, they were this morning.'

He gave me a doubtful look. My claim of acquaintanceship with the Browns had done nothing for my status. I tried to improve it. 'Do you have a cottage vacant?'

'Ten of them. Take your pick.'

'How much?'

'Depends on if you rent by the day or the week. They're three-fifty a day, sixteen a week.'

'I'd better check with the Browns first, see if they're planning to stay.'

'I wouldn't know about that. They been here three weeks.' He had a flexible worried mouth in conflict with a stupid stubborn chin. He stroked his chin as if to educate it. 'I can let you have number eight for twelve a week single. That's right next door to the Browns' place.'

'I'll check with them.'

'I don't believe they're there. You can always try.'

I went outside and down the dreary line of cottages. The door of number seven was locked. Nobody answered my repeated rapping.

When I turned away, the old man was standing in front of number eight. He beckoned to me and opened the door with a flourish:

'Take a look. I can let you have it for ten if you really like it.'

I stepped inside. The room was cold and cheerless. The inside walls were concrete block, and the same unnatural green as the outside. Through a crack in the drawn blind, yellow light slashed at the hollow bed, the threadbare carpet. I'd spent too many nights in places like it to want to spend another.

'It's clean,' the old man said.

'I'm sure it is, Mr Dack.'

'I cleaned it myself. But I'm not Dack, I'm Stanislaus. Dack sold out to me years ago. I just never got around to having the signs changed. What's the use? They'll be tearing everything down and putting up high-rise apartments pretty soon.' He smiled and stroked his bald skull as if it was a kind of golden egg. 'Well, you want the cottage?'

'It really depends on Brown's plans.'

'If I was you,' he said, 'I wouldn't let too much depend on him.'

'How is that, Mr Stanislaus?'

'He's kind of a blowtop, ain't he? I mean, the way he treats that little blonde wife. I always say these things are between a man *and* his wife. But it rankles me,' he said. 'I got a deep respect for women.'

'So have I. I've never liked the way he treated women.'

'I'm glad to hear that. A man should treat his wife with love and friendship. I lost my own wife several years ago, and I know what I'm talking about. I tried to tell him that, he told me to mind my own business. I know he's a friend of yours—'

'He's not exactly a friend. Is he getting worse?'

'Depends what you mean, *worse*. This very day he was slapping her around. I felt like kicking him out of my place. Only, how would that help *her?* And all she did was make a little phone call. He tries to keep her cooped up like she was in jail.' He paused, listening, as if the word *jail* had associations for him. 'How long have you known this Brown?'

'Not so long,' I said vaguely. 'I ran into him in Los Angeles.'

'In Hollywood?'

'Yeah. In Hollywood.'

'Is it true she was in the movies? She mentioned one day she used to be in the movies. He told her to shut up.'

'Their marriage seems to be deteriorating.'

'You can say that again.' He leaned toward me in the

doorway. 'I bet you she's the one you're interested in. I see a lot of couples, one way and another, and I'm willing to bet you she's just about had her fill of him. If I was a young fellow like you, I'd be tempted to make her an offer.' He nudged me; the friction seemed to warm him. 'She's a red-hot little bundle.'

'I'm not young enough.'

'Sure you are.' He handled my arm, and chuckled. 'It's true she likes 'em young. I been seeing her off and on with a teen-ager, even.'

I produced the photograph of Tom that Elaine Hillman had given me. 'This one?'

The old man lifted it to the daylight, at arm's length. 'Yeah. That's a mighty good picture of him. He's a good-looking boy.' He handed the photograph back to me, and fondled his chin. 'How do you come to have a picture of him?'

I told him the truth, or part of it: 'He's a runaway from a boarding school. I'm a private detective representing the school.'

The moist gleam of lechery faded out of Stanislaus's eyes. Something bleaker took its place, a fantasy of punishment perhaps. His whole face underwent a transformation, like quick-setting concrete.

'You can't make me responsible for what the renters do.'

'Nobody said I could.'

He didn't seem to hear me. 'Let's see that picture again.' I showed it to him. He shook his head over it. 'I made a mistake. My eyes ain't what they used to be. I never seen him before.'

'You made a positive identification.'

'I take it back. You were talking to me under false pretenses, trying to suck me in and get something on me. Well, you got nothing on me. It's been tried before,' he said darkly. 'And you can march yourself off my property.'

'Aren't you going to rent me the cottage?'

He hesitated a moment, saying a silent goodbye to the ten dollars. 'No sir, I want no spies and peepers in my place.'

'You may be harboring something worse.'

I think he suspected it, and the suspicion was the source of his anger.

'I'll take my chances. Now you git. If you're not off my

property in one minute, I'm going to call the sheriff.'

That was the last thing I wanted. I'd already done enough to endanger the ransom payment and Tom's return. I got.

VIII

A BLUE SPORTS car stood in the drive behind the Hillman Cadillac. An athletic-looking young man who looked as if he belonged in the sports car came out of the house and confronted me on the front steps. He wore an Ivy League suit and had an alligator coat slung over his arm and hand, with something bulky and gun-shaped under it.

'Point that thing away from me. I'm not armed.'

'I w-want to know who you are.' He had a faint stammer.

'Lew Archer. Who are you?'

'I'm Dick Leandro.' He spoke the words almost questioningly, as if he didn't quite know what it meant to be Dick Leandro.

'Lower that gun,' I reminded him. 'Try pointing it at your leg.'

He dropped his arm. The alligator coat slid off it, onto the flagstone steps, and I saw that he was holding a heavy old revolver. He picked up the coat and looked at me in a rather confused way. He was a handsome boy in his early twenties, with brown eyes and dark curly hair. A certain little dancing light in his eyes told me that he was aware of being handsome.

'Since you're here,' I said, 'I take it the money's here, too.'

'Yes. I brought it out from the office several hours ago.'

'Has Hillman been given instructions for delivering it?'

He shook his head. 'We're still waiting.'

I found Ralph and Elaine Hillman in the downstairs room where the telephone was. They were sitting close together as if for warmth, on a chesterfield near the front window. The waiting had aged them both.

The evening light fell like gray paint across their faces. She was knitting something out of red wool. Her hands moved rapidly and precisely as if they had independent life.

Hillman got to his feet. He had been holding a newspaper-wrapped parcel in his lap, and he laid it down on the chesterfield, gently, like a father handling an infant.

'Hello, Archer,' he said in a monotone.

I moved toward him with some idea of comforting him. But the expression in his eyes, hurt and proud and lonely, discouraged me from touching him or saying anything very personal.

'You've had a long hard day.'

He nodded slowly, once. His wife let out a sound like a dry sob. 'Why haven't we heard anything from that man?'

'It's hard to say. He seems to be putting on the screws deliberately.'

She pushed her knitting to one side, and it fell on the floor unnoticed. Her faded pretty face wrinkled up as if she could feel the physical pressure of torture instruments. 'He's keeping us in hell, in absolute hell. But why?'

'He's probably waiting for dark,' I said. 'I'm sure you'll be hearing from him soon. Twenty-five thousand dollars is a powerful attraction.'

'He's welcome to the money, five times over. Why doesn't he simply take it and give us back our boy?' Her hand flung itself out, rattling the newspaper parcel beside her.

'Don't fret yourself, Ellie.' Hillman leaned over her and touched her pale gold hair. 'There's no use asking questions that can't be answered. Remember, this will pass.' His words of comfort sounded hollow and forced.

'So will I,' she said wryly and bitterly, 'if this keeps up much longer.'

She smoothed her face with both hands and stayed with her hands in a prayerful position at her chin. She was trembling. I was afraid she might snap like a violin string. I said to Hillman:

'May I speak to you in private? I've uncovered some facts you should know.'

'You can tell me in front of Elaine, and Dick for that matter.'

I noticed that Leandro was standing just inside the door.

'I prefer not to.'

'You're not calling the shots, however.' It was a curious echo of the man on the telephone. 'Let's have your facts.'

I let him have them: 'Your son has been seen consorting with a married woman named Brown. She's a blonde, show-business type, a good deal older than he is, and she seems to have been after him for money. The chances are better than even that Mrs Brown and her husband are involved in this extortion bid. They seem to be on their uppers—'

Elaine raised her open hands in front of her face, as if too many words were confusing her. 'What do you mean, consorting?'

'He's been hanging around with the woman, publicly and privately. They were seen together yesterday afternoon.'

'Where?' Hillman said.

'At The Barroom Floor.'

'Who says so?'

'One of their employees. He's seen them before, and he referred to Mrs Brown as 'Tom's girl friend, the older one.' I've had corroborating evidence from the man who owns the court where the Browns are living. Tom has been hanging around there, too.'

'How old is this woman?'

'Thirty or more. She's quite an attractive dish, apparently.'

Elaine Hillman lifted her eyes. There seemed to be real horror in them. 'Are you implying that Tom has been having an affair with her?'

'I'm simply reporting facts.'

'I don't believe your facts, not any of them.'

'Do you think I'm lying to you?'

'Maybe not deliberately. But there must be some ghastly mistake.'

'I agree,' Dick Leandro said from the doorway. 'Tom has always been a very clean-living boy.'

Hillman was silent. Perhaps he knew something about his son that the others didn't. He sat down beside his wife and hugged the paper parcel defensively.

'His virtue isn't the main thing right now,' I said. 'The question is what kind of people he's mixed up with and what they're doing to him. Or possibly what they're doing to you with his cooperation.'

'What is that supposed to mean?' Hillman said.

'We have to reconsider the possibility that Tom is in on the extortion deal. He was with Mrs Brown yesterday. The man on the telephone, who may be Brown, said Tom came to them voluntarily.'

Elaine Hillman peered up into my face as if she was trying to grasp such a possibility. It seemed to be too much for her to accept. She closed her eyes and shook her head so hard that her hair fell untidily over her forehead. Pushing it back with spread fingers, she said in a small voice that sent chills through me:

'You're lying, I know my son, he's an innocent victim. You're trying to do something terrible, coming to us in our affliction with such a filthy rotten smear.'

Her husband tried to quiet her against his shoulder. 'Hush now, Elaine. Mr Archer is only trying to help.'

She pushed him away from her. 'We don't want that kind of help. He has no right. Tom is an innocent victim, and God knows what is happening to him.' Her hand was still at her head, with her pale hair sprouting up between her fingers. 'I can't take any more of this, Ralph—this dreadful man with his dreadful stories.'

'I'm sorry, Mrs Hillman. I didn't want you to hear them.'

'I know. You wanted to malign my son without anyone to defend him.'

'That's nonsense, Ellie,' Hillman said. 'I think you better come upstairs and let me give you a sedative.'

He helped her to her feet and walked her out past me, looking at me sorrowfully across her rumpled head. She moved like an invalid leaning on his strength.

Dick Leandro drifted into the room after they had left it, and sat on the chesterfield to keep the money company. He said in a slightly nagging way:

'You hit Elaine pretty hard with all that stuff. She's a sensitive woman, very puritanical about sex and such. And incidentally she's crazy about Tommy. She won't listen to a word against him.'

'*Are* there words against him?'

'Not that I know about. But he has been getting into trouble lately. You know, with the car wreck and all. And now you t-tell me he's been dipping into the fleshpots.'

'I didn't say that.'

'Yeah, but I got the message. Where does the g-girl live, anyway? Somebody ought to go and question her.'

'You're full of ideas.'

He had a tin ear for tone. 'Well, how about it? I'm game.'

'You're doing more good here, guarding the money. How did Hillman happen to pick you to bring the money, by the way? Are you an old family friend?'

'I guess you could say that. I've been crewing for Mr Hillman since I was yay-high.' He held out his hand at knee level. 'Mr Hillman is a terrific guy. Did you know he made Captain in the Navy? But he won't let anybody call him Captain except when we're at sea.

'And generous,' the young man said. 'As a matter of fact, he helped me through college and got me a job at his broker's. I owe him a lot. He's treated me like a father.' He spoke with some emotion, real but intended, like an actor's. 'I'm an orphan, you might say. My family broke up when I was yay-high, and my father left town. He used to work for Mr Hillman at the plant.'

'Do you know Tom Hillman well?'

'Sure. He's a pretty good kid. But a little too much of an egghead in my book. Which keeps him from being popular. No wonder he has his troubles.' Leandro tapped his temple with his knuckles. 'Is it true that Mr Hillman put him in the booby—I mean, in a sanatorium?'

'Ask him yourself.'

The young man bored me. I went into the alcove and made myself a drink. Night was closing in. The garish bullfight posters on the walls had faded into darkness like long-forgotten *corridas*. There were shadows huddling with shadows behind the bar. I raised my glass to them in a gesture I didn't quite understand, except that there was relief in darkness and silence and whisky.

I could hear Hillman's footsteps dragging down the stairs. The telephone on the bar went off like an alarm. Hillman's descending footsteps became louder. He came trotting into the room as the telephone rang a second time. He elbowed me out of his way.

I started for the extension phone in the pantry. He called after me:

'No! I'll handle this myself.'

There was command in his voice. I stood and watched him pick up the receiver, hold it to his head like a black scorpion, and listen to what it said.

'Yes, this is Mr Hillman. Just a minute.' He brought a business envelope and a ballpoint pen out of his inside pocket, turned on an overhead light, and got ready to write on the bar. 'Go ahead.'

For about half a minute he listened and wrote. Then he said: 'I think so. Aren't there steps going down to the beach?'

He listened and wrote. 'Where shall I walk to?' He turned the envelope over and wrote some more. 'Yes,' he said. 'I park two blocks away, at Seneca, and approach the steps on foot. I put the money under the right side of the top step. Then I go down to the beach for half an hour. Is that all?'

There was a little more. He listened to it. Finally he said: 'Yes. But the deal is very much on as far as I'm concerned. I'll be there at nine sharp.'

There was a pathetic note in his voice, the note of a salesman trying to nail down an appointment with a refractory client.

'Wait,' he said, and groaned into the dead receiver.

Dick Leandro, moving like a cat, was in the alcove ahead of me. 'What is it, Mr Hillman? What's the trouble?'

'I wanted to ask about Tom. He didn't give me a chance.' He lifted his face to the plaster ceiling. 'I don't know if he's alive or dead.'

'They wouldn't *kill* him, would they?' the young man said. He sounded as though he'd had a first frightening hint of his own mortality.

'I don't know, Dick. I don't know.' Hillman's head rolled from one side to the other.

The young man put his arm around his shoulder. 'Take it easy now, Skipper. We'll get him back.'

Hillman poured himself a heavy slug of bourbon and tossed it down. It brought a little color into his face. I said:

'Same man?'

'Yes.'

'And he told you where to make the money-drop.'

'Yes.'

'Do you want company?'

'I have to go there alone. He said he'd be watching.'

'Where are you to go?'

Hillman looked at each of our faces in turn, lingeringly, as if he was saying goodbye. 'I'll keep that to myself. I don't want anything to wreck the arrangements.'

'Somebody should know about them, though, in case anything does go wrong. You're taking a chance.'

'I'd rather take a chance with my own life than my son's.' He said it as if he meant it, and the words seemed to renew his courage. He glanced at his wristwatch. 'It's twenty-five to nine. It will take me up to twenty minutes to get there. He didn't give me much leeway.'

'Can you drive okay?' Leandro said.

'Yes. I'm all right. I'll just go up and tell Ellie that I'm leaving. You stay in the house with her, won't you, Dick?'

'I'll be glad to.'

Hillman went upstairs, still clutching his scribbled-over envelope. I said to Leandro: 'Where is Seneca Street?'

'Seneca Road. In Ocean View.'

'Are there steps going down to the beach anywhere near there?'

'Yeah, but you're not supposed to go there. You heard Mr Hillman.'

'I heard him.'

Hillman came down and took the parcel of money out of Leandro's hands. He thanked the young man, and his voice was deep and gentle as well as melancholy.

We stood on the flagstone steps and watched him drive away into the darkness under the trees. In the hole in the dark west a little light still persisted, like the last light there was ever going to be.

IX

I WENT THROUGH the house to the kitchen and asked Mrs Perez to make me a plain cheese sandwich. She grumbled, but she made it. I ate it leaning against the refrigerator. Mrs Perez wouldn't talk about the trouble in the family. She seemed to have a superstitious feeling that trouble was only amplified by words. When I tried to question her about Tom's habits, she gradually lost her ability to understand my English.

Dick Leandro had gone upstairs to sit with Elaine. He seemed more at home than Tom appeared to have been with his own family. I went out through the reception hall. It was nine o'clock, and I couldn't wait any longer.

Driving along the highway to Ocean View, I argued jesuitically with myself that I had stayed clear of the money-drop, I wasn't double-dealing with Hillman, who wasn't my client in any case, and besides I had no proof that Mrs Brown and her husband were connected with the extortion attempt.

It was deep night over the sea, moonless and starless. I left my car at a view-point near Dack's Auto Court. The sea was a hollow presence with a voice. I hiked down the access road to the court, not using the flashlight that I carried with me.

The office was lighted and had a neon 'Vacancy' sign above the door. Avoiding the spill of light from it, I went straight to cottage number seven. It was dark. I knocked, and got no answer. I let myself in with the key I had and closed the self-locking door behind me.

Mrs Brown was waiting, I stumbled over her foot and almost fell on top of her before I switched on my flashlight. She lay in her winking sequined gown under the jittery beam. Blood was tangled like tar in her bright hair. Her face was mottled with bruises, and misshapen. She looked as though she had been beaten to death.

I touched her hand. She was cold. I turned the light away from her lopsided grin.

The beam jumped around the green walls, the newspaper-littered floor. It found a large strapped canvas suitcase standing at the foot of the bed with two paper bags beside it. One of the bags contained a bottle of cheap wine, the other sandwiches that were drying out.

I unstrapped the suitcase and opened it. An odor rose from its contents like sour regret. Men's and women's things were bundled indiscriminately together, dirty shirts and soiled slips, a rusting safety razor and a dabbled jar of cold cream and a bottle of mascara, a couple of dresses and some lingerie, a man's worn blue suit with a chain-store label and nothing in the pockets but tobacco powder and, tucked far down in the outer breast pocket, a creased yellow business card poorly printed on cheap paper:

HAROLD 'HAR' HARLEY

Application Photos Our Specialty

I found the woman's imitation snakeskin purse on a chair by the side window. It contained a jumble of cosmetics and some frayed blue chip stamps. No wallet, no identification, no money except for a single silver dollar in the bottom of the bag. There were also a pack of cards, slick with the oil of human hands, and a dice which came up six all three times I rolled it.

I heard a car approaching, and headlights swept the window on the far side. I switched off my flashlight. The wheels of the car crunched in the gravel and came to a halt directly in front of the cottage. Someone got out of the car and turned the cottage doorknob. When the door refused to open, a man's voice said:

'Let me in.'

It was the slightly wheezing, whining voice I'd heard that afternoon on Hillman's phone. I moved toward the door with the dark flashlight raised in my hand. The man outside rattled the knob.

'I know you're in there, I saw the light. This is no time to carry a grudge, hon.'

The woman lay in her deep waiting silence. I stepped around her and stood against the wall beside the door. I shifted the flash to my left hand and fumbled for the spring lock with my right.

'I hear you, damn you. You want another taste of what you had today?' He waited, and then said: 'If you won't open the door, I'll shoot the lock out.'

I heard the click of a hammer. I stayed where I was beside the door, holding the flashlight like a club. But he didn't fire.

'On the other hand,' he said, 'there's nothing in there I need, including you. You can stay here on your can if you want to. Make up your mind right now.'

He waited. He couldn't outwait her.

'This is your last chance. I'll count to three. If you don't open up, I'm traveling alone.' He counted, one, two, three, but it would take bigger magic to reach her. 'Good riddance to bad rubbish,' he said.

His footsteps moved away on the stones. The car door creaked. I couldn't let him go.

I snapped back the lock and opened the door and rushed him. His shadowy hatted figure was halfway into his car, with one foot on the ground. He whirled. The gun was still in his hand. It gave out a hot little flame. I could feel it sear me.

I staggered across the gravel and got hold of his twisting body. He hammered my hands loose with the butt of his gun. I had blood in my eyes, and I couldn't avoid the gun butt when it smashed into my skull. A kind of chandelier lit up in my head and then crashed down into darkness.

Next thing I was a VIP traveling with a police guard in the back of a chauffeured car. The turban I could feel on my head suggested to the joggled brain under it that I was a rajah or a maharajah. We turned into a driveway under a red light, which excited me. Perhaps I was being taken to see one of my various concubines.

I raised the question with the uniformed men sitting on either side of me. Gently but firmly, they helped me out of the patrol car and walked me through swinging doors, which a man in white held open, into a glaring place that smelled of disinfectants.

They persuaded me to sit down on a padded table and then to lie down. My heart hurt. I felt it with my hands. It had a towel around it, sticky with blood.

A large young face with a moustache leaned over me upside down. Large hairy hands removed the towel and did some probing and scouring in my scalp. It stung.

'You're a lucky man. It parted your hair for you, kind of permanently.'

'How bad is it, Doctor?'

'The bullet wound isn't serious, just a crease. As I said, you're lucky. This other lesion is going to take longer to heal. What did you get hit with?'

'Gun butt. I think.'

'More fun and games,' he said.

'Did they catch him?'

'You'll have to ask them. They haven't told me a thing.'

He clipped parts of my head and put some clamps in it and gave me a drink of water and an aspirin. Then he left me lying alone in the white-partitioned cubicle. My two guards moved rapidly into the vacuum.

They were sheriff's men, wearing peaked hats and tan uniforms. They were young and hearty, with fine animal bodies and rather animal, not so fine, faces. Good earnest boys, but a little dull. They said they wanted to help me.

'Why did you kill her?' the dark one said.

'I didn't. She'd been dead for some time when I found her.'

'That doesn't let you out. Mr Stanislaus said you were there earlier in the day.'

'He was with me all the time.'

'That's what you say,' the fair one said.

This repartee went on for some time, like a recording of an old vaudeville act which some collector had unwisely preserved. I tried to question them. They wouldn't tell me anything. My head was feeling worse, but oddly enough I began to think better with it. I even managed to get up on my elbows and look at them on the level.

'I'm a licensed private detective from Los Angeles.'

'We know that,' the dark one said.

I felt for my wallet. It was missing. 'Give me my wallet.'

'You'll get it back all in good time. Nobody's going to steal it.'

'I want to talk to the sheriff.'

'He's in bed asleep.'

'Is there a captain or lieutenant on duty?'

'The lieutenant is busy at the scene of the crime. You can talk to him in the morning. The doctor says you stay here overnight. Concussion. What did the woman hit you with, anyway?'

'Her husband hit me, with a gun butt.'

'I hardly blame him,' the fair one said emotionally, 'after what you did to his wife.'

'Were you shacked up with her?' the dark one said.

I looked from one healthy smooth face to the other. They didn't look sadistic, or sound corrupt, and I wasn't afraid for myself. Sooner or later the mess would be straightened out. But I was afraid.

'Listen,' I said, 'you're wasting time on me. I had legitimate business at the court. I was investigating—' The fear came up in my throat and choked off the rest of the sentence. It was fear for the boy.

'Investigating what?' the dark one said.

'Law enforcement in this country. It stinks.' I wasn't feeling too articulate.

'We'll law-enforcement you,' the dark one said. He was broad, with muscular shoulders. He moved them around in the air a little bit and pretended to catch a fly just in front of my face.

'Lay off, muscle,' I said.

The large, moustached face of the doctor appeared in the entrance to the cubicle. 'Everything okay in here?'

I said above the deputies' smiling assurances: 'I want to make a phone call.'

The doctor looked doubtfully from me to the officers. 'I don't know about that.'

'I'm a private detective investigating a crime. I'm not free to talk about it without the permission of my principal. I want to call him.'

'There's no facilities for that,' the dark deputy said.

'How about it, Doctor? You're in charge here, and I have a legal right to make a phone call.'

He was a very young man behind his moustache. 'I don't know. There's a telephone booth down the hall. Do you think you can make it?'

'I never felt better in my life.'

But when I swung my legs down, the floor seemed distant and undulant. The deputies had to help me to the booth and prop me up on the stool inside of it. I pulled the folding door shut. Their faces floated outside the wired glass like bulbous fishes, a dark one and a fair one, nosing around a bathyscaphe on the deep ocean floor.

Technically Dr Sponti was my principal, but it was Ralph Hillman's number I asked Information for. I had a dime in my pocket, fortunately, and Hillman was there. He answered the phone himself on the first ring:

'Yes?'

'This is Archer.'

He groaned.

'Have you heard anything from Tom?' I said.

'No. I followed instructions to the letter, and when I came up from the beach the money was gone. He's double-crossed me,' he said bitterly.

'Did you see him?'

'No. I made no attempt to.'

'I did.' I told Hillman what had happened, to me and to Mrs Brown.

His voice came thin and bleak over the wire. 'And you think these are the same people?'

'I think Brown's your man. Brown is probably an alias. Does the name Harold Harley mean anything to you?'

'What was that again?'

'Harold or "Har" Harley. He's a photographer.'

'I never heard of him.'

I wasn't surprised. Harley's yellow card was the kind that businessmen distributed by the hundred, and had no necessary connection with Brown.

'Is that all you wanted?' Hillman said. 'I'm trying to

keep this line open.'

'I haven't got to the main thing. The police are on my back. I can't explain what I was doing at the auto court without dragging in the extortion bit, and your son.'

'Can't you give them a story?'

'It wouldn't be wise. This is a capital case, a double one.'

'Are you trying to tell me that Tom is dead?'

'I meant that kidnapping is a capital crime. But you are dealing with a killer. I think at this point you should level with the police, and get their help. Sooner or later I'm going to have to level with them.'

'I forbid—' He changed his tone, and started the sentence over: 'I beg of you, please hold off. Give him until morning to come home. He's my only son.'

'All right. Till morning. We can't bottle it up any longer than that, and we shouldn't.'

I hung up and stepped out into the corridor. Instead of taking me back to the emergency ward, my escort took me up in an elevator to a special room with heavy screens on the windows. They let me lie down on the bed, and took turns questioning me. It would be tedious to recount the dialogue. It was tedious at the time, and I didn't listen to all of it.

Some time around midnight a sheriff's lieutenant named Bastian came into the room and ordered the deputies out into the hall. He was a tall man, with iron-gray hair clipped short. The vertical grooves in his cheeks looked like the scars inflicted by a personal discipline harsher than saber cuts.

He stood over me frowning. 'Dr Murphy says you're feeling critical of law enforcement in this county.'

'I've had reason.'

'It isn't easy recruiting men at the salaries the supervisors are willing to pay. We can hardly compete with the wages for unskilled labor. And this is a *tough* job.'

'It has its little extra compensations.'

'What does that mean?'

'I seem to be missing my wallet.'

Bastian's face went grim. He marched out into the hall, made some remarks in a voice that buzzed like a hornet, and came back carrying my wallet. I counted the money in it, rather obtrusively.

'It was used to check you out,' Bastian said. 'LA County gives you a good rating, and I'm sorry if you weren't treated right.'

'Think nothing of it. I'm used to being pushed around by unskilled labor.'

'You heard me apologize,' he said, in a tone that closed the subject.

Bastian asked me a number of questions about Mrs Brown and the reason for my interest in her. I told him I'd have to check with my client in the morning, before I could open up. Then he wanted everything I could give him about Brown's appearance and car.

The moments before and after the shot were vague in my memory. I dredged up what I could. Brown was a man of better than medium size, physically powerful, not young, not old. He was wearing a dark gray or blue jacket and a wide-brimmed grayish hat which shadowed his eyes. The lower part of his face was heavy-jawed. His voice was rough, with a slight wheeze in it. The car was a dirty white or tan two-door sedan, probably a Ford, about eight years old.

I learned two facts from Lieutenant Bastian: the car had an Idaho license, according to other tenants of the court, and Stanislaus was in trouble for keeping no record of the license number. I think Bastian gave me these facts in the hope of loosening my tongue. But he finally agreed to wait till morning.

They shifted me to another room on the same floor, unguarded. I spent a good part of the night, waking and sleeping, watching a turning wheel of faces. The faces were interspersed from time to time with brilliant visions of Dack's Auto Court. Its green ugliness was held in the selective sunset glare, as if it was under a judgment, and so was I.

X

MORNING WAS WELCOME, in spite of the pain in my head. I

couldn't remember eating anything but Mrs Perez's cheese sandwich since the previous morning. The tepid coffee and overscrambled eggs tasted like nectar and ambrosia.

I was finishing breakfast when Dr Sponti arrived, breathing rapidly and audibly. His plump face bore the marks of a bad night. He had sleepless bruises around the eyes, and a gash in his upper lip where his razor had slipped. The chilly hand he offered me reminded me of the dead woman's, and I dropped it.

'I'm surprised you knew I was here.'

'I found out in a rather circuitous way. A Lieutenant Bastian phoned me in the middle of the night. Evidently he saw the check I gave you yesterday morning. He asked me a great many questions.'

'About me?'

'About the whole situation involving you and Tom Hillman.'

'You told him about Tom Hillman?'

'I had no choice, really.' He picked at the fresh scab on his lip. 'A woman has been murdered in Ocean View. I was honor bound to provide the authorities with all the information I could. After all—'

'Does this include the business of the ransom money?'

'Naturally it does. Lieutenant Bastian considered it highly important. He thanked me effusively, and promised that the name of the school would be kept out of the papers.'

'Which is the main thing.'

'It is to me,' Sponti said. 'I'm in the school business.'

It was frustrating to have held out for nothing, and to have no secrets to trade with Bastian. But it was relieving, too, that the thing was out in the open. Hillman's imposition of silence had made it hard for me to do my job. I said:

'Have you had any repercussions from Ralph Hillman?'

'He phoned early this morning. The boy is still on the missing list.' Sponti's voice was lugubrious, and his eyes rolled heavily toward me. 'The parents are naturally quite frantic by this time. Mr Hillman said things I'm sure he'll regret later.'

'Is he still blaming you for the kidnapping?'

'Yes, and he blames me for bringing you into the case. He seems to feel you broke faith with him, shall we say.'

'By going to the auto court and getting myself shot?'

'You frightened off the kidnappers, in his opinion, and prevented them from returning his son to him. I'm very much afraid he wants nothing more to do with you, Mr Archer.'

'And neither do you?'

Dr Sponti pursed his lips and brought his ten fingers together in the air. They made a Norman arch and then a Gothic one. 'I'm sure you understand the pressures I'm under. I'm virtually obliged to do as Mr Hillman wishes in his extremity.'

'Sure.'

'And I'm not going to ask you to refund any part of your check. The entire two hundred and fifty dollars is yours, even though you've been in my employ'—he looked at his watch—'considerably less than twenty-four hours. The unearned surplus will take care of your medical expenses, I'm sure.' He was backing toward the door. 'Well, I have to run.'

'Go to hell,' I said as he went out.

He poked his head in again: 'You may regret saying that. I'm tempted to stop payment on that check after all.'

I made an obscene suggestion as to the disposition of the check. Dr Sponti turned as blue as a Santa Clara plum and went away. I lay and enjoyed my anger for a while. It went so nicely with the reciprocating ache in my head. And it helped to cover over the fact that I had let myself in for this. I shouldn't have gone the second time to Dack's Auto Court, at least not when I did.

A nurse's aide came in and took away my tray. Later a doctor palpated my skull, looked into my eyes with a tiny light, and told me I probably had a slight concussion but so had a lot of other people walking around. I borrowed a safety razor from an orderly, shaved and dressed, and went down to the cashier's window and paid my bill with Sponti's check.

I got over two hundred dollars change. Riding downtown in a taxi, I decided I could afford to spend another day on the case, whether Dr Sponti liked it or not. I told the driver to let me off at the telephone company.

'You said the courthouse.'

'The telephone company. We've had a change of plan.'

'You should have said so in the first place.'

'Forgive my failure of leadership.'

I was feeling bitter and bright. It had to do with the weather, which had turned sunny, but more to do with my decision to spend my own time on a boy I'd never seen. I didn't tip the driver.

One end of the main public room in the telephone building was lined with long-distance booths and shelves of out-of-town directories. Only the main cities in Idaho, like Boise and Pocatello and Idaho Falls, were represented. I looked through their directories, for a photographer named Harold Harley. He wasn't listed. Robert Brown was, by the legion, but the name was almost certainly an alias.

I installed myself in one of the booths and placed a long-distance call to Arnie Walters, a Reno detective who often worked with me. I had no Idaho contact, and Reno was on the fastest route to Idaho. Reno itself had a powerful attraction for thieves with sudden money.

'Walters Agency,' Arnie said.

'This is Lew.' I told him where I was calling from, and why.

'You come up with some dillies. Murder and kidnapping, eh?'

'The kidnapping may be a phony. Tom Hillman, the supposed victim, has been palling around with the murdered woman for a couple of weeks.'

'How old did you say he was?'

'Seventeen. He's big for his age.' I described Tom Hillman in detail. 'He may be traveling with Brown either voluntarily or involuntarily.'

'Or not traveling at all?' Arnie said.

'Or not traveling at all.'

'You know this boy?'

'No.'

'I thought maybe you knew him. Okay. Where does this photographer Harold Harley come in?'

'Harley may be Brown himself, or he may know Brown. His card is the only real lead I have so far. That and the Idaho license. I want you to do two things. Check Idaho and adjoining states for Harley. You have the business directories, don't you?'

'Yeah, I'll get Phyllis on them.' She was his wife and partner.

'The other thing, I want you to look out for Brown and the boy, you and your informers in Tahoe and Vegas.'

'What makes you think they're headed in this direction?'

'It's a hunch. The woman had a silver dollar and a loaded dice in her purse.'

'And no identification?'

'Whoever did her in got rid of everything she had in that line. But we'll identify her. We have *her*.'

'Let me know when you do.'

I walked across down to the courthouse, under a sky that yesterday's rain had washed clean. I asked the deputy on duty in the sheriff's department where to find Lieutenant Bastian. He directed me to the identification laboratory on the second floor.

It was more office than laboratory, a spacious room with pigeons murmuring on the window ledges. The walls were crowded with filing cabinets and hung with maps of the city and county and state. A large adjacent closet was fitted out as a darkroom, with drying racks and a long metal sink.

Bastian got up smiling. His smile wasn't greatly different from last night's frown. He laid down a rectangular magnifying glass on top of the photograph he had been studying. Leaning across the desk to take his outstretched hand, I could see that it was a picture of Mrs Brown in death.

'What killed her, Lieutenant?' I said when we were seated.

'This.' He held up his right hand and clenched it. His face clenched with it. 'The human hand.'

'Robert Brown's?'

'It looks like it. He gave her a beating early yesterday afternoon, according to Stanislaus. The deputy coroner says she's been dead that long.'

'Stanislaus told me they quarreled over a telephone call she made.'

'That's right. We haven't been able to trace the call, which means it was probably local. She used the phone in Stanislaus's office, but he claims to know nothing more about it.'

'How does he know Brown gave her a beating?' I said.

'He says a neighbor woman told him. That checks out.' Bastian wiped his left hand across his tense angry face, without really changing his expression. 'It's terrible the way some people live, that a woman could be killed within a neighbor's hearing and nobody knows or cares.'

'Not even Brown,' I said. 'He thought she was alive at nine-thirty last night. He talked to her through the door, trying to get her to open up. Or he may have been trying to con himself into thinking he hadn't killed her after all. I don't think he's too stable.'

Bastian looked up sharply. 'Were you in the cottage when Brown was talking through the door?'

'I was. Incidentally, I recognized his voice. He's the same man who extorted twenty-five thousand dollars from Ralph Hillman last night. I listened in on a phone call he made to Hillman yesterday.'

Bastian's right fist was still clenched. He used it to strike the desk top, savagely. The pigeons on the window ledge flew away.

'It's too damn bad,' he said, 'you didn't bring us in on this yesterday. You might have saved a life, not to mention twenty-five thousand dollars.'

'Tell that to Hillman.'

'I intend to. This morning. Right now I'm telling you.'

'The decision wasn't mine. I tried to change it. Anyway, I entered the case after the woman was killed.'

'That's a good place to begin,' Bastian said after a pause. 'Go on from there. I want the full record.'

He reached down beside his desk and turned on a recorder. For an hour or more the tape slithered quietly from wheel to wheel as I talked into it. I was clientless and free and I didn't suppress anything. Not even the possibility that Tom Hillman had cooperated with Brown in extorting money from his father.

'I'd almost like to think that that was true,' Bastian said. 'It would mean that the kid is still alive, anyway. But it isn't likely.'

'Which isn't likely?'

'Both things. I doubt that he hoaxed his old man, and I doubt that he's still alive. It looks as if the woman was used as a decoy to get him in position for the kill. We'll probably find his body in the ocean week after next.'

His words had the weight of experience behind them. Kidnap victims were poor actuarial risks. But I said:

'I'm working on the assumption that he's alive.'

Bastian raised his eyebrows. 'I thought Dr Sponti took you off the case.'

'I still have some of his money.'

Bastian gave me a long cool appraising look. 'LA was right. You're not the usual peeper.'

'I hope not.'

'If you're staying with it, you can do something for me, as well as for yourself. Help me to get this woman identified.' He slid the picture of Mrs Brown out from under the magnifying glass. 'This postmortem photo is too rough to circularize. But you could show it around in the right circles. I'm having a police artist make a composite portrait, but that takes time.'

'What about fingerprints?'

'We're trying that, too, but a lot of women have never been fingerprinted. Meantime, will you try and get an identification? You're a Hollywood man, and the woman claimed that she was in pictures at one time.'

'That doesn't mean a thing.'

'It might.'

'But I was planning to try and pick up Brown's trail in Nevada. If the boy's alive, Brown knows where to find him.'

'The Nevada police already have our APB on Brown. And you have a private operative on the spot. Frankly, I'd appreciate it if you'll take this picture to Hollywood with you. I don't have a man I can spare. By the way, I had your car brought into the county garage.'

Cooperation breeds cooperation. Besides, the woman's identity was important, if only because the killer had tried to hide it. I accepted the picture, along with several others taken from various angles, and put them in the same pocket as my picture of Tom.

'You can reverse any telephone charges,' Bastian said in farewell.

Halfway down the stairs I ran into Ralph Hillman. At first glance he looked fresher than he had the previous evening. But it was an illusory freshness. The color in his cheeks was hectic, and the sparkle in his eyes was the glint of desperation. He sort of reared back when he saw me, like a spooked horse.

'Can you give me a minute, Mr Hillman?'

'Sorry. I have an appointment.'

'The lieutenant can wait. I want to say this. I admit I made a mistake last night. But you made a mistake in getting Sponti to drop me.'

He looked at me down his patrician nose. '*You'd* naturally think so. It's costing you money.'

'Look, I'm sorry about last night. I was overeager. That's the defect of a virtue. I want to carry on with the search for your son.'

'What's the use? He's probably dead. Thanks to you.'

'That's a fairly massive accusation, Mr Hillman.'

'Take it. It's yours. And please get out of my way.' He looked compulsively at his wristwatch. 'I'm already late.'

He brushed past me and ran upstairs as if I might pursue him. It wasn't a pleasant interview. The unpleasantness stuck in my crop all the way to Los Angeles.

XI

I BOUGHT A hat a size too large, to accommodate my bandages, and paid a brief visit to the Hollywood division of the LAPD. None of the detective-sergeants in the upstairs offices recognized Mrs Brown in her deathly disguise. I went from the station to the news room of the Hollywood *Reporter*. Most of the people at work there resented being shown such pictures. The ones who gave them an honest examination failed to identify Mrs Brown.

I tried a number of flesh peddlers long the Strip, with the same lack of success and the same effect. The photographs made me unpopular. These guys and dolls pursuing the rapid buck hated to be reminded of what was waiting on the far side of the last dollar. The violence of the woman's death only made it worse. It could happen to anybody, any time.

I started back to my office. I intended to call Bastian and ask him to rush me a Xerox copy of the composite sketch as soon as his artist had completed it. Then I thought of Joey Sylvester.

Joey was an old agent who maintained an office of sorts two blocks off Sunset and two flights up. He hadn't been able to adapt to the shift of economic power from the major studios to the independent producers. He lived mainly on his share of residuals from old television movies, and on his memories.

I knocked on the door of his cubbyhole and heard him hiding his bottle, as if I might be the ghost of Louis B. Mayer or an emissary from J. Arthur Rank. Joey looked a little disappointed when he opened the door and it was only me. But he resurrected the bottle and offered me a drink in a paper cup. He had a glass tumbler for his own use, and I happened to know that nearly every day he sat at his desk and absorbed a quart of bourbon and sometimes a quart and a half.

He was a baby-faced old man with innocent white hair and crafty eyes. His mind was like an old-fashioned lamp with its wick in alcohol, focused so as to light up the past and its chauffeur-driven Packard, and cast the third-floor-walkup present into cool shadow.

It wasn't long past noon, and Joey was still in fair shape. 'It's good to see you, Lew boy. I drink to your health.' He did so, with one fatherly hand on my shoulder.

'I drink to yours.'

The hand on my shoulder reached up and took my hat off. 'What did you do to your head?'

'I was slightly shot last night.'

'You mean you got drunk and fell down?'

'Shot with a gun,' I said.

He clucked. 'You shouldn't expose yourself the way you do. Know what you ought to do, Lew boy? Retire and write your memoirs. The unvarnished sensational truth about Hollywood.'

'It's been done a thousand times, Joey. Now they're even doing it in the fan mags.'

'Not the way you could do it. Give 'em the worm's-eye view. There's a title!' He snapped his fingers. 'I bet I could sell your story for twenty-five G's, make it part of a package with Steve

McQueen. Give some thought to it, Lew boy. I could open up a lovely jar of olives for you.'

'I just opened a can of peas, Joey, and I wonder if you can help me with it. How is your tolerance for pictures of dead people?'

'I've seen a lot of them die.' His free hand fluttered toward the wall above his desk. It was prepared with inscribed photographs of vanished players. His other hand raised his tumbler. 'I drink to them.'

I cluttered his desk top with the angry pictures. He looked them over mournfully. 'Ach!' he said. 'What the human animal does to itself! Am I supposed to know her?'

'She's supposed to have worked in pictures. You know more actors than anybody.'

'I did at one time. No more.'

'I doubt that she's done any acting recently. She was on the skids.'

'It can happen overnight.' In a sense, it had happened to him. He put on his glasses, turned on a desk lamp, and studied the pictures intensively. After a while he said: 'Carol?'

'You know her.'

He looked at me over his glasses. 'I couldn't swear to it in court. I once knew a little blonde girl, natural blonde, with ears like that. Notice that they're small and close to the head and rather pointed. Unusual ears for a girl.'

'Carol who?'

'I can't remember. It was a long time ago, back in the forties. I don't think she was using her own name, anyway.'

'Why not?'

'She had a very stuffy family back in Podunk. They disapproved of the acting bit. I seem to remember she told me she ran away from home.'

'In Podunk?'

'I didn't mean that literally. Matter of fact, I think she came from some place in Idaho.'

'Say that again.'

'Idaho. Is your dead lady from Idaho?'

'Her husband drives a car with an Idaho license. Tell me more about Carol. When and where did you know her?'

'Right here in Hollywood. A friend of mine took an interest in the girl and brought her to me. She was a lovely child. Untouched.' His hands flew apart in the air, untouching her. 'All she had was high-school acting experience, but I got her a little work. It wasn't hard in those days, with the war still going on. And I had a personal in with all the casting directors on all the lots.'

'What year was it, Joey?'

He took off his glasses and squinted into the past. 'She came to me in the spring of '45, the last year of the war.'

Mrs Brown, if she was Carol, had been around longer than I'd thought. 'How old was she then?'

'Very young. Just a child, like I said. Maybe sixteen.'

'And who was the friend who took an interest in her?'

'It isn't like you think. It was a woman, one of the girls in the story department at Warner's. She's producing a series now at Television City. But she was just a script girl back in the days I'm talking about.'

'You wouldn't be talking about Susanna Drew?'

'Yeah. Do you know Susanna?'

'Thanks to you. I met her at a party at your house, when you were living in Beverly Hills.'

Joey looked startled, as though the shift from one level of the past to another had caught him unawares. 'I remember. That must have been ten years ago.'

He sat and thought about ten years ago, and so did I. I had taken Susanna home from Joey's party, and we met at other parties, by agreement. We had things to talk about. She picked my brains for what I knew about people, and I picked hers for what she knew about books. I was crazy about her insane sense of humor.

The physical thing came more slowly, as it often does when it promises to be real. I think we tried to force it. We'd both been drinking, and a lot of stuff boiled up from Susanna's childhood. Her father had been a professor at UCLA, who lost his wife young, and he had supervised Susanna's studies. Her father was dead, but she could still feel his breath on the back of her neck.

We had a bad passage, and Susanna stopped going to parties,

at least the ones I went to. I heard she had a marriage which didn't take. Then she had a career, which took.

'How did she happen to know Carol?' I said to Joey.

'You'll have to ask her yourself. She told me at the time, but I don't remember. My memory isn't what it was.' The present was depressing him. He poured himself a drink.

I refused the offer of one. 'What happened to Carol?'

'She dropped out of sight. I think she ran off with a sailor, or something like that. She didn't have what it takes, anyway, after the first bloom.' Joey sighed deeply. 'If you see Susanna, mention my name, will you, Lew? I mean, if you can do it gracefully.' He moved one hand in an undulating horizontal curve. 'She acts like she thought I was dead.'

I used Joey's phone to make a call to Susanna Drew's office. Her secretary let me talk to her:

'This is Lew Archer, Susanna.'

'How nice to hear from you.'

'The occasion isn't so nice,' I said bluntly. 'I'm investigating a murder. The victim may or may not be a girl you knew back in the forties, named Carol.'

'Not Carol Harley?'

'I'm afraid she's the one.'

Her voice roughened. 'And you say she's dead?'

'Yes. She was murdered yesterday in a place called Ocean View.'

She was silent for a moment. When she spoke again, her voice was softer and younger. 'What can I do?'

'Tell me about your friend Carol.'

'Not on the telephone, *please*. The telephone dehumanizes everything.'

'A personal meeting would suit me much better,' I said rather formally. 'I have some pictures to show you, to make the identification positive. It should be soon. We're twenty-four hours behind—'

'Come over now. I'll send your name out front.'

I thanked Joey and drove to Television City. A guard from the front office escorted me through the building to Susanna Drew's office. It was large and bright, with flowers on the desk and explosive-looking abstract expressionist paintings on the walls. Susanna was standing at the window, crying. She was a slim woman with short straight hair so black the eye stayed on it. She kept her back to me for some time after her secretary went out and closed the door. Finally she turned to face me, still dabbing at her wet cheeks with a piece of yellow Kleenex.

She was fortyish now, and not exactly pretty, but neither did she look like anybody else. Her black eyes, even in sorrow, were furiously alive. She had style, and intelligence in the lines and contours of her face. Legs still good. Mouth still good. It said:

'I don't know why I'm carrying on like this. I haven't seen or heard from Carol in seventeen or eighteen years.' She paused. 'I really do know, though. "It is Margaret I mourn for." Do you know Hopkins's poem?'

'You know I don't. Who's Margaret?'

'The girl in the poem,' she said. 'She's grieving over the fallen autumn leaves. And Hopkins tells her she's grieving for herself. Which is what I'm doing.' She breathed deeply. 'I used to be so *young*.'

'You're not exactly over the hill now.'

'Don't flatter me. I'm old old old. I was twenty in 1945 when I knew Carol. Back in the pre-atomic era.' On the way to her desk she paused in front of one of the abstract paintings, as if it represented what had happened to the world since. She sat down with an air of great efficiency. 'Well, let me look at your pictures.'

'You won't like them. She was beaten to death.'

'God. Who would do that?'

'Her husband is the prime suspect.'

'Harley? Is she—was she still with that *schmo*?'

'Evidently she still was.'

'I knew he'd do her in sooner or later.'

I leaned on the end of her desk. 'How did you know that?'

'It was one of those fated things. Elective affinities with a reverse twist. She was a really nice child, as tender as a soft-boiled egg, and he was a psychopathic personality. He just couldn't leave her alone.'

'How do you know he was a psychopathic personality?'

'I know a psychopathic personality when I see one,' she said, lifting her chin. 'I was married to one, briefly, back in the fabulous fifties. Which constitutes me an authority. If you want a definition, a psychopathic personality is a man you can't depend on for anything except trouble.'

'And that's the way Harley was?'

'Oh yes.'

'What was his first name?'

'Mike. He was a sailor, a sailor in the Navy.'

'And what was the name of his ship?'

She opened her mouth to tell me, I believe. But something shifted rapidly and heavily in her mind, and closed off communication. 'I'm afraid I don't remember.' She looked up at me with black opaque eyes.

'What did he do before he went into the Navy? Was he a photographer?'

She looked back over the years. 'I think he had been a boxer, a professional boxer, not a very successful one. He may have been a photographer, too. He was the sort of person who had been a number of things, none of them successfully.'

'Are you sure his name wasn't Harold?'

'Everybody *called* him Mike. It may have been a *nom de guerre*.'

'A what?'

'A fighting name. You know.' She breathed deeply. 'You were going to show me some pictures, Lew.'

'They can wait. You could help me most right now by telling me what you can remember about Carol and Harley and how you got to know them.'

Tensely, she looked at her watch. 'I'm due in a story conference in one minute.'

'This is a more important story conference.'

She breathed in and out. 'I suppose it is. Well, I'll make it short and simple. It's a simple story, anyway, so simple I couldn't use it in my series. Carol was a country girl from Idaho. She ran away from home with an awol sailor. Mike Harley came from the same hick town, I think, but he'd already been in the Navy for a couple of years and seen the world. He promised to take her out to the coast and get her into the movies. She was about sixteen and so naïve it made you want to weep or burst out laughing.'

'I can hear you laughing. When and where did you happen to meet her?'

'In the early spring of 1945. I was working at Warner's in Burbank and spending weekends in various places. You know the old Barcelona Hotel near Santa Monica? Carol and Harley were staying there, and it's where I—well, I got interested in her.'

'Were they married?'

'Carol and Harley? I think they'd gone through some sort of ceremony in Tia Juana. At least Carol thought they were married. She was also thought Harley was on extended leave, until the Shore Patrol picked him up. They whisked him back to his ship and Carol was left with nothing to live on, literally nothing. Harley hadn't bothered to make an allotment or anything. So I took her under my wing.'

'And brought her to see Joe Sylvester.'

'Why not? She was pretty enough, and she wasn't a stupid girl. Joey got her a couple of jobs, and I spent a lot of time with her on grooming and diction and posture. I'd just been through an unhappy love affair, in my blue period, and I was glad to have somebody to occupy my mind with. I let Carol share my apartment, and I actually think I could have made something out of her. A really wholesome Marilyn, perhaps.' She caught herself going into Hollywood patter, and stopped abruptly. 'But it all went blah.'

'What happened?'

'Harley had left her pregnant, and it began to show. Instead of grooming a starlet, I found myself nursing a pregnant teen-ager with a bad case of homesickness. But she refused to go home. She said her father would kill her.'

'Do you remember her father's name?'

'I'm afraid not. She was using the name Carol Cooper for professional purposes, but that wasn't her true surname. I *think* her father lived in Pocatello, if that's any help.'

'It may be. You say she was pregnant. What happened to the baby?'

'I don't know. Harley turned up before the baby was born—

the Navy had finally kicked him out, I believe—and she went back to him. This was in spite of everything I could say or do. They were elective affinities, as I said. The Patient Griselda and the nothing man. So seventeen years later he had to kill her.'

'Was he violent when you knew him?'

'Was he not.' She crossed her arms over her breast. 'He knocked me down when I tried to prevent her from going back to him. I went out to find help. When I got back to my apartment with a policeman they were both gone, with all the money in my purse. I didn't press charges, and that was the last I saw of them.'

'But you still care about Carol.'

'She was nice to have around. I never had a sister, or a daughter. In fact, when I think back, *feel* back, I never had a happier time than that spring and summer in Burbank when Carol was pregnant. We didn't know how lucky we were.'

'How so?'

'Well, it was a terribly hot summer and the refrigerator kept breaking down and we only had the one bedroom and Carol got bigger and bigger and we had no men in our lives. We thought we were suffering many deprivations. Actually all the deprivations came later.' She looked around her fairly lavish office as if it was a jail cell, then at her watch. 'I really have to go now. My writers and director will be committing mayhem on each other.'

'Speaking of mayhem,' I said, 'I'll ask you to look at these pictures if you can stand it. The identification should be nailed down.'

'Yes.'

I spread the photographs out for her. She looked them over carefully.

'Yes. It's Carol. The poor child.'

She had become very pale. Her black eyes stood out like the coal eyes of a snowgirl. She got to her feet and walked rather blindly into an adjoining room, shutting the door behind her.

I sat at her desk, pinched by her contour chair, and used the phone to ask her secretary to get me Lieutenant Bastian. He was on the line in less than a minute. I told him everything Susanna Drew had told me.

She came out of the next room and listened to the end of the conversation. 'You don't waste any time,' she said when I hung up.

'Your evidence is important.'

'That's good. I'm afraid it's taken all I've got.' She was still very pale. She moved toward me as if the floor under her feet was teetering. 'Will you drive me home?'

Home was an apartment on Beverly Glen Boulevard. It had a mezzanine and a patio and African masks on the walls. She invited me to make us both a drink, and we sat and talked about Carol and then about Tom Hillman. She seemed to be very interested in Tom Hillman.

I was becoming interested in Susanna. Something about her dark intensity bit into me as deep as memory. Sitting close beside her, looking into her face, I began to ask myself whether, in my present physical and financial and moral condition, I could take on a woman with all those African masks.

The damn telephone rang in the next room. She got up, using my knee as a place to rest her hand. I heard her say:

'So it's you. What do you want from me now?'

That was all I heard. She closed the door. Five minutes later, when she came out, her face had changed again. A kind of angry fear had taken the place of sorrow in her eyes, as if they had learned of something worse than death.

'Who was that, Susanna?'

'You'll never know.'

I drove downtown in a bitter mood and bullyragged my friend Colton, the DA's investigator, into asking Sacramento for Harold or Mike Harley's record, if any. While I was waiting for an answer I went downstairs to the newsstand and bought an early evening paper.

The murder and the kidnapping were front-page news, but there was nothing in the newspaper story I didn't already know, except that Ralph Hillman had had a distinguished combat record as a naval aviator and later (after Newport Line School) as a line officer. He was also described as a millionaire.

I sat in Colton's outer office trying to argue away my feeling that Bastian had shoved me onto the fringes of the case. The feeling deepened when the word came back from Sacramento that neither a Harold nor a Mike Harley had a California record, not even for a traffic violation. I began to wonder if I was on the track of the right man.

I drove back to the Strip through late afternoon traffic. It was nearly dusk when I reached my office. I didn't bother turning on the light for a while, but sat and watched the green sky at the window lose its color. Stars and neons came out. A plane like a moving group of stars circled far out beyond Santa Monica.

I closed the venetian blind, to foil snipers, and turned on the desk lamp and went through the day's mail. It consisted of three bills, and a proposition from the Motel Institute of St Louis. The Institute offered me, in effect, a job at twenty thousand a year managing a million-dollar convention motel. All I had to do was fill out a registration form for the Institute's mail-order course in motel management and send it to the Institute's registrar. If I had a wife, we could register as a couple.

I sat toying with the idea of filling out the form, but decided to go out for dinner first. I was making very incisive decisions. I decided to call Susanna Drew and ask her to have dinner with me, telling myself that it was in line of business. I could even deduct the tab from my income tax.

She wasn't in the telephone book. I tried Information. Unlisted number. I couldn't afford her anyway.

Before I went out for dinner by myself, I checked my answering service. Susanna Drew had left her number for me.

'I've been trying to get you,' I said to her.

'I've been right here in my apartment.'

'I mean before I knew you left your number.'

'Oh? What did you have in mind?'

'The Motel Institute of St Louis is making a very nice offer to couples who want to register for their course in motel management.'

'It sounds inviting. I've always wanted to go out to sunny California and manage a motel.'

'Good. We'll have dinner and talk strategy. Television won't last, you know that in your heart. None of these avant-garde movements last.'

'Sorry, Lew. I'd love dinner, another night. Tonight I'm not up to it. But I did want to thank you for looking after me this afternoon. I was in a bad way for a while.'

'I'm afraid I did it to you.'

'No. My whole lousy life reared up and did it to me. You and your pictures were just the catalytic agent.'

'Could you stand a visit from a slightly catalytic agent? I'll bring dinner from the delicatessen. I'll buy you a gardenia.'

'No. I don't want to see you tonight.'

'And you haven't changed your mind about that telephone call you wouldn't tell me about?'

'No. There are things about me you needn't know.'

'I suppose that's encouraging in a way. Why did you leave your number for me, then?'

'I found something that might help you—a picture of Carol taken in 1945.'

'I'll come and get it. You haven't really told me how you met her, you know.'

'Please don't come. I'll send a messenger with it.'

'If you insist. I'll wait in my office.' I gave her the address.

'Lew?' Her voice was lighter and sweeter, almost poignant. 'You're not just putting on an act, are you? To try and pry out my personal secrets, I mean?'

'It's no act,' I said.

'Likewise,' she said. 'Thank you.'

I sat in the echoing silence thinking that she had been badly treated by a man or men. It made me angry to think of it. I didn't go out for dinner after all. I sat and nursed my anger until Susanna's messenger arrived.

He was a young Negro in uniform who talked like a college graduate. He handed me a sealed manila envelope, which I ripped open.

It contained a single glossy print, preserved between two sheets of corrugated cardboard, of a young blonde girl wearing a pageboy bob and a bathing suit. You couldn't pin down the reason for her beauty. It was partly in her clear low forehead, the high curve of her cheek, her perfect round chin; partly in the absolute femaleness that looked out of her eyes and informed her body.

Wondering idly who had taken the photograph, I turned it over. Rubber-stamped in purple ink on the back was the legend: 'Photo Credit: Harold "Har" Harley, Barcelona Hotel.'

'Will that be all?' the messenger said at the door.

'No.' I gave him ten dollars.

'This is too much, sir. I've already been paid.'

'I know. But I want you to buy a gardenia and deliver it back to Miss Drew.'

He said he would.

XII

1945 WAS A long time ago, as time went in California. The Barcelona Hotel was still standing, but I seemed to remember hearing that it was closed. I took the long drive down Sunset to the coastal highway on the off-chance of developing my lead to Harold Harley. Also I wanted to take another look at the building where Harley and Carol had lived.

It was a huge old building, Early Hollywood Byzantine, with stucco domes and minarets, and curved verandahs where famous faces of the silent days had sipped their bootleg rum. Now it stood abandoned under the bluff. The bright lights of a service station across the highway showed that its white paint was flaking off and some of the windows were broken.

I parked on the weed-ruptured concrete of the driveway and walked up to the front door. Taped to the glass was a notice of bankruptcy, with an announcement that the building was going to be sold at public auction in September.

I flashed my light through the glass into the lobby. It was still completely furnished, but the furnishings looked as though they hadn't been replaced in a generation. The carpet was worn threadbare, the chairs were gutted. But the place still had atmosphere, enough of it to summon up a flock of ghosts.

I moved along the curving verandah, picking my way among the rain-warped wicker furniture, and shone my light through a french window into the dining room. The tables were set, complete with cocked-hat napkins, but there was dust lying thick on the napery. A good place for ghosts to feed, I thought, but not for me.

Just for the hell of it, though, and as a way of asserting myself against the numerous past, I went back to the front door and tapped loudly with my flashlight on the glass. Deep inside the building, at the far end of a corridor, a light showed itself. It was a moving light, which came toward me.

The man who was carrying it was big, and he walked as if he had sore feet or legs. I could see his face now in the upward glow of his electric lantern. A crude upturned nose, a bulging forehead, a thirsty mouth. It was the face of a horribly ravaged baby who had never been weaned from the bottle. I could also see that he had a revolver in his other hand.

He pointed it at me and flashed the light in my eyes. 'This place is closed. Can't you read?' he shouted through the glass.

'I want to talk to you.'

'I don't want to talk to you. Beat it. Amscray.'

He waved the gun at me. I could tell from his voice and look that he had been drinking hard. A drunk with a gun and an excuse to use it can be murder, literally. I made one more attempt:

'Do you know a photographer named Harold Harley who used to be here?'

'Never heard of him. Now you get out of here before I blow a hole in you. You're trespashing.'

He lifted the heavy revolver. I withdrew, as far as the service station across the street. A quick-moving man in stained white coveralls came out from under a car on a hoist and offered to sell me gas.

'It ought to take ten,' I said. 'Who's the character in the Barcelona Hotel? He acts like he was bitten by a bear.'

The man gave me a one-sided smile. 'You run into Otto Sipe?'

'If that's the watchman's name.'

'Yeah. He worked there so long he thinks he owns the place.'

'How long?'

'Twenty years or more. I been here since the war myself, and he goes back before me. He was their dick.'

'Hotel detective?'

'Yeah. He told me once he used to be an officer of the law. If he was, he didn't learn much. Check your oil?'

'Don't bother, I just had it changed. Were you here in 1945?'

'That's the year I opened. I went into the service early and got out early. Why?'

'I'm a private detective. The name is Archer.' I offered him my hand.

He wiped his on his coveralls before he took it. 'Daly. Ben Daly.'

'A man named Harold Harley used to stay at the Barcelona in 1945. He was a photographer.'

Daly's face opened. 'Yeah. I remember him. He took a picture of me and the wife to pay for his gas bill once. We still have it in the house.'

'You wouldn't know where he is now?'

'Sorry, I haven't seen him in ten years.'

'What was the last you saw of him?'

'He had a little studio in Pacific Palisades. I dropped in once or twice to say hello. I don't think he's there any more.'

'I gather you liked him.'

'Sure. There's no harm in Harold.'

Men could change. I showed Carol's picture to Daly. He didn't know her.

'You couldn't pin down the address in Pacific Palisades for me?'

He rubbed the side of his face. It needed retreading, but it was a good face. 'I can tell you where it is.'

He told me where it was, on a side street just off Sunset, next door to a short-order restaurant. I thanked him, and paid him for the gas.

The short-order restaurant was easy to find, but the building next door to it was occupied by a paperback bookstore. A young woman wearing pink stockings and a ponytail presided over the cash register. She looked at me pensively through her eye makeup when I asked her about Harold Harley.

'It seems to me I heard there was a photographer in here at one time.'

'Where would he be now?'

'I haven't the slightest idea, honestly. We've only been here less than a year ourselves—a year in September.'

'How are you doing?'

'We're making the rent, at least.'

'Who do you pay it to?'

'The man who runs the lunch counter. Mr Vernon. He ought to give us free meals for what he charges. Only don't quote me if you talk to him. We're a month behind now on the rent.'

I bought a book and went next door for dinner. It was a place where I could eat with my hat on. While I was waiting for my steak, I asked the waitress for Mr Vernon. She turned to the white-hatted short-order cook who had just tossed my steak onto the grill.

'Mr Vernon, gentleman wants to speak to you.'

He came over to the counter, an unsmiling thin-faced man with glints of gray beard showing on his chin. 'You said you wanted it bloody. You'll get it bloody.' He brandished his spatula.

'Good. I understand you own the store next door.'

'That and the next one to it.' The thought encouraged him a little. 'You looking for a place to rent?'

'I'm looking for a man, a photographer named Harold Harley.'

'He rented that store for a long time. But he couldn't quite make a go of it. There's too many photographers in this town. He held on for seven or eight years after the war and then gave up on it.'

'You don't know where he is now?'

'No sir, I do not.'

The sizzling of my steak reached a certain intensity, and he heard it. He went and flipped it with his spatula and came back to me. 'You want french fries?'

'All right. What's the last you saw of Harley?'

'The last I heard of him he moved out to the Valley. That was a good ten years ago. He was trying to run his business out of the front room of his house in Van Nuys. He's a pretty good photographer—he took a fine picture of my boy's christening party—but he's got no head for business. I ought to know, he still owes me three months' rent.'

Six young people came in and lined up along the counter. They had wind in their hair, sand in their ears, and the word 'Surfbirds' stenciled across the backs of their identical yellow sweatshirts. All of them, girls and boys, ordered two hamburgers apiece.

One of the boys put a quarter in the jukebox and played 'Surfin' ain't no sin.' Mr Vernon got twelve hamburger patties out of the refrigerator and lined them up on the grill. He put my steak on a plate with a handful of fried potatoes and brought it to me personally.

'I could look up that Van Nuys address if it's important. I kept it on account of the rent he owed me.'

'It's important.' I showed him Carol's picture, the young one Harley had taken. 'Do you recognize his wife?'

'I didn't even know he had a wife. I didn't think he'd rate a girl like that.'

'Why not?'

'He's no ladies' man. He never was. Harold's the quiet type.'

Doubt was slipping in again that I was on the right track. It made my head ache. 'Can you describe him to me?'

'He's just an ordinary-looking fellow, about my size, five foot ten. Kind of a long nose. Blue eyes. Sandy hair. There's nothing special about him. Of course he'd be older now.'

'How old?'

'Fifty at least. I'm fifty-nine myself, due to retire next year. Excuse me, mister.'

He flipped the twelve hamburger patties over, distributed twelve half-buns on top of them and went out through a swinging door at the back. I ate my steak. Mr Vernon returned with a slip of paper on which he had written Harley's Van Nuys address: 956 Elmhurst.

The waitress delivered the hamburgers to the surfbirds. They munched them in time to the music. The song the jukebox was playing as I went out had a refrain about 'the day that I caught the big wave and made you my slave.' I drove up Sunset onto the San Diego Freeway headed north.

Elmhurst was a working-class street of prewar bungalows built too close together. It was a warm night in the Valley, and some people were still out on their porches and lawns. A fat man drinking beer on the porch of 956 told me that Harley had sold him the house in 1960. He had his present address because he was still paying Harley monthly installments on a second trust deed.

That didn't sound like the Harley I knew. I asked him for a description.

'He's kind of a sad character,' the fat man said. 'One of these guys that wouldn't say "boo" to a goose. He's had his troubles, I guess.'

'What kind of troubles?'

'Search me. I don't know him well. I only saw him the twice when I bought the house from him. He wanted out in a hurry, and he gave me a good buy. He had this chance for a job in Long Beach, developing film, and he didn't want to commute.'

He gave me Harley's address in Long Beach, which is a long way from Van Nuys. It was close to midnight when I found the house, a tract house near Long Beach Boulevard. It had brown weeds in the front yard, and was lightless, like most of the houses in the street.

I drove past a street light to the end of the block and walked back. The all-night traffic on the boulevard filled the air with a kind of excitement, rough and forlorn. I was raised in Long Beach, and I used to cruise its boulevards in a model-A Ford. Their sound, whining, threatening, rising, fading, spoke to something deep in my mind which I loved and hated. I didn't want to knock on Harley's door. I was almost certain I had the wrong man.

The overhead door of the attached garage was closed but not locked. I opened it quietly. The street light down the block shone on the rear of a dirty white Ford sedan with an Idaho license plate.

I went to the lefthand door of the car and opened it. The dome light came on. The car was registered in the name of Robert Brown, with an address in Pocatello. My heart was pounding so hard I could scarcely breathe.

The door from the garage into the house was suddenly

outlined up light. The door sprung open. The light slapped me across the eyes and drenched me.

'Mike?' said the voice of a man I didn't know. He looked around the corner of the door frame. 'Is that you, Mike?'

'I saw Mike yesterday.'

'Who are you?'

'A friend.' I didn't say whose friend. 'He left his car for you, I see.'

'That's between him and I.'

His defensive tone encouraged me. I moved across the lighted space between us and stepped up into his kitchen, closing the door behind me. He didn't try to keep me out. He stood barefoot in his pajamas facing me, gray-haired and haggard-faced, with drooping hound eyes.

'My brother didn't tell me about a partner.'

'Oh? What did he tell you?'

'Nothing. I mean—' He tried to bite his lower lip. His teeth were false, and slipped. Until he sucked them back into place he looked as if I had scared him literally to death. 'He didn't tell me a thing about you or anything. I don't know why you come to me. That car is mine. I traded him my crate for it.'

'Was that wise?'

'I dunno, maybe not.' He glanced at the unwashed dishes piled in the sink as if they shared responsibility for his lack of wisdom. 'Anyway, it's none of your business.'

'It's everybody's business, Harold. You must know that by now.'

His lips formed the word 'Yes' without quite saying it. Tears came into his eyes. It was Harold he mourned for. He named the most terrible fear he could conjure up:

'Are you from the FBI?'

'I'm a police agent. We need to have a talk.'

'Here?'

'This is as good a place as any.'

He looked around the dingy little room as if he was seeing it with new eyes. We sat on opposite sides of the kitchen table. The checkered oilcloth that covered it was threadbare in places.

'I didn't want any part of this,' he said.

'Who would?'

'And it isn't the first time he got me into trouble, not by a long shot. This has been going on for the last thirty-five years, ever since Mike got old enough to walk and talk. I kid you not.'

'Just what do you mean when you say he's got you into trouble? This time.'

He shrugged crookedly and raised his open hands as if I should plainly be able to see the stigmata in his palms. 'He's mixed up in a kidnapping, isn't he?'

'Did he tell you that?'

'He never told me anything straight in his life. But I can read. Since I saw the papers today I've been scared to go out of the house. And you know what my wife did? She left me. She took a taxi to the bus station and went back to her mother in Oxnard. She didn't even wash last night's dishes.'

'When was your brother here?'

'Last night. He got here around ten-thirty. We were on our way to bed but I got up again. I talked to him right here where we're sitting. I thought there was something screwy going on—he had that wild look in his eye—but I didn't know what. He gave me one of his stories, that he won a lot of money in a poker game from some sailors in Dago, and they were after him to take the money back. That's why he wanted to change cars with me. He said.'

'Why did you agree to it?'

'I dunno. It's hard to say no when Mike wants something.'

'Did he threaten you?'

'Not in so many words. I knew he had a gun with him. I saw him take it out of his car.' He lifted his eyes to mine. 'You always feel sort of under a threat when Mike has something going. Stand in his way and he'll clobber you soon as look at you.'

I had reason to believe him. 'What was the make and model and license number of your car?'

'1958 Plymouth two-door, license IKT 449.'

'Color?'

'Two-tone blue.'

I made some notes. 'I'm going to ask you a very important question. Was the boy with Mike? This boy?'

I showed him Tom's picture. He shook his head over it. 'No sir.'

'Did he say where the boy was?'

'He didn't mention any boy, and I didn't know about it, then.'

'Did you know he was coming here last night?'

'In a way. He phoned me from Los Angeles yesterday afternoon. He said he might be dropping by but I wasn't to tell anybody.'

'Did he say anything about changing cars when he phoned you?'

'No *sir.*'

'Did you and your brother have any previous agreement to change cars?'

'*No* sir.'

'And you didn't know about the kidnapping until you read about it in the paper today?'

'That's correct. Or the murder either.'

'Do you know who was murdered?'

His head hung forward, moving up and down slightly on the cords of his neck. He covered the back of his neck with his hand as if he feared a blow there from behind. 'I guess—it sounded like Carol.'

'It was Carol.'

'I'm sorry to hear about that. She was a good kid, a lot better than he deserved.'

'You should have come forward with information, Harold.'

'I know that. Lila said so. It's why she left me. She said I was setting myself up for a patsy again.'

'I gather it's happened before.'

'Not this bad, though. The worst he ever did to me before was when he sold me a camera he stole from the Navy. He turned around and claimed I stole it when I visited him on his ship on visiting day.'

'What was the name of the ship?'

'The *Perry Bay*. It was one of those jeep carriers. I went aboard her in Dago the last year of the war, but I wisht I never set foot on her. The way they talked to me, I thought I was gonna end up in the federal pen. But they finally took my word that I didn't know the camera was hot.'

'I'm taking your word now about several things, or have you noticed?'

'I didn't know what to think.'

'I believe you're an honest man in a bind, Harold.'

My spoken sympathy was too much for him. It made his eyes water again. He removed his hand from the back of his neck and wiped his eyes with his fingers.

'I'm not the only one you have to convince, of course. But I think you can probably work your way out of this bind by telling the whole truth.'

'You mean in court?'

'Right now.'

'I want to tell the truth,' he said earnestly. 'I would have come forward, only I was ascared to. I was ascared they'd send me up for life.'

'And Mike too?'

'It wasn't him I was worried about,' he said. 'I'm through with my brother. When I found out about Carol—' He shook his head.

'Were you fond of her?'

'Sure I was. I didn't see much of her these last years when they were in Nevada. But Carol and me, we always got along.'

'They were living in Nevada?'

'Yeah. Mike had a job bartending in one of the clubs on the South Shore. Only he lost it. I had to—' His slow mind overtook his words and stopped them.

'You had to—?'

'Nothing. I mean. I had to help him out a little these last few months since he lost his job.'

'How much money did you give them?'

'I dunno. What I could spare. A couple of hundred dollars.' He looked up guiltily.

'Did Mike pay you back last night by any chance?'

He hung his head. The old refrigerator in the corner behind him woke up and started to throb. Above it I could still hear the sound of the boulevard rising and falling, coming and going.

'No he didn't,' Harold said.

'How much did he give you?'

'He didn't *give* me anything.'

'You mean he was only paying you back?'

'That's right.'

'How much?'

'He gave me five hundred dollars,' he said in horror.

'Where is it?'

'Under my mattress. You're welcome *to* it. I don't want any part of it.'

I followed him into the bedroom. The room was in disarray, with bureau drawers pulled out, hangers scattered on the floor.

'Lila took off in a hurry,' he said, 'soon as she saw the paper. She probably filed suit for divorce already. It wouldn't be the first time she got a divorce.'

'From you?'

'From the other ones.'

Lila's picture stood on top of the bureau. Her face was dark and plump and stubborn-looking, and it supported an insubstantial dome of upswept black hair.

Harold stood disconsolately by the unmade bed. I helped him to lift up the mattress. Flattened under it was an oilskin tobacco pouch containing paper money visible through the oilskin. He handed it to me.

'Did you see where this came from, Harold?'

'He got it out of the car. I heard him unwrapping some paper.'

I put the pouch in my pocket without opening it. 'And you honestly didn't know it was hot?'

He sat on the bed. 'I guess I knew there was something the matter with it. He couldn't win that much in a poker game, I mean and keep it. He always keeps trying for the one more pot until he loses his wad. But I didn't think about *kidnapping*, for gosh sake.' He struck himself rather feebly on the knee. 'Or murder.'

'Do you think he murdered the boy?'

'I meant poor little Carol.'

'I meant the boy.'

'He wouldn't do that to a young kid,' Harold said in a small hushed voice. He seemed not to want the statement to be heard, for fear it would be denied.

'Have you searched the car?'

'No sir. Why would I do that?'

'For blood or money. You haven't opened the trunk?'

'No. I never went near the lousy car.' He looked sick, as if its mere presence in his garage had infected him with criminality.

'Give me the keys to it.'

He picked up his limp trousers, groped in the pockets, and handed me an old leather holder containing the keys to the car. I advised him to put on his clothes while I went out to the garage.

I found the garage light and turned it on, unlocked the trunk, and with some trepidation, lifted the turtleback. The space inside was empty, except for a rusty jack and a balding spare tire. No body.

But before I closed the trunk I found something in it that I didn't like. A raveled piece of black yarn was caught in the lock. I remembered Sam Jackman telling me that Tom had been wearing a black sweater on Sunday. I jerked the yarn loose, angrily, and put it away in an envelope in my pocket. I slammed the turtleback down on the possibility which the black yarn suggested to my mind.

XIII

I WENT BACK into the house. The bedroom door was closed. I knocked and got no answer and flung it open. Harold was sitting on the edge of the bed in his underwear and socks. He was holding a ·22 rifle upright between his knees. He didn't point it at me. I took it away from him and unloaded the single shell.

'I don't have the nerve to kill myself,' he said.

'You're lucky.'

'Yeah, very lucky.'

'I mean it, Harold. When I was a kid I knew a man who lost his undertaking business in the depression. He decided to blow out his brains with a twenty-two. But all it did was blind him. He's been sitting around in the dark for the last thirty years. And his sons have the biggest mortuary in town.'

'So I should be in the mortuary business.' He sighed. 'Or anything but the brother business. I know what I have to go through.'

'It's like a sickness. It'll pass.'

'My brother,' he said, 'is a sickness that never passes.'

'He's going to, this time, Harold. He'll be taken care of for the rest of his life.'

'If you catch him.'

'We'll catch him. Where did he head from here?'

'He didn't tell me.'

'Where do you think?'

'Nevada, I guess. It's always been his favorite hangout. When he has money he can't stay away from the tables.'

'Where did he live when he worked on the South Shore of Tahoe?'

'They were buying a trailer but he lost that when he lost his barkeep job. His boss said he got too rough with the drunks. After that they moved from one place to another, mostly motels and lodges around the lake. I couldn't give you any definite address.'

'What was the name of the club he worked at?'

'The Jet. Carol worked there, too, off and on. She was sort of a singing waitress. We went to hear her sing there once. Lila thought she was lousy, but I thought she was okay. She sang pretty sexy songs, and that's why Lila—'

I interrupted him. 'Do you have a phone? I want to make a couple of collect calls.'

'It's in the front room.'

I took the rifle with me, in case he got further ideas about shooting himself, or me. The walls of the front room were as crowded as the walls of a picture gallery with Harold's photographs. Old Man, Old Woman, Young Woman, Sunset, Wildflowers, Mountain, Seascape; and Lila. Most of them had been hand-tinted, and three portraits of Lila smiled at me from various angles, so that I felt surrounded by toothy, flesh-colored face.

I went back to the bedroom. Harold was putting on his shoes. He looked up rather resentfully.

'I'm okay. You don't have to keep checking up on me.'

'I was wondering if you had a picture of Mike.'

'I have one. It's nearly twenty years old. After he got into trouble he never let me take him.'

'Let's see it.'

'I wouldn't know where to find it. Anyway, it was done when he was a kid and he doesn't look like that anymore. It's an art study, like, of his muscles, in boxing trunks.'

'What does he look like now?'

'I thought you saw him.'

'It was dark at the time.'

'Well, he's still a fairly nice-looking man, I mean his features. He quit fighting before he got banged up too bad. He has brown hair—no gray—he parts it on the side. Mike always did have a fine head of hair.' He scratched at his own thin hair. 'Greenish-gray eyes, with kind of a wild look in them when he's got something going. Thin mouth. I always thought it was kind of a cruel mouth. Teeth not so good. But I dunno, he's still a nice-looking fellow, and well set-up. He keeps himself in pretty good physical shape.'

'Height and weight?'

'He's an inch or so under six feet. He used to fight light-heavy, but he must be heavier now. Maybe one eighty-five.'

'Any scars or distinguishing marks?'

Harold jerked his head up. 'Yeah. He's got scars on his back where Dad used to beat him. I got some of my own.' He pulled up his undershirt and showed me the white scars all up and down his back, like hieroglyphs recording history. Harold seemed to take his scars as a matter of course.

'Are your parents still living?'

'Sure. Dad's still running the farm. It's on the Snake River,' he said without nostalgia. 'Pocatello Rural Route 7. But Mike wouldn't be going there. He hates Idaho.'

'You never can tell, though,' I said as I made some notes.

'Take my word. He broke with Dad over twenty years ago.' As an afterthought, he said: 'There's a portrait I did of Dad in the front room. I call it "Old Man." '

Before I sat down with the telephone I looked more closely at the portrait: a grizzled farmer with flat angry eyes and a mouth like a bear trap. Then I called Arnie Walters in Reno and gave him a rundown on the old man's son, Mike Harley, ex-sailor, ex-fighter, ex-bartender, gambler, kidnapper, wife-beater, putative murderer and driver of a 1958 Plymouth two-door, California license number IKT 449.

'You've been busy,' Arnie said when he finished recording my facts. 'We have, too, but we haven't come up with anything. We will now.' He hesitated. 'Just how much muscle do you want put into the operation?'

'You mean how much can I pay for?'

'Your client.'

'I lost my client. I'm hoping this stuff I've uncovered will get me another one, but it hasn't yet.'

Arnie whistled. 'What you're doing isn't ethical.'

'Yes it is. I'm temporarily an investigator for the local sheriff's office.'

'Now I know you've flipped. I hate to bring this up, Lew, but you owe me three hundred dollars and that's a charity price for what we've done. Tomorrow at this time it'll be six hundred anyway, if we stay with it. With our overhead we just can't work for nothing.'

'I know that. You'll be paid.'

'When?'

'Soon. I'll talk to you in the morning.'

'What do we do in the meantime?'

'Carry on.'

'If you say so.'

Arnie hung up on me and left me feeling a little shaky. Six hundred dollars was what I got for working a full week, and I didn't work every week. I had about three hundred dollars in the bank, about two hundred in cash. I owned an equity in the car and some clothes and furniture. My total net worth, after nearly twenty years in the detective business, was in the neighbourhood of thirty-five hundred dollars. And Ralph Hillman, with his money, was letting me finance my own search for his son.

On the other hand, I answered my self-pity, I was doing what I wanted to be doing. I wanted to take the man who had taken me.

I wanted to find Tom. I couldn't drop the case just as it was breaking. And I needed Arnie to backstop me in Nevada. Carry on.

I made a second collect call, to Lieutenant Bastian. It was long past midnight, but he was still on duty in his office. I told him I was bringing in a witness, and I gave him a capsule summary of what the witness was going to say. Bastian expressed a proper degree of surprise and delight.

Harold was still in the bedroom, standing pensively beside the tie rack attached to the closet door. He was fully dressed except for a tie.

'What kind of a tie do you think I ought to wear? Lila always picks out the tie I wear.'

'You don't need a tie.'

'They'll be taking my picture, won't they? I've got to be properly dressed.' He fingered the tie rack distraughtly.

I chose one for him, a dark blue tie with a conservative pattern, the kind you wear to the funerals of friends. We closed up the house and garage and drove south out of Long Beach.

It was less than an hour's drive to Pacific Point. Harold was intermittently talkative, but his silences grew longer. I asked him about his and his brother's early life in Idaho. It had been a hard life, in an area subject to blizzards in the winter and floods in the spring and extreme heat in the summer. Their father believed that boys were a kind of domestic animal that ought to be put to work soon after weaning. They were hoeing corn and digging potatoes when they were six, and milking the cows at eight or nine.

They could have stood the work, if it hadn't been for the punishment that went with it. I'd seen Harold's scars. The old man used a piece of knotted wire on them. Mike was the first to run away. He lived in Pocatello for a couple of years with a man named Robert Brown, a high-school coach and counselor who took him in and tried to give him a chance.

Robert Brown was Carol's father. Mike paid him back for his kindness eventually by running away with his daughter.

'How old was Mike then?'

'Twenty or so. Let's see, it was about a year after they drafted him into the Navy. Yeah, he'd be about twenty. Carol was only sixteen.'

'Where were you at the time?'

'Working here in Los Angeles. I was 4-F. I had a job taking pictures for a hotel.'

'The Barcelona Hotel,' I said.

'That's right.' He sounded a little startled by my knowledge of his life. 'It wasn't much of a job, but it gave me a chance to freelance on the side.'

'I understand that Carol and your brother stayed there, too.'

'For a little. That was when he was awol and hiding out. I let them use my room for a couple of weeks.'

'You've done a lot for your brother in your time.'

'Yeah. He paid me back by trying to frame me for stealing a Navy camera. There's one extra thing I could have done for him.'

'What was that?'

'I could have drowned him in the river when he was a kid. That's all the use he's been to anybody. Especially Carol.'

'Why did she stick to him?'

He groaned. 'She wanted to, I guess.'

'Were they married?'

He answered slowly. 'I think so. She thought so. But I never saw any papers to prove it.'

'Lately,' I said, 'they've been calling themselves Mr and Mrs Robert Brown. The car he left with you is registered to Robert Brown.'

'I wondered where he got it. Now I suppose I'll have to give it back to the old guy.'

'First the police will be wanting it.'

'Yeah. I guess they will at that.'

The thought of the police seemed to depress him profoundly. He sat without speaking for a while. I caught a glimpse of him in the headlights of a passing car. He was sitting with his chin on his chest. His body appeared to be resisting the movement which was carrying him toward his meeting with the police.

'Do you know Carol's father?' I asked him finally.

'I've met Mr Brown. Naturally he holds Mike against me. God

knows what he'll think of me now, with Carol dead and all.'

'You're not your brother, Harold. You can't go on blaming yourself for what he's done.'

'It's my fault, though.'

'Carol's death?'

'That, too, but I meant the kidnapping. I set it up for Mike without meaning to. I gave him the idea of the whole thing.'

'How did you do that?'

'I don't want to talk about it.'

'You brought it up, Harold. You seem to want to get it off your chest.'

'I've changed my mind.'

I couldn't get him to change it back. He had a passive stubbornness which wouldn't be moved. We drove in complete silence the rest of the way.

I delivered Harold and the five hundred dollars to Lieutenant Bastian, who was waiting in his office in the courthouse, and checked in at the first hotel I came to.

XIV

AT NINE O'CLOCK in the morning, with the taste of coffee still fresh in my mouth, I was back at the door of the lieutenant's office. He was waiting for me.

'Did you get any sleep at all?' I said.

'Not much.' The loss of sleep had affected him hardly at all, except that his voice and bearing were less personal and more official. 'You've had an active twenty-four hours. I have to thank you for turning up the brother. His evidence is important, especially if this case ever gets into court.'

'I have some other evidence to show you.'

But Bastian hadn't finished what he was saying: 'I talked the sheriff into paying you twenty-five dollars per diem plus ten cents a mile, if you will submit a statement.'

'Thanks, but it can wait. You could do me a bigger favor by talking Ralph Hillman into bankrolling me.'

'I can't do that, Archer.'

'You could tell him the facts. I've spent several hundred dollars of my own money, and I've been getting results.'

'Maybe, if I have an opportunity.' He changed the subject abruptly: 'The pathologist who did the autopsy on Mrs Brown has come up with something that will interest you. Actual cause of death was a stab wound in the heart. It wasn't noticed at first because it was under the breast.'

'That does interest me. It could let Harley out.'

'I don't see it that way. He beat her and then stabbed her.'

'Do you have the weapon?'

'No. The doctor says it was a good-sized blade, thin but quite broad, and very sharp, with a sharp point. It went into her like butter, the doctor says.' He took no pleasure in the image. His face was saturnine. 'Now what was the evidence you referred to just now?'

I showed Bastian the piece of black yarn and told him where I had found it. He picked up the implication right away:

'The trunk, eh? I'm afraid it doesn't look too promising for the boy. He was last seen wearing a black sweater. I believe his mother knitted it for him.' He studied the scrap of wool under his magnifying glass. 'This looks like knitting yarn to me, too. Mrs Hillman ought to be shown this.'

He put the piece of yarn under glass on an evidence board. Then he picked up the phone and made an appointment with the Hillmans at their house in El Rancho, an appointment for both of us. We drove out through morning fog in two cars. At the foot of the Hillmans' driveway a man in plain clothes came out of the fog-webbed bushes and waved us on.

Mrs Perez, wearing black shiny Sunday clothes, admitted us to the reception hall. Hillman came out of the room where the bar was. His movements were somnambulistic and precise, as if they were controlled by some external power. His eyes were still too bright.

He shook hands with Bastian and, after some hesitation, with me. 'Come into the sitting room, gentlemen. It's good of you to make the trip out here. Elaine simply wasn't up to going downtown. If I could only get her to eat,' he said.

She was sitting on the chesterfield near the front window. The morning light was unkind to her parched blonde face. It was two full days and nights since the first telephone call on Monday morning. She looked as if all the minutes in those forty-eight hours had passed through her body like knots in wire. The red piece of knitting on the seat beside her hadn't grown since I'd seen it last.

She managed a rather wizened smile and extended her hand to Bastian. 'Ralph says you have something to show me.'

'Yes. It's a piece of yarn which may or may not have come off your boy's sweater.'

'The black one I knitted for him?'

'It may be. We want to know if you recognize the yarn.' Bastian handed her the evidence board. She put on reading glasses and examined it. Then she put it aside, rose abruptly, and left the room. Hillman made a move to follow her. He stopped with his hands out in a helpless pose which he was still in when she returned.

She was carrying a large, figured linen knitting bag. Crouching on the chesterfield, she rummaged among its contents and tossed out balls of wool of various colors. Her furiously active hand came to rest holding a half-used ball of black wool.

'This is what I had left over from Tom's sweater. I think it's the same. Can you tell?'

Bastian broke off a piece of yarn from the ball and compared it under a glass with my piece. He turned from the window:

'The specimens appear identical to me. If they are, we can establish it under the miscroscope.'

'What does it mean if they are identical?' Ralph Hillman said.

'I prefer not to say until we have microscopic confirmation.'

Hillman took hold of Bastian's arm and shook him. 'Don't double-talk me, Lieutenant.'

Bastian broke loose and stepped back. There were white frozen-looking patches around his nose and mouth. His eyes were somber.

'Very well, I'll tell you what I know. This piece of yarn was found by Mr Archer here, caught in the lock of a car trunk. The car was one driven by the alleged kidnapper, Harley.'

'You mean that Tom was riding in the trunk?'

'He may have been, yes.'

'But he wouldn't do that if—' Hillman's mouth worked. 'You mean Tom is dead?'

'He may be. We won't jump to any conclusions.'

Elaine Hillman produced a noise, a strangled gasp, which made her the center of attention. She spoke in a thin voice, halfway between a child's and an old woman's: 'I wish I had never recognized the yarn.'

'It wouldn't change the facts, Mrs Hillman.'

'Well, I don't want any more of your dreadful facts. The waiting is bad enough, without these refinements of torment.'

Hillman bent over and tried to quiet her. 'That isn't fair, Elaine. Lieutenant Bastian is trying to help us.' He had said the same thing about me. It gave me the queer feeling that time was repeating itself and would go on endlessly repeating itself, as it does in hell.

She said: 'He's going about it in a strange way. Look what he's made me do. All my balls of yarn are spilled on the floor.' She kicked at them with her tiny slippered feet.

Hillman got down on his knees to pick them up. She kicked at him, without quite touching him. 'Get away, you're no help, either. If you'd been a decent father, this would never have happened.'

Bastian picked up the evidence board and turned to me. 'We'd better go.'

Nobody asked us not to. But Hillman followed us out into the hall.

'Please forgive us, we're not ourselves. You haven't really *told* me anything.'

Bastian answered him coolly: 'We have no definite conclusions to report.'

'But you think Tom's dead.'

'I'm afraid he may be. We'll learn more from an analysis of the contents of that car trunk. If you'll excuse me, Mr Hillman, I don't have time for further explanations now.'

'I do,' I said.

For the first time that morning Hillman looked at me as if I might be good for something more than a scapegoat. 'Are you willing to tell me what's been going on?'

'So far as I understand it.'

'I'll leave you men together then,' Bastian said. He went out, and a minute later I heard his car go down the drive.

Hillman deputed Mrs Perez to stay with his wife. He led me into a wing of the house I hadn't visited, down an arching corridor like a tunnel carved through chalk, to a spacious study. Two of the oak-paneled walls were lined with books, most of them in calfbound sets, as if Hillman had bought or inherited a library. A third wall was broken by a large deep window overlooking the distant sea.

The fourth wall was hung with a number of framed photographs. One was a blownup snapshot of Dick Leandro crouching in the cockpit of a racing yacht with his hand on the helm and the white wake boiling at his back. One showed a group of Navy fliers posing together on a flight deck. I recognized a younger Hillman on the far right of the group. There were other similar pictures, taken ashore and afloat; one of a torpedo-bomber squadron flying formation in old World War II Devastators; one of an escort carrier photographed from far overhead, so that it lay like a shingle on the bright, scarified water.

It seemed to me that Hillman had brought me to this specific room, this wall, for a purpose. The somnambulistic precision of his movements was probably controlled by the deep unconscious. At any rate, we were developing the same idea at the same time, and the photographer of the escort carrier was the catalyst.

'That was my last ship,' Hillman said. 'The fact is, for a few weeks at the end I commanded her.'

'A few weeks at the end of the war?'

'A few weeks at *her* end. The war was long since over. We took her from Dago through the Canal to Boston and put her in mothballs.' His voice was tender and regretful. He might have been talking about the death of a woman.

'She wasn't the *Perry Bay* by any chance?'

'Yes.' He swung around to look at me. 'You've heard of her?'

'Just last night. This whole things is coming together, Mr Hillman. Does the name Mike Harley mean anything to you?'

His eyes blurred. 'I'm afraid you're confusing me. The name you mentioned earlier was Harold Harley.'

'I had the wrong name. Harold is Mike's brother, and he's the one I talked to last night. He told me Mike served on the *Perry Bay*.'

Hillman nodded slowly. 'I remember Mike Harley. I have reason to. He caused me a lot of trouble. In the end I had to recommend an undesirable discharge.'

'For stealing a Navy camera.'

He gave me a swift responsive look. 'You do your homework thoroughly, Mr Archer. Actually we let him off easy, because he wasn't quite responsible. He could have been sent to Portsmouth for stealing that expensive camera.' He backed up into a chair and sat down suddenly, as if he'd been struck by the full impact of the past. 'So eighteen years later he has to steal my son.'

I stood by the window and waited for him to master the immense coincidence. It was no coincidence in the usual sense, of course. Hillman had been in authority over Harley, and had given Harley reason to hate him. I had heard the hatred speak on the telephone Monday.

The fog over the sea was burning off. Ragged blue holes opened and closed in the grayness. Hillman came to the window and stood beside me. His face was more composed, except for the fierce glitter of his eyes.

'When I think of what that man has done to me,' he said. 'Tell me the rest of it, Archer. All you know.'

I told him the rest of it. He listened as if I was an oracle telling him the story of his future life. He seemed particularly interested in the murdered woman, Carol, and I asked him if he had ever met her.

He shook his head. 'I didn't know Harley was married.'

'The marriage may not have been legal. But it lasted.'

'Did Harley have children?'

'One at least.'

'How could a man with a child of his own—?' He didn't finish the thought. Another thought rushed in on his excited mind: 'At any rate this disposes of the notion that Tom was mixed up with the woman.'

'Not necessarily. Harley could have been using her as bait.'

'But that's fantastic. The woman must be—have been old enough to be his mother.'

'Still, she wasn't an old woman. She was born about 1930.'

'And you're seriously suggesting that Tom had an affair with her?'

'It's an academic question under the circumstances, Mr Hillman.'

His patrician head turned slowly toward me, catching the light on its flat handsome planes. The days were carving him like sculpture. 'You mean the fact that Tom is dead.'

'It isn't a fact yet. It is a strong possibility.'

'If my boy were alive, wouldn't he have come home by now?'

'Not if he's deliberately staying away.'

'Do you have reason to believe that he is?'

'Nothing conclusive, but several facts suggest the possibility. He was seen with the woman on Sunday, under his own power. And he did run away in the first place.'

'From Laguna Perdida School. Not from us.'

'He may expect to be clapped back into the school if he returns.'

'Good Lord, I'd never do that.'

'You did it once.'

'I was forced to by circumstances.'

'What were the circumstances, Mr Hillman?'

'There's no need to go into them. As you would say, the question is academic.'

'Did he attempt suicide?'

'No.'

'Homicide?'

His eyes flickered. 'Certainly not.' He changed the subject hurriedly: 'We shouldn't be standing here talking. If Thomas is alive, he's got to be found. Harley is the one man who must know where he is, and you tell me Harley is probably on his way to Nevada.'

'He's probably there by now.'

'Why aren't you? I'd fly you myself if I could leave my wife. But you can charter a plane.'

I explained that this took money, of which I'd already spent a fair amount in his behalf.

'I'm sorry, I didn't realize.'

He produced the two-thousand-dollar check that Dr Sponti and Mr Squerry had given him on Monday, and endorsed it to me. I was back in business.

XV

STELLA, IN HER hooded blue jacket, was waiting for me part way down the driveway. The girl had a heavy pair of binoculars hung around her neck on a strap. Her face was bloodless and thin, as if it had provided sustenance for her eyes.

When I stopped the car, she climbed uninvited into the seat beside me. 'I've been watching for you.'

'Is that what the field glasses are for?'

She nodded gravely. 'I watch everybody who comes in or goes out of Tommy's house. Mother thinks I'm bird-watching, which she lets me do because it's a status-symbol activity. Actually I am doing a bird study for next year's biology class, on the nesting habits of the acorn woodpeckers. Only they all look so much alike they're hard to keep track of.'

'So are people.'

'I'm finding that out.' She leaned toward me. Her small breast brushed my shoulder like a gift of trust. 'But you know what, Mr Archer? Tommy tried to call me this morning, I'm almost certain.'

'Tell me about it.'

'There isn't much to tell, really. It was one of those calls with nobody on the other end of the line. My mother answered the phone, and that's why Tommy didn't speak. He wanted me to answer it.' Her eyes were luminous with hope.

'What makes you think it was Tommy?'

'I just know it was. Besides, he called at five to eight, which is the exact same time he always used to call me in the morning. He used to pick me up and drive me to school.'

'That isn't too much to go on, Stella. More likely it was a wrong number.'

'No. I believe it was Tommy. And he'll be trying again.'

'Why would he call you instead of his parents?'

'He's probably afraid to call them. He must be in serious trouble.'

'You can be sure of that, one way or another.'

I was only trying to moderate her hopefulness, but I frightened her. She said in a hushed voice: 'You've found out something.'

'Nothing definite. We're on the track of the kidnapper. And incidentally, I have to be on my way.'

She held me with her eyes. 'He really was kidnapped then? He didn't go to them of his own accord or anything like that?'

'He may have in the first place. After that, I don't know. Did Tommy ever mention a woman named Carol?'

'The woman who was killed?'

'Yes.'

'He never did. Why? Did he know her?'

'He knew her very well.'

She caught my implication and shook her head. 'I don't believe it.'

'That doesn't prevent it from being true, Stella. Didn't you ever see them together?'

I got out my collection of pictures and selected the one that Harold Harley had taken of Carol in 1945. The girl studied it. She said with something like awe in her voice:

'She's—she was very beautiful. She couldn't have been much older than I am.'

'She wasn't, when the picture was taken. But that was a long time ago, and you should make allowances for that.'

'I've never seen her. I'm sure. And Tommy never said a word about her.' She looked at me glumly. 'People *are* hard to keep track of.' She handed me the picture as if it was heavy and hot and would spill if it was tilted.

At this point a female moose deprived of her calf, or something closely resembling her, came crashing through the oak woods. It was Stella's mother. Her handsome red head was tousled and her face was brutalized by anxiety. She spotted Stella and charged around to her side of the car. Stella turned up the window and snapped the lock.

Rhea Carlson rapped on the glass with her fist. 'Come out of there. What do you think you're doing?'

'Talking to Mr Archer.'

'You must be crazy. Are you trying to ruin yourself?'

'I don't care what happens to me, that's true.'

'You have no right to talk like that. You're ungrateful!'

'Ungrateful for what?'

'I gave you life, didn't I? Your father and I have given you everything.'

'I don't want everything. I just want to be alone, Mother.'

'No! You come out of there.'

'I don't have to.'

'Yes you do,' I said.

Stella looked at me as if I had betrayed her to the enemy.

'She's your mother,' I said, 'and you're a minor, and if you don't obey her you're out of control, and I'm contributing to the delinquency of a minor.'

'*You* are?'

'Reluctantly,' I said.

The word persuaded her. She even gave me a little half-smile. Then she unlocked the door and climbed out of the car. I got out and walked around to their side. Rhea Carlson looked at me as if I might be on the point of assaulting her.

'Calm down, Mrs Carlson. Nothing's happened.'

'Oh? Would you know?'

'I know that no harm will ever come to Stella if I'm around. May I ask you a question?'

She hesitated. 'I won't promise to answer it.'

'You received a phone call this morning at five to eight. Was it local or long distance?'

'I don't know. Most of our long-distance calls are dialed direct.'

'Was anything said?'

'I said hello.'

'I mean on the other end of the line.'

'No. Not a word.'

'Did whoever it was hang up?'

'Yes, and I'm sure it wasn't the Hillman boy. It was just another stupid mistake in dialing. We get them all the time.'

'It was so Tommy,' Stella said. 'I *know* it.'

'Don't believe her. She's always making things up.'

'I am not.' Stella looked ready to cry.

'Don't contradict me, Stella. Why do you always have to contradict me?'

'I don't.'

'You do.'

I stepped between them. 'Your daughter's a good girl, and she's almost a woman. Please try to bear that in mind, and treat her gently.'

Mrs Carlson said in scornful desperation: 'What do you know about mothers and daughters? Who are you, anyway?'

'I've been a private detective since the war. In the course of time you pick up a few primitive ideas about people, and you develop an instinct for the good ones. Like Stella.'

Stella blushed. Her mother peered at me without understanding. In my rear-view mirror, as I started away, I saw them walking down the driveway, far apart. It seemed a pity. For all I knew, Rhea Carlson was a good girl, too.

I drove downtown and took Sponti's two-thousand-dollar check to the bank it was drawn on. I endorsed it, under Ralph Hillman's signature: 'With many thanks, Lew Archer.' It was a weak riposte for being fired, but it gave me some satisfaction to think that it might bring out the purple in Dr Sponti's face.

The transfusion of cash made me feel mobile and imaginative. Just on a hunch, I drove back to Harold Harley's place in Long Beach. It was a good hunch. Lila answered the door.

She had on an apron and a dusting cap, and she pushed a strand of black hair up under the cap. Her breast rose with the gesture. Lila wasn't a pretty woman, but she had vitality.

'Are you another one of them?' she said.

'Yes. I thought you left Harold.'

'So did I. But I decided to come back.'

'I'm glad you did. He needs your support.'

'Yeah.' Her voice softened. 'What's going to happen to

Harold? Are they going to lock him up and throw the key away?'

'Not if I can help it.'

'Are you with the FBI?'

'I'm more of a free lance.'

'I was wondering. They came this morning and took the car away. No Harold. Now no car. Next they'll be taking the house from over my head. All on account of that lousy brother of his. It isn't fair.'

'It'll be straightened out. I'll tell you the same thing I told Harold. His best chance of getting free and clear is to tell the truth.'

'The truth is, he let his brother take advantage of him. He always has. Mike is still—' She clapped her hand to her mouth and looked at me over it with alarm in her brown eyes.

'What is Mike still doing, Mrs Harley?'

She glanced up and down the dingy street. A few young children were playing in the yards, with their mothers watching them. Lila plucked at my sleeve.

'Come inside, will you? Maybe we can make some kind of a deal.'

The front door opened directly into the living room. I stepped over a vacuum-cleaner hose just inside the door.

'I've been cleaning the house,' she said. 'I had to do something and that was all I could think of.'

'I hope Harold will be coming home to appreciate it soon.'

'Yeah. It would help him, wouldn't it, if I helped you to nail his brother?'

'It certainly would.'

'Would you let him go if you got Mike in his place?'

'I can't promise that. I think it would probably happen.'

'Why can't you promise?'

'I'm just a local investigator. But Mike is the one we really want. Do you know where he is, Mrs Harley?'

For a long moment she stood perfectly still, her face as unchanging as one of her photographs hanging on the wall. Then she nodded slightly.

'I know where he was at three a.m. this morning.' She jabbed a thumb toward the telephone. 'He called here from Las Vegas at three a.m. He wanted Harold. I told him I didn't know where Harold was—he was gone when I came home last night.'

'You're sure it was Mike who called?'

'It couldn't have been anybody else. I know his voice. And it isn't the first time he called here, whining and wheedling for some of our hard-earned money.'

'He wanted money?'

'That's right. I was to wire him five hundred dollars to the Western Union office in Las Vegas.'

'But he was carrying over twenty thousand.'

Her face closed, and became impassive. 'I wouldn't know about that. All I know is what he said. He needed money bad, and I was to wire him five hundred, which he would pay back double in twenty-four hours. I told him I'd see him in the hot place first. He was gambling.'

'It sounds like it, doesn't it?'

'He's a crazy gambler,' she said. 'I hate a gambler.'

I called the Walters Agency in Reno. Arnie's wife and partner Phyllis told me that Arnie had taken an early plane to Vegas. Harold Harley's two-tone Plymouth had been spotted at a motel on the Vegas Strip.

Not more than two hours later, after a plane ride of my own, I was sitting in a room of the motel talking with Arnie and the Plymouth's new owner. He was a man named Fletcher who said he was from Phoenix, Arizona, although his accent sounded more like Texas. He was dressed up in a western dude costume, with high-heeled boots, a matching belt with a fancy silver buckle, and an amethyst instead of a tie. His Stetson lay on one of the twin beds, some women's clothes on the other. The woman was in the bathroom taking a bath, Arnie told me, and I never did see her.

Mr Fletcher was large and self-assured and very rough-looking. His face had been chopped rather carelessly from granite, then put out to weather for fifty or fifty-five years.

'I didn't want to buy his heap,' he said. 'I have a new Cadillac in Phoenix, you can check that. He didn't even have a pink slip for it. I paid him five hundred for the heap because he was broke, desperate to stay in the game.'

'What game was that?' I asked him.

'Poker.'

'It was a floating game,' Arnie said, 'in one of the big hotels. Mr Fletcher refuses to name the hotel, or the other players. It went on all day yesterday and most of last night. There's no telling how much Harley lost, but he lost everything he had.'

'Over twenty thousand, probably. Was the game rigged?'

Fletcher turned his head and looked at me the way a statue looks at a man. 'It was an honest game, friend. It had to be. I was the big winner.'

'I wasn't questioning your honesty.'

'No sir. Some of the finest people in Phoenix visit the little woman and I in our residence and we visit them in their residences. Honest Jack Fletcher, they call me.'

There was a silence in which the three of us sat and listened to the air-conditioner. I said: 'That's fine, Mr Fletcher. How much did you win?'

'That's between I and the tax collector, friend. I won a bundle. Which is why I gave him five hundred for his heap. I have no use for the heap. You can take it away.' He lifted his arm in an imperial gesture.

'We'll be doing just that,' Arnie said.

'You're welcome to it. Anything I can do to cooperate.'

'You can answer a few more questions, Mr Fletcher.' I got out my picture of Tom. 'Did you see this boy with Harley at any time?'

He examined the picture as if it was a card he had drawn, then passed it back to me. 'I did not.'

'Hear any mention of him?'

'I never did. Harley came and went by himself and he didn't talk. You could see he didn't belong in a high-stakes game, but he had the money, and he wanted to lose it.'

'He wanted to lose it?' Arnie said.

'That's right, the same way I wanted to win. He's a born loser, I'm a born winner.'

Fletcher got up and strutted back and forth across the room. He lit a Brazilian cigar, not offering any around. As fast as he blew it out, the smoke disappeared in the draft from the air-conditioner. 'What time did the game break up this morning?' I said.

'Around three, when I took my last big pot.' His mouth savored the recollection. 'I was willing to stay, but the other people weren't. Harley wanted to stay, naturally, but he didn't have the money to back it up. He isn't much of a poker player, frankly.'

'Did he give you any trouble?'

'No sir. The gentleman who runs the game discourages that sort of thing. No trouble. Harley did put the bite on me at the end. I gave him a hundred dollars ding money to get home.'

'Home where?'

'He said he came from Idaho.'

I took a taxi back to the airport and made a reservation on a plane that stopped in Pocatello. Before sundown I was driving a rented car out of Pocatello along Rural Route Seven, where the elder Harleys lived.

XVI

THEIR FARM, GREEN and golden in the slanting light, lay in a curve of the river. I drove down a dusty lane to the farmhouse. It was built of white brick, without ornament of any kind. The barn, unpainted, was weathered gray and in poor repair.

The late afternoon was windless. The trees surrounding the fenced yard were as still as watercolors. The heat was oppressive, in spite of the river nearby, even worse than it had been in Vegas.

It was a far cry from Vegas to here, and difficult to believe that Harley had come home, or ever would. But the possibility had to be checked out.

A black and white farm collie with just one eye barked at me through the yard fence when I stepped out of the car. I tried to calm him down by talking to him, but he was afraid of me and he wouldn't be calmed. Eventually an old woman wearing an apron came out of the house and silenced the dog with a word. She called to me:

'Mr Harley's in the barn.'

I let myself in through the wire gate. 'May I talk to you?'

'That depends what the talk's about.'

'Family matters.'

'If that's another way to sell insurance, Mr Harley doesn't believe in insurance.'

'I'm not selling anything. Are you Mrs Harley?'

'I am.'

She was a gaunt woman of seventy, square-shouldered in a long-sleeved, striped shirtwaist. Her gray hair was drawn back severely from her face. I liked her face, in spite of the brokenness in and around the eyes. There was humor in it, and suffering half transformed into understanding.

'Who are you?' she said.

'A friend of your son Harold's. My name is Archer.'

'Isn't that nice? We're going to sit down to supper as soon as Mr Harley finishes up the milking. Why don't you stay and have some supper with us?'

'You're very kind.' But I didn't want to eat with them.

'How is Harold?' she said. 'We don't hear from him so often since he married his wife. Lila.'

Evidently she hadn't heard the trouble her sons were in. I hesitated to tell her, and she noticed my hesitation.

'Is something the matter with Harold?' she said sharply.

'The matter is with Mike. Have you seen him?'

Her large rough hands began to wipe themselves over and over on the front of her apron. 'We haven't seen Mike in twenty years. We don't expect to see him again in this life.'

'You may, though. He told a man he was coming home.'

'This is not his home. It hasn't been since he was a boy. He turned his back on us then. He went off to Pocatello to live with a man named Brown, and that was his downfall.'

'How so?'

'That daughter of Brown was a Jezebel. She ruined my son. She taught him all the filthy ways of the world.'

Her voice had changed. It sounded as if the voice of somebody slightly crazy was ranting ventriloquially through her. I said with deliberate intent to stop it:

'Carol's been paid back for whatever she did to him. She was murdered in California on Monday.'

Her hands stopped wiping themselves and flew up in front of her. She looked at their raw ugliness with her broken eyes.

'Did Mike do it to her?'

'We think so. We're not sure.'

'And you're a policeman,' she stated.

'More or less.'

'Why do you come to us? We did our best, but we couldn't control him. He passed out of our control long ago.' Her hands dropped to her sides.

'If he gets desperate enough, he may head this way.'

'No, he never will. Mr Harley said he would kill him if he ever set foot on our property again. That was twenty years ago, when he ran away from the Navy. Mr Harley meant it, too. Mr Harley never could abide a lawbreaker. It isn't true that Mr Harley treated him cruelly. Mr Harley was only trying to save him from the Devil.'

The ranting, ventriloquial note had entered her voice again. Apparently she knew nothing about her son, and if she did she couldn't talk about him in realistic terms. It was beginning to look like a dry run.

I left her and went to the barn to find her husband. He was in the stable under the barn, sitting on a milking stool with his forehead against the black and white flank of a Holstein cow. His hands were busy at her teats, and her milk surged in the pail between his knees. Its sweet fresh smell penetrated the smell of dung that hung like corruption in the heated air.

'Mr Harley?'

'I'm busy,' he said morosely. 'This is the last one, if you want to wait.'

I backed away and looked at the other cows. There were ten or twelve of them, moving uneasily in their stanchions as I moved. Somewhere out of sight a horse blew and stamped.

'You're disturbing the livestock,' Mr Harley said. 'Stand still if you want to stay.'

I stood still for five minutes. The one-eyed collie drifted into the stable and did a thorough job of smelling my shoes. But he still wouldn't let me touch him. When I reached down, he moved back.

Mr Harley got up and emptied his pail into a ten-gallon can; the foaming milk almost overflowed. He was a tall old man wearing overalls and a straw hat which almost brushed the low rafters. His eyes were as flat and angry and his mouth as sternly righteous as in Harold's portrait of him. The dog retreated whining as he came near.

'You're not from around here. Are you on the road?'

'No.' I told him who I was. 'And I'll get to the point right away. Your son Mike's in very serious trouble.'

'Mike is not my son,' he intoned solemnly, 'and I have no wish to hear about him or his trouble.'

'But he may be coming here. He said he was. If he does, you'll have to inform the police.'

'You don't have to instruct me in what I ought to do. I get my instructions from a higher power. He gives me my instructions direct in my heart.' He thumped his chest with a gnarled fist.

'That must be convenient.'

'Don't blaspheme or make mock, or you'll regret it. I can call down the punishment.'

He reached for a pitchfork leaning against the wall. The dog ran out of the stable with his tail down. I became aware suddenly that my shirt was sticking to my back and I was intensely uncomfortable. The three tines of the pitchfork were sharp and gleaming, and they were pointed at my stomach.

'Get out of here,' the old man said. 'I've been fighting the Devil all my life, and I know one of his cohorts when I see one.'

So do I, I said, but not out loud. I backed as far as the door, stumbled on the high threshold, and went out. Mrs Harley was standing near my car, just inside the wire gate. Her hands were quiet on her meager breast.

'I'm sorry,' she said to me. 'I'm sorry for Carol Brown. She wasn't a bad little girl, but I hardened my heart against her.'

'It doesn't matter now. She's dead.'

'It matters in the sight of heaven.'

She raised her eyes to the arching sky as if she imagined a literal heaven like a second story above it. Just now it was easier for me to imagine a literal hell, just over the horizon, where the sunset fires were burning.

'I've done so many wrong things,' she said, 'and closed my eyes to so many others. But don't you see, I had to make a choice.'

'I don't understand you.'

'A choice between Mr Harley and my sons. I knew that he was a hard man. A cruel man, maybe not quite right in the head. But what could I do? I had to stick with my husband. And I wasn't strong enough to stand up to him. Nobody is. I had to stand by while he drove our sons out of our home. Harold was the soft one, he forgave us in the end. But Mike never did. He's like his father. I never even got to see my grandson.'

Tears ran in the gullies of her face. Her husband came out of the barn carrying the ten-gallon can in his left hand and the pitchfork in his right.

'Go in the house, Martha. This man is a cohort of the Devil. I won't allow you to talk to him.'

'Don't hurt him. Please.'

'Go in the house,' he repeated.

She went, with her gray head down and her feet dragging.

'As for you, cohort,' he said, 'you get off my farm or I'll call down the punishment on you.'

He shook his pitchfork at the reddening sky. I was already in the car and turning up the windows.

I turned them down again as soon as I got a few hundred yards up the lane. My shirt was wet through now, and I could feel sweat running down my legs. Looking back, I caught a glimpse of the river, flowing sleek and solid in the failing light, and it refreshed me.

XVII

BEFORE DRIVING OUT to the Harley farm, I had made an evening appointment with Robert Brown and his wife. They already knew what had happened to their daughter. I didn't have to tell them.

I found their house in the north end of the city, on a pleasant, tree-lined street parallel to Arthur Street. Night had fallen almost completely, and the street lights were shining under the clotted masses of the trees. It was still very warm. The earth itself seemed to exude heat like a hot-blooded animal.

Robert Brown had been watching for me. He hailed me from his front porch and came out to the curb. A big man with short gray hair, vigorous in his movements, he still seemed to be wading in some invisible substance, age or sorrow. We shook hands solemnly.

He spoke with more apparent gentleness than force: 'I was planning to fly out to California tomorrow. It might have saved you a trip if you had known.'

'I wanted to talk to the Harleys, anyway.'

'I see.' He cocked his head on one side in a birdlike movement which seemed odd in such a big man. 'Did you get any sense out of them?'

'Mrs Harley made a good deal of sense. Harley didn't.'

'I'm not surprised. He's a pretty good farmer, they say, but he's been in and out of the mental hospital. I took—my wife and I took care of his son Mike during one of his bouts. We took him into our home.' He sounded ashamed of the act.

'That was a generous thing to do.'

'I'm afraid it was misguided generosity. But who can prophesy the future? Anyway, it's over now. All over.' He forgot about me completely for a moment, then came to himself with a start. 'Come in, Mr Archer. My wife will want to talk to you.'

He took me into the living room. It had group and family photos on the walls, and a claustrophobic wallpaper, which lent it some of the stuffiness of an old-fashioned country parlor. The room was sedately furnished with well-cared-for maple pieces. Across the mantel marched a phalanx of sports trophies gleaming gold and silver in the harsh overhead light.

Mrs Brown was sitting in an armchair under the light. She was a strikingly handsome woman a few years younger than her husband, maybe fifty-five. She had chosen to disguise herself in a stiff and rather dowdy black dress. Her too precisely marcelled brown hair had specks of gray in it. Her fine eyes were confused, and surrounded by dark patches. When she gave me her hand, the gesture seemed less like a greeting than a bid for help.

She made me sit down on a footstool near her. 'Tell us all about poor Carol, Mr Archer.'

All about Carol. I glanced around the safe, middle-class room, with the pictures of Carol's ancestors on the walls, and back at her parents' living faces. Where did Carol come in? I could see the source of her beauty in her mother's undisguisable good looks. But I couldn't see how one life led to the other, or why Carol's life had ended as it had.

Brown said: 'We know she's dead, murdered, and that Mike probably did it, and that's about all.' His face was like a Roman general's, a late Roman general's, after a long series of defeats by barbarian hordes.

'It's about all I know. Mike seems to have been using her as a decoy in an extortion attempt. You know about the Hillman boy?'

He nodded. 'I read about it before I knew that my daughter—' His voice receded.

'They say he may be dead, too,' his wife said.

'He may be, Mrs Brown.'

'And Mike did these things? I knew he was far gone, but I didn't know he was a monster.'

'He's not a monster,' Brown said wearily. 'He's a sick man. His father was a sick man. He still is, after all the mental hospital could do for him.'

'If Mike was so sick, why did you bring him into this house and expose your daughter to him?'

'She's your daughter, too.'

'I know that. I'm not allowed to forget it. But I'm not the one that ruined her for life.'

'You certainly had a hand in it. You were the one, for instance, who encouraged her to enter that beauty contest.'

'She didn't win, did she?'

'That was the trouble.'

'Was it? The trouble was the way you felt about that Harley boy.'

'I wanted to help him. He needed help, and he had talent.'

'Talent?'

'As an athlete. I thought I could develop him.'

'You developed him all right.'

They were talking across me, not really oblivious of me, using me as a fulcrum for leverage, or a kind of stand-in for reality. I guessed that the argument had been going on for twenty years.

'I wanted a son,' Brown said.

'Well, you got a son. A fine upstanding son.'

He looked as if he was about to strike her. He didn't, though. He turned to me:

'Forgive us. We shouldn't do this. It's embarrassing.'

His wife stared at him in unforgiving silence. I tried to think of something that would break or at least soften the tension between them:

'I didn't come here to start a quarrel.'

'You didn't start it, let me assure you.' Brown snickered remorsefully. 'It started the day Carol ran off with Mike. It was something I didn't foresee—'

His wife's bitter voice cut in: 'It started when she was born, Rob. You wanted a son. You didn't want a daughter. You rejected her and you rejected me.'

'I did nothing of the sort.'

'He doesn't remember,' she said to me. 'He has one of these convenient memories that men have. You blot out anything that doesn't suit your upright idea of yourself. My husband is a very dishonest man.' She had a peculiar angry gnawing smile.

'That's nonsense,' he protested. 'I've been faithful to you all my life.'

'Except in ways I couldn't cope with. Like when you brought the Harley boy into our home. The great altruist. The noble counselor.'

'You have no right to jeer at me,' he said. 'I wanted to help him. I had no way of knowing that he couldn't be reached.'

'Go on. You wanted a son any way you could get one.'

He said stubbornly: 'You don't understand. A man gets natural pleasure from raising a boy, teaching him what he knows.'

'All you succeeded in teaching Mike was your dishonesty.'

He turned to me with a helpless gesture, his hands swinging out. 'She blames me for everything.' Walking rather aimlessly, he went out to the back part of the house.

I felt as if I'd been left alone with a far from toothless lioness. She stirred in her chair:

'I blame myself as well for being a fool. I married a man who has the feelings of a little boy. He still gets excited about his high-school football teams. The boys adore him. Everybody adores him. They talk about him as if he was some kind of a plaster saint. And he couldn't even keep his own daughter out of trouble.'

'You and your husband should be pulling together.'

'It's a little late to start, isn't it?'

Her glance came up to my face, probed at it for a moment, moved restlessly from side to side.

'It may be that you'll kill him if you go on like this.'

'No. He'll live to be eighty, like his father.'

She jerked her marcelled head toward one of the pictures on the wall. Seen from varying angles, her head was such a handsome object I could hardly take my eyes off it. It was hard to believe that such a finely shaped container could be full of cold boiling trouble.

I said, partly because I wanted to, and partly to appease her: 'You must have been a very beautiful girl.'

'Yes. I was.'

She seemed to take no pleasure even from her vanity. I began to suspect that she didn't relate to men. It happened sometimes to girls who were too good-looking. They were treated as beautiful objects until they felt like that and nothing more.

'I could have married anybody,' she said, 'any man I went to college with. Some of them are bank presidents and big corporation executives now. But I had to fall in love with a football player.'

'Your husband is a little more than that.'

'Don't *sell* him to me,' she said. 'I know what he is, and I know what my life has been. I've been defrauded. I gave everything I had to marriage and motherhood, and what have I got to show for it? Do you know I never even saw my grandson?'

Mrs Harley had said the same thing. I didn't mention the coincidence.

'What happened to your grandson?'

'Carol put him out for adoption, can you imagine? Actually I know why she did it. She didn't trust her husband not to harm the baby. That's the kind of a man she married.'

'Did she tell you this?'

'More or less. Mike is a sadist, among other things. He used to swing cats by their tails. He lived in this house for over a year and all the time I was afraid of him. He was terribly strong, and I never was certain what he was going to do.'

'Did he ever attack you?'

'No. He never dared to.'

'How old was he when he left?'

'Let me see, Carol was fifteen at the time. That would make him seventeen or eighteen.'

'And he left to join the Navy, is that correct?'

'He didn't go into the Navy right away. He left town with an older man, a policeman who used to be on the local force. I forgot his name. Anyway, this man lost his position on the force through bribery, and left town, taking Mike with him. He said he was going to make a boxer out of him. They went out to the west coast. I think Mike joined the Navy a few months later. Carol could—' She stopped in dismay.

'What about Carol?'

'I was going to say that Carol could tell you.' The angry smile twisted and insulted her mouth. 'I must be losing my mind.'

'I doubt that, Mrs Brown. It takes time to get used to these shocks and changes.'

'More time than I have. More time than I'll ever have.' She rose impatiently and went to the mantelpiece. One of the trophies standing on it was out of line with the others. She reached up and adjusted its position. 'I wonder what Rob thinks he's doing in the kitchen.'

She didn't go and find out what he was doing. She stood in an awkward position, one hip out, in front of the empty fireplace. Under the dowdy black dress, the slopes and masses of her body were angry. But nothing that she could do with her body, or her face, could change the essential beauty of the structure. She was trapped in it, as her daughter had been.

'I wish you'd go on with your story, Mrs Brown.'

'It hardly qualifies as a story.'

'Whatever you want to call it, then. I'm very grateful for the chance to talk to you. It's the first decent chance I've had to get any information about the background of this case.'

'The background hardly matters now, or the foreground either.'

'It does, though. You may tell me something that will help me to find Harley. I take it you've seen him and Carol from time to time over the years.'

'I saw *him* just once more—after that, I wouldn't give him house room—when he came home from the Navy in the winter 1944-45. He claimed to be on leave. Actually he was absent without leave. He talked himself back into Rob's good graces. Rob had been terribly let down when he left town with that ex-policeman, the bribery artist. But my gullible husband fell for his line all over again. He even gave him money. Which Mike used to elope with my only daughter.'

'Why did Carol go with him?'

She scratched at her forehead, leaving faint weals in the clear skin. 'I asked her that, the last time she was home, just a couple of months ago. I asked her why she went and why she stuck with him. She didn't really know. Of course she wanted to get out of Pocatello. She hated Pocatello. She wanted to go out to the coast and break into the movies. I'm afraid my daughter had very childish dreams.'

'Girls of fifteen do.' With a pang, I thought of Stella. The pang became a vaguely formed idea in an unattended area of my mind. Generation after generation had to start from scratch and learn the world over again. It changed so rapidly that children couldn't learn from their parents or parents from their children. The generations were like alien tribes islanded in time.

'The fact is,' I said, 'Carol did make it into the movies.'

'Really? She told me that once, but I didn't believe her.'

'Was she a chronic liar?'

'No. Mike was the chronic liar. I simply didn't believe that she could succeed at anything. She never had.'

The woman's bitterness was getting me down. She seemed to have an inexhaustible reservoir of the stuff. If she had been like this twenty years before, I could understand why Carol had left home at the first opportunity, and stayed away.

'You say you saw Carol just a couple of months ago.'

'Yes. She rode the bus from Lake Tahoe in June. I hadn't seen her for quite a long time. She was looking pretty bedraggled. God knows what kind of a life he was leading her. She didn't talk much.'

'It was a chancy life. Harley seems to have lost his job, and they were on their uppers.'

'So she told me. There was the usual plea for money. I guess Rob gave her money. He always did. He tried to pretend afterwards, to me, that he gave her the car, too, but I know better. She took it. Apparently their old car had broken down, and they couldn't live at Tahoe without a car.'

'How do you know she took it if your husband says she didn't?'

She showed signs of embarrassment. 'It doesn't matter. They were welcome to the car.' It was her first generous word. She half-spoiled it: 'We needed a new one, anyway, and I'm sure she did it on the spur of the moment. Carol always was a very impulsive girl.

'The point is,' she said, 'she left without saying goodbye. She took the car to go downtown to the movies and simply never came back. She even left her suitcase in her room.'

'Had there been trouble?'

'No more than the usual trouble. We did have an argument at supper.'

'What about?'

'My grandson. She had no right to put him out for adoption. She said he was her baby to do with as she pleased. But she had no right. If she couldn't keep him, she should have brought him to us. We could have given him opportunities, an education.' She breathed heavily and audibly. 'She said an unforgivable thing to me that evening. She said, did I mean the kind of opportunities she had? And she walked out. I never saw her again. Neither did her father.' Her head jerked forward in emphatic affirmation: 'We *did* give her opportunities. It's not our fault if she didn't take advantage of them. It isn't fair to blame us.'

'You blame each other,' I said. 'You're tearing each other to pieces.'

'Don't give me that sort of talk. I've had enough of it from my husband.'

'I'm merely calling your attention to an obvious fact. You need some kind of intermediary, a third party, to help straighten out your thinking.'

'And you're electing yourself, are you?'

'Far from it. You need an expert counselor.'

'My husband *is* a counselor,' she said. 'What good has it done him? Anyway, I don't believe in seeking that kind of help. People should be able to handle their own problems.'

She composed her face and sat down in the armchair again, with great calm, to show me how well she was handling hers.

'But what if they can't, Mrs Brown?'

'Then they can't, that's all.'

I made one more attempt. 'Do you go to church?'

'Naturally I do.'

'You could talk these problems over with your minister.'

'What problems? I'm not aware of any outstanding problems.' She was in despair so deep that she wouldn't even look up toward the light. I think she was afraid it would reveal her to herself.

I turned to other matters. 'You mentioned a suitcase that your daughter left behind. Is it still here in the house?'

'It's up in her room. There isn't much in it. I almost threw it out with the trash, but there was always the chance that she would come back for it.'

'May I see it?'

'I'll go and get it.'

'If you don't mind, I'd sooner go up to her room.'

'I don't mind.'

We went upstairs together, Mrs Brown leading the way. She turned on the light in a rear bedroom and stood back to let me enter.

The room provided the first clear evidence that she had been hit very hard by Carol's running away. It was the bedroom of a high-school girl. The flouncy yellow cover on the French provincial bed matched the yellow flounces on the dressing table, where a pair of Kewpie-doll lamps smiled vacantly at each other. A floppy cloth dog with his red felt tongue hanging out watched me from the yellow lamb's wool rug. A little bookcase, painted white like the bed, was filled with high-school texts and hospital novels and juvenile mysteries. There were college pennants tacked around the walls.

'I kept her room as she left it,' Mrs Brown said behind me.

'Why?'

'I don't know. I guess I always thought that she'd come home in the end. Well, she did a few times. The suitcase is in the closet.'

The closet smelled faintly of sachet. It was full of skirts and dresses, the kind girls wore in high school a half-generation before. I began to suspect that the room and its contents had less to do with Carol than with some secret fantasy of her mother's. Her mother said, as if in answer to my thought:

'I spend a lot of time here in this room. I feel very close to her here. We really were quite close at one time. She used to tell me everything, all about the boys she dated and so on. It was like living my own high school days over again.'

'Is that good?'

'I don't know.' Her lips gnawed at each other. 'I guess not, because she suddenly turned against me. Suddenly she closed up completely. I didn't know what went on in her life, but I could see her changing, coarsening. She was such a pretty girl, such a pure-looking girl.' Her mouth was wrenched far off center and it remained that way, as if the knowledge of her loss had fallen on her like a cerebral stroke.

The suitcase was an old scuffed cowhide one with Rob Brown's initials on it. I pulled it out into the middle of the floor and opened it. Suddenly I was back in Dack's Auto Court opening Carol's other suitcase. The same sour odor of regret rose from the contents of this one and seemed to permeate the room.

There was the same tangle of clothes, this time all of them women's skirts and dresses and underthings and stockings, a few cosmetics, a paperback book on the divination of dreams. A hand-scrawled piece of paper was stuck in this as a bookmark. I pulled it out and looked at it. It was signed 'Your Brother "Har." '

DEAR MIKE,

I'm sorry you and Carole are haveing a 'tough time' and I enclose a money order for fifty which I hope will help out you have to cash it at a postoffice. I would send more but things are a little 'tight' since I got married to Lila shes a good girl but does not believe that blood is thicker than water which it is. You asked me do I like bing married well in some ways I really like it in other ways I dont Lila has very strong ideas of her own. Shes no 'sinsational' beauty like Carole is but we get long.

Im sorry you lost your job Mike unskilled jobs are hard to come by in these times I know you are a good bartender and that is a skill you should be able to pick up something in that line even if they are prejudiced like you say. I did look up Mr Sipe like you asked me to but he is in no position to do anything for anybody hes on the skids himself the Barcelona went bankrupt last winter and now old Sipe is just watchman on the place but he sent his best regards for old time sake he wanted to know if you ever developed a left.

I saw another 'friend' of yours last week I mean Captain Hillman I know you bear a grudge there but after all he treated you pretty good he could have sent you to prison for ten years. No Im not rakeing up old recrimations because Hillman could do something for you if he wanted you ought to see the raceing yacht he has thats how I saw him went down to Newport to take some sailing pictures. I bet he has twenty-five thousand in that yacht the guy is loaded. I found out he lives with his wife and boy in Pacific Point if you want to try him for a job hes head of some kind of 'smogless industry.'

Well thats about all for now if you deside to come out to 'sunny Cal' you know where we live and dont worry Lila will make you welcome shes a good soul 'at heart.'

SINCERELY YOURS

Mrs Brown had come out of her trance and moved toward me with a curious look. 'What is that?'

'A letter to Mike from his brother Harold. May I have it?'

'You're welcome to it.'

'Thank you. I believe it's evidence. It seems to have started Mike thinking about the possibility of bleeding the Hillmans for money.' And it explained, I thought, why Harold had blamed himself for instigating the crime.

'May I read it?'

I handed it to her. She held it at arm's length, squinting.

'I'm afraid I need my glasses.'

We went downstairs to the living room, where she put on horn-rimmed reading glasses and sat in her armchair with the letter. 'Sipe,' she said when she finished reading it. 'That's the name I was trying to think of before.' She raised her voice and called: 'Robert! Come in here.'

Rob Brown answered from the back of the house: 'I was just coming.'

He appeared in the doorway carrying a clinking pitcher and three glasses on a tray. He said with a placatory look at his wife: 'I thought I'd make some fresh lemonade for the three of us. It's a warm night.'

'That was thoughtful, Robert. Put it down on the coffee table. Now, what was the name of the ex-policeman that Mike left town with, the first time?'

'Sipe. Otto Sipe.' He flushed slightly. 'That man was a bad influence, I can tell you.'

I wondered if he still was. The question seemed so urgent that I drove right back to the airport and caught the first plane out, to Salt Lake City. A late jet from Minneapolis rescued me from a night in the Salt Lake City airport and deposited me at Los Angeles International, not many miles from the Barcelona Hotel, where a man named Sipe was watchman.

XVIII

I HAD A gun in a locked desk drawer in my apartment, and one in my office. The apartment in West Los Angeles was nearer. I went there.

It was in a fairly new, two-story building with a long roofed gallery on which the second-floor apartments opened directly. Mine was the second-floor back. I parked in the street and climbed the outside stairs.

It was the dead dull middle of the night, the static hour when yesterday ended and tomorrow gathered its forces to begin. My own forces were running rather low, but I wasn't tired. I had slept on the planes. And my case was breaking, my beautiful terrible mess of a case was breaking.

A light shone dimly behind my draped front window, and when I tried the door it was unlocked. I had no family, no wife, no girl. I turned the knob quietly, and slowly and tentatively opened the door.

It seemed I had a girl after all. She was curled up on the studio couch under a blanket which came from my bed. The light from a standing lamp shone down on her sleeping face. She looked so young I felt a hundred years old.

I closed the door. 'Hey, Stella.'

Her body jerked under the blanket. Throwing it off, she sat up. She was wearing a blue sweater and a skirt. 'Oh,' she said. 'It's you.'

'Who were you expecting?'

'I don't know. But don't be cross with me. I was just dreaming something, I forget what, but it was depressing.' Her eyes were still dark with the dream.

'How in the world did you get in here?'

'The manager let me in. I told him I was a witness. He understood.'

'I don't. A witness to what?'

'Quite a few things,' she said with some spirit. 'If you want me to tell you, you can stop treating me like a mentally retarded delinquent. Nobody else does, except my parents.'

I sat on the edge of the studio couch beside her. I liked the girl but at the moment she was an obstruction, and could turn into a serious embarrassment. 'Do your parents know you're here?'

'Of course not. How could I tell them? They wouldn't have let me come, and I had to come. You *ordered* me to get in touch with you if I ever heard from Tommy. Your answering service couldn't find you and finally they gave me your home address.'

'Are you telling me you've heard from him?'

She nodded. Her eyes held steady on my face. They were brimming with complex feelings, more womanly than girlish. 'He phoned around four o'clock this afternoon. Mother was at the store, and I had a chance to answer the phone myself.'

'Where was he, did he say?'

'Here in—' She hesitated. 'He made me promise not to tell anyone. And I've already broken my promise once.'

'How did you do that?'

'I put a little note in Mr Hillman's mailbox, before I left El Rancho. I couldn't just leave him dangling, when I *knew*.'

'What did you tell him?'

'Just that I'd heard from Tommy, and he was alive.'

'It was a kind thing to do.'

'But it broke my promise. He said I wasn't to tell anyone, especially not his parents.'

'Promises have to be broken sometimes, when there are higher considerations.'

'What do you mean?'

'His safety. I've been afraid that Tom was dead. Are you absolutely certain you talked to him?'

'I'm not telling a lie.'

'I mean, you're sure it wasn't an imposter, or a tape recording?'

'I'm sure. We talked back and forth.'

'Where was he calling from?'

'I don't know, but I think it was long distance.'

'What did he say?'

She hesitated again, with her finger raised. 'Is it all right for me to tell you, even after I promised?'

'It would be all wrong if you didn't. You know that, don't you? You didn't come all the way here to hold it back.'

'No.' She smiled a little. 'He didn't tell me too much. He didn't say a word about the kidnappers. Anyway, the fact that he's alive is the important thing. He said he was sorry I'd been worried about him, but he couldn't help it. Then he asked me to meet him and bring some money.'

I was relieved. Tom's need for money implied that he had no part of the payoff. 'How much money?'

'As much as I could get hold of in a hurry. He knew it wouldn't amount to a great deal. I borrowed some from the people at the beach club. The secretary of the club gave me a hundred dollars of her own money—she knows I'm honest. I took a taxi to the bus station. You know, I never rode on a bus before, except the school bus.'

I cut in impatiently: 'Did you meet him here in Los Angeles?'

'No. I was supposed to meet him in the Santa Monica bus station at nine o'clock. The bus was a few minutes late, and I may have missed him. He did say on the phone that he mightn't be able to make it tonight. In which case I was to meet him tomorrow night. He said he generally only goes out at night.'

'Did he tell you where he's staying?'

'No. That's the trouble. I hung around the bus station for about an hour and then I tried to phone you and when I couldn't I took a taxi here. I had to spend the night somewhere.'

'So you did. It's too bad Tom didn't think of that.'

'He probably has other things on his mind,' she said in a defensive tone. 'He's been having a terrible time.'

'Did he say so?'

'I could tell by the way he talked to me. He sounded—I don't know—so upset.'

'Emotionally upset, or just plain scared?'

Her brow knit. 'More worried than scared. But he wouldn't say what about. He wouldn't tell me anything that happened. I asked him if he was okay, you know, physically okay, and he said he was. So I asked him why he didn't come home. He said on account of his parents, only he didn't call them his parents. He called them his anti-parents. He said they could probably hardly wait to put him back in Laguna Perdida School.'

Her eyes were very dark. 'I remember now what I was dreaming before you woke me up. Tommy was in that school and they wouldn't let him out and they wouldn't let me see him. I went around to all the doors and windows, trying to get in. All I could see was the terrible faces leering at me through the windows.'

'The faces aren't so terrible. I was there.'

'Yes, but you weren't locked up there. Tommy says it's a terrible place. His parents had no right to put him there. I don't blame him for staying away.'

'Neither do I, Stella. But, under the circumstances, he has to be brought in. You understand that, don't you?'

'I guess I do.'

'It would be a rotten anticlimax if something happened to him now. You don't want that.'

She shook her head.

'Then will you help me get him?'

'It's why I came here, really. I couldn't sic the police on him. But you're different.' She touched the back of my hand. 'You won't let them put him back in Laguna Perdida.'

'It won't happen if I can possibly help it. I think I can. If Tom needs treatment, he should be able to get it as an outpatient.'

'He isn't sick!'

'His father must have had a reason for putting him there. Something happened that Sunday, he wouldn't tell me what.'

'It happened long before that Sunday,' she said. 'His father turned against him, that's what happened. Tommy isn't the hairy-chested type, and he preferred music to trap-shooting and sailing and such things. So his father turned against him. It's as simple as that.'

'Nothing ever is, but we won't argue. If you'll excuse me for a minute, Stella, I have to make a phone call.'

The phone was on the desk under the window. I sat down there and dialed Susanna Drew's unlisted number. She answered on the first ring.

'Hello.'

'Lew Archer. You sound very alert for three o'clock in the morning.'

'I've been lying awake thinking, about you among other things and people. Somebody said—I think it was Scott Fitzgerald—something to the effect that in the real dark night of the soul it's always three o'clock in the morning. I have a reverse twist on that. At three o'clock in the morning it's always the real dark night of the soul.'

'The thought of me depresses you?'

'In certain contexts it does. In others, not.'

'You're talking in riddles, Sphinx.'

'I mean to be, Oedipus. But you're not the source of my depression. That goes back a long way.'

'Do you want to tell me about it?'

'Another time, doctor.' Her footwork was very skittish. 'You didn't call me at this hour for snatches of autobiography.'

'No, though I'd still like to know who that telephone call was from the other day.'

'And that's why you called me?' There was disappointment in her voice, ready to turn into anger.

'It isn't why I called you. I need your help.'

'Really?' She sounded surprised, and rather pleased. But she said guardedly: 'You mean by telling you all I know and like that?'

'We don't have time. I think this case is breaking. Anyway I have to make a move, now. A very nice high-school girl named Stella has turned up on my doorstep.' I was speaking to the girl in the room as well as to the woman on the line; as I did so, I realized that they were rapidly becoming my favorite girl and woman. 'I need a safe place to keep her for the rest of the night.'

'I'm not that safe.' A rough note in her voice suggested that she meant it.

Stella said quickly behind me: 'I could stay here.'

'She can't stay here. Her parents would probably try to hang a child-stealing rap on me.'

'Are you serious?'

'The situation is serious, yes.'

'All right. Where do you live?'

'Stella and I will come there. We're less than half an hour from you at this time of night.'

Stella said when I hung up: 'You didn't have to do it behind my back.'

'I did it right in front of your face. And I don't have time to argue.'

To underline the urgency I took off my jacket, got my gun and its harness out of the drawer, and put it on in front of her. She watched me with wide eyes. The ugly ritual didn't quite silence her.

'But I didn't want to *meet* anybody tonight.'

'You'll like Susanna Drew. She's very stylish and hep.'

'But I never *do* like people when adults tell me I will.'

After the big effort of the night, she was relapsing into childishness. I said, to buck her up:

'Forget your war with the adults. You're going to be an adult pretty soon yourself. Then who will you have to blame for everything?'

'That isn't fair.'

It wasn't, but it held her all the way to the apartment house on Beverly Glen. Susanna came to the door in silk pajamas, not the kind anyone slept in. Her hair was brushed. She hadn't bothered with makeup. Her face was extraordinarily and nakedly handsome, with eyes as real and dark as any night.

'Come in, Lew. It's nice to see you, Stella. I'm Susanna. I have a bed made up for you upstairs.' She indicated the indoor balcony which hung halfway up the wall of the big central studio, and on which an upstairs room opened. 'Do you want something to eat?'

'No, thank you,' Stella said. 'I had a hamburger at the bus station.'

'I'll be glad to make you a sandwich.'

'No. Really. I'm not hungry.' The girl looked pale and a little sick.

'Would you like to go to bed then?'

'I have no choice.' Stella heard herself, and added: 'That was rude, wasn't it? I didn't mean it to be. It's awfully kind of you to take me in. It was Mr Archer who gave me no choice.'

'I had no choice, either,' I said. 'What would you do if you had one?'

'I'd be with Tommy, wherever he is.'

Her mouth began to work, and so did the delicate flesh around her eyes and mouth. The mask of a crying child seemed to be struggling for possession of her face. She ran away from it, or from our eyes, up the circular stairs to the balcony.

Susanna called after her before she closed the door: 'Pajamas on the bed, new toothbrush in the bathroom.'

'You're an efficient hostess,' I said.

'Thank you. Have a drink before you go.'

'It wouldn't do anything for me.'

'Do you want to go into where you're going and what you have to do?'

'I'm on my way to the Barcelona Hotel, but I keep running into detours.'

She reacted more sharply than she had any apparent reason to. 'Is that what I am, a detour?'

'Stella was the detour. You're the United States Cavalry.'

'I love your imagery.' She made a face. 'What on earth are you planning to do at the old Barcelona? Isn't it closed down?'

'There's at least one man living there, a watchman who used to be the hotel detective, named Otto Sipe.'

'Good Lord, I think I know him. Is he a big red-faced character with a whisky breath?'

'That's probably the man. How do you happen to know him?'

She hesitated before she answered, in a careful voice: 'I sort of frequented the Barcelona at one time, way back at the end of the war. That was where I met Carol.'

'And Mr Sipe.'

'And Mr Sipe.'

She wouldn't tell me any more.

'You have no right to cross-question me,' she said finally. 'Leave me alone.'

'I'll be glad to.'

She followed me to the door. 'Don't leave on that note. Please.

I'm not holding back for the fun of it. Why do you think I've been lying awake all night?'

'Guilt?'

'Nonsense. I'm not ashamed of anything.' But there was shame in her eyes, deeper than her knowledge of herself. 'Anyway, the little I know can't be of any importance.'

'You're not being fair. You're trying to use my personal feeling for you—'

'I didn't know it existed. If it does, I ought to have a right to use it any way I need to.'

'You don't have that right, though. My privacy is a very precious thing to me, and you have no right to violate it.'

'Even to save a life?'

Stella opened her door and came out on the balcony. She looked like a young, pajamaed saint in a very large niche.

'If you *adults*,' she said, 'will lower your voices a few decibels, it might be possible to get a little sleep.'

'Sorry,' I said to both of them.

Stella retreated. Susanna said: 'Whose life is in danger, Lew?'

'Tom Hillman's for one. Possibly others, including mine.'

She touched the front of my jacket. 'You're wearing a shoulder holster. Is Otto Sipe one of the kidnappers?'

I countered with a question: 'Was he a man in your life?'

She was offended. 'Of course not. Go away now.' She pushed me out. 'Take care.'

The night air was chilly on my face.

XIX

TRAFFIC WAS SPARSE on the coastal highway. Occasional night-crawling trucks went by, blazing with red and yellow lights. This stretch of highway was an ugly oilstained place, fouled by petroleum fumes and rubbed barren by tires. Even the sea below it had a used-dishwater odor.

Ben Daly's service station was dark, except for an inside bulb left on to discourage burglars. I left my car in his lot, beside an outside telephone booth, and crossed the highway to the Barcelona Hotel.

It was as dead as Nineveh. In the gardens behind the main building a mockingbird tried a few throbbing notes, like a tiny heart of sound attempting to beat, and then subsided. The intermittent mechanical movement of the highway was the only life in the inert black night.

I went up to the front door where the bankruptcy notice was posted and knocked on the glass with my flashlight. I knocked repeatedly, and got no answer. I was about to punch out a pane of glass and let myself in. Then I noticed that the door was unlocked. It opened under my hand.

I entered the lobby, jostling a couple of ghosts. They were Susanna, twenty years old, and a man without a face. I told them to get the hell out of my way.

I went down the corridor where Mr Sipe had first appeared with his light, past the closed, numbered doors, to a door at the end which was standing slightly ajar. I could hear breathing inside the dark room, the heavy sighing breathing of a man in sleep or stupor. The odor of whisky was strong.

I reached inside the door and found the light switch with my right hand. I turned it on and shifted my hand to my gun butt. There was no need. Sipe was lying on the bed, fully clothed, with his ugly nostrils glaring and his loose mouth sighing at the ceiling. He was alone.

There was hardly space for anyone else. The room had never been large, and it was jammed with stuff which looked as if it had been accumulating for decades. Cartons and packing cases, piles of rugs, magazines and newspapers, suitcases and foot lockers, were heaped at the back of the room almost to the ceiling. On the visible parts of the walls were pictures of young men in boxing stance, interspersed with a few girlie pictures.

Empty whisky bottles were ranged along the wall beside the door. A half-full bottle stood by the bed where Sipe was lying. I turned the key that was in the lock of the door and took a closer look at the sleeping man.

He wasn't just sleeping. He was out, far out and possibly far gone. If I had put a match to his lips, his breath would have ignited like an alcohol burner. Even the front of his shirt seemed to be saturated with whisky, as though he'd poured it over himself in one last wild libation before he passed out.

His gun was stuck in the greasy waistband of his trousers. I transferred it to my jacket pocket before I tried to rouse him. He wouldn't wake up. I shook him. He was inert as a side of beef, and his big head rolled loosely on the pillow. I slapped his pitted red cheeks. He didn't even groan.

I went into the adjoining bathroom—it was also a kind of kitchen fitted out with an electric plate and a percolator that smelled of burned coffee—and filled the percolator with cold water from the bathtub faucet. This I poured over Sipe's head and face, being careful not to drown him. He didn't wake up.

I was getting a little worried, not so much about Sipe as about the possibility that he might never be able to give me his story. There was no way of telling how many of the bottles in the room had been emptied recently. I felt his pulse: laboriously slow. I lifted one of his eyelids. It was like looking down into a red oyster.

I had noticed that the bathroom was one of those with two doors, serving two rooms, that you find in older hotels. I went through it into the adjoining bedroom and shone my light around. It was a room similar in shape and size to the other, but almost bare. A brass double bed with a single blanket covering the mattress was just about the only furniture. The blanket lay in the tumbled folds that a man, or a boy, leaves behind when he gets up.

Hung over the head of the bed, like a limp truncated shadow of a boy, was a black sweater. It was a knitted sweater, and it had a raveled sleeve. Where the yarn was snarled and broken I could see traces of light-colored grease, the kind they use on the locks of automobile trunks. In the wastebasket I found several cardboard baskets containing the remains of hamburgers and french fries.

My heart was beating in my ears. The sweater was pretty good physical evidence that Stella had not been conned. Tom was alive.

I found Sipe's keys and locked him in his room and went through every other room in the building. There were nearly a hundred guest and service rooms, and it took a long time. I felt like an archaeologist exploring the interior of a pyramid. The Barcelona's palmy days seemed that long ago.

All I got for my efforts was a noseful of dust. If Tom was in the building, he was hiding. I had a feeling that he wasn't there, that he had left the Barcelona for good. Anybody would if he had the chance.

I went back across the highway to Daly's station. My flashlight found a notice pasted to the lower righthand corner of the front door: 'In case of emergency call owner,' with Daly's home number. I called it from the outside booth, and after a while got an answer:

'Daly here.'

'Lew Archer. I'm the detective who was looking for Harold Harley.'

'This is a heck of a time to be looking for anybody.'

'I found Harley, thanks to you. Now I need your help in some more important business.'

'What's the business?'

'I'll tell you when you get here. I'm at your station.'

Daly had the habit of serviceability. 'Okay. I'll be there in fifteen minutes.'

I waited for him in my car, trying to put the case together in my mind. It was fairly clear that Sipe and Mike Harley had been working together, and had used the Barcelona as a hideout. It didn't look as if Tom had been a prisoner; more likely a willing guest, as Harley had said from the start. Even with Laguna Perdida School in the background, it was hard to figure out why a boy would do this to his parents and himself.

Daly came off the highway with a flourish and parked his pickup beside me. He got out and slammed the door, which had his name on it. He gave me a frowzy sardonic pre-dawn look.

'What's on your mind, Mr Archer?'

'Get in. I'll show you a picture.'

He climbed in beside me. I turned on the dome light and got out Tom's photograph. Every time I looked at it it had changed, gathering ambiguities on the mouth and in the eyes.

I put it in Daly's oil-grained hands. 'Have you seen him?'

'Yeah. I have. I saw him two or three times over the last couple of days. He made some telephone calls from the booth there. He made one yesterday afternoon.'

'What time?'

'I didn't notice, I was busy. It was along toward the end of the afternoon. Then I saw him again last night waiting for the bus.' He pointed down the road toward Santa Monica. 'The bus stops at the intersection if you flag it down. Otherwise it don't.'

'Which bus is that?'

'Any of the intercity buses, expecting the express ones.'

'Did you see him get on a bus?'

'No. I was getting ready to close up. Next time I looked he was gone.'

'What time was this?'

'Around eight-thirty last night.'

'What was he wearing?'

'White skirt, dark slacks.'

'What made you interested enough to watch him?'

Daly fidgeted. 'I dunno. I didn't *watch* him exactly. I saw him come out of the grounds of the Barcelona and I wondered what he was doing there, naturally. I'd hate to see such a nice-looking boy mixed up with a man like Sipe.' He glanced at the photograph and handed it back to me, as if to relieve himself of the responsibility of explaining Tom.

'What's the matter with Sipe?'

'What isn't? I've got boys of my own, and I hate to see a man like Sipe teaching the boys to drink and—other things. He ought to be in jail, if you want my opinion.'

'I agree. Let's put him there.'

'You're kidding.'

'I'm serious, Ben. Right now Sipe is in his hotel room, passed out. He probably won't wake up for a long time. Just in case he does, will you stay here and watch for him to come out?'

'What do I do if he *comes* out?'

'Call the police and tell them to arrest him.'

'I can't do that,' he said uneasily. 'I know he's a bad actor, but I got nothing definite to go on.'

'I have. If you're forced to call the police, tell them Sipe is wanted in Pacific Point on suspicion of kidnapping. But don't call them unless you have to. Sipe is my best witness, and once he's arrested I'll never see him again.'

'Where are you going?'

'To see if I can trace the boy.'

His eyes brightened. 'Is he the one that's been in all the papers? What's his name? Hillman?'

'He's the one.'

'I should have recognized him. I dunno, I don't pay too much attention to people's faces. But I can tell you what kind of a car they drive.'

'Does Sipe have a car?'

'Yeah. It's a '53 Ford with a cracked engine. I put some goop in it for him, but it's due to die any day.'

Before I left, I asked Daly if he had seen anyone else around the hotel. He had, and he remembered. Mike Harley had been there Monday morning, driving the car with the Idaho license. I guessed that Tom had been riding in the trunk.

'And just last night,' he said, 'there was this other young fellow driving a brand-new Chevvy. I think he had a girl with him, or maybe a smaller fellow. I was just closed up, and my bright lights were off.'

'Did you get a good look at the driver?'

'Not so good, no. I think he was dark-haired, a nice-looking boy. What he was doing with that crumb-bum—' Shaking his head some more, Ben started to get out of my car. He froze in mid-action: 'Come to think of it, what's the Hillman boy been doing walking around? I thought he was a prisoner and everybody in Southern California was looking for him.'

'We are.'

It took me a couple of hours, with the help of several bus-company employees, to sort out the driver who had picked Tom up last night. His name was Albertson and he lived far out on La Cienaga in an apartment over a bakery. The sweet yeasty smell of freshly made bread permeated his small front room.

It was still very early in the morning. Albertson had pulled on trousers over his pajamas. He was a square-shouldered man of about forty, with alert eyes. He nodded briskly over the picture:

'Yessir. I remember him. He got on my bus at the Barcelona

intersection and bought a ticket into Santa Monica. He didn't get off at Santa Monica, though.'

'Why not?'

He rubbed his heavily bearded chin. The sound rasped on my nerves. 'Would he be wanted for something?' Albertson said.

'He would.'

'That's what I thought at the time. He started to get off and then he saw somebody inside the station and the kid went back to his seat. I got off for a rest stop and it turned out there was a cop inside. When I came back the boy was still on the bus. I told him this was as far as his fare would take him. So he asked me to sell him a ticket to LA I was all set to go and I didn't make an issue. If the kid was in trouble, it wasn't up to me to turn him in. I've been in trouble myself. Did I do wrong?'

'You'll find out on Judgment Day.'

He smiled. 'That's a long time to wait. What's the pitch on the kid?'

'Read it in the papers, Mr Albertson. Did he ride all the way downtown?'

'Yeah. I'm sure he did. He was one of the last ones to get off the bus.'

I went downtown and did some bird-dogging in and around the bus station. Nobody remembered seeing the boy. Of course, the wrong people were on duty at this time in the morning. I'd stand a better chance if I tried again in the evening. And it was time I got back to Otto Sipe.

Ben Daly said he hadn't come out of the hotel. But when we went to Sipe's room the door was standing open and he was gone. Before he left he had finished the bottle of whisky by his bed.

'He must have had a master key, Ben. Is there any way out of here except the front?'

'No sir. He has to be on the grounds some place.'

We went around to the back of the sprawling building, past a dry swimming pool with a drift of brown leaves in the deep end. Under the raw bluff which rose a couple of hundred feet behind the hotel were the employees' dormitories, garages, and other outbuildings. The two rear wings of the hotel contained a formal garden whose clipped shrubs and box hedges were growing back into natural shapes. Swaying on the topmost spray of a blue plumbago bush, a mockingbird was scolding like a jay.

I stood still and made a silencing gesture to Daly. Someone was digging on the far side of the bush. I could see some of his movements and hear the scrape of the spade, the thump of earth. I took out the gun and showed myself.

Otto Sipe looked up from his work. He was standing in a shallow hole about five feet long and two feet wide. There was dirt on his clothes. His face was muddy with sweat.

In the grass beside the hole a man in a gray jacket was lying on his back. The striped handle of a knife protruded from his chest. The man looked like Mike Harley, and he lay as if the knife had nailed him permanently to the earth.

'What are you doing, Otto?'

'Planting petunias.' He bared his teeth in a doggish grin. The man seemed to be in that detached state of drunkenness where everything appears surreal or funny.

'Planting dead men, you mean.'

He turned and looked at Harley's body as if it had just fallen from the sky. 'Did he come with you?'

'You know who he is. You and Mike have been buddies ever since he left Pocatello with you in the early forties.'

'All right, I got a right to give a buddy a decent burial. You just can't leave them lying around in the open for the vultures.'

'The only vultures I see around here are human ones. Did you kill him?'

'Naw. Why would I kill my buddy?'

'Who did?'

Leaning on his spade, he gave me a queer cunning look.

'Where's Tom Hillman, Otto?'

'I'm gonna save my talk for when it counts.'

I turned to Ben Daly. 'Can you handle a gun?'

'Hell no, I was only at Guadal.'

'Hold this on him.'

I handed him my revolver and went to look at Harley. His face when I touched it was cold as the night had been. This and the advanced coagulation of the blood that stained his shirt front told me he had been dead for many hours, probably all night.

I didn't try to pull the knife out of his ribs. I examined it closely without touching it. The handle was padded with rubber, striped black and white, and moulded to fit the hand. It looked new and fairly expensive.

The knife was the only thing of any value that had attached itself to Mike Harley. I went through his pockets and found the stub of a Las Vegas to Los Angeles plane ticket issued the day before, and three dollars and forty-two cents.

Ben Daly let out a yell. Several things happened at once. At the edge of my vision metal flashed and the mockingbird flew up out of the bush. The gun went off. A gash opened in the side of Daly's head where Otto Sipe had hit him with the spade. Otto Sipe's face became contorted. He clutched at his abdomen and fell forward, with the lower part of his body in the grave.

Ben Daly said: 'I didn't mean to shoot him. The gun went off when he swung the spade at me. After the war I never wanted to shoot anything.'

The gash in the side of his head was beginning to bleed. I tied my handkerchief around it and told him to go and call the police and an ambulance. He ran. He was surprisingly light on his feet for a man of middle age.

I was feeling surprisingly heavy on mine. I went to Sipe and turned him onto his back and opened his clothes. The wound in his belly was just below the umbilicus. It wasn't bleeding much, externally, but he must have been bleeding inside. The life was draining visibly from his face.

It was Archer I mourned for. It had been a hard three days. All I had to show for them was a dead man and a man who was probably dying. The fact that the bullet in Sipe had come from my gun made it worse.

Compunction didn't prevent me from going through Sipe's pockets. His wallet was fat with bills, all of them twenties. But his share of the Hillman payoff wasn't going to do him any good. He was dead before the ambulance came shrieking down the highway.

XX

A LOT OF talking was done, some on the scene and some in the sheriff's office. With my support, and a phone call from Lieutenant Bastian, and the fairly nasty cut in the side of his head, Ben was able to convince the sheriff's and the DA's men that he had committed justifiable homicide. But they weren't happy about it. Neither was I. I had let him kill my witness.

There was still another witness, if she would talk. By the middle of the morning I was back at the door of Susanna Drew's apartment. Stella said through the door:

'Who is it, please?'

'Lew Archer.'

She let me in. The girl had bluish patches under her eyes, as if their color had run. There was hardly any other color in her face.

'You look scared,' I said. 'Has anything happened?'

'No. It's one of the things that scares me. And I have to call my parents and I don't want to. They'll make me go home.'

'You have to go home.'

'No.'

'Yes. Think of them for a minute. You're putting them through a bad time for no good reason.'

'But I do have a good reason. I want to try and meet Tommy again tonight. He said if he didn't make it last night he'd be at the bus station tonight.'

'What time?'

'The same time. Nine o'clock.'

'I'll meet him for you.'

She didn't argue, but her look was evasive.

'Where's Miss Drew, Stella?'

'She went out for breakfast. I was still in bed, and she left me a note. She said she'd be back soon, but she's been gone for at least two hours.' She clenched her fists and rapped her knuckles together in front of her. 'I'm worried.'

'About Susanna Drew?'

'About everything. About me. Things keep getting worse. I keep expecting it to end, but it keeps getting worse. I'm changing, too. There's hardly anybody I like any more.'

'The thing will end, Stella, and you'll change back.'

'Will I? It doesn't feel like a reversible change. I don't see how Tommy and I are ever going to be happy.'

'Survival is the main thing.' It was a hard saying to offer a young girl. 'Happiness come in fits and snatches. I'm having more of it as I get older. The teens were my worst time.'

'Really?' Her brow puckered. 'Do you mind if I ask you a personal question, Mr Archer?'

'Go ahead.'

'Are you interested in Miss Drew? You know what I mean. Seriously.'

'I think I am. Why?'

'I don't know whether I should tell you this or not. She went out for breakfast with another man.'

'That's legitimate.'

'I don't know. I didn't actually see him but I heard his voice and I'm very good on voices. I think it was a married man.'

'How can you tell that from a man's voice?'

'It was Tommy's father,' she said. 'Mr Hillman.'

I sat down. For a minute I couldn't think of anything to say. The African masks on the sunlit wall seemed to be making faces at me.

Stella approached me with an anxious expression. 'Shouldn't I have told you? Ordinarily I'm not a tattletale. I feel like a spy in her house.'

'You should have told me. But don't tell anyone else, please.'

'I won't.' Having passed the information on to me, she seemed relieved.

'Did the two of them seem friendly, Stella?'

'Not exactly. I didn't see them together. I stayed in my room because I didn't want him to see *me*. She wasn't glad to have him come here, I could tell. But they did sound kind of—intimate.'

'Just what do you mean by "intimate"?'

She thought about her answer. 'It was something about the

way they talked, as if they were used to talking back and forth. There wasn't any politeness or formality.'

'What did they say to each other?'

'Do you want me to try and tell you word for word?'

'Exactly, from the moment he came to the door.'

'I didn't hear all of it. Anyway, when he came in, she said: "I thought you had more discretion than this, Ralph." She called him Ralph. He said: "Don't give me that. The situation is getting desperate." I don't know what he meant by that.'

'What do you think he meant?'

'Tommy and all, but there may have been more to it. They didn't say. He said: "I thought I could expect a little sympathy from you." She said she was all out of sympathy, and he said she was a hard woman and then he did something—I think he tried to kiss her—and she said: "Don't do that!" '

'Did she sound angry?'

Stella assumed a listening attitude and looked at the high ceiling. 'Not so very. Just not interested. He said: "You don't seem to like me very much." She said that the question was a complicated one and she didn't think now was the time to go into it, especially with somebody in the guest room, meaning me. He said: "Why didn't you say so in the first place? Is it a man?" After that they lowered their voices. I don't know what she told him. They went out for breakfast in a few minutes.'

'You have a very good memory,' I said.

She nodded, without self-consciousness. 'It helps me in school, but in other ways it isn't so fabulous. I remember all the bad things along with the good things.'

'And the conversation you heard this morning was one of the bad things?'

'Yes, it was. It frightened me. I don't know why.'

It frightened me, too, to learn that Hillman might have been the faceless man with Susanna when she was twenty. In different degrees I cared about them both. They were people with enough feeling to be hurt, and enough complexity to do wrong. Susanna I cared about in ways I hadn't even begun to explore.

Now the case was taking hold of her skirt like the cogs of an automated machine that nobody knew how to stop. I have to admit that I wouldn't have stopped it even if I knew how. Which is the peculiar hell of being a pro.

'Let's see the note she left you.'

Stella fetched it from the kitchen, a penciled note scrawled on an interoffice memo form: 'Dear Stella: I am going out for breakfast and will be back soon. Help yourself to the contents of the refrig. S. Drew.'

'Did you have anything to eat?' I said to Stella.

'I drank a glass of milk.'

'And a hamburger last night for dinner. No wonder you look pinched. Come on, I'll take you out for breakfast. It's the going thing.'

'All right. Thank you. But then what?'

'I drive you home.'

She turned and walked to the sliding glass doors that opened onto the patio, as far away in the room as she could get from me. A little wind was blowing, and I could hear it rustling in the fronds of a miniature palm. Stella turned back to me decisively, as if the wind and the sunlight had influenced her through the glass.

'I guess I have to go home. I can't go on *scaring* my mother.'

'Good girl. Now call her and tell her you're on your way.'

She considered my suggestion, standing in the sunlight with her head down, the white straight part of her hair bisecting her brown head. 'I will if you won't listen.'

'How will I know you've done it?'

'I never lied to you yet,' she said with feeling. 'That's because you don't tell lies to me. Not even for my own good.' She produced her first smile of the morning.

I think I produced mine. It had been a bad morning.

I immured myself in a large elaborate bathroom with fuzzy blue carpeting and did some washing, ritual and otherwise. I found a safety razor among the cosmetics and sleeping pills in the medicine cabinet, and used it to shave with. I was planning an important interview, a series of them if I could set them up.

Stella's cheeks were flushed when I came out. 'I called home. We better not stop for breakfast on the way.'

'Your mother's pretty excited, is she?'

'Dad was the one I talked to. He blames you. I'm sorry.'

'It was my bad judgment,' I said. 'I should have taken you home last night. But I had something else to do.' Get a man killed.

'It was *my* bad judgment,' she said. 'I was *punishing* them for lying about Tommy and me and the car.'

'I'm glad you know that. How upset is your father?'

'Very upset. He even said something about Laguna Perdida School. He didn't really mean it, though.' But a shadow crossed her face.

About an hour later, driving south with Stella toward El Rancho, I caught a distant glimpse of the school. The rising wind had blown away all trace of the overcast, but even in unobstructed sunlight its buildings had a desolate look about them. I found myself straining my eyes for the lonely blue heron. He wasn't on the water or in the sky.

On impulse, I turned off the highway and took the access road to Laguna Perdida. My car passed over the treadle. The automatic gates rose.

Stella said in a tiny voice: 'You're not going to put me in here?'

'Of course not. I want to ask a certain person a question. I won't be long.'

'They better not try to put me in here,' she said. 'I'll run away for good.'

'You've had more mature ideas.'

'What else can I do?' she said a little wildly.

'Stay inside the safety ropes, with your own kind of people. You're much too young to step outside, and I don't think your parents are so bad. They're probably better than average.'

'You don't know them.'

'I know you. You didn't just happen.'

The old guard came out of his kiosk and limped up to my side of the car. 'Dr Sponti isn't here just now.'

'How about Mrs Mallow?'

'Yeah. You'll find her down the line in East Hall.' He pointed toward the building with the ungenerous windows.

Leaving Stella in the car, I knocked on the front door of East Hall. After what seemed a long time, Mrs Mallow answered. She was wearing the same dark formal costume that she had been wearing on Monday, and the same rather informal smell of gin.

She smiled at me, at the same time flinching away from the daylight. 'Mr Archer, isn't it?'

'How are you, Mrs Mallow?'

'Don't ever ask me that question in the morning. Or any other time, now that I come to think of it. I'm surviving.'

'Good.'

'But you didn't come here to inquire after my health.'

'I'd like to have a few minutes with Fred Tyndal.'

'I'm sorry,' she said, 'the boys are all in class.'

'It could be important.'

'You want to ask Fred some questions, is that it?'

'Just one, really. It wouldn't have to take long.'

'And it won't be anything disturbing?'

'I don't think so.'

She left me in the lounge and went into Patch's office to make a telephone call. I wandered around the big battered homeless room, imagining how it would feel to be a boy whose parents had left him here. Mrs Mallow came back into the room:

'Fred will be right over.'

While I was waiting, I listened to the story of her marriages, including the one that had lasted, her marriage to the bottle. Then Fred came in out of the sunlight, none of which adhered to him. He sort of loitered just inside the door, pulling at the hairs on his chin and waiting to be told what he had done wrong this time.

I got up and moved toward him, not too quickly. 'Hello, Fred.'

'Hello.'

'You remember the talk we had the other day?'

'There's nothing the matter with my memory.' He added with his quick evanescent smile: 'You're Lew Archer the First. Did you find Tom yet?'

'Not yet. I think you can help me find him.'

He scuffed the door frame with the side of his shoe. 'I don't see how.'

'By telling me everything you know. One thing I can promise—they won't put him back in here.'

'What good will that do me?' he said forlornly.

I had no answer ready. After a moment the boy said, 'What do you want me to tell you?'

'I think you were holding back a little the other day. I don't blame you. You didn't know me from Adam. You still don't, but it's three days later now, and Tom is still missing.'

His face reflected the seriousness of this. He couldn't stand such seriousness for very long. He said with a touch of parody:

'Okay, I'll talk, I'll spill everything.'

'I want to ask you this. When Tom broke out of here Saturday night, did he have any definite person or place in mind that he intended to go to?'

He ducked his head quickly in the affirmative. 'Yeah, I think so.'

'Do you know where he was going?'

'Tom didn't say. He did say something else, though, something about finding his true father.' The boy's voice broke through into feeling he couldn't handle. He said: 'Big deal.'

'What did he mean by that, Fred?'

'He said he was adopted.'

'Was he really?'

'I don't know. A lot of the kids here want to think they're adopted. My therapist calls it a typical Freudian family romance.'

'Do you think Tom was serious?'

'Sure he was.' Once again the boy's face reflected seriousness, and I caught a glimpse there of the maturity that he might reach yet. 'He said he couldn't know who he was until he knew for sure who his father was.' He grinned wryly. 'I'm trying to forget who my father is.'

'You can't.'

'I can try.'

'Get interested in something else.'

'There isn't anything else.'

'There will be.'

'When?' he said.

Mrs Mallow interrupted us. 'Have you found out what you need to know, Mr Archer? Fred really should be going back to class now.'

I said to him: 'Is there anything else you can tell me?'

'No, sir. Honestly. We didn't talk much.'

The boy started out. He turned in the doorway suddenly, and spoke to me in a voice different from the one he had been using, a voice more deep and measured:

'I wish you were my father.'

He turned away into the bleak sunlight.

Back in the car, I said to Stella: 'Did Tom ever tell you that he was adopted?'

'Adopted? He can't be.'

'Why not?'

'He can't be, that's all.' The road curved around a reedy marsh where the red-winged blackbirds sounded like woodwinds tuning up, and violins. Stella added after a while: 'For one thing, he looks like his father.'

'Adopted children often do. They're picked to match the parents.'

'How awful. How *commercial.* Who *told* you he was adopted?'

'He told a friend at the school.'

'A girl?'

'A boy.'

'I'm sure he was making it up.'

'Did he often make things up?'

'Not often. But he did—he does have some funny ideas about some things. He told me just this summer that he was probably a changeling, you know? That they got him mixed up with some other baby in the hospital, and Mr and Mrs Hillman weren't his real parents.' She turned toward me, crouching on the seat with her legs under her. 'Do you think that could be true?'

'It could be. Almost anything can happen.'

'But you don't believe it.'

'I don't know what I believe, Stella.'

'You're an adult,' she said with a hint of mockery. 'You're supposed to know.'

I let it drop. We rode in silence to the gate of El Rancho. Stella said:

'I wonder what my father is going to do to me.' She hesitated. 'I apologize for getting you into this.'

'It's all right. You've been the best help I've had.'

Jay Carlson, whom I hadn't met and wasn't looking forward to meeting, was standing out in front of his house when we got there. He was a well-fed, youngish man with sensitive blue eyes resembling Stella's. At the moment he looked sick with anger, gray and shuddering with it.

Rhea Carlson, her red hair flaring like a danger signal, came out of the house and rushed up to the car, with her husband trudging behind her. He acted like a man who disliked trouble and couldn't handle it well. The woman spoke first:

'What have you been doing with my daughter?'

'Protecting her as well as I could. She spent the night with a woman friend of mine. This morning I talked her into coming home.'

'I intend to check that story very carefully,' Carlson said. 'What was the name of this alleged woman friend?'

'Susanna Drew.'

'Is he telling the truth, Stella?'

She nodded.

'Can't you talk?' he cried. 'You've been gone all night and you won't even speak to us.'

'Don't get so excited, Daddy. He's telling the truth. I'm sorry I went to Los Angeles but—'

He couldn't wait for her to finish. 'I've got a right to get excited, after what you've done. We didn't even know if you were alive.'

Stella bowed her head. 'I'm sorry, Daddy.'

'You're a cruel, unfeeling girl,' her mother said. 'And I'll never be able to believe you again. Never.'

'You know better than that, Mrs Carlson.'

Her husband turned on me fiercely. 'You stay out of it.' He probably wanted to hit me. In lieu of this, he grasped Stella by the shoulders and shook her. 'Are you out of your mind, to do a thing like this?'

'Lay off her, Carlson.'

'She's my daughter!'

'Treat her like one. Stella's had a rough night—'

'She's had a rough night, has she? What happened?'

'She's been trying to grow up, under difficulties, and you're not giving her much help.'

'What she needs is discipline. And I know where she can get it.'

'If you're thinking of Laguna Perdida, your thinking is way out of line. Stella is one of the good ones, one of the best—'

'I'm not interested in your opinion. I suggest you get off my place before I call the police.'

I left them together, three well-intentioned people who couldn't seem to stop hurting each other. Stella had the courage to lift her hand to me in farewell.

XXI

I WENT NEXT door to the Hillmans'. Turning in past their mailbox, I heard the noise of a sports car coming down the driveway. I stopped in the middle of the narrow blacktop so that Dick Leandro had to stop, too.

He sat there looking at me rather sulkily from under his hair, as if I'd halted him in the middle of a Grand Prix. I got out and walked over to the side of his car and patted the hood.

'Nice car.'

'I like it.'

'You have any other cars?'

'Just this one,' he said. 'Listen, I hear they f-found Tom, is that the true word?'

'He hasn't been found yet, but he's running free.'

'Hey, that's great,' he said without enthusiasm. 'Listen, do you know where Skipper is? Mrs Hillman says he hasn't been home all night.' He looked up at me with puzzled anxiety.

'I wouldn't worry about him. He can look after himself.'

'Yeah, sure, but do you know where he *is*? I want to ta-talk to him.'

'What about?'

'That's between him and I. It's a personal matter.'

I said unpleasantly: 'Do you and Mr Hillman share a lot of secrets?'

'I w-wouldn't say that. He *advises* me. He gives me g-good advice.'

The young man was almost babbling with fear and hostility. I let him go and drove up to the house. Elaine Hillman was the one I wanted to see, and she let me in herself.

She looked better than she had the last time I'd seen her. She was well groomed and well dressed, in a tailored sharkskin suit which concealed the shrinkage of her body. She was even able to smile at me.

'I got your good news, Mr Archer.'

'Good news?' I couldn't think of any.

'That Tom is definitely alive. Lieutenant Bastian passed the word to me. Come in and tell me more.'

She led me across the reception hall, making a detour to avoid the area under the chandelier, and into the sitting room. She said almost brightly, as if she was determined to be cheerful:

'I call this the waiting room. It's like a dentist's waiting room. But the waiting is almost over, don't you think?' Her voice curled up thinly at the end, betraying her tension.

'Yes. I really think so.'

'Good. I couldn't stand much more of this. None of us could. These days have been very difficult.'

'I know. I'm sorry.'

'Don't be sorry. You've brought us good news.' She perched on the chesterfield. 'Now sit down and tell me the rest of it.'

I sat beside her. 'There isn't much more, and not all of it is good. But Tom is alive, and free, and very likely still in Los Angeles. I traced him from the Barcelona Hotel, where he was hiding, to downtown Los Angeles. He was seen getting off a bus in the main station around ten o'clock last night. I'm going back there this afternoon to see if I can find him.'

'I wish my husband was here to share this,' she said. 'I'm a little worried about him. He left the house early last evening and hasn't been back since.' She looked around the room as if it felt strange without him.

I said: 'He probably got word that Tom was alive.'

'From whom?'

I left the question unanswered.

'But he wouldn't go without telling me.'

'Not unless he had a reason.'

'What possible reason could he have for keeping me in the dark?'

'I don't know, Mrs Hillman.'

'Is he going out of his mind, do you think?'

'I doubt it. He probably spent the night in Los Angeles searching for Tom. I know he had breakfast this morning with Susanna Drew.'

I'd dropped the name deliberately, without preparation, and got the reaction I was looking for. Elaine's delicate blonde face crumpled like tissue paper. 'Good Lord,' she said, 'is that still going on? Even in the midst of these horrors?'

'I don't know exactly what *is* going on.'

'They're lovers,' she said bitterly, 'for twenty years. He swore to me it was over long ago. He begged me to stay with him, and gave me his word of honor that he would never go near her again. But he has no honor.' She raised her eyes to mine. 'My husband is a man without honor.'

'He didn't strike me that way.'

'Perhaps men can trust him. I know a woman can't. I'm rather an expert on the subject. I've been married to him for over twenty-five years. It wasn't loyalty that kept him with me. I know that. It was my family's money, which has been useful to him in his business, and in his hobbies. Including,' she added in a disgusted tone, 'his dirty little bed-hopping hobby.'

She covered her mouth with her hand, as if to hide the anguish twisting it. 'I shouldn't be talking this way. It isn't like me. It's very much against my New England grain. My mother, who had a similar problem with my father, taught me by precept and example always to suffer in silence. And I have. Except for Ralph himself, you're the only person I've spoken to about it.'

'You haven't told me much. It might be a good idea to ventilate it.'

'Do you believe it may be connected in some way with—all this?' She flung out her arm, with the fingers spread at the end of it.

'Very likely it is. I think that's why your husband and Miss Drew got together this morning. He probably phoned her early in the week. Tuesday afternoon.'

'He did! I remember now. He was phoning from the bar, and I came into the room. He cut it short. But I heard him say something to the effect that they must absolutely keep quiet. It must have been that Drew woman he was talking to.'

The scornful phrase made me wince. It was a painful, strange colloquy, but we were both engrossed in it. The intimacy of the people we were talking about forced intimacy on us.

'It probably was her,' I said. 'I'd just told Lieutenant Bastian that she was a witness, and Bastian must have passed it on to your husband.'

'You're right again, Mr Archer. My husband had just heard from the lieutenant. How can you possibly know so much about the details of other people's lives?'

'Other people's lives are my business.'

'And your passion?'

'And my passion. And my obsession, too, I guess. I've never been able to see much in the world besides the people in it.'

'But how could you possibly find out about that phone call? You weren't here. My husband wouldn't tell you.'

'I was in Miss Drew's apartment when the call came. I didn't hear what was said, but it shook her up.'

'I hope so.' She glanced at my face, and her eyes softened. She reached out and touched my arm with gentle fingers. 'She isn't a friend of yours?'

'She is, in a way.'

'You're not in love with her?'

'Not if I can help it.'

'That's a puzzling answer.'

'It puzzles me, too. If she's still in love with your husband it would tend to chill one's interest. But I don't think she is.'

'Then what are they trying to conceal?'

'Something in the past.' I hoped it was entirely in the past. Susanna, I had learned in the course of the morning, could still hurt me where I lived. 'It would help if you'd go into it a little deeper. I know it will also hurt,' I said to myself and her.

'I can stand pain if there's any purpose in it. It's the meaningless pain I can't stand. The pain for Tom, for instance.' She didn't explain what she meant, but she touched her blue-veined temple with her fingertips.

'I'll try to make it short, Mrs Hillman. You said the affair has been going on for twenty years. That would take it back to around the end of the war.'

'Yes. The spring of 1945. I was living alone, or rather with a woman companion, in a house in Brentwood. My husband was in the Navy. He had been a squadron commander, but at the time I'm talking about he was executive officer of an escort carrier. Later they made him captain of the same ship.' She spoke with a kind of forlorn pride, and very carefully, as if the precise facts of the past were all she had to hold on to.

'In January or February of 1945 my husband's ship was damaged by a kamikaze plane. They had to bring it back to San Diego for repairs. Ralph had some days of leave, of course, and of course he visited me. But I didn't see as much of him as I wanted to, or expected to. I found out later why. He was spending some of his nights, whole weekends, with Susanna Drew.'

'In the Barcelona Hotel?'

'Did she tell you?'

'In a way.' She had given me Harold Harley's picture of Carol, and the printing on the back of the picture had sent me to the Barcelona Hotel. 'About herself she told me, not about your husband. She's a loyal girl, anyway.'

'I don't want to hear her praised. She's caused me too much suffering.'

'I'm sorry. But she was only twenty, remember.'

'She's closer to forty now. The fact that she was twenty then only made it worse. I was still in my twenties myself, but my husband had already discarded me. Do you have any idea how a woman feels when her husband leaves her for a younger woman? Can you imagine the crawling of the flesh?'

She was suffering intense remembered pain. Her eyes were bright and dry, as if there was fire behind them. The cheerfullest thing I could think of to say was:

'But he didn't leave you.'

'No. He came back. It wasn't me he cared for. There was the money, you see, and his postwar plans for his engineering firm. He was quite frank on the subject, and quite impenitent. In fact, he seemed to feel that he was doing me an enormous favor. He felt that any couple who couldn't have a child—' Her hand went to her mouth again.

I prompted her: 'But you had Tom.'

'Tom came later,' she said, 'too late to save us.' Her voice broke into a deeper range. 'Too late to save my husband. He's a tragically unhappy man. But I can't find it in my heart to pity him.' Her hand touched her thin breast and lingered there.

'What's the source of the trouble between him and Tom?'

'The falsity,' she said in her deeper voice.

'The falsity?'

'I might as well tell you, Mr Archer. You're going to find out about it sooner or later, anyway. And it may be important. Certainly it's psychologically important.'

'Was Tom—is Tom an adopted son?'

She nodded slowly. 'It may have to come out publicly, I don't know. For the present I'll ask you not to divulge it to anyone. No one in town here knows it. Tom doesn't know it himself. We adopted him in Los Angeles shortly after my husband left the Navy and before we moved here.'

'But he resembles your husband.'

'Ralph chose him for that reason. He's a very vain man, Mr Archer. He's ashamed to admit even to our friends that we were incapable of producing a child of our own. Actually Ralph is the one who is sterile. I'm telling you this so you'll understand why he has insisted from the beginning on the great pretense. His desire to have a son was so powerful, I think he has actually believed at times that Tom is his own flesh and blood.'

'And he hasn't told Tom he isn't?'

'No. Neither have I. Ralph wouldn't let me.'

'Isn't that supposed to be a poor idea, with an adopted child?'

'I told my husband that from the beginning. He had to be honest with Tom, or Tom would not be honest with him. There would be falsity at the center of the household.' Her voice trembled, and she looked down at the carpet as if there was no floor under it. 'Well, you see what the consequence has been. A ruined boyhood for Tom and a breakdown of the family and now this tragedy.'

'This almost-tragedy. He's still alive and we're going to get him back.'

'But can we ever put the family back together?'

'That will depend on all three of you. I've seen worse fractures mended, but not without competent help. I don't mean Laguna Perdida. And I don't mean just help for Tom.'

'I know. I've been wretchedly unhappy, and my husband has been quite—quite irrational on this subject for many years. Actually I think it goes back to Midway. Ralph's squadron was virtually massacred in that dreadful battle. Of course he blamed himself, since he was leading them. He felt as though he had lost a dozen sons.'

'How do you know?'

'He was still writing to me then,' she said, 'freely and fully, as one human being to another. He wrote me a number of very poignant letters about our having children, sons of our own. I *know* the thought was connected with his lost fliers, although he never said so. And when he found out he couldn't have a son of his own, and decided to adopt Tom, well—' She dropped her hands in her lap. Her hands seemed restless without knitting to occupy them.

'What were you going to say, Mrs Hillman?'

'I hardly know. I'm not a psychologist, though I once had some training in philosophy. I've felt that Ralph was trying to live out some sort of a fantasy with Tom—perhaps relive those terrible war years and make good his losses somehow. But you can't use people in that way, as figures in a fantasy. The whole thing broke down between Tom and his father.'

'And Tom caught on that your husband wasn't his father.'

She looked at me nervously. 'You think he did?'

'I'm reasonably certain of it,' I said, remembering what Fred Tyndal had told me. 'Mrs Hillman, what happened on the Sunday morning that you put Tom in Laguna Perdida?'

She said quickly: 'It was Ralph's doing, not mine.'

'Had they quarreled?'

'Yes. Ralph was horribly angry with him.'

'What about?'

She bowed her head. 'My husband has forbidden me to speak of it.'

'Did Tom say something or do something very wrong?'

She sat with her head bowed and wouldn't answer me. 'I've told you more than I should have,' she said eventually, 'in the hope of getting to the bottom of this mess. Now will you tell me something? You mentioned a hotel called the Barcelona, and you said that Tom had been hiding there. You used the word "hiding." '

'Yes.'

'Wasn't he being held?'

'I don't know. There may have been some duress, possibly psychological duress. But I doubt that he was held in the ordinary sense.'

She looked at me with distaste. I'd brought her some very tough pieces of information to chew on, and probably this was the hardest one of all. 'You've hinted from the beginning that Tom cooperated willingly with the kidnappers.'

'It was a possibility that had to be considered. It still is.'

'Please don't sidestep the question. I can stand a direct answer.' She smiled dimly. 'At this point I couldn't stand anything else.'

'All right. I think Tom went with Harley of his own free will, rode in the trunk of Harley's car to the Barcelona Hotel, and stayed there without anybody having to hold a gun on him. I don't understand his reasons, and I won't until I talk to him. But he probably didn't know about the extortion angle. There's no evidence that he profited from it, anyway. He's broke.'

'How do you know? Have you seen him?'

'I've talked to somebody who talked to him. Tom said he needed money.'

'I suppose that's good news in a way.'

'I thought it was.'

I made a move to go, but she detained me. There was more on her mind:

'This Barcelona Hotel you speak of, is it the big old rundown place on the coast highway?'

'Yes. It's closed up now.'

'And Tom hid, or was hidden, there?'

I nodded. 'The watchman at the hotel, a man named Sipe, was a partner in the extortion. He may have been the brains behind it, to the extent that it took any brains. He was shot to death this morning. The other partner, Harley, was stabbed to death last night.'

Her face was open, uncomprehending, as if she couldn't quite take in these terrible events.

'How extraordinary,' she breathed.

'Not so very. They were heavy thieves, and they came to a heavy end.'

'I don't mean those violent deaths, although they're part of it. I mean the deep connections you get in life, the coming together of the past and the present.'

'What do you have in mind?'

She grimaced. 'Something ugly, but I'm afraid it has to be said. You see, the Barcelona Hotel, where my son, my adopted son, has been staying with criminals, apparently'—she took a shuddering breath—'that very place was the scene of Ralph's affair with Susanna Drew. And did you say that the watchman's name was Sipe, the one who was shot?'

'Yes. Otto Sipe.'

'Did he once work as a detective in the hotel?'

'Yes. He was the kind of detective who gives our trade a bad name.'

'I have reason to know that,' she said. 'I knew Mr Sipe. That is, I talked to him once, and he left an impression that I haven't been able to wipe out of my memory. He was a gross, corrupt man. He came to my house in Brentwood in the spring of 1945.

He was the one who told me about Ralph's affair with Miss Drew.'

'He wanted money, of course.'

'Yes, and I gave him money. Two hundred dollars, he asked for, and when he saw that I was willing to pay he raised it to five hundred, all the cash I had on hand. Well, the money part is unimportant. It always is,' she said, reminding me that she had never needed money.

'What did Sipe have to say to you?'

'That my husband was committing adultery—he had a snapshot to prove it—and it was his duty under the law to arrest him. I don't know now if there was ever such a law on the books—'

'There was. I don't think it's been enforced lately, or an awful lot of people would be in jail.'

'He mentioned jail, and the effect it would have on my husband's reputation. This was just about the time when Ralph began to believe he could make Captain. I know from this height and distance it sounds childish, but it was the biggest thing in his life at that time. He came from an undistinguished family, you see—his father was just an unsuccessful small businessman—and he felt he had to shine in so many ways to match my family's distinction.' She looked at me with sad intelligence. 'We all need something to buttress our pride, don't we, fragments to shore against our ruins.'

'You were telling me about your interview with Otto Sipe.'

'So I was. My mind tends to veer away from scenes like that. In spite of the pain and shock I felt—it was my first inkling that Ralph was unfaithful to me—I didn't want to see all his bright ambitions wrecked. So I paid the dreadful man his dirty money— and he gave me his filthy snapshot.'

'Did you hear from him again?'

'No.'

'I'm surprised he didn't attach himself to you for life.'

'Perhaps he intended to. But Ralph stopped him. I told Ralph about his visit, naturally.' She added: 'I didn't show him the snapshot. That I destroyed.'

'How did Ralph stop him?'

'I believe he knocked him down and frightened him off. I didn't get a very clear account from Ralph. By then we weren't communicating freely. I went home to Boston and I didn't see Ralph again until the end of the year, when he brought his ship to Boston harbor. We had a reconciliation of sorts. It was then we decided to adopt a child.'

I wasn't listening too closely. The meanings of the case were emerging. Ralph Hillman had had earlier transactions with both of the extortionists. He had been Mike Harley's superior officer, and had thrown him out of the Navy. He had knocked down Otto Sipe. And they had made him pay for his superiority and his power.

Elaine was thinking along the same lines. She said in a soft, despondent voice:

'Mr Sipe would never have entered our lives if Ralph hadn't used that crummy hotel for his crummy little purposes.'

'You mustn't blame your husband for everything. No doubt he did wrong. We all do. But the things he did nineteen or twenty years ago aren't solely responsible for this kidnapping, or whatever it was. It isn't that simple.'

'I know. I don't blame him for everything.'

'Sipe, for instance, would probably have been involved anyway. His partner Mike Harley knew your husband and had a grievance against him.'

'But why did Tom, my poor dear Tom, end up at that same hotel? Isn't there a fatality in it?'

'Maybe there is. To Sipe and Harley it was simply a convenient place to keep him.'

'Why would Tom stay with them? They must be—have been outrageous creatures.'

'Teen-age boys sometimes go for the outrageous.'

'Do they not,' she said. 'But I can't really blame Tom for anything he's done. Ralph and I have given him little enough reality to hold on to. Tom's a sensitive, artistic, introverted boy. My husband didn't want him to be those things—perhaps they reminded Ralph that he wasn't our son, really. So he kept trying to change him. And when he couldn't, he withdrew his interest. Not his love, I'm sure. He's still profoundly concerned with Tom.'

'But he spends his time with Dick Leandro.'

One corner of her mouth lifted, wrinkling her cheek and eye, as if age and disillusion had taken sudden possession of that side of her face. 'You're quite a noticer, Mr Archer.'

'You have to be, in my job. Not that Dick Leandro makes any secret of his role. I met him coming out of your driveway.'

'Yes. He was looking for Ralph. He's very dependent on Ralph,' she added dryly.

'How would you describe the relationship, Mrs Hillman? Substitute son?'

'I suppose I would. Dick's mother and father broke up some years ago. His father left town, and of course his mother got custody of Dick. He needed a substitute father. And Ralph needed someone to crew for him on the sloop—I sometimes think it's the most urgent need he has, or had. Someone to share the lusty gusty things he likes to do, and would like a son to do.'

'He could do better than Dick, couldn't he?'

She was silent for a while. 'Perhaps he could. But when you have an urgent need, you tend to hook up with people who have urgent needs of their own. Poor Dick has a great many urgent needs.'

'Some of which have been met. He told me that your husband put him through college.'

'He did. But don't forget that Dick's father used to work for Ralph's firm. Ralph is very strong on loyalty up and down.'

'Is Dick?'

'He's fanatically loyal to Ralph,' she said with emphasis.

'Let me ask you a hypothetical question, without prejudice, as they say in court. If your husband disinherited Tom, would Dick be a likely heir?'

'That's excessively hypothetical, isn't it?'

'But the answer might have practical consequences. What's your answer?'

'Dick might be left something. He probably will be in any case. But please don't imagine that poor stupid Dick, with his curly hair and his muscles, is capable of plotting—'

'I wasn't suggesting that.'

'And you mustn't embarrass Dick. He's come through nobly in this crisis. Both of us have leaned on him.'

'I know. I'll leave him alone.' I got up to go. 'Thank you for being frank with me.'

'There's not much point in pretending at this late date. If there's anything else you need to know—'

'There is one thing that might help. If you could give me the name of the agency through which you adopted Tom?'

'It wasn't done through an agency. It was handled privately.'

'Through a lawyer, or a doctor?'

'A doctor,' she said. 'I don't recall his name, but he delivered Tom at Cedars of Lebanon. We paid the expenses, you understand, as part of the bargain that we made with the mother.'

'Who was she?'

'Some poor woman who'd got herself in trouble. I didn't actually meet her, nor did I want to. I wanted to feel that Tom was my own son.'

'I understand.'

'Does it matter who his parents were? I mean, in the current situation?'

'It does if he's wandering around Los Angeles looking for them. Which I have reason to think he may be doing. You should have a record somewhere of that doctor's name.'

'My husband could tell you.'

'But he isn't available.'

'It may be in his desk in the library.'

I followed her to the library and while she rummaged in the desk I looked at the pictures on the wall again. The group photo taken on the flight deck must have been Hillman's squadron. I looked closely at their faces, wondering which of the young men had died at Midway.

Next I studied the yachting picture of Dick Leandro. His handsome, healthy, empty face told me nothing. Perhaps it would have meaning for somebody else. I took it off the wall and slipped it into the side pocket of my jacket.

Elaine Hillman didn't notice. She had found the name she was looking for.

'Elijah Weintraub,' she said, 'was the doctor's name.'

XXII

I PHONED DR Weintraub long-distance. He confirmed the fact that he had arranged for Thomas Hillman's adoption, but he refused to discuss it over the phone. I made an appointment to see him in his office that afternoon.

Before I drove back to Los Angeles I checked in with Lieutenant Bastian. He'd been working on the case for nearly three days, and the experience hadn't improved his disposition. The scarlike lines in his face seemed to have deepened. His voice was hoarse and harsh, made harsher by irony:

'It's nice of you to drop by every few days.'

'I'm working for Ralph Hillman now.'

'I know that, and it gives you certain advantages. Which you seize. But you and I are working on the same case, and we're supposed to be cooperating. That means periodic exchanges of information.'

'Why do you think I'm here?'

His eyes flared down. 'Fine. What have you found out about the Hillman boy?'

I told Bastian nearly all of it, enough to satisfy both him and my conscience. I left out the adoption and Dr Weintraub, and the possibility that Tom might turn up at the Santa Monica bus station at nine that night. About his other movements, and the fact that he had probably been a voluntary captive in the Barcelona Hotel, I was quite frank.

'It's too bad Otto Sipe had to die,' Bastian grumbled. 'He could have cleared up a lot of things.'

I agreed.

'Exactly what happened to Sipe? You were a witness.'

'He attacked Ben Daly with a spade. Daly was holding my gun while I examined Harley's body. The gun went off.'

Bastian made a disgusted noise with his lips. 'What do you know about Daly?'

'Not much. He has a service station across from the Barcelona. He struck me as dependable. He's a war veteran—'

'So was Hitler. L A says Daly had previous dealings with Sipe. Sipe bought secondhand cars through him, for instance.'

'That would be natural enough. Daly ran the nearest service station to where Sipe worked.'

'So you don't think Daly killed him to shut him up?'

'No, but I'll bear it in mind. I'm more interested in the other killing. Have you seen the knife that Harley was stabbed with?'

'Not yet. I have a description.' Bastin moved some papers around on top of his desk. 'It's what they call a hunting knife, made by the Oregon firm of Forstmann, with their name on it. It has a broad blade about six inches long, is very sharp and pointed, has a striped rubber handle, black and white, with finger mouldings on it. Practically brand new. Is that an accurate description?'

'I only saw the striped rubber handle. The fact that the blade is quite broad, sharp, and pointed suggests that it's the same knife that stabbed Carol.'

'So I told L A They're going to send me the knife for identification work.'

'That's what I was going to suggest.'

Bastian leaned forward, bringing his arms down heavily among the papers on his desk top. 'You think somebody in town here stabbed him?'

'It's an idea worth considering.'

'Why? For his share of the money?'

'It couldn't have been that. Harley had nothing left by the time he left Las Vegas. I talked to the high-roller who cleaned him out.'

'I'm surprised Harley didn't shoot him.'

'I gather there were professional guns around. Harley was never more than a semi-pro.'

'Why then?' Bastian said, his eyebrows arched. 'Why was Harley killed if it wasn't for money?'

'I don't think we'll know until we put our finger on the killer.'

'Do you have any nominations?' he said.

'No. Do you?'

'I have some thoughts on the subject, but I'd better not think them out loud.'

'Because I'm working for Hillman?'

'I didn't say that.' His dark eyes veiled themselves, and he changed the subject. 'A man named Robert Brown, the victim's father, was here asking for you. He's at the City Hotel.'

'I'll look him up tomorrow. Treat him gently, eh?'

'I treat 'em all gently. Harold Harley called me a few minutes ago. He's taking his brother's death hard.'

'He would. When did you let him go?'

'Yesterday. We had no good reason to hold him in custody. There's no law that says you have to inform on your own brother.'

'Is he back home in Long Beach?'

'Yes. He'll be available for the trial, if there's anybody left to prosecute.'

He was needling me about the death of Otto Sipe. On that note I left.

I made a detour up the coast highway on the way to my appointment with Dr Weintraub, and stopped at Ben Daly's service station. Ben was there by the pump, with a bandage around his head. When he saw me he went into the office and didn't come out. A boy who looked like a teen-aged version of Ben emerged after a while. He asked in an unfriendly way if there was anything he could do for me.

'I'd like to talk to Mr Daly for a minute.'

'I'm sorry. Dad doesn't want to talk to you. He's very upset, about this morning.'

'So am I. Tell him that. And ask him if he'll look at a picture for identification purposes.'

The boy went into the office, closing the door behind him. Across the roaring highway, the Barcelona Hotel asserted itself in the sunlight like a monument of a dead civilization. In the driveway I could see a number of county cars, and a man in deputy's uniform keeping back a crowd of onlookers.

Daly's boy came back with a grim look on his face. 'Dad says he doesn't want to look at any more of your pictures. He says you and your pictures brought him bad luck.'

'Tell him I'm sorry.'

The boy retreated formally, like an emissary. He didn't show himself again, and neither did his father. I gave up on Daly for the present.

Dr Weintraub's office was in one of the new medical buildings on Wilshire, near Cedars of Lebanon Hospital. I went up in a self-service elevator to a waiting room on the fifth floor. This was handsomely furnished in California Danish and had soothing music piped in, which got on my nerves before I had time to sit down. Two pregnant women on opposite sides of the room caught me, a mere man, in a crossfire of pitying glances.

The highly made-up girl behind the counter in one corner said:

'Mr Archer?'

'Yes.'

'Dr Weintraub will see you in a few minutes. You're not a patient, are you? So we needn't bother taking your history, need we?'

'It would give you the horrors, honey.'

She moved her eyelashes up and down a few times, to indicate shocked surprise. Her eyelashes were long and thick and phony, and they waved clumsily in the air like tarantula legs.

Dr Weintraub opened a door and beckoned me into his consulting room. He was a man about my age, perhaps a few years older. Like a lot of other doctors, he hadn't looked after himself. His shoulders were stooped under his white smock, and he was putting on weight. The curly black hair was retreating from his forehead.

But the dark eyes behind his glasses were extraordinarily alive. I could practically feel their impact as we shook hands. I recognized his face, but I couldn't place it.

'You look as though you could use a rest,' he said. 'That's free advice.'

'Thanks. It will have to come later.' I didn't tell him he needed exercise.

He sat down rather heavily at his desk, and I took the patient's chair facing him. One whole wall of the room was occupied by bookshelves. The books seemed to cover several branches of medicine, with special emphasis on psychiatry and gynecology.

'Are you a psychiatrist, doctor?'

'No, I am not.' His eyes were melancholy. 'I studied for the Boards at one time but then the war came along. Afterwards I chose another specialty, delivering babies.' He smiled, and his eyes lit up. 'It's so very satisfying, and the incidence of success is so very much higher. I mean, I seldom lose a baby.'

'You delivered Thomas Hillman.'

'Yes. I told you so on the telephone.'

'Have you refreshed your memory about the date?'

'I had my secretary look it up. Thomas was born on December 12, 1945. A week later, on December 20 to be exact, I arranged for the baby's adoption by Captain and Mrs Ralph Hillman. He made a wonderful Christmas present for them,' he said warmly.

'How did his real mother feel about it?'

'She didn't want him,' he said.

'Wasn't she married?'

'As a matter of fact, she was a young married woman. Neither she nor her husband wanted a child at that time.'

'Are you willing to tell me their name?'

'It wouldn't be professional, Mr Archer.'

'Not even to help solve a crime, or find a missing boy?'

'I'd have to know all the facts, and then have time to consider them. I don't have time. I'm stealing time from my other—from my patients now.'

'You haven't heard from Thomas Hillman this week?'

'Neither this week nor any other time.' He got up bulkily and moved past me to the door, where he waited with courteous impatience till I went out past him.

XXIII

WITH ITS PORTICO supported by fluted columns, the front of Susanna's apartment house was a cross between a Greek temple and a Southern plantation mansion. It was painted blue instead of white. Diminished by the columns, I went into the cold marble lobby. Miss Drew was out. She had been out all day.

I looked at my watch. It was nearly five. The chances were she had gone to work after her breakfast with Hillman. I went out and sat in my car at the curb and watched the rush-hour traffic crawling by.

Shortly after five a yellow cab veered out of the traffic stream and pulled up behind my car. Susanna got out. I went up to her as she was paying the driver. She dropped a five-dollar bill when she saw me. The driver scooped it up.

'I've been hoping you'd come to see me, Lew,' she said without much conviction. 'Do come in.'

She had trouble fitting her key into the lock. I helped her. Her handsome central room appeared a little shabby to my eyes, like a stage set where too many scenes had been enacted. Even the natural light at the windows, the fading afternoon light, seemed stale and secondhand.

She flung herself down on a sofa, her fine long legs sprawling. 'I'm bushed. Make yourself a drink.'

'I couldn't use one. There's a long night ahead.'

'That sounds ominous. Make me one then. Make me a Journey to the End of the Night cocktail, with a dash of henbane. Or just dip me a cup of Lethe, that will do.'

'You're tired.'

'I've been working all day. For men must weep and women must work, though the harbor bar be moaning.'

'If you'll be quiet for a bit, I want to talk to you seriously.'

'What fun.'

'Shut up.'

I made her a drink and brought it to her. She sipped it. 'Thank you, Lew. You're really a dear man.'

'Stop talking like a phony.'

She looked up at me with hurt dark eyes. 'Nothing I say is right. You're mad at me. Maybe I shouldn't have left Stella by herself, but she was still sleeping and I had to go to work. Anyway, she got home all right. Her father called, to thank me, just before I left the office.'

'To thank you?'

'And to cross-examine me about you and a few other things. Stella seems to have left home again. Mr Carlson asked me to get in touch with him if she comes here. Should I?'

'I don't care. Stella isn't the problem.'

'And I am?'

'You're part of it. You didn't leave Stella this morning because you had to go to work. You had breakfast with Ralph Hillman, and you ought to know that I know it.'

'It was in a public place,' she said irrelevantly.

'That's not the point. I wouldn't care if it was breakfast in bed. The point is you tried to slur over the fact, and it's a damned important fact.'

The hurt in her eyes tried to erupt into anger, but didn't quite succeed. Anger was just another evasion, and she probably knew that she was coming to the end of her evasions. She finished her drink and said in a very poignant female voice:

'Do you mean important to you personally, or for other reasons?'

'Both. I talked to Mrs Hillman today. Actually she did most of the talking.'

'About Ralph and me?'

'Yes. It wasn't a very pleasant conversation, for either of us. I'd rather have heard it from you.'

She averted her face. Her black head absorbed the light almost completely. It was like looking into a small head-shaped area of almost total darkness.

'It's a passage in my life that I'm not proud of.'

'Because he was so much older?'

'That's one reason. Also, now that I'm older myself, I know how wretchedly mean it is to try and steal another woman's husband.'

'Then why go on doing it?'

'I'm not!' she cried in resentment. 'It was over almost as soon as it started. If Mrs Hillman thinks otherwise, she's imagining things.'

'I'm the one who thinks otherwise,' I said. 'You had breakfast with him this morning. You had a phone call from him the other day, which you refused to discuss.'

Slowly she turned and looked up at my face. 'But it doesn't *mean* anything. I didn't *ask* him to phone me. I only went out with him this morning because he was desperate to talk to someone and I didn't want to disturb Stella. Also, if you want the truth, so he couldn't make a pass at me.'

'Does he go in rather heavily for that?'

'I don't know. I hadn't seen him in about eighteen years. Honestly. I was appalled by the change in him. He was in a bad way this morning. He'd been drinking, and he said he'd been up all night, wandering around Los Angeles, searching for his son.'

'I've been doing a little searching myself, but nobody goes out to breakfast with me and holds my hand.'

'Are you really jealous of him, Lew? You can't be. He's *old.* He's a broken-down old man.'

'You're protesting too much.'

'I mean it, though. I had an enormous sense of revulsion this morning. Not just against Ralph Hillman. Against my whole misguided little life.' She looked around the room as if she perceived the shabbiness I had seen. 'I'm liable to spill over into my autobiography at any moment.'

'That's what I've been waiting for, Susanna. How did you meet him?'

'Make me another drink.'

I made it and brought it to her. 'When and how did you meet him?'

'It was in March of 1945, when I was working at Warner's. A group of Navy officers came out to the studio to see a preview of a war movie. They were planning a party afterwards, and I went along. Ralph got me drunk and took me to the Barcelona Hotel, where he introduced me to the stolen delights of illicit romance. It was my first time on both counts. First time drunk, first time bedded.' Her voice was harsh. 'If you wouldn't stand over me, Lew, it would be easier.'

I pulled up a hassock to her feet. 'But it didn't go on, you say?'

'It went on for a few weeks. I'll be honest with you. I was in love with Ralph. He was handsome and brave and all the other things.'

'And married.'

'That's why I quit him,' she said, 'essentially. Mrs Hillman—Elaine Hillman got wind of the affair and came to my apartment in Burbank. We had quite a scene. I don't know what would have happened if Carol hadn't been there. But she got the two of us quieted down, and even talking sensibly to each other.' She paused, and added elegiacally: 'Carol had troubles of her own, but she was always good at easing situations.'

'What was Carol doing in that situation?'

'She was living with me, didn't I tell you that? I took her into my home. Anyway, Carol sat there like a little doll while Elaine Hillman laid out for me in detail just what I was doing to her and her marriage. The ugliness of it. I saw I couldn't go on doing it to her. I told her so, and she was satisfied. She's quite an impressive woman, you know, at least she was then.'

'She still is, when you get under the surface. And Ralph Hillman is an impressive man.'

'He was in those days, anyway.'

I said to test her honesty: 'Didn't you have any other reason for dropping him, besides Elaine Hillman's visit?'

'I don't know what you mean,' she said, failing the honesty test, or perhaps the memory test.

'How did Elaine Hillman find out about you?'

'Oh. That.' The shame that lay beneath her knowledge of herself came up into her face and took possession of it. She whispered: 'Mrs Hillman told you, I suppose?'

'She mentioned a picture.'

'Did she show it to you?'

'She's too much of a lady.'

'That was a nasty crack!'

'It wasn't intended to be. You're getting paranoid.'

'Yes, Doctor. Shall I stretch out on this convenient couch and tell you a dream?'

'I can think of better uses for a couch.'

'Not now,' she said quickly.

'No. Not now.' But in the darkest part of our transaction we had reached a point of intimacy, understanding at least. 'I'm sorry I have to drag all this stuff out.'

'I know. I know that much about you. I also know you haven't finished.'

'Who took the picture? Otto Sipe?'

'He was there. I heard his voice.'

'You didn't see him?'

'I hid my face,' she said. 'A flashbulb popped. It was like reality exploding.' She passed her hand over her eyes. 'I think it was another man in the doorway who took the picture.'

'Harold Harley?'

'It must have been. I didn't see him.'

'What was the date?'

'It's in my memory book. April 14, 1945. Why does it matter?'

'Because you can't explode reality. Life hangs together in one piece. Everything is connected with everything else. The problem is to find the connections.'

She said with some irony: 'That's your mission in life, isn't it? You're not interested in people, you're only interested in the connections between them. Like a—' she searched for an insulting word—'a plumber.'

I laughed at her. She smiled a little. Her eyes remained somber.

'There's another connection we have to go into,' I said. 'This one involves the telephone, not the plumbing.'

'You mean Ralph's call the other day.'

'Yes. He wanted you to keep quiet about something. What was it?'

She squirmed a little, and gathered her feet under her. 'I don't want to get him into trouble. I owe him that much.'

'Spare me the warmed-over sentiment. This is for real.'

'You needn't sound so insulting.'

'I apologize. Now let's have it.'

'Well, he knew you had seen me, and he said we had to keep our stories straight. It seems there was a discrepancy in the story he told you. He told you he hadn't met Carol, but actually he had. After Mike Harley was arrested, she made an appeal to him and he did what he could. I wasn't to tell you about his interest in Carol.'

'He was interested in Carol?'

'Not in the way you mean,' she said with a lift of her head. 'I was his girl. He simply didn't like the idea of leaving a child bride like Carol alone in the Barcelona Hotel. He asked me to take her under my wing. My slightly broken wing. Which I did, as you know.'

'It all sounds very innocent.'

'It was. I swear it. Besides, I liked Carol, I loved her, that summer in Burbank. I felt as if the baby in her womb belonged to both of us.'

'Have you ever had a child?'

She shook her head rather sadly. 'I never will have now. I was sure I was pregnant once, that very spring we've been talking about, but the doctor said it was false, caused by wistful thinking.'

'Was Carol seeing a doctor when she lived with you?'

'Yes, I made her go. She went to the same doctor, actually. Weintraub, his name was.'

'Did he deliver her baby?'

'I wouldn't know. She'd already left me, remember, and gone off with Mike Harley. And I didn't go back to Dr Weintraub on account of the unpleasant associations.'

'Was he unpleasant to you?'

'I mean the association with Ralph Hillman. Ralph sent me to Dr Weintraub. I think they were buddies in the Navy.'

Dr Weintraub's plump face came into my mind. At the same time I remembered where I had seen a younger version of it, stripped of excess flesh, that very day. Weintraub was a member of the group on the flight deck, in the picture hanging on Hillman's library wall.

'It's funny,' Susanna was saying, 'how a name you haven't heard for seventeen or eighteen years will crop up, and then a couple of hours or a couple of days later, it will crop up again. Like Weintraub.'

'Has the name been cropping up in other contexts?'

'Just this afternoon at the office. I had a rather peculiar caller whom I meant to tell you about, but all these other matters pushed him out of my mind. He was interested in Dr Weintraub, too.'

'Who was he?'

'He didn't want to say. When I pressed him, he said his name was Jackman.'

'Sam Jackman?'

'He didn't mention his first name.'

'Sam Jackman is a middle-aged Negro with very light skin who looks and talks like a jazz musician on his uppers, which he is.'

'This boy seemed to be on his uppers, all right, but he certainly isn't Sam's. Maybe he's Sam son. He can't be more than eighteen or nineteen.'

'Describe him.'

'Thin-faced, very good features, very intense dark eyes, so intense he scared me a little. He seemed intelligent, but he was too excited to make much sense.'

'What was he excited about?' I said with a mounting excitement of my own.

'Carol's death, I think. He didn't refer to it directly, but he asked me if I had known Carol in 1945. Apparently he'd been all the way out to Burbank trying to find me. He came across an old secretary at Warner's whom I still keep in touch with, and used her name to get past my secretary. He wanted to know what I could tell him about the Harley baby, and when I couldn't tell him anything he asked me what doctor Carol had gone to. I dredged up Weintraub's name—Elijah Weintraub isn't exactly a forgettable name—and it satisfied him. I was quite relieved to get rid of him.'

'I'm sorry you did.'

She looked at me curiously. 'Do you suppose he could be the Harley baby himself?'

I didn't answer her. I got out my collection of photographs and shuffled them. There was an electric tremor in my hands, as if time was short-circuiting through me.

Susanna whispered fearfully: 'He isn't dead, is he, Lew? I couldn't bear to look at another dead picture.'

'He's alive. At least, I hope he is.'

I showed her Tom Hillman's face. She said: 'That's the boy I talked to. But he's very much the worse for wear now. *Is* he the Harley baby?'

'I think so. He's also the baby that Ralph and Elaine Hillman adopted through Dr Weintraub. Did you get the impression that he was on his way to see Weintraub?'

'Yes. I did.' She was getting excited, too. 'It's like an ancient identity myth. He's searching for his lost parentage.'

'The hell of it is, both of his parents are dead. What time did you see him?'

'Around four o'clock.'

It was nearly six now. I went to the phone and called Weintraub's office. His answering service said it was closed for the night. The switchboard girl wouldn't give me Weintraub's home address or his unlisted number, and neither would the manager of the answering service. I had to settle for leaving my name and Susanna's number and waiting for Weintraub to call me, if he was willing.

An hour went by. Susanna broiled me a steak, and chewed unhungrily on a piece of it. We sat at a marble table in the patio and she told me all about identity myths and how they grew. Oedipus. Hamlet. Stephen Dedalus. Her father had taught courses in such subjects. It passed the time, but it didn't relieve my anxiety for the boy. Hamlet came to a bloody end. Oedipus killed his father and married his mother, and then blinded himself.

'Thomas Harley,' I said aloud. 'Thomas Harley Hillman Jackman. He knew he wasn't the Hillmans' son. He thought he was a changeling.'

'You get that in the myths, too.'

'I'm talking about real life. He turned on his foster parents and went for his real parents. It's too bloody bad they had to be the Harleys.'

'You're very certain that he is the Harley child.'

'It fits in with everything I know about him. Incidentally, it explains why Ralph Hillman tried to hush up the fact that he'd taken an interest in Carol. He didn't want the facts of the adoption to come out.'

'Why, though?'

'He's kept it a secret all these years, even from Tom. He seems to be a little crazy on the subject.'

'I got that impression this morning.' She leaned across the corner of the table and touched my fingers. 'Lew? You don't think he went off his rocker and murdered Carol himself?'

'It's a possibility, but a remote one. What was on his mind at breakfast?'

'Him, mostly. He felt his life was collapsing around his ears. He thought I might be interested in helping him to pick up the pieces. After eighteen years he was offering me my second big break.' Her scorn touched herself as well as Hillman.

'I don't quite understand.'

'He asked me to marry him, Lew. I suppose that's in line with contemporary *mores*. You get your future set up ahead of time, before you terminate your present marriage.'

'I don't like that word "terminate." Did he say what he intended to do with Elaine?'

'No.' She looked quite pale and haunted.

'I hope divorce was all he had in mind. What was your answer?'

'My answer?'

'Your response to his proposal.'

'Oh. I told him I was waiting for a better offer.'

Her dark meaningful eyes were on my face. I sat there trying to frame a balanced answer. The telephone rang inside before I had a chance to deliver it.

I went in through the door we had left open and picked up the receiver. 'Archer speaking.'

'This is Dr Weintraub.' His voice had lost its calmness. 'I've just had a thoroughly upsetting experience—'

'Have you seen the Hillman boy?'

'Yes. He came to me just as I was leaving. He asked me essentially the same question you did.'

'What did you tell him, Doctor?'

'I told him the truth. He already knew it, anyway. He wanted to know if Mike and Carol Harley were his parents. They were.'

'How did he react to the information?'

'Violently, I'm afraid. He hit me and broke my glasses. I'm practically blind without them. He got away from me.'

'Have you told the police?'

'No.'

'Tell them, now. And tell them who he is.'

'But his father—his adoptive father wouldn't want me—'

'I know how it is when you're dealing with an old commander, Doctor. He was your commander at one time, wasn't he?'

'Yes. I was his flight surgeon.'

'You aren't any more, and you can't let Hillman do your thinking for you. Do you tell the police, or do I?'

'I will. I realize we can't let the boy run loose in his condition.'

'Just what is his condition?'

'He's very upset and, as I said, violently acting out.'

With his heredity, I thought, that was hardly surprising.

XXIV

I KISSED SUSANNA goodbye and drove down Wilshire through Westwood. I wanted to be at the Santa Monica bus station at nine, just in case Tom showed up, but there was still time for another crack at Ben Daly. I turned down San Vicente toward the coastal highway.

The sun was half down on the horizon, bleeding color into the sea and the sky. Even the front of the Barcelona Hotel was touched with factitious Mediterranean pink. The crowd of onlookers in the driveway had changed and dwindled. There were still a few waiting for something more interesting than their lives to happen.

It was a warm night, and most of them were in beach costume. One man was dressed formally in a dark gray business suit and dark gray felt hat. He looked familiar.

I pulled up the drive on impulse and got out. The man in the dark gray suit was Harold Harley. He was wearing a black tie, which Lila had doubtless chosen for him, and a woebegone expression.

It deepened when he saw me. 'Mr Archer?'

'You can't have forgotten me, Harold.'

'No. It's just that everything looks different, even people's faces. Or that hotel there. It's just a caved-in old dump, and I used to think it was a pretty ritzy place. Even the sky looks different.' He raised his eyes to the red-stretched sky. 'It looks hand-tinted, phony, like there was nothing behind it.'

The little man talked like an artist. He might have become one, I thought, with a different childhood.

'I didn't realize you were so fond of your brother.'

'Neither did I. But it isn't just that. I hate California. Nothing really good ever happened to me in California. Or Mike either.' He gestured vaguely toward the cluster of official cars. 'I wisht I was back in Idaho.'

I drew him away from the little group of onlookers, from the women in slacks and halters which their flesh overflowed, the younger girls with haystacks of hair slipping down their foreheads into their blue-shadowed eyes, the tanned alert-looking boys with bleached heads and bleached futures. We stood under a magnolia tree that needed water.

'What happened to your brother started in Idaho, Harold.' And also what happened to you, or failed to happen.

'You think I don't know that? The old man always said Mike would die on the gallows. Anyway, he cheated the gallows.'

'I talked to your father yesterday.'

Harold started violently, and glanced behind him. 'Is he in town?'

'I was in Pocatello yesterday.'

He looked both relieved and anxious. 'How is he?'

'Much the same, I gather. You didn't tell me he was one step ahead of the butterfly nets.'

'You didn't ask me. Anyway, he isn't like that all the time.'

'But he had to be committed more than once.'

'Yeah.' He hung his head. In the final glare of day I could see the old closet dust in the groove of his hat, and the new sweat staining the hatband.

'It's nothing to blame yourself for,' I said. 'It explains a lot about Mike.'

'I know. The old man was a terror when Mike was a kid. Maw finally had him committed for what he did to Mike and her. Mike left home and never came back, and who could blame him?'

'But you stayed.'

'For a while. I had a trick of pretending I was some place else, like here in California. I finally came out here and went to photography school.'

I returned to the question that interested me. It was really a series of questions about the interlinked lives that brought Mike Harley and Carol Brown from their beginnings in Idaho to their ends in California. Their beginnings and ends had become clear enough. The middle still puzzled me, as well as the ultimate end that lay ahead in darkness.

'I talked to Carol's parents, too,' I said. 'Carol was there earlier in the summer, and she left a suitcase in her room. A letter in it explained to me why you blamed yourself for the Hillman extortion.'

'You saw my letter, eh? I should never have written a letter like that to Mike. I should have known better.' He was hanging his head again.

'It's hard to see ahead and figure what the little things we do will lead to. And you weren't intending to suggest anything wrong.'

'Gosh, no.'

'Anyway, your letter helped me. It led me back here to Otto Sipe, and I hope eventually to the Hillman boy. The boy was holed up here with Sipe from Monday morning till Wednesday night, last night.'

'No kidding.'

'How well did you know Otto Sipe?'

Harold winced away from the question. If he could, he would have disappeared entirely, leaving his dark business suit and black tie and dusty hat suspended between the crisp brown grass and the dry leaves of the magnolia. He said in a voice that didn't want to be heard:

'He was Mike's friend. I got to know him that way. He trained Mike for a boxing career.'

'What kind of a career did he train you for, Harold?'

'Me?'

'You. Didn't Sipe get you the job as hotel photographer here?'

'On account of—I was Mike's brother.'

'I'm sure that had something to do with it. But didn't Sipe want you to help him with his sideline?'

'What sideline was that?'

'Blackmail.'

He shook his head so vehemently that his hat almost fell off. 'I never had any part of the rake-off, honest. He paid me standard rates to take those pictures, a measly buck a throw, and if I didn't do it I'd lose my job. I quit anyway, as soon as I had the chance. It was a dirty business.' He peered up the driveway at the bland decaying face of the hotel. It was stark white now in the twilight. 'I never took any benefit from it. I never even knew who the people were.'

'Not even once?'

'I don't know what you mean.'

'Didn't you take a picture of Captain Hillman and his girl?'

His face was pale and wet. 'I don't know. I never knew their names.'

'Last spring at Newport you recognized Hillman.'

'Sure, he was the exec of Mike's ship. I met him when I went aboard that time.'

'And no other time?'

'No sir.'

'When were you and Mike arrested? In the spring of 1945?'

He nodded. 'The fifth of March. I'm not likely to forget it. It was the only time I ever got arrested. After they let me go I never came back here. Until now.' He looked around at the place as if it had betrayed him a second time.

'If you're telling the truth about the date, you didn't take the picture I'm interested in. It was taken in April.'

'I'm not lying. By that time Otto Sipe had another boy.'

'What gave him so much power around the hotel?'

'I think he had something on the management. He hushed up something for them, long ago, something about a movie star who stayed here.'

'Was Mike staying here at the time he was picked up?'

'Yeah. I let him and Carol use my room, the one that went with the job. I slept in the employees' dormitory. I think Otto

Sipe let Carol stay on in the room for a while after me and Mike were arrested.'

'Was it the room next door to his, at the end of the corridor?'

'Yeah.'

'Did it have a brass bed in it?'

'Yeah. Why?'

'I was just wondering. They haven't changed the furnishings since the war. That interconnecting bathroom would have been handy for Sipe, if he liked Carol.'

He shook his head. 'Not him. He had no use for women. And Carol had no use for him. She got out of there as soon as she could make other arrangements. She went to live with a woman friend in Burbank.'

'Susanna.'

Harold blinked. 'Yeah. That was her name, Susanna. I never met her, but she must have been a nice person.'

'What kind of a girl was Carol?'

'Carol? She was a beauty. When a girl has her looks, you don't think much about going deeper. I mean, there she *was*. I always thought she was an innocent young girl. But Lila says you could fill a book with what I don't know about women.'

I looked at my watch. It was past eight, and Harold had probably taken me as far as he could. Partly to make sure of this, I asked him to come across the highway and see his old acquaintance, Ben Daly. He didn't hang back.

Daly scowled at us from the doorway of his lighted office. Then he recognized Harold, and his brow cleared. He came out and shook hands with him, disregarding me.

'Long time no see, Har.'

'You can say that again.'

They talked to each other across a distance of years, with some warmth and without embarrassment. There was no sign of guilty involvement between them. It didn't follow necessarily, but I pretty well gave up on the idea that either of them was involved in any way with the recent crimes.

I broke in on their conversation: 'Will you give me one minute, Ben? You may be able to help me solve that murder.'

'How? By killing somebody else?'

'By making another identification, if you can.' I brought out Dick Leandro's picture and forced it into his hand. 'Have you ever seen this man?'

He studied the picture for a minute. His hand was unsteady. 'I may have. I'm not sure.'

'When?'

'Last night. He may be the one who came to the hotel last night.'

'The one with the girl, in the new blue Chevvy?'

'Yeah. He could be the one. But I wouldn't want to swear to it in court.'

XXV

THE SANTA MONICA bus station is on a side street off lower Wilshire. At a quarter to nine I left my car at the curb and went in. Stella, that incredible child, was there. She was sitting at the lunch counter at the rear in a position from which she could watch all the doors.

She saw me, of course, and swung around to hide her face in a cup of coffee. I sat beside her. She put down her cup with an impatient rap. The coffee in it looked cold, and had a grayish film on it.

She spoke without looking directly at me, like somebody in a spy movie. 'Go away. You'll frighten Tommy off.'

'He doesn't know me.'

'But I'm supposed to be alone. Besides, you look like a policeman or something.'

'Why is Tommy allergic to policemen?'

'You would be, too, if they locked you up the way they locked him up.'

'If you keep running away, they'll be locking you up, Stella.'

'They're not going to get the chance,' she said, with a sharp sideways glance at me. 'My father took me to a psychiatrist today, to see if I needed to be sent to Laguna Perdida. I told her everything, just as I've told you. She said there was nothing the matter with me at all. So when my father went in to talk to her I walked out the front door and took a taxi to the bus station, and there was a bus just leaving.'

'I'm going to have to drive you home again.'

She said in a very young voice: 'Don't teen-agers have any rights?'

'Yes, including the right to adult protection.'

'I won't go without Tommy!'

Her voice rose and broke on his name. Half the people in the small station were looking at us. The woman behind the lunch counter came over to Stella.

'Is he bothering you, miss?'

She shook her head. 'He's a very good friend.'

This only deepened the woman's suspicions, but it silenced her. I ordered a cup of coffee. When she went to draw it, I said to Stella:

'I won't go without Tommy, either. What did your psychiatrist friend think about him, by the way?'

'She didn't tell me. Why?'

'I was just wondering.'

The waitress brought my coffee. I carried it to the far end of the counter and drank it slowly. It was eight minutes to nine. People were lining up at the loading door, which meant that a bus was expected.

I went out the front, and almost walked into Tommy. He had on slacks and a dirty white shirt. His face was a dirty white, except where a fuzz of beard showed.

'Excuse me, sir,' he said, and stepped around me.

I didn't want to let him get inside, where taking him would create a public scene that would bring in the police. I needed a chance to talk to him before anyone else did. There wasn't much use in trying to persuade him to come with me. He was lean and quick and could certainly outrun me.

These thoughts went through my head in the second before he reached the door of the station. I put both arms around his waist from behind, lifted him off his feet, and carried him wildly struggling to my car. I pushed him into the front seat and got in beside him. Other cars were going by in the road, but nobody stopped to ask me any questions. They never do any more.

Tom let out a single dry sob or whimper, high in his nose. He must have known that this was the end of running.

'My name is Lew Archer,' I said. 'I'm a private detective employed by your father.'

'He isn't my father.'

'An adoptive father is a father, too.'

'Not to me he isn't. I don't want any part of Captain Hillman,' he said with the cold distance of injured youth. 'Or you either.'

I noticed a cut on the knuckle of his right hand. It had been bleeding. He put the knuckle in his mouth and sucked it, looking at me over it. It was hard to take him seriously at that moment. But he was a very serious young man.

'I'm not going back to my cruddy so-called parents.'

'You have nobody else.'

'I have myself.'

'You haven't been handling yourself too well.'

'Another lecture.'

'I'm pointing out a fact. If you could look after yourself decently, you might make out a case for independence. But you've been rampaging around clobbering middle-aged doctors—'

'He tried to make me go home.'

'You're going home. The alternative seems to be a life with bums and criminals.'

'You're talking about my parents, my real parents.' He spoke with conscious drama, but there was also a kind of bitter awe in his voice. 'My mother wasn't a bum and she wasn't a criminal. She was—nice.'

'I didn't mean her.'

'And my father wasn't so bad, either,' he said without conviction.

'Who killed them, Tom?'

His face became blank and tight. It looked like a wooden mask used to fend off suffering.

'I don't know anything about it,' he said in a monotone. 'I didn't know Carol was dead, even, till I saw the papers last night.

I didn't know Mike was dead till I saw the papers today. Next question.'

'Don't be like that, Tom. I'm not a cop, and I'm not your enemy.'

'With the so-called parents I've got, who needs enemies? All my—all Captain Hillman ever wanted was a pet boy around the house, somebody to do tricks. I'm tired to doing tricks for him.'

'You *should* be tired, after this last trick. It was a honey of a trick.'

He gave me his first direct look, half in anger and half in fear. 'I had a right to go with my real parents.'

'Maybe. We won't argue about that. But you certainly had no right to help them extort money from your father.'

'He's not my father.'

'I know that. Do you have to keep saying it?'

'Do you have to keep calling him my father?'

He was a difficult boy. I felt good, anyway. I had him.

'Okay,' I said. 'We'll call him Mr X and we'll call your mother Madam X and we'll call you the Lost Dauphin of France.'

'That isn't so funny.'

He was right. It wasn't.

'Getting back to the twenty-five thousand dollars you helped to take them for, I suppose you know you're an accomplice in a major felony.'

'I didn't know about the money. They didn't tell me. I don't think Carol knew about it, either.'

'That's hard to believe, Tom.'

'It's true. Mike didn't tell us. He just said he had a deal cooking.'

'If you didn't know about the extortion, why did you ride away in the trunk of his car?'

'So I wouldn't be seen. Mike said my dad—' he swallowed the word, with disgust—'he said that Captain Hillman had all the police looking for me, to put me back in Laguna—'

He became aware of his present situation. He peered around furtively, scrambled under the wheel to the far door. I pulled him back into the middle of the seat and put an armlock on him.

'You're staying with me, Tom, if I have to use handcuffs.'

'Fuzz!'

The jeering word came strangely from him, like a foreign word he was trying to make his own. It bothered me. Boys, like men, have to belong to something. Tom had felt betrayed by one world, the plush deceptive world of Ralph Hillman, with schools like Laguna Perdida on the underside of the weave. He had plunged blindly into another world, and now he had lost that. His mind must be desperate for a place to rest, I thought, and I wasn't doing much of a job of providing one.

A bus came down the street. As it turned into the loading area, I caught a glimpse of passengers at the windows, travel-drugged and blasé. California here we come, right back where we started from.

I relaxed my grip on Tom. 'I couldn't let you go,' I said, 'even if I wanted to. You're not stupid. Try for once to figure out how this looks to other people.'

'This?'

'The whole charade. Your running away from school—for which I certainly don't blame you—'

'Thanks a lot.'

I disregarded his irony. 'And the phony kidnapping and all the rest of it. An adopted son is just as important as a real one to his parents. Yours have been worried sick about you.'

'I bet.'

'Neither one of them gave a damn about the money, incidentally. It's you they cared about, and care about.'

'There's something missing,' he said.

'What?'

'The violin accompaniment.'

'You're a hard boy to talk to, Tom.'

'My *friends* don't think so.'

'What's a friend? Somebody who lets you run wild?'

'Somebody who doesn't want to throw me into the Black Hole of Calcutta, otherwise known as Laguna Perdida School.'

'I don't.'

'You say you don't. But you're working for Captain Hillman, and he does.'

'Not any more.'

The boy shook his head. 'I don't believe you, and I don't believe him. After a few things *happen* to you, you start to believe what people do, not what they say. People like the Hillmans would think that a person like Carol was a nothing, a nothing woman. But she wasn't to me. She liked me. She treated me well. Even my real father never raised his hand to me. The only trouble we had was about the way he treated Carol.'

He had dropped his brittle sardonic front and was talking to me in a human voice. Stella chose this moment to come out of the loading area onto the sidewalk. Her faced was pinched with disappointment.

Tom caught sight of her almost as soon as I did. His eyes lit up as if she was an angel from some lost paradise. He leaned across me.

'Hey! Stell!'

She came running. I got out of the car and let her take my place beside the boy. They didn't embrace or kiss. Perhaps their hands met briefly. I got in behind the wheel.

Stella was saying: 'It *feels* as though you've been gone for ages.'

'It does to me, too.'

'You should have called me sooner.'

'I did.'

'I mean, right away.'

'I was afraid you'd—do what you did.' He jerked his chin in my direction.

'I didn't, though. Not really. It was his idea. Anyway, you have to go home. We both do.'

'I have no home.'

'Neither have I, then. Mine's just as bad as yours.'

'No, it isn't.'

'Yes, it is. Anyway,' she said to clinch the argument, 'you need a bath. I can smell you. And a shave.'

I glanced at his face. It had a pleased silly embarrassed expression.

The street was empty of traffic at the moment. I started the car and made a U-turn toward the south. Tom offered no objection.

Once on the freeway, in that anonymous world of rushing lights and darkness, he began to talk in his human voice to Stella.

Carol had phoned him, using his personal number, several weeks before. She wanted to arrange a meeting with him. That night, driving Ralph Hillman's Cadillac, he picked her up at the view-point overlooking the sea near Dack's Auto Court.

He parked in an orange grove that smelled of weddings and listened to the story of her life. Even though he'd often doubted that he belonged to the Hillmans, it was hard for him to believe that he was Carol's son. But he was strongly drawn to her. The relationship was like an escape hatch in Captain Hillman's tight little ship. He kept going back to Carol, and eventually he believed her. He even began to love her in a way.

'Why didn't you tell me about her?' Stella said. 'I would have liked to know her.'

'No, you wouldn't.' His voice was rough. 'Anyway, I had to get to know her myself first. I had to get adjusted to the whole idea of my mother. And then I had to decide what to do. You see, she wanted to leave my father. He gave her a hard time, he always had. She said if she didn't get away from him soon, she'd never be able to. She wasn't good at standing up for herself, and she wanted my help. Besides, I think she knew he was up to something.'

'You mean the kidnapping and all?' she said.

'I think she knew it and she didn't know it. You know how women are.'

'I know my mother,' she answered sagely.

They had forgotten me. I was the friendly chauffer, good old graying Lew Archer, and we would go on driving like this forever through a night so dangerous that it had to feel secure. I remembered a kind of poem or parable that Susanna had quoted to me years before. A bird came in through a window at one end of a lighted hall, flew the length of the hall, and out through another window into darkness: that was the span of a human life. The headlights that rose in the distance and swooped by and fell away behind us reminded me of Susanna's briefly lighted bird. I wished that she was with me.

Tom was telling Stella how he first met his father. Mike had been kept in the background the first week; he was supposed to be in Los Angeles looking for work. Finally, on the Saturday night, Tom met him at the auto court.

'That was the night you borrowed our car, wasn't it?'

'Yeah. My fa—Ralph had me grounded, you know. Carol spilled some wine on the front seat of the car and he smelled it. He thought I was driving and drinking.'

'Did Carol drink much?'

'Quite a bit. She drank a lot that Saturday night. So did he. I had some wine, too.'

'You're not old enough.'

'It was with dinner,' he said. 'Carol cooked spaghetti. Spaghetti à la Pocatello, she called it. She sang some of the old songs for me, like "Sentimental Journey." It was kind of fun,' he said doubtfully.

'Is that why you didn't come home?'

'No. I—' The word caught in his throat. 'I—' His face, which I could see in the rear-view mirror, became contorted with effort. He couldn't finish the sentence.

'Did you want to stay with them?' Stella said after a while.

'No. I don't know.'

'How did you like your father?'

'He was all right, I guess, until he got drunk. We played some gin rummy and he didn't win, so he broke up the game. He started to take it out on Carol. I almost had a fight with him. He said he used to be a boxer and I'd be crazy to try it, that his fists could kill.'

'It sounds like a terrible evening.'

'That part of it wasn't so good.'

'What part of it was?'

'When she sang the old songs. And she told me about my grandfather in Pocatello.'

'Did that take all night?' she said a little tartly.

'I didn't *stay* with them all night. I left around ten o'clock, when we almost had the fight. I—' The same word stuck in his throat again, as if it was involved with secret meanings that wouldn't let it be spoken.

'What did you do?'

'I went and parked on the view-point where I picked her up

the first time. I sat there until nearly two o'clock, watching the stars and listening, you know, to the sea. The sea and the highway. I was trying to figure out what I should do, where I belonged. I still haven't got it figured out.' He added, in a voice that was conscious of me: 'Now I guess I don't have any choice. They'll put me back in the Black Hole of Calcutta.'

'Me too,' she said with a nervous giggle. 'We can send each other secret notes. Tap out messages on the bars and stuff.'

'It isn't funny, Stell. Everybody out there is crazy, even some of the staff. They get that way.'

'You're changing the subject,' she said. 'What did you do at two a.m.?'

'I went to see Sam Jackman when he got off work. I thought I could ask him what to do, but I found out that I couldn't. I just couldn't tell him that they were my parents. So I went out in the country, and drove around for a few hours. I didn't want to go home, and I didn't want to go back to the auto court.'

'So you turned the car over and tried to kill yourself.'

'I—' Silence set in again, and this time it lasted. He sat bolt upright, staring ahead, watching the headlights rise out of the darkness. After a time I noticed that Stella's arm was across his shoulders. His face was streaked with tears.

XXVI

I DROPPED STELLA off first. She refused to get out of the car until Tom promised that he wouldn't go away again, ever, without telling her.

Her father came out of the house, walking on his heels. He put his arms around her. With a kind of resigned affection, she laid her head neatly against his shoulder. Maybe they had learned something, or were learning. People sometimes do.

They went inside, and I turned down the driveway.

'He's just a fake,' Tom said. 'Stella lent me the car, and then he turned around and told the police I stole it.'

'I believe he thought so at the time.'

'But he found out the truth later, from Stella, and went right on claiming I stole it.'

'Dishonesty keeps creeping in,' I said. 'We all have to watch it.'

He thought this over, and decided that I had insulted him. 'Is that supposed to be a crack at me?'

'No. I think you're honest, so far as you understand what you're talking about. But you only see one side, your own, and it seems to consist mainly of grievances.'

'I have a lot of them,' he admitted. After a moment he said: 'You're wrong about me only seeing one side, though. I know how my—my adoptive parents are supposed to feel, but I know how I feel, too. I can't go on being split down the middle. That's how I felt, you know, these last few nights, like somebody took a cleaver and split me down the middle. I lay awake on that old brass bed, where Mike and Carol, you know, conceived me—with old Sipe snoring in the other room, and I was there and I wasn't there. You know? I mean I couldn't believe that I was me and this was my life and those people were my parents. I never believed the Hillmans were, either. They always seemed to be putting on an act. Maybe,' he said half-seriously, 'I was dropped from another planet.'

'You've been reading too much science fiction.'

'I don't *really* believe that. I *know* who my parents were. Carol told me. Mike told me. The doctor told me, and that made it official. But I still have a hard time telling my*self*.'

'Stop trying to force it. It doesn't matter so much who your parents were.'

'It does to me,' he said earnestly. 'It's the most important thing in my life.'

We were approaching the Hillmans' mailbox. I had been driving slowly, immersed in the conversation, and now I pulled into the driveway and stopped entirely.

'I sometimes think children should be anonymous.'

'How do you mean, Mr Archer?' It was the first time he had called me by my name.

'I have no plan. I'd just like to change the emphasis slightly. People are trying so hard to live through their children. And the children keep trying so hard to live up to their parents, or live them down. Everybody's living through or for or against somebody else. It doesn't make too much sense, and it isn't working too well.'

I was trying to free his mind a little, before he had to face the next big change. I didn't succeed. 'It doesn't work when they lie to you,' he said. 'They lied to me. They pretended I was their own flesh and blood. I thought there was something missing in me when I couldn't feel like their son.'

'I've talked to your mother about this—Elaine—and she bitterly regrets it.'

'I bet.'

'Let's not get off on that routine, Tom.'

He was silent for a while. 'I suppose I have to go and talk to them, but I don't want to live with them, and I'm not going to put on any phony feelings.'

No phoniness, I thought, was the code of the new generation, at least the ones who were worth anything. It was a fairly decent ideal, but it sometimes worked out cruelly in practice.

'You can't forgive them for Laguna Perdida.'

'Could you?'

I had to think about my answer. 'It would depend on their reasons. I imagine some pretty desperate parents end up there as a last resort with some pretty wild sons and daughters.'

'They're desperate, all right,' he said. 'Ralph and Elaine get desperate very easily. They can't stand trouble. Sweep it under the rug. All they wanted to do was get me out of sight, when I stopped being their performing boy. And I had all these terrible things on my mind.' He put his hands to his head, to calm the terrible things. He was close to breaking down.

'I'm sorry, Tom. But didn't something crucial happen that Sunday morning?'

He peered at me under his raised arm. 'They told you, eh?'

'No. I'm asking you to tell me.'

'Ask them.'

It was all he would say.

I drove up the winding blacktop lane to the top of the knoll. Lights were blazing outside and inside the house. The harsh white floods made the stucco walls look ugly and unreal. Black shadows lurked under the melodramatic Moorish arches.

There was something a little melodramatic in the way Ralph Hillman stepped out from one of the arches into the light. He wasn't the wreck Susanna had described, at least not superficially. His handsome silver head was sleekly brushed. His face was tightly composed. He held himself erect, and even trotted a few steps as he came toward my side of the car. He was wearing a wine-colored jacket with a rolled collar.

'Prodigal son returneth,' Tom was saying beside me in scared bravado. 'But they didn't kill the fatted calf, they killed the prodigal son.'

Hillman said: 'I thought you were Lieutenant Bastian.'

'Are you expecting him?'

'Yes. He says he has something to show me.'

He stooped to look in the window and saw Tom. His eyes dilated.

'My boy!' His hoarse, whisky-laden voice hardly dared to believe what it was saying. 'You've come back.'

'Yeah. I'm here.'

Hillman trotted around to the other side of the car and opened the door. 'Come out and let me look at you.'

With a brief, noncommittal glance in my direction, Tom climbed out. His movements were stiff and tentative, like a much older man's. Hillman put his hands on the boy's shoulders and held him at arm's length, turning him so that his face was in the light.

'How *are* you, Tom?'

'I'm okay. How are you?'

'Wonderful, now that you're here.' I didn't doubt that Hillman's feeling was sincere, but his expression of it was somehow wrong. Phony. And I could see Tom wince under his hands.

Elaine Hillman came out of the house. I went to meet her. The floodlights multiplied the lines in her face and leached it of any color it might have had. She was pared so thin that she reminded me vaguely of concentration camps. Her eyes were brilliantly alive.

'You've brought him back, Mr Archer. Bless you.'

She slipped her hand through my arm and let me take her to him. He stood like a dutiful son while she stood on her toes and kissed him on his grimy tear-runneled cheek.

Then he backed away from both of them. He stood leaning against the side of my car with his thumbs in the waistband of his slacks. I'd seen a hundred boys standing as he was standing against cars both hot and cold, on the curb of a street or the shoulder of a highway, while men in uniform questioned them. The sound of the distant highway faintly disturbed the edges of the silence I was listening to now.

Tom said: 'I don't want to hurt anybody. I never did. Or maybe I did, I don't know. Anyway, there's no use going on pretending. You see, I know who I am. Mike and Carol Harley were my father and mother. You knew it, too, didn't you?'

'I didn't,' Elaine said quickly.

'But you knew *you* weren't my mother.'

'Yes. Of course I knew that.'

She glanced down at her body and then, almost wistfully, at her husband. He turned away from both of them. His face had momentarily come apart. He seemed to be in pain, which he wanted to hide.

'One of you must have known who I really was.' Tom said to Hillman: 'You knew, didn't you?'

Hillman didn't answer. Tom said in a high desperate voice: 'I can't stay here. You're both a couple of phonies. You put on a big act for all these years, and as soon as I step out of line you give me the shaft.'

Hillman found his voice. 'I should think it was the other way around.'

'Okay, so I did wrong. Stand me up against a wall and shoot me.'

The boy's voice was slightly hysterical, but it wasn't that that bothered me so much. He seemed to be shifting from attitude to attitude, even from class to class, trying to find a place where he could stand. I went and stood beside him.

'Nobody's talking about punishing you,' Hillman said. 'But a homicidal attack is something that can't be laughed off.'

'You're talking crap,' the boy said.

Hillman's chin came up. 'Don't *speak* to me like that!'

'Or what will you do? Lock me up with a bunch of psychos and throw away the key?'

'I didn't *say* that.'

'No. You just went ahead and did it.'

'Perhaps I acted hastily.'

'Yes,' Elaine put in. 'Your father acted hastily. Now let's forget the whole thing and go inside and be friends.'

'He isn't my father,' Tom said stubbornly.

'But we can all be friends, anyway. Can't we, Tom?' Her voice and look were imploring. 'Can't we forget the bad things and simply be glad they're over and that we're all together?'

'I don't know. I'd like to go away for a while and live by myself and think things through. What would be wrong with it? I'm old enough.'

'That's nonsense.' Hillman shouldn't have said it. A second later his eyes showed that he knew he shouldn't have. He stepped forward and put his hand on the boy's shoulder. 'Maybe that isn't such a bad idea, after all. We're intelligent people, we ought to be able to work something out between us. There's the lodge in Oregon, for example, where you and I were planning to go next month. We could step up our schedule and synch our watches, eh?'

The performance was forced. Tom listened to it without interest or hope. After a bit Elaine put her hand inside her husband's arm and drew him toward the house. Tom and I followed along.

Mrs Perez was waiting at the door. There was warmth in her greeting, and even some in Tom's response. They had a discussion about food. Tom said he would like a hamburger sandwich with pea soup. Mrs Perez darted jouncily away.

Hillman surveyed the boy in the light of the chandelier. 'You'd better go up and bathe and change your clothes.'

'Now?'

'It's just a suggestion,' Hillman said placatingly. 'Lieutenant Bastian of the sheriff's department is on his way over. I'd like you—you should be looking more like yourself.'

'Is he going to take me away? Is that the idea?'

'Not if I can help it,' Hillman said. 'Look, I'll come up with you.'

'I can dress myself, Dad!' The word slipped out, irretrievable and undeniable.

'But we ought to go over what you're going to say to him. There's no use putting your neck in a noose—I mean—'

'I'll just tell him the truth.'

The boy walked away from him toward the stairs. Ralph and Elaine Hillman followed him with their eyes until he was out of sight, and then they followed his footsteps with their ears. The difficult god of the household had returned and the household was functioning again, in its difficult way.

We went into the sitting room. Hillman continued across it into the bar alcove. He made himself a drink, absently, as if he was simply trying to find something to do with his hands and then with his mouth.

When we came out with the drink in his hand, he reminded me of an actor stepping out through a proscenium arch to join the audience.

'Ungrateful sons are like a serpent's tooth,' he said, not very conversationally.

Elaine spoke up distinctly from the chesterfield: 'If you're attempting to quote from *King Lear*, the correct quotation is: "How sharper than a serpent's tooth it is to have a thankless child!" But it isn't terribly appropriate, since Tom is not your child. A more apt quotation from the same work would be Edmund's line, "Now, gods, stand up for bastards!" '

He knocked back his drink and moved towards her, lurching just a little. 'I resent your saying that.'

'That's your privilege, and your habit.'

'Tom is not a bastard. His parents were legally married.'

'It hardly matters, considering their background. Did you and your precious Dr Weintraub have to choose the offspring of criminals?'

Her voice was cold and bitter. She seemed, after years of silence, to be speaking out and striking back at him.

'Look,' he said, 'he's back. I'm glad he's back. You are,

too. And we want him to stay with us, don't we?'

'I want what's best for him.'

'I *know* what's best for him.' He spread his arms, swinging them a little from side to side, as if he was making Tom a gift of the house and the life that went on inside it.

'You don't know what's best for anybody, Ralph. Having men under you, you got into the habit of thinking you knew. But you really don't. I'm interested in Mr Archer's opinion. Come and sit here beside me,' she said to me, 'and tell me what you think.'

'What exactly is the subject?' I said as I sat down.

'Tom. What kind of a future should we plan for him?'

'I don't think you can do it for him. Let him do his own planning.'

Hillman said across the room: 'But all he wants to do is go away by himself.'

'I admit that isn't such a good idea. We should be able to persuade him to tone it down. Let him live with another family for a year. Or send him to prep school. After that, he'll be going away to college, anyway.'

'Good Lord, do you think he'll make it to college?'

'Of course he will, Ralph.' She turned to me. 'But is he ready now for any ordinary prep school? Could he survive it?'

'He survived the last two weeks.'

'Yes. We have to thank God for that. And you.'

Hillman came and stood over me, shaking the ice in his glass. 'Just what was the situation with those people? Was Tom in league with them against us? Understand me, I don't intend to punish him or do anything at all about it. I just want to know.'

I answered him slowly and carefully. 'You can hardly talk about a boy being in league with his mother and father. He was confused. He still is. He believed you had turned against him when you put him in Laguna Perdida School. You don't have to be a psychiatrist to know that that isn't the kind of school he needs.'

'I'm afraid you aren't conversant with all the facts.'

'What are they?'

He shook his head. 'Go on with what you were saying. Was he in cahoots with those people?'

'Not in the way you mean. But they offered him an out, physically and emotionally, and he took it. Apparently his mother was kind to him.'

'*I* was always kind to him,' Elaine said. She shot a fierce upward glance at her husband. 'But there was falsity in the house, undermining everything.'

I said: 'There was falseness in the other house, too, at Dack's Auto Court. There's no doubt that Mike Harley was conning him, setting him up for the phony kidnapping. He didn't let his paternal feelings interfere. Carol was another matter. If she was conning Tom, she was conning herself, too. Tom put it something like this: she knew Harley was up to something, but she didn't let herself know. You get that way after twenty years of living with a man like Harley.'

Elaine nodded slightly. I think it was a comment on her own marriage. She said. 'I'm worried about Tom's heredity, with such parents.'

The blood rushed into Hillman's face. 'For God's sake, that's really reaching for trouble.'

'I hardly need to reach for it,' she said quietly. 'It's in my lap.' She looked at him as if he had placed it there.

He turned and walked the length of the room, returned part way, and went into the bar. He poured more whisky over the ice in his glass, and drank it down. Elaine watched him with critical eyes, which he was aware of.

'It settles my nerves,' he said.

'I hadn't noticed.'

He looked at his watch and paced up and down the room. He lost his balance once and had to make a side step.

'Why doesn't Bastian come and get it over with?' he said. It's getting late. I was expecting Dick tonight, but I guess he found something more interesting to do.' He burst out at his wife: 'This is a dismal household, you know that?'

'I've been aware of it for many years. I tried to keep it together for Tom's sake. That's rather funny, isn't it?'

'I don't see anything funny about it.'

I didn't, either. The broken edges of their marriage were rubbing together like the unset ends of a bone that had been fractured but was still living.

Bastian arrived at last. He came into the reception hall carrying a black metal evidence case, and he was dark-faced and grim. Even the news that Tom was safe at home failed to cheer him much.

'Where is he?'

'Taking a bath,' Hillman said.

'I've got to talk to him. I want a full statement.'

'Not tonight, Lieutenant. The boy's been through the wringer.'

'But he's the most important witness we have.'

'I know that. He'll give you his full story tomorrow.'

Bastian glanced from him to me. We were just inside the front door, and Hillman seemed unwilling to let him come in any farther.

'I expected better cooperation, Mr Hillman. You've had cooperation from us. But come to think of it, we haven't had it from you at any time.'

'Don't give me any lectures, Lieutenant. My son is home, and it wasn't thanks to you that we got him back.'

'A lot of police work went into it,' I said. 'Lieutenant Bastian and I have been working closely together. We still are, I hope.'

Hillman transferred his glare to me. He looked ready to order us both out. I said to Bastian:

'You've got something to show us, Lieutenant, is that right?'

'Yes.' He held up his evidence case. 'You've already seen it, Archer. I'm not sure if Mr Hillman has or not.'

'What is it?'

'I'll show you. I prefer not to describe it beforehand. Could we sit down at a table?'

Hillman led us to the library and seated us at a table with a green-shaded reading lamp in the middle, which he switched on. It lit up the tablecloth brilliantly and cast the rest of the room, including our faces, into greenish shadow. Bastian opened the evidence box. It contained the hunting knife with the striped handle which I had found stuck in Mike Harley's ribs.

Hillman drew in his breath sharply.

'You recognize it, do you?' Bastian said.

'No. I do not.'

'Pick it up and examine it more closely. It's quite all right to handle it. It's already been processed for fingerprints and blood.'

Hillman didn't move. 'Blood?'

'This is the knife that was used to kill Mike Harley. We're almost certain that it was also used to kill the other decedent, Carol Harley. Blood of her type was found on it, as well as her husband's type. Also it fits her wound, the autopsist tells me. Pick it up, Mr Hillman.'

In a gingerly movement Hillman reached out and took it from the box. He turned it over and read the maker's name on the broad shining blade.

'It looks like a good knife,' he said. 'But I'm afraid I don't recognize it.'

'Would you say that under oath?'

'I'd have to. I never saw it before.'

Bastian, with the air of a parent removing a dangerous toy, lifted the knife from his hands. 'I don't want to say you're lying, Mr Hillman. I do have a witness who contradicts you on this. Mr Botkin, who owns the surplus goods store on lower Main, says that he sold you this knife.' He shook the knife, point foremost, at Hillman's face.

Hillman looked scared and sick and obstinate. 'It must have been somebody else. He must be mistaken.'

'No. He knows you personally.'

'I don't know him.'

'You're a very well known man, sir, and Mr Botkin is certain that you were in his store early this month. Perhaps I can refresh your recollection. You mentioned to Mr Botkin, in connection with the purchase of this knife, that you were planning a little trip to Oregon with your son. You also complained to Botkin, as a lower Main Street businessman, about an alleged laxness at The Barroom Floor. It had to do with selling liquor to minors, I believe. Do you remember the conversation now?'

'No,' Hillman said. 'I do not. The man is lying.'

'Why would he be lying?'

'I have no idea. Go and find out. It's not my job to do your police work for you.'

He stood up, dismissing Bastian. Bastian was unwilling to be dismissed. 'I don't think you're well advised to take this attitude, Mr Hillman. If you purchased this knife from Mr Botkin, now is the time to say so. Your previous denial need never go out of this room.'

Bastian looked to me for support. I remembered what Botkin had said to me about The Barroom Floor. It was practically certain that his conversation with Hillman had taken place. It didn't follow necessarily that Hillman had bought the knife, but he probably had.

I said: 'It's time all the facts were laid out on the table, Mr Hillman.'

'I can't tell him what isn't so, can I?'

'No. I wouldn't advise that. Have you thought of talking this over with your attorney?'

'I'm thinking about it now.' Hillman had sobered. Droplets of clear liquid stood on his forehead as if the press of the situation had squeezed the alcohol out of him. He said to Bastian: 'I gather you're more or less accusing me of murder.'

'No, I am not.' Bastian added in a formal tone: 'You can, of course, stand on your constitutional rights.'

Hillman shook his head angrily. Some of his fine light hair fell over his forehead. Under it his eyes glittered like metal triangles. He was an extraordinarily handsome man. His unremitting knowledge of this showed in the caressive movement of the hand with which he pushed his hair back into place.

'Look,' he said, 'could we continue this séance in the morning? I've had a hard week, and I'd like a chance to sleep on this business. I've had no real sleep since Monday.'

'Neither have I,' Bastian said.

'Maybe you need some sleep, too. This harassing approach isn't really such a good idea.'

'There was no harassment.'

'I'll be the judge of that.' Hillman's voice rose. 'You brought that knife into my home and shook it in my face. I have a witness to that,' he added, meaning me.

I said: 'Let's not get bogged down in petty arguments. Lieutenant Bastian and I have some business to discuss.'

'Anything you say to him you'll have to say in front of me.'

'All right.'

'After I talk to the boy,' Bastian said.

Hillman made a curt gesture with his hand. 'You're not talking to him. I don't believe I'll let you talk to him tomorrow, either. There are, after all, medical considerations.'

'Are you a medical man?'

'I have medical men at my disposal.'

'I'm sure you do. So do we.'

The two men faced each other in quiet fury. They were opposites in many ways. Bastian was a saturnine Puritan, absolutely honest, a stickler for detail, a policeman before he was a man. Hillman's personality was less clear. It had romantic and actorish elements, which often mask deep evasions. His career had been meteoric, but it was the kind of career that sometimes left a man empty-handed in middle life.

'Do you have something to say to the lieutenant?' Hillman asked me. 'Before he leaves?'

'Yes. You may not like this, Mr Hillman. I don't. Last night a young man driving a late-model blue Chevrolet was seen in the driveway of the Barcelona Hotel. It's where Mike Harley was found stabbed, with that knife.' I pointed to the evidence box on the table. 'The young man has been tentatively identified as Dick Leandro.'

'Who made the identification?' Bastian said.

'Ben Daly, the service-station operator.'

'The man who killed Sipe.'

'Yes.'

'He's either mistaken or lying,' Hillman said. 'Dick drives a blue car, but it's a small sports car, a Triumph.'

'Does he have access to a blue Chevrolet?'

'Not to my knowledge. You're surely not trying to involve Dick in this mess.'

'If he's involved, we have to know about it.' I said to Bastian: 'Maybe you can determine whether he borrowed or rented a blue Chevrolet last night. Or it's barely possible that he stole one.'

'Will do,' Bastian said.

Hillman said nothing.

XXVII

BASTIAN PICKED UP his evidence case and shut it with a click. He walked out without a sign to either of us. He was treating Hillman as if he no longer existed. He was treating me in such a way that I could stay with Hillman.

Hillman watched him from the entrance to the library until he was safely across the reception hall and out the front door. Then he came back into the room. Instead of returning to the table where I was, he went to the wall of photographs where the squadron on the flight deck hung in green deep-sea light.

'What goes on around here?' he said. 'Somebody took down Dick's picture.'

'I did, for identification purposes.'

I got it out of my pocket. Hillman came and took it away from me. The glass was smudged by fingers, and he rubbed it with the sleeve of his jacket.

'You had no right to take it. What are you trying to do to Dick, anyway?'

'Get at the truth about him.'

'There *is* no mysterious truth about him. He's a perfectly nice ordinary kid.'

'I hope so.'

'Look here,' he said, 'you've accomplished what I hired you to do. Don't think I'm ungrateful—I'm planning to give you a substantial bonus. But I didn't hire you to investigate those murders.'

'And I don't get the bonus unless I stop?'

'I didn't say that.'

'You didn't have to.'

He spread his hands on the table and leaned above me, heavy-faced and powerful. 'Just how do you get to talk to your betters the way you've been talking to me?'

'By my betters you mean people with more money?'

'Roughly, yes.'

'I'll tell you, Mr Hillman. I rather like you. I'm trying to talk straight to you because somebody has to. You're headed on a collision course with the law. If you stay on it, you're going to get hurt.'

His face stiffened and his eyes narrowed. He didn't like to be told anything. He liked to do the telling.

'I could buy and sell Bastian.'

'You can't if he's not for sale. You know damn well he isn't.'

He straightened, raising his head out of the light into the greenish shadow. His face resembled old bronze, except that it was working. After a time he said:

'What do you think I ought to do?'

'Start telling the truth.'

'Dammit, you imply I haven't been.'

'I'm doing more than imply it, Mr Hillman.'

He turned on me with his fists clenched, ready to hit me. I remained sitting. He walked away and came back. Without whisky, he was getting very jumpy.

'I suppose you think I killed them.'

'I'm not doing any speculating. I am morally certain you bought that knife from Botkin.'

'How can you be certain?'

'I've talked to the man.'

'Who authorized you to? I'm not paying you to gather evidence against me.'

I said, rather wearily: 'Couldn't we forget about your wonderful money for a while, and just sit here and talk like a couple of human beings? A couple of human beings in a bind?'

He considered this. Eventually he said: 'You're not in a bind. I am.'

'Tell me about it. Unless you actually did commit those murders. In which case you should tell your lawyer and nobody else.'

'I didn't. I almost wish I had.' He sat down across from me, slumping forward a little, with his arms resting on the tabletop. 'I admit I bought the knife. I don't intend to admit it to anyone else. Botkin will have to be persuaded to change his story.'

'How?'

'He can't make anything out of that store of his. I ought to know, my father owned one like it in South Boston. I can give Botkin enough money to retire to Mexico.'

I was a bit appalled, not so much by the suggestion of crude subornation—I'd often heard it before—as by the fact that Hillman was making it. In the decades since he commanded a squadron at Midway, he must have bumped down quite a few moral steps.

I said: 'You better forget about that approach, Mr Hillman. It's part of the collision course with the law I was talking about. And you'll end up sunk.'

'I'm sunk now,' he said in an even voice.

He laid his head down on his arms. His hair spilled forward like a broken white sheaf. I could see the naked pink circle on the crown which was ordinarily hidden. It was like a tonsure of mortality.

'What did you do with the knife?' I said to him. 'Did you give it to Dick Leandro?'

'No.' Spreading his hands on the tablecloth, he pushed himself upright. His moist palms slipped and squeaked on the polished surface. 'I wish I had.'

'Was Tom the one you gave it to?'

He groaned. 'I not only gave it to him. I told Botkin I was buying the bloody thing as a gift for him. Bastian must be aware of that, but he's holding it back.'

'Bastian would,' I said. 'It still doesn't follow that Tom used it on his father and mother. He certainly had no reason to kill his mother.'

'He doesn't need a rational motive. You don't know Tom.'

'You keep telling me that. At the same time you keep refusing to fill in the picture.'

'It's a fairly ugly picture.'

'Something was said tonight about a homicidal attack.'

'I didn't mean to let that slip out.'

'Who attacked whom and why?'

'Tom threatened Elaine with a loaded gun. He wasn't kidding, either.'

'Was this the Sunday-morning episode you've been suppressing?'

He nodded. 'I think the accident must have affected his mind. When I got home from the judge's house, he had her in his room. He was holding my revolver with the muzzle against her head'—Hillman pressed his fingertip into his temple—'and he had her down on her knees, begging for mercy. Literally begging. I didn't know whether he was going to give me the gun, either. For a minute he held it on me. I half expected him to shoot me.'

I could feel the hairs prickling at the nape of my neck. It was an ugly picture, all right. What was worse, it was a classic one: the schizophrenic execution killer.

'Did he say anything when you took the gun?'

'Not a word. He handed it over in a rather formal way. He acted like a kind of automaton. He didn't seem to realize what he'd done, or tried to do.'

'Had he said anything to your wife?'

'Yes. He said he would kill her if she didn't leave him alone. She'd simply gone to his room to offer him some food, and he went into this silent white rage of his.'

'He had a lot of things on his mind,' I said, 'and he'd been up all night. He told me something about it. You might say it was the crucial night of his young life. He met his real father for the first time'—Hillman grimaced—'which must have been a fairly shattering experience. You might say he was lost between two worlds, and blaming you and your wife for not preparing him. You should have, you know. You had no right to cheat him of the facts, whether you liked them or not. When the facts finally hit him, it was more than he could handle. He deliberately turned the car over that morning.'

'You mean he attempted suicide?' Hillman said.

'He made a stab at it. I think it was more a signal that his life was out of control. He didn't let go of the steering wheel, and he wasn't badly hurt. Nobody got hurt in the gun incident, either.'

'You've got to take it seriously, though. He was in dead earnest.'

'Maybe. I'm not trying to brush it off. Have you talked it over with a psychiatrist?'

'I have not. There are certain things you don't let out of the family.'

'That depends on the family.'

'Look,' he said, 'I was afraid they wouldn't admit him to the school if they knew he was that violent.'

'Would that have been such a tragedy?'

'I had to do something with him. I don't know what I'm going to do with him now.' He bowed his disheveled head.

'You need better advice than I can give you, legal and psychiatric.'

'You're assuming he killed those two people.'

'Not necessarily. Why don't you ask Dr Weintraub to recommend somebody?'

Hillman jerked himself upright. 'That old woman?'

'I understood he was an old friend of yours, and he knows something about psychiatry.'

'Weinie has a worm's-eye knowledge, I suppose.' His voice rasped with contempt. 'He had a nervous breakdown after Midway. We had to send him stateside to recuperate, while men were dying. While men were dying,' Hillman repeated. Then he seemed to surround himself with silence.

He sat in a listening attitude. I waited. His angry face became smooth and his voice changed with it. 'Jesus, that was a day. We lost more than half of our TBD's. The Zekes took them like sitting ducks. I couldn't bring them back. I don't blame Weinie for breaking down, so many men died on him.'

His voice was hushed. His eyes were distant. He didn't even seem aware of my presence. His mind was over the edge of the world where his men had died, and he had died more than a little.

'The hell of it is,' he was saying, 'I love Tom. We haven't been close for years, and he's been hard to handle. But he's my son, and I love him.'

'I'm sure you do. But maybe you want more than Tom can give you. He can't give you back your dead pilots.'

Hillman didn't understand me. He seemed bewildered. His gray eyes were clouded.

'What did you say?'

'Perhaps you were expecting too much from the boy.'

'In what way?'

'Forget it,' I said.

Hillman was hurt. 'You think I expect too much? I've been getting damn little. And look what I'm willing to give him.' He spread his arms again, to embrace the house and everything he owned. 'Why, he can have every nickel I possess for his defense. We'll get him off and go to another country to live.'

'You're away ahead of yourself, Mr Hillman. He hasn't been charged with anything yet.'

'He will be.' His voice sounded both fatalistic and defiant.

'Maybe. Let's consider the possibilities. The only evidence against him is the knife, and that's pretty dubious if you think about it. He didn't take it with him, surely, when you put him in Laguna Perdida.'

'He may have. I didn't search him.'

'I'm willing to bet they did.'

Hillman narrowed his eyes until they were just a glitter between the folded lids. 'You're right, Archer. He didn't have the knife when he left the house. I remember seeing it afterwards, that same day.'

'Where was it?'

'In his room, in one of the chests of drawers.'

'And you left it in the drawer?'

'There was no reason not to.'

'Then anybody with access to the house could have got hold of it?'

'Yes. Unfortunately that includes Tom. He could have sneaked in after he escaped from the school.'

'It also includes Dick Leandro, who wouldn't have had to sneak in. He's in and out of the house all the time, isn't he?'

'I suppose he is. That doesn't prove anything.'

'No, but when you put it together with the fact that Dick was probably seen at the Barcelona Hotel last night, it starts you thinking about him. There's still something missing in this case, you know. The equations don't balance.'

'Dick isn't your missing quantity,' he said hastily.

'You're quite protective about Dick.'

'I'm fond of him. Why shouldn't I be? He's a nice boy, and I've been able to help him. Dammit, Archer.' His voice deepened. 'When a fellow reaches a certain age, he needs to pass on what he knows, or part of it, to a younger fellow.'

'Are you thinking of passing on some money, too?'

'We may eventually. It will depend on Elaine. She controls the main money. But I can assure you it couldn't matter to Dick.'

'It matters to everybody. I think it matters very much to Dick. He's a pleaser.'

'What is that supposed to mean?'

'You know what it means. He lives by pleasing people, mainly you. Tell me this. Does Dick know about the gun incident in Tom's room?'

'Yes. He was with me that Sunday morning. He drove me to the judge's house and home again.'

'He gets in on a lot of things,' I said.

'That's natural. He's virtually a member of the family. As a matter of fact, I expected him tonight. He said he had something he wanted to talk over with me.' He looked at his watch. 'But it's too late now. It's past eleven o'clock.'

'Get him out here anyway, will you?'

'Not tonight. I've had it. I don't want to have to pull my face together and put on a front for Dick now.'

He looked at me a little sheepishly. He had revealed himself to me, a vain man who couldn't forget his face, a secret man who lived behind a front. He pushed his silver mane back and patted it in place.

'Tonight is all the time we have,' I said. 'In the morning you can expect Bastian and the sheriff and probably the DA pounding on your door. You won't be able to put them off by simply denying that you bought that knife. You're going to have to explain it.'

'Do you really think Dick took it?'

'He's a better suspect than Tom, in my opinion.'

'Very well, I'll call him.' He rose and went to the telephone on the desk.

'Don't tell him what you want him for. He might break and run.'

'Naturally I won't.' He dialed a number from memory, and waited. When he spoke, his voice had changed again. It was lighter and younger. 'Dick? You said something to Elaine about dropping by tonight. I was wondering if I was to expect you . . . I know it's late. I'm sorry you're not too well. What's the trouble? . . . I'm sorry. Look, why don't you come out anyway, just for a minute? Tom came home tonight, isn't that great? He'll want to see you. And I particularly want to see you . . . Yep, it's an order. . . . Fine, I'll look for you then.' He hung up.

'What's the matter with him?' I asked.

'He says he doesn't feel well.'

'Sick?'

'Depressed. But he cheered up when I told him Tom was home. He'll be out shortly.'

'Good. In the meantime I want to talk to Tom.'

Hillman came and stood over me. His face was rather obscure in the green penumbra. 'Before you talk to him again, there's something you ought to know.'

I waited for him to go on. Finally I asked him: 'Is it about Tom?'

'It has to do with both of us.' He hesitated, his eyes intent on my face. 'On second thought, I don't think I'll let my back hair down any further tonight.'

'You may never have another chance,' I said, 'before it gets let down for you, the hard way.'

'That's where you're wrong. Nobody knows this particular thing but me.'

'And it has to do with you and Tom?'

'That's right. Now let's forget it.'

He didn't want to forget it, though. He wanted to share his secret, without taking the responsibility of speaking out. He lingered by the table, looking down at my face with his stainless-steel eyes.

I thought of the feeling in Hillman's voice when he spoke of his love for Tom. Perhaps that feeling was the element which would balance the equation.

'Is Tom your natural son?' I said.

He didn't hesitate in answering. 'Yes. He's my own flesh and blood.'

'And you're the only one who knows?'

'Carol knew, of course, and Mike Harley knew. He agreed to the arrangement in exchange for certain favors I was able to do him.'

'You kept him out of Portsmouth.'

'I helped to. You mustn't imagine I was trying to mastermind some kind of plot. It all happened quite naturally. Carol came to me after Mike and his brother were arrested. She begged me to intervene on their behalf. I said I would. She was a lovely girl, and she expressed her gratitude in a natural way.'

'By going to bed with you.'

'Yes. She gave me one night. I went to her room in the Barcelona Hotel. You should have seen her, Archer, when she took off her clothes for me. She lit up that shabby room with the brass bed—'

I cut in on his excitement: 'The brass bed is still there, and so was Otto Sipe, until last night. Did Sipe know about your big night on the brass bed?'

'Sipe?'

'The hotel detective.'

'Carol said he was gone that night.'

'And you say you only went there once.'

'Only once with Carol. I spent some nights in the Barcelona later with another girl. I suppose I was trying to recapture the rapture or something. She was a willing girl, but she was no substitute for Carol.'

I got up. He saw the look on my face and backed away. 'What's the matter with you, is something wrong?'

'Susanna Drew is a friend of mine. A good friend.'

'How could I know that?' he said with his mouth lifted on one side.

'You don't know much,' I said. 'You don't know how sick it makes me to sit here and listen to you while you dabble around in your dirty little warmed-over affairs.'

He was astonished. I was astonished myself. Angry shouting at witnesses is something reserved for second-rate prosecutors in courtrooms.

'Nobody talks to me like that,' Hillman said in a shaking voice. 'Get out of my house and stay out.'

'I'll be delighted to.'

I got as far as the front door. It was like walking through deep, clinging mud. Then Hillman spoke behind me from the far side of the reception hall.

'Look here.' It was his favorite phrase.

I looked there. He walked toward me under the perilous chandelier. He said with his hands slightly lifted and turned outward:

'I can't go on by myself, Archer. I'm sorry if I stepped on your personal toes.'

'It's all right.'

'No, it isn't. Are you in love with Susanna?'

I didn't answer him.

'In case you're wondering,' he said, 'I haven't touched her since 1945. I ran into some trouble with that house detective, Sipe—'

I said impatiently: 'I know. You knocked him down.'

'I gave him the beating of his life,' he said with a kind of naïve pride. 'It was the last time he tried to pry any money out of me.'

'Until this week.'

He was jolted into temporary silence. 'Anyway, Susanna lost interest—'

'I don't want to talk about Susanna.'

'That suits me.'

We had moved back into the corridor that led to the library, out of hearing of the room where Elaine was. Hillman leaned on the wall like a bystander in an alley. His posture made me realize how transient and insecure he felt in his own house.

'There are one or two things I don't understand,' I said. 'You tell me you spent one night with Carol, and yet you're certain that you fathered her son.'

'He was born just nine months later, December the twelfth.'

'That doesn't prove you're his father. Pregnancies often last longer, especially first ones. Mike Harley could have fathered him before the Shore Patrol took him. Or any other man.'

'There was no other man. She was a virgin.'

'You're kidding.'

'I am not. Her marriage to Mike Harley was never consummated. Mike was impotent, which was one reason he was willing to have the boy pass as his.'

'Why was that so necessary, Hillman? Why didn't you take the boy and raise him yourself?'

'I did that.'

'I mean, raise him openly as your own son.'

'I couldn't. I had other commitments. I was already married to Elaine. She's a New Englander, a Puritan of the first water.'

'With a fortune of the first water.'

'I admit I needed her help to start my business. A man has to make choices.'

He looked up at the chandelier. Its light fell starkly on his hollow bronze face. He turned his face away from the light.

'Who told you Mike Harley was impotent?'

'Carol did, and she wasn't lying. She was a virgin, I tell you. She did a lot of talking in the course of the night. Her whole life. She told me Mike got what sex he got by being spanked, or beaten with a strap.'

'By her?'

'Yes. She didn't enjoy it, of course, but she did it for him willingly enough. She seemed to feel that it was less dangerous than sex, than normal sex.'

A wave of sickness went through me. It wasn't physical. But I could smell the old man's cow barn and hear the whining of his one-eyed dog.

'I thought you were the one who was supposed to be impotent,' I said, 'or sterile.'

He glanced at me sharply. 'Who have you been talking to?'

'Your wife. She did the talking.'

'And she still thinks I'm sterile?'

'Yes.'

'Good.' He turned his face away from the light again and let out a little chuckle of relief. 'Maybe we can pull this out yet. I told Elaine at the time we adopted Tom that Weintraub gave me a test and found that I was sterile. I was afraid she'd catch on to the fact of my paternity.'

'You may be sterile at that.'

He didn't know what I meant. 'No. It's Elaine who is. I didn't need to take any test. I have Tom to prove I'm a man.'

He didn't have Tom.

XXVIII

WE WENT INTO the sitting room, the waiting room. Though Tom was in the house the waiting seemed to go on, as if it had somehow coalesced with time. Elaine was in her place on the chesterfield. She had taken up her knitting, and her stainless-steel needles glinted along the edge of the red wool. She looked up brightly at her husband.

'Where's Tom?' he said. 'Is he still upstairs?'

'I heard him go down the back stairs. I imagine Mrs Perez is feeding him in the kitchen. He seems to prefer the kitchen to the sitting room. I suppose that's natural, considering his heredity.'

'We won't go into the subject of that, eh?'

Hillman went into the bar alcove and made himself a very dark-looking highball. He remembered to offer me one, which I declined.

'What did that policeman want?' Elaine asked him.

'He had some stupid questions on his mind. I prefer not to go into them.'

'So you've been telling me for the past twenty-five years. You prefer not to go into things. Save the surface. Never mind the dry rot at the heart.'

'Could we dispense with the melodrama?'

'The word is tragedy, not melodrama. A tragedy has gone through this house and you don't have the mind to grasp it. You live in a world of appearances, like a fool.'

'I know. I know.' His voice was light, but he looked ready to throw his drink in her face. 'I'm an ignorant engineer, and I never studied philosophy.'

Her needles went on clicking. 'I could stand your ignorance, but I can't stand your evasions any longer.'

He drank part of his drink, and waved his free hand loosely over his head. 'Good heavens, Elaine, how much do I have to take from you? This isn't the time or place for one of those.'

'There never is a time or place,' she said. 'If there's time, you change the clocks—this is known as crossing the International Ralph Line—and suddenly it's six o'clock in the morning, in Tokyo. If there's a place, you find an escape hatch. I see your wriggling legs and then you're off and away, into the wild Ralph yonder. You never faced up to anything in your life.'

He winced under her bitter broken eloquence. 'That isn't true,' he said uneasily. 'Archer and I have been really dredging tonight.'

'Dredging in the warm shallows of your nature? I thought you reserved that pastime for your women. Like Susanna Drew.'

Her name sent a pang through me. It was a nice name, innocent and bold and slightly absurd, and it didn't deserve to be bandied about by these people. If the Hillmans had ever been innocent, their innocence had been frittered away in a marrige of pretenses. It struck me suddenly that Hillman's affair with Susanna had also been one of pretenses. He had persuaded her to take care of Carol without any hint that he was the father of the child she was carrying.

'Good Lord,' he was saying now, 'are we back on the Drew girl again after all these years?'

'Well, are we?' Elaine said.

Fortunately the telephone rang. Hillman went into the alcove to answer it, and turned to me with his hand clapped over the mouthpiece.

'It's Bastian, for you. You can take the call in the pantry. I'm going to listen on this line.'

There wasn't much use arguing. I crossed the music room and the dining room to the butler's pantry and fumbled around in the dark for the telephone. I could hear Mrs Perez in the kitchen, talking to Tom in musical sentences about her native province of Sinaloa. Bastian's voice in the receiver sounded harsh and inhuman by comparison:

'Archer?'

'I'm here.'

'Good. I checked the matter of Dick Leandro's transportation, in fact I've just been talking to a girl friend of his. She's a senior at the college, named Katie Ogilvie, and she owns a Chevrolet sedan, this year's model, blue in color. She finally admitted she lent it to him last night. He put over a hundred miles on the odometer.'

'Are you sure she wasn't with him? He had a girl with him, or another boy, Daly wasn't quite sure.'

'It wasn't Miss Ogilvie,' Bastian said. 'She was peeved about the fact that he used her car to take another girl for a long ride.'

'How does she know it was a girl?'

'The lady dropped a lipstick in the front seat. A very nice white gold lipstick, fourteen carat. I don't think,' he added dryly, 'that Miss Ogilvie would have testified so readily if it wasn't for that lipstick. Apparently Leandro impressed the need for secrecy on her.'

'Did he say why?'

'It had something to do with the Hillman kidnapping. That was all she knew. Well, do we pick up Leandro? You seem to be calling the shots.'

'He's on his way out here. Maybe you better follow along.'

'You sound as if things are building up to a climax.'

'Yeah.'

I could see its outlines. They burned on my eyeballs like the lights of Dack's Auto Court. I sat in the dark after Bastian hung up, and tried to blink them away. But they spread out into the darkness around me and became integrated with the actual world.

Sinaloa, Mrs Perez was saying or kind of singing to Tom in the kitchen, Sinaloa was a land of many rivers. There were eleven rivers in all, and she and her family lived so close to one of them that her brothers would put on their bathing suits and run down for a swim every day. Her father used to go down to the river on Sunday and catch fish with a net and distribute them to the neighbors. All the neighbors had fish for Sunday lunch.

Tom said it sounded like fun.

Ah yes, it was like Paradise, she said, and her father was a highly regarded man in their *barrio.* Of course it was hot in summer, that was the chief drawback, a hundred and twenty degrees in the shade sometimes. Then big black clouds would pile up along the Sierra Madre Occidental, and it would rain so hard, inches in just two hours. Then it would be sunny again. Sunny, sunny, sunny! That was how life went in Sinaloa.

Tom wanted to know if her father was still alive. She replied with joy that her father lived on, past eighty now, in good health. Perez was visiting him on his present trip to Mexico.

'I'd like to visit your father.'

'Maybe you will some day.'

I opened the door. Tom was at the kitchen table, eating the last of his soup. Mrs Perez was leaning over him with a smiling maternal mouth and faraway eyes. She looked distrustfully at me. I was an alien in their land of Sinaloa.

'What do you want?'

'A word with Tom. I'll have to ask you to leave for a bit.'

She stiffened.

'On second thought, there won't be any more secrets in this house. You might as well stay, Mrs Perez.'

'*Thank* you.'

She picked up the soup bowl and walked switching to the sink, where she turned the hot water full on. Tom regarded me across the table with the infinite boredom of the young. He was very clean and pale.

'I hate to drag you back over the details,' I said, 'but you're the only one who can answer some of these questions.'

'It's okay.'

'I'm not clear about yesterday, especially last night. Were you still at the Barcelona Hotel when Mike Harley got back from Vegas?'

'Yes. He was in a very mean mood. He told me to beat it before he killed me. I was intending to leave, anyway.'

'And nobody stopped you?'

'He wanted to get rid of me.'

'What about Sipe?'

'He was so drunk he hardly knew what he was doing. He passed out before I left.'

'What time did you leave?'

'A little after eight. It wasn't dark yet. I caught a bus at the corner.'

'You weren't there when Dick Leandro arrived?'

'No sir.' His eyes widened. 'Was he at the hotel?'

'Evidently he was. Did Sipe or Harley ever mention him?'

'No sir.'

'Do you know what he might have been doing there?'

'No sir. I don't know much about him. He's *their* friend.' He shrugged one shoulder and arm toward the front of the house.

'Whose friend in particular? His or hers?'

'His. But she uses him, too.'

'To drive her places?'

'For anything she wants.' He spoke with the hurt ineffectual anger of a displaced son. 'When he does something she wants, she says she'll leave him money in her will. If he doesn't, like when he has a date, she says she'll cut him out. So usually he breaks the date.'

'Would he kill someone for her?'

Mrs Perez had turned off the hot water. In the steamy silence at her end of the kitchen, she made an explosive noise that sounded like 'Chuh!'

'I don't know what he'd do,' Tom said deliberately. 'He's a yacht bum and they're all the same, but they're all different, too. It would depend on how much risk there was in it. And how much money.'

'Harley,' I said, 'was stabbed with the knife your father gave you, the hunting knife with the striped handle.'

'I didn't stab him.'

'Where did you last see the knife?'

He considered the question. 'It was in my room, in the top drawer with the handkerchiefs and stuff.'

'Did Dick Leandro know where it was?'

'I never showed him. He never came to my room.'

'Did your mother—did Elaine Hillman know where it was?'

'I guess so. She's always— she was always coming into my room, and checking on my things.'

'That's true,' Mrs Perez said.

I acknowledged her comment with a look which discouraged further comment.

'I understand on a certain Sunday morning she came into your room once too often. You threatened to shoot her with your father's gun.'

Mrs Perez made her explosive noise. Tom bit hard on the tip of his right thumb. His look was slanting, over my head and to one side, as if there was someone behind me.

'Is that the story they're telling?' he said.

Mrs Perez burst out: 'It isn't true. I heard her yelling up there. She came downstairs and got the gun out of the library desk and went upstairs with it.'

'Why didn't you stop her?'

'I was afraid,' she said. 'Anyway, Mr Hillman was coming—I heard his car—and I went outside and told him there was trouble upstairs. What else could I do, with Perez away in Mexico?'

'It doesn't matter,' Tom said. 'Nothing happened. I took the gun away from her.'

'Did she try to shoot you?'

'She said she would if I didn't take back what I said.'

'And what did you say?'

'That I'd rather live in an auto court with my real mother than in this house with her. She blew her top and ran downstairs and got the gun.'

'Why didn't you tell your father about this?'

'He isn't my father.'

I didn't argue. It took more than genes to establish fatherhood. 'Why didn't you tell him, Tom?'

He made an impatient gesture with his hand. 'What was the use? He wouldn't have believed me. Anyway, I *was* mad at her, for lying to me about who I was. I did take the gun and point it at her head.'

'And want to kill her?'

He nodded. His head seemed very heavy on his neck. Mrs Perez invented a sudden errand and bustled past him, pressing his shoulder with her hand as she went. As if to signalize this gesture, an electric bell rang over the pantry door.

'That's the front door,' she said to nobody in particular.

I got there in a dead heat with Ralph Hillman. He let Dick Leandro in. The week's accelerated aging process was working in Leandro now. Only his dark hair seemed lively. His face was drawn and slightly yellowish. He gave me a lackluster glance, and appealed to Hillman:

'Could I talk to you alone, Skipper? It's important.' He was almost chattering.

Elaine spoke from the doorway of the sitting room: 'It can't be so important that you'd forget your manners. Come in and be sociable, Dick. I've been alone all evening, or so it seems.'

'We'll join you later,' Hillman said.

'It's very late already.' Her voice was edgy.

Leandro's dim brown glance moved back and forth between them like a spectator's at a tennis game on which he had bet everything he owned.

'If you're not nice to me,' she said lightly, 'I won't be nice to you, Dick.'

'I do-don't care about that.' There was strained defiance in his voice.

'You will.' Stiff-backed, she retreated into the sitting room.

I said to Leandro: 'We won't waste any more time. Did you do some driving for Mrs Hillman last night?'

He turned away from me and almost leaned on Hillman, speaking in a hushed rapid voice. 'I've *got* to talk to you alone. Something's come up that you don't know about.'

'We'll go into the library,' Hillman said.

'If you do, I go along,' I said. 'But we might as well talk here. I don't want to get too far from Mrs Hillman.'

The young man turned and looked at me in a different way, both lost and relieved. He knew I knew.

Hillman also knew, I thought. His proposal to Susanna tended to prove it; his confession that Tom was his natural son had provided me with evidence of motive. He leaned now on the wall beside the door, heavy and mysterious as a statue, with half-closed eyes.

I said to the younger man: 'Did you drive her to the Barcelona Hotel, Dick?'

'Yessir.' With one shoulder high and his head on one side, he held himself in an awkward pose which gave the effect of writhing. 'I had no w-way of knowing what was on her mind. I *still* don't know.'

'But you have a pretty good idea. Why all the secrecy?'

'She said I should borrow a car, that they had phoned for more money and Skipper wasn't here so we would have to deliver it. Or else they'd kill him. We were to keep it secret from the police, and afterwards she said I must never tell anyone.'

'And you believed her story?'

'I c-certainly did.'

'When did you start to doubt it?'

'Well, I couldn't figure out how she could get hold of all that c-cash.'

'How much?'

'Another twenty-five thousand, she said. She said it was in her bag—she was carrying her big knitting bag—but I didn't actually see the money.'

'What did you see?'

'I didn't actually *see* anything.' Like a stealthy animal that would eventually take over his entire forehead, his hair was creeping down toward his eyes. 'I mean, I saw this character, the one she—I saw this character come out of the hotel and they went around the back and I heard this scream.' He scratched the front of his throat.

'What did you do?'

'I stayed in the car. She told me to stay in the car. When she came back, she said it was an owl.'

'And you believed her?'

'I don't know much about birds. Do I, Skipper?'

Elaine cried out very brightly from her doorway: 'What under heaven are you men talking about?'

I walked toward her. 'You. The owl you heard last night in the hotel garden. What kind of an owl was it?'

'A screech—' Her hand flew up and pressed against her lips.

'He looked human to me. He wasn't a very good specimen, but he was human.'

She stopped breathing, and then gasped for breath. 'He was a devil,' she said, 'the scum of the earth.'

'Because he wanted more money?'

'It would have gone on and on. I had to stop him.' She stood shuddering in the doorway. With a fierce effort of will, she brought her emotions under control. 'Speaking of money, I can take care of you. I'm sure the police would understand my position, but there's no need to connect me with this—this—' She couldn't think of a noun. 'I can take care of you and I can take care of Dick.'

'How much are you offering?'

'She looked at me imperiously, from the moral stilts of inherited wealth.

'Come into the sitting room,' she said, 'and we'll talk about it.'

The three of us followed her into the room and took up positions around her chesterfield. Hillman looked at me curiously. He was very silent and subdued, but the calculator behind his eyes was still working. Dick Leandro was coming back to life. His eyes had brightened. Perhaps he still imagined that somehow, sometime, there would be Hillman money coming to him.

'How much?' I said to her.

'Twenty-five thousand.'

'That's better than a knife between the ribs. Does that mean twenty-five thousand overall or twenty-five thousand for each murder?'

'Each murder?'

'There were two, done with the same knife, almost certainly by the same person. You.'

She moved her head away from my pointing finger, like a stage-shy girl. A stage-shy girl playing the role of an aging woman with monkey wrinkles and fading fine blonde hair.

'Fifty thousand then,' she said.

'He's playing with you,' Hillman said. 'You can't buy him.'

She turned toward him. 'My late father once said that you can buy anyone, anyone at all. I proved that when I bought you.' She made a gesture of repugnance. 'I wish I hadn't. You turned out to be a bad bargain.'

'You didn't buy me. You merely leased my services.'

They faced each other as implacably as two skulls. She said: 'Did you have to palm her bastard off on me?'

'I wanted a son. I didn't plan it. It happened.'

'You made it happen. You connived to bring her baby into my house. You let me feed and nurture him and call him mine. How could you be such a living falsity?'

'Don't talk to me about falsity, Elaine. It seemed the best way to handle the problem.'

'Stallion,' she said. 'Filth.'

I heard a faint movement in the adjoining room. Straining my eyes into the darkness, I could see Tom sitting on the bench in front of the grand piano. I was tempted to shut the door, but it was too late, really. He might as well hear it all.

Hillman said in a surprisingly calm voice: 'I never could understand the Puritan mind, Ellie. You think a little fun in bed is the ultimate sin, worse than murder. Christ, I remember our wedding night. You'd have thought I was murdering you.'

'I wish you had.'

'I almost wish I had. You murdered Carol, didn't you, Ellie?'

'Of course I did. She phoned here Monday morning, after you left. Tom had given her his telephone number. I took the call in his room, and she spilled out everything. She *said* she had just caught on to her husband's plans, and she was afraid he would harm Tom, who wasn't really his son. I'm sure it was just an excuse she used to get her knife into me.'

'Her knife?' I said.

'That was a badly chosen image, wasn't it? I mean that she was glorying over me, annulling the whole meaning of my existence.'

'I think she was simply trying to save her son.'

'*Her* son, not mine. Her son and Ralph's. That was the point, don't you see? I felt as if she had killed me. I was just a fading ghost in the world, with only enough life left to strike back. Walking from where I left the Cadillac, I could feel the rain fall through me. I was no solider than the rain.

'Apparently her husband had caught her phoning me. He

took her back to their cottage and beat her and left her unconscious on the floor. She was easy for me to kill. The knife slipped in and out. I hadn't realized how easy it would be.

'But the second time wasn't easy,' she said. 'The knife caught in his ribs. I couldn't pull it out of him.'

Her voice was high and childish in complaint. The little girl behind her wrinkles had been caught in a malign world where even things no longer cooperated and even men could not be bought.

'Why did you have to stick it into him?' I said.

'He suspected that I killed Carol. He used Tom's number to call me and accuse me. Of course he wanted *money*.' She spoke as if her possession of money had given her a special contemptuous insight into other people's hunger for it. 'It would have gone on and on.'

It was going on and on. Tom came blinking out of the darkness. He looked around in pity and confusion. Elaine turned her face away from him, as if she had an unprepossessing disease.

The boy said to Hillman: 'Why didn't you tell me? It could have made a difference.'

'It still can,' Hillman said with a hopefulness more grinding than despair. 'Son?'

He moved toward Tom, who evaded his outstretched hands and left the room. Walking rather unsteadily, Hillman followed him. I could hear them mounting the stairs, on different levels, out of step.

Dick Leandro got up from his place, rather tentatively, as if he had been liberated from an obscure bondage. He went into the alcove, where I heard him making himself a drink.

Elaine Hillman was still thinking about money. 'What about it, Mr Archer? Can you be bought?' Her voice was quite calm. The engines of her anger had run down.

'I can't be bought with anything you've offered.'

'Will you have mercy on me, then?'

'I don't have that much mercy.'

'I'm not asking for a great deal. Just let me sleep one more night in my own house.'

'What good would that do you?'

'This good. I'll be frank with you. I've been saving sleeping pills for a considerable time—'

'How long?'

'Nearly a year, actually. I've been in despair for at least that long—'

'You should have taken your pills sooner.'

'Before all this, you mean?' She waved her hand at the empty room as if it was a tragic stage littered with corpses.

'Before all this,' I said.

'But I couldn't die without knowing. I knew my life was empty and meaningless. I had to find out why.'

'And now it's full and meaningful?'

'It's over,' she said. 'Look, Mr Archer, I was frank with you today. Give me a *quid pro quo*. All I'm asking for is time to use my pills.'

'No.'

'You owe me something. I helped you as much as I dared this afternoon.'

'You weren't trying to help me, Mrs Hillman. You only told me what I already knew, or what I was about to find out. You gave me the fact that Tom was adopted in such a way that it would conceal the more important fact that he was your husband's natural son. You kept alive the lie that your husband was sterile because it hid your motive for murdering Carol Harley.'

'I'm afraid your reasoning is much too subtle for me.'

'I hardly think so. You're a subtle woman.'

'I? Subtle? I'm a ninny, a poor booby. The people in the streets, the scum of the earth knew more about my life than I—' She broke off. 'So you won't help me.'

'I can't. I'm sorry. The police are on their way now.'

She regarded me thoughtfully. 'There would still be time for me to use the gun.'

'No.'

'You're very hard.'

'It isn't me, really, Mrs Hillman. It's just reality catching up.'

The sheriff's car was in the driveway now. I rose and went as far as the sitting-room door and called out to Bastian to come in. Elaine sighed behind me like a woman in passion.

Her passion was a solitary one. She had picked up her knitting in both hands and pressed both steel needles into her breast. She struck them into herself again before I reached her. By the middle of the following day she had succeeded in dying.